AT FAITH'S END

BOOK TWO OF THE HAUNTED SHADOWS

CHRIS GALFORD

Edited by Nathan Hartley

Cover Illustration by Matthew Watts

By Chris Galford

First Edition: October 2013.

For my Brother,

For reminding me that a passion for writing never dies

come days or months or years;

one must merely have the courage to embrace it.

"In every breath, laughter. In every life, love, such that even death will weep."

~Asanti proverb

<u>Prologue</u>

Outside, a dull, resonant clang issued from the gates. A dozen times a day that sound repeated through the courtyard. They were never simply open any more. One never knew what might blow in on the wind.

Sword and smoke and always ash, rising in the east.

Outside, they were rattling the last bit of frost from the hinges. Pikes and bows bristled along the walls as soldiers stalked the battlements. They had been lax, at a time, but no more. The snow had gone, or near enough, yet the world never seemed to thaw. As the poets cried, the Winter King was nearly overthrown, but the young Spring Prince crept only slowly from his hole. The first flowers would be long in coming.

Seasons marched, like men, like countries. But there were no countries, and in time there would be no men.

Outside, they went about as if all the world was still the same—and so it was, and it wasn't. They said an emperor was dead. Others had died before him. Those that lived on shedded tears wiped them on their sleeves and stepped over the graves into the twilight of their lives. Old men passed so new could arise. So this one had, and even now she could smell the stink of him, close her eyes and feel the horror of his ringing pulse battering her heart—the fervor of his face, looming orthodoxy sneer behind the thin veneer of snow and emeralds, and gryphons, as shepherds gliding beneath the setting sun.

All this Usuri saw and felt, and all the while the world went on pretending she no longer was a part of it.

There was no country and no king, and all the fire in Hell tittered.

Yet inside, she couldn't feel the tumultuous summer's pull. The walls assailed her. When she breathed, there was frost in her lungs. When she touched the glass, there was nothing but a mirror of herself, in all its horror.

Usuri had grown haggard over the months spent in Vissering Castle. She scarcely ate. Only when her body cried out agonized gasps for life did she oblige, and always questioningly. In rebellion against the eastern styles of longer hair, she had carved what little she had close to the scalp. There was something satisfying in the motion. Her father gnawed at her waking thoughts and Rurik at her dreams. Each mocked her from the flames. Both gagged her days with brimstone and stole her breath away.

For months her father had laid beneath the earth, but his blood was no longer the only thing coursing in her. There were other faces, other names, ghosts without homes save her own tormented mind. It was only right. She had done them. All of them. She had plucked the chords of their life away and forever silenced their notes in life's song.

Three tunes for three dead princes.

It was their deaths that racked her, not their lives. Names. She did not like to think of them with names—merely featureless ghouls, stalking the periphery of her soul.

The soul—a fevered thing. It was breaking every day, piece by piece, bringing a skeletal paleness to the olive life of her body. When she killed, pieces of her died with them. Not literally. Will. A slow and purposeful dying within. Inside: blackness. She loathed to look into it, lest it become all she saw. A step or a bound—she did not know how far away she was, yet she was getting closer every day.

How long since she had killed? The princely pair were last in mind—the villain king and his dolled-up brother. She had kissed the one, felt his touch on her skin. It wouldn't come out no matter how hard she tried. The stain was on her. It bubbled inside with her father's voice, tormenting her.

"I see you," it said, *"I know what you did,"* and she could not hide, no matter how deep she buried herself. Her hands were still wrapped from when she tried to dig the voices out. The blood had stopped flowing, but the bandages held—she knew the danger as well as they did. Yet the danger to herself was the least of her worries.

Somewhere down below, the blood stirred like a poison, threatening her sanity.

They were not alone in the castle anymore. There were others. Those *things*. They had its blood and they had its eyes, and they were laughing inside, where only her father could laugh now because they had taken him, as they took Kasimir, as they would take her. There was an empress and a prince, and it was their presence that saw her locked within a tower.

Before, she had been allowed to roam a little. She had her watchers, but so long as she was calm, she could roam. Then she had tried to put her claws upon the Cullick wench, the lying creature-creature-creature that had taken Rurik inside her and—they didn't like that. Cullick saw her to the tower. She was too weak to object. Her deprivations took their toll on her body, as the killings peeled at the innards. They locked her in a tower, ostensibly for her own good, but she knew better.

Cullick couldn't let her be seen. Cullick couldn't risk what she would do if she saw them. Yet she did see them. In the yard. On the walls. They were everywhere.

"Father," she cried as she had when she was small. "Father, I am weak! I have not the strength! I have seen the Sunrise! I have seen the Shadow, and the Lion's mouth, but it is wide and it is terrible and what am I? Who am I to tip the storms? They will not change!"

Killer! The word barked back at her and she could not deny, but there were words in her head, pounding with the force of a thousand-thousand cannon, and she could not turn aside from them.

Everything slid slowly into place, piece by piece. Little pieces on the board, moving to fruition. Everywhere the kings and queens, riding onto glory and to death.

Their devil-angel rode on southron wings. That was what they said. She could hear it, when she wanted. It haunted her dreams. The terrible shadow in his robes of white—they could not see him for what he was. She ran from him, but he only grew and grew, fangs falling from his malformed cheeks as his body bloated and distorted. He would laugh at her, arms outstretched as the darkness spread around him. He was a devil, and in her dreams she would round the circle three times, and he would catch her, pin her, devour her in white, and she would be falling into pyre flames, and everywhere was her father, tortured in innumerable ways, and always by the same faceless woman, wearing her husband's crown.

And as she screamed, the choirs sang—the children's dirge, from little bodies without tongues. Sometimes, she saw Rurik there, and she would call out to him, but he could not hear her. Then it would be him on the scaffold where his father met his end, and it would be his head put before the chopping block, and

Essa with the blade. Singers sang, the head rolled, and at her feet, Charlotte would raise it to her lips and the head would ask:

"Can you see the glory?"

Of the coming, of the coming—

The door rattled and she twisted back, watching how the shadows spread across the twilit planes. The room was always brightest this time of day. Keys jangled, real voices gossiped. Her prison didn't feel quite so small in these moments. Yet it wasn't small, not really. Not terribly, at least. She had a bed and pillows, two mirrors—thrice broken each—and all the space for walking, wandering, twisting, dining on the open air—and the purity of that air was a marvel. There were no cobwebs. Not anywhere. She saw to that, day in and day out.

One day, she caught a spider weaving webs above the door. Spider-little-spider-May, she never saw it coming. Then there was no more spider above the chamber door.

If only *she* were just as squishy.

Aren't they all?

Light broke from the hall beyond, in ringing dust. Usuri tried not to cringe. In the ring—a scream—then nothing, never.

Would that she could pluck her wings.

Charlotte filled the silence with her doll-like form—no ruffled wrinkles, no miscombed hair; curled, gold as the coins bitter men exchanged. Her skin—like porcelain. The light struck her angelic.

Tray in hand, the angel moved parallel to her, to place her meal beside the bed. Usuri inched a pace, on hand and foot, marveling at the novelty. Little Charlotte was not a rarity in her presence, for all the ill-will she bade her, but the girl never brought her food. Whether that was her desire or her father's, Usuri could not say. *All Cullicks are as kings before the servile—above, beyond, mere men with lofty heads.* She watched, but she moved no nearer. A shadow lurked behind the angel, filling the doorway, then the room. She did not shrink from it, but she did not goad it.

It had struck her. It would have no problem doing so again.

She cringed, reveled—perhaps, again.

"A mess. As ever." The angel did not look at her as she set each item on the bed. "How might a woman become a beast?" She paused. Usuri could imagine her smiling. "You teach us every day, bit-by-bit."

Usuri kept her silence. Charlotte moved on, handing the tray off to her shadow as she gathered some unseen strength into herself. Charlotte turned, steadied, drank her in. Usuri waited, shrinking—she did not like it when those eyes were on her, when they would meet her as a person. She advanced, a river rushing on to swallow her whole. Usuri felt her breaths quicken, felt the tightening in her chest. Angel wings, all too near. False promises taking flight. She shut her eyes, tried to close out the voices.

"Can you see the glory," her dead father asked.

"Go away," she whispered as the body crouched beside her. Tiny angel wings, like a fly's—she could crush them if she wanted. Just needed to reach out and...

"Usuri, please look at me." She did not want to look. *Hell is in the eyes, and in Hell you can see and you don't want to see and everything is...*"Please."

Usuri lashed at her, crying "Out!" but the hand caught her wrist, Usuri's shaking wrist. Another was on her arm and she did not want to look but Charlotte was there, and she was not leaving. They never left. Not really. They were everywhere and all around—but their walls, their halls, they could not hold her. Even with body broken, the spirit rose and swam in the deep recesses of the forgotten—self.

Usuri looked at her with eyes hollowed in the flame's of man's hate, watched the mirrors of the angel and the monster in their reflection. Her or *her*, she could not say. There was compassion there, though, staring back at the remnants of her life. The hand on her arm moved slowly, purposefully. She felt it, did not watch it, but it came to her, stroked the hair from her face and flecks of dirt from her skin. She must have been so thin.

Charlotte's face shrank at the sight. Her eyes left Usuri's momentarily. They found the floor, then back, creasing with care. "What is it like?" Charlotte whispered. Her touch lingered on Usuri's cheek.

"There are things out there, you know. Waiting. We do not want to push you. You are so..."

Dead?

"Frail," said Charlotte. A line of worry creased the woman's brow. "Surely this does not…" *Need to be?* Apparently, Charlotte thought better of her path. Usuri could see the shift. "But you did this to yourself. And before that: them." Charlotte's hands folded in her lap. A place where so few things fell. Usuri would have thought her virginal, but all was poison there. Rurik was poisoned there. "It will get worse now. Our lord's inquisitor would sit the throne. Ring about his neck, with bastard children in tow. There will be burnings, you know. Of course you know. Do you care?"

Underlying: would you have them do unto others as they have done unto you? She could imagine Charlotte burning, but the pretty locks always fell away until it was her father's grimacing, screaming face—but she had not been there. The moment when the Inquisition's flames finally split his screams. She could only imagine it now.

"Father wishes to see you. With them, between them—it grows dangerous. It's just a matter of time before—it's worse now. Much worse. We would end it. And you—I know you do." *Justifying, clarifying, always mitigating to the sound of its own sullen ring! A beast! A beast! Father, how of this breast, or of this beast, might any word yet change?* "We could not spare Matair, but the rest— they still breathe, you know. Would you like to see them?"

And say what? Usuri looked at herself and in a moment's clarity saw what they saw: the disheveled monster, in fine but ratted gowns; bound hands, black feet, hair crusted wet. All of House Matair was dead. She could smile for them and twirl in her little gown, as this creature did, but they would never know her as anything more than their father's novelty.

"You will lie again," she whispered.

Charlotte smiled faintly. "All men lie. Should we wish against it, we should not speak at all."

"Does it sing? When no one is around to hear it?" Usuri watched the confusion settle about the lady. "Take heart. He moves in you. Never…I cannot touch them if I know not what to touch. I see them, but I do not know them."

More than once, she had heard Rurik's voice ringing in the dark. That faint cry from fields choked with frosted death. She tried to shut him out. To close her mind and her ears against it and pretend she couldn't hear his pain.

"We can piece them for you. Or bring you to them. This is bigger now. You're not a shadow, Usuri. You're not," Charlotte said.

"It says, the songbird without wings. In its cage, it speaks of wind. What does it know that she does not?" Usuri touched the hand and the hand faltered. She traced it down the wrist, felt it yield until the shadow stirred its steel. Such lines, such grace, majesty in a vase—the design was fickle. It never knew. They never did. It took something larger. "If it comes, then so will I."

She released her grip on Charlotte's skin, and the girl drew up and away. They always did. They had their purpose, and once they saw it done there was no other. Usuri folded her hands into her lap, watched the way the veins creased along the knuckles. So frail.

Rurik might have said that to the lamara whore, as he caressed her at night.

"Will you eat?"

Usuri smiled toothily at the woman until she left. *Eat is the wrong word*, she thought, as she looked over the bread Charlotte had left behind. She would consume—until she had grown fat on all the vagaries of her odium and burst forth in a requiem of deconstruction. How sweet the sugared tune that would sing them all to silence.

Chapter 1

There is nothing like a fire to stir the passions of a young man's heart. That, or a young woman to share it with. Yet the space beside Rurik Matair was empty, as it had been lo those many moons afield. As ice mingled with snow and the skies clouded overhead. The sun, only lately, began to beat them all into the sodden drudgery of not-quite-spring.

All around him the camp bustled with the same mundane stirrings he had come to know over the long months since he had left his family's home in Verdan. His family's home, not his, he kept reminding himself. For all an old man's promises, that hope had died alongside him in the dust and the snow.

Rurik, the exile, cocked his head to the music of the camp's appointed bards—some little more than soldiers with pipes or improvised drums. Most, however, came from the litter of camp followers that still swarmed about the outskirts. Their tunes mingled with the raucous tenor of rousing soldiers and the grinding ring of smiths putting hammer to steel.

Although the soldiers talked of their commander like he was Assal's gift to men, the man they called the Bastard took great care to see his people didn't mingle with his soldiers. Despite a few riotous days after the Emperor's death, he had kept the two camps more or less distinct from one another. Soldiers often visited the camp followers in daylight for a tumble or a trade, but come sundown every man was expected at his place, on pain of whipping. Of course some still braved it. Some nights, Rurik even envied their scars.

But he had his duties. The thought rang unpleasantly to mind as he drifted over the rations. Someone had been pilfering from the lot. Soldiers had already taken the wayward supplyman into custody, but it was his duty to catalogue the stores to figure exactly how much was missing. At his count, they were down an entire sack of bread and a quarter pound of cheese.

He worried most about the cheese. Hard as that stuff was, an aspiring criminal might bludgeon someone to death with it.

Since the pigeons had first carried news of the Emperor's demise back to Anscharde—the Imperial capital—the supply trains had slowed. What wagons pressed through bore no luxuries, only the austere pickings of a soldier's diet. It wouldn't have been enough if the army had kept up its march—and was scarcely enough as is—but with the passing of their monarch, the men of Idasia had settled into the uncomfortable lull of winter.

In the three months since their bloody victory at Leitzen, the army had been split and split again, and their own segment had gained perhaps ten miles. It was enough to carry them to the walled town of Pasłówska to winter. Mankałd, the thrice-forsaken capital of Effise, and their one-time goal for the march, lay but several days to the north. There it would remain.

Even so, Rurik could not say his lord had made a poor decision. The army didn't have the heart for another winter siege, and in spite of their proximity to their enemy's heart the winter months had been largely quiet. Aside from a few skirmishes with raiders, neither their scouts, nor those locals in their employ, had seen any sign of the battered Effisian army.

Rurik took it as a blessing. He had seen enough of the bloodshed—its lilting ring still terrorized the occasional dream.

As he marked the last tally in his head, he felt the unsettling sensation on the back of his neck of being watched. He sighed, "Stop it, Voren," and turned wearily toward the pale brown eyes squinting out at him from the door flap. The skinny baker snorted, snatched up a loaf of bread from one of the tables, and let the echoing pound of his footsteps carry him out of the tent.

That seemed to be the extent of their conversations these days. Since the…incident with Essa, their one-time associate always seemed to be lurking or scowling about. Whenever he wasn't coddling the girl that was to say. It was an added little dagger in Rurik's heart whenever he spied them together. Ever-watchful, the scrawny baker always seemed to have a smile ready for just those moments.

But there was nothing he could do about that. For all his efforts, if there was one thing he took away from his father, it was that one couldn't change the past. And he had muddled that up enough. Sometimes, as he sat alone, Rurik tried to remember the little things—the scent of her hair, the warmth of a kiss. It agonized him every time those senses failed him.

Tying up the last of the bags, Rurik called the guards posted outside, and together with them, hastened into the crowded lanes of the camp. It was much reduced from that brightly-colored mass the exile had first beheld at Erkitz, but it was still enough to dizzy a man. Though many soldiers had been moved into the town itself, thousands of idle, homesick, and restless armed men remained trapped within canvas walls. They grouped around the fires and roved anxiously about the paths patrols had worn, but the whole place buzzed in a way that always left Rurik unsettled. He did not like to spend much time there.

Passing between its wooden gates, they started into the streets of quaint Pasłówska. The town was about what one could expect from such a place. When he breathed in, frost mingled with manure. Cobbled streets clacked beneath their feet, but it still had the air of a farmers market. For miles beyond the town's walls, farms were all the eye could see. Any number of hamlets catered to the same folk, but Pasłówska was simply the biggest gathering place for such people so near to the Effisians' capital. Even with soldiers roving the streets, its people came and went as they always had, albeit a bit more warily. More than a few shot uncertain or spiteful looks at the troupe as they hurried along.

Low moans ran as undercurrent in the air as they rounded Pasłówska's only church. Rurik winced away. Within the dome of its low stone walls, the Bastard had turned the holy structure into one of several makeshift homes for the army's doctors. They treated the townsfolk with the same candor as the soldiers, but all they seemed to take anymore were cases of disease. Mostly the Bloody Flux. Even so, Rurik found himself pawing at the arm a knight's mace had broken in the field. The place was a reminder he didn't need. Still cradled in its sling, his arm's throbbing always seemed worst in the damp mornings.

The first day after Leitzen remained a blur. A different sort of battle, he supposed. Rowan told him later that he had nearly lost the arm. It was only Alviss, their towering Kuric guardian, that had politely persuaded the doctors the quickest course was not always the best, and that his arm wasn't as bad as all that.

Rurik himself had spent most the day asleep, feverish and out of wits. Flashes would come to him, of people and words, and cries for water, but that was all. Men danced from flames, leaving only hollow eyes in their ash. He saw Essa's face, contorted in fear, leaning over him with her green-green eyes leaking tears, but then it was gone. He couldn't say if either were real. Sometimes, a voice called to him in whispers, and seemed to stir the shape of his visions, but he could never recall it when he woke. He hoped the sound was Essa.

By the time he came around, she was gone, and as distant as ever. He had known her since they were children, and she wouldn't even speak to him. Every time she looked at him, all he ever saw in her was horror. All she ever saw in him was a monster.

A monster he had not created.

In that time beyond knowing, when they had coupled in the night and Essa did not know who she was.

His brother Ivon called to him as they neared the mayoral estate, which the Bastard had taken for his own. The troupe halted at the call, and Rurik cast back down the street, watching his brother stride toward him, his regular train of sycophants in tow. In truth, they were one of the few signs of the man he had known months before. Though the voice was the same, and the motions behind them, the long black warrior's tail of his brother's hair had been lopped off in mourning—a tradition older than the Empire itself. Oddly—and hauntingly—it made him look even more like their father. Yet he was thinner than he once had been, and all his clothes stank of the same overuse as everyone else. In war, even nobles were not excepted from hardship.

They clasped arms, awkwardly, and stepped apart. Ivon's eyes roamed him as they always did, as though sizing him up—or searching for a sibling somewhere in Rurik's pitiful mask. At his side, Ivon's latest page kept glancing between them, smiling broadly, stupidly. Even so, he looked sturdier than the last had been. Even before the Bloody Flux took him.

"How may I be of assistance, brother?" Rurik asked, his manner emphasizing urgency. He glanced over his shoulder, toward the hall, and back. "Tessel will be needing me shortly."

Wolfish. That was how his brother's smiles always looked. "I have no doubt. Merely passing along a kind word. Alviss sought you at the dawning. I gave promise to set you his way."

"Alviss?" Rurik could not keep hopefulness from warming his voice. "What did he want?"

Ivon shrugged. "Same as ever, I would suppose. He left no message."

"I see." He shifted, licking his lips. He wanted to ask, but could not find the courage. Besides, he doubted his brother would have the answer he sought. More tribulations to stack his morning with. Instead, "Any sign of forage?"

"Same as ever. War and winter leave little to pluck."

"I see." Rurik repeated. Hemmed and hawed and thought of asking after the other missing link. The hunger more ravenous than even food: coin. His eyes wandered to his brother's hunched shadow, the Brickheart—Vardick, his father's captain of the guard, now his brother's man wholly—and lingered over the scars and the gnarled fingers on the hilt of a sword, and wondered if he didn't miss his pupil, and those long nights thwacking Rurik in the gloom of winter. Then his eyes crossed the man's dead-set own and he ceased to wonder.

Thinking of nothing else to add, he smiled his sweetest smile and dipped his head to his brother. "I'll let Tessel know."

"Go serve your lord, lad."

Your lord. Much was to be made of specificity. They parted ways, each striding their own lane through the town. Many shared his brother's views on their newfound commander. An upstart. A brash fool. Tessel. The bastard saint of common men and common dreams, revered for his prowess and loathed for the birth no man could change.

To Rurik, he was simply Tessel.

The guards lazily admitted them at the door. Rurik parted ways with his guardians then and wheedled his way down a vacant entrance hall. In that hall, soldiers out of garb milled about, having turned the place from reception area into their personal barracks. The youth paused there to rub some of the pain from his bundled arm. He gasped and bit it back, trying not to appear out of sorts among the settled soldiers.

But of course, he was. He smiled at them, trying to play it off like some childish game. A few nodded. Most continued their conversations or their light meals. Pain they understood. It was the exile in him they didn't trust. *Deserter,* their looks seemed to say. *Traitorkin.*

From among them, however, a blond head bobbed toward him, only to rise a moment later. Boderoy was one of the Bastard's attendants, as he had attended the Emperor before him. Whereas most of the Emperor's company had departed with his body, Boderoy, out of some odd sense of devotion, had chosen to remain. The man had all of the grace one might expect from such a creature, though his sharp eyes and robust limbs told of a man far from unfamiliar with a good tussle. Rurik guessed him at about thirty summers. Of an age with their bastard. His mannerisms often painted him far younger, though.

"Where is he," Rurik asked as the man drew near.

Smilingly, Boderoy led him through an adjacent hall to the house's sitting room. There he knocked once and called out their presence, waiting for a reply before admitting him. When the Bastard's gravelly voice beckoned, Rurik stepped inside. The door clacked shut behind him.

Kyler Tessel was in rare form. The man his soldiers called the Bastard sat alone. He hunched over the room's small table, scribbling ink across a parchment, heedless of how much smeared the others beneath it.

Tessel looked remarkably like his late father must have when he was of that age. Tall and slender—in the lean and agile way of warriors, rather than boys—with the grassy green Durvalle eyes that looked *at* a man, as a man, and guaranteed none could second guess his birthright. His curled brown hair was trimmed short, which only seemed to emphasize his long, predatory nose. His features, Rurik marveled, were fine, and war only seemed to chisel them further into refinement, rather than weariness. He dressed simply, for his air alone commanded obedience. Like the alpha in a pack of wolves.

He scarcely glanced up as Rurik entered, but Rurik could feel the sigh of contentment at his presence. Tessel was rarely alone and he liked it that way.

"Were I meant for solitude," the commander had once confided in Rurik, "I should have been born an owl. A man is nothing without others to share life with."

Yet he was undeniably alone. They both were. The Bastard and the exile. Fate had pressed the one apart from his fellow man by blood, and chance had stolen the other away with the blood of a cold woman.

Rurik lingered in the doorway until Tessel gestured him into a chair across from him. "Sit," the man bade, and the exile obeyed, sitting up straight and steady. While he waited for his lord to speak, he found his eyes roaming the bits of parchment spread before him. The one being signed was addressed to Huwcyn, Count Ibin's nephew, and from what language Rurik glimpsed, their commander was none too pleased. Another looked to be a petition from the town's council. It would hardly be the first.

Curious, Rurik thought, *to surrender one moment, and demand so heartily in the next...*

It would be neglected, he decided. Such things often were. For Tessel, the army always came first.

After silence stretched long enough to make it apparent Rurik wouldn't speak, Tessel, still not looking up from his scribbling, grunted, "Must you always be so dreadfully formal, lad? Speak. Speak!" He paused there, his quill faltering long enough to leave a growing stain on his signature. "Unless I come to suspect bad word. It is not bad, is it?"

Grimacing, Rurik tried to ease some of the tension from his shoulders. "Well, it's not good."

Tessel considered that a moment, then shrugged back into his writing. "If it were good you shouldn't have been sent at all."

"I suppose."

"How much is missing?"

"A whole sack of our tasteless bread and about a quarter pound of the frostbit cheese."

"A pity."

Sprinkling a touch of dust onto the ink to help it dry faster, Tessel at last eased back in his seat, though not without a sigh. Setting the quill aside, he shook out his right hand. The scraggly scar across the palm—earned by the curious curvature of a kris dagger, Rurik was told—always bothered him after extended use. Most would never know it, though.

"And where do we stand?"

"Well..." Rurik cleared his throat, uncertain of how to say it. As the Effisian mayor was all too keen on lecturing him: he who speaks truth had best be swift of foot. "If we cut rations again, we should have enough for another two octaves. Maybe three." His own stomach growled at the prospect. Half-rations were already the order of the day.

If the idea phased the general, Tessel didn't show it. "With luck, one of the trains will break through by then." The barest wisp of a smile curled the edges of his thin lips. "And with luck, our betters won't break us by then."

Their betters, as Tessel liked to call them, were the nobles at the heart of his army. His generals. The supposed voices of his whims. Men like Ivon, and men much higher. While their soldiers might have had much love for Tessel, the nobles did not. A bastard, even a royal bastard, was nothing to blooded men.

There had always been a certain tension to the air from the very moment the Emperor called up his levies. Armies did not march in winter, and for good reason. Preparation aside, an army inevitably outran its supply trains and a winter army could scarcely forage for supplements. Starvation, and the diseases it brought with it, was a greater killer than swords ever were.

Things bards never sang about. Things Rurik had only lately learned.

Trouble had bloomed in earnest with the Emperor's death, however. After Leitzen, there was a split. In spite of his incompetence in the months leading up to their march, many turned to Lord Marshall Othmann as their commander, and he, for one, advocated cutting loose the majority of their levies for the remainder of the winter months. Small forces would be left to hold their earnings and the rest could return with the thaw.

Through the window, he saw a man bellowing from the stocks. Though the words were lost, their gist was easily deciphered. Across from him, another pair wriggled against the same fate. Had they been back home, people would have hurled fruit at them. Here, they could afford no such loss.

Tessel caught him staring. "Do not mind the rabble, Rurik. More feuding." He gave a dismissive flick of the wrist. "They will keep until morn."

Hoping to ease winter's burden, Tessel had divided the army. Many of the nearly 10,000 souls Othmann had originally commanded were sent north, ostensibly to burn and pillage and link up with Idasian forces scouring the coast, while others were sent south, to likewise plunder their way through the countryside to a beleaguered General Ernseldt. The rest scattered in a choking semi-circle about the lands approaching the Effisian capital, but Tessel would not release a single man from duty.

Men allowed the grace of home could scarce be expected to return, especially when the force of the call was in doubt.

Meanwhile, the Lord Marshall and the Bastard clashed, and not always privately. As yet, the will of the latter prevailed. But the only thing shielding him was the promise of a dead man and the thin assurance of promises made to that same corpse.

Rurik thought of the old man, wrinkled, pale, utterly ruined and fragile in death. No man could have looked less an emperor. More like a skeleton in armor. By now, he had probably reached Anscharde. He and the remnants of his guardsmen.

"What of Ivon? What news does he bring of the lot?"

"Would that I could say."

He thought of Ivon standing before him that morning and all the things that brothers might have said. Then—nothing. They shared a mother and a father. They no longer shared a name. For all the false smiles the man now showered him with, that fact always seemed to creep into the fore. When his brother looked on him, all Ivon saw was their father's end. The coward that should have ended in his place. Rurik had no doubt Ivon was glad the Bastard had taken such an interest in him. So he didn't have to.

It only hurt when he thought about it.

But his brother bloomed into brothers. His brothers spawned sisters. Sisters melded into wives, sons, daughters, and all that webbing of thoughts careened on the hand of a dead man, still watching him, still judging him, through all those beckoning eyes.

"Why did you come back?" he asked, in the dead of dreams.

"Well," Tessel ventured uneasily. "Men will what they will." A trace of jurti: the art of saying nothing yet sounding grandiose in the same breath. Perhaps moved by the uncertainty in Rurik's own eyes, though, the Bastard reached out and clapped him on the hand. "Besides, you're the only noble blood I should ever need."

Three months ago, he hadn't even known Rurik existed. In those days when blood still ruled day-to-day. Now, especially on Rurik's darker days, things like this had become commonplace, as if to say: *You are not just a part of something great. You belong,* and this was more than he could ever hope.

As he fumbled for a suitable reply, a knock on the door interrupted his thoughts.

Tessel eased back from him and barked entrance. A messenger entered without hesitation, a note gripped tight between greasy fingers. At a time, when the old man sat in Tessel's place, such a soul would have had to prostrate himself three times just to be given the right to speak.

"A rider, ser," the man said, offering the note with only the slightest inclination of his head. Bastards fell beyond the realms of the courts' archaic jurti. "Bearing the Imperial Seal, and with word from the capital."

Both men perked considerably. Only inklings had crept in from Anscharde over these long months.

Tessel reached out to take the message, but let it hang a moment, asking, "Didn't come with food did he?" His tone was only half-serious, but the messenger gravely shook his head all the same. Tessel muttered a disappointed "of course" under his breath and promptly dismissed the messenger. The young man looked only too glad to go. Rurik decided to join him.

Begging off by leave of matters to attend in camp, he rose to depart. Halfway to the door, however, Rurik was startled by the sound of Tessel's voice.

"Hold that thought, my friend." The Bastard's smile spread from ear to ear as his eyes leapt across the page. "Best say your vows. Our new emperor calls us home."

Chapter 2

He would forever after remember the smell of cinnamon and clove for the day they put his father to the flame. Cinnamon and clove. The perfumed court-stink of the dead and the dying and the weeping.

He stood in the grey-cast gloom, caressed by the warmth of the pyres, ringed by the wrinkled faces of the court's functionaries, courtiers, and sons. Mired in mud. He followed the procession with the son's dutiful eye, for all to see, but even then he knew the mud would stain his sandals. It would stain his sandals and the southron sway of his robes, and he would not look the emperor his colors deserved. Yet he would seem the bereaved, and the people would love him for it. So sayeth his wife. So mote it be.

All pomp for a people he knew nothing of. It seemed he was eight years old all over again, but Zelnig, his tutor, was no longer around to take him by the hand and whisper that his father would not do him harm. They were both dead now. The master and the servant.

Thirty years. Has it been so long?

He looked at his wife, bundled in the mourning layers, and still somehow resplendent for it. A tiny sable column, dark and fair and utterly possessed of the moment. His sacrilegious heart. No eyes turned back to him. Her voice, needling through his head, ordered him away, and he did, knowing she knew best. She wrapped herself a little tighter about his arm and leaned her head against his shoulder, like a widow might weep for her husband.

Everywhere, they always made the pair. The white prelate's robe hung loose about his thick form, weighted by the heaviness to the air. He wore no crown, save the pointed tower of a holy man's hat. Only the felt cloak, laced in eagles' splendor, burdened him as anything more than a man of the Patriarch's court. That and the eyes. The fawning, uncertain glimpses men always quailed before a god.

Thirty years they had kept him beyond the Empire. It was a second son's duty.

The first, they had the blood. They would bear the crown and the weight of nations on their shoulders.

The second took Assal into his heart and traded steel and gold for shields of psalms and jewels of the divine's own word. The second son always went into the south, where Assal spread his hands and kissed four corners of the ragged earth to make Ravonno—the princely states, his pact with man.

Then, his boy's eyes had looked at his new home with terror. Now, he looked on his old home with wonder.

But they didn't come here for him.

Every turn of the streets revealed still more people, spreading out in congregation. From rich to poor, the mob knew no boundaries, massing in the shadows of the buildings, hanging heads from windows and roofs, clambering over one another for a glimpse. Just a glimpse. Their eyes were bleary with wonder, and they crowded one another with abandon, but the true power of it, the unsettling horror of it, was how the man's body made them share the silence of the grave. The whole city seemed soundless, vacant, drained.

He could but wonder if it had been the same for his brothers. Shrouded in silk and pressed through the haunting eyes of the crowd. Yet somehow, he doubted it.

Gerome and Molin might have had their mourners. Joseph would have been given the solemn march of soldiers. Neither could have stolen them both, as their father had.

The procession stretched for hours. A stone-faced column of palace guardsmen formed its bulwark, dour and brooding in their black armor and dull, gold-trimmed capes. At the sides of the white-draped wagon that bore the Emperor came the pair that had seen his body safely home, Sers Viltenz and Seppelt, members of the distinguished Imperial Guard, scarcely distinguishable save for the white capes that marked their station. A third lay draped across the coffin. It was a monument to their place beside their lord, even in death. A monument to the one that had fallen beside him in battle—Ser Ettore.

When he thought hard enough, he could almost picture the man, white-haired long before age truly struck. A memento of his mother's time. Her brother, her guardian, her friend. A solid, dependable Ravonnen. Dead—ascended for it.

He glanced down the line of faces atop the high steps—the Hinnlisch Stairs—of the Imperial palace. Portly Portir, his father's youngest brother and regent for the crown, stood sweating beneath the sun. Beside him stood the general, Mauritz, wild-eyed and bearded in the way of the eastern provinces, the eldest of their trio, and the most dangerous. His eyes were spear points, ticking out over the ocean of souls.

Beyond and behind them were his own legion—brothers, sisters, nieces, nephews, all watching, all waiting. Had she been alive, their mother would have been among them, stout as any castle wall.

One child stood apart from the rest, "protected" by another pair of palace guardsmen. A veil of brown curls hung about her soft face. She had what the others assured him were *her* mother's eyes, tear-struck and amber and utterly uncomprehending.

Her mother could not be burdened to attend.

Her mother still hid after the death of *his* brothers.

The heathen empress.

Still, he did not let it consume him. As the holy Vorges intoned, all things with time would come.

Noon held the sun high in the clouds by the time the body reached the foot of the stairs. At the urging of Mauritz, he joined his family in the great descent, until the casket loomed before him, and the guardsmen spread away from them, to stand at rapt attention. Normally, a priest would say the holy words, the heads would bow, and the deed would be done. Now, Ingricus, his father's consul-priest, watched him with a mix of awe and indecision. His wife squeezed his hand. Mauritz turned to him, beckoning, as Portir started to move forward, only to catch himself, squinting, as though suddenly aware of a great wrong.

And then the eyes were watching him, truly watching him. Standing alone above the blackness, he took the torch from Ser Viltenz's outstretched hand. None of the Marindi nations bade their men be wasted in the earth.

"With dust," he cried to the crowd, surprised at the fervor of his own voice, "we are all! Of dust, we breathe! In dust, we may return!"

The cycle. Unbidden. Unbroken. It killed and it raised anew. It cast sons out and drew them back. One did not understand the Circle. They merely walked it.

He never even knew his father as he committed his body to the torch.

But when Leopold looked out on his people, he knew. Then the wailing began.

Chapter 3

The first days were the hardest. Essa woke in a cold sweat almost every night, though her body felt aflame. She curled in her covers and tried to hide from the night, but everything prickled and chided her, and no matter how she turned everything bubbled down to the simple, insatiable sense of need.

It was the most vicious part of arasyl. It worked its way into the bowels and made the body clamor for more. The higher the dose, the worse the craving.

There were hands in her dreams. Touching. Probing. She bade them to stop, but they did not listen to her. They touched her until her blood flowed, and it wouldn't stop. She did not want it, but she could feel the wetness, the incendiary itch of the drug bubbling up against her veins, and the voice in her ear would whisper: *"Flesh doesn't lie."*

She could see her body arch, but she could not look away. It wasn't her. The hands were on her and she didn't know who she was.

The clergy called it the Great Beast. Doctors sufficed to call it addiction. All Essa knew was that it made her very bones shudder. She ground her teeth even as she slept—when she was able to sleep—and woke with a mouth that felt like distant desert sands.

But Essa weathered it, as she weathered everything else. She huddled in her cousin's arms in the long winter nights, buried her head in his chest, and tried not to think. It was all she could do. She was not her father's child. It was not in her to simply lie down and die when the world reared its ugly head at her.

That did not mean she had the strength to look it in the eye.

Nor Rurik.

Months came and went, trickling into the holes of her being like so much rain. She might have hid beneath the clouds, had the others not forced her back into the light of life. They understood, as only family of the heart could, but they also knew what no victim could remember: the world kept moving.

Their camp grew to include another woman—a novelty not lost on her. Roswitte, the woman named herself, and she moved with an animal ease Essa found at first compelling. Like an uncertain puppy, however, she had lurked at the edge of her space, observing, waiting.

Roswitte—the Little Bear, as she heard the soldiers call her—was the first to break the silence. "Eyes like them are like enough to bleed a girl, she's not so careful," she quipped over the crackle of a dinner fire. "Go back to hiding, or say what you've a mind to say. No right soul can manage both."

After that, it was Roswitte that continued to push, prodding for time with her where the others offered only space. Any words they shared were forced, though, for Essa saw in her too much of the wild. She was a brute walked out of the gloom, thrust forcibly on society. She reminded Essa of home. Her true home. Yet she was Ivon's pet. That alone made her circumspect.

Regrettably, the bear came not alone. Falcons circled its trail, and it was not long before their lord Ivon extended a hand of friendship to them and bid them land. From the ranks of the Bloody Gorjes—sellswords that encircled the Company's camp—emerged three souls with which Ivon bade them make friendship and partnership. All served the same banner, he said. It was time they acted it.

She tried to avoid them as one might the plague, but one was persistent. Viveld, his name was. Where the others danced about with their questions and jibes, he established himself early, walking straight through the bad blood and the interrogations between the groups to offer his hand to her, and introduce himself.

"Killers need little introduction," she said, eyeing the hand waggling in her face.

It pulled the corners of his mouth higher. "Killer? Not yet, if'n it please. These here hands are set for horse flesh, starlight, and when you get caught riding some other fellow's horses, you don't have many options."

It was more candid than she was used to. She was taken aback by the honesty, as well, and struggled to maintain the mask of indifference too many tavern nights had taught her.

The man was young, with a beard yet shaping under the lengthening days, and a demeanor that oozed determination. She suspected it was not merely quick hands that had made his trade, while he had it.

"So what gave you wings?" she countered, sneering at the badge of a bloody falcon pinned to his breast.

"Alas," he said, in the same breath he dropped to the earth beside her. She scooted back, but he simply rolled onto his side to watch her. "There comes a time a man with an axe shouts: will it be the hand or will it be the time? I chose time and these fine sorts bought me up right quick."

She rolled her eyes. "For your hands?"

"My hands can do many things, but it's my head they wanted. Takes a special sort to work with animals. You have to be observant." With a knowing pride, he emphasized this with a prod of her knee. It was horribly forward. "Much like you, I should suspect."

The man proved an enigma. But a good one. His humor was easy, his demeanor unoffensive; where his friends needled and pried, he straddled the line, doing his best to play middle man and defuse any arguments between camps. What's more: he obviously sensed the hurt within her and greeted it with a childishness that disarmed her.

Only Voren did not take to him, and there were moments she caught the two in awkward silence, not so much weighing the measure of one another, but as if deciphering how best to be rid of a troublesome rat. Viveld laughed it off. Voren warned her off.

Essa huddled away from the lights of the camp, swaying to the gentle motions of the night. When the watery remnants of the night's soup had left her, she staggered back for the maze, reminding herself all the while to breathe.

She hated it. There was not a moment spent within those shadows she felt safe, or welcome. It felt better in the daylight—the whole camp did. When one could make out faces, one could bring humanity to them. Without, they were nothing but a churning nest of angry hornets, stinging eachother in addled disarray, for lack of anyone else to rage against.

It was nothing more than a feeling that gave her followers away. The undeniable, preternatural sense of being watched.

With forced ease, she slowed her steps and shrank against a canvas wall, concealing herself in the snores of the men therein. No one else was around. Yet she knew how to train her ears and to pick out the sounds that preceded men. Most would not have heard them. Their foot falls were like bare feet on cotton threads. Yet the thrum of them beat through her, accompanied by the whispering sashay of leather rubbing against leather. Between the baying of the crickets and the gawking chimes of men at play, such deliberate softness tweaked at the hairs of her neck.

She tensed, drawing into herself with the knives she kept close. She would have preferred to shoot from afar—with a bow, in a place more rooted in her element—but one could not pick all their battles. She drew down as deep into the shadows as she could, waiting until a figure shimmied down her trail and into view.

It was Viveld. He cast about for a moment and then, his eyes catching the barest glimpse of her silhouette, lit with such a fire as to be unmistakable as anything but pleasure. "Starlight!" he cried, and stepped toward her.

Essa eased the daggers back and stood upright. She craned her head, listening for more of the sounds, but as he neared, she could not be certain. He smothered all beneath his boisterousness.

"Why are you—"

Even as she stepped toward him, she saw the error of her trust. His fist snapped out and hooked her down. On instinct, an arm swung up to shield her from the worst of the blow, and she bent back, hoping for distance, but it was not alcohol on the man's breath, and he was quick. He snared her wrist and yanked her forward as she staggered, then flung her forward into the mud.

Essa kicked out at Viveld's shin, and screamed as loud as she could—the more bodies, she dared to hope, the more witnesses to deny him. Viveld grabbed at her leg with each successive kick, and lunged over the last, falling on top of her and wrestling her down.

It was in that same moment the others appeared, intent on taking their petty toll. A pair of Gorjes—in the flash of faces and fists and boots, she could make out shapes, register that she had seen them before, but nothing more. They beat her. She struggled and bit and screamed at them as they beat her, but they were relentless.

"Easy, girl. You already gave it away. What's another go of it, yeah?"

They had her hands down, over her head. Viveld craned over her like a ghoul, his boyish teeth gleaming even in the dark. "Some mares just have to be saddled before they calm the hell down, you know?" Then he started to work his pants down over milky legs.

There was rage—but the fear didn't truly hit until they covered her mouth. Because she realized in that moment that all her screams had been for nothing. Not ten feet away, a whole group of men had surely woken with the fury of that wail, and not one stirred.

This—this is the conviction of men among men.

The bodies bowed over her like trees bent to the rain. They closed her in, and there was nothing beyond them. The rattle of a belt buckle struck her as sharp as a logger's axe. Her senses wrapped around the sound, blind to all beyond, sectioning her off from the pain. There was only the fight. No matter how hard they struck her, she kicked and she writhed, determined not to submit.

For there were two deaths to die. There was a death of the body and a death of the self. They could take the one but she would not let them have the other.

Thunder pounded the air. Hot ash showered her as sparks of daylight scattered like coals among across the bowed men. In that instant, the pressure increased on her left arm. She started to scream again, but as abruptly it, and the pressure on her mouth, vanished. A dark shape whipped over her head. She heard its curses as it crashed.

As Viveld looked up in horror, the pressure on her legs let up as well. She curled in like a snake and kicked out, taking him square in the chest with both booted feet, satisfaction thrusting wind against her soles as she heaved him into the dust. The last man had risen. Essa rolled away and staggered to her feet. The bruises pulsed, but something deeper carried her.

Matted braids glanced between the turning of a broad hunter's knife. The third Gorjes man struggled with something on his belt as Roswitte swung in on him. When he backpedalled she snapped her foot into the crook of his knee. He lost his grip, swung instead. She drove the blade in and carved down. A spatter of blood struck Essa's cheek. The man howled, but his other arm snapped against the woman's gut. It drew back to swing again, but in the space a normal person should have stumbled, Roswitte only grunted, tore her blade free and swung it around into the tendons of the man's other arm.

It sawed through the flesh as a tanner to his trade. Yet it was the look that cooled the blood against Essa's skin. As Roswitte kicked the man down, she all but snarled as she leapt after him. The eyes were hot as the campfire ash still

29

flickering in the dirt, but ringed by ghosts as grim as any starving man. Rage danced there. Raw, unfiltered hate. The blade rose and fell. Rose and fell.

By then there were shouts rising all around them. Death broke what little covenant this place held and sent even cowards scurrying to do what was right.

The blond mountain that had sloughed off the other man traded blows with him still. They struggled, the Gorjes now a withered branch of the great mountain, and Alviss breaking it more with every rumbling gesture. Alviss caught him and twisted a limb down sharp. She heard the snap. Heard the man cry out.

She moved of her body's own accord, for Viveld, her hands shaking with the promise of what was to come. He had moved, though. Her mind, as though asleep, could not register the shift. Dazed, she twisted and saw him running as best as his drooping pants allowed. Running for Alviss.

She cried out to him, and Alviss turned, but the little man leapt on him, wrapping arms about his neck and pulling up hard. Alviss coughed and heaved an elbow back. Viveld folded like a reed, and Alviss swung an arm up behind his head in turn, then used the angle to pitch Viveld over his shoulder, on top of his squirming compatriot.

"They won't touch you 'gain, girl."

It took her a moment to realize it was Roswitte speaking. She was mere feet away, scarlet dripping off her blade. Essa stepped back, her mouth opening and closing against a soundless dread. In the huntress's face, no recognition of what she had just done.

The huntress stalked toward the others as Alviss anchored himself on Viveld's writhing form. "Please," the boy kept whispering. Every utterance was punctuated with a fist. They hammered his chest. Hammered his neck. "Please." They smashed his comely face and stole his words away. "Pease. Pease." Lips so swollen he couldn't even form the sound anymore, but still the punches fell. Until he stopped squirming. Until the fists were punching nothing but the emptiness of the grave.

Only then did Alviss stop. He wavered, as though the weight of his own breaths swayed him. He turned, meeting her eyes, and the blue of his seemed deeper then, like the blackest depths of a lake in the aftermath of rain. An empty reflection from which even the ripples had faded. Pain no battlefield could bring him. She knew that look was for her.

"Roswitte," he said, without turning from Essa. The huntress ignored him, advancing on the one man still crawling away. "Stop now. This is done."

Essa stepped toward her, bruises swelling into existence with every step. Only in the span of breaths recognized did the pain become real again.

Still Roswitte moved.

She would have killed again, feasting on the kills of that animal night, but for the thunder of the air. Armed and armored men of the Ulneberg fell on them from two directions, forcing themselves between the killers and the dead. Their line was interspersed with the curious and the newly emboldened, creeping from their tents, forming a mass of crowing, gawking whispers. Sound swam the space between tents, and as long guns leveled on Roswitte, Essa thought the crescendo of blood would go on.

A step backward. Then another. The woman scowled defiantly at all around her before she let her blade slip and topple to the earth. Alviss closed his eyes and bowed his head as if to prayer.

"What in the Maker's name happened here tonight? What happened?"

"Animals," Essa answered as she sank to her knees in the dirt, hands pressed to the back of her head. "They circle the herd, searching for the weakest. But sometimes the herd won't let them go."

The arrival of Ivon's men were the only thing that saved that final Gorjes.

The next day, Alviss and Roswitte were flogged for the crime. Publicly. The huntress had Ivon's ear and Rurik had Tessel's. For anyone else, the punishment might have been death.

Strung up beside them was the surviving Gorjes man, his back torn to pieces by a whip. When the time came to pull him down, it was other Gorjes that did it, and there was not one among them that didn't turn looks like ice upon her distant observation. It only furthered her sense of isolation.

Part of her asked if there weren't something about her that attracted such madness.

All around her, the world bloomed brown and muddied with the noon, and Starlet bayed beneath her, disagreeably grinding a hoof through the muck. The gesture was enough to make her wince. Ever since Essa's recovery, Starlet had gained a terrible stubborn streak, rebelling, no doubt, over the perceived snub her master had delivered through the long bout of confinement to bridled walks or stall-based imprisonment.

If only one could explain vertigo to a horse.

She stroked her horse's neck to calm her and whispered assurance in her ear even as she bade the little black mare on. Like her, she was a wild thing, unused to such keeping. She did not like the stalls, and she was not particularly fond of the other horses. Some of the fault of those manners likely lay with her, but Essa did what she could, when she could. Still, Starlet wanted to run the open plains. She wanted to stretch her legs and feel the wind rustling through her hair. It did not particularly seem to matter what her master wanted.

But she listened, in the end. She bowed her head to Essa's coaxing and twisted around in the frost-licked field, back toward the farms. It was early in the season yet, but the farmers had begun their toiling. The farmers and no one else. There were no steel lines on the horizon. No dust clouds stirred by marching hordes.

"Where are you, little sparrow?" Rowan called.

Her cousin walked beside her, tugging his scarf a little tighter as the wind kicked up. He followed her eyes, but no longer her thoughts. Too much chaos, she supposed.

"Far and away," she muttered. Yet she still had the piece of mind to study the plains for crags, lest her horse meet the same fate as Rowan's.

Further back, Alviss and Chigenda loped after them, and beyond them, the idiot wardens Gunther and Marvelle—Bloody Gorjes, headstrong and tight-lipped, and always smiling like they shared a joke between them. Thieves, she suspected, with a relationship likely older and more profitable than the war had shown them.

She was the only one ahorse. Alviss preferred to walk. Gunther and Marvelle had never been able to afford such a creature in their miserable lives—which was not to say, of course, that Essa had actually paid for Starlet. Chigenda had lost his to battle and Rowan to lamed foot. The men of the camp had seen Rowan's carved up and served, as they did with any dead animal. At the time, Rowan had looked as though he would be sickened by it. Essa still was.

One hand gently patted her thigh and she tried her best to smile for her cousin. Rowan's amber eyes shone back, even as he gave her a playful pinch. Love, she supposed.

"You know," Rowan prodded her, "somewhere under there is a beautiful woman that remembers the worth of her cousin's gestures. I would settle for the child that laughs at the absurdity of those gestures."

He often hid heart behind his jokes. Just as she did. A dear heart—it was a shame it was confined to such a frail form. Months of rationing had not done him well.

Frowning, she called back over her shoulder. "Alviss, have you any more of that jerky?"

The deep lines of the Kuric's weathered face twitched thoughtfully beneath his thick, gray-blond beard. He wiggled a finger at her and reached into one of his satchels, for the remnants of Rowan's beloved steed. Marvelle and Gunther looked on greedily all the while. She scowled back at them, but so long as they only looked…

Rowan shook his head. "Darling—"

"Shush now," Essa snipped.

Alviss walked up to them and held out a hand in offering. She took it in hers, gingerly, but disappointment blossomed swiftly. It was little more than a bite. She looked to Alviss expectantly, but his face took on a severe quality as he cast away.

"Only one bit left. That—tomorrow."

The man knew how to stretch things out, to be sure, but Essa couldn't help but ponder the virtue of it. Today or tomorrow, it made little difference. The hunger would come all the same. Regardless, she clapped the old man's broad hand between her tiny fingers and graced him with sincere thanks. Unphased, he nodded, and swiftly turned back to their trailing Zuti. Marvelle called after him, begging. Essa didn't look, but she could imagine the dark gaze that followed.

Nothing like the frigid stare of a Kuric berserker to catch a man's breath.

She passed the bit of jerky to Rowan, all the while ignoring his protests. He took, eventually, as he always did. He ate it and he savored it, and then he still looked pale.

Better than the roasted dog the camp followers had taken to selling, at any rate.

Overhead, grey clouds stirred a heaviness to the air. It bristled, with that energetic tingle that so often set her head to pounding. Sunlight pressed through in fleeting rays, illuminating the wide expanse of flat land. There was nothing quite so seemingly barren as fields mired between growths. Nothing quite so empty feeling as a land with nothing hidden—a place of plains and gentle hills. One could have gone for miles and it would have been the same. Clusters of civilization broke the monotony—made it worse. One could see them spread about the horizon.

Sometimes, she dreamed of the Ulneberg—of stretching out beneath its great boughs. A person could lose themselves there. It had been too long. It would be longer still.

Most of Idasia shared this present visage. The great expanse, they called it. Walk between the borders, and one would never know it. Idasia and Effise, they were not so different. It was only men that made them so. Always men.

They trotted past the farmers and they trudged past their homesteads, most stripped bare of anything more than necessity. That was the foraging of the grand army of the Empire, now. She tried not to make eye contact as they went. She did not like the pity that stared back. Pity and hate.

Powerlessness was never becoming.

Essa bundled her cloak about herself and tried not to think of sleep. She rubbed the crow's feet from the corners of her eyes and closed them to the feeling of frost gathering along her arms. Wet frost, for it all stank of the rain to come. The smell of insomnia.

Nights in camp were always the hardest.

At a time, fire would have warmed her, but with the melting of the snows, Tessel had forbid any fire to preserve grass and hay for the gryphons and horses. They had long since run out of any wood, and though some men whispered of smashing homes for kindling, their general had outlawed mistreatment of the townspeople. Pasłówska, he said, was a proving ground for all that would come. Men bettered themselves not in women's blood, but in steel and tribulation.

As she opened her eyes, Essa found her gaze drifting beyond the ring of their own tents. A pair of sellsword Gorjes roamed one of the footpaths nearby. One of them hooked her with his gaze, elbowing his compatriot as they shared some barb. Bloody-taloned falcons loping through the dark. If any wished to dirty their hands in the honey of their enemies, it was probably they. She looked away, to icy laughter. She suppressed a shudder.

Caught between such birds of prey and their kills she felt, to some extent, as though sailing down the Marali Sea to walk oneself into a Zuti city. Which was to say, utterly foreign. There was no hiding. Soldiers of all colors looked at her like something less than what she was—and eyed with intentions somewhat more than what she desired. They saw the swell of her hips and pointedly ignored the rest.

The camp followers helped ease the tension, but some men's eyes still wandered.

Somewhat absentmindedly, she brushed the gangly lengths of her hair over her ears and tried her best not to scratch at the growing itch beneath the rough texture of her skin.

As if being a half-breed weren't trouble enough.

At least the Gorjes knew their place. Or had learned it.

All men, it seemed, had dark possibility within them.

When she closed her eyes, she could still feel his touch. She could still hear his voice. The eyes—they said they loved her. Even as Rurik's hands shed her dignity.

Alviss stood beside her in the grass. She cocked her chin just high enough to catch the bottom of his. He held a cloak to her, the lakes of his eyes warmly beckoning.

"Come," he said. "Dreams before darkness."

Without a word, she took his cloak and she took his hand, and let him guide her back to her tent. To nightmares.

Morning, unlike night, brooked routine. They rose with the horns. They ate en masse. They hungered for more but were not given it, and spoke with Captain Haruld to see if they drew lots for the day's scouts. If they did, they trudged again across the empty plains. If they did not, they spent their hours trying not to think of their stomachs.

With this morning came word that rations would be cut again. It did not go over well in camp. Men fell to bickering long before the supplymen ever reached them all. Voices shouted over the din of the camp such that the air sweltered. Rain drizzled on the tensions and the canvas, and made mockery of their paths. Essa breathed it in and tried to let it wash her away.

"It's a mite pissy out there," Roswitte eloquently noted as she stepped into their camp late that morning. She shook out the hood of her cloak and stood slogged and sodden before them. Like a drowned rat, in her way.

The rest of the the Company were splayed around what might have been, in gentler times, the foundations of a campfire. Some nights, Rowan stared so hard into those unused lines, Essa suspected he wished to test the capacity for mental kindling. Suffice to say, while some—as she—were content for a morning without labors, others all but leapt for the break in the monotony that the forester's visits brought, as infrequent as they were.

Rowan strangled a dry laugh. "As though it were good before. Starvation has that effect."

"More'n that," the forester said, largely ignoring him. "Lot of folk scurrying for Tessel's door. There's something else, something—"

"Effise?" Alviss asked. He paused from whetting the head of his bardiche.

"Battel?" their dark-skinned compatriot asked from beside him.

For Chigenda, the word almost seemed to come with a sort of divisive pleasure. He, more than anyone else, had chafed from idleness. But it wasn't the food, or disease, or any of the countless things that plagued the other soldiers. For Chigenda, Essa sometimes thought, it was earnest disappointment in the prevailing of logic in their war.

"No. Mayhaps. They said there was a messenger—" Roswitte turned, twisting her gaze on Essa mid-sentence. "And how're you this morning, child? Speaking?"

Essa never knew quite how to reply to the woman's jibes. So instead, she stared. The forester's sharp smile faltered after a moment. "Well," she said, "comes and goes, I suppose."

"Like a little somethin' else I know," Marvelle's high voice called. Essa turned to find the squat man loping into camp alongside his long-faced associate. They didn't sleep in the Company's camp, but they were never far. Not while the Gorjes' camp encircled their own. Grins in place, the pair moved toward them with all the grace and poise of Kalavri jackals. "How's the errant knight-lord, eh? Pull youself from his coattails for little ol' us?"

"Fine," Roswitte said tightly. She flicked her gaze to Alviss, seemed to share some dark thought, and twisted back on Essa again. The woman caught her by the wrist, nearly yanking Essa off her feet in her haste to go. "But I'm taking this one for a touch."

"If you—"

"Alone," Roswitte snapped through Rowan's interruption. Its vehemence was enough to stay him. "We won't be long."

Roswitte wasted no time in camp and Essa couldn't rightly blame the woman. Behind them, she could hear the Gorjes moving in, and Gunther's distinctly throaty tones as he inquired after what he dubbed "the peaches." The grind of Alviss's axe began anew.

But if the air was tense in camp, it was little better between the pair of them. Essa found her times with Roswitte to be awkward. Silence pervaded the space between them, despite the forester's occasional efforts, and Essa was often left with the distinct feeling that the woman was forcing it. She sensed Alviss's hand in it, but she would never say as much.

Officially, Roswitte was sworn to Ivon Matair, ostensibly the lord of Verdan since his father's execution. She slept in his household's tents and could often be seen going about his work. Many of the men snickered about it—some of those from Verdan liked to call her Matair's bear—but no one doubted her dedication. Nor did they trade their barbs with her directly. Still, between her duties, she could occasionally be found at their own camp. What drew her there time and again since Rurik had left was beyond Essa.

Grudgingly, however, she had to admit the extra feminine presence was appreciated, at times. Though calling Roswitte a woman was a…stretch.

For her part, Essa never knew quite how to address the woman. She guessed Roswitte was at least twice her age, if not older—she certainly looked older. Time had little to do with it, however. The way she moved. The way she acted.

There was a perpetual tension to her that often left her seeming wearied and worn. She never spoke of it, though. A testament to her strength, perhaps. Or something of a shield. For all that the woman was, she never spoke of herself.

She could also pull a longbow back to full draw. A feat, to say the least. And Essa had already seen her skill with a knife.

Sometimes, she seemed to look at Essa as though she were very far away, or as though she saw someone else in her eyes. It was unsettling.

"So," the forester ventured as they breached the ring of Gorjes tents, "how are we feeling today?"

The question they always asked. Essa shrugged her shoulders and focused on a man playing fetch with one of the camp hounds. It seemed absurd, watching a grown man in rings running laps with a bloodhound. *Best take care of it*, she thought regardless. If there was one thing to be said for the starvation it was this: it had certainly cut down on the number of wild dogs.

They went on. A man emptied his waste bucket at their feet. Near the gates of Pasłówska, another man fell to bickering with his brother over a tack of tasteless ikir.

"Should we stop them?" Essa asked quietly. All around them, their brothers-at-arms either watched with a grim sort of bloodthirstiness or turned away in disgust.

Roswitte cocked her head at the men, then rolled her eyes past Essa. "No." She stepped around them and continued on into the row of tents. Essa lingered a moment, hesitant, then trotted after her. When she caught her, the forester only shook her head. "Soldiers will be, child."

There was something in the way she said it. A snap of rebuke. Essa bit her tongue against a venomous retort and narrowed her eyes to the trail.

"Where are we going?"

It was Roswitte's turn to shrug. "Where ears find no purchase."

At first, she thought they were headed to town. To her lord, perhaps, and the blistering tongues of his men-at-arms. The thought left her stomach lurching. Rurik was oft nearby, like a lovesick puppy, and unlike him the rest of his family couldn't stand her.

But they passed the gates and skirted the majority of the tents, cutting toward the stables that formed the western edge of camp. Pages loitered there, mostly, to tend their lords' steeds. A few guards lingered.

As they headed inside, the forester grabbed a pair of brushes from a pot near the door and led Essa toward her own horse, Starlet.

Roswitte paused before the stall, holding out one of the brushes to her. "Lord Ivon set me to tend his horse and check his accounts this morning," Roswitte explained. "Yours seemed in need of the company." She reached out a hand and plucked the lock on the gate.

They spent nearly the next hour brushing out the tangles in Starlet's hair, washing her, and checking her for fleas. Every now and then, Roswitte tried to work a question into the routine, asking after the others, after the Gorjes, and most importantly, after herself. She asked about her distance from Rurik, about the fights—mostly the fights, and the tone of it seemed to indicate worry. Again, Essa had the impression she was being spied upon. For whom, exactly, she could not say, but given that she was Ivon's creature, and Ivon was Rurik's brother, she had a dark assumption, and that assumption bid only terse answers.

When she asked the forester, in turn, about her interest, Roswitte only scowled and returned to brushing. "Curiosity," Roswitte answered, "need not always rise from darkness."

Essa put herself into her task, tried to feel comfort in the closeness of her steed, and pointedly ignored the woman.

"You…fancied him, didn't you?" Roswitte eventually asked. By then, they were coaxing the last tangles from Starlet's tail.

It was a struggle not to scream.

"I ask only because of what I see, girl. And Alviss, you know, when the old man speaks of you…"

She thrust her brush into the bucket of growing slop, wetted it in the dirty water, and thrust the bristles hard against a particularly thick knot. Starlet whinnied unappreciatively.

"Girl. Look at me." Essa made it a point not to look up. She coiled her fingers in the tuft of hair and tried to unthread it. "You have to know he asks after you. In his sheepish way. And the way he hangs—you're being overly cruel, aren't you?"

Essa felt her hand shake. She had to narrow her breaths. The woman knew nothing, she kept telling herself. *Nothing-nothing-nothing.* If she did, she wouldn't have asked that. No one would have asked that.

"You're both pups and he's a fine one to hitch a star to. What could he have possibly done?"

Another voice saved her from having to answer that. Even as she glared up at the flustered woman, Essa heard her name rise an octave above the bustle of the stables. She followed its contours to the long lane between the stalls and settled on the lanky baker-savior hastening toward them. Roswitte followed her gaze, but said nothing, contemplating.

She decided then to a play a card from her watcher's own hand.

"Essa," Voren repeated as he neared, a smile stretched from cheek to cheek. "I—"

Before he could say another world, she launched herself at him. Catching him mid-stride, she threw her arms around him, crying "Voren" and clasping him tight. "Oh, I told you to meet me hours ago. This just won't do." Stepping between the boy and her watcher, Essa meant to keep his confused look from giving her away. Then, twisting back to Roswitte, she exclaimed, "Oh we simply must be off. You will lock the stall when you go, yes?"

The forester's jaw clenched, but she nodded sternly. Her dark eyes fastened on Voren, as though searching out a weak link.

"If you wish," she muttered.

"Thank you for the morning, all the same," Essa said. Then, squeezing at her savior's arm, she bid him flee. Resisting only long enough to part a hailing farewell to Roswitte, Voren trailed her like a limp rag doll, without question.

"I don't think she likes me," Voren murmured as they stepped back into the light.

With a snort, she replied, "She doesn't like anyone. Now—what is it?"

"I—" Voren started, fidgeted, and took her by the hand. She flinched away and he spread his hands in apology, but motioned all the same toward the other side of the stables. Following his lead, she slipped with him into the shadows, bathing them in the chill of the gloom. She shuddered softly, looking away as the baker took a spot against the wall.

"I came to tell you they're cutting rations again. If you've got any leftovers, I'd horde them well. And—and they're putting extra guards on the tents, just in case. I can't—that is to say, I don't think I can get us anymore."

That he had managed under already staunch scrutiny—and Rurik's undoubtedly knowing scrutiny, no less—was testament enough to his dedication. Such that she had never asked him to take.

She flicked her feline gaze on him. "That? That's all over camp, Voren. Is that all?"

The baker flinched a bit at the bite in her words. She didn't mean to be so snappish with him. Roswitte's words had her on edge.

"I'm sorry. I don't mean to be—"

"It's alright," he interjected, waving it off as though it were nothing. As he always did. That only made it worse. "And—no. I wanted to say—" Voren leaned close, swallowing hard against the sodden air. "I want you to take extra care. It's getting—well, they're getting rowdy. Restless. There's talk some of the nobles might…" He paused. "Desert."

Essa became suddenly very self-conscious. She glanced over her shoulder, feeling the eyes already on her. Several of the stable hands were watching them, all wolfish grins. Rolling her eyes against the implication, she took the baker once more in hand and dragged him toward the outskirts of camp.

Rain had swamped the trail to the tents of the camp followers. It stood as a muddy river, rolling perpetually downhill and undoubtedly flooding more than a few out of any semblance of a home. Nature always found a way, messy as it was. Standing there, at the edge of the trail, Essa sighed and turned back to Voren. A few guardsmen loitered near the river as well, watching and commenting on the plight. For once, she was glad their own tents were pitched much further afield.

"What do you mean desert?"

"I mean just that. I-I've been in their tents, I mean, handing out the rations. I heard the talk. It's—"

"It's rumor is what it is, and if things are really as bad as you make them rumor's like to get you killed."

Forcing her voice to a whisper, she asked, "Where? Who said these things?"

"People," he blubbered. When her stare lengthened to points, however, he tentatively added, "You're the one that told me rumor'd get me killed!"

"You're learning," she added without mirth. "But now's hardly the time. Did you—did you take this to Rurik, at least?"

Exasperation flashed into lines of anger before the boy's eyes flicked away. He rolled his jaw, started to say something, then simply shook his head. He had never said anything about that night with Rurik, but Essa had the sneaking suspicion he knew. Some men had perfected poker faces—Voren didn't. And since then he had been there as only Rowan had before. Sitting by her through the long nights—even if she never said a word. He brought her compresses when she took to fever. Apologized for things he had no hand in, simply because he was a man.

Alviss, she knew, was not so overly fond of the boy, but she was grateful for him. He helped her through the hate and he never questioned. He let her move at her own pace. Even if it sometimes drew her ire on him. Rowan said Voren loved her. Sometimes she wondered if that weren't true. Though she questioned the form it took.

Rurik—she couldn't even begin. When her eyes met his, she did not see the apology. She saw hurt, certainly, and confusion—mostly confusion. Like all men, he could not understand the nature of his crime, but held the wherewithal to blame it on someone else.

Perhaps that was why she took to Voren so heavily. Try as he might, and age as he would, when he looked on her it was not with a man's eyes—but a boy's.

"Voren…"

"Es. Listen. Perhaps I would but Ivon—"

Words trailed to the sloppy clop of horses' hooves. Of beckoning shouts. Voren strained to hear, to see—Essa strained only to tell where they came from. There were many, she knew. The hooves were like wet thunder. It was more enthusiasm than she had heard in a moon's turn.

Craning onto the tips of her toes, she caught a glimmer beyond the tents. As the whores crept to bear, hoping for sight of new fare, she saw the glint of armor coming around the other side, moving in a broad arc to take them nearer to the town in the quickest manner. They bore no banners, but the horses marked them as outriders—scouts. Fear cramped in her stomach at the thought of such fury. It could only mean one thing.

"Get back to the mess, Voren."

He gaped at her, undaunted. "What is it?"

"I think the war's found us."

She could see her sentiments echoed in the faces of more than a few. Without any word from those riders, anxious men pawed at wet steel or grabbed for their long guns—guns that would be useless in such swamp. Essa remained, even as Voren tugged at her. She stared out beyond the camp, scanning the hills for any sign.

It was not a big thing—and that's what caught her. A train less than a dozen strong strung itself out along one of the low rises, plunged on, and disappeared again beneath the canvas walls. She cursed, for such a fleeting glimpse. But she had seen all she needed to see. Banners. Banners and men to hold them, but not enough to issue a battle cry. Less than a dozen against all the might of Idasia. In that moment, the knots in her stomach twisted into something else entirely.

It wasn't war, she realized. It was a parley.

* *

Nothing made old wounds throb like the thunder and the rain. Be they man or men.

Rurik flexed his shoulder, wincing against the throb it produced. It was like he had simply slept wrong, tensed the muscles—but it was an ache that would not abate. When the doctor had proposed it was time to remove his sling, he had looked on incredulously. Berric—one of Tessel's appointed guards—had distracted him with a smile and a pilfer of his blade. Even as he turned to grab at it, he realized his mistake. It was Berric's eyes—they were the giveaway.

Rather than simply remove the sling, the doctor gave his arm a straightening yank. There was a little pop and a large flare—but it was gone, mercifully gone, even before his yelp had subsided. The bones were nearly settled, the man informed him. The remainder just needed a little stretch. A pat on his back and a grunt of thanks, and the doctor sent him on his way. But it still throbbed with the storm. He suspected it would throb long after.

Berric was in the midst of trying to make it up to him—alcohol mercifully involved—when word of the riders came in. Ten in all, bearing the colors of

Effise's bandit-prince himself—Leszek. The white horse's head, stretched above the bloodied red of his people's sea seemed an ominous marker to Rurik, as did the thunder marking their approach, but he had hastened all the same to meet them on behalf of his lord.

Several of the nobles had intercepted them, however, and stood poised to make terms without their commander. The Effisians had been herded into the town's tavern, the occupying soldiers ejected for the time being. What men remained were the lords' own men-at-arms, Rurik noted with a grimace, and they tried their best to bar his way. There was something to be said for a boy's stubbornness, however, and he raised offense loud enough to draw some of Berric's fellows.

Yet even as the men-at-arms were circled, they hemmed and hawed before him, brandishing pikes and swords and obstinately refusing to move. It was only the timely arrival of his brother Ivon that at last broke the stalemate. With all the air of a high nobleman, the handsome knight ordered the men aside—and they did it, whether they wished to or not. Rurik pressed in after him, nearly clutching at his heel, though Ivon only grudgingly acknowledged it.

Inside, the hearth had been lit to compensate for the gloom outdoors. Windows had been shuttered and the Effisian party had filed into the back of the room, with a host of tables, chairs, and bitter Idasian noblemen between them and the door.

Rurik might have expected Ser Huwcyn Ibin. A bull of a man, his orange-red hair made him shine among the rest of his grungy fellows, even more so than his girth. His father's title made him one of the greatest of the assembly in camp, and what was worse was that he knew it.

It was the presence of another, more stubbly figure that set him immediately on edge, however. Ser Falk of Torruck. The man was neither high nobility nor a diplomat, and his cleft chin was lasting memory of the battle at Leitzen, where the army had lost its emperor and he had lost both of his sons. For the moment, the knight stood scowling and ringed by men of hopefully better sense, but for how long Rurik could not say. And in a room of nearly two dozen members of the Imperial nobility, he doubted Falk was the only one with an axe to grind.

Who he did not see—and more's the pity for it—was Lord Marshall Othmann. Surely with so many nobles cloistered around like baying hens, even that high fool could not have missed the Effisians' approach. What's worse: he suspected it was, like so many of the man's petty ploys, somehow meant to be a dig at Tessel. If anything happened to these men, after all, it would be on Tessel's head, as acting commander.

Noting who stood armed and who, sensibly, did not, Rurik hastily pressed from his brother's side. Swallowing, he found it difficult to wet his throat, but resolved to speak his piece in spite of the many eyes leveling on him. Here, in this camp, he kept trying to tell himself they were as equals. It didn't stop his hands from shaking.

Peaceably as could be, he announced himself, all the while inching nearer to the embassy. "Lords, good men of Effise, it is a pleasure. On behalf of Lord Kyler Tessel, I welcome you to our camp. I trust our reception has been—" He hesitated as Huwcyn's great bulk shifted first into, then from his path. Inclining his head to the man, he finished, "graciously delivered."

One of the soldiers—Rurik quickly identified this as the captain for the way the other men looked to him—leaned over to a squirrely, robed man, whispering something in their own take on the Marindi tongue. The fidgeting ambassador, curiously devoid of any of the gold or other fineries that typified his station, cocked his head slightly to the side, nodding and watching. His eyes roamed Rurik, unabashedly appraising him. He whispered something back to the guardsman and, straightening, stepped forward from the protection of steel.

The man was tall. Rurik was not the tallest of people, but he was a man grown, and yet the Effisian ambassador stood a head—if not more—above his own, nearly of a height with Alviss, though with none of the bulk behind it. He looked down his long nose at Rurik—deliberately, as it turned out.

"Does his lordship send a page to do his diplomacy?" he asked in Idasia's own grizzled tongue. A mad flush seized Rurik. To his dismay, he heard the question answered by a few snickers from the crowd of noblemen. The Effisians, however, stood still as stone.

Before Rurik could answer, Huwcyn of all people stepped to his defense, further undermining him.

"This is Rurik Matair. And on the word of Huwcyn of Thorinde, I do attest he is the attendant of the marshall. You can be certain he speaks with his tongue. We all speak for the Empire, grace. And we all listen to Effise."

Huwcyn's frog-like eyes flickered down on him, and back to the diplomat, glittering with amusement. *Well, I walked into that*, Rurik brooded bitterly. Behind those eyes, though, there was no sign of any support forthcoming. While he spied Berric fingering the hilt of his blade, no one else seemed terribly appalled. Rurik thought he saw his brother move a step closer, but it might as easily have been his imagination.

The diplomat nodded his assent, and bowed low in accordance with jurti. "A pleasure, Your Grace." Straightening, he beamed a yellow-toothed smile as he continued. "Serene Effise and His Highness, the High Prince Leszek, send their blessings to you, noble warriors. I, Franciszek Bazylski do bear them to you. Much blood have you spilt, and seen spilt in turn. You have come deep into Effise and her soil has welcomed many of your children to her womb. Yet His Highness has seen your mercy to his cities, and in honor of the great Emperor Matthias Durvalle, He Who Rides wishes to discuss terms."

It was like the air was sucked clean from the lips of every man of the room. It went dead. Then murmurs seeded, a little tide rolling back from the brink. Rurik blinked, looked first to his brother—cold, rigid, unmoved—then to Huwcyn, and back. The lanky diplomat was smiling.

"This best, perhaps, conducted in private. I am sure—"

"Terms?" a voice blurted from the back of the room. "I'll show them their goddamned terms!"

Damn that man. Ser Falk was already moving.

One of his fellow noblemen stretched out an arm to hold the bereaved father, but Falk struck him with a mailed fist and barreled through two other idle men in his path. In him, Rurik had a vision of a bull with head and horns lowered.

A shape slid in front of him, shielding him, hand going to steel, and Rurik hesitated for a fleeting second on this brother's gesture. *Too long*, he cursed. Falk closed fast. "Berric," Rurik cried, while lamenting his own lack of blade.

Berric, too, was already on the move. Sword sweeping, the soldier shoved through other nobles to thrust himself squarely in Falk's path. Falk didn't hesitate. His saber clattered against Berric's guard, but the soldier held his ground. The calm soldier's blade danced circles around the furious swipes of its opponent, bringing Berric close enough to smash Falk's face with the hilt. The grayed veteran staggered, bloodied, but still he might have gone on, had not two of his fellows seized him. They bore him to the ground, shouting curses, and tore the blade from his grip.

Shoulders sagging with shallow breaths, Berric only slowly resumed his posture. Stepping close to Rurik, he sheathed his blade in accordance with jurti, but he never took his eyes off Falk. Not even as they bundled him toward the door. The curses stalked him out.

Breath broke in a tense flood from Ivon, and without a spared glance for his brother, the young lord eased back into the crowd. The ambassador, for his part, looked mortified by the display. Grimacing, Rurik couldn't help but wonder if the fool had damned any hope for talks. Not that reconciliation seemed quite possible in his mind.

Even as he apologized, however, one interruption begot another, and one of Tessel's messengers arrived to announce him. Rurik felt the words slip right from his tongue as everyone turned to address the proper commander. Those same words sank down as heavy knots into his gut. *Perfect.* He no longer had any place, and given how badly the last few moments had gone it was probably for the best.

Demeaned as a child. Blades to parley. Imagine if I had a whole hour to command.

Tessel, in spite of the bagged eyes, looked almost regal in his cavalry cuirass and gryphon-embroidered tabard. He watched them all in the remote manner more befitting of an owl, but he marched straight through the crowd for the diplomat without pause. His soldiers loitered at the door, but two other men accompanied him to the meeting. To his left, aged and crooked beneath his linens, Rurik recognized Pasłówska's chief burgher and mayor. Erim—Baron Pordill of Lucretsia—stood sleek and silvered to Tessel's right, time having stricken the black strands from his soft features, but none of his fatherly qualities.

At the diplomat's feet, Tessel bowed precisely as low as jurti commanded. "It is my honor to receive you, Your Grace," he said. Only then, under a strict eye, did he take in the rest of the Effisians men, terminating on Messar Bazylski with a straight smile. "My condolences I was not here to meet you myself. I was delayed en route, but I trust between them my emissaries were more than capable." He spared a glance for Huwcyn, the men trading soldiers' curt nods.

"Would that all your noblemen were so…disposed," Bazylski bobbed uncertainly.

Tessel, nodding as much to himself as to the diplomat, turned his unyielding gaze to Rurik. "You may go now, Rurik. Knights, lords, you shall all go as well. My lord Huwcyn, if you would be so kind as to join me, we shall retire these discussions upstairs."

Curtly, cleanly, he dismissed them all. Some of the men seemed less than obliged to go, but none honestly raised the specter of doubt. For that, Rurik was glad. There were only so many embarrassments a man could take. One man had already made a mockery of them for the day—another would make it seem the whole army stood upon the brink. For that matter, Rurik would not have put it past Othmann to have guaranteed Falk's presence here. That Tessel had come without him, well…he hoped the slight fit the crime.

Hardly the image of unity one needed for such discussions.

Whether they understood that, or feared Tessel's rage, or even Berric's skill with a blade, the noblemen filed back into the rain under a veil of darkly worded gossip, and Rurik with them. He looked for Ivon, but through some manner of foresight, his brother was one of the first out the door. He might have sought him, but Berric caught him first, patting his good shoulder as he leaned in close.

"Watch your back. That one's not like to be sated," Berric whispered, before he shut him out into the rain. Him and all the other nobles, with all their whispers between them.

With the spring came rain, with the rain came mud, and with the mud came war's greatest killer: disease.

Throughout the camp there was evidence of it, but nowhere more than the grey-backed canvas with its doctors and its wailing dead-to-be. The fact of it terrified Rurik as little else could. For it was more than mere death. It was the thought of otherwise strong men, terrifying men, who could plunge into a sea of lead and steel and rise still human, suddenly reduced to infants. Crying out in their sleep. Clutching for those toiling over them. Crumbling, inch by human inch.

Again the dark days came to him. Flashes of substance, taken in too many scattered lumps to mean anything as one. Teeth loomed above his shoulder in the guise of saws, and behind them the dark eyes, hushed tones. Alviss sat before his bedside, holding his hand and snarling wolf-like into their midst, and the phantoms scattered as sheep. The voice, continuous through his mind: *Return to the muck. Return.* Ghost-like spasms of sympathy curled through his shoulder. A hand idly fingered at the old coin he always kept in his pocket.

That voice was known to him.

Accursed nostalgia. Yet was it not nostalgia that called him to the Eagles' camp? He slunk past the sprawling tent like a dog with its tail between its legs. When he glanced inside, he envisioned his mother reaching out to him, pale-faced, blood still slick between her thighs. There were some ghosts he could not face. Say what men would.

It was midday, so most were well and truly about the work of the camp. For its size, the camp was surprisingly simple in layout, its lanes easily navigable. Martial priorities, he supposed. Sections were divvied up by province of origin, with companies of sellswords attached to whichever lords had made the acquaintance of their services. Naturally, these twenty some odd sections were then split into the myriad regions that made up each province, but one truth always held: the attending lords always lay pretty-as-you-please packed into the center of their people's mass. Some of these places were fortified encampments in their own right, but most were open, so long as one held no blood feud with any therein.

The Company of the Eagles—though one could hardly call so few a company—remained settled in the boundaries of the Jaritz contingent, near the eastern boundaries of the larger encampment. They were not close to Ivon and his fellow bannermen. They remained instead where they always had been: smack in the center of another camp of sellswords, the Gorjes. Originally, it had been a ploy by Rurik's father to keep them out of sight. Now it was merely that no one knew where else to put them.

Few troubled about his path home and he kept his eyes from those who did. Rurik found he preferred it that way.

He wove between the walls of canvas, quickening his pace as he stepped amidst the lands of the bloody falcon. Men gambled brazenly with whatever they had at hand. One roared at a loss, others laughed with the man that robbed him. A few pikemen trailed him with their eyes as he stopped to consider the loss. Rurik hurried on, tipping his head and doing his best to be as one with the shadows. Clouds churned overhead and the mud slopped at his deteriorating boots.

"Why the rush, boy-o?"

A hundred feet. Maybe less. He could see the drooping visage of his eagle perched atop the tent, like an island in shark-infested waters. Yet the voice seemed to slither from the alleys themselves and it seized him as sure as any hand. When he turned, he found himself eye to eye with Orif of Kellsly, the vile captain of the Gorjes. He stepped casually from the flap of the tent Rurik had just passed, smiling his battered smile. Many of the teeth had long been plucked—an image that should have rendered the fierce comical, but only served to fuel the ghoul's malevolence.

Behind him, yellow eyes and sickly grayish skin marked one of his enigmatic bodyguards. A hunched but menacing wraith, the orjuk bore no weapons that Rurik could see, but the trunks that formed his arms left doubt as to whether he needed them. One hand idly fingered the long, single black braid that was the hallmark of his people. It was the first Rurik had ever encountered. From the first, he had hoped it would be the last.

"Orif," Rurik said tightly.

A hundred feet. He tried to spy out Alviss from afar, but with the rain, he was undoubtedly inside. All the while he tried to suppress that squawking voice reminding him that Ivon may have been their nominal commander, but only that. Sellswords kept their own company, and what happened in the heart of their own domain was generally left to their own business. Ivon and Alviss both might as well have been miles away.

"Hear the crag-hoppers have come to ground. As a *representative* of our good commander, mind telling me what that might mean for our wages?"

Rurik swallowed. It was not a conversation he wished to have at the best of times. While most soldiers had been paid by the crown for outfitting and the right of levy, most had yet to be paid for services rendered. For Tessel, the majority waited. Some, like Orif and his greedy band, were not so patient.

"I'm sure I couldn't begin, at the moment."

Orif gave a dry chuckle. "Oh, I'm sure."

Rurik flushed at his tone. "It's a parley. When he's—I'm sure I'll know more in the days to come. If you'll excuse—"

But Orif took a step closer in his need to relieve Rurik. "Woah, woah. Easy, lad. Wasn't so long ago we was goodly neighbors, you know. Did I know a speckled mare from a rabid gryph? Certainly. Did I spare a word? Of course not. So a man's inclined to ask: where's the trust? And me and your pa—well. *Really.*" Orif's grin took on a decided edge. No few of those gaping gums had been caused by men at Kasimir's beck and call. Rurik's father had not abided thieves. "But we really gots to talk soon, you and me. Your girl's seriously edging my boys. War's no place for a woman with her britches up, and camp's no place for a lamara."

"Excuse me?"

"I'm not forgetting my dead boy, devil-eyes. At the least, Tessel owes me for the loss of hands. You hear me?"

Though it was Rurik who took a step back, he tried to hold firm as he mastered himself, demanding: "What did you call her?"

Orif rolled his eyes, smile fading. "I knew her father, you twit. Think I'm blind, too? Aren't nothing so tight what's human."

Rurik could feel the twitch in his hand. He also became acutely aware of just how close his blade was. *One sweep,* he told himself, thinking of Rowan's quick-draws. Orif was watching him from the recesses of his dark eyes, waiting for something. Both hands rested surely before him, and Rurik became steadily aware of other eyes lurking. The orjuk at his back was prepared for sudden death. He needed to go. Before they goaded him into doing something stupid.

And with them, it was a matter of when. Not if.

"Think of this as a courtesy I been meaning to have with you some time now, boy," Orif whispered.

"I'll speak with Alviss, and with Lord Tessel. It's all I can do."

Orif scoffed, but some of the tension seemed to go out of his shoulders. Disappointment, perhaps, hedged through his eyes. "See that you do."

Rurik was off before the words had even left his mouth. As he went, he could feel the eyes following him, but he resolved not to look back. Not for the first time, he resolved to broach the topic of the company's reassignment with Ivon. Only fear of drawing other unwanted eyes had stopped him in the past. That, and the fear that he would insult his friends' capabilities.

Slow breaths sought to steady his heart. Nothing stirred the blood, however, like an assault upon one's kin.

Lamara, they called her—the old Asanti term for "half-bloods." Literally, the union of man and Aswari. It was derogatory, but it was all they had for blood such as Essa's. Sighing, he tried to imagine Essa's mother, but it only came out as the cobbled patchwork of stories and legends. What of the Aswari remained, he knew, were mostly confined to designated villages, tightly governed by often less-than-sympathetic lords. The Vorges spoke of the Aswari like phantoms, a nimble people past their time and far beyond man's salvation. People reborn as men, to reign anew.

Essa's all-too-human father had belittled her simply for asking. He drank away his life remembering. And Essa—she learned only through his sobering insults. Her mother had left them both before Essa was even a year old.

Given the nature of Essa's father, it wasn't hard for him to imagine why.

Nor was it hard, then, to reckon why the thought of alcohol's hand in her corruption made it all the more difficult for her to bear. That night. That horrible night. It came to the fore whenever Rurik neared the threshold of their memory, and as his steps slowed, he knew it would haunt him until the end of days. He still wasn't certain what had happened. Arasyl rang in his mind and haunted his thoughts. It was the only thing, shouted in Essa's rage, that he had to go on. Where it had come from, though, was another matter entirely.

It was somewhat unsettling that, as he stepped amidst the triangle of tents marking the grounds of the Company of the Eagles, the only ones there to greet him were the pair of Gorjes Orif had leant at Ivon's command. One of the pair hooked him with a smile as he glanced around, but the other was bent to a wood carving. He couldn't say he remembered either of their names.

"Lost?" asked the shorter of the pair. He tipped the rim of his hat with the question, letting accumulated water run.

"Alviss about? I was supposed to speak with him." Frowning, Rurik bent toward Essa's tent, peering through the open flap, but neither she nor Rowan were there. "Where is she?"

At the sound of chains rattling, Rurik turned toward the northern point of the triangle—Alviss's fur-laden tent. Pulling himself up to his full height, the sight of the rising northman was like watching a bear rise from its den. Alviss's blue eyes immediately locked on his former ward and all but ignored the others. It set a pang through Rurik's own heart. They saw too little of one another these days and that, as much as anything, he knew for his own fault.

"Well the mountain's hard to miss," the Gorjes man jibed. "As to the peach, it's sad to say the other'n took her. Prolly to teach her the fine art of castration."

Rurik stared. Alviss glared. Putting up his hands in innocence, the man traded a sheepish smile between them.

"Ey, she's a bear for a reason. Little wolf just don't quite do it. If either of you still had your stones, it'd be more terrifying, I swear you." His partner grinned as he bent into another stroke of the wood, but added nothing from between tobacco-stained teeth. Rurik, shaking his head, did his best to ignore it as he moved to greet Alviss.

Both burrowed into Alviss's crowded tent—made so not for any abundance of goods, but simply by the presence of the Kuric himself. Nosing in somewhere between a deer's hide and the flap, Rurik tried his best to make himself comfortable. It was not easy. Nor was it easy to look the old man in the eye, as once he had.

Expressionless, Alviss nevertheless met him with the bearing of a father regarding his child. Rurik swallowed through a smile, trying to recapture the myriad thoughts he had held before he stepped foot into the tent. Scattered, they had, and all with a look. It had been as such for months. The old man loved him, to be sure, but there was a hurt there that went deeper than words. Essa's hurt. Such pains never touched just one.

"So," Rurik said quietly. "Ivon said you were looking for me the other day. I should have come sooner but…" *But I was too afraid to risk it.* He squirmed. "I've a little time, between Effisians and nobles. Will they…?" He hooked a thumb over his shoulder, indicating the men outside. He did not like the thought of them listening in.

Alviss dismissed the worry with a wave of his calloused hand. It hooked the open flap and yanked it shut. "Aye. I thought it time we had a piece."

"A—a piece?"

The Kuric eased back against one of the poles of the tent, crossing his arms over his chest. "About Essa, Rurik."

Rurik felt hope swell past his reservations. "Has she—has she asked of me?"

If he thought the fates had finally shown him a kindness, however, the dampening look the Kuric shot him struck any thought of it from mind.

"She asks often, but means little. I've enough of pain. You will tell me of that night."

He could feel the color draining from his cheeks. "I don't think—"

"All of it, child."

So he did. Skirting the details of their coupling, he recanted the night in detail, or as much of it as he could remember. He tried his best to keep theory from the mix and tell it only as he saw it. It wasn't until he came to the morning after, though, that he choked.

Boyish pride is a frail thing. It wounds easily and scars deeply. His heart was much the same, for all his shows to the contrary. Even that brief telling was as salt in the wounds, and by the end, Rurik's eyes were cast firmly to the earth, like a beaten dog, his thoughts circling around the woman that had scorned him.

"Why, Alviss? Why won't she speak to me? You-you see, I did nothing wrong."

The Kuric sighed deeply at that, but there was no sympathy in it. He dragged a hand through the gnarls of his beard and looked pointedly away. When he looked up, Rurik could see another night not so long ago, Essa curled against Alviss in the dark, weeping. The old man held her and let her fade into the furs, far from any hurt. He took it all in so that its burden might pass from her. There was never any falter in the solemn watch of those owlish eyes.

"I do not doubt you," Alviss said finally. "Still. Drug. No drug. There is more. Hurt as such—no heart could stir it, did not love. She loved you."

Loved. Past. No word could have hurt him more. Rurik felt himself falling as he blurted, "And I her! Then why does she torture me so? I—I was kind. I didn't, that is to say—"

"Why." The word snapped from Alviss like the crack of a whip. Rurik blinked up at him, startled by the harshness in his tone. "There is a whole side you do not see. I can live with boy that makes mistake. Such is youth. But this hurts not you only, Rurik. Think. What if she took to child? Would she ever look to it with mother's eyes—even if she survived the birthing?"

"But Aswari don't—" He bit down on his tongue to keep himself from finishing. Nevertheless, the Kuric took his meaning.

"Take human child?" their guardian remarked mirthlessly. "Clearly. So she stands before us." Rurik hung his head, trying not to look at him, but Alviss bulled on. "Every time she looked at that child, she would see only mistake. Or deception. Little matters. Youth is her curse, as yours. Youth cannot raise youth. Don't tell yourself otherwise. You cannot even take care of yourself.

"You Idasians. Always say—boy, he has man's blood at fifteenth year. You thought it manhood when you taste your first…peach. Is not age does it. Is not *making love* does it. This is your problem. Still think like boy. Think: why she hates me? Why she does this? Not: what have *I* done to *her*? What can I do *for* her? Did you mean hurt? No. But you did."

Rurik sat, stunned to silence. Calm disintegrated into ashes. He tasted many things—anger, sadness, shame. His fist clenched and unclenched at the thought. How had he not seen it before? Before, he had worried only that she thought he had drugged her. That he had raped her. Intentionally. Not that intention mattered in such a thing. In her eyes, he feared a mirror. One that would cast him for a monster.

It was there, still, but now it spider-webbed into so many other fears he never would have thought to consider. He felt vacant, and dizzy, and he wanted desperately to be anywhere but there. Yet he sat riveted, unable to speak and unable to flee.

Outside, one of the Gorjes was laughing. He heard it, but only just. *Essa,* he thought, *how will you ever forgive me?* It was not just the action. It was the willful selfishness of fear. No wonder she would not look him in the eye. He had not once gone to her, taken her hand in his, and asked, free of any conditions, why she cried when she thought no one was looking.

Perhaps now the time was far too late. Better than most, he understood that one most terrible lesson of youth: the heart may want, but it will gladly move to find it. Only fools could name themselves solitary.

Beyond family—both blooded and adopted—Essa had spent the long days since in the company of but one man. It drew his eyes down to the muck just to think it, but he had to know. Yet to tell himself to leave well enough alone if truth it was proved much the harder.

"Is she with him?"

There was a slight pause before the Kuric's answer came. "What matters?"

"You—you know why it matters to me. She's always on my mind. Every day. And when I see her with him…I wasn't half so scared when they were pulling knives on me, Alviss."

"All boys feel such. You don't want to hear. Fine. But fact is this: her life is hers. Let her make choice. *That* choice is not yours." He started to interject, but Alviss held up one massive hand to stay him. "Are you sure this is love? Not lust?"

"Alviss! I of all people should know the difference."

"You of…" The giant shuddered once, then barked out a single laugh as dry and biting as an arctic wind. "Boy, you are. These things—they jumble. We see what we want seen, all too true, when someone else has them. Calm. Treat her as you always have. She will come around." Alviss stared over Rurik's head, watching their shapes move in the distance. Rurik longed so badly to turn and to look as well, but he could not help feeling this was a test. He fidgeted. "Or she won't," the Kuric said at last.

"I can't accept that, Alviss."

"Then more the fool, you." The Kuric's gaze leveled back on him, heavy as a weighted pike. "Choice, as I say, not yours to make."

The sky outside was grey and white above them, and it rumbled with the chill. Heavy eyes watched him as only a father could. *Pescha,* he thought—he was no better than Essa's father. For once, he could honestly read Alviss's face. The Kuric pitied him.

Rurik waited until light was but a thousand tiny fires burning against an oil-slicked canvas. Men walked the periphery of the camp, but they did not see him, nor care to see him. He wandered far as he might dare from the town walls and boisterous politick, into the mud and muck he and his friends had once shared. Then he sat in the cool night, clutching to an old gift coin as he prayed his fears away.

Where only one would hear. Where only one would weep.

Chapter 4

"The delay is regrettable, Your Highness, but what is a year? With the coffers drained as they are, it is the only course I can see for us."

Leopold rimmed the cup with the tip of his finger, trying to reproduce the sound. The wine had been drained away. They were still waiting for the boy to return with more. It was a travesty of a thing. In Ravonno, no one would have thought to let the cups run dry. All his years there had laid this lesson plain: priests, like princes, were all but insufferable sober.

"My lord?"

Leopold stared just as dryly over the rim of the cup, at the red-faced figure of Lord Hinslen. The blowhard was one of the court's many relics. Brother to one of Idasia's quaint "palatines" and the voice to matters foreign—or as close as one might come—for the breadth of an empire, Hinslen was a man done grievous wrong by time. Whereas age bloated some men, it had withered the one-time soldier to a husk. Though he sat still with a soldier's repose, his black beard was shot with streaks of grey, and the palest of cataracts hazed his intemperate gaze.

Yet time had done little to temper the man's propensity for speech. This latest bundle was but the tail-end of his hour-long play for domination of the small chamber. A chamber that was, despite the sun pouring in from outside and the hot air blowing from within, unseemly chill. This was the Lord's Council. Leopold could hardly see why they needed him to suffer through it.

"And when we do have the coin? How long?" For all his minimal effort, Leopold could not keep the boredom from seeping in.

Straightening his crooked jaw, the old man croaked, "Two octaves, perhaps. Three if the rains come early. The spring showers can be a touch…unpredictable."

"My father is dead," Leopold sighed, "and the succession clear. None dispute it. We have the crown. We have the capital. We have the bishops. At a word, even the Patriarch will come with his blessing. Why must I wait? You would not ask such things of Joseph."

No one had given voice to the question of why the foreign minister was assuming the voice for local affairs. Leopold presumed it was by virtue of his age. Exasperated, his gaze flicked to the empty chair beside him where, he was told, had once sat their venerable chancellor. He, it would seem, had passed as suddenly as that guiding fatherly hand, left to drown under the same unsavory circumstances as had claimed too many of his own family.

If there was one thing Leopold had learned from Ravonno it was this: every man was friend only so long as it suited their interests. He could look out on these men now and see the regard they paid to this dead one, but he doubted any of them truly called him friend. More like than not, at least one of them had been involved in his "accident." Or so his wife kept reminding him.

At last, another voice arose, and this being the stuffed crowing of the Empire's actual treasurer, Portir. "Consider the country from whence you came, Leopold. Ours is not so different in its courses. Yet until you have the blessing of the electors, you can be nothing more than prince. Royalty may be birthed, but a ruler—a ruler is raised…"

Portir, called "the Devout" brother Durvalle among the southern halls to taunt Leopold, was his uncle. A bulbous, nervous sort with a tiring propensity for soft-spoken lecture, he was one of the few pieces of family whom had taken the time for contact in Leopold's long years abroad, though sometimes Leopold wished he hadn't. Of the gathered men, he was probably one of the most powerful now, in the wake of everything. He was certainly the richest.

It was he that had sent the letter for Leopold's return, and it was he that greeted their carriage on that fateful morn, the palace guardsmen arrayed about him like a personal army. Their meaning had not been lost. After, Ersili had taken Leopold by the shoulder and whispered in his ear: "You watch that one. He knows what it is to be regent and he should come to slaver for more, should words not ease. Should chancellor not sate."

It did tend to put the man in a new light.

"Spare me the tired epithets. I know the demagoguery of ritual. Just tell me—can these men take the crown from me?"

The room shifted uneasily around the question. Already he could see the weasel thoughts scrambling through their heads. Not one of them wished to confront the truth. Save his uncle Mauritz.

"They can. It does not mean they will. But it's more than that. Coffers or no—Hinslen, you neglect a fact. We need a replacement for the Veldharts, or there will never *be* a vote."

The general, with his long white hair and beard, stood beside his brother Portir, opposite Leopold. His hand was on his wider brother's shoulder, as though to steady him. It was like watching a wolf guide an antelope.

"What about Lord Ittenbeck?" Hinslen countered, turning it toward the group. "He is more than loyal—to the true family, mind you—and he is—"

"A pig, a philanderer, and far too severe. Even his fellow lords divine the need to wash after an hour with him." Lord Turgitz, the youngest man of the council, interrupted.

Under scrutiny, Leopold supposed this was one man he could come to like. A duke's son, he nevertheless kept his opinions to the considerate silence not of the witless inheritor, but the discerning merchant. Though short, he had a voice like liquid iron, and the courtesy—unlike too many Idasians—to bathe on a regular basis. A pity he was nothing more than their Minister of Ships.

"A pig with vast shores of grain. Given the harvests we've had the last few years—"

"There are any number of suitable knights on the crown's own lands," Portir said, with all the warmth of a father trying to appease his struggling spawn, "Men Matthias drew close to him. I should think it would be a fair concession to the new bloods among the court, no?"

"New does not always translate to better," Hinslen interceded, with all the candor of a pricked boar. "One should not forget the old families that first set the crown here. A middle ground is well and good, but bear in mind what many of these others have to bring forward. Proven loyalty foremost among them."

It was only after this tired lecture that Hinslen seemed to realize the potential fault in it, and he hastily turned himself back to Leopold. "Which is not to demean your own circumstances, Your Highness. I meant only—"

"I know what you meant."

In truth, he didn't. It sufficed to cow the braggart, but the names slid over his head. The intricacies and familiarities between these men that were supposed to be his hands left him as one entombed without a light, and he could only hope they did not note it. Half of politics was bluff, but it never hurt to buoy it with actual knowledge.

Damn Ersili for setting me here. This was her place.

More importantly: damn that boy with the wine. Did he run all the way to the vineyard for another cup?

Turgitz flicked his attention to Ser Ontlaus, the only one of the council—save Mauritz—still armed with a blade. In his leather cuirass and greaves, he was as much guardian to the council as member. With his thick arms contrasted by grey, drooping eyes, one had to wonder how much fire this dog still had in him, though.

"Honorable Ontlaus, surely there's someone close to the court you might recommend."

But the head of the Imperial Guard shook his head resolutely and addressed Leopold, "I am here to counsel the decisions proposed of others. I do not begin them."

"What about Lord Gorrowsly?" Portir slid into the conversation. "He has been—"

"I grow weary," Leopold cut in.

Portir choked on his words and floundered like a dying fish. Mauritz smiled as the others fell to silence.

"But—my lord? We have much more still to discuss. Palatines aside, there is the matter of the Chancellery."

Leopold, already half-way to his feet, snorted derisively. "Would you like it?"

"Would I—" The dying fish paled like one too. Hinslen's face registered shock, while the pair of military men gave only stony masks. Turgitz alone gave the slightest hint of a smile.

Yes, he definitely liked that one.

"Highness," Hinslen sputtered. "This is most irregular. This is a matter for discussion. Debate. It is not for—"

"I have thought long and hard," Leopold answered seriously. Untruthfully. "There is no better man for it. But I do have one last question, sers, before I'll hear no more of it. If you think this country can get along without an emperor for a year, pray tell who do you think shall rule in my stead? Who shall keep Assal's peace?"

Puffing up, Portir gaped as he answered, "With you, my lord nephew. I shall rule with you. As your father's lord regent and—that is to say, if your most gracious words be genuine, chancellor—I shall help guide you, and the year shall be good. We shall use it to make you Idasian again, my boy. We know you are at heart, but to the people—I dare say you will seem as a foreign conqueror."

Hinslen nodded to that, at least, but Turgitz and Ontlaus, while paying Portir his due, seemed slightly more concerned with his brother. Mauritz smiled through it, patting his brother on the shoulder and nodding his quiet assent.

The most dangerous men, Ersili once told him in bed, were those that gave nothing away. Naturally, she was the most dangerous of all.

"Of course," Mauritz said. "And my soldiers will keep the peace in the meanwhile. When the levees return from Effise, well, we should have more than enough men between you and any…" For a flicker of a second, the general's eyes drifted to the regent. "…naysayers."

"We have also dispatched messengers to Effise itself," Portir added. "We would see this monster of a blight done before you take to your office. The people—they grow weary of it."

With that, Leopold was finished. Hoisting himself onto his aching feet, the heir apparent graced the rising nobles with a single, curt nod and twisted away from the heart of his nation's politics. The men bowed to him as he went, but his disgust bid no hesitation. Already it felt as though he were walking on needles, and this was only his second meeting of the council. As far as he could see, they were just a ragged troupe of gossipy old men—save Turgitz, of course—utterly incapable of certainty, and utterly disposed to dragging him from his valuable time. In all the months since his demise, one chair of their number still sat empty, since they could not even agree to appoint a new chancellor for their fragile state. That alone told volumes.

The Lord's Council ran most of the day-to-day operations of the Empire, and Leopold was determined to let them. How his father had ever sat among them he would never know, but they were beneath his time. As he saw it, no emperor should have to be second-guessed and bogged down with the menial.

If she would have it, he would appoint his wife to the council in his stead. *How they would love that*, he mused. It was a pleasant thought. A woman had never served there and his wife was more than capable of putting the men in line. *Backward slugs like these could certainly use the injection of new blood.*

The more he thought about it, in fact, the more convinced he was of its merits. Ersili thrived on these sorts of things, anyway.

When he emerged from the council chamber, Bertold was waiting for him like his own personal shadow. He stood at the threshold, beside the men of the palace guard, at once enigmatic and malevolent in the smooth silver sheen of his mask. Strands of brown poked out from the deep lip of his cowl as the sunlight through the windows flashed deep lines across his red and brown robes. Only his bare hands hinted at one of the true curiosities of the man—like the lightest of chocolates, the result of a mixed heritage of Zuti and Marindi.

"My own dog," Leopold mused aloud.

Bertold said nothing in reply. He bowed his head to the heir apparent and followed obediently in his wake. Leopold had no other guards—at least that he could see. He had little doubt one court hound or another stalked their wake, and it was only right. Men sought to keep tabs on him. To stalk his movements and to know—for better or worse—what manner of being stepped so surely between their foreign halls. And he was more than man.

In the Vorges, it was said a man once asked his lord, "In all the land, might there be such a king that only heaven could divine his ways?" At the time, there had been no answer. Kings, be they fair or foul, ruled of might or fear or birth. Assal had little to do with it.

Yet divinity was the only way Leopold could describe the whirl of months behind him. His beloved Ersili had whispered to him as such from the moment the letter came of Joseph's end. She had mounted him in the sanctity of their chambers, wrapped in his own hallowed robes, whispering Grace into his ear as she took him inside her. The God's own, she had cried.

Strictly speaking, there had been some perks to being a prelate of the Church—perks those lower in the pecking order were not nearly so free to endulge.

"Tell me, Bertold, what is my wife about today?"

The masked man shrugged, turned away. Leopold could imagine him scowling down one of the corridors, peering out their pursuers. "She went to town. I am told a hedge witch caught her eye."

He could hear the derision in the man's voice, and it made him smile. "Is that right?"

"I am told she is returned."

In some ways, he collected his oddities. Ersili and her children might have been scoffed by another man. They had been, in fact, by many men. The willful youngest daughter of a Ravonnen nobleman, she had been married young to one too old, and though he had gotten her with two children, it did not take him long to die. Leopold had given him his rites. But from the moment he first spoke with Ersili, he had forsaken his own.

He was hardly the first priest to say the same, and though it provided a great many avenues for the other prelates to strike at him, he warded them, as any content man may. They were as two parts of a whole, their minds carved from the same bedrock, though hers he dared say was all the sharper.

Sucking a little at his gut, the would-be emperor pressed at the doors to his personal chambers, intending to show the woman his appreciation. Instead, he and Bertold were met with smoke, spice, and smiles.

The massive room had been converted, from the profligate manner of kings, to the sleek substance of eastern mystery. All the windows had been drawn and covered, such that the only light came from the torches and chandelier that blazed about the room's central table. The fires cast long shadows over the receded furniture, leaving a sense of emptiness to the room that seemed utterly unnatural. At the heart of it all sat his wife, clothed in damask and divinity, her white smile beckoning. The only piece of this entire palace with any meaning to him.

"Husband," she announced him warmly, "come, come. Tonight we set your demons to rights, and settle this blood-letting."

Joseph, it was said, had burst into flames from a fire that had no right to be. Molin died with him, choking, it would seem, on his fear. His father's chancellor had drowned, when there were nearly a dozen men on hand to save him. There was no denying something dark hunted his family. Even Bertold, skeptical as the foreign sorcerer could be, had spoken to him of a gloom over the castle—a pall, he said, of eyes and ears and bitter flames. Ersili often found her own ways of dealing with such things.

She wore the fire like a mask. Its warm light smoothed the already soft lines of her cheeks, accentuated the golden allure of her eyes. Their children were not there. Smoke issued from a censer the witch had set to dangling over the table.

Her hand parted it, reaching for him, and he went to it as a man wanting. Around him, the circlets and artifices of his holy office lay in shadow, comforted by empty goblets and discarded bits of food.

Gods were not the sum of their possessions. Lines far deeper than the realms of men guided the paths of life, and while many of the robed men saw fire and brimstone in the avenues of the unexplained, Leopold was not bound by such mundane fears.

Gods knew there was more to the world than mere men. There were angels and there were demons and all the myriad powers that walked the earth between them. Gods saw beyond, and they took precautions where they might.

"This is Elfi. She will draw out the spirit and banish it."

Bertold, stepping soundlessly from the doorway, let out an uncertain wheeze from behind his mask. "Were you seen?"

Ersili met him blandly. "It does not matter who bears witness to a god's desires. Men can but let them come to pass."

Yes, he told himself, *men worry. Gods take.* Leopold took his wife's hand and stepped into the ring of smoke. His legs wobbled against the soothing texture of it, sleeked as they were with the sweat of his walk. Behind him, he could hear the silence of Bertold's condemnation, feel the pitched numbness of his song. Somewhere far away, there was an energy crackling, and not for the first time, Leopold found himself asking if he did not have a touch of the tingles Bertold spoke of. Rare, the man said they were, and rarer every day, yet it seemed only right for one such as he to have something so old, so indescribably unique.

Its blasphemy only added edges to the pleasure no other power could caress. Church men burned those creatures out—but then, it was the nature of men to fear that which they did not understand. Childish reasoning, really. Yet he had bandied to their games in Ravonno and he would do the same here. Bertold was most valuable for his discretion. He never entered into the light. It would have damned them all.

"My sweet," her voice beckoned in the dark.

Blue eyes glimpsed them both from across the table. Bound in simple cloth, the dark curls of their guide spilt before them as she offered her hands across the oaken altar. Leopold's eyes flicked across her sizeable bust, and the delicacy of her fingertips, and he caught himself plumbing the hedonistic depths of the other motivations his wife may have held. The crescent of the woman's teeth opened to them in beckoning, and he knew this was the way.

She would break the shackles of his earthly fears and set him truly free.

He kissed his wife's hand and delivered himself into the old magicks. From the corner of the room, his wife's body servants watched and cowed away, whispering as frightened children might, when one asks devils into the room. Bertold snorted, whispering the enrapture of his wards about them, in the thrum of white, as the witch, turning up her palms to them, touched their skin and sank away into her spirits, calling on Assal to guide them.

Chapter 5

Leverage was one of those precious things no man could teach. It had to be taken. Yet in so doing it had to be delicately handled, for its art, blackmail, was as a double-edged sword. Improperly wielded, one might lop off their own arm.

Which made a child's role in the affair ever so tedious.

The cells of Vissering Castle were quiet in the night, in that manner of graveyards. Silhouettes danced along the walls where her accompaniment's torches flicked them. Dartrek kept his quiet, and the others mimicked him. Only little Kana, hand clutched tight in Charlotte's own, would break the monotony of boots on stone. They were sobering, her tears.

Charlotte was the first in when the keys rattled open the appropriate cage. Her phantom sat huddled on the floor. No chains bound him. Only stone and memories. Once, his father had sat as he, just beyond those walls.

If only stones could speak. Then again, they probably wouldn't have anything kind to say about her or her dear family. But then again, people never did, so why should stones?

Isaak Matair's eyes had fixed her long before the irons rattled shut. A smile broke his lips as he beckoned, "Good eventide, whore." She met his gaze, and his words, in stony silence. For all that was whispered of this one, she had never met the gentleman others claimed in him. Only his steely remains.

She liked to think of it as their game—the absence of all life's little formalities. Its little lies. It was nice not to have to act for once.

"Does it ever sleep?" she countered. Never once had she beheld his dark eyes shut. "Or are my visits just so enticing?"

He ignored her jibes. "I believe I heard dear Witold in the yard today, just as I believe she comes to jest at my good wife's departure?"

"To the contrary. I come with a proposal. It seems you will be able to join her, soon."

Not a shred of interest broke his mask. Charlotte might have admired it, if it didn't so remind her of Boyce, her father's spider. At a time, she had dared hope he would break himself. Some men deprived themselves, hoping their sacrifice might make some grand statement of defiance. Yet it was the men who took and ate, and drank, and said nothing of, which lasted. Starvation destroyed captives, not their captors.

The only thing she found that turned this particular creature's head were the whimpers beyond the door. In those fleeting glances, she thought she caught the scent of uncertainty. So she went after it as a bloodhound.

Dartrek brought the child at her beck and call. Five name days to the mark, and weeping like a newborn. But Charlotte had eyes only for Isaak. She almost smiled at the twitch of anger when it slipped.

"Papa!" the little one squealed. Her hands reached for him as she sprang, but Dartrek had her by the scruff and yanked her right back.

Isaak started, but held himself at that last crossroads of reaction and reason. Ever the impressive specimen. His face was a war on a battlefield she knew well.

Whoever said the world was won in steel had apparently never mastered the graces of Jurti.

"Witold did not take her," Isaak softly spoke.

She would keep the one in his place, as she would keep the other.

"He did not, for all your wife's objections. His own granddaughter. Do not think too harshly of him—it was our whims that stayed her. We felt her safer here, with her father. And she has playmates of an age. Why, my own brother—"

Isaak's dark eyes pinioned on her. "I have little doubt. And how would the House Cullick desire me to express my gratitude?"

My, how quick we are. "Oh come now, do not be like that." She even pouted, enjoying a flare of showmanship. The middle brother Matair's eyes never moved, though. "In truth, we want the same thing. Or at least, things that lead to the same ends. You wish for your family," she said, reaching a hand to fuss with Kana's hair. The girl flinched away from her, scowling. "Undoubtedly for your lands, as well. Well, this isn't the time to have so many unknowns scrambling for your scraps. It promotes chaos. People like their familiarity.

"So we would like you to have those things, too. Nearly all your relatives have now gone, save your pair. Yet you see, there are still some…uncertainties that need to be dealt with. Your brother Ivon, for example. As I understand it, he is still afield with the Emperor's bastard, with an army at his back. Now that's a fine thing, for a fine soldier. Yet we fear the rumors he may have heard. The…whispers. Things like that are like to drive a man to rashness, and that would benefit no one. We would like for you to explain things to him. Help him see how things truly are. Then take him home—back where he belongs."

"An awful long leash," Isaak snorted. "Particularly given the duke's own words: we have no land. What's to keep me from returning with that same army at my back?"

He was direct. Charlotte had to give him that. "Nothing, I suppose. Save little Kana here. And that drakkon Anelie above." This time, she did not hold back her smile. "All you need do is help your brother see reason."

As for Ivon, Charlotte's father might have used that one's own wife and child to blackmail him, if he could have. Unfortunately, when Duke Rusthöffen departed in the wake of the trial, he took that pair with him, as well as the eldest daughter, Liesa. To protect the heirs of House Matair, he said. A noble's duty. He never said aloud that it was House Cullick he sought to shield them from.

That Lotte—Ivon's wife—had been eventually released to the custody of her own father was a fact they knew too well, however. Lord Urill Insley was as sly as he was decrepit, and one of the many men that had benefited from the Cullicks' generosity in the wake of the Matairs' downfall. It was in a terribly humbling letter that he had sought to thank Charlotte's family for their kindnesses—the silver nature of which was of course not put to writing, and she hoped he choked on it—and for the good conduct in returning his daughter to him.

Its mockery had been enough to pucker an entire room of Cullicks up like sour lemons. It was rare one managed to so effectively undermine one of her father's plans. It was even less advisable. The black fury it had put her father into would be revenged a hundredfold. Of that, there could be no doubt. The feud was a custom old and dear to Idasia, and for Walthere Cullick, it took far less than blood to invoke. Nothing less would sate it.

The rest of the Matair brood was secured through equal parts threat and bribery, and Walthere gave up Isaak's dear wife only as a kindness from one nobleman to another. Some gentile show of honor. Or, more accurately, to make himself the better man, and indebt his rival to him. After all, the Empress herself had practically perched upon Walthere's shoulder at the trial. She may have never said a word in favor of their present course, but she did not have to. Threat of presence was evidence enough to most.

Such scheming was the only reason Charlotte had come here again. Why she had brought this offer, when good sense told her otherwise. Isaak's use only lessened here, in this cell. Though his name bore trouble with it, and he stood a dangerous man besides, out there he could strike where their own blades yet found no purchase. And they still had the bargaining power.

Kana made little sounds, occasionally squirming against her fleshy bonds. Her father gave a solemn shake of his head.

"Tessel is not likely to just let one of the banners walk away. The Emperor called them. It would take the Emperor to draw them back." His hard gaze flicked to his daughter and his lips tightened just so. "Or lack of coin."

She batted a hand at him dismissively. "Worry not for the Bastard, ser. That one has his own travails. And it is Lord Marshall Othmann that has the command. We shall give you a letter to him, from our own hand. Its seal will give you both leave enough. The rest is your own matter."

Long legs twisted under Isaak's deceptively huddled frame, twisting until he had a footing on which to stand. Kana tried to jerk forward again, but Dartrek's grip was firm. He drifted a few steps closer to Charlotte, and though his left hand did not touch the hilt of his sword, the fingers tensed. She pretended not to notice. It was an expected gesture, but she didn't rightly fear anything from Isaak. He was no fool.

He answered Dartrek's bluff, though, drawing himself forward several paces until he was carefully within the man's own bubble of space. Dark eyes stared her towering shieldman down, though neither blinked. Kana caught her father's hand with a squeal. Charlotte only rolled her eyes. *Men and their displays.* But for Isaak, she knew it was more. Bravado had little to do with it. Distraction lay in those motions. Perhaps he thought she wouldn't see him squeeze his daughter's hand. Surely he knew neither would care in such a moment. All they saw was defiance.

At least, that was all they should have seen. *A lion's eyes miss nothing.*

"Is that all?" Isaak asked coolly.

"Not by half. For there is another, more…" She tapped at her chin, baiting him. "Delicate matter we would ask that you—"

Hard eyes snapped back on her. "No," he said. Dartrek started forward and Isaak's hand loosed his daughter's as he gave ground.

Charlotte parted with an annoyed huff. "You did not even hear what I had to say."

"You mean Rurik of course," he returned, not missing a beat.

That actually took her aback. She hadn't expected that, but then, he was a clever sort. If they wanted one brother dealt with, surely they would not leave the other scurrying about.

"An astute observation. But I do ask that you reconsider your stance." She paused there, waiting, but he offered no further interruption. Hatred broiled in that stare, but there was something, still—some glimmer that bid her on. Not entirely unreasonable, perhaps. "He is kin, it is true. Yet in that same regard, is he not kinslayer?"

"He did not take an axe to my father's neck."

"But you are a logical man. He may as well have. He knew what would come of returning home. What it would mean. He led us to your father's door and fled before the punishment." Charlotte shook her head with a small sigh. "As he has escaped so many things. A small man, growing ever smaller.

"Tell me, do you ever sit here at night wondering why? Why your house? Why your family? The answer should be plain. It is him. He wronged me, tis true, but nothing so stark as what he has wrought on you and yours. Wantonly. Unnecessarily. Would you—"

Again he cut her off, saying, "I will go, if that is what you need."

She stumbled, hesitant. An eyebrow rose in question. *Another game?* "And you know what we ask? Of you? Of…him?"

Rurik's brother nodded, not turning away from it. There was a chill there even she had not expected to see. Hatred, yes but—not for her. Not all of it. It was the chill portents of a creature more shadow than man. Logical, not emotional. She might have shuddered, if he weren't watching. As it were, she only smiled anew.

"If such is the case, I shall return to you on the morrow, and at that, you may go. Let the guards know what you need and it will be so."

"And the child will be released to my wife when it is done." He said "the child" like one would say "the horse," or "the gold," and Isaak was careful not to look at her.

70

Charlotte might have smiled for the misplaced effort, but she did not bother, for "the child's" hurt sucks of air were sound enough of her victory. "And the child will be released when it is done."

The shade bowed its head in a farce of respect, and Charlotte twisted back for the door. She waved at her guardian and Dartrek began to back after her, yanking Kana away from her loitering father. A hollow gaze stalked them to the entrance. She could feel it boring into her back.

All men were tools, as she saw it. Dangerous tools, when roused, but that was why one took care in efforts of control. It all came back to leverage. It wasn't enough to ask a man if he would kill his brother. One had to make him see the consequences if he did not. Then one could only ask, which would he choose: brother or daughter? For all that kin might mean, most would choose the daughter.

Of course, if her own father met the question, she had little doubt which he would choose. Some men had different priorities, and an extra child to spare.

Behind them, Charlotte heard Isaak rattling something around. "Lady whore, you forgot something," he called. She half-turned, letting his tone glance off her. There was nothing to break her now. She had won, and for all his petty words there was no sight sweeter to her eyes than a man destroyed.

Yet he had scooped a bowl off the floor, its contents rotting in the flickers of the light. Isaak offered it to her with an empty face. "The slop, if you would be so kind? It is that hour."

There was no escaping the Empress's moods. Not for Charlotte. Not for anyone, she had found, save her father.

By afternoon's pallid light, they moved through Fürlangen's bustling streets, hoping to indulge one of the woman's "last remaining pleasures," as she put them. One of many, to be sure. Today it was jewelry. Tomorrow it could be embroidery. Spinning or song. Or stitching. The very thought gave Charlotte a shudder. Her governess was gone—it would have looked poor for a grown woman to require one in the presence of such high nobility—but she could still feel her cold presence lurking in this. The woman had always tried to make her appreciate such—though she hesitated to name them so—arts.

71

Charlotte had never quite managed to convince her that her interests lay in other arts. That creature was of the traditional school, wherein women dared not touch politick or theology, and the height of feminine grace was to bewitch some simple, noble man with equally simple smiles, and to spread one's chaste legs for him as wife and do the bed duty that would bring the children, and the grandchildren, and all the while never saying a word that did not do them all the best.

However, she did learn to play along. To indulge others.

In truth, that was probably why the Empress looked so fondly on her. Though others appeased, Charlotte engaged, even when the very thought of doing so sickened her. Yet it was the fondness her father saw, and he trusted delicacy more to her than to his wife.

The Empress was one of those simple creatures. Yet in the months since the burning, her need for escape became paramount. The Empress's moods were not solely whimsies of materialistic drive. She had taken a darker complexion since her return, proving prone to spouts of depression. Or madness, if the keep's whispers were to be believed.

It was hardly surprising. Death was always a shock to the privileged, but this was a woman that had suddenly seen the whole course of her life unsaddled. Soldiers had delivered the three of them—the Empress, Princess Sara, and the young prince Lothen—from harm, but one child remained beyond their grasp, still locked in the viper's nest that was Anscharde.

Rosamine. The name twinkled in every tear the woman shed, and rightly so. No one had made their move as yet, but when the new emperor was crowned, all knew what little Rosamine would become: hostage, bargaining chip, and outright threat. Emperor Matthias's other heirs had little need for this empress's children, but she and they alike were a threat to their stability. As of the moment, Rosamine was their only means to get to her.

Thus the Empress walked the streets of her new home with Charlotte and her mother as guides.

Fürlangen was a hold town. With the figure of Vissering Castle looming over it and thick, low walls surrounding the old, inner city, it was a respectable specter of a profitable past. Iron once ran rich in the veins beneath its earth. It grew fat on those profits, and had, in another age, commanded great respect for it. Though those particular prospects had since moved far to the west, Fürlangen kept up appearance well enough. It was a marketing haven, far from the largest in the Empire—it lacked the river or sea access that could have made it so—but large enough to remain as the capital of Usteroy.

At least, until the Cullicks decided to make some other city their hold. If her father ever got his wish, and Cullick blood drifted back into the Imperial capital, Fürlangen probably would not last more than a few years.

She wasn't sure how she felt about that.

A glance at the two women with her saw yet another terrified jeweler drape a broach across the Empress's neck. Charlotte's mother shook her head at some indiscriminate flaw, face scrunching distastefully at her royal cousin. Karlene Cullick fussed more than the Empress. She always had.

More sisters than cousins. Odd, considering how many years it had been. Both carried their Banurian heritage through their pinched faces, soft skin, and altogether bright hair, traits which, pinched faces aside, Charlotte herself had gratefully inherited. Yet neither still had the accent. Surelia had been away from her homeland for more than a decade, and Charlotte's mother, Karlene, since her first bleedings. Up until the last year, Charlotte had never even met this so-called relative.

Yet people had a tendency to cling to the past. Charlotte supposed that had something to do with the women's sudden fondness, but she also suspected more than a little of it was built with pity as its mortar.

First impressions had painted Surelia Durvalle as nothing more than an air-headed, excitable woman of eccentric tastes. Since she had returned to Vissering Castle in the snow and the slush, the Empress had grown somewhat more...demure. On that day, that first, bleeding look she had spared Charlotte had nearly turned her stomach.

Pity was not something she felt for that woman. But Charlotte did feel a touch of her pain. She had caused it, after all. They all had. Clueless woman that she was, Surelia likely never could have wished those dead men ill, no matter what they might have done to her in life. *Flower of a thing.* Outside of executions, she had probably never seen death up close.

Fire, Charlotte understood, did terrible things to one's looks. Not to mention the smell.

This was to say, it probably made the former heir apparent as grim on the outside as he had always been inside. With luck, he was still roasting in the abyss.

"No, no I've quite enough of these. Come, majesty, to Nissa. You've been too long without a new gown, and my girl is simply the best."

Karlene snapped her fingers as if she were empress, and the guardsmen snapped with her, pressing into the crowd. Surelia only nodded, sedate as a cow, and shared a whisper with her cousin. Normally, she flourished in numbers. Now she shied from them.

Fortunately their guards were as the prow of a great ship, cutting the crowds as waves before them. The only sound to compete with the vendors' howls were the Empress and her cousin, yammering at this and that like each were nothing but a pound of flesh. Empress or no, few bowed—only inclined their heads or averted their eyes and went about their toils.

Some of the guards held to Cullick's colors—like Dartrek—but most bore the soft blacks and dull golds of the palace guard. They neither needed nor bore standards. Their full dress armor and carriage besides announced all that need be said. It was not as if the royals' dalliance was a secret. The only question for most was how long they intended to remain.

Wide streets allowed them easy movement through the market that formed the heart of the city. Colored tents painted the sunlit afternoon, butting up against old walls of slanting stone—the oldest parts of Fürlangen. Beyond the defensive wall lay newer homes, more shoddily rendered—mixes of wood and stone and even clay bricks, their roofs woven of sagging thatch, straw, or whatever else they could gather. Even inside, there were none of the ostentatious towers and domes some of the larger cities commanded, but the place bore its age with dignity, its vaulted roofs and gables only adding to its apparent size.

As they headed west, out of the village of tents and stalls and into the old market proper, storefronts leapt alive in the daylight. Polished stone gleamed, glass panes of varying size and shape and color reflecting images of their little train as it meandered through lines of other figures, some in leather, some in cotton, coats and gowns and cloaks brushing against the cobbles. Theirs was the only carriage, however, its rich, ornate markings distinguishing them despite the fact that none of them rode within.

Surelia smiled distantly as her eyes flitted from post to post, making her appear entirely out of place.

"It is a lovely place, no? Not like Sayerne, not like Old Banur, but it is…home," Karlene mused aloud.

"It is so—" Surelia nodded vacantly. "Peaceful. Not at all like Anscharde. But tell me, where is the Church? The Circle?"

"Just us, darling. Only us. They have their place here, sure as any, but I assure you this is home. Their people do not wander here." Karlene patted Surelia's hand. "Walthere is so sweetly thorough."

The shop they were looking for was near the westernmost edge of the district, the last building in a row. Little distinguished it but the dresses lined outside its door. Yet even through the window, one could spy the dangling silk. Outside was for the littlefolk. Inside was for the rest.

A hunched man in mail sat on a stool outside the door, warily eying the racks of clothes and the women that walked them. They shied away from the approaching caravan. He stood and bowed his bald head to them.

"Fine work as ever, Ebelard," Karlene jibed as they stepped inside. The man smiled back at her, as few dared to do.

There were certain perks one gained with a noble house's favor.

Charlotte, however, held little interest in the lot. As the guardsmen took up position outside the shop, she moved with Dartrek into a small corner of Tajiman silks and other gentle weaves—a place where she could watch the window and the streets beyond.

She did not like the thought of this. Any of it.

Day and night, it seemed, her father schemed with his attendants, and more and more frequently shut her out of the discussions. For more than an octave, her dear uncle and cousin had been abroad, dealing with border issues. The witch had been confined. Even worse, the matter of the Matair children had been left in Charlotte's hands, as had many of the more local affairs, and she found herself increasingly hard-pressed for time, even when she wasn't being dragged out for more baubles. Her father assured her it was good practice. It was not a tune she liked to hear. Quite the contrary, it worried her as to exactly what he was plotting.

Worse still: Sara would not leave the castle, and her absence was a hole in Charlotte's heart. That woman was earnest and gentle for all her sharp wits, in a way she had not expected of another noblewoman. Or she had been. Two months they had taken shelter in the castle, and for two months, Sara had hardly spoken a word to anyone.

Her brother Molin, the white cloak said, had died in her arms. Tears reddened her face, though they never showed when Charlotte called on her. She went through the motions, but the spark—that inner fire of life—had snuffed itself. Even the Empress's vaunted hope that Sara's husband would come for her at that hour of need went unanswered.

Walthere had been eager to add that count to his web of allies. But the man never answered a letter.

Meanwhile, his wife sat mere stones away from her brother's killer. That thought worked a chill up Charlotte's spine like little else could. The mad woman who cut herself in the dark.

Still, Charlotte had her own part to play. She nodded at her mother's suggestions, parted with base words for the fineries brought before her. The Empress, meanwhile, stood amidst a flock of supplicants, blushing through their ministrations at a new gown.

It was hardly the figure Charlotte had expected when she first turned up at their door. Walthere had sent a column of soldiers for her, and nary a letter for the crown. One of the white cloaks had forsaken them at an inn beside the road, taking half their men and both the bodies, and heading north for Anscharde itself. The other bore the tortured royals to them gladly, all the while speaking of fire and ash and sorcery on the wind.

Godlessness. The man had shuddered through the thought. *There is a devil on the wind.* The aged knight brooked no other blade but his to guard the Empress's son, and had not left him since their return. He guarded him still, somewhere back at the keep. Charlotte caught Surelia staring out the window more than a couple times herself, her eyes lost in the distance. Lost, undoubtedly, to her son.

She had clutched him like a mad woman, on that day. Held him tight to her breast and would not turn away.

A shout from outside drew Dartrek's attention. "Rider," the man grunted. Charlotte turned at that, sidling up for a better look and leaving her mother rummaging through a host of fabrics.

The crowd jostled this way and that, needling out of the path of some unseen figure. One of her father's bannermen, perhaps. Charlotte did her best to peek without demeaning her station.

Sometimes, she longed for a peasant's life. Rarely, but it did happen. A peasant was rarely cuffed for the simple crime of standing on their tip toes.

"Charlotte? What do you think?"

She tried not to. Without looking at her mother, Charlotte appraised, "A touch too bold, I think. Something darker, perhaps?" Only the frustrated gasp that followed turned her back from the shuffling crowd. She found her mother staring at her, hands on the hips of her dress and a sour look crinkling her cheeks. The dress Charlotte had thought she would be hoisting was nowhere in sight.

Damn.

"I say, girl. Really."

"Apologies, mother," she said, fighting down her annoyance.

The Empress, likely catching dignity's fleeting scent, turned back to them with a dress in hand. She parted her lips to speak, but it was Karlene that continued. "Of *Vande*." She hissed between drawn teeth. Charlotte's own breath wavered at the name—for its implications to her brother. It was marriage, of course. Ten, twelve years off, with a war in between, and still her mother was set upon a purpose. "Highness, no, I'll not hear words on this," her mother added quickly, waving off her cousin's pointed attempt to enter the conversation. In their brief time together, Surelia had already made her dislike of that particular child well-apparent.

Vande's parents—barons—had apparently snubbed Surelia at court before she gained the lofty title, and that was one thing that had never left the airy boundaries of her blonde head.

Before she could answer with a lie, Charlotte found herself saved by the motions of the crowd. All eyes were drawn to the nearing figure of a man astride a gryphon, its feather tips colored to the Cullick shades. A messenger. The crowd flowed around him as he passed, nearer and nearer. Charlotte called out to him when he was close enough for her to keep civil tones, and he bowed his head in hastened subjugation.

"His Highness requests your presence immediately, Lady Charlotte," the man squawked when he was close enough. He hopped promptly down from his gryphon and stepped aside, brushing a hand along the saddle. "You are to take my beast, lady. Your man should follow as quickly as he may."

She spared a glance for her mother and the Empress. "Did he say what this is for?" But the man only shook his head. Apparently, her father couldn't be bothered with *whats*. Letting out an exasperated sigh, she nevertheless tipped her head to the man and moved to the beast's stirrups. She tried her best to ignore the smell. Gryphons, like camels, were grungy creatures. Dartrek helped her up, repeating the soldier's note: he would follow as soon as he was able.

"Should we return together?" Apparently no one had told Surelia that empresses need not ask the obvious.

"It is probably Maynard. No doubt we've had a Lievklaus pecking at our grains again," Karlene said drily. "Besides, we still need to see to your dress, my dear. Go, Charlotte, and you help your father however you may." This last came out as a sort of gracious dismissal, and Charlotte very much wished to tell her she did not need the permission, though of course she did.

She did not wish to force her bodyguard to walk, however. "Might Dartrek borrow one of the men's steeds? We shall be sure it awaits him in the stables."

Karlene wobbled her head back and forth and finally turned to Surelia, but the Empress's face grew long with the request, until it seemed to pull her head into a most vehement shake. "I am sorry, dear, but then there would be only eleven horses, and you should not wish the men to look uneven."

Somehow, that undoubtedly made sense in Surelia's head, and that was the frightening part. Charlotte did not push the point, but she did spare a sympathetic look for her dour shadow. The man looked away, but she thought she caught some crooked warmth in him.

"Tell your father to send one of the boys out with some of that burgundy fabric, Charlotte. You know the roll. Nissa, here, she needs to see what we mean, for our Empress's gown," Karlene lectured as Charlotte settled into the saddle, pulling herself up by a bundle of the gryphon's long feathers. "And if you see your brother, you tell him I shall be having a word with him tonight. That spectacle at breakfast this morning was unacceptable."

Charlotte flicked her mother the faintest of smiles, and bowed low for her and her cousin both as she drew the gryphon around in a broad circle. The street cleared for her. There was nothing quite so dangerous as a gryphon's claws, and they did have a tendency to startle. It squawked once, and as the Empress's shaking hands descended for a customary curtsy, Charlotte was already riding back into the crowd.

When she was finally free from the thick of it, she gave the gryphon a tug of the reins and a sharp cry of enthusiasm that set it bounding. Horses had a longer stride—and rightly so, for most outsized their feathered compatriots by several hand lengths—but this creature had an easy sort of spring to its canters, and its clawed feet seemed to fling its momentum forward. Charlotte bent low to it, letting the wind rustle her hair with its feathers, and urged it to spread its wings. At the northern tower of the city's watch, it sprang up and caught the stones by the mortar, and with a shout from one of the horrified guards, pressed off into the wind and cast itself afloat.

On the plains, horses were unmatched, but in the woods, the gryphon was an unmatched beast. The way it could climb—one might almost call it a cat. Yet here on the plains was perhaps the only place one could truly bask in their ways of old. Charlotte closed her eyes and let her arms go slack, letting the hiss of the air carry her aloft. Flight was not meant for man, but one could steal glimpses. The gryphon held itself in a glide for perhaps twenty feet before the illusion snapped. Then its wings tucked and its feet cracked back into the dirt, and they were off again along the trail.

How bitter the tragedy Assal wrote when he put men's fates to ink. Instead of wings, he gave them thought and with thought came concern, worry, and doubt. That alone could have weighted down even the lightest of birds. These little moments were all she had now, and she paced them throughout her days, and cherished them dearly. Yet in truth they were all she needed. Glimpses of freedom kept the soul alive. Too much and one would float too high, and the sun would burn them up and leave them only ashes.

Conspiracy had its bright sides, too.

By the time she arrived back at the castle, there was a small gathering of gawking souls about the yard.

Dismounting, she took her steed's lead in hand and guided it toward the stalls, where the commotion seemed to settle. It was a smattering of littlefolk, mostly—a few loitering guardsmen, some servants, and a few of the stableboys. Among them, however, was a golden-haired figure cut from a knight's old tale: the robust figure of Ser Edwin, one of her father's knights. The man was always prodding around the stables, but for him to gawk as such—it leant a certain air to the already curious spectacle.

She headed straight for Edwin. The crowd obliged her, though most merely angled around her, still hoping for a look at whatever lurked within the stables.

Edwin smiled at her approach and dipped his head in greeting, beckoning with a call to "his fair lady." Charlotte had always liked Edwin as a girl. Tragedy was that Edwin preferred the stableboys.

She maneuvered alongside him and peered inside. The doorway was dark, though many small shapes clearly scurried within. "What are we looking at?" she asked, as the knight pulled a hand through her ride's feathers. It shuddered affectionately.

"A first for most, my lady. Your father's put a call to someone with a Curii."

"A Curii? Here?" Excitement followed bewilderment hand in hand at that. Everyone had heard of the fabled horses, but outside of Naran, they were a rare commodity. One was said to be worth a king's ransom, and that would be just, since that was whom they were raised for. "Would you be so kind, ser?" Her hand already held the reins to the man, but Edwin, in turn, was already reaching for them. He waved her along with a few terse words, and she readily slipped into the stalls.

Inside, the other horses were in a fury. Stablehands rushed between them, coaxing with gentle words while bribing with oats and hay. Charlotte followed the trail of maddened stallions to the back, stepping lightly along the dirt path of the building's hall, to one of the few quiet stalls.

A red mare pulled loosely at its snare, snorting indignantly. She stepped a little closer, scarcely believing her eyes. The beast was not the largest in the room, but the flared black nostrils and equally black mane gave it away as something wholly fiercer than the rest. *Curii*, she swallowed. Some people called

80

them a devil breed. They were fleet creatures, said to be kin to the wind itself—and just as wild.

A trainer once told her a man could work such a horse five years before it knew him well enough to trust him. Understandably, few had such patience. Trained Curii were highly sought as station items among the nobility, but only a few small ranches on the borders of Naran and Asantil still bred them. Most were purged alongside the orjuks, who first rode them out of those mountains and used them to burn a swath across Marindis.

One day, both would likely be nothing more than tales.

The horse seemed to sense her approach at the last moment and began to redouble its struggles accordingly. A series of long, high whinnies drew her back from the stalls as a stable boy rushed to his task.

Vissering was becoming something of a gallery for freaks.

Sparing a final, lingering glance for the beauty, Charlotte gathered her skirts and bundled herself back into the cool air. Edwin greeted her with a grin.

"A wonder, isn't it?"

"Truly," she answered, leveling her gaze on the keep before them. "Any idea who rides it?" She pictured a foreigner, or a messenger—one of the royal family's, perhaps. Maybe they had finally decided the Empress had tarried long enough. Maybe the electors were finally called to vote.

"Would that I did, lady. The guards spoke only of a lout—some dark man, of low character. A shade, truly, to hear them tell it. I fear perhaps your father is hiring out."

She smiled grimly at the thought, but offered nothing in reply. They left it at that, Charlotte leaving her steed in his care as she headed for the keep.

Inside, she skirted the great hall and made promptly for the spiraling steps of the adjoining tower's ascent, intuition her sole guide. While her father tended to receive guests in the solar, he did not entrust conspiracy to it, and if he had sent for her specifically, that likely meant a very private encounter indeed. The library held her guess and guided her steps three flights above the earth, taking them one at a time despite her father's haste.

A lady did not rush herself.

All the while, her thoughts turned to the omen of the horse. There were swords within that line of thought. Guns. But most of all: blood. The children of the blood were on the move, and her father knew that better than anyone. Days of his life had been lost to letters between him and the other electors—the dukes and palatines of the Altengard.

It was a pity to think such men, so solid in their own right, could cave so easily to fear of what had befallen the Veldharts. Everything had seemed to backfire then. By all manner of logic, they should have turned their eyes to others of the blood, nearer, younger, more easily controllable. Instead, they turned their voices to one beyond Idasian borders for an emperor. An outsider, they said, proven in his leadership, and bearing with him the friendship of the southern states.

A circled man. One every bit as dangerous as the brother they had slain, but with none of his knowledge of the realm. It was enough to turn a person's stomach.

Maybe that was it. Mayhaps they had finally sought to put the vote to paper and make the man official. *Assal be good, let us hope they have not so suddenly found efficiency.* Walthere would have to agree, lest he be scrutinized. They had all already made the decision. The rest was just detail—tradition. It would certainly twist her father's stomach though.

But just before the library, another thought stilled Charlotte.

Something watched her.

It was less a presence than a sensation. Eyes prickled like needles along the skin of her neck. She was being watched, where only shadows should have lurked. Only one spider could and would have at that.

"Boyce, if you think—"

She stopped. Shadows broke along the slim, high cheeked face, nestled into the eclipse of a cowl. He seemed as thin as a willow branch to her, but something about him belied a hidden strength. There was no hint of steel about his person. It seemed unnecessary. Burdensome, even, for a man that could set himself out of sight and out of mind behind walls he had never before graced. Gloved hands remained perched—delicately, almost—against crossed legs. This...man, was the only other soul in the alcove.

"It sees," the shadow said, without question. Silver eyes, hammered and battered to the points of blades, swept the distance between them and sought to cut her down. Yet nothing of the man itself so much as moved.

She held, but not without a backward step. No sign of acknowledgement of that small retreat broke that man's face, however. His black face. Black as the horses in the yard. Black as the moonless night. Unnatural, and disturbingly feminine.

"It—I see much, dark blood," she replied, catching herself. "But not what brings you to our home."

It wasn't human. She could tell that much. Still…

It didn't unnerve her like she thought it should, and that only proved all the more disturbing.

Breaths passed long and silent between them, until Charlotte caught herself lamenting the absence of her shield. Dartrek served his purpose. Still, she began to pull her long gloves free, intending to confront this shade fully. Her father's men were always in distance of a shout, and sometimes there were no better ways to gauge a man. Fear was no excuse to act afraid.

A step forward was all she gained.

Dull, wooden raps echoed amidst the room as Walthere and his entourage wobbled through the open door at the other end of the room. The dark one's eyes, however, remained fixed on her. Not a smile or even a frown to break the air. Charlotte pulled herself away, to the men that would burn an empire. Old, out of shape, swaddled in fortune. They looked beyond her, to the dark man coddled in their wealth.

Most looked as startled as she felt.

"So you have met," Walthere wheezed. Cane leading, he shuffled for a chair. Recent months had seemed to exact physical vengeance for his political successes. While out hawking one morning, his horse had startled and bucked him from the saddle. He'd had the cane ever since. "Good. This saves us some trouble. Names? Dreams? Aspirations? Have we moved to those at least?" His eyes provided the mirth his lips never would.

Charlotte followed her father's smarmy gaze back to their guest. The creature only cocked its head in something resembling curiosity. Long fingers slid the length of its thighs.

"No? Pity. Charlotte, darling, this is what you would call a sellsword. A very good one."

Purple lips finally curled, ever-so-slightly.

"It has come to my attention our northern holdings have need of such—protection. Thieves, you know. Always looking to take what isn't theirs." A sad shake of his head seemed to dismiss the danger, adding, "The people beckon, and I think it time—"

"Talks too much," the dark man observed with the softest of yawns. His eyes flicked, fleetingly, to the sidling specter of Boyce. An eyebrow rose. "Silk and lies, they say."

Boyce did not smile. Sleeves weighted with daggers, he crossed his arms against his chest.

Charlotte rather liked this man already.

Charlotte's father was a man unaccustomed to interruption. His dark eyes narrowed to slits and his lips pursed distastefully.

The guardsmen that accompanied him fanned out slowly about the hall, looking aside with practiced disinterest. Mardel and Kamps, two of her father's closest fops, turned as if to find a place to sit, but realizing their place, turned away in noted discomfort. Theirs was not a place from which to speak. Only Boyce advanced, scuffing the carpet under polished boots, with eyes for the sellsword alone. It was his hands Charlotte watched, the conciliatory motion—open, empty, palms extended. Diplomats moved as such. Snakes moved as such.

He began to say something, but the sellsword shifted, violence tilting his hands back toward some unseen threat at his hip. Boyce was the only one that stopped outright, though the others tensed about the shoulders and the wrists, weapons brandishing more readily, more uncertainly. Boyce's own hands folded inward.

They all stood dressed as if for a ball, and only the sellsword seemed discontent to play along. His dark clothing hardly complimented his already dark complexion, and it was ragged, beaten, and torn. Beneath, she caught glimpses of skin that struck her as more hide than flesh, leathery in bearing and doubtless scarred. There were few men she could truly posit of the title "grim." This was one.

"The mark?"

It broke the rules. All the more reason for amusement. Politics was a vulgar thing, its foundations the coarse dung of mankind. People didn't discuss it in such open terms.

One of the guardsmen crossed in front of her and Charlotte brushed aside, musing on the look that waited at the other end. It was Usuri's look: death and madness. Where did her father find such people?

"A high-flown bird—a craven and a crow," Walthere ultimately replied through a thin scowl. "You'll find its name in your saddlebags. Boyce has your p—"

"Payment when done. No others?"

The startled look on Walthere's face earned a cocked eyebrow from the sellsword.

"Other what?" Boyce answered for his lord.

The sellsword's bright eyes fell, and his face answered in kind: competition. Whoever they were sending him after, he wanted no competition for it. Walthere shook his head quickly.

"Father!"

"One crow. One hawk. That should be enough."

There was scrutiny in the hunter's stare, but he shrugged after a moment and made to rise. "If more come, they will not return." He seemed to follow Boyce's feet—the backward slide. A smile teased out, and though his words were offered to Cullick, his gaze shifted up for Boyce alone. It was like watching two spiders circle the same mate. There was an accounting in that look.

But Charlotte had heard enough. They already tended to one mad soul beneath their roof; she would not abide another. Pressing past her father's man, she made for him, howling anew. "Father, you cannot possibly consider this." She did not slow even at the darkening of his glance—the terse flick of a man that did not want to be disturbed. Mardel stepped forth to intercept her, despite a dismayed shake of the head from Boyce, and he started to speak, but Charlotte swept past him as one might cattle.

She was aware of the eyes that watched her from every corner of the room. She did not care. Charlotte stood before her father, even as his hand took her arm. "Not now," he hissed, but she shook him off, pressing him back with a sharp, "Then never, ser." She had been called for a reason. She was not some passive witness and she would not bear another grievance with tight lips. Stiff steps carried her into her father's space, such that he was forced to either give ground or meet her eye to eye.

He gave, taking her by the hand and drawing her into his web. Boyce stepped up to fill their space.

"Unbelievable," he snapped and whispered in the same breath. "You would undermine me? Now? You cannot imagine the words—"

She stilled him with a hand against his chest, breathing through his anger. "Father," she said, thinning her tone. It shook him, but he wheezed out the final words and let them go. "Forget you so soon your contract to another? Already you saddle us with a killer. One we already risked much to court. You would send another?"

"You said yourself that she is broken. She refused. And besides, her woman's craft stands upon our own capabilities. Some things even her ways cannot reach. This is practical."

"It is asinine. And what of that other? Do her as you did the rest? You know what may happen if you cross her." Little dolls all burned to ash.

Scarlet flushed the man's cheeks. Backtalk was a sin, but the mention of the girl in front of others... "I will not be called to account. Not by you. I know the risks. She has her uses yet. I can talk her back from that hole she digs herself. But this—this is different. A letter came for me, and I think you know its worth." Her heart sank. The measured look he gave her confirmed its nature. So the electors had been measured. "I simply have not the time any longer for her moods. And if she—if she doesn't come to it, if she won't, then yes, dear heart, this world shall be done a kindness."

Breaths could not suffice. Charlotte wanted to scream, but the air gathered in her lungs and burst forth in an exasperated creak. She turned away. *They will burn.* Practiced muscles eased, made a mask of her face. *It's all she wants. Can't you see?* Humanity numbed her.

They had a witch. They had a mad little witch, caught in the highest strands of their web, mad as a poisoned little fly. On her back they flew the fires of their hate. Then they denied her. They wondered why the fly would foam. It twisted, raged. No use. No use. A fly without wings was no use to them. But how could a web ever snuff the flames?

The sellsword chuckled. "A penny for the moat, where all the ashen song be wrote—a tune for man, so long eloped in hours of decision and derisive hope.

Flutter, flutter heart, beyond your base and noble part. All eyes behold the passing."

The words, poetic in their way, slipped away into the cracks of the hall, and they all met them dumbly. No one knew quite what to make of them, Charlotte least of all, for the man said them straight at her. Or through her, as seemed more the man's wont.

"Yes, thank you for that," Boyce breathed a moment later. "But I believe it is time."

The sellsword only vaguely seemed to note this fact, nodding slowly to the sound of Boyce's voice. Then the creature turned, sharply, to bow before him—a smooth sort of half-tilt, as one might begrudge an elder. He turned and repeated the same to Walthere, and adjusted only slightly to make for Charlotte. He did not bow. Rather, the sellsword came forward. He stopped when he was nearly foot for foot with Boyce, where his slender frame became all the more apparent beside the bulging spider. He swept his cloak back and bent down, while extending a hand to take her own. She slid her own out to meet it, as jurti demanded.

Audacious creature. The guardsmen shifted, uncertain whether to take offense. Leather coiled about her fingers like a vice.

As he bent before her, hand clasped tight, she had a premonition. Of foreboding. Of uncertainty. She shifted and he—sniffed her. Even Boyce started at that, but Charlotte only stood there, lips parting with the shock of it. For a heartbeat, she had a glimpse of herself tipping to a prince, only to take his hair in hand. Again, it all came down to the dolls. *Beast,* she very nearly snapped. Purpled lips laid a kiss against the flesh and the sellsword retracted a pace, the fainted flicker of a smile curling the edges of those lips.

"It smells."

She yanked her hand back in disgust, but the smile remained. "I say," her father barked, though he said no more, and did less, making no move for the man. Charlotte wanted to slap them both.

"How dare you," she settled for instead. "This perfume—"

But the creature clucked his tongue at her, interrupting her fury. "Not *that. The* smell. It smothers you." His head cocked slightly to the side, appraising her under a new light. "It has been touched. A curious thing."

He is insane, she thought with horror. It was the only explanation. Perhaps that was what happened when one outlived his people. Or perhaps there was a reason the aswari burned them from the world, in their infancy.

Yes, Charlotte knew him then. "Iruwen," Boyce called to him in that moment. Children's tales and monsters even to the Vorges, the people that came before *the People*, that were looked on as freaks even by their cousin aswari, whose open hearts had so damned them in so many other things. They were the guilt, the Vorges named them simply, on which all love was built. "Come," he said, "I will walk you to the stables." She heard the words, and numbly watched the shadow rise, and for this she was glad, for in spite of how the Vorges named them, Charlotte felt no heart in this creature before her.

The assassin bowed in parting, and with a whistle of a hum he was off. Though his legs were longer, he kept his strides measured, to walk perfectly side-by-side Boyce out the door.

And hopefully, Charlotte shuddered, *out of our lives.*

She stared after the two men and made that her prayer. "If you summoned me to ask advice, I give it freely father: be rid of that one. Be rid of him and be glad you did." This was one wolf she truly feared. At a glance of the others gathered, she knew it was a common sentiment. "Your courtyard is already a-wag about his coming."

"And let them wag," Walthere said curtly. "Such is the wont of such people, as the blade is his. Only the holy man needs preaching, child, and you remember that proverb."

"Without shame, without conscience."

Walthere's lip curled into a wolfish snarl, but he held it back. A snap of his fingers and a bark of that wrath sent Martel scrambling to their side, though, with a paper in hand. "In politics, there is no conscience. Grow up and stop pretending to something I did not teach you. Instead, take that woman's mind of yours and put it to this damnable script. They've made an elector of a priest and set this vote to our hands." He shook the letter from Martel's hand as he spoke, thrusting it at her.

She took it, but she did not bother to read it. It was not as though it would hold revelation. "We will need to have a rider afoot before day's end, then." But she was not yet done with lecture. "And does this priest have something to do with your dark knight?"

Walthere all but choked on his rage, so one of his fops danced in along the high road. "My lady, please. This is hardly the place."

"And who is our dear priest at least?" she countered, thrusting the note back at Martel.

"Bishop Hargrove of Tennesburg. A gracious half-wit, and a giving suckle of the patriarchal teat. It's said he likes a good drink." The fop shrugged. "Not a bad man, but he is a fiery one for the circle."

"They did it without question or concession," Walthere snapped. "That is not done, not without an emperor to do it."

Charlotte looked at him crossly. "And it is hardly unexpected. So father, as you have often counseled me: chew on it. It is. As is another priest's crowning. Send them your acceptance and be done, and all the while, turn to that which you lock away, before it turns its hand to us. Mind your cultivation: it's a weed you watered, and a weed will choke another weed down as sure as any flower, should that weed suddenly thrust itself amongst the wrangling. I cannot be the only one to whom she speaks."

"No one asked you to."

"Someone has to."

Martel squirmed from one foot to the other. "Lord, lady, perhaps this is a discussion best held elsewheres."

"You get the tongue on you, child. I do not particularly like it." Walthere swatted at Martel, and the fop had the sense to skitter out of their path. "For too long you have been playing the wild part, and that will not suit. Not now. But if it appeases you, I will make that climb, if you see to that damnable letter, and to Sara. Her mother bleats at me daily with her worries and I will not have her locked in her room much longer. Get her out."

She scoffed. "And Lothen? Would you have me cuddle up with his bladesman next and see to it he gets his proper sunlight as well?"

The cane shook when Walthere's fist closed against its head. "Be silent and do your duty. That is one thing well in hand, so don't you mind it. It was your aunt that set him to that and he has been rightly dealt. If you must learn something it is this: learn the hearts of the people to whom you speak before your actually open your lips. He will be attending our empress again in short time, and Lothen will be joining Gerold with his tutors. Martel! You have the men?"

"Aye, highness. A squirrely lot, and not a one of them Idasian, and I swear one or more of them may eat the kitchen from under us but—"

"Squirrely." Walthere snapped the word and, only when Martel shrank, did he twist it into a barking laugh. "Squirrels are ones to talk." Then he twisted back to Charlotte, and by then the mirth was already gone. Yet he reached out all the same and put a hand against her shoulder. She was surprised by the warmth of it, even through her shawl. He was sweating. "I trust this is agreeable?"

She bowed her head. "I will see it done, father. And if I may…?"

"There is more?" She could hear the tension in him, and she aspired to make her voice quick, lest his mood change anew before all the words were out.

"I wondered if we might see to a tutor for the girls, as well." She dared a glance up to measure his reply, but saw only stone there, and cast back down. "The Matairs, I mean to say."

"They are well, are they not?"

"They are," she said, though in truth they were not.

Kana, the little Matair, was all tears and longing. She spoke of her father and her mother and asked for little else. Charlotte could not bear to be around the shrill of it. Anelise, the youngest of Kasimir's daughters, was another matter. She watched her niece and guarded her dearly, but to others she was about as icy as Charlotte herself. What she found a virtue in herself, however, was hardly met the same in another. The girl was rebellious, and worse, she was smart. If she was not already twisting at the window screws and tapping at the panes, Charlotte would be terribly disappointed.

"But I fear the days of silence will not do them, or us, well. They need something to better occupy their day. Only so much joy can be had from pulling at a soldier's beard. Children are difficult enough inherently. One needs not fuel the fire."

Walthere seemed to consider the idea a moment before he gave his consent to it. She thanked him for it and hoped that would be all, but his hand remained on her shoulder, and neither stirred. After a moment, he leaned close and laid a kiss upon her cheek. Were she anyone but his daughter, she might have mistaken it for a kiss of death. The other was just as stunning.

"I have not thanked you for all of it, child. Know I do appreciate your efforts. If you do so well with them as you have with the Empress and with that Matair boy, well…"

She did not know what to say. So all she said was: "I will try my best, ser."

"I am sure you will." His thumb rubbed at her and she thought he might say something more, but then he was moving past her, to other matters. His fops scrabbled at his heels, and the guardsmen picked up their blades and followed. When she looked back at them, she caught Martel in turn looking back at her, face scrunched in confusion.

For a moment, she stood there in the hallway, pondering how to proceed. Too much at one time. The hairs of her head still tingled where her father had touched her. *An Iruwen walks out of the mists of time, and father kisses me.* If this was one of those signs of the gods people so liked to get on about, she was certain it took wiser souls than her to read them. She looked up into the stoneworks, wondering. *If you could make our enemies so dysfunctional as we, then this tune might play itself out to the quick.* If only she were a bird, life would be simpler, it was true. Yet this, troubles on troubles, were what set her to her best. A breath to steady herself, and she was off—she had not the time to wait for Dartrek. Their enemies would surely not.

Their enemies had a kingdom to wield. Maker help them, they had but lies and assassins and madmen, and none of these were a fortress. The only recourse was to attack.

Chapter 6

Rurik watched the sunlight curl through the fans of the maidenhair leaves, the branches lively and brown even in the twisting shade. Petals spiraled to the sound of the wind's sighs. The trees towered over all, even the town's walls, nestled between rocks as old and moss-covered as they. At a time, men might have gathered beneath their boughs to ponder those secret things only peace could breed.

Yet even at noon, the camp was restless.

The sights passed. The notions with them. Rurik and Berric hastened to the general's call.

Riders had probed the lines at dawn. They wore no colors and they fled when spied, but their intent was not in doubt. With the coming of spring and the indecision of their embassy, the Effisians were gauging them, and only a single train of new supplies had arrived from the west.

While the foraging parties roamed farther and farther afield, some men had resolved to boil their own bootstraps in order to supplement their hungry bellies—a fate typically befalling only those sailors too long at sea.

Another octave of this and they would not be fit to fight. They needed to move. No one doubted it. The only question was where.

Tessel and his council were discussing that very topic as Rurik loomed. As usual, the mass of men—and it was a mass, for Tessel had been ever enthused to the notion of hearing the reports and representatives of all beneath his banners, making for a great many aggrieved nobles and many more bemused captains— met in the gardens behind the church, where some semblance of privacy had been reserved. Annoyed and expectant stares flicked Rurik's way as he skittered to a stop among them. They turned away again as quick, briefly mollified by a salute and a fleeting explanation. He had been sent for his brother. He returned alone.

Fortunately, Tessel had greater matters on his mind. Of the host that clung to his words, three men had been drawn into his closest council, the rest hovering at the outskirts like children peeping in the window. Baron Pordill and Lord Marshall Othmann represented the titled folk, and though they could not have stood further apart in personality, they were the souls to whom Tessel most had to answer.

Othmann—who never let the rest of them forget it—was the man who, by all rights, should have held the power that Tessel wielded, while Pordill was a respected and experienced leader, and the highest ranked man afield, Othmann aside. Joining them was the largely silent specter of Vogel, a severe man whose most defining feature was the paralysis that had seized his left side as the result of a riding accident. He was commonborn, he could not even read, but he stood most valued to Tessel for his worth to the men and the wealth of his knowledge of all things war-like. Unlike some, though, he only spoke when he had something to say.

The conversation, such as it was, had changed remarkably little since Rurik had left.

"I say we move south," Pordill said. The only silver-haired officer left in the wake of the Emperor's death, this man, with his habits of soft speech, seemed more the attending grandfather to this mass of men. Though his sigil was a black goat, there were reasons some called him the "Black Sheep" behind his back. No few among the camp would have stabbed the man that so insulted him, though. "We have heard no more of Ernseldt. Our soldiers arrived. It's all we know. We should join our forces, sack Cardase, and press from there."

"Cardase has been under siege for months, even if Ernseldt remains. There will be no victory in its stores," Othmann countered. Months of rationing had done the lord marshall as well as everyone else, and his skin had begun to take on an almost bony, emaciated sort of sheen. He also spoke softly, but harshly.

"A point," the Bastard added, "and even if there were, how much longer might we last for it? We starve at half the numbers we would have if our two armies joined. No city in the land could feed us. We would only be forced to break anew, and further."

"Aye. But that's true regardless. The land lies barren. The Effisians want it that way. These people barely feed themselves. They can hardly feed us as well."

The Bastard spared a studious look for Othmann, and Rurik shared it. It was not usual for the man to part with wisdom—even if he possessed it. "Then what would you suggest?"

"Back and forth we have danced this issue of where to push, where to keep this fight alive. Well I tell you this, and I mean no offense—ludicrous, is all it is. Salvation lies only in the north, Kyler. We broke the crag-hoppers at sea for just this reason. The fleet can do what the wagons cannot. Reach the sea, and they will see us fed. I have letters to the plenty from Turgitz, telling of our men along the coast, and I tell you they live in paradise compared to we."

They drifted gradually as they spoke. Tessel, though a man of many qualities, had never found patience among them. He preferred his discussions in the open air for that very reason—it allowed him the opportunity to move, to pace, to work out the tension that might otherwise burst undesirably. Rurik found it an amusing enough quirk—a steady contrast to his father, who had always been something of a statue. Others found it less endearing.

They halted again under the boughs of one of the great, crooked trees, Tessel nodding to himself all the while.

"It is funny to me, Othmann, that you always speak so of such letters, yet never until these meetings of ours."

Othmann scoffed. "I bring matters to attention when those matters are of import, and you have made it clear the method by which you like to discuss. One does not trivialize councils of war with every scrap of personal correspondence."

"Up to our arses in it," Berric muttered into Rurik's ear as he shuffled for a better spot among the crowd.

This was not the first quarrel over the matter of letters. Though the army recognized Tessel for its leader, both the court and the nobility back west had made it plain whom they assumed was in charge. Rumor said Othmann was hiding things from Tessel. Knowing the man only made that more believable.

"No," Tessel added after a sour moment. "No, I think not. We press north, but we will continue east as well."

"East!"

"Yes, Othmann, east. This journey was the Emperor's will and testament, and I'll not shirk it now that he has passed."

Pordill and Othmann shared an anxious glance, and Pordill was left licking his own lips in the aftermath. "A noble gesture, to be sure, but if I might?" Tessel inclined his head, and Pordill pressed on. "Lend me two companies and I will head to the sea myself, and take us back supplies. If you are intent upon

Mankałd, from there I can sail them down the Ipsen, to wherever you may camp."

Before Tessel could reply, Othmann all but snarled. "Already the horse prince watches our camp. You think he will not piece together your plan when you ride from here? They will follow you, and once they know we are bogged down by siege, they will see those supplies razed on the river. They have logjams there, dams and bridges to block all but the smallest craft, and they have proven they are not above clogging the rivers to deny us. There is a reason we do not already use those bloody streams."

"It could simply divide their attentions," Pordill said. "They haven't the men for two fronts if they suppose we shall divide and conquer."

"Too much of a gamble. If we do not—"

"Enough. I have heard enough." Tessel nodded again, more severely, before he turned to face them all. "We will continue to Mankałd. This is not to be debated. Vogel, you will see a bird sent for Anscharde every night until the wagons break through, that they may be aware of our progress, and our intent."

The thin captain, swallowed as ever in his oversized tunic, hastily assured the general it would be done. Tessel, however, was already swiveling on another of his captains—a sparsely-haired giant of a man and a soldier-priest whom Rurik readily despised. One of the growing multitudes of Farrens that seemed to be clamoring to Tessel's confidence.

"Narve, you will dispatch orders to each of the company captains, and to the lords. We will divide the army before we march. Stagger things out. Five armies. Three in front, like curling wings; one in reserve, trailing; the fifth remains here, to guard any trains. Count Pordill, you are welcome to whatever men you wish for your expedition north—you tell it true, we need that food if we are to make the press, there is no way around it. Vogel, you will lead the left wing, Othmann you will lead the right, while—"

"Excuse my impertinence, but this is ludicrous," Othmann snapped. Tessel's own words petered out into icy silence. Rurik all but groaned. *Up to our arses indeed.* "We starve, and you seek to press us deeper into enemy terrain? These farcical hopes aside, on what do you expect us to march, exactly?"

"Your patriotism, clearly," Tessel jibed.

Several of his captains let out low, if uncertain chuckles. Rurik was not among them. Nor was Vogel. "In this, I must agree with the marshall," Vogel grumbled. "We couldn't support ourselves. It could take the lord count more'n a oct to return, even if the fates be kind to him. Leszek would harry us the whole way, and we'd wear ourselves into the dirt."

Berric elbowed Rurik in the side. "Well that's a piss of a thing, when Vogel takes the marshall's side. Portent, I'd say."

"Of?" Rurik asked quietly, trying not to be heard over the arguing generals.

"Drakkons and hellspawn, most like."

"What of the messenger? Does not Leszek seek peace?" another of Tessel's captains asked. This started a certain amount of murmuring among the assembled. In the wake of the embassy for peace, many now dared to hope on it.

"No," Tessel answered with practiced certainty. "Would that it were so. Merely his father. Leszek would heed no peace of ours and I fear his countrymen would more readily follow him than any of his father's decrees."

Peace with Mordazz and his deeps, would be more like. Rurik had to fight down the scowl his face wished to form. If anyone could find Leszek, let alone reason with the man, he was sure the soldiers would name him Assal incarnate. The Effisian prince was a devil made flesh, and he fought for his land as the old stories said men should. They could conquer every Effisian stone from west to east, but if that man still drew breath they would never own Effise. *Peace. Would that we were so lucky!*

"Leszek's nothing but a kuree turd," Othmann spat. "But you, Kyler. You ignore the obvious. Word of those messengers should have been sent immediately for Anscharde! Even the prospect of peace...and what of the summons from our own court? You and half this army should be headed back for the border by now. We should not even be having this discussion, in truth. Not you and I."

The words struck a chord that set Rurik ill at ease. The others shifted uncomfortably—disquieted by the marshall's lack of decorum, but also every bit as eager to know the answer. Rurik twisted an anxious glance over his shoulder, that he might look to the guards following twenty paces at their backs.

Do your ears perk to this, friends? The letter to which the marshall referred—the letter Rurik had watched Tessel smile down on—had been quietly tucked away after its reading. Tessel had shared its contents only with Rurik and his fellow captains, seeking to keep Othmann and his nobles from the truth. But somehow they had found out anyway.

Doubtless, it had not been the only letter. That would have implied trust. *And it is the duty of a soldier*, Rurik's father always said, *to trust no one when the steel stirs.*

Tessel met the man eye-to-eye, unflinching before the challenge. "The court's words were, as intended, put to me for weighing and interpretation. As commander here, it is my purview to decide what is best for the army. If we break now, the Effisians will roll back all the gains we made over the course of the last year, and come next spring, we will have nothing to show for it. We have an opportunity to strike now, to subjugate Effise and restore it to the Empire's care, so that they too may have the joy of Imperial decrees." His lips curled, mirthlessly. "I will return to the court when the Emperor's will is done."

Still, Othmann scoffed angrily. "The men are like enough to riot if you go this route, Kyler. I do not say it lightly. But you know as well as I that all men have their limits, and they are nearly there."

"So it is, marshall, so it is. But of what men do you speak? Our soldiers or their betters?"

"Easy, sers," Pordill cautioned, trying to put himself between the pair. "There is no need to let hot heads—"

Othmann ignored him. "The hands move where the head leads. All are one in this."

"Are you certain? I have heard the moans of the men, but I have heard none of this rabble-rousing. Though I have heard of certain whispers between our goodly nobles. I hear any number of them have been attending your tent, of late, as point of fact. A more distrusting man might ponder what you were sharing that you did not see fit to tell your commander."

Othmann tightened at that, while beside him the Black Sheep murmured "Assal be good." Othmann waved off the accusation with a derogatory puff of air. "Silk and lies. My men come to me with questions as to our next moves. I answer them, and in turn answer to you. Would you have every soul mucking about your flaps in the middle of the night?"

This was getting out of hand. "Should I?" Berric nodded toward the trailing guardsmen, who seemed as yet unperturbed by the display. Given the rumbles among the captains, though, wise men might have begun to fear another Falk. At least none of these were armed.

"Leave it. They're not such great fools as that." Even as he said it, Rurik cast another apprehensive glance to the guardsmen all the same. He did not quite believe it himself.

Across the yard, Tessel frowned. "Of course. I meant no insinuation, marshall. Yet for all that, and since you seem so set upon laundering our dirty airs this day, I might also ask as to why so many of these same men are bandying letters through my aide-de-camp's own brother. It was my understanding all letters were to go through Boderoy, but these always go to your tent before they reach the birds. Might you speak on that? I had no notions the two of you were so close."

The marshall's gaze leveled on Rurik, and he swallowed, shrinking before it. *Poncy scum*, he thought, but as much as he hated Othmann, that was one soul he dared not cross. He was high nobility, and a general at that, and for all the ill will men slung at his character, none besmirched his ferocity with a blade. It was Tajiman steel, they said, and even in the poorest hands it severed heads like a knife to butter. And Othmann's hand was like a guiding wind. Rurik felt its flutter on his neck contained even within the darkness of the man's look.

"Ser Ivon was a confidante of His Majesty, and is a confidante of my own, Kyler. His friendships can be helped no more than his unfortunate relations to certain less-than-honored kin."

"Or their arrogant toadies," the soldier-priest muttered.

Tessel fixed his steely gaze on the priest, but addressed his words to Othmann. "Of course. Far be it from me to besmirch the man. I had hoped he might join us to speak on the matter himself." Rurik swallowed as the man's searching gaze swung his way. "Rurik?" All other eyes quickly followed.

Rurik fidgeted. When he had managed to slip in without a fuss, he had dared to hope he might escape unscathed. He might have known better. The meeting with his brother had, in truth, not gone well. He had met Ivon at his tent, under the scrutiny of a dozen knights and men-at-arms, all spoiling for a fight.

Their words had been mercifully brief. Rurik had delivered the summons and asked, exactly as he had been told to, after the nature of Ivon's recent whispers.

"Whispers? You make it sound as if I skulk through the streets like a back-alley blade."

"Nevertheless, I would know what it is the nobles have been sharing, Ivon. We are to be one front. Not many, squabbling."

Ivon had laughed at that, openly and coldly. "You have no authority to question a nobleman."

"On Lord Tessel's authority, I do."

"A bastard's authority, executed by an exile. It's worth less than the dirt I piss on. Get out, and take your summons with you. I think we have played your master's game long enough. If you must tell him something, tell him thus: the noble lords that constitute this army are in agreement. It is time we headed home. To remain is murder and disobedience."

Rurik had stood there, riveted as much by shock as anger. The wheels turned in his head and he reeled for something, anything to hit back at his brother with, but there was nothing. *Traitor,* he felt his own mind hiss. He thought of the kindness his brother had shown him since Tessel took him under his wing, and he realized it had all been a farce. Respect? There was none of it there. Not in front of other men. Only anger, though how much of it was for his own foul soul he could not say.

Ivon's guards had escorted him out, while Ivon remained behind.

Some things were beyond even blood. "The nobles and their houses are restless, ser. They wish to return home," Rurik spoke quickly to the assembled, leaving out his brother's colorful additions.

"As is their right, by Assal!" Othmann beamed. It was like watching a ferret gloat over a silver coin.

"Is this true?" Tessel twisted a hard gaze on Pordill.

The baron consented with a heavy sigh. "It is. I could not give names of all that share the opinion, but I would say the majority of us wish for home. Many have been from their lands for more than a year, and when news of your letter went about, the rest—well, in the wake of His Majesty…"

Tessel dismissed him wordlessly, turning back to Rurik. "You will tell your brother, and these dissenters, precisely what I've told these men here. This army will march. I appreciate their concerns, but they were beckoned here for a purpose."

"Who are you to refuse Imperial decree?" Othmann cut in once more.

Tessel grimaced. "Refuse? I follow Imperial decree. From the lips of the Emperor himself. Twenty thousand men, and the lot of you quail at a bit of parchment from a man yet uncrowned?"

"Watch your tongue, ser," Othmann snarled. "That is the heir you speak of."

"An heir that has never seen his country. An heir raised in the excesses of—" Tessel bit himself off there, refusing to let Othmann goad him into a fight. All present knew his feelings on the Church, and the Orthodox Visaj. Through gritted teeth, he continued, seething, "When a man speaks with Imperial authority again, I will listen. Not before." Then he strode forward, toward Rurik and his other gathered captains. "And what of you all? Do you quail as well? Do you lose heart in your emperor's wishes?"

"Never, ser," one man answered.

"Matthias!" another shouted.

The rest seemed to share the opinion, nodding and praising and offering assent. One even asked for the courtesy of rooting out the dissenters. Though Tessel shook his head at that, it seemed to strike some spark in his eye all the same, and he twisted sharply back to the nobles. "It seems we reach an impasse, marshall. Some say yes, some say no. And I say yes. Tell your men to prepare for march." He held the marshall's gaze a moment longer, then started to turn away.

Othmann wouldn't let it go. "I warn you, Kyler, as friend and councilor, that these men are your commanders. The heads that guide the limbs. If you isolate them, you set this army in danger of mutiny. You know as I do we follow you for the Emperor's affections toward you—but I pray you remember he is dead, and without those affections, there is little shielding you."

A specter of a far greater darkness crossed Tessel's eyes in that moment. His was not a face accustomed to rage. Rurik cringed. He realized then how thin the ground was that the marshall walked. "Is that right," Tessel asked, softly. "And have they offered any names?"

"I pray you tread careful, lord," Vogel rumbled.

Othmann hesitated, seemingly catching a hint of his own peril. "Many. They all have their opinions on whom might best serve." He looked to Baron Pordill for support, but there was nothing there for him.

At that, Tessel actually smiled. "I'm sure, marshall." His eyes turned on Rurik, purposefully softening. But even in the quiet breaths that followed, Rurik felt the lingering touch of the shade, and he could not help but wonder what else might lurk beneath the image of the man. Somewhere in the space between masks, humanity lurked.

"Unfortunately you fail to realize one very important thing. Perilous as you paint the mood here, what do you think happens when the armed masses behold the destruction of their voice?" Tessel shook his head, growing older for the effort. The marshall's frown thinned into blackness. "A hundred voices rise to take its place, but twenty thousand more would stand to drown them in noise."

Sleep would not come to Rurik that night. When he closed his eyes, the screams followed, and all was noise and blood. Men died in the gloom between—shapeless masses, armed and armored, falling by the thousands through a ring of opaque twilight. The noise of which Tessel spoke rang in his ears and drowned the voice of all.

They fell on one another in the darkness. He feared it in waking, and it would brook him no rest.

Outside, stars rained through the night sky. He drew aside the canvas flap of the window for a better look. They blazed, a dozen, two dozen, three dozen tiny fires blurring the luminescent figure of Havreth, one of the twin moons. None fell. They merely streamed across the sky and disappeared beyond the walls. Other men would wish on them, as was the custom. The star rains were a sporadic thing, as old as time itself, lighting a night here and there every few years. The last time Rurik had seen them he was on the road, huddled beneath the celestial flames and the dewy grass, with a woman coiled beside him and friends all around him and a fire burning itself to embers at their feet. There were no screams, then. Merely the endless journey.

There is no one. No one but you, and them, and all the other corpses in the field. You are alone. No one watches. No one waits. He rubbed his eyes and tipped his head against a knee. *He does not see you. He is dead and gone and you are alone.* Yet he could not convince himself, so he surrendered to this as well.

Bundling some of the hay beneath him into a ball, he pressed it up against the wall and scrunched tighter into the corner. Around him, four other men slept in the blissful throes of dreamlessness. One murmured, smiled, and rolled away with a grunt. *Or the dreams of the lucky.*

He folded, grinding his nails against his skull and praying for the dawn. After hours lost to tossing and twisting off the itchy woolen sheet, Rurik surrendered to his insomnia. Prayers came and went from mind without ever being uttered. He looked at the ceiling of the old hut, ignoring the nasally rasps of snores around him, and tried to form a picture of Assal in his mind. All he ever saw were boards. There was no face in them. Not even the shape of one. A curse sputtered from his lips and he tried to brace the impending emptiness with a renewed dedication to the atheistic. A dull coin taunted him with the ache and he could feel it weighing him down.

He let the flap fall flat again and repeated the ritual of these long nights. They had been happy. All of them but he. So he, in his childishness, had naturally seen it stricken away, his own foolish sense of what happiness needed to be drifting further all the while.

He drew the coin from the pocket of his tunic. It was a rusted thing, completely unremarkable in every way. That did not keep him from cupping it in his hand and whispering his heart into its depths.

Why? A soothing sort of cave whisper. He knew no one could hear him. A woman had promised him different, but the memory of her had grown as dim as the visage of the coin itself. If she even lived, what could remain?

Even in the midst of war, they draw rank and draw steel, thinking only of the blood and the name and the glitter of it all. Pointless. Don't they see? They would kill us all. Ivon and all the rest like him. Arrogant. Thoughtless hate.

It was something to vent his frustration on. A focus. And Usuri knew the pain. She knew horror. If only he could have helped her, too, but—as in all things, he was ever too late.

Yet I'm no better than the mud on their boots. They look at me and through me and they just laugh. They look at Tessel, but all they see is danger. Blood. They don't care what his blood says. They'll stab him down in the street and let it run, and they'll stab me down too just for standing at his side. Blood is all that ever matters. Not words. Not intent.

But the chaos of his thoughts coalesced upon a single note. *Why did he have to hide that letter?* It had gnawed at him all day and still he had no answer. Such things would always out.

He folded his legs inward, cradling against them the way he used to as a child. There were no worries then—not like now, anyways. As long as he listened to his tutors and he listened to his father and he kept all his nonsense quiet, he could run where he would and play as he would. He could wander the streets of Verdan, tall and proud and unafraid, and call to Essa through the trees. Children would flock and play between the shadows of the setting sun.

And they would laugh. He and Essa and all the rest. They would eventually go away. But her image remained. It still remained, even if she didn't want it.

How? How can I make her see?

Silence answered, cold and uninvited. He rubbed his thumb against the faded profile of the coin and thought of another girl, another pain, another fire in the gut. Iñigo, the old pagan, stood framed against a stake, eyes closed to the light. It burned and burned and stole them both away. Rurik shook his head. He still couldn't believe the old man was dead. In his mind he formed the looks the old man shared with his daughter. He focused on the smile, on the laughter of a joke beside the fireplace, and the faces slowly came into focus.

She disappeared into the darkness of his wake. Then the world went to hell. All Rurik had left to remember her by was the coin.

Usuri? he asked the cold, ignoring the snort of a sleeping soldier's answer. *Where did you go? It's all gone wrong. So very wrong.* The coin thrummed against his fingers. A chill blossomed through him with the whistle of the wind. She had said she would answer, but the coin never answered. It was only his voice. His fears.

In the darkness of the night, it was not enough.

* *

Though the night had been lit with the falling fires, dawn was a gray affair. Sky was nothing more than a notion between clouds, their dark canopy rolling taut above the sodden earth. It was the sort of morning that soaked the clothes without ever spilling a drop. It sank through the sink and settled deep in the bones. Even the plains felt small, boxed in by boundless walls.

For hours of the aurora light, Roswitte hunched against the damp and waited. Nothing stirred. No game. No scouts. Even the traps lay bare. All that walked the brush was a hunter and her unused bow. She returned empty-handed, as frustrated with herself as with the wildlife.

There was nothing like a good hunt to bring the self together again. Likewise, there was nothing so infuriating as the waste of that precious time.

The camp was just beginning its rounds when she strode behind the cordon. She ignored the polite nods of the guardsmen, eyes glued to the road ahead.

A well sat at the outskirts of the town. Studni, the townsfolk called it. Or stuzni. Something like that. While Roswitte was aware their language shared many similarities with the Corva tongue that was the standard of the Empire, the intricacies of the Effisian language were lost on her, and what's more, they infuriated her. Its thick, guttural nature wrapped around the tongue and left it hissing in displeasure, and she had long since given up trying. The well was what she sought, whatever the name.

A handful of other men clustered around the hole in the earth, but they paid her no heed. One pulled a drink with an exaggerated gasp, then grunted off a bucket to her as she held a hand for the pleasure. She let it fall back into the deep with little care, then pulled the full bucket up into the light again. She tipped her head back to savor the taste of the cool water on her dry throat. Then she plunged face and hands alike into the chill and savored the tiny bites it scattered across her skin.

When she pulled back into the world, she nearly started at the sight of the knight staring down at her. Mere paces separated them, the man's fingers at easy rest on the hilt of a sheathed sword. The eyes were warm, even if the rest bespoke of violence. He smiled at her. She ignored him in turn.

Drawing back her hair with one hand, Roswitte lowered the bucket again with the other, pulling water for her return to Ivon. Still, the knight waited patiently, making a seat of the well's stones.

On the day Roswitte rode into the war, she had thought herself removed from Ser Ensil the dust knight and the rest of his sellswords. In the days since, however, the man had made a habit of his presence. He and his company had been staked beside this well, and he always came out to greet her as a consequence. Always he smiled, and whispered good tidings, possessed of a grin that had little reason to be. He ate as poorly as the rest of them, now. The difference was: he seemed impervious to the infection of defeatism that seemed to accompany it in everyone else.

"Good morn, ranger," the man eventually called. The jovial lilt to his voice set her hairs on edge, involuntary though she knew it was.

"Good morn," she called in turn.

Would that she could leave it at that. He asked after the woods, oblivious to her torment. *A man should have the sense to know an empty haul when he sees one.* She looked at him crossly and continued to raise the pail. When it was safe in hand, she began to unwind the rope that bound it to the well. Ensil leaned forward, heedless. "Do your charges keep the peace so well?"

She hefted the pail onto her hip and started off. Ensil rose to follow her. "They sleep," she answered at length, anxious to be rid of him. "As most should 'bout these early hours." She kept her eyes to the path ahead.

Beyond the flags and the banners of the individual houses and companies, the army was a scattered beast. Men sprawled and staked where they would until some higher power pointed them somewhere else. They spent their days stewing, or patrolling a broad and chaotic ring about the town's more sensible walls. More than a few would look on their camp and see nothing but a senseless maze.

Time and repetition drilled home all things, though. Even the formless gained shape with endless replication. Roswitte might have shut her eyes at this point and let her feet carry her the rest of the way. Ivon's tent was east, and east she went, secretly loathing the growing sounds of the waking masses.

"Might I escort you to your tent, lady?" Ensil had asked that first day beside the well, as gallant a figure as one could cut. A pity, because one could never quite trust a man that was prettier than most girls.

Even then she had felt the burgeoning scowl—distrust. "If I can stalk them woods, knight, I can wander a camp unaided."

He had given her that, but followed regardless, like a lost puppy—no concept of where else to go. She didn't stop him. So it became routine, day after day. The penniless warder of the woods and the honorless knight of the roads, navigating the lanes together.

It was only after each walk, when she stood a moment in the tumult of the teeming city of their camp, that the little voice would whisper: *Be kind to this man. Be good. This is the man that saved your life.* All the same, their walks repeated. *Only bitter tastes come of bitter deeds.*

They were nearly to the limits of Witold's ranks before the dust knight spoke again. "When you speak to your lord, you should tell him there is some foul talk about the fires these nights. Many are worried as to the tension between the lord commanders."

"Gossip's the nature of men. Let them have it. It's foul deeds I fear."

"One may beget the other, if things do not resolve themselves soon, lady."

She stopped, acutely aware of the curious rivermen—those souls of Verdan and the Ulneberg at large that formed the bulk of Witold's conscripts—watching from afar. "And you, ser? You and yours share such rumor?"

"A man would be a fool to ignore the voices of his peers." Ensil said easily. He never took offense. "All men are disconsolate when put to war. More so when they cannot find the war for which they march. It takes so little to push them into the ultimate miscalculations."

"Duty demands."

"For members of a house, perhaps. Their bondsmen. Duty means nothing to baser sorts, for it cannot see family fed, nor fields harvested, particularly if coin does not come. And for your sellswords, and your free companies, that coin is the only note. As I am sure you well know, duty and honor are oft enough realm only for those with security to afford them."

She studied the man's eyes as he spoke. Wide and gentle, she beheld no sign of treachery tightening them. They did not look away, nor did they shrink before her gaze. *A good man, in truth,* she decided, shying away from him at length. Honesty—perhaps the man's most redeeming quality. Unfortunately, it was as dangerous as everything else.

"Thanks for 'scorting me."

He touched a hand to his breast as he bowed. "Ever a pleasure, lady."

"And for your counsel. I'll share it with milord."

"It is the duty of the eyes to forever watch the motions of others. Some are merely better at it than others."

With that, they bid farewell and broke their separate ways. *A good man indeed,* she told herself with a sigh. It changed little. Her coldness was, she reasoned, perhaps undeserved, but it was what it was. In his face she saw still the bald and bearded faces leering back at her. Smelled that male stink of sweat and ale. Hot breath. She saw a knife and blood and...Fallit. Most of all, she saw Fallit. She couldn't forget, and she held Ensil at fault for her memory.

Not for the first time, she told herself tomorrow she would smile. Tomorrow she would answer him with the mirth he seemed to seek. Tomorrow she would set aside death's call, and play a human again.

One look at his face and it would die, though, as sure as any concept of the flesh.

He knew. That was enough to damn him.

She handed the bucket to Ivon's quartermaster and made straight for her lord's tent. The guards there did not bar her way, though she waited with them long enough for one to announce her. Etiquette maintained, she drew the flap aside and stepped inside.

Ivon was leaned against his desk, arms crossed to her approach. Tall, proud, he would have been the perfect union of mother and father, had his long hair survived his grief. His father's muddied eyes watched her narrowly, though without guile. She bowed beneath them, pretending for a moment she was a lady she was not. *Dogs,* her master's voice rang through her head. *All men are dogs.* She set her bow beside the entrance and turned to meet him properly.

"Any luck?"

She shook her head and raised unmarred hands for his inspection.

"Pity. I should have liked some deer. Or a nice elk. It's been too long." His shoulders sank with a soft sigh, and the tension seemed to roll easily off him. The young lord parted with a smile, though the rest of him remained defensive as ever—a trait he shared with his father. "Just as well. I suppose the mess would seem unbecoming, at this point."

Her thoughts wandered to Verdan and the wealth of animals loping beneath the canopies of the trees. Fish in the stream. Deer amongst the tall grass. Wild goose and pheasant and turkey wallowing in their flightless fancy. She could nearly taste them.

Her stomach turned. In ten days, she had known nothing but paltry bites of hard bread and the dull tack of leather.

"Anyone?"

"Nothing, ser. The hills are as devoid of men as beasts."

Would that there were more of a difference between the two, she thought bitterly.

"Good. I would trust your eyes above a hundred outriders ahorse, Ros." Such praise might have had more of an impact if his voice had flecked itself with an ounce of emotion. She bowed regardless. Then, before he could dismiss her, she told him all of what Ensil had said, and all that she herself had heard.

The very basis of the feudal structure was that men looked to their leaders for guidance. Men looked to their nobles and their nobles looked to the royals, and all was simple, if not always easy. Unfortunately, the present discourse within the camp presented a unique and terrifying dilemma. In war, commanders superseded all other authority beside the royal authority. To serve them was to serve the crown. To disobey one's captain was to invite the sting of death.

Even in their own camp there were those that would no longer meet one another's gaze. The lords of the homeland said it was time to go. Some preached—more openly than others—that the Bastard sought to disobey the royal family. There were whispers of letters and birds and riders in the night, though Roswitte put little enough stock in any of it. The men that followed these lords, however, receded deeper into their camps, like fortresses of cloth and iron. To disobey nobility—and especially the royal family—was death for any peasant. One's loyalty, and one's life, was to their lord.

Yet the Bastard had called for the march. He was the son of the late emperor, lending him credence in the eyes of the people, if not in the eyes of the nobility. Bastard or no, he had led men before his father's death; it seemed only natural that he should lead them after, while Othmann, for all his many qualities, was castrated by spiteful humor. If not for his failures, many of these men need never have come east to fight at all. To leave their families in the bitter winter and to remain through the beginnings of a planting season. The Bastard appointed men even from the peasant ranks to advise and support him. It endeared him to some.

Which was right to follow? For Roswitte it was easy. Wherever her own lord walked, she would follow.

108

"Men will do what is right, in the end." Ivon said eventually. Fervidly. "Might I trust myself to you, Ros? A secret on my father's name?"

"On your—" She stirred at that. A certain heat rang through her ears. Not a light thing, this. *Careful, girl.* Such words were iron. "Always, ser."

"The Bastard oversteps himself. It is the curse of his breed to be consumed by blood. Theirs. Others. To prove themselves. I think that is what he would do here, with this fool's march. Othmann may be a fool, but he is the fool we know.

"We have made great gains here. We choke their rivers, anchor in their bays, and ride unopposed across vast tracts of their land. Yet what should it take to hold them? Not so many, I think. So few of them remain. Great gains—we might go home, content in that—and I would rather die in my own bed, at home, than in this forsaken waste."

Home. The word fanned the heat. It caught in her throat and she felt herself unconsciously tug away from her lord. The ghost of an old man and his cane walked the halls, an inquisition smile stretching pillar to pillar in the great room. There was a touch on her shoulder—a friendly touch—and a flirtatious laugh. A man strode through memory, and took her hands in his. *Little bear,* it whispered. *Fallit.*

"As you say, milord." Her eyes rose again to his. She kept the memories at bay.

No lord should burden his people so with such a casual tongue. In this, more than anything, she knew Ivon for his father's son.

Ivon didn't notice. He stared off into his own thoughts, occasionally tapping a finger against his arm. For a long moment, nothing more passed between them, until Roswitte began to wonder if she weren't supposed to leave.

Finally, Ivon scrutinized her as he had before. "We've all lost something in coming here. Such is the nature of war, but by Assal, I know I should have been at my lord's side." His gaze thinned and he leaned back against his desk. "So it is. There is nothing for it now."

So she was not the only one to suffer the clawing of demons. Still, there were other itches that gnawed at her, and given how candid her lord's mood seemed to carry itself now, Roswitte found her own sense of kind stepping out of line. Such opportunities were rare, and for all her obedience, not a man could name her apathetic to curiosity.

109

Rumors were plenty. The truthbearers few. Given how Ivon spoke of Tessel and the war…

"Milord—if you don't mind my asking—what about the Effisians? Word's to the plenty that peace looms…don't it?"

It had been the talk of the camp. An honest hope. While other hatreds flickered in the dark, that one point burned like a guiding star. The men of the army saw only an out—an answer to their prayers. In this, Ensil had spoken true. They had not asked to come here. While even the lowest sot felt the heat of anger for their emperor's death, it was an abstract burn, and the long months of idleness had cooled its heat, dulling the sense of their cause.

All they saw now was an opportunity for home. Any affront the Effisians had once called seemed nothing more than a distant dream. Whatever they had done had hardly affronted them personally. They were the eyes that would forever haunt the living—pale, human eyes that raged and waned that they themselves might persevere. Truly, many of them stood more human than their own masters. Did not both suffer for the greed of the "higher" men?

It had been years since any man had been given leave to speak for Effise within Idasian bounds. Those higher sorts didn't see the point. So for these beleaguered men, the sight of that small troop riding into their camp had been as good a sign of home as any.

We done well, we tell ourselves. Others have died that I might live but now— now I can live. I'm going home. Sometimes she pitied the weak hearts of her countrymen. *Do we dare to hope?* How many times before it was beaten out of them entirely?

Rather than roar for the injustice of the call to march, there was only discontent in it misunderstanding. They knew they had to march if they were called, but that little spark inside still questioned: *Why do we do so?*

Ivon regarded her sternly. "Not so long as Tessel answers. If you people hang your hopes on that, well—know he rejected that outright." A woman of Ivon's station might have asked in turn that immortal: *Why?* Roswitte only nodded, eyes answering: *I see.* It did not matter whether she did or not.

"Therein, the injustice." She winced. She did not wish to hear this. "They said letters have already been sent to Anscharde. So Tessel would see us march before the crown can issue its replies. Clever and stupid in one."

She spared him a bemused look.

"If the crown cannot reach him, whatever he does in the meanwhile is legitimate. Supposing he were commander. Of course, the crown has already decided on that as well."

She smelled blood lurking at the edge of Ivon's voice. "Milord?"

Only then did he smile. Whatever had possessed the soldier to his moment of whimsy fled before the reality of where they stood. Ivon leaned off his desk and cleared the darkness from his tongue. "Fear not. It is a threat we shall soon remove." Then he dismissed her.

Four of them sat in the yard, surrounded by men of the watch and men of the Word. The stink of man was greatest at the heart, though Roswitte scarcely smelled it anymore. Months in the damp and the cold had long since drowned it out. Even before the war, none of them bathed. It was, after all, a privileged thing—a thing for nobles and for royals, not for the men and women of the earth.

"Repent!" The word cracked like a cannonball across the fallow yard. "Repent all ye sinners, before ye be bound eternal to this soil—the aimless wanderer, the lost sheep, the broken step in the almighty cycle…"

Alviss, Vardick, and the Zuti heathen joined her for the Word. None of them were terribly religious sorts. Still, Roswitte had always found a certain morbid fascination for men such as these—the dueling priests, so content in their humanity in so many other aspects of life, yet equally content to rain hellfire and destruction on the crossroads of faith.

Across the yard, the crowds edged around the words of four men with faces ripe as tomatoes. Three stood in robes of varying hue, while their opponent was clad in the strict blues and the silver-trimmed sash of the Orthodox. There was no denying the fanaticism of either side, but if there was any fear that three would drown the one, the Orthodox man's voice seemed to have time and training on its side, and proved more than ample competition for the Farrens.

They had been going on for near an hour. Roswitte and the rest had not been there at its inception, but the shouts were close enough to the Verdanite camp that it was hard to hear anything else. At first, the Brickheart had brought her there in the hope of discussing her work—which she took to mean discussing his concerns of the camp's discontent. When they had spied the foreign pair, however, that plan was quickly discarded. It brought her little grief. Besides, it wasn't as if they didn't have the time. In all likelihood, the priests could rattle for an hour more.

And how they rattle!

All spoke with passion and with zeal uncontested. They played to fears before they played to anger. Bits of logic tempered the fanatical whole—just enough to get the crowd talking—but there was no mention of any humanist tendencies. The Orthodox damned the Farrens to the abyss by virtue of the Word. The Farrens damned the Church to the abyss for usurping Assal's will. Men's souls, hanging in the balance, gaped lamely, occasionally shouting.

"Is it like this in the north, Alviss?" Roswitte asked over the din of the crowd.

Alviss's eyes did not waver from the speakers. "In Kuruse?"

"The oceans, damned fool," Vardick snapped. "What's fire matter, place to place?"

"Orthodox are there. No Farren. Kuric keep their own gods. And our priests fight as sure as the rest. These? Talk," Alviss said, emphasizing the point with a dismissive flick of the hand. "Too little we see of it."

There rose an image to Roswitte's mind of a dozen Alvisses screaming across a frozen waste. Robes rattled about their ankles, circlets upon their necks, battle axes raised high in prayer, offering, and lustful sacrifice to the Maker. It took effort to suppress a shudder.

Holy men were monstrous enough with word and voice. The thought of battle hardened berserkers, steeled still further by religious conviction—it made her wonder at the greater questions in life. Foremost among them: how Marinidis had ever survived the Kuric raids of centuries past. Some would, naturally, chalk it up to the triumph of one faith over another—in this case, the Visaj over the multitude of pantheistic faiths that stole their northern neighbors' souls. Roswitte, however, was a more practical soul.

Luck was their divine wind. That was all.

Her eyes shifted to the Zuti. The squat, broad-chested man sat apart even in this, legs and arms crossed, as if to section him off from the rest of the world. Beneath the pregnant light, his dark skin gleamed, and with it, the fires in his equally dark eyes. Time would prove if luck would be enough to stem his

112

people's tide as well. In the meantime, the people of Marindis would cling to their gunpowder and hope it was enough.

Faith. Men would swing it where they would.

"The less you see, the better it is." Vardick groaned. Yet his eyes swept the lines as surely as a hawk, trying to pick out men of his own lord's camp. If anyone had skirted duty for this, Roswitte had little doubt they would soon discover how Vardick had earned the name "Brickheart."

"True," Alviss consented. "There are better places for faith."

"For you, Alvise," the Zuti snipped. The man's foreign tongue still couldn't get the Kuric's name right.

Man, the Farrens claimed, was the only proper place in which to put one's faith. Assal—God—had shown them the path. He watched. But He also waited. The divine was to be found within man, which was to say, all men. Not to be dictated by one man on a seat of veiled mysticism, a man who thought faith a mere extension of politics.

Men make faith. It's their right to sully it good, Roswitte mused. She tipped back against the sound and the fury.

"Folk cheer it loud enough," Roswitte said.

"Not your noble. They're smart to dread it," Alviss countered.

True enough, there were scant few of theirs among the ranks. *Who could trust a faith of freedom?*

"Why such fire?" the Zuti asked. "Dey all just spirit."

"Spirit?"

"Spirit. How you say—piece of world. Of people. Of…more spirit. All stem from Uhnashanti. Holy Zutam tell it true. No spirit greater than other."

"But that's faith," Roswitte said. *Mysterious. Pointless. All-consuming.* Faith—the path to truth without the travails of reason. "When you believe strong enough in a thing, you can't allow no rival. Muddles the water too much. To say: you're just as right as I while believing something elsewise, makes for too many questions."

Vardick grunted. "Mother Church is as much a foundation as any."

"Aye. And for it to grow and to control the shape, your builders got to be of one mind."

"Law's growth, self's demise." Alviss said softly.

"More those pillars a-tumble, more uppity those selves get, yeah." She whistled, even, feeling a little looser with herself than she had in months. Conversations still made her uneasy. "Look'it these," she offered, hooking a thumb to the crowd. "Your lead dogs start to bark at one another and it's like the whole pack's gone rabid."

"Order's vital. Think what these idiots might do if lords and faith weren't there to tell them 'stay.'" Vardick's laugh was a coarse, barking thing. Several of the crowd turned nervously at its sound.

The Orthodox voice rose to a fevered pitch. Red lines streaked the bearded old face as the man waved his arms to the sound. Death awaited the non-believer. In soul as well as body. Farre was naught but Mordazz—the Devil King—made flesh, in the priest's eyes. His servants—no better than the heathen Zuti that would sweep them beneath the sands of time.

As Roswitte watched, she slowly realized that no one defended these men. Farren or Orthodox. As they stoked the flames of hate, and the hate broiled in the eyes of the listening masses, the only thing that protected the individuals was the balance of that mass—one mass against the other. It was bravery Roswitte could admire—or arrogance she could not.

There was no mirth in the Zuti's own voice as he denounced the lot. "This why you fight—you weak. All one—is joke. One be all, you hope. Stupid. Holy Zutam let man be man. Own man. So when man fight, he know he fight for self, and in fight, for Zutam too. This fire—it burn only you."

The Brickheart bristled at the words. "Strong piece from thems what seek to gobble up the world, mudman. Keep 'em to yourself."

"It's all nonsense," Alviss added, silencing the lot. "What matters who says it?"

Did it matter? Roswitte had never been devout, but she knew what she believed. She looked at Alviss, wondering of the lines that moved beneath the scars. *What do you believe?* For her, it was the Orthodox path. Assal was Assal. Man was man. One lived their lives, walked the circle, moved on. Done—dead and gone.

Yet death stirred questions. Fallit's death. Kasimir's. If all was so simple, why was there no simple point or course to agony? Why this one, not that one?

"Like bastard," the Zuti concluded, turning away. "What matter?"

Careful, she wanted to say. But Roswitte would never defend Tessel. He was a usurper, nothing more. He may have used his silver tongue to snare the young lord Rurik, but it wasn't as though that was difficult. *Feed a boy love, coddle the dog in him with respect, and slap a sword in the man's hand, and his will is for the taking.* Lost and lonely souls were merely easier to win.

A frown creased her face as she thought of him and Essa. "Perhaps the children have the right of it," Vardick said at the same moment. All three of them regarded the master-at-arms with the same skeptical stare. He remained trained on the speaker, however—a Farren again. "They're idiots, but they know: what's it matter? This is all that matters." He ground his foot against the dirt for emphasis.

The Zuti's eyes rolled his head away. Alviss laughed. "True. Blood and earth. That is the whole."

"Blood and earth," Vardick grunted. "And a good piss besides."

Faith and fire or blood and earth—Roswitte couldn't say which struck her worse. She kept her silence as the old men reminisced, but her mind secretly raced. The world was screwed up enough on its own without considering the otherworldly, true—and the children? Hardly an example to aspire to. They put the beyond behind them, and took the brunt of the blood instead.

They dwelt on one another. Sand shifted beneath their feet and they hated just as quick. None would tell Roswitte why—not that it was any of her business. Truth be told, she knew not why she was so concerned for Essa, in particular. The girl was Pescha's spawn—as far as she should be concerned, the girl and the rest of her brood could burn in the abyss.

But there was something there. Something more. Perhaps she saw a bit of herself in the girl, though in truth, the two of them were nothing alike. That beauty of a thing—the only woes Essa had ever suffered were those brought on by other people. *A fortunate whelp.*

Of the pair, should not her heart go out to Rurik? Her servant's loyalty? True, she used him often enough as excuse to call upon the girl, but it was only that. She could feign devotion all she liked; the honest thought of it failed to excite. For all his father's hopes, the boy was nothing but a ponce. He tried, but that meant little. He was incompetent. He was flighty. He was lost. She saw the way he looked at his friends. Even when they spoke to him, when they listened to him, there was a darkness there that would not sleep. He smiled, but the eyes were poor liars. Even power did not suit him, and the Bastard seemed content to heap it on his shoulders.

More importantly: there was something he held back. She did not like secrets.

The children were not a lot to follow. They were a lesson against.

Shouts unsteadied the crowd as several men pressed toward the fore. Fists lanced against flesh, and Roswitte frowned for the predictability of men. Vardick rose to his feet with a beleaguered grunt, one hand dangling loose and dangerous against his blade. He was looking for an excuse, as ever. Training Rurik was not enough. The man's blood bubbled too hot—her master's foul-tempered dog.

"Sit, Vardick. They will hold," Alviss cautioned.

The men came close, but the Kuric told it true. Men shouted, raged, but others held them back, for all the want that drank in their eyes. The noise of it nearly smothered the camp, but Roswitte pricked at something deeper, something beyond. She squinted over her shoulder, feeling a sick sensation creep up her spine.

A few banners waved. Other soldiers, uninterested in the speech, loped on.

The Zuti and the Brickheart bickered over nothing. Silent time had taken its toll on the both of them. The waiting—it got all men eventually. She breathed. Yes, there was something there. She rose up on one knee, peering between the rows of men. Shapes moved in a line of flickering shadows between the tents further back. Not a patrol—there was too much color to the motion.

There were no shouts, no trumpet calls, but as she squinted the shapes into existence, she started. *All men are dogs.* She thought of the Bastard and Rurik, and wondered if even he could be so foolish. A few richly colored and heavily armed riders broke ahead of a line of men, shouting at the soldiers to halt. Men held pistols openly. The black parade pressed on, heedless, as the man at their heart dismissed the riders with a shake of the head, and words too far to hear.

The speech cracked, fell apart. The fire rose and fell and rose again, but the crowd no longer listened. They looked to the west and to the clank of armor on the march, and there, every one of them beheld the fall.

The vitality of order.

Hands bound at his back, the lord marshall moved between a column of soldiers. They waded through the mass with little trouble, the gaping men parting as easily as wheat in the field. The column was like an arrow driving through the mass, and not one among them wore his colors. Roswitte stood, squinting at them, scrutinizing. Other men moved around the column, harping. Noblemen, she realized. The soldiers kept them at bay, however, with the tips of pikes.

Her eyes deadened on the colors, but Alviss leant them voice. "Bastard's men." They marched for the town, damnation and hellfire resuming in their wake.

* *

They came for him as the sun sank toward its nightly oblivion. There was no warning. Apparently, even for the captain that would be blamed.

"Even you, Tessel, even you cannot do this. Tell me you are not so, so…" Rurik shouted his damnation, until the anger touched so deeply the words themselves began to catch.

He had not intended to rage. All the way to Tessel's post, he had tried to calm his fears. To breathe and to think. Yet the words left his mouth as soon as the door opened and their eyes met. He did not regret it. Not like he should.

It was one of the few things he didn't.

Soldiers had taken Lord Marshall Othmann as the sun set and bore him into a southern exile. He and a scarce 300 men were supposedly reassigned to the aid of General Ernseldt's forces in the south. There was no question of the truth in Rurik's mind, however: it was meant to be a death march. It seemed that even Tessel had a breaking point, and Othmann had poked and prodded his way right over the edge.

All the camp was in an uproar of confusion and uncertainty—a tense debacle of men all armed and ready and too long spent starving and spoiling without a fight. Every soul seemed to know. Yet Rurik had to hear of it from Othmann's nobles. Furious nobles, rightly terrified by the insinuations of the event: a titleless man with the whims and means to kill the untouchable.

Tessel met him with blank apathy. The other captains scoffed for him. The *other* captains. Further proof of the grand deception—as though the locked gates and swarms of men crawling like ants across the walls had not been sign enough. This was planned.

Fury stole him away. He could not take any more lies. Their indifference only barreled Rurik on. "You must send for him. Bring him back, Tessel. Assal above, the man was an ass but you cannot—he is a *lord*, ser. Old blood. Old lord. Do you even realize…?"

"I cannot do that," Tessel answered swiftly, his curtness as much a dismissal as anything. But a smile eased his harsh features, and a breath settled him. He did not *want* to be angry. "It is done."

"Done? Ser, you—done?" Anger stumbled headlong into fear. If Othmann was truly dead, there was nothing anyone here could do to save their heads. The men outside would surely take them. "Tell me he still breathes."

Ten good men stood between the pair. Rurik's gaze shifted past every one. At a time, he had been proud to have them, even if he didn't agree with or trust them all. These were men strong enough to pull themselves up on their own merits—men Tessel put to use not for title or blood, but for usefulness.

That made them no less yes-men. The difference was: they were yes-men loyal to a man, rather than a name. As all of them looked to him, riled and affronted at his lack of kind, Rurik felt a sinking feeling in the pit of his stomach. There was no appealing to these. Tessel owned them, heart and soul.

Tessel batted a hand at him. "He lives. He simply goes to do his duty. Away from me and away from them. Without its head, what is the writhing serpent?" He looked away from Rurik, focusing, it seemed, on the hands folded in his lap. "The rest will fall in line. Then, at last, we will march."

"He did right." Vogel chose that moment to assert himself as Tessel's dog. Veins sprouted thick webs across his vulture's neck as the man became animate, flinging his one good hand at Rurik. "Do you realize what they planned?"

Yet that captain's threat had ever been in his silence and his tact. Rurik found himself emboldened by the snap in demeanor, and it drew him forward. "Planning? What does it matter? I dread more what the passion of fear will wreak."

"Hold your tongue, boy!"

The priest, Narve, degraded him with a loud snort. "Naturally, the lordling sides with their ilk."

Rurik's hands faintly shook, but neither made a move for his sword. Several of the others, plainly, maintained no such restraint. For an instant, Rurik toyed with the consequences, wondered even if the railing crowd of lesser nobles outside the house would take the clang of steel as a rallying cry. Passion—it was always the greater force, between it and logic.

Reluctantly, he tried to breathe the tension from his fingers.

It was a mistake. A calculated mistake, but a mistake nonetheless. He had to believe that. Tessel had not seen the violence in *their* eyes as they shook him back into the waking world.

Hands descended on him. Outside, Berric cried out like a cock at the dawning, but no one brandished steel. Rurik twisted in his sheet, the day dying around him as his eyes opened to shadows and to men. Bright colors. Weary resignation. Scabbards and swords and the rattle of so many chains. Gnarled hands took him by the collar and dragged him to his feet.

Rurik stumbled. He was surrounded by nobles, the mark of the twilight making gargoyles of their faces. Berric and the others stood still as statues at the door, hands on their swords but surrounded by men-at-arms. Rurik was alone.

Amidst the sweat and the flush, they demanded Othmann's release. I don't know. Can't you see I don't know? Cold eyes, darkening stances. Death—so close. Where is the lie? What happened? Othmann was taken to Tessel and taken away and his court stood in anxious disarray around Rurik. Nothing was known. The world had been subverted to guesses—questions of faith.

I am too young.

Why?

The only blood I'll ever need.

They didn't matter. He didn't tell them that, though. Where, they asked? Where has he gone? What does he intend? Advisor, confidante—in the dark. He had to turn out his palms and plead ignorance, like a beggar at confession.

A man could flout convention only so long. The Farren stain would listen. So mote it be. They left him, trembling, in the cold.

The memory passed, but he stood still in the cold. Different faces, but the anger was all too familiar.

"These people are not peasants, Kyler."

"How dare you," shouted a bald, slant-nosed man. Bonsweid—a farmer from the eastern marches. His fire was matched only by the priest. Fortunately, one of the others put a hand against his shoulder—a subtle barrier.

119

Tyler's eyes rose narrowly. "Meaning?"

"They are men of substance. Of power. In their minds, if not in fact. We have marginalized them. Put them to a nameless power—"

Bonsweid nearly choked. "Nameless! Nameless, you say! The Emperor's own."

"…They see neither respect nor—nor compromise. They fear and they can see the anger. Now you've taken the greatest among them. Who among them would not fear a purge? These are sensible men. They came to fight for Idasia, but this—"

"Then they will fight. Put them to the front and let them taste the war we've all fed," Narve snarled.

"You're not even—"

Tessel raised a hand. The room seethed into silence, smoke and flame circling one another through thin eyes. "Go," he commanded, but the room hesitated. "All of you save Rurik," he snapped, louder this time, and the men shuffled reluctantly from the room.

Dark stares lingered at Rurik's back. Even those he liked, they did not trust him. They did not see an exile. They saw a nobleman. They saw a weakling and a coward that could not even be true to his own.

What is there to trust?

When they were alone, Tessel gestured to a chair. "Sit," he commanded, and Rurik obeyed. Then the long fingers settled. He seemed to gather the emptiness of the wide room about him like a cloak, to beat back the chill. "You forget yourself, Rurik."

"And I fear you forget the art of politick."

There was silence between them.

Tessel's chair creaked as he shifted forward. "You fear, my friend. You are not the first. Breathe. You are safe here. Just answer me this: what makes one man different from another?"

Rurik sensed a trap. The general, his friend, leaned forward like a hawk to the kill. There was a subtle menace to the folded claws of his hands, in spite of the soothing tone of his voice and the misleading submission in his eyes. It was a kingly bearing, he realized. This man, this bastard, had he been born simply of a different mother—this man might have borne a crown.

How fickle, fate.

"Any number of things."

Tessel stared.

"Blood. Coin. Power. Fate, I suppose."

A soft smile teased across the general's features. Rurik knew he had said exactly what the man hoped for.

"But are we not all one flesh? One mind? A sword brings power. Knowledge brings coin. With either, one can make blood reckoned, can earn names. The only thing that differs between a noble man and a working man is that they have *now*, while the other does not have it *yet*. Such things can be taken. They are always taken."

"And that—that is what they fear, Kyler. The—the taking." Rurik's mind reeled. Tessel's ideas were not healthy, no matter how he felt. "Think of this from their perspective—"

"A shallow enough prospect."

"Humor me." Tessel rolled his eyes, but waved him on. "They resist the most because they have the most to lose here, in their way. All men fear for homes and families, but these must fear for many homes, many families. Some know not what they'll return to—my brother, as an example—and now you take away what little assurances they have left. Now you speak of taking and taking is what they think you hope to do. Take from them. Take from the crown.

"They want to go home! And not just them—the only thing working in your favor is that your men don't see that common bond yet. Bonds with a noble?" He let out a short, frail laugh. "Assal's bleeding cock, Kyler, I know you wish to honor your father, but this—men can only be pushed so far. To tell it true, I don't even know what you hope to achieve here. And many," again, he thought, of Ivon and Verdan and a father's blade in his chest, "many were promised by the Emperor. With his death, there is no promise. No certainty of reward. When this is done—"

"But it is not done. That is the point."

"That's not how they see it. Your father—"

"Is all the more reason to march. What would the world think of a people that refused to avenge their master? Especially one such as him. We owe him and Idasia this war, and I'll not have anyone second guess it."

"And if they resist?"

Tessel's gaze grew grim. "Disloyalty is death. You know this."

He lowered his head. Death was the burden. For so many things—or it was supposed to be. A night far and away danced to mind, with a woman and a cell and a man calling for blood. It was disloyalty then, too. Only fate had been merciful.

No, not fate, he thought as quickly, and with it, found the strength to look up again. *Father.*

"This questioning, Rurik—what guides it truly? Would you leave with them—these men that care so little for you?"

"No," he nearly shouted. "No. What they do matters little to me. It is concern, Kyler. Your father promised me freedom long ago but…it is done. I am where I belong."

Freedom seemed naught but a ripple of a notion. It disrupted the reflections of the world, only to break upon the distant shore, unchanged. It was enough for some men to chase after. Rurik tried to tell himself he was no longer one of those men.

Truth be told, Rurik would not have known what to do with such bounty if he had it. Essa couldn't stand to look at him. His brother barely tolerated him. The people of Verdan knew him only as a rapist and an exile.

But most important was the taint. Blood would have stained such a gift, for it was the blood of pity that earned it. Matair would have been a name rooted in the corpse of a dead man, for even emperors could not raise fathers from the grave.

Such thoughts settled like weights in his gut—parts mixed with sorrow, and with anger. Duty was best. Freedom would not have been right, and hope was too far gone to care.

Still, something in the way Tessel took the news unsettled Rurik further. Dark eyes seemed to sink into themselves, searching inward. The long face slackened, shifted.

When Tessel's voice came again, it was barely above a whisper. "He said this?"

"Assal be my witness. But death changes all."

Tessel always looked a man in the eyes when he spoke to them. Yet this time, he turned away all the same. "Why are you here, Rurik? For glory? Or phantoms?" When Rurik did not answer, Tessel looked pointedly to his knee. "I do not mean it harshly, my friend."

It was a question he had long asked himself, in the darkest hours of the night. All the way to Verdan, it had stalked the purpose of his blade. When war found him, he found himself no better prepared to answer it. The truth was, as often as he looked inside himself for answers, his own hands never guided the truth. Life was something others always decided for him.

"It wasn't my choice."

"Choice?" A sharp, bitter laugh cracked the general's demeanor. "Who spoke anything of choice? Few ever have that. But all men have thought, my friend, and it is yours I seek, to reach my point. Why do you think you are here?

"To hide," Rurik answered belatedly.

"I see. Cheer, then—I do not begrudge you it. You would not be the first. But my father, well…he came for the opposite."

Rurik could not keep the confusion from his face.

"I tell you, my father came here to die, Rurik."

Death, the priests said, was the final path. Ademius had seen it long ago, and worked its trails to the fruit at their core. Death was the path to new beginnings. The path to Assal. The path to freedom. It was why, they said, all men moved inevitably toward death. Not only was it predetermined, but each was predisposed.

Life moved in circles. Such was the path. What came would come again, breath to breath, until each riddled out the truth within. War was a path to the next, as sure as any, but lies gained nothing. Rurik twisted the concept around, unable to find words.

The Emperor had smiled as they spoke. He was not a man toward death. He promised life, and Rurik had to believe. Anything else just didn't make sense.

Tessel's gaze returned to him, murky but observant. "People ask why I did not stop him. Why I let him ride that vainglorious charge. Well, that is the truth of it. Our good marshall may be incompetent but, sooner or later, his sieges would have worked. His march would have gone on. Months. Years down the line. But my father would not have lived to see it, and one of those hounds at the capital would have taken all the glory.

"I know not the truth of things between you, but I know thus: my father was a great man whittled by time. The world is too sick to notice, but he rode here to die as a man should. With the wind beneath his knees and a sword in his hand."

All at once, Rurik beheld a boy limping across a field. A horse whirled, spears and long guns baiting it round and round about. An emperor reared. His sword flashed. And he died in the dust, with vultures pecking at his flesh.

Glory? It echoed hollow. A hollowness that struck and spread within, and left him cold.

"He was already dead. For all that he had tried, the world burned around him. For seventy years he had built it up, but he would need another seventy to keep it. And his body ate at him in ways time seemed incapable. At a time, he could barely breathe.

"Tell me Rurik, do you understand what I am saying? A man has a right to die a man, and yet, it's a secret thing." Tessel's eyes fell to his hands. "Secret that this dread nonsense burned through his lungs and through his gut; secret that he rode to meet death on his own terms. No man…no man should suffer." His hands curled, and he looked to meet Rurik again, defeat and pride mingling in the shadows.

It was a long moment before Rurik could find the words to speak.

"You tell me, you say, so many dead, so many lives…this march—it was all for one man?"

"Aren't they all? One man. One nation. One faith." Tessel added the last with a sarcastic roll of the eyes. "That is the nature of the world."

We shall see these evil things undone, the man had said.

Lies, all of it. Sickness burbled in Rurik's gut, deeper and more profoundly than any flu. *Why should it hurt?* He had said it himself—it no longer mattered. Dead was dead. *It's just another lie.* But it wasn't just another lie. It was the greatest of deceptions—a play upon a child's hopes, and fears, to make an oath upon a dead man while pissing on his grave.

It was one thing to lose hope. It was quite another to learn it was nothing more than a fever dream.

Even emperors were men. Men lied. Men died. Words moved between them, but these were naught but air. What meaning did they really have? Matair—it was only a name. It could be invoked, and discarded, and the world would go on, unmoved.

Always, he would remain Rurik, but Matthias, he would go to eternity as the bold, and the brave. No one told stories of the dark things brave men did to stir others to that same goodly death. A family may have waited on the sons' return, but they were to be sacrifices before the martyr's name.

Air, blood, and dust. That was all he ever had.

Rurik was very glad he was already sitting down.

"If they knew, his enemies would call it cowardice…"

In the confines of his heart, Rurik took up the cry as well. *Coward! Coward! Coward!* Like a rooster's cries. He struggled to smooth his hands against his legs—to give nothing.

Just like the dead man.

"All men have flaws," Tessel repeated, more quietly this time. "But do you know what he told me before we broke camp that day?" He let it hang, as if he himself could scarcely believe it. "Son, he says, I do not care if anyone else could hear it, save you, but you are mine, and a fine one at that. The greatest wrong I ever did you was to whelp you on a baseborn woman. Were it all different—and this is the thing—I should have set the crown to you myself.

"And yet…and yet I am expected to take heed of a man that has never laid eyes on him? On greedy uncles? *That* is true injustice."

Rurik was too numb to feel anything more than the barest edges of the general's passion.

Still, he answered: "And what would you do of it?"

At this, a solemn smile made a foreshadow of Tessel. "As I said: I know not the truth of things between you. Truly, I know only the shape of my own heart, and it would tell you this: stay with me, Rurik. Stay with me and you shall have the blood you seek."

* *

Motion defined the night. Subtle motion. Most would not distinguish it. A few men moved horses into the center of the camp, one or two at a time, while others hoisted saddlebags and arms. Others drifted along the perimeter edges, pikes or swords tensed for blows, wandering heavily but purposefully and turning away all that did not belong.

For a young hunter, the obvious thought surrendered the horsemen to a raid and the blades to a camp laid nervous by the turning of the day's events.

Yet there was more to it. If the raiders were knights, as the bearing and—in many cases—the faces gave these to be, they left their preparations to their pages and their squires alone. These men shared the burden with them, though all took great care to wear footmen's garb. This was not to say, however, that they were bad at it. Most would not have second-guessed the effort, but Roswitte had seen many of these men before, and their boys too. Their faces didn't fool her.

Raiders kept their horses to the stables until the last, for it allowed a quicker departure with fresher, rested steeds. This was an act of silence, or treachery, or both. Something not meant for unknown eyes.

Raiders also traveled light. The weapons and armor were common fair for this, but these men loaded sheets, coin, clothes, and food—an act more suited to refugees than to warriors.

As they meandered toward their lord's tent, Roswitte could not help but wonder if this was why she had been summoned. To fight or to flee.

Brickheart's presence among the packers leaned her toward fight. When Othmann had been taken, Brickheart had slipped away like a mouse in the night, to rally Witold's banners into a marshaled ring of steel. None had relented and none had been permitted entrance—Roswitte included—until Ivon had returned and ordered the camp at ease.

Now, the grizzled master-at-arms of Verdan stood with Jörg—Ivon's shieldman—hands at their sides and voices low. Both nodded to her, quieting briefly as she passed.

So it was that the utter lack in Ivon's tent surprised her little. Everything had been stripped, packed, and taken. Only Ivon remained attired, his squire fussing at the buckles of his armor as he himself worked to tie his dark hair back into a tail. If he started at her entrance, he let nothing slip. He dismissed her accompanying guards, but left the squire to his affairs.

After a moment of awkward silence, he glanced over his shoulder again, regarding her. "Do words fail you, warden?"

She shrugged. "Not my place to speak first."

There was a sigh in the way he sagged and shrugged off, but it found no sound. He stepped away from his squire, hefting a piece of glass to admire the boy's work. The child trembled when a hand reached for him. It clapped him on the shoulder.

Like father and son, she mused. It was always the quiet moments like this, away from men and steel, that one could see the mother in him. Even then, few did. Precious few words could adequately capture this scion of the Matairs. Careless was not among them.

"Just as well. For Ros, I need you to listen to me now."

Roswitte snapped back to attention and drew upright, tensing at the familiar stress in her master's tone. The last time such a tune had played, Fallit's life had been the call of the curtain. Yet the servant in her bid her only say: "Your burdens are my own, lord. Speak, and bid them gone."

Ivon started to speak, frowned, and turned away, tapping his fingers up the plates of his armor. Indecision was unbecoming on the man, she decided then. Nor could he mask it, as his father had, unaccustomed to it as he was.

But there was always something to break a man. One merely had to find it.

"What if I were to tell you something terrible will soon sweep this camp?"

She felt her throat tighten. *Danger*, a little voice cried. "Are you in danger?" she asked, just a little too quickly. Ivon quirked an eyebrow at her familiar tone, but she remained as she was.

Ivon's frown deepened into a sigh. His head gave a shake. "No, it's nothing like that. It's just..." His knuckles rapped against the metal. "This isn't the place for me anymore, Ros. Not the war. No one's talking. No one's moving. Yet my home—it calls. Calls me back from the silence. And—I fear if I do not go tonight, I may never live to see it."

"And what of your brother?"

"Rurik?" With a nod, she cast him back to a rueful sort of silence. His stance stiffened, and Ivon slowly shook the thought out. "That one is at home here. Let him be. We were never meant for the same roof anyhow." His knuckles rapped a final note, and the lord gave his head another shake. She knew the tune, and it did not settle her. Nerves held that chord, and Ivon Matair was not one for anxiety. "All the same, the ears I trust to this are few. You were a confidante of my father. I trust in that. As such, I asked you here tonight to offer: will you come with us?"

Her own eagerness surprised her. "Yes," she answered immediately. "Gladly."

Fallit's hand fell heavy on her shoulder. Visions of trees and deer and a little cabin in the woods mingled with the words and tainted the taste of them. All the while she wondered what she really wanted—but then again, some things were never meant to be known, and never would.

Oaths were but words men hid behind at the end of the day. They passed as easy from one to another. Let them call her a bear all they wished. Now, she wished to hide in her words. There were no other dens left to her.

Chapter 7

On the same morning the last dredges of slush finally dissolved into mud, a rider bearing royal colors called on Vissering Castle with a message for Walthere and the Empress both. The man came without escort, a fact Charlotte took as somewhat ludicrous in the present political air, but her father adhered well enough to the old codes of how to treat an envoy, even if that messenger did not make the process easy.

He was a young man, the salty pepperings of a beard attesting to how recently manhood had graced him. An unlikely figure for the task, Charlotte supposed. But than, so many of their fighting men had gone east with the old emperor, and it was better the young than the infirm.

When ushered into the castle's solar, he waved both food and drink, and refused the offering of a seat. He was of a single mind, and to his credit, he read his message faithfully: a demand for the presence of Charlotte's father and the Empress both at the coronation of Prelate Leopold, to become Emperor Leopold II. Bare octaves had passed since Walthere had lent his voice to the other electors of the Altengard and given the man his approval.

A flicker of amusement crossed the count's eyes just long enough for Charlotte's watchful gaze to catch, but his poise remained otherwise intact, and their guest did not seem to notice. The dear empress was not likewise composed, but fortunately she deferred to Walthere, who respectfully declined, claiming both his wife and Princess Sara as too ill to travel. At this, the messenger scoffed, claiming it was not a request, but a duty.

"The Lady Mother and the princess have tarried here too long, at any rate," the messenger babbled to deaf ears. "His Majesty asks that she return in all haste. She will be well cared for, I am to assure you."

But the Empress would have none of it. "As I am here," she countered. "And I would not leave my coz's side at so dark an hour."

For most, that answer, delivered with Imperial weight, should have been enough. Yet at this, the messenger dared cross another step between himself and the high lords, eyes blazing with arrogant defiance. "And by Assal, my lady, His Highness says such tarrying ushers your empire into a far darker hour at that. If you do not come, he has said he will be forced to remove you at a later date. So too the princess, and your son as well."

It was nothing short of a miracle that spared the man the sword of any one of the men-at-arms huddled with them in the room. As it was, it did not spare him the spearing gaze of her uncle, nor the harsh rebuke of her father.

"You would threaten an empress?" Walthere calmly balked. "Tell me, in Anscharde, do they still teach boys to use their heads, or merely to wag their tongues?"

The man left shortly thereafter, red-faced. Charlotte watched him through a window as he put his spurs to his horse and kicked it through the gates in a scantly-suppressed fury. If their new emperor were half so bold as he, she had little doubt they would soon regret that child's wounded pride.

Supposing, of course, his daggers were swifter than their own.

"Was that—was that good?" The Empress's hands remained folded about each other in her lap. They were hands that wanted to tremble. Her gaze did not rise from them, even to address the count. "He will be back, I think."

Charlotte glanced to her father, a perfect portrait of resolute distance—a perfect portrait of jurti's disassociation with reality—but when it became apparent he had nothing to say, she crossed the room to take the damaged woman's hands in hers.

"You did well, majesty. Considering how fast that one ran from here, I dare say pride will not let him back again."

This was no longer a woman playing games. Surelia was a woman that did not know how to play the game in the first place. For all her splendor, she was a simple mind—all she had ever wanted was for people to love her and her family, and now the honesty that many didn't, that many would even dare to disrespect her openly, laid open a wound Charlotte suspected had long festered within her. There was a certain way to deal with such a creature, and Walthere's hard manners were not it.

A shocked sort of innocence flared in Surelia's eyes at Charlotte's placating words, and a grateful smile passed between them.

It died as Walthere turned on them. "I had hoped for a month before such trivialities," he spoke sourly. "This priest is restless."

"And it would not become you to grow unmanned by a clod such as that." Charlotte gave Surelia's hands a squeeze, and tried to turn from her, only to find those hands had not in turn released her. It gave her words an unnecessary sort of hesitancy that she tried to force her way around. "If he moves quick, you will move quicker."

"So you say," he said flatly. Then he turned his attentions at last to Surelia. "Will you be alright, my lady?"

She had, by then, regained some of her regal composure, but only, Charlotte suspected, by leeching it off of her. "I shall want my son brought to me. At once."

"I imagine he is playing with Gerold," Charlotte said, trying to be helpful.

Walthere frowned. "They are not with the Matair girls again, are they?"

She wished that she could say no, but she could not see through walls, and she could thusly only guess, and the guess would not be one Walthere would want to hear. Children did not see the boundaries their parents often did, and for his imagination's part, it did little Gerold well to have damsels for his knightly fantasies. If it kept the lot of them happy, so far as Charlotte was concerned, it made everyone's lot better. There was no reason Walthere needed to know it, though.

As she floundered, Walthere pushed on regardless. "I shall send for Bidderick, as I shall send for my attendants. Do you think you shall be up for a show later? I think today would be a splendid time for a certain unveiling."

Charlotte stirred at this. Art? She had seen no artists about the keep of late. Suspicion crooked her gaze back sharply to the Empress, but it fell quickly. Innuendo was unlikely. She doubted the woman would have caught it if Walthere had offered it.

"An unveiling?" Surelia looked as puzzled as Charlotte felt. "How will…how would that attend your men?"

"It does well to greet revelations with reassurances, particularly before our new emperor begins declarations. In youth rests the very best of hopes—is it not so?"

Surelia's eyes shuffled nervously to Charlotte and back. It rekindled suspicion's embers. "It is so. I—I think I shall remain, however. Send Bidderick to my quarters. I shall meet them there." As though an afterthought, she gave

Charlotte's hand another doting squeeze, and made a point of meeting her gaze plainly. "Thank you for all you have done to make us welcome, dear. You are a true treasure."

She might have winced. Deflection. Painfully plain deflection. This did not bode well at all.

"Very well," Walthere said with a flourish. "Your presence will be missed, but I understand. Rest. I shall have Karlene attend you as well. You do one another well." As if dismissing the woman, his gaze flicked back to his daughter. "Charlotte. I shall need you to attend me today as well. Come along while I make arrangements."

As they passed into the hall, Dartrek and Walthere's own shieldmen sidling into their wake, Walthere made a pointed effort not to look at her. She sensed it quickly. The Empress's words had put her on edge, but it was the motions of Walthere's rush that unsettled her. Men like him kept their eyes away for one of two reasons: either to make a point or to hide one. Even among family, Walthere made no habit of carelessness; jurti demanded constant observation.

That he still spoke, and in clearer voice than he had dared with their dear guest, only reinforced her suspicions of the latter option. He did it with a smile, though, and a nod for any of the blooded folk sifting through his halls. It may have been an act, but in him, she beheld none of the viciousness the messenger had left.

There was a certain lift to his shoulders. A quickness to the step his recovering limb should have made him check. He seemed…happy.

"We need more time in Anscharde." There was such a thing as too observant. It took her a moment to realize the statement was barked at her. "Don't look so slack-jawed. Are you a peasant? Smile, girl. Smile, like I taught you." Hesitantly, she let his words infect her lips. He wanted something—it was in the note of his demand. "Good." It was only here, ever so briefly, that he turned his own smile to her. "Ustrit, go fetch Boyce, would you? He is just down the hall. Tell him the arrangements are in order." He paused there, leaving room for the shieldman to veer off down a side hall before resuming their own stride. "Now listen. What happens today is part of the act. The great act. You know what I mean."

"Thrones and crowns and certain men in dark clothing. I have an idea."

"Very good. Boyce has things at work there. But we all have our parts to play, and eyes must always be on us, never on their own two feet. I do not tell you this enough, but I am proud of you, Charlotte. Proud of all that you are. I ask only that you know that, and you trust me, as you have always trusted me, as we go into this day."

She nearly missed a step. "Father?"

Walthere kept walking. Their conversation was at an end, though only in practicality. In thought, it and all its worrying suppositions and lines of inquiry would go on and on a thousand fold through Charlotte's mind until the first of their noble kind slithered into their graces, and she found herself turning to Dartrek for answers, only to be met with her shadow's unwavering stare. He looked to her. He wanted to speak, but he knew as little of its course as she.

Though the time Charlotte and her father spent in one another's company that day was great, they never again spoke as he had begun to in the hall. It made its nature almost perverse to her. Walthere talked in whispers, but he never spoke of love. Certainly not respect. That something should so unnerve him that he might bring it to her ears and turn away again as quick—it made her wonder if death was all his ghastly Iruwen sellsword was about. Even the thought of the creature set her skin to a crawl.

And still he hadn't spoken of Usuri again—of the magic they had unleashed, only to cork again as soon as its usefulness waned. For hours, she questioned how to put that girl's condition to him, but he busied her time with too many other things.

As he read and wrote and dressed, he had her scurrying to her mother with the Empress's request, then to Sara to fetch her for their coming strides, and dictating for him after that. Sara tried hard to coax them to conversation—bless her—with talk of Gerold and Lothen, for she doted on the little ones, and of the messenger, for she craved knowledge of Anscharde, but while Walthere bandied with her, Charlotte's responses were muted. She was distracted, and she knew her friend saw it, and she smiled in thanks to her, but it was what it was.

They sat in the same room, her father and she, but they could not have been further apart.

By early evening, they had their assembly prepared. Torches flickered through the castle to make a maze of glittering lights, and a small feast had been laid out in the great hall. Walthere and Sara and she all descended to that room together, proclaimed by the Empress's own herald. After Walthere addressed their guests, and bid them welcome, he took them all for a walk.

Most men were simple enough. A good life to them was a peaceful life—a place to raise food and family, a good lord that did not skim so much extra every month, and one that likewise kept a force of arm to see the first secured. So long as these few matters were provided, such people could suffer any number of other indignities with eyes to task alone. They were sheep.

Nobility, Charlotte had found, came with haughtier senses of the self, but the majority were still sheep to be led. Take a stick firm in hand and swat them down the paths one wished, filling their heads with promises of green pastures at the other end, and most would follow. Walthere knew the worth of his sheep. He took them well in hand and he used her to go among them and hear their concerns and to lead them willingly down his trail.

In truth, few liked Charlotte. All whispers traveled to their victim eventually, and she had heard them all. They thought her a whore or a fool or at the least a precocious child, and for that, it was good to have Sara afoot. People felt at greater ease, spoke more freely, when it was not just Charlotte lurking in their ranks, and Sara struck to the core of most people. The woman had one of those easy demeanors that could disarm all but the cleverest of men, and make friends of many more, and when she took Charlotte's side, it gave another message. This was her father's court, and she hated it, but they would have to accept her.

For a time, they walked the predictable courses of speech. Nobles were by nature curious sorts, and gatherings such as this were excused to gossip as much as any. Most had already heard of the messenger's arrival at their gates, and more than a few had already inferred his meaning. They asked after it in a way that made them seem as though casually stumbling into it, and beyond him, the Empress, the princess, and the little prince. They hungered, and Walthere baited them, ready as she was—with an answer to all their questions.

If only she might have said the same for her own.

"It was only a matter of time. We knew he would send for her eventually. If he has half a brain in his head, he knows he cannot ignore her."

"And the Empress? Where is she now?"

134

"Retired. The petulant whelp nearly set the shakes about her. At the least, we no longer need to *feign* illness."

Walthere shook his head and grumbled aside. The train of courtiers followed in their wake, passing beneath the portraits of the dead and wise, their sabers rattling the cobbles. Half the men, Charlotte mused, should never have shared a room. Now they shared a thin hall, and their master's chill favor all at once.

But this was the purpose of a castle's galleries—so as the walls were to defend, the galleries were to humble and to awe. Men gathered in their solars and their studies, but the walk showed the possibilities, mingled effortlessly with the lines of the past.

Her great grandfather's face on the wall, for example, was not merely a memorial to the dead—it was to remind the living that even a century past it was the wealth and prestige of House Cullick that stirred the fortunes of these lands and guided its people to their purpose. There were men that called history a poem and those that called it a song, and the bards certainly heralded it so. The simple truth? History was never simply history. If it was anything it was another collar—another means to control.

Her father pivoted back on his crowd, halting them beneath a tapestry of the battle of Ferrise—the battle where Cullick and their Curderoy forebears both had nearly been extinguished from the face of Lecura. In this, Charlotte heard the lion roar: *We will survive.*

"I would hear of the readiness of our men. If need be true, how soon could they march?"

Ser Kobulle, a knight of the Western Reaches, was quick to answer. "Planting season slows the process, but it goes at that. And it is no small feat to gather so many under bandits' guise."

"Aye. You have our blades, lord, but give us the time to see them properly sharpened." More than a few men deferred to Lord Gardesl's swagger. The bald, broad titan of a man was one of those rare characters whose mere bearing could earn him such. To be called a knight, and to look as though you could twist a man's head clean off with bared hands was no small thing.

But not all men were so moved. "It goes—they tell it true enough. But lord, not all of us have the means to support such."

There were a few scandalous whispers at that. It even managed to cock one of Walthere's brows. Poor though the speaker was, it was not a "noble" thing to lay it quite so plain.

"A balance must be struck. Too many of our men are already afield in Effise. If we do not take care with our summons…" The leather-skinned Lord Surrel's shoulders slumped with a weight only hearts could bring. "We shall find no food to support our armies come autumn."

"Tut, tut," another tongue clucked into the fray. At this one's sound, Charlotte nearly groaned for all his pleasant air. The slender, rat-haired viscount Hamoelet had never seen war, nor likely ever would. He kept one hand on his wife's arm—though all knew it was she that steadied him. "All men pass beneath your brother's own eye, my lord. He will see them to their purpose, if any a man may. Perhaps…even before autumn?"

There was a general clamoring of assent at that. Even Walthere smiled. If ever there were a man respected in Usteroy, it was his brother, Maynard. Were the bards to be believed, he spit steel and breathed fire. Pity so few would ever know the side of him that Charlotte held close to heart. The side that doted on the little children, and wandered the evening halls in worry for their blood.

Men knew the figure. Few knew the weight of the soul behind it.

"All save one. Messar Kamps," her father said, turning on the shrew of a figure, "you will take a delegation to Anscharde, with gifts of horse and linen. Make sure they know the depth of my apologies for my absence at our lord's coronation. I trust that you shall also bring word of this day's events. They will be notable, I assure you." With this, some of the slyness came into his voice, and the whispers rose with it, for all men knew when Walthere grew playful, there was ample reason. It puzzled Charlotte further.

"And fair lady Argenne, I would have you write your brother. Assure him any motions at his borders are but exercise against the rising acts of banditry there. As a fact, it would do nicely to ask of him any troops he might spare for the task. Surely he, after all, is as burdened by the villains as we."

Both assured him it would be done. Content, the lord of the castle then motioned them forward anew. Walthere moved on, ignoring the grapevine secrets slithering through the gaggle at his back, no few in part fanned by Sara, who pressed and parried with the gossip as a grandmother at her knitting.

136

This was Charlotte's purpose, though: to watch and to listen as tittered behind a fan, and most importantly, to remember.

Above their heads, the passing tapestry whispered: *put fortune to me and you shall survive as well.*

"My lord, if I might be so bold," Kobulle called over the clamor of booted feet, "Would we not best be served in recalling our men from the east? Many of the very best of us remain abroad…"

A fan began to flutter at Charlotte's side. "Oh, I do so miss my Geoffrey. He's sent word of terrible things afoot in that bastard's cold…" Young Lindie Ipsvend whispered far too loudly under the gust.

Much hot air rode that gust. The trick was to find which of it had worth beyond its uttering. Yet Charlotte was shrewd.

Geoffrey. Ser Geoffrey. Ten men-at-arms beneath him. Beholden to a sodden marsh, but fierce with a spear. He has a son…Geoffrey as well, isn't it? The son was old enough to fight, and inherit; he could call his littlefolk to them for he was well-liked, and as much a Farren as the father. There was a nephew as well if memory served, south of their border, in Sorbia, likely as eager to inherit as Geoffrey. That, too, could be useful. *If Geoffrey the Elder does not return, we will be fine for it.*

Names struck images, images reverberated into chords of possibility and present and past, and those without worth were shut out while the others tumbled on, and the connections consumed her. All this came and went as the others spoke, and she set her face to stone—the warrior's face, her uncle called it—and let none of it show. Memory was as key to jurti as anything.

"It is already done," Walthere answered without breaking stride. "They will be here within the month."

"Far be it for me to pick, lord, but is that so wise? The people see our just war in Effise—Assal wills it—and will no doubt fall upon our men as turncoats." Ser Hanvedt, another of the western banners, ducked his dark eyes even as he asked, in the manner of one unaccustomed to being heard.

"And what of the Bastard?" Hamoelet interjected. "He holds not the emperor title, but I am told he has as little love for certain birds of the nest as we. Might we not have words?"

"No," Cullick answered firmly.

"But it's my understanding the soldiers there march to his call, now. That makes him…"

Children hold more commonsense than this one. If she were his wife, Charlotte surely would have dug her nails into the fool's arm until his own blood cowed him, but neither lord nor lady Hamoelet seemed to possess any sense of the madness they offered. Oh, it was good detail, but the craft of it was all wrong. *What fool—even among friends—reveals so plainly such detail?* This was what jurti was made for.

Instead, he all but wailed the presence of his own spies. *Tactless.*

"I said no, Hamoelet. Leave it alone. The man is baseborn, and ill-tempered besides. He's as like to a bull's charge, if someone goads him, and I'll not ruin our lots with such."

The Bastard, it was said, was an impressive man by all counts—physically. Unfortunately, though he once held the Emperor's favor, he had never been a man of the court. To tell it truly, rumor held him to more than one quarrel with the nobility of the city Nirsburg, where his father long saw him housed, and all knew of his bloody duel with Baron Keffl, for insults slung upon his whore mother. What's more, he had a penchant for plain talk and crass tongue—neither of which endeared a man to the creatures of silk.

In all, the man lacked finesse. He lacked layers. Even his faith was so dreadfully plain, so rigid, Charlotte could not help but greet it with disdain. The man's fervent press of the reformed word was admirable, she supposed, but his bluntness in its regard had been what finally forced him to the field in a more permanent sense. Fanatics of any breed were, after all, a terrible burden to the status quo. Especially given people's tendency to follow them.

Passion often overran logic, unfortunately. If only the man weren't so intractable, he might have been a useful pawn. The early days of any faith were meant for the clever, not the angry. She sighed into her fan. *Pity.*

Guards parted the heavy doors to their statue garden—a place Charlotte had almost come to fathom as religious for its silence and its grace. Sara slunk back at last, extricating herself with a giggle and a parting quip, to come to Charlotte's side. Her hand caught Charlotte's, and offered a smile so infectiously conspiratorial Charlotte could not help but share it.

"Do you weary, princess?" she teased.

Sara's face knitted into a perfect frown. "I am now equipped with the knowledge of five more children than I began, and a sound idea of who here flatters, who here desires, and whose lecherous eyes or mind do not quite match their tongues. I can also tell you that you and I are the best attired, and that not one of these fears my pretty skirts half so much as they do your father."

"Is that proper?"

"It is perfectly proper, and good." She gave Charlotte's skin a pinch, and her grin widened when she did not so much as flinch. "And best used in conjunction with pretty skirt, that if the one does not cow, the other might awe."

Perhaps it had been her eldest brother—dear, deceased Joseph—that had taught Sara her initial lessons on fear. Mayhap she had simply watched and learned the walk from the capital's own streets. Sara's intelligence could not be denied, however. *If only she had ever found a husband to match her wits, we might well be hailing an empress now.* It was a pleasurable thought to dwell on.

Armed men stalked the periphery of the group's destination. Most bore the badge of Usteroy, but one or two kept royal colors. Men and women fanned out between them, but all continued to follow Walthere's lead down the carpet.

True to the garden's name, sculptures of marble and granite towered over their guests in intricate arrays. Not to honor the dead or mark some living man's glory, but for art in and of itself. At the end of this expansive courtyard, a saint looked down on them through stained color, the red and yellow glass making a prism of the room's dim trails.

Beneath the saint there stood another that caught Charlotte's eye. Draped in canvas, a broad portrait was supported on easels, a squirrely waif of a man just beside, his long and perfumed hair giving Charlotte pause—a reminder of another artist from younger days. She chewed her lip and turned aside, turning the swell of her attentions on the others' reactions. She assumed her father had called them together to discuss the coming strife. Not art.

From the pleasant, if uncertain faces, most his nobles had believed the same.

Walthere rose up before his crowd and gestured like a Ravonnen maestro readying himself for the chords. Her father loved a good show. "My lords, my friends, in these dark times, it is the duty of men to preserve some piece of the light. Put aside your grim visions a moment. I called you here tonight to share a piece of beauty." Turning to the artist, Walthere snapped his fingers. "Adamu, if you'd be so good."

The artist snapped forward with a few bobs of his womanish head, two previously unseen boys stepping from behind the portrait to assist. Between them, they grappled the ropes and edges of the canvas, and pulled it down into a heap.

Charlotte's own gasp was lost in a chorus of them. Before their eyes, the Emperor rose anew, the oil still slick upon his eyes, so wild and proud as they turned upon their end. The man was astride his rearing, snowy mare, sword craned high above his head, captured in the moment before the circling ghouls brought his body to its end. Smoke coiled about the scene. Horses circled him. Bodies lay beneath his feet. Sunlight struck him, and he was more. Hands reached for him, as steel, as God. In more ways than one, Charlotte felt as though they all stepped over his grave. She could feel Sara bristle beside her, though her face gave nothing away.

Playing on his nobles' captive attention, Walthere's own voice took on a delicate edge. "I call it simply, 'The Battle of Leitzen.' I made its commission with the Empress's blessing, and I intend to dedicate it to her in feast for our late emperor's honor, two octaves hence. It is my intent to make it a day of festivity for all manner of folk in Usteroy, unless, of course…"

No one took the bait—a fact Charlotte was immeasurably thankful for. Heads bobbed and the women fawned accordingly, praising the man in silence for his virtues, even if not all held her father's goodwill toward the peasants in such high regard. It was all part of the game. Bodies were bodies, after all, and word would quickly spread of their generosity. Nobles would admire his dedication to *a* man. The littlefolk would admire its application to *all*.

The benefits of a generous Farren, they would say.

"I will spare no expense in the festivities, and I would put calls to all your brothers and sisters abroad, to welcome them for this day. It is, after all, more than the mere sum of a man's life, but the extension of his legacy."

Walthere turned then, inexplicably, to her. His smile broadened unnaturally, and his white teeth shone as he stepped toward her. There was, in that moment, the little voice in her head that cried: *run, run*. But ladies did not run. She stood her ground and returned his smile with the grace and kind required. All eyes turned to them both, as he took her hand in his, patting it affectionately.

"We all know the importance of legacy. It is what remains when the man has faded. For some, it is an idea. For others, a place. For most, it is as simple as a child. Family. So it is for me, and so it is I hope to share my family's bliss with you all.

"I intend this day to formally announce as well the bond of union between my dearest daughter and our youngest lord, the little Lothen, who our gracious empress has agreed to us."

Dimly, Charlotte was aware of the crowd's reactions. For a moment she felt forced beyond her own body—a disembodied thought, or a notion of a thought, peering down at some other girl's fate from the rafters. Everyone else was smiles and awe—and none of them faked.

At some point, Sara drew close—almost imperceptibly close—and her hand shifted from her hand to her back, as though guiding her. *Is she as shocked as the rest?* Charlotte was not certain when the normally glass-like woman had grown unreadable.

Walthere Cullick had always had a thing of surprises, and this was the surprise to top them all. With a showman's flare, he offered her forward, and she blundered her way, absent thought, through a most regal curtsy, to the praise of all.

There has to be something. Something. But her mind was blank. There was nothing to use. Nothing to break the hold of this rude awakening.

She heard the words, but she was helpless to process them. The word "union" kept ringing through her head, like a pauper's tune. No small part of her wanted to turn on the man at her arm and tear into him with word and nail. Yet the same part knew the glory held within those words. With such a thing, she would be one of the most powerful women in the land—never mind the questions of how the count could have secured such a thing.

Only hours before, that same woman had turned round and round about the reality that she would never likely marry. All knew of her deflowering, her supposed rape at the bumpkin lordling's hands. Men passed her by, for all the beauty that had not changed in her. Women turned up their noses at her, for all the grace she had not lost. And in truth, she had come to terms with it. For all her father's rage, she had an inch of herself in that freedom.

Now, she would be a woman wed to a boy, scarcely free of wet nurse. She would know marriage, without ever *knowing* marriage for years to come. A tool. She remained a tool. She turned on the smile, and it sank deep into her gut, to ill stirrings. It was a play, and Lothen too would be an unwitting part.

If ever there were a woman to know her feeling, it was Sara, but Sara took her hands in hers, plucking her from her father, and instead of salvation, kissed them and squealed with wetness in her eyes, exclaiming her joy for all to see. This would mean so much. A sister, the woman said. *A sister.*

Charlotte's head spun. What she wouldn't have done for a moment's breath. She leaned heavily on her father's arm for support, even as the other women started forward to congratulate her. Nervously, her eyes found the portrait, and they all fell away.

Choice, the eyes of a dead man whispered, *is but an illusion.*

* *

In Leopold's eyes, the purpose of a council was to advise, never to instruct. Emperors, like gods, were supposed to be above the beck and call of such base men.

Then again, even gods were only words without swords to back them up—and Mauritz Durvalle had all the swords. It might have been less unsettling if uncle and nephew had felt any bonds of kinship to one another. Few enough men in this decrepit empire even knew who Leopold was.

They were as two foreigners set upon the same squalid vessel. It was a reality that came with no small distaste. When they looked at one another, they saw nothing but the sum of a people and a life lost to the other, and no shared strand of hair or shapely jaw could change that fact. At least Mauritz was Orthodox. Leopold clung anxiously to the hope that would be enough.

"What is this? And where is the rest of the council?"

They stepped together into the council's chambers—Leopold and his wife, Ersili. It was her voice that led them, almost before they were even through the doors. The summons had been from the council, but only Mauritz awaited them and it was his soldiers at the door.

A veteran of many wars, Mauritz's bearing cast him larger than he truly was, even as time had weathered him into an edged old man. He was the soldier brother, the second son of the last generation of Durvalles, and it carried in him still, despite the slight hunch to his back. Nearly eight feet tall in his prime, time had battered the scarred warrior of his height and of his fine red hair, but the eyes still held the fire that the rest of his seventy-five-year-old body did not. The blade still at his side—even in this hallowed hall—certainly helped foster the image.

A crooked smile broke the general into a bow. "Unnecessary," he countered, without missing a beat. "As I might have imagined, well—" His tongue fumbled around the landscape of his lips, grasping for the right insult. "His Highness's lady should be."

Fury pinched Ersili's lips. "Empress would be the term, lordship."

"Politics is a messy business, mum. A man's business. In the future, do remember that in the north, my lady, jurti demands we use the terms our blood has earned."

Only Leopold's hand on hers restrained the outburst lurking just beneath the surface. It was a pity, really. In truth the pair of them held more in common than either might have realized. Not birth, certainly, but fire—*Oh, the fire*.

Whereas Mauritz had his embers tempered in the fires of war, Ersili had hers stoked on the streets of Ravonno. A fact, he knew all too well, which would forever haunt her bearing.

Nails clenched against Leopold's hand, and he flinched. He tried to assert himself to hide it, but as his uncle rose, he knew he fooled no one. The man made a sweeping gesture, indicating the table and their readied seats. Say what he might, Mauritz had expected the two of them together.

Perhaps because it was always so. All men had their secrets, but for Leopold, Ersili was not one of them. In Ravonno, his enemies in the Prelatory had whispered against her as a witch, but he ignored them. He was not the only prelate to take a woman. If priests could, there was no reason he shouldn't, after all.

Of course, that did leave the thorny business of their marriage up for debate. She claimed the title, and he more than happily gave it to her.

But they had never been married. Not by paper and not by the Church. It meant little to him. It could mean the world to the people. It could mean death for the nobility.

As he slid into his chair, Leopold tried to turn his sternest glare upon his uncle. "Where she goes, I go. Remember that."

Mauritz's head cocked to one side. "I believe you mean that the other way around, highness." He remained standing—a fact that Ersili, if not Leopold, noted, and matched. Leopold's eyes drifted between them and, cursing, immediately regretted his decision.

"Majesty," he advised, trying to keep the distaste from his voice.

"Not yet, highness. But if we play our cards correct, I should say so, yes."

"Enough of the small talk," Ersili interjected. To the point, as ever. "You summoned us, Mauritz. We would know the why of it."

They had clashed all month long. People had thought Ersili a bauble, a cute amusement to be dismissed while they gnawed on Leopold's bones. Instead, she had been the one to gnaw. Feelers had been cast into Anscharde's various districts nearly from the day of their arrival, and Ersili had grown emboldened by the work Leopold so willingly offered her, but it was only after the electors' confirmation that she had deemed it time enough to teach the court its place.

In private talks with Portir, she had put the fat man in his place before rounding on the Emperor's treasury. Together with a hastily assembled entourage of local aristocrats and commoners alike, she had hunted for strands of corruption about the capital and seen both noblemen and soldiers alike jailed for it. Portir had demurely—if grudgingly—accepted the state of things. Mauritz, however, had argued against her before the council. Without his brother's support.

Ersili had shone when she spoke of such things, for she loved to outfox those who thought themselves superior. She had been doing it her whole life. Yet Leopold had his doubts. Perhaps she had moved too quickly.

Mauritz's hand drifted to a bottle of wine at his side. He plucked it as one might pluck the points of a feather, pouring himself a glass before passing it on. He took a sip and positioned himself like the eagle he was, perched against one of the broad-backed chairs of the councilmen.

Not for the first time, Leopold wondered if it wouldn't be best to have the man killed.

144

He might have, but for the fact that the general knew all his assassins. *A nest of vipers, our family.*

"It is with regret that I must inform you of Lord Portir's humble resignation of the council."

Leopold started from the bottom of his glass. "His what?"

"We have received no such letter."

Mauritz's smile was wide enough to swallow a tiger. "Perhaps that was because he did not intend it. I imagine the decision caught him as much unawares as it did you."

There was a game being played here, and for as many bawdy words as he had traded with his fellow robes in Turnina—that petulant gem of the world, and of Ravonno—Leopold had little patience for such things. It was the part of politics that bored him.

One of the parts, anyways.

"I am afraid we do not follow. We simple Ravonnens, perhaps, were not meant for your country's double-speak."

All the more reason for his wife's ever-vigilant presence. She was the diplomatic one—and the poisonous one, if a blade crossed them.

"Pity. You had best learn it. We do love our jests." Mauritz raised his glass to the both of them. "In one of the world's great and many tragedies, he has withdrawn to the Tower."

The Tower, as it was colloquially known, was the place naughty nobles went to die. It was a crumbling husk of a thing to the north of the palace, part of an older structure that had long since fallen into history. That the city clung to it was bad enough. That they had to make it a symbol was all the worse. It had been pointed out to Leopold on one of their many forays into the city. He had endeavored not to consider it again.

"To the Tower? But why?"

"I fear you never knew my brother in his prime, Your Highness." Mauritz craned his head away as he speared an apple with his fork. "A fine mind, once. Tragically, it fails him. Age is but one of the many issues your council faces, but it is a heavy one. Besides, as your wife's own investigations proved—" Leopold thought he caught a sneer there. "—there were too many willing to take advantage of that weakness. This was for his own good, I assure you."

"Does he see it that way?"

"How very unkingly of you, sire."

Leopold sighed into his hand. "Why should *I* see it this way?"

"Much better. And to answer your question," Mauritz punctuated with the crunch of his teeth on the apple's flesh, "because power-hungry men do not suit your cause unless they are *your* power-hungry men. Portir is not well-loved by the people, but he is by our fellows on the council, and while some of us fight wars for the glory of this nation, he has spent his years amassing coin. Far more than you or I could boast, I am afraid."

"Coin that, under the law, I would imagine, now falls to the crown," Ersili concluded, catching the insinuation. There was some small awe in even her venomous tones.

Mauritz shrugged. "If you should say so, my lady. I am but a simple soldier. I would have no knowledge of that."

"Well. You are to be commended for your dedication to the law—few would commend even family to it."

"A dedication I trust the court shall remember, in time." Mauritz watched Ersili without mirth, but the way he nodded to her offered some hope of respect, at least. "And I hope it shall put aside our own quarrels—though they have been for the good of all, I have no doubt."

So it was a bargain then. Leopold might have groaned aloud. Big or small, no deed came without its strings, it seemed. Though bribery was, perhaps, a lesser sin. Especially on so grand a scale, even Assal could look aside. Yet Assal was a man. Women, he had found, did not often bind their anger up in circles and let the fates make what they would of it. They remembered, and bribery, he had likewise found, only went so far to allaying it. And only for a time, at that.

While he cringed, Ersili had no hesitation. "And what of Portir's grandson? I shouldn't imagine he will be pleased at his father's condition."

Grandson? As if he did not feel old enough! Leopold turned to his wife, examining her for trace of jest. She glanced back at him, her eyes softening like those of a master patting down a distraught pup. Well, the man was eight years younger than his brother, but that still gave him more than seventy years, so there was certainly time for a family. That said, Leopold would have expected such a creature loitering about the court, if he existed. *More relatives. Goody.*

Warily, he looked across the table to Mauritz. Were there little generals running around as well? The thought was enough to give any reasonable man the shakes.

"He has a grandson?" Leopold asked lightly.

"And two daughters," his wife answered, placating. He should have expected—she never went to any place without its notions firmly scoured. Of course, he shouldn't have let that slip to Mauritz. "Duke Urtz, you'll recall?"

He had never met the man, or even heard the name, but he was grateful for the attempt to spare his dignity. With an "o" of remembrance, he feigned knowledge.

"Yes, of course. Urtz. A good man and…" He mouthed at the air, trying to sort out the right term. "Devout?" His wife's smile, at least, told him he had guessed that correctly.

Mauritz developed a sudden interest in picking at a scab. "Well in hand. Truth be told, they have not gotten along in many a year. Portir banished him from court when he was but his father's boy. A drinker in youth, you see. Dueled another lordling one night. Killed him. Caused a bit of a scandal in its day. The court paid the family off, and the boy was sent home. But the point is, neither ever forgave the other the offense."

From outside, Leopold caught the rattle of mailed boots—of marching men, set to purpose. It drew him off. Boards creaked. Voices swam the air in low murmurs. He imagined a sword rattled in its sheath.

It was a common enough sound in the castle, but his mind wandered, and he entertained the notion—however brief—that these would be the men to carry him off, to carry him to a similar fate as his uncle. Towers were very tall after all, with plenty of prisons in the sky for heads both noble and divine. Regicide was a crime most heinous, and kinslayer as well—but who was there to second guess, especially when it was not death they wrought? There were no crimes against imprisoning unlawful men—and it was generally the usurper that made the justifications.

Of every man, he knew, on some level he had to ask the same question: are you Mauritz's man, or the crown's?

If only he had his own men. Alas, he came into his crown but a humble priest, with only Bertold at his side. In the eyes of the Church, prelates were but

147

priests after all, and no man of Assal's cloth was permitted such dominance over men. Of course, the Church itself wielded a rather sizable army, but this was for the almost exclusive use of the Patriarch—for the good of the Faith, naturally. This didn't even mention the princes and *their* armies.

Leopold could count on them, if push came to shove. But there was a difference between having an army and having an army at hand. Many miles separated Anscharde from Ravonno. Swords-in-theory did him little good if he was dead-in-fact.

Then again, there were the palace guards—but these were admittedly for show. Men knew and respected the soldiers of the crown for the authority they represented, not for any particular martial skill. Bodyguards at best, illusions of bodyguards more accurately.

Even ignoring that, they were much reduced in number since his father's absconding of them into his futile efforts in Effise.

And where had that gotten him? An army barely 200 strong, that's where.

What Leopold really wanted was to call upon his brother's men, but as his wife continually reminded him, what was his brother's was not necessarily his own. Soldiers followed generals, or they followed coin. Joseph had drawn upon both sympathies. Leopold could boast neither. At court, Portir controlled the revenue—among hundreds of other scheming nobles with private funds—and Mauritz remained the only general. He had also been the man closest to Joseph before his death. It was Joseph, after all, that had beckoned Mauritz to Anscharde.

Ostensibly, Leopold's older brother had hoped to bolster his own position with fresh troops—and inevitably left Leopold's own more precarious. His heart fell to think it. Even in death, his family could spite him.

No, Joseph's men were as good as Mauritz's men. And a sizeable addition, at that.

"Praise be that even in the darkest corners, Assal will find some light."

Mauritz raised his cup to that and tipped it to the both of them. "Praise be," he repeated.

At the least, Mauritz was devout. It was a small thing, but it was something.

"Will this affect my husband's coronation?"

"Our coronation," Leopold corrected with a gentle smile.

"In two octaves the crown will rest upon your head. Mark my words, at that."

"And shall we have an empress to grace the event?"

"My lady?"

"An empress. Your men sent for this Cullick and his brood, did they not? Along with the Empress Dowager? I would have them at our ascendance." Ersili's eyes twinkled, bright and cruel and innocent all at once. "For their blessing."

For the first time that day, Mauritz appeared perturbed. His feet shuffled uncomfortably against his chair, and he turned his attention briefly to his apple, from which he took another bite, using the action to cover his uncertainty. "In honesty, I should think not."

Leopold leaned forward. "Surely we are not to be troubled by one irksome count, grace? What manner of man should defy royal edict?"

"A smart man, I should think."

"Are you mere tribesmen, to so brook dissent? The man is a cretin," Ersili snapped.

"And no more the fool for it. He has the people's ears, fertile soil beneath his feet, and a good many blades in hand. Only a fool would disregard him."

The word set a ringing in Leopold's own ears. A sheepish glance turned from Mauritz to his wife. Her fingers spread against the table, thin and pale and violent, but her voice, when it came, lacked even the slightest hint of venom.

"And what would you propose, then?"

"Propose?" Mauritz shrugged. "I propose we continue acting as though we are the ignorant noblemen we are, and carve out his throat when he makes his move." There was the barest trace of whimsy to the elderly soldier's tone.

Sellswords, Leopold decided. They needed to hire sellswords. Mauritz said it himself: they had the coin now, didn't they?

But then, only a fool would surrender such bounty. He watched his uncle in a new and increasingly wary light. Soldiers could be bought, certainly. But who was to say the wild general couldn't simply buy them out from under him again?

"Easier said than done."

"Until Othmann returns our soldiers from Effise, we can do no more. Do not concern yourself with such small matters."

It seemed as good a time as any. With an exaggerated effort, Leopold drew back his chair and sauntered to his feet. In accordance with protocol, Mauritz bowed his head to him, though Ersili kept her gaze flat. Leopold took her hand in his regardless, kissing each knuckle tenderly before addressing his uncle.

"Then I leave it in your capable hands, uncle. Let Ersili assist you in any arrangements you need—and it shall fall to her to go over poor Portir's ledgers. I trust you do not mind?"

There was a flicker of annoyance in the old man's eyes. "Without offense, highness, perhaps you might share with me your dear heart's qualifications for such things? I find numbers often lie beyond our women's…rather delicate sensibilities."

Leopold opened his mouth to speak, but Ersili cut him off. "I have managed my father's estate since I was nine years old, *my lord*. I served as chequer to the coin for Prince Massimo, of our fair south's northern principality. And I dare say I can count the threads upon your tunic and find spare thread enough to feed a small town's hungry bellies for a year.

"Let us not speak of qualifications, lord." She gave Leopold's hand a squeeze, only to let it drop thereafter. "I suggest we speak of inheritance."

With a smile and a nod to his dear and writhing uncle, Leopold gladly turned and left them to their ledgers.

War was a nasty business. As were politics, religion, and the hard northern cuisine.

There was but one recourse for Leopold to take from it all while his wife battled on his behalf, and it awaited him in the throne room. Even as the guardsmen pressed open the heavy-plated doors, his ears burned to the squeal of his preferred name: "Papa!" On instinct, his arms dropped with his knees, and the emperor-to-be became all too human for an instant.

Fiore threw herself into his arms with abandon, her tiny hands tugging at the loose skin of his face. She was a portly little thing, and he winced at the thought that soon he might not be able to pick her up at all, but he was still a man of middle years, strong and proud as any knight, and for the moment, he lifted her high.

"Ani said I'm not a princess, papa! Is that true?"

150

Anatole skulked just beyond, scuffing a shoe against the cobbles and very pointedly not looking at either his sister or his father. Fiore turned back to stick her tongue out at him. She was ever the proud child, and at just six years, spiritedly curious, while her brother—well, too old now, perhaps, to envision himself a knight—had long since settled for the jester's role.

In response to his daughter's tongue, Leopold gave one of her long pig tails a hearty tug, until she had bent back far enough for their eyes to meet anew. She giggled.

"And you believe everything your brother tells you, sweetling?"

She tottered. "No…"

By which, of course, she meant yes.

"Good. Because he takes far too much after his papa to be honest." Balancing his daughter on one arm, the Emperor crooked a free finger toward his son. The boy's eyes flickered, and lowered, and he only reluctantly sloughed forward. "What do you have to say for yourself, my boy?"

"I'm not a liar."

"I never said you were. I simply said you weren't honest." The boy's face scrunched in confusion, and Leopold laughed.

"Aren't those the same?"

"If it were, I suppose we should all be liars, in which case, we are quite damned, and you've nothing to worry about."

Alarm dug Fiore's fingers tighter into the crook of his neck. "We're damned, papa?" Her little arms quivered, and she snuggled deeper against him. Sighing, Leopold bounced her slightly as he shook his head at Anatole—a look of man to man, which spoke of battles lost. The boy mimicked his sigh, his shaggy blond mane making his own gesture somewhat lighter in character. He grinned like a fool, a fool-boy, and it stirred Leopold's heart.

They were both as such: blond angels, neither yet a decade's turn upon the earth. Both loved him unconditionally, in the manner only children could muster. Both obeyed him unquestioningly, and took his words to heart. All this, when neither looked at all like him.

Sometimes, one had to marvel at how the heart could overcome the blood. Another man's flesh and blood could be every bit one's own children if only the heart made room for them, as Leopold's had. They were, he tried to tell himself, his only vice.

But then again, that simply wouldn't have been true. At the least, the other vices complimented them nicely.

"Princess, papa is a joking man. It is a gift the Lord did bless me with."

Fiore's arms crossed in impudent fury, and her lips pouted at the notion that someone—anyone—would cross her with half-truths. "It was not funny."

He prodded her button nose with one chubby finger. "No, I suppose it wasn't. Forgive me?"

"Maybe…"

The tone promised a cost. What's more: he already knew he would pay it. He always paid it. Children were, after all, as close a thing to the divine as one could come. Or the demonic. Though Leopold reckoned he could probably name a half dozen members of his own family to put any child's tantrum to shame.

Gathering his daughter in his arms, Leopold began to lope and loop his way toward the throne, Anatole trailing the sounds of their laughter and conspiracy.

Beyond that sound, there was nothing in the room to give it note. Without the courtiers and councilors, the place might as well have been a tomb. It was short, with none of the pomp of the southern courts—a plain room of few tapestries, little light, and only two chairs. These at least struck one with an imperial bearing—a necessary offering of the mother and father of the Empire. The white-cloaked Imperial Guardsmen he had left to watch the children remained at the base of these, little more than ornaments for the room. They stepped aside for them.

"Eventide…" Leopold meant to add their names in passing, but for the life of him, he could not remember them. The only Ravonnen among them had died with his father. "…I trust all goes well?" he added awkwardly instead.

"Aye, highness."

"Your Highness," the second man greeted him. "Lord Heinrich was about, looking for you."

Leopold paused atop the last step of the dais, turning awkwardly with his daughter on his knee. "And what, pray tell, did my brother want of me?"

"I—"

"Uncle Heinrich smells of cows!" Fiore bellowed overtop of the guard. "And I hate his face."

He raised an eyebrow and turned it on Anatole. "Is that so?"

The boy grinned again. "It is a rather ugly face."

Leopold smirked into his hand. "And while I will neither confirm nor deny that, sweetling, let us never again say it aloud, shall we? Hm? As you will, ser."

"He said something of Lord Portir…"

"And offered us sweets to tell him more," Anatole said with no small measure of disgust. "I told him we should spy for nothing less than a horse apiece."

Leopold looked on his son with disbelief. The boy only shrugged. "He didn't seem to think it much of a deal. He was gone before I could tell him what color I wanted."

"White! I want a white horse!" Fiore clapped her hands together excitedly. "We shall be as the wind!"

The guardsman coughed pointedly. "He should like to speak with you before the day is out, Your Highness."

"As would they all, I'm sure. When you find my wife about, do tell her. She shall endeavor to mend this. Meanwhile we, I do believe," Leopold said, switching to a slightly higher scale as he addressed his still excited daughter, "should have a date with the court menagerie."

"Will there be horses?" Fiore asked.

"Oh, sweetling, nothing so mundane. There are plenty of those afoot in these very halls. But what is your position on two-headed gryphons?"

Chapter 8

By the time they pulled the two men from one another's throats, Rurik was sporting a swollen lip, and one of the brawlers had earned himself a broken arm. Even so, it took three other soldiers to separate them, and these spent plenty of time eying the crowd as well, for fear some other rabble-rouser would get it in his head to join the squabble. Thankfully today such was not to be the case.

"And what was this one about," Berric said, sidling up in the aftermath of the departing men's shouts.

Rurik wiped a spot of blood from his chin, then tried to sort that out for himself. "Idiocy," he offered.

"A great deal of that going around."

This was the sixth such fight in an octave. At least this incident lacked a blade. In the last fight, one man had poked the other in the ribs with a dagger. He had bled like a speared boar, ostensibly over a spot of the watered down swill they still passed as wine. Then, it had been Rurik's duty to hang the man with the knife. That made two. Two dead over less wine than it would take to make a child tipsy.

Rurik's role—as confidante for Tessel—was becoming increasingly devoted to policing the unruly. It was a heavy task considering the fact that they were *all* unruly. In a time when the leather off one's shoes was becoming viewed as an all-too viable alternative to the grumblings of one's belly, hunger was turning braggarts into outright swine.

The camp's followers were leaving every day. Even reports that many trains of the departed were attacked by Prince Leszek's raiding parties did little to stymie this. Raiders could only rob or kill. It was widely viewed as a much sounder alternative to the slow wasting of starvation. As the cost of the ones that remained increased, however, the soldiers were increasingly set upon their flight as well—save for the whores, of course.

With spring, the army was sifting further and further out from itself, rather than coalesce. Though it reduced the strain on supplies, it was also leaving them increasingly open at a time that Tessel seemed to be growing more and more paranoid of the world around him.

154

Plucking a skin of the ratswill from his own pack, Rurik stomached a swig, wincing as it ran between raw gums. In the time it took him to look up again, another onlooker had sidled into their midst, though this one held himself carefully apart from the rest, and looked straight at him. Boderoy's patient smile captured him.

"Well what is it," Rurik snapped at Tessel's attendant.

"Ser Tessel wants a word. Marching orders, I take it."

That, at least, did something to lighten his mood. "About damned time."

Berric patted him earnestly on the shoulder. "Go, my friend. I'll wipe this down."

Rurik was only too content to let Berric do so. With a token show of reluctance, he thanked his friend and headed for the town proper, Boderoy leading.

Few wandered the lanes as freely as he anymore. Perimeters seemed to have sprung up as much around clumps of tents and wafting pennants as the more solid wooden structures of the camp's edges. Suspicious eyes turned inward, and no one went any longer without their steel. Even Rurik was no longer allowed to move without the protection of his station—men that followed him still, their pikes and bright attire making him feel more a peacock than a shade.

A hundred camps in one. That was what their grand army of the Empire had been reduced to. With the abrupt departure of Marshall Othmann, and the consequential refusal of Tessel to meet with any of the nobles and their representatives, the camp had been polarized. As it was, Leszek and the Effisians wouldn't need to harry their trains. If simply left to their own devices long enough, they would likely tear themselves apart.

Yet even in this, Rurik walked a singular path. Noble men scowled at his passing. Ivon would not spare a word with him. The common men were no better. Each viewed him as a traitor to the other. Like a half-breed. A Lamara.

The thought of it pulled him toward the Eagles' company, but though his steps were swift, they were never swift enough. The true Lamara no longer awaited him. Essa was never there. A few times he had caught the scant passing of her shadow at his approach, but this was as close as he had ever gotten. These days if it wasn't Gorjes men, it was the little bear's all-too-knowing stare that greeted his trouble. Something had turned Roswitte's surly glares upon him.

Alviss had warned him off. There was reason to that call. But even so: it was so very hard. After all, could a man who had once tasted of the sea's fair breeze ever convince himself a pond would do? Essa had been a daily part of his life for so many months—and now? Now there was only pity, and work, and even he hated himself for how they painted him.

At the edge of camp, a woman caught his eye. She stood before the tents, red hair askew, cloak-smothered but shapely. She was a pale mirage that enticed men with wanton looks. She caught his eye and held it. Purpling lips pursed into a smile and she tipped back the folds of her cloak, revealing merely cloth, cold and grime having pulled it tight to ample features. A finger hooked toward him, as she openly ogled.

What women might tempt us to. For a moment, he wavered. Then he hurried on, temptation's laughter haunting him through the man-made alleys of the tent city.

"Ser? The commander?" one of his guardsmen asked.

The Gorjes watched them hasten on. More than one blew him a mocking kiss.

Without worry of horses or men upon their paths, the trek to the town gates was swift. Within their embrace, it also seemed as though he had crossed the threshold of one world into another. Peasants mingled amiably enough with the soldiers, and hoes and sickles were more commonplace here than blades. Here, all the able-bodied men were of like mind—bound, as they were, in dedication to the Bastard.

With Othmann's departure, not one noble soul remained housed within Pasłówska's walls.

Polarized. *They fear a revolution of a sort, and so you give them a symbol for the effort.*

He knew that he would die, the Bastard had said. *Even emperors lie. Why should good men be any different?*

Boderoy stopped them just inside the gates, his thinning features bowing ever-so-slightly to a more proper greeting. As good as his master's orders, the man put a hand to Rurik's chest as he tried to continue on. "Tessel has gone to meet with Lord Pordill in the chapel," he informed them. "No steel."

Only once Rurik relinquished his blade and pistol both did the attendant turn to guide him on.

Unmistakable amidst the stone hovels that surrounded it, the town's small church lay open to their arrival. Two soldiers stood outside the doors, their own steel as unmistakable as the church. Joining them was a tawdry assembly of men-at-arms, their emblazoned surcoats and surly demeanors leaving no doubt that these were nobles' men, or lesser nobles themselves. No three wore the same sigil, save the half-dozen bearing Pordill's goat.

While it was comforting to know that Tessel hadn't forsaken safety entirely, it was somewhat distressing to think how tipped the numbers were. A word from Rurik added his own guards to the door as he tugged Boderoy aside.

The meeting was planned. The crowd was not. "I thought we were meeting with Pordill."

"You are. It would seem others came along for the pleasure."

Casting a wary glance over his shoulder, Rurik added, "So should some of ours. I would have you bring some of the men from the gates to—"

"All the other captains are inside already, young master. There are more than enough bodies. I would suggest you go to join them. You fret too much over details."

"I fret too much over my neck, Boderoy. Would you…?"

"Go, go," the man said, making shooing gestures with his hands. "I will see who I can wrangle."

Appeased, but far from settled, Rurik crossed the icy glares of the nobles' men and mounted the church's stairs. Even from outside, he could smell the stench of disinfectant and rot alike. Sickness. Blood. His nose curled at the thought of all the sick, but if the nobles could brave it, he supposed he could as well. Truth be told, the thought of seeing his brother again was more unnerving than the blood.

Assal give me the strength. A foot inside the door, he hastily added: *And the wisdom to carry a closed mouth.*

Cots lined the circling wall, to provide relief to those overflowing pews that had survived the hunt for firewood. Even so, the floor held the excess, forming a macabre scene of wracked lungs and twisting flesh. It was a sea of horrid, bloodshot eyes, and Rurik felt his stomach lurch involuntarily at the sight. *You can do this,* he reminded himself. Even so, he made it a point to hurry down the aisle.

A short walk through the chapel made Tessel's choice of venue all too clear. If sickness didn't deter any unnecessary guests, the altar likely would. Ringed in the manner of all such homes to Assal, the altar was bound by silver—or painted to look like it—with white linen covering its broad expanse. The statue of the prophet at its center would call any Orthodox to peace. Tessel may have been a Farren, but most of the nobles were pure Visaj.

A perfect, if distressing setting.

Though the altar did not have its own separate room, it was set in a sizeable alcove that formed the rear of the chapel. Larger samples of the sort often came with confessionals, as well as back rooms for the priests, and even classrooms, in certain cities. This, however, was extravagant enough for Pasłówska.

True to Boderoy's word, Tessel stood beside the altar, ringed by his other captains, save one—Narve—who had the day's watch in camp. By Rurik's opinion, they were none the less for the priest's absence. A few additional guardsmen stood clustered about the dais, apart from the gathering, but Pordill and a small train of nobles were entwined with Tessel and his, arguing, apparently, over a large map. On closer inspection, it was Effise.

As he approached, the normally calm Pordill slammed a gauntleted fist into the wood. "Reason is the cornerstone of the great. Take the chip from your shoulder and open your ears. You cannot arrest people in the night."

"And I have told you before, Erim. I did not arrest the Lord Marshall. I reassigned him. He is in good health," Tessel replied, not pausing even as his head dipped in greeting to Rurik.

"The Lord Marshall is answerable only to the crown. Remember your own title, *ser*," one of the younger nobles snipped. One of Huwcyn's admirers. "Which ranks higher before Assal?"

"I should presume all men are equal, Gerrin, for we are all of us flesh and bone," Tessel said testily, "But so too do I remind you that as appointed by an emperor, my own station temporarily supersedes his own. For that matter, as acting commander, I do have the right of lawgiver. And I act—"

"Carelessly," Pordill grunted. "What of Ferrigus? Or Matair? You discard our advice. You bar us from your quarters. Yet you meet with thieves and exiles and all manner of filth." This he added with a wave across Tessel's captains.

"Ivon?" Rurik asked, alarmed. All octave his brother had evaded him. For eight days, only silence greeted him from the reduced camp of Verdan's men. He had assumed there had been desertions, just as he had assumed his brother merely didn't wish to speak to him. He stepped toward the table, though no eyes turned at his approach. "What happened to Ivon?"

They ignored him. Talked around him.

"I had nothing to do with Matair. He deserted. Far from the first—"

"An honorable man! So either it's a sign our army is truly forsaken, or a lie," Huwcyn Ibin boomed, to make himself heard. He stood at the center of the gathered nobles, and raised his warrior's hands theatrically. "Ivon Matair is not the sort to cut and run. While you cannot even tell his brother."

Pordill nodded assertively. "And you expect us to believe this? Even as your knives wander our night?"

"What happened to Ivon?" Rurik asked again, louder.

There was a knife in his gut. His father's death had planted it there. Essa's turn had twisted it. He felt it digging deeper now, and though he felt his sense of calm slipping with it, he feared the worst, and could not hold himself back. Absently, he wished that Berric were here to advise him, but Berric was doing his duty, and he was alone, and none of these men listened.

Tessel waved them off. "I find we've many nobles afoot here, but tragically few noble men."

This jab drew Huwcyn forward. Even without a blade, the man cut an imposing figure. He looked like one of the northmen, and singly among his lot, like a man born to war. Wisely, two of the captains drew between him and Tessel, jaws squared for a fight. They sized one another up over the long moments.

"I did not call this meeting to trade barbs," Tessel sighed, falling back to his diplomatic nature. He gestured his own men off—a command obeyed with reluctance. Only Boderoy remained close at hand, having sidled more-or-less silently up to his master while everyone else stood distracted. "Pordill. Please. Be reasonable. This camp is becoming armed camps, and the divisions of necessity do not aid matters. Do not blame me for vigilantes, as I do not blame you and yours for the vigilantes among your own names. We need to make plans for Mankałd. We *need* to march."

Pordill stared down at the map on the table. He shook his head, mumbling something under his breath. Rurik turned between them, still confused. *Ivon? Where are you?* He thought of his conversation with Tessel, of the rage and the lies and the wavering of certainty—would he lie about his brother too? He looked into the general's eyes and hoped he could see something, some flicker of knowing, but all he saw was doubt and anger.

A new voice beckoned from the throng of nobles. "My lord, please, hear me out." The speaker was a slip of a man, probably only a few scant years older than Rurik. He had no hair, but his eyes, puffed and reddened by an obvious lack of sleep, made him appear even more the boy—a fact accentuated by the robes he bore. Robes that clearly did not fit him. Rurik didn't recognize him—a remarkable feature in its own right.

And yet, he had a familiar quality. A certain vulture-like figure Rurik did not particularly admire. One of the man's own companions laid a hand against his arm as he stepped forward, and he shrunk like a wilted flower, uncertain.

"I am no lord, Ser Frechauf."

The name was more telling than the features. It lifted the man back to the general, and drew Rurik's eyes in scrutiny. *Haber's brother.* A hunched bull of a man from the south. He could picture him from the training grounds, snarling commands without ever having to raise his voice. Gruff—far more peasant than noble—but one of Othmann's staunch courtiers. One of Ivon's friends.

The hand fell from Frechauf's arm. He stepped forward, brushing past Pordill with such uncalculated fervor it seemed as if he would throw himself to Tessel's knees. But he hesitated, hands shaking.

"Lord, ser, whatever you will have, Tessel! But please, I beg you, release my brother. At least let me see him. I was there when your men took him away." He took another step forward, hands coiling together. "I saw the crest they bore." Another step. His head snapped back on his party—a plea as much to them as any. "They said he was a traitor!" A hand flung, frantic and true, and his sleeves shook beneath the fervor.

Tessel's eyes did not waver as his did. "A question only the man himself could answer. Could you name the ones that took him?"

"Could any name a peasant for a man?"

By a trick of light, something flickered as a sleeve stirred. *That's not his arm.*

Frechauf had crossed within a breath of Tessel when the dagger flashed from the folds of his robes.

* *

By the time they pulled the two men from one another's throats, Essa was wondering if Rurik realized he was not cut out for his lot in life. There had been nearly a dozen brawls over the course of the octave—only half of which the Bastard's aide-de-camp had actually caught.

But he tried. As he tried with her. As he tried with his brother. It was more than she could say of most.

She had to wonder if he knew his brother was gone. He went to the edge of that camp every day, and every day the guardsmen turned him away. Orders were orders. They were not to speak of Ivon's departure. They were to turn aside any that did not belong. They were to do as they were told.

Which was just as well, considering they didn't know anything. Not really. Ivon had simply slipped away in the night, along with Vardick, a token assembly of soldiers, and a handful of Witold's bannermen. There had been no word, and as far as she could tell, nothing but their horses removed. In brighter times, it should have never gone unnoticed. With everyone else making islands of themselves, the fool could be gone a month before anyone noticed.

Unfortunately, this left Witold's retainers with few visible commanders. While most were loyal to Ivon, few had any desire to stay if he wasn't. Men trickled out daily. And then there were the Gorjes.

Marvelle leered out of the crowd at her. "See something you like?"

With eyes of carefully shaped ice, she slid out and carefully wiggled a dagger at the would-be Eagle. The man's grin only widened, before he turned away again.

"Charming creatures, those," Rowan quipped, laying a comforting hand against her shoulder. "I should say you could have him for dinner, if I didn't think he'd give us all the pox." His hand slid down, following her arm to the dagger, and gently lowering it toward her belt. "Rats always do, you know."

She let him guide her back to caution. This time. There was a day she would kill them all. Men such as these wished to be lords of war, armed and armored, and glittering like peacocks. She was content to be a dagger in the night. It could wait, but it would always fall. So help her, not one of them would escape when it did. There were crimes she needed to right, and if they so willingly strode into the role of scapegoat, the problem was not hers.

With a huff, Essa slid the dagger into its place and leaned back into her cousin. Her eyes rolled down his length, and a frown was the result. For once, he was dressed in something more akin to their place: dark, damp, and not the least bit ostentatious. It felt remarkably out of self.

"Some things simply make a good mantelpiece."

"And that's called wasteful, girl. Come now. There's nothing more for us here. Let us go before the young master sees."

She lingered longer than she should have. She always did, in moments like this. Half of her wanted to beat the boy senseless—to take him by the hair and pull until he felt as she had felt in the long nights after the rape. Even the word was enough to poison her spit. The other half hoped simply that he would see her. A morbid, somewhat masochistic side perhaps, but all the same, she hoped it. What would happen if he did, though—that she could not say.

Nor could she say if she hoped to see sorrow or pain in his eyes. All she knew is she wanted him to see the same in her.

Betrayal sowed only bitter oats.

Which was precisely why she did not trust the Gorjes. Looking around, nearly half the crowd was Gorjes—appropriate, considering it was one of theirs that started today's beating. Though they allegedly owed their oaths to Count Witold, they were sellswords at heart. And sellswords, with nothing to fight and no coin to pay them, were nothing more than murderers in wait.

Ivon was the man with the coin. He was their broker, their wrangler. Without anyone to give them orders, they would make their own—and that would likely mean selling out the rest of them as soon as the reward grew shiny enough. Thankfully, they were not privy to Ivon's departure. They, like the rest of the camp, seemed appropriately duped.

It would be easy to know the day they learned the truth. If they didn't sell out the rest of Witold's men, they would certainly string the Eagles up. Threat of intervention from proper law was about the only thing that kept those vultures from their door.

What they needed was to go. Go like Ivon. Go like Roswitte. Go from this place and leave them to die or live and see the world and to never look back. But they wouldn't. For some reason they couldn't. Sense demanded it, but still she loitered, looking for something that did not exist. Yet that only infuriated her more, because she knew it was illogical, but she did it anyways. The gods were cruel.

She rubbed her eyes against the latest migraine. Sometimes it seemed she could scarcely go a day without them any longer. Hunger, most likely. It made her almost miss the numbness of appetite that had followed the arasyl. Talking helped. Not that she did much of that. Roswitte would have made her. She blinked away spots and stared skyward. But Roswitte was gone. That notion gathered more weight in her gut than she would have expected.

Overhead, the sky shone blue and wide and clear, like a reflection of the sea. Somewhere in the distance, a gryphon's warbling cry split her head anew. Were they younger days, she might have saddled the creature. She might have mounted it, and through it, mounted the sky and the world and left it all behind.

Dreams—they were troubling things.

"Need attendance?" Marvelle called after them as they walked away. He often proved more observant than his lousy demeanor implied.

"With walking? I think we have the gist of it. Boots and everything." Rowan did not stop, even as he answered.

In spite of the sarcasm, she could hear Marvelle share words with his brothers. There was laughter—they would follow in time. She groaned inwardly at the thought. Time alone was far too precious to waste on fools.

They paralleled Rurik's own path through the early part of his trek, splitting from it as a whore caught his eye. *So that is love now, is it?* She wanted to spit on him. Rowan, noticing the redhead, guided her skillfully away from that particular shipwreck, and straight back for their own end of camp. To food, and to company.

Or at least, to company. Essa's stomach growled. It had been three days since her last solid meal. Far from the longest ever, but still not desirable. When she made water now, even her body's leavings seemed to reflect that fact.

"He'll have nothing for us, Rowan."

Her cousin shrugged his slender shoulders. "I trust the smell shall give us strength."

"The smell of tack?"

"The strength to know there's worse things than starvation, darling."

At least they weren't dying of thirst. Even the shit-laced waters around the camp were better than the cracked flesh and bloodied organs that came without. She thought of an old man she had seen in the followers' camp, not long after the Emperor's death. This one was already dead, but he was a shriveled thing. He and his dog—and the dog, still howling.

She shuddered. The stores were breaking down. Portions were becoming scarcer and scarcer and there were rumors of hoarding.

And still the wagons grew scarcer still. Men looked for them on every horizon, but it seemed as if their own country had abandoned them.

Civilization, she had always said. Too much of it was the real killer. Give her the woods and she would never starve.

Some did not need even that luxury. The Zuti, by every truth there was, should have ground them all up and spit them out and rendered the whole of their petty squabbles to nothing years ago. Truth be told, they puzzled her. As she looked out on her own kind—and that, in and of itself, a laughable note—she could not help but think the Marindi had somehow failed themselves. The Zuti were a people that hailed from a continent of sand and glass, or so the sailors said. A land of fire and brimstone, if the priestly sort were to be asked. Either way, it was not a thing one found bounty in. If they could survive that, well, it was no wonder they had taken over the continent's west coast. The only real wonder was that they had been stopped.

Unconsciously, she glanced behind her, looking for sign of their own southerner. The man had a way of disappearing for hours at a time, only to show up at the worst. She still didn't know what to make of him, good or bad. But he earned her respect by being the one soul to utterly avoid talking to her of Rurik. A boon, to be sure.

But names had a power. Usuri had taught her that. She bit her tongue as they crossed an open path, and a killer moved into it.

Chigenda caught them half-way to the stores, a disheveled-looking baker held by one arm. When he reached them, he gave the boy a shove forward and folded his arms against his bare chest. The boy looked first to the Zuti, rubbing his arm, then to the befuddled pair before him. He licked thin lips, made thinner by the lack of food.

"Essa," he murmured.

"Voren."

"Lord," Rowan groaned. "Don't tell me our dear Zuti has made you his voice now. You do still speak, don't you, Chigenda?"

The brown man's lips spread into a pale imitation of a smile.

"Well, at least he's not deaf. Yet. Probably."

"Voren?" Essa repeated, ignoring the others. She did not like the nervous tick to his eyes.

"I-I was looking for you. He was there. At-at camp I mean. Your camp. C-came to t-tell you…"

"Little man much speak me like dis," the Zuti said crossly, leaning over his ward. "Is funny, no?"

Essa scowled at him. Voren took an unconscious step in her direction.

"Something's happening. Lindie said she saw armed men in camp." Lindie was one of the other workers at the stores. She was skittish, like Voren, but Essa had not found her prone to overreaction.

Rowan rolled his eyes. "All the men in camp are armed, child. It's part of war."

"Weapons drawn, Rowan. With eyes what like fire."

Cousins exchanged a look. As one, they turned to Chigenda. The Zuti was staring off into the camp, scrutinizing the crowd of Gorjes still jeering between the tents. "Heard no ting. But people—dey move. Little men. Little sword."

"How many?"

Without looking at them, the Zuti tapped one finger against his temple. "That is ting. No move as one. Many little men. Each to self, each own way."

As if to prove his point, a shout rose in the distance—but in a gathering so large, this was not an unusual occurrence, and it was quickly lost to the other sounds of camp.

Armed men. As Rowan said, there were always armed men. And with Tessel's recent incursions in the night…who was to say what their purpose was? It could have been another brawl. Or a grudge. There were more than enough of those to go around.

There were many things it might have been. But few could make so stark a turning of Essa's stomach.

Rowan apparently shared her feeling.

"There is a foulness on the air. Let us to camp, little birds."

* *

Chaos. The dagger kissed air. Tessel seized Frechauf by the wrist, to wide eyes. Then he cracked his knuckles on the side of the assassin's head. As they shrugged off the moment's confusion, many of the other nobles produced smuggled steel as well and swung at anyone close at hand. Cries shattered the sanctity of the temple, mingling with the moans of the sick and the dying.

Rurik froze. *They will kill you. If you do not fight, they will carve you like a piece of meat regardless.* But was the only one who couldn't react.

A scattered roar went up as the captains scrambled to meet the traitorous nobles. Rurik heard their cries rumble further still. Pordill was shouting. The men at his side shoved at the other nobles, shoved at the captains and at Rurik. They tried to shout down the chaos but blood had already fueled it. Metal rang beyond the door even as the old wood slammed shut.

Rurik saw steel. He knew he should flee or fight with tooth and nail, but his hands were as meat dangling from the hooks of his arms. In the shuffle for Tessel's life, one of the nobles knocked him aside even as Pordill fled past, he and another man making for the door. Bonsweid—the farmer—surged in turn, to meet the oncoming nobleman.

Boderoy was dead by then. Rurik nearly stumbled over his corpse. Another of the captains staggered into Rurik, and as he pushed him back into his fight, sense jarred the would-be corpse to mind.

Tessel spun between four other men, dagger in one hand, club in the other. There was no sign of where he had gathered the club, but between the two,

Tessel was as a whirling dervish. Every time a man garnered the courage to strike, he struck faster, harder, and first, driving them back.

There was a pounding at the doors. Shouts. Sick men wavered and howled, uncertain as to whether all was real or nightmare. Tessel's trusted captains moved to aid him, or died in the effort—two more already lagged back, nursing knife wounds. Somewhere, Vogel of Caslau had snatched up a sword, and though one-armed, he still threw himself into the fray with abandon, but Rurik could see blood streaming. Soldiers moved with shield and sword and drove the nobles before them, but they were as disorganized as any, having been the first fallen upon, and now, shock had ruined them.

No guns at least, Rurik noted. No guns, and only thin layers of cloth and leather to protect the lot.

With a cry, Rurik launched himself at the noble squaring off with Vogel. In hindsight, a poor move. The cry alerted the man, and he twisted just in time, catching Rurik square in the jaw with a hard jab of his elbow. Rurik was shunted aside, clattering against the table. But it gave Vogel the chance he needed to plunge steel through the assassin's surcoat.

Death was a strangled cry. Its final circle closed upon them.

* *

Blood was in the streets. Armored men rattled down the lines between the tents and pitched battle in the frost.

At first, Essa couldn't make sense of it. Shouts preceded steel, and she assumed there had been a brawl. Then came the screams. The ring of blades. She stepped from the circle of their tents into a world consumed by war. *Raid,* she thought. That is, until she saw the stables.

Gorjes poured through the camp in a stampede, and true to the herd, none seemed to know from what they were running. Alviss, waiting for them at the campsite, had taken charge as soon as Essa and the others reached him. With a few confused Gorjes, Gunther and Marvelle among them, he set a ring about the camp, kicking the fire into ashes and waiting for the screams to find shape.

Essa slipped past at the baying of a distant horse. *Starlet,* she thought. *Gods above, they're killing the horses.* Chigenda twisted at the last moment, and he saw her, but she put a finger to her lips and he looked first beyond her, then he turned away again without a sound.

167

The nearest stables weren't far from Witold's share of the encampment. Outside, a stable boy lay amidst a pile of hay, quiet now. Skewered. Bloodied. With a face warped not in fear, but shock. She knew the wide eyes, the vacant, gasping part of the lips. Two stab wounds had taken him quickly in the chest. Dagger thrusts. Swift. Messy. Someone had walked right up to him, with a smile or a wave, and stabbed him through the heart.

Nor was he the only one. Stalls had been hacked open. The horses were gone. Stablehands were scattered among the mud and the stones, blood pooling between them. Some still groaned. Most didn't.

Dead children, tossed to the mud. She didn't scream. It seemed too far beyond that. She waded through the bodies of the dead, and never said a word. Steel answered regardless.

* *

When Rurik was a boy, one of his father's rare gestures to his children was to take them all to hunt. Only rarely did he catch anything, though his brother Isaak almost always flushed a deer. Some people had all the luck.

One day, they happened upon another hunt in progress. Having forsaken their horses for the day—to young Rurik's ever-lasting complaint—they moved low and silent to the earth, mimicking their father and his wardens. Through the brush they heard a low howl, and the gnashing of many teeth. Rurik was scared, but Ivon goaded him. Isaak teased him. Their father motioned them on.

In a clearing of the woods, a large old elk had been separated from its herd. Bent to the earth, it kept backing up with the large rack of bone protecting its fore. From wolves, as it would happen—four large hounds, all matted and grey, circling and waiting for their chance. The elk already limped. Kasimir pointed out the blood. Rurik felt sick to watch it.

Time and again the beast warded their attempts to assail it, but time slowed it, time wore it, and time undid it.

A joke, Rurik surmised—the things people think of when death faces them. Tessel was the elk. The nobles were his wolves.

Even the greatest brawler was but a man. And all men tired.

One man twisted him. Another stabbed in. Tessel turned his club for a backhanded swipe and caught the enterprising assassin clean across the nose. From the blood, Rurik judged he broke it, too.

But the motion left him open. Vogel turned to him even as Rurik lumbered to his feet, fingering the welt already growing across his numb and shuddering vision.

The blade pierced him through the side. Tessel grunted and staggered under the force of it, but held his ground. As other daggers loomed, he coiled and stabbed that blooded traitor down. The rest seemed to lack that one's fire, at least before the warding wave of steel that Tessel brought to bear, but they had his hate, and they had time.

Blood stained Tessel's tunic. Wear creased the lines of his face, and though his blade still danced, when he tried to rise to full, the weight of the blow struck against him became apparent.

The general winced, and wilted. But still he stood. Two men advanced on him, but so did the soldiers and the captains. Only Huwcyn Ibin held before them, wielding one of the soldiers' swords. It was he, ever the practical man, who made the call above the din: "The Bastard bleeds. Run you fools, run!"

* *

Fire spread quickly, despite the water-soaked canvas. Tightly packed, the tents were ample fuel to the leaping sparks. Essa moved with one of the bucket teams, heaping water onto the swell until the food stores were secure.

Voren sat at the edge of the blackened disasters, hands raw and flaked. He did not watch her. He did not even say a word. His own tent had caught as he tried to save the stores. Nothing had been lost to him, so far as she could tell, save the flesh it took to pull his living from the tent.

It was the death that stilled him. Essa could understand that. It stilled her too. Yet he still breathed and that—that was something she could build on.

She bound his hands with some of the torn canvas strips. She poured water in his wounds and sat him upright, ordering him to remain. Numb nods returned. Not enough. She set a knife in his lap before she left him.

Then she put herself to the hunt.

Ash drifted on the wind. It reminded her of Lieven—of broiling streets and wailing wives; of crumbling walls and bloodied eyes. Death. Every breath was a choking struggle against it, built on others' ends.

Alviss and the others were trying to save the Gorjes' camp—a flailing effort, she gathered, by the lack of well water. Captain Haruld had come with a dozen other men and ordered them to it. Then he had gone, barking orders too few seemed to hear, and even she could no longer catch his sound.

And they—they were too far, the fires too fast.

Some were less fortunate than others.

Rurik was in there somewhere, too. She looked to Pasłówska, where the crowds ran thickest. Too far. Trying not to think of him, she moved into the west, where the shouts were faintest and the tracks the heaviest. Mud held the truth of their passing.

Yet there she saw her second sign of disillusion. Beyond the stakes and trenches of their camp, there was no fear. Or at least, no flight. Prostitutes gawked from their hide-lined homes, painted lips drawn wide. Swindlers craned over ragged carts. Dogs howled as the beggars hid.

But there were no fires, and no one fled. No blood swam the camp followers' lanes—just the same old spring chill. Her hands knotted against the implication.

They asked her questions as she passed, but Essa never parted with a word. A horse whinnied on the horizon, and the plains held black and brown specks against the dappled green.

In the distance, Starlet, with a dead man dangling from her stirrups.

* *

In Tessel's fall, there was a glimmer of another man—an older man, but every bit as brash, rounding the world on a braying steed, as everyone and everything descended into death around him.

There was so much blood.

He staggered against the altar, dropping his club as he clawed the sheets, struggling just to keep upright. The last of the nobles loomed over him, ignoring the pleas of his fleeing partner. "This is for my brother," the man snarled, as he raised another dagger high. Only Vogel's shoulder kept it from the fall, jolting Frechauf into the spears of the guardsmen.

Tessel rolled so his back was against the altar, that he could see savior and assassin both, and slid to the cobbles.

The soldiers stammered after Huwcyn and the last of his conspirators, even as the doors to the temple shrieked. Men in surcoats appeared in the leaking daylight, blades in hand. Nobles' men, all of them. Blood seeped at their feet, for

170

the guardsmen Tessel had left on the door had been hacked down. The soldiers skidded, stopped; forward led only into the arms of death. Huwcyn shouted to his saviors. The count's son flung himself into their ranks and disappeared into the sun. For a moment, the soldiers lingered, stretching arms and legs as if to charge.

If they had, they would all have died.

But the sound was greater than the fury. Eyes on the dais, the men-at-arms slipped back the way they had come, and the soldiers chased them to the door. From beyond, the noise spilled back into their desecrated hall, and all knew that the disease of madness had spread far.

It was all coming apart. In the camp, there would be only confusion, and if the nobles had the foresight to kill Narve, it could well fall to massacre. Rurik, however, joined the other captains around Tessel. "Kill them," the man spat. Blood flecked his phlegm, his eyes narrow slits. "Hunt the bastards. I won't—I won't have them go." But he howled like a man damned when Vogel pressed a heavy hand against his side. The captain's brows knitted, and he twisted on his fellows.

"Get a medicus. Now."

* *

A bullet was the end of the thief. Or, if it wasn't, it had jarred him enough to let Starlet do the rest.

Saltpeter cracked sharp through the air as Essa bent to the body. Blood—still warm—reddened the tips of her fingers. What was left of the man's face was tranquil, but it was enough.

She knew him. In memory, he rode stoically. Astride a horse, the man had been as any other, tending to his master's needs, brandishing colors and steel wherever war beckoned. There was no name with it. No deed. Just—a face.

Essa closed his eyes and turned back toward the camp. Horses grazed among the pastures, nibbling at those buds untouched by frost. The shouts had dimmed, fallen silent.

A pair of riders broke from the western gate, riding hard. One could fall. Slumped in his saddle, she could see red spraying from between clenched fingers. On their saddles, she caught glimpses of silver rattling out of the bags. Blood money. Earned and paid.

There were lions on their chests. Yellow lions. Cullick's lions. The omen stilled her.

In memory, she saw the young man's lord. A hold, not far from Verdan. Lenesby. That was the man's name. One of Witold's banners. One of Ivon's retinue.

Noble men killed peasant men. Peasant men killed noble men. The stench of both drowned in ash as they died on foreign soil. Blood, like the winter, was never done as soon as one might think.

A body tumbled from its saddle with a groan, as his partner shouted to the sky.

Flames flickered off the steeples of the town, as Essa leaned into the muck. Brown eyes swam in it. They mingled with the blood and were lost. Dark hands—her hands—shook against her breeches.

She knew where the killers had come from. Voren had warned her.

Yet she had never thought to warn *him*.

* *

"To hell with it. You—sew. You—speak," Tessel snarled. He snapped at each in turn.

As the doctor bent to his work with needle and thread, Vogel sagged. "Thirty-some dead, ser. Half again that number bloodied. They caught us unawares. Stabbed men as they ate. Most the dead was gone before we knew what was what."

Rurik winced for his general as the needle yanked back through the skin. Thoughts of limbs and blood and war set his stomach burbling. Tessel only grunted. Once they had gotten him off the floor of the church and staunched the initial bleeding, he had come around well enough. An open-air tent had since been staked outside the doors, and Tessel had insisted he be taken there, where he might better survey the damage.

"How many left?"

"Most the nobles fled, and I'd say most has only their house guard what to follow them. Cut a swath out the west edge of camp, they did."

The men posted at Pasłówska's gates, Rurik had discovered after, had realized too late what was happening. Men had sown fire in the town as well as the camp, and many soldiers—fearing fire as all are taught to fear it—had left their posts to aid the locals and put out the flames. They had shut the gates, lest danger flee or more gain entry, but there had been no orders beyond that. When Huwcyn and his ilk had fallen upon the western gate it had been scarcely manned, and unsuspecting. They had butchered the guards and thrown open the gates, and thus fled with all the rest.

"There's some of the household folk, sure, and men-at-arms, but as prisoners go, I'd doubt they've much to know."

"How many left?" Tessel repeated, through grated teeth.

"Three, ser. Knights is all. Can't speak to it, though. A lot of men are out for blood."

"And there's been enough of it!" Even Tessel winced at last as his voice hit that crescendo. Ignoring the doctor's frown, he continued, more softly. "Stop it, stop them, and get these men under guard, or so help me, I'll feed your stones to the dogs. I want them at my tent by day's end. We'll have this out. Organize the men. Get them riding. Horses. Gryphons. Whatever's left. Hell, do anything to get their minds off…this. But they need to be ready to move."

"Milord?"

"What?"

"Several bands set after the nobles a'ready, if it please you. I sent riders b—"

"Madness," Tessel huffed, sinking deeper into his chair. The thread made a fifth line within his blood, and a sixth. "Everything's gone mad."

Having bided his words long enough, Rurik seized the opportunity to interject himself. "Just so, ser, just so, and all the more reason we need to get you on your feet."

"Excuse me? This man seems very determined to keep me *off* my feet." Tessel waved a hand derisively at the doctor. Frowning, the man took another good stab at him, hard enough to earn a shudder of acknowledgement.

"And you should ask him which is better, then: a bloodied man, or a bloodied army? These men look up to you—hell, they stayed, didn't they? The longer they're left to stew, imagining what was done to you, the darker this will get."

"Makes sense," Vogel agreed. There was a spark of pride in his eyes as he said it, too.

173

"And what shall I tell them of this?" Tessel grumbled, waving the same hand at the doctor and his wound.

"I expect you'll tell them it's a flesh wound."

"And the blood?"

"Someone else's." Rurik's nose wrinkled as his eyes drifted over the body of Ser Frechauf. The eyes kept staring back, as though they could disbelieve their own demise. He, and the rest of the would-be assassins had been unceremoniously heaped in the street. "His, for example. Can't imagine he'll mind."

There was ice in Tessel's gaze when it fell upon the corpse. "Nor I. Thrice damn the man, and all of them. For what they did to Boderoy, I…" His eyes glazed and his fist faintly shook as the memory took him. For a man so accustomed to war, Rurik was stunned by how much it unmanned him. Fury gathered and bore him on. "I should cut off his head and bury the pieces leagues apart. Let his ghost forever haunt this forsaken place, headless and alone. They do not deserve to go on." As though realizing his own grim tiding, the general swung back with all the fury of the battle-blooded. So wroth was it that Rurik found a backward step.

"Let Pordill and Huwcyn join him. Do you hear me? Run them down and stake them down, and leave their heads for me. That Pordill, he is old and he is wily—together as the two so often are—and I damn only myself for not seeing it sooner. A sheep, they say! A snake I name him! Damn him. Damn them both. If he thinks he can but shift the blame to others, and slither away before the blood flies…"

It was painful to see Tessel seethe so. Anger came and went to him, same as any man, but he prided himself on his calm. For Rurik, and any number of other men, it would have come to blows long ago. The prodding, the sneering and the jeering and the whole useless nature of arrogance in the camp. Yet frustration and ire should have been the end of it.

Rurik shook for how close death had come to them all, but the numbness remained. *An octave before.* His brother had fled an octave before. *Had he known?* The timing could not be ignored. Would he have cared? If he did, he hadn't told Rurik, and that was damnable in and of itself. If he wasn't a kinslayer, he was at least an oathbreaker. But Rurik couldn't hate. It made him feel nothing at all; if anything, it emptied him of feeling's very concept.

His brother had left him to die. And Tessel, flush with the fury of Hell and the devil-god Mordazz himself, would surely not distinguish for the man.

Moments like these planted seeds. He wanted to reach out, to catch Tessel by the shoulders and shake sense back into his pale face, screaming no, no, it mustn't be let in, but it would be let in, and the darkness would build, no matter what others would say. So it had been with his own blades in the dark. Cullick had ordered those, no doubt, but at the time, he had thought them for his father's own. It had driven him for a time. Seen his father's time end.

And this? In the child's logic stamping through his recovering mind, he could not help but ponder, fearful as that same dear child, if this too were not some consequence, some ripple off the circle he walked down into Hell.

This was about men. Tessel turned his wrath on Vogel next, venting orders with emotion, not logic, and all the while cringing as the needle bit deep. Vogel did not shudder under it. He took the words and turned them calmly back, and though blood rested him, he dared to question Pordill's role in vengeance. It was not heard. This was about men, but Tessel would be blind to it. The blood would pool and the seed would suck and grow until it bloomed into a multitude, and they named wrath not Huwcyn, nor Pordill, but nobility—the same nobility that had shunned the general all his life. As Rurik had done to the family he had thought abandoned him.

Children. The world was stocked with children.

"Sers! Sers!"

It was a child's cry, but loud enough to rattle the whole of the tent. There was a shuffle outside, as the men's attentions turned to the line of soldiers. Jagged, bleary motions animated the figures of the guards, followed by a soft shriek and the repetition of the title. Vogel cast an awkward eye to his fellows, then drew the nearest man aside and bore open the scene to them.

A blond-haired youth struggled with several guards, who were in the process of dragging him away. He bore no colors of marking, but all knew the face.

"God be good, men. Let that boy go," Vogel snapped at them, aghast.

When they did, the boy raked them with a scowl, but scampered away as quickly as he could, straight for the tent.

"We tried to tell 'em no visitors, captain, but he was an insistent little—" one of the guards attempted to explain.

Vogel did not let him. "Truly? And you suppose Tessel's page has a knife hidden up his arse? Watch for men, idiots."

The flap fell shut again as Vogel ushered the boy in, apologizing all the while. The youth, for his part, shrugged it off without a second thought. The way he shook as he gathered himself suggested excitement stood him far above a child's fear, or fury. He strode proudly toward Tessel, the eagerness plain within his bright eyes—only to hesitate when his eyes drank in the full scope of his master's injury.

At sight of the boy, anger's flames were snuffed as if by the snap of a hand, and Tessel became another man. He smiled, in spite of himself. "Easy, Jonas. What is it? What's happened?"

"I…" The youth swallowed, trying to regain some of his former swagger. He shook, looking between them, and wrung his hands. "We caught one, ser."

"Caught?"

"He was ahorse, ser, and the men—Borgen's men—they took him from his horse wit staves and drug him off."

"Which of the bastards was it?"

"None of them, ser."

"What?"

The boy squirmed beneath the attentive gazes of his masters. "This one was riding in, not out. It's why we was able to nab him."

Vogal gawked. "You must be—"

The boy, retrieving his excitement, redoubled the speed of his words, and simply talked over him. "Says he be a messenger. Flew Imperial colors. Given who was doing the stabbing hereabouts, I thought it right-wise…well, what I means to say is, we searched him. Found this little number." Jonas held out a rolled bit of parchment. "Seal's official, and all."

True to the boy's word, the double-gryphon seal of the Empire had been affixed to the tattered edges of the roll. Rurik was aghast. "You seized an Imperial messenger?"

Regardless, Tessel reached out and plucked the roll, tearing the wax seal without hesitation. From over his shoulder, Rurik could make out a short letter, crisp, succinct, and gracefully rendered. Professionally scribbled.

Harsh laughter followed, such that the now scowling doctor was forced to put a second hand upon the general's chest and force his rocking body still. Tessel tossed the paper to the earth and ran his hands over his face and through his hair, smothering his own fatalistic sounds. Nervousness shifted his attendants, uneasy looks the only motion within the otherwise still tent.

After a while, Tessel's hands simply fell limp at his side. The very force about him stilled. It left him staring skyward, slack. "Apparently, we should not take umbrage with our dearly departed noblemen." The words—whispered—held their weight in poison.

"Ser?"

"It would seem I am a prisoner. Your man there came for Othmann—to order me an outlaw, to place me in chains, and to take this army home." With a dark humor, he struck up his hands and offered them to the doctor. "Come, come, dear man, bind me up to the quick. There could well be a knighthood in it for you."

"A forgery, surely!" For a fleeting breath of a moment, Rurik swallowed his own anger, his own fear. "What reason would the Emperor have to order such a thing?"

"We have no emperor. Only princes. Princes in need of armies, and princes with the ears of far too many nobles. Do you think they'd really want a bastard in charge of the army's bulk? This is not their first letter, Rurik, and you know it well enough. Yet they meant it for the last."

Slumped in his chair, the Bastard's head swiveled back on them, eyes dark as emeralds. He licked his lips, turning from one man to the other until they fell quiet as the dead. Never had the lines of his cheeks and the swelling beneath his eyes been more apparent. He looked almost skeletal—fierce and dreadfully unmoved.

"Well. Othmann got his wish, I'd say. I'll not—God, but you're a butcher!" This last he barked in vehemence at the doctor. "I'll not have our empire without the soldiers it so *desperately* needs. Get this mess cleaned, and order the companies drawn up by afternoon's light. Put messengers to our camps—our army must reassemble. I would have words."

Truth would die in those words. Rurik knew it before the order was drawn to its final thread. Truth would die and still they would march, and sure as he drew breath, that man's anger would find its out at last, and unbridled, descend on those for whom he had so long drawn it in. On the vagueness of a hope, Rurik looked to Vogel for support, but the man only bowed as men would bow, and before he left, Rurik did the same, wondering all the while how starving men could march. It only took a turn to prophecy. A look at the dying and the dead.

By night, the camp had lost none of its confusion, and their leaders shared none of their truths. Lies swung around him and lies poured from him, and for all his reticence he was a wanton partner to the crime. Dried blood clung in spatters to Rurik's tunic. It seemed older than it was, and his soul all the darker.

His eyes were heavy as he turned them through the shapes rendered unfamiliar by night. Bodies churned into the west and were gone. Ink consumed the moon. It consumed rope and bodies, and left both dangling beneath the haze. There was no godliness afoot, no sign of celestial touch upon this barren waste. He longed for the comfort of his brother's camp, but that place was closed to him, now more than ever. Scavengers stalked its wake, the Gorjes foremost among them, and what was once orderly was picked to pieces.

Berric had been sent to find the Company of the Eagles, but as yet there stood no answer.

And with that, the only creature left to Rurik for guidance was the Bastard. *Tessel.* One voice in a sea of discontent. A man he no longer trusted. *A voice of lies, sure as any.* None of it made any sense. So he whispered his madness to the only place that still offered peace in its silence.

Yet as he clutched the rusted coin, Rurik had the feeling of a stare fixing him. He looked back, but no one lurked in the shadows. Sighing at his own foolishness, he wrapped his legs in his arms and sank deeper into the warmth of the fire.

Then, like a crack of thunder, a voice: *"Months pass by the silver back, and only now it sings."* He was not alone.

The timber of the voice nearly cracked Rurik from his perch. As it was, he bolted to his feet, spinning round to track his old friend's voice. It seemed to ring between tent and wall like.

Yet there was nothing. A sigh split his cracked lips.

Usuri? I did not think—

"*It would do you best, stop there.*"

He sank slowly back down onto the log, staring at the coin in his palm. Not even a vibration—such as it had always been before. Had he—it seemed so foolish now—had he honestly thought her dead? Yet implication seized him. *You heard it? All that I have said?* In thought, one becomes too loose with the truth, he realized, and the realization made his stomach twist at the thought of all the sorceress might have heard. At a time, he might have thought himself mad. He stole a glance around the vacant fire pit. Most still would.

But now, it was the rest of the world that had grown silent. There was no mirth in camp on this dark night. Nothing but a boy and a coin rendered by a girl, so many years ago, who cupped his hand and dared to whisper: "Whenever a voice is needed."

"*Whines of hearts. Whines of flesh. Comfort… always seeks it in the shadows.*" A breathless pause, shuddering perhaps beneath its own bitterness. "*Away, flesh. You're not welcome here anymore.*"

Usuri? You're not making sense. Please—

"*One thing. It's all they ever care about.*"

He called to her again, but it was as if the woman—so briefly touched—had closed a door against their words. Only quiet greeted him, leaving him distinctly colder than before.

She was alive. She hadn't been burned.

But what was left?

Chapter 9

Everything burned, everyone lied, and no one paid for it but the ones in the muck. They might as well have *been* muck, the way the world trod on them. The way it took them all for granted, so far as Voren saw it.

"Freedom!" shouted the Bastard. "Freedom for the father, freedom for the son, yes, let freedom ring for the daughter and the slave and all the fools arrayed before the Gray Hills. There is no us and them but we, and we-we-we will teach them what it means to defy an emperor. Blood—what is blood but the blood that is spilt? All men bleed. Breeding and birthing mean nothing to the circle and the cycle churns regardless of the form—no!"

They would hunt these men as sure as any other.

Loyalty—it was to be put aside, as they had put aside their own. They were men. They had loyalty to a higher providence than to titled animals. Titled men that would dare to kill another with a greater title than their own. The Emperor had made this an army of the people, and they had sought to make it an army of their people. Even now the so-called nobles fled their crimes, hoping for safety in the walls of their homes.

"They and their princes. Princes from afar, princes that dishonored the memory of their father, bickering over scraps and men before the dust had even settled on his tomb. Men that would not fight as the people had fought, as he had fought. Men that beckoned some southern priest to guide them, to delude them into collusion of a broken system, to bind them all not to god or right, but to a church of corrupt men and bedeviled fools, who sure as any other men of privilege sought land, sought wealth, not the higher faith they so preached. Oh yes, oh yes, how many bishops stand common born?

We-we-we are the people. We are the breath of Idasia. They would make us fight and die in foreign lands, only to kill us for surviving. When they show fear, they call us mad for honor. When they seek to flee with tail twixt legs they seek to beat us to submission, and name us all for traitors. We will show them this is not the case. Not the right that we have earned.

And they would dishonor our dead by allying with the very men what once assailed us. They would undo all our hard-won gains simply to fuel their own internal avarice. An alliance with the devil! What they think they cannot take by force, they seek to take by wile, yea, they seek to take by sacrifice—our sacrifice! Idasia and Ravonno and Effise to be as one against the people! No more. We will not let them usher us into the night.

Time-it-is-time-it-is-now. Let the world see. Let all know.

We are the coming-of-the-coming-of-the-coming-of-the-right."

A new order. These words rang in Voren's ears and on his tongue, and tasted of bread and flour and sweet summer honey. He could see home—Idasia—and his heart burned at the visage of a twenty thousand man liberation.

Peasants could not bear arms, save in their lord's good name. Peasants could not voice opinion, save at their good lord's asking.

But they still bore arms. They heard their grievances voiced. *Well, this is the flaw isn't it? You can give a man a sword but it's altogether another thing to take it from him.* Nobles were simply men with power. Always had been. One could give it or one could take it or one could die beneath it. Peasants were simply without.

But men were men. Get enough of them, and they were no different from any other horde. They did not cease to be an army simply because the nobles ceased with orders.

A pity such a horde would do precisely as the nobles feared—they would burn and pillage and rape their own land into oblivion, until it was a desert every bit as wasted as heathen Zutam. For men of a crowd were men of emotion, and though they would fight for their land, and die for their general, bloodying themselves against the invisible shackles that had always been attached, killing, yes, for a dream, the hate and the rage and the sadness would well inside them until everyone and everything was noble, was resistant, and they would kill them all to drink that precious blood. They would lose themselves. It was the nature of war.

As he had lost himself.

Voren breathed heavy. He could not smell the throng any longer. Months had dulled the stench, such that the whole world was simply foul. His clothes, muddied, washed, and soiled anew, clung to him now in the same stench, and he knew he was ever one of these, and he hated all the more for it.

Water fell sharp and cold and bitter across the palms of his hands, washing the char away. It no longer stung at the juncture on his left hand where a pinky once lay, but the fireborn ash of his flesh burned deep into the muscle. He recoiled from it. He reveled in it. He was making himself clean again.

Everything was safe—his meager possessions, his meager flesh. Dozens lay bleeding in the muck and dozens more graced the air on wings of flame. Nothing purified quite so sweetly. But they were all men of the earth. The nobles had been denied even this good death, their heads hacked off and their bodies dumped in shallow pits. Blood always begot more blood.

The circle is broken. The covenant lost. We must reclaim what is the right of all.

There she had been! Before his eyes she had walked as an angel of vengeance, like a pagan goddess of old. The huntress. She pulled him from the flames. She lay him down in a ring of steel and bade him safely remain.

Essa. Ever the guardian.

He longed to be stronger for her, so she did not have to be. But he was what he was, and she was a broken thing, broken at the hands of a creature so much lower than them all. And the family was all the same! Was not his brother one of the traitors that would have doomed their general? Ever, ever, always and ever, it was a Matair at the heart of despair.

He stood at the well and tried not to drift. The army churned around him, tents stripped, food stored for march. What of it remained. Little enough had been left to them anyway, and the fire snipped a fair chunk of the rest. He was blamed, of course, as were all the kitchen staff. More attentive, Irdlin roared at them, his bulbous nostrils flared, hands raised in anger. How the fool crowed! They should have been more attentive—food was the life of an army. Without, they might as well be dead.

"Move along, baker. There's more'n you what needs that pail."

Voren handed off the empty bucket and stepped along into the sunken lanes of the camp. The question from there was one of where to go. He no longer had a home, for it too had gone to ashes. Then again, had he ever? *A silly question.* Of course he had. A nice, warm home in Verdan—four sturdy walls, clean, with enough space for a second room. Enough to make a man respectable, if not respected. A palace of the littlefolk.

Now? Nothing. He hadn't even the canvas to sew another—supposing he knew how to sew. A luckier man might have turned to the camp's followers with

182

coin and tack to craft another, but that was no longer an option either. Not since Tessel had run the last of them off.

For the people! For the people! Not that a starving army could afford to feed the people.

Steadily, it all slipped away. A heavy sigh carried him through the motions, back across the familiar lines to the little swath of tents the Company called their own. Not home, perhaps, but a path all the same. He would not lie in the muck. *No, not the dirty dirt, not that, never, no.* Essa would give him room. Two miserable nights he had already spent in the holes of the storage. He would not do so again.

"Who goes?" an unfamiliar voice called out, in that barren waste between an army and civilization.

The Company had moved, but some among even the wildest of dogs, once caught up by a scent, could scarce leave it be until it lay but bleeding in the muck. Oh, he knew the sound's weight. It lurked behind a dozen eyes, wherever Essa and the rest lay.

He stopped cold. Eyes were on him. Icicles dangled from such sight and drilled holes into his head. Always watching. Always waiting. Spears and swords, a band of Gorjes moved to bar him. Not peasants, them, no. Not peasants and not nobles—something lower, far lower.

"Well that's a baker it is." One of the other men grinned. Wolfish—it was a hard trait to master when one had but a single tooth to bare. Eddie, he'd heard the others name him. Some islander waif. Certainly not Idasian.

"And what's a baker doing here?"

"Bringing bread, if he knows what's good for 'em."

"Stale bread. No. He's here for tarts. Always is." A third man—the man Essa called Marvelle—jabbed him with the butt of his spear. He stumbled. "Right, baker? Here for the owl's scraps, right?"

She's not scraps. She's a woman. She's a strong woman. A proud woman. A woman greater than you could ever—

"Answer me, runt."

Panic settled in him in such moments. It brought a stutter to his answer. "N-no. Not sc-scraps. I'm—that is to say—this is…"

The lot of them pelted him with laughter. "Get on with it, boy. And just be glad you weren't a little closer to them Matairs."

"C-closer?"

The man grinned a wicked little grin, and yanked his thumb promptly across his throat. Trailing from his skin, he used that same thumb to gesture behind. Makeshift gallows stuck out from beyond the folding canvas, complete with dead men swaying in the breeze. They had been stripped, and beaten, and he doubted any of it had come at the Bastard's orders, but the real horror came from the fact that Voren recognized one of the faces. The armor was gone, but these dead men were soldiers of Verdan—soldiers Ivon had left behind, in his cowardly flight.

Mercy, Assal, I beg you mercy. Knows the world no end to Matair treachery?

"Hid the lord's flight they did. Rather big up on the no-no pile." Marvelle ground the butt of his spear in the muck, and leered. "Bastard says there's no more place for them noble types here, and it's not like they had the coin to do much convincing to the contrares."

Animals. Voren wished little more than to turn and flee, but the little man's hand caught him by the shoulder. Images of daggers and swords and all manner of things that could cut his delicate flesh danced to mind, but the sellsword sufficed to lean a little closer.

"Now you ask that girl o'yours—little miss frost bitch—if we might render her any services now that both her bear and her title are heels to wind, yeah?" Laughter poured from the others' mouths as Marvelle propelled him forward with a shove to the back. He scrambled for safety, the laughter swelling at his back.

This is salvation? Men like this? Cutthroats and thieves, liars and rapists all—an army of the bottom rung, a new society of the meek. Would that he could damn them all with fetid curse alone. He should bare his breast and cut deep, so deep, and shout to all the hounds of Hell to damn the lot. Yet, *I am better, and you will know, as all shall know, the follies of a man pushed far and farther yond his bearing,* and he bore it deep, as he did all things. Hoarding it.

He stumbled into the ring of the Company's camp, only to be promptly caught by the other shoulder. When he looked up, however, it was no grimy Gorjes hand, but the massive, wrinkled paw of a *kuree*. From beneath coarse beard, the one called Alviss glowered down at him—or stared, simply, for he could never tell which with the barbarian—but let him go as soon as he had righted himself. Brushing at his shoulder, Voren mumbled a half-hearted thank you, but the kuree only grunted.

"Gorjes hospitality I see!" The high voice beckoned him across the spent fire, to the colorful figure of Essa's cousin. "Ever since the stabbing—and the running of the bulls, as I like to call it—they've been mighty on edge." He grinned at the sound of his own voice and wiggled the point of his rapier at them. "Edge, get it?"

Voren paused. He was never quite certain what to make of the duelist. A good man, no doubt, but a strange one. Too colorful. Too…elegant. He tried far too hard to be what he was not. Yet he genuinely cared for Essa. Genuinely protected her. Even though that that meant he was perpetually on the hunt.

For men like him. Men like the man he had been before he had poured every last drop of the arasyl into the bowels of the frozen earth.

He shook his head. "They had a message for Essa."

Rowan turned aside. "I'm sure they did. It's why we don't leave home without our pointy bits, neither."

Would that we all had…pointy bits, to that end. A rustle at his back brought the hairs on his neck end-to-end. He turned cautiously, and nearly leapt. For the second time in such few days, the Zuti simply materialized from the tents, spear in hand. No emotion marked his face. It was unnecessary, he thought, and should only detract. For a man so obvious, so out of place, to so handily vanish in plain sight—well, it spoke volumes. This one watched the watchers.

"No danger would befall you, bacher," Alviss said. "Chigenda made you from the cross. They would not act."

"Cessful," the southerner concluded.

Voren spared a glance between them, shored up a breath, and turned to the fire pit. Behind Rowan, another shape—a slender shape—tore at the foundations of civilization. The tent crumbled with a whoosh of dust, and Essa, her long hair wild and slick against her face, was revealed to the light.

Even broken, there was no force on all Lecura so wild.

"As you can see, the lady's in," Rowan chimed.

As if hearing them for the first time, Essa glanced up. Softly panting, she wiped her hands against her leggings and hopped around the mess toward them. "Finish up," she said to Rowan, with a pointed kick to his shin. The grown man groaned like a sullen child, but he twisted up and away before she could fix him with a scowl. Swiping the stray strands from her eyes, she went to them, choosing Alviss over him as the old man extended an arm.

Essa did not like to appear weak to others, but the old man had a certain way about him. She folded against him like a girl-child, letting his arm enwrap her. His other leaned their frames against the pike-like heft of his bardiche axe. Frightening relics, both, of a people best left to dark and tundra. The lands, some claimed, where men had birthed; where other folk had sensibly dared not walk.

Neither the axe, nor Alviss, appeared the least bit unsteady. And they, all eyes upon his tiny frame, reminded him all too clearly that Alviss, at the least, had always been firmly in Rurik's court. His stomach churned at the thought.

"Do you need help packing, Voren?" Essa asked.

He shook his head. "No, Es. I actually came to inquire—"

"Your hands. Have you made use of the Keltis root?" Alviss interrupted, with a nod in his direction.

He looked down to the ashes of his hands. The cuts still tingled where the breeze touched them. Irdlin wouldn't have him at the stores because of it. But it was not as bad as it could have been. The Kuree had been there, and Essa too, and they had taken him by the arms and squeezed herbs into the wounds, bandaging him so infections would not take hold.

Bandages he had since removed. Why? He dared not voice it. Could not voice the venom that swam for him, and so many others. Sometimes scorn bubbled up like a hot spring from the depths of his heart.

"I have. It numbs it. But—"

Essa's pretty face scrunched into a glower. "What happened to your bandages?"

"I—"

"Scars fit." Chigenda leaned over his shoulder, the concept of personal boundaries apparently foreign to him. "Is good. Brave ting did."

"Not a baker," Essa scolded. "He needs his soft hands."

He was not sure whether to sing or scowl at that. She knew his hands—knew the downy texture—but at the same time, no one would let him speak. Another breath to steady himself. Then: "Irdlin cast me out of the stores."

Essa leaned away from Alviss. "He did what?"

"Probably all that thievery!" Rowan chimed from the remains of their tent.

"Cast me out. And without the Brickheart or-or Ivon here I've—that is to say, nothing binds me there."

"You mean to leave?" Surprise laid the girl's mouth open wide.

"No! I means to ask if I might…stay here. I would be no burden."

That shut her mouth again as quick. An eyebrow rose, then her eyes turned from one friend to the other, making a circle of the camp. They only stared back. When she settled again on Voren, her hands smoothed against her tunic. Then she stepped forward and took him by the arm, turning him about with the intent of departure.

She leaned close as she guided him a few steps away. "Surely they can get you another tent, no?" His heart sank even as the whisper left her. *After everything…*"I mean, that's not to say no, but—"

"You do not want me?" He blurted. Someone snickered—Rowan, perhaps, or the Gorjes beyond. Gallows trees still set a creaking tune in the shallow distance, and they seemed too apt a symbol for him now.

"No!" She blanched. "No. Voren. You've been a wonder. For everything. Truly. I…I couldn't ask for a better friend." Her fingers slipped from the crook of his elbow to the fragile palm, the rough skin touching his own tenderly. "It's just since—"

He clasped her hand in both of his. "Essa—I would never let him hurt you."

And that was what hurt the most. He could see it in the darkening lines of her face. Rurik had stolen what, at one time, she might have freely given. He stole something precious to her—something she could never take back. Lungs clouded with the frosted air, Essa coughed it out, and used it as an excuse to twist away. Innocence. When she looked him in the eye, he still saw it in his reflection. There was still some doubt, some isolated hope.

There came then a single coarse laugh, like a wolf's yowling note—the Zuti, looming at their backs. "Wit bread and bone?" the man asked, as Voren rounded on him. "De fire good, little backer, but de kindle could use work."

Before he could say a word in reply, a great shout went up as one of the larger tents crumbled. Men swarmed over the remnants like buzzards, picking clean the supports and fabric pooled in the aftermath. A priest's chants rose higher still; somewhere, men were kneeling to the words of Tessel's new devoted. Farrens—the word of the people, Tessel called it.

"Alviss?" Essa said.

"If you wish this, little bird, I am no lord to deny you."

She nodded, awkwardly, then pulled him along to the south, where the Gorjes' strides were thinnest. They broke that barrier swiftly, sparing not a glance for man or beast. Out of the corner of his eye, however, Voren caught the Kuric nodding—not to Essa, certainly, but to the Zuti. Even as his eyes curved that way, he saw the Zuti was already gone. A shadow in the day. One he could only guess was trailing them.

Even knowing, he pried only flickers of the demon, tense as a bow string, and for the barest of moments, Voren had the irrational fear that they were being hunted.

In that moment, he knew pity for the killer's victims.

Essa spun on him suddenly, seizing both his arms to steady him. "We're on the move, Voren. Alviss watches me like a hawk, and for good reason—the Gorjes do, too. I come and go and oft-times I've nary a word for any about me. I'm not exactly good company."

He thought of kisses in the night. Of darkness. Of drinks shared and laughter with them—two boys, worlds and tables apart, all eyes for a girl deeply drowned. The headaches, she cried, they lasted two octaves after all was said and done.

Blood had stained the sheets.

"Rurik isn't exactly the height of my troubles, Voren."

But Rurik was the height of his. Even still, in the dark places of the world, he could see his face. Waiting. "Then why do you tell me the rest?"

"So you understand. Living with us? 'Specially now? Honestly I would not blame you if you fled. This whole venture is mad."

"Then why do you remain?"

She stared at him for a long moment, with a face curdled like sour fish. "Some people have nothing else." But there was hesitation. Doubt. He watched her eyes, defiant though they were, and he knew a certainty. There was something she held back.

"As long as you stay, Essa, I would be a coward to flee."

"You would be a fool."

"Seven years you were gone. Seven years. And that was for a drunk. If I left you to a war?" His own demand animated him, a surging anger heating his words to the quick. "How long should it be?"

"Voren—"

"Friends are rare in this life, Essa. Rare and rarer. This," he said, waggling the missing pinky of his left hand for her, "is proof enough of mortality. And I want to—to protect you. You always protected me. It's—it's only right. But you can't keep closing up, you can't—I means to say…"

To hell with it.

She was close. It was not so hard to close the gap, to put lips to lips and take her breath away. Salty was the flesh—sweat and mud and mulled wine. He closed his eyes, to let the moment sink. *It's her—it's her—it's her.* Footsteps in the grass. Long shadows. He tasted her and felt his palms sweat. Her skin! It was under his hands and on his lips and they were one.

As it should be.

When his eyes took in the light again, she stood, still as she ever had, and quiet—so quiet. Her eyes were dark, unreadable, but her lips hung slightly. There were no words. Shock or bliss, he could not say. A woman's heart was her own, as a man's mind should be. He swallowed, leaned back. Their arms fell away.

"It's how I—"

A hand took him by the shoulder and yanked him back. The Zuti. He started to explain but the Zuti only shook his head. "Time goes, little backer." His eyes flickered to the west, and Voren glanced there and back, to the girl, wavering graceful as a willow tree. He spread beneath the boughs with a hasty bow his ownself, and started to move.

There was a whisper at his back, a soft and gentle release. He longed to turn for it, but he knew his time had passed. The Zuti's hand pressed harder into his back, and he tried to straighten, breathing himself to new heights.

He stepped more fully into the light and drank the heady air. The world moved before them, a churn of horses and gryphons and men beneath the flags.

Dust was everywhere, painting the world with a muddied eye. They moved—to death or salvation, he could not say which.

* *

Plains heaved unto plains, as the day surrendered unto night; the world spread before them and was bare. There was no marker to denote one land from the other, save the exhaustion that weighted their bodies and souls alike. Plains heaved unto plains, and the daystar curled into the half-light of the waning and waxing twins.

No one said a word.

One had to beware of crags in the flatness—hidden holes or sudden dips that could lame a horse as surely as an arrow. Yet the further west they drew, the more safely they could let their horses stretch their legs.

It was the land for which their steeds were bred. Numbering just six and ten, the band moved swiftly across the open stretch. Though the opening scramble had lost them good, solid steeds, Ivon was insistent. Even now they rested only long enough to keep their remaining horses fresh, and they moved mostly at night to better mask their movements. For their own part, they moved on adrenaline, fueled by the knowledge of hunters at their backs.

Yet as the days lengthened and farms gave way to villages and ringed hamlets, they began to worry less of pursuit. They had distance and they had speed—a full two days' advance on their hunters, and horses, where their pursuers had only gryphons. The oversized birds might have been prized by scouts for their maneuverability and their flexibility, and truthfully, it did them well in close-knit spaces or treacherous climbs, but they could not match a horse for speed. The openness was their advantage.

Twice they saw and passed the smoke of not so distant towers. The watchfires, Ivon called these, the outermost shield of the Empire's settled boundaries. Or at least, Scheyer's hold. Though each lay within a day's march of the next, each held but a few dozen men, and certainly none of Margrave Scheyer's court. They symbolized hope, but not their destination.

Yet this hope was tested but shortly after, when the plains were swallowed up in trees. Old things they were, but dead with the winter, and the wind caught in them and howled and set them ill at ease. This—all of it, from the broad plains to the bowels of this forest—was the place called Neunhagen. New Field. Trails here were hardier than the beaten paths of the Ulneberg, but they could no longer let their horses to full stride. They bunched and bundled and kept their steel close upon their slumber.

A full octave of riding finally put them beneath the walls of Ungerührt Tor, the capital of Momeny province. It was more like Verdan than any proper city. Its walls were high, but wrought of wood, with roads still trudged in dirt, rather than stone. It had a keep where the margrave—Dustan Scheyer—made nominal residence, and this was of stone, but the thatched and wooden huts of the townsfolk were vulnerable and scattered. It was a town of farmers and soldiers thrust together, devoid of commercial value, and deprived of strategic worth.

It was no wonder the margrave spent so much of his time afield. But then, Roswitte supposed, that was probably half the trouble.

Momeny was the newest of the Idasian provinces. Parts further to the west had been pieces of Lucretsia and Usteroy for decades, but with the gains in the war with Effise, the Emperor had seen it time to raise the place up on its own two feet. The baron Dustan Scheyer had been set as its head, but Scheyer was first and foremost a warrior. As the people back home encouraged settlement to "weed out the Effisian blood," Scheyer took on the mantle of margrave and pushed ever further east, content to rule outpost to outpost, rather than from any one seat.

She knew this for one reason: because Ivon, in his restlessness, spoke on of such detail. It was strange to hear him talk. Stranger not to care.

The gates were already open to them when they arrived, but the soldiers were less inviting. Though accustomed to the motions of armies, they seemed less keen on the authoritative notion of provincial knights. The local steward was at first warm and receptive, only to sharply adopt his men's concerns when he realized they were not messengers from the Imperial march.

Rather, from the look in the man's squinty eyes, she guessed he had them pegged for deserters. The muck the long nights had made of them likely didn't help the image.

Spreading his hands against the light of the setting sun, the steward murmured apology. "You must understand, this is all a bit…difficult." He looked to his men arrayed about the gates, to them, and back to the keep. Deciding what to do with them.

191

More than anything, this is the problem with politicians, Roswitte disdained. They were suited to a certain element. They were even good within the confines of that element. But when you cast new factors, new twists into their orderly role, they floundered.

"Truly, I understand how it must sound," Ivon replied, still attempting diplomacy. "We ask only for riders to be sent, and stables for our horses—some provisions for the short trek ahead. We make for Verdan, and from there, to Count Witold. But the Emperor must be warned, and he surely must be advised. It is true—we do have a new emperor, do we not?"

"Forgive me. But if what you say is true, why do but five haggard knights come with the word, a paltry sum between them—no offense to your station, sers. And with the same due respect: why a Matair? If you had some sign from Lord Scheyer, perhaps, but, as it stands…"

"Good master, what would you have me do? I come to you as a knight of the realm, with word of great danger to it—and to you, in particular, as you are our *border*, man."

The man's head shook pitiably. "Be that as it may. I will see what we may do. In the meantime, I hope that you and yours will accept our hospitality."

The pikes of the guards fanned out around them, even as pages reached out for the reins of their horses.

As if we have a choice.

Their host's "hospitality" proved nigh another octave in the keeping, with Ivon and his brother knights sequestered in the keep, while Roswitte and the rest were kept in less extravagant cells—one of the common rooms the soldiers used. Exhausted, deprived of their horses, and roundly "attended," they were caught as fish in the net. All they could do was wait, and hope.

On the second day of captivity, they were informed that certain messengers had been turned away at the gates, after asking for them. There had been four in all, astride gryphons, and they had identified themselves as servants of Marshall Othmann himself, with orders to seize deserters and bear them back for proper punishment. Had they been bearing the Imperial seal, the steward might have acquiesced. As it was, Roswitte had to thank Assal for small favors.

At noon on the third day, they were startled by the cacophonous ringing of the church bells, and the clamor of crowds in the street. From their window, they

192

could see little, but it was apparent the guards held the people's concern, rushing in armored lines down the dirt paths.

Roswitte's first thought was that the Bastard had come for them. It was dismissed as quickly as it had come, however, for logic dictated no army could move so fast—and certainly not one as bloated as his. It might have been more hunters, but they would not have earned so great a fuss. In truth, she could not imagine anything less than royalty would.

From their vantage, the captives could but barely see the gates, opened and inviting to whomever called. The crowd bloomed around them, cheering and crying out, and littering the street with the petals of flowers. Whoever it was, they were treating him as one might a triumphant general. Even those who could not join the crowd did so in spirit, leaning from their windows or slouched within open doors.

Gradually, a small train of men appeared to push through the crowd. At their head was a wedge of exhausted-looking pikemen, followed by what could only be knights. It was the horses more so than the men that gave them away, for the men were as battered and weary as they, with none of the banners of their station.

"They come as poor as we," one of her companions snipped. "Why should they earn such noise?"

They leaned close. "Who comes, who comes?" But as soon as her eyes narrowed on the surcoat of the riders' head-wedge, Roswitte eased to hear the laughter of the Brickheart. Even from afar, that one could not mistake the red-struck gate, dangling from three Visaji rings.

Baron Scheyer had returned, and he did not look pleased.

"You are lucky I do not have you flogged, Carmile. Get out, and let me not see you slinking about these halls before day's end."

Scheyer's steward bowed as low as his honor would allow—though not so low as Roswitte wished to lay him—and skittered from the room without a word of protest. The baron-margrave was not pleased, and there was nothing anyone could have said to appease him.

Though his troubles clearly extended far beyond his own walls, Scheyer had fallen into a red fury when informed of the captives in his keep. All had heard it. Never had Roswitte beheld a calm man so readily sundered, the margrave even going so far as to strike one of his soldiers as the man tried desperately to explain *why* they had been detained. When he had summoned them all to a consequential meeting with his steward, there was no doubt it was for the sole reason of furthering the man's embarrassment.

By Roswitte's reckoning, it was about as comfortable as watching a wolf tear down the straggling youth from a herd of deer.

"My sincerest apologies, again. He is a good man. He meant well. But meanings and actions…" Scheyer shook his head, and hung it in his hand, looking suddenly weary.

Ivon, for his part, seemed content to simply push on. In his mind, she supposed, they had already lost too much time. "Think nothing of it, grace. A misunderstanding anyone could have made."

Their giant of a host rubbed his temples as he settled back into his wicker throne. They were in the keep's dining hall, a hall which doubled as its place of meeting. The chairs, the table, the windows—all were simple things, wood and air, without hint of courtly arrogance. The only concession to station was a tapestry hung over the room's hearthfire, depicting some ancient hunt. Slender Aswari picking at gryphons with spears.

She squinted. How they might have managed to hit the things in flight was beyond her.

"I admire your calm, but I fear it has little place anymore."

This tipped Ivon's head to acceptance. "Still. There is no need to mistreat your man on my account. We were not harmed, or any such thing."

"Merely our prides," the Brickheart grumbled. He stood at Roswitte's side, behind their lord, arms crossed and body leaned away defensively, searching ever for the hidden blade that seemed to stalk his dreams of men. He looked aside when Ivon thrust a glance at him, however.

At least he didn't choose to share his true feelings. She still snickered at his first thoughts of Scheyer's initial approach. Something about sheep and cunts.

Scheyer scoffed, his face crooked. "I fear you don't understand the half of it, Ivon. The Bastard's on the hunt."

"I did somewhat put him on the spot. But we could bear no more. Please, I need but to return—"

"A moment, would you?" Scheyer waved off his concerns as if they were nothing. "It's not just you he's hunting, lads. Did you not wonder at my own return?"

"I…" Ivon began, only to fall silent. He did not like to presuppose, but the baron put him on the spot. Dark brows knitted instead, and he only offered: "My concerns were elsewhere, I will confess."

Scheyer smiled. "Honesty. Admirable. Still—you need to broaden the scope of your sight. A bird came for me days ago, from Anscharde. Imperial decree told me I was to await the Bastard's arrival here, and to accept him in chains."

All heads clustered around the table perked, Ivon not excepted. "What?"

"There was no word at camp," Ser Lorenn quipped, seated opposite Ivon. The man may have looked like the wrong end of a pig, but he was one of the young lord Matair's closest company.

"Seems there has been a change of notion, regardless," Scheyer barked. "That damned fool Ibin and his pups took steel to the Bastard."

Roswitte might have gasped, if she had expected anything different. Truth be told, she could have seen it coming. There was only so far men could be pushed, and titled men were more likely to act. The lowborn had everything to gain, but the titled had everything to lose.

It was a butting of heads, of male bravado, insofar as she was concerned—and they were all idiots for it.

But then, dead was dead. Corpses rarely had a chance for regret. But Imperial decree. What had the Bastard done to them?

Yet even still, another question begged: how came he to such information? A note could scarce suffice, and a rider as little likely—there had been nothing as they left, and none had passed them save farmers on their way to Ungerührt Tor. If spies were this man's wont, though, than Tessel stood still and ever the losing man, for Scheyer was a warrior—he wore it on him like a cloak—and he would surely see the man laid down for any such crime as treason.

"Where come you to this?" Ser Lorenn challenged.

Ivon and the others blanched, and started to question, but Scheyer held them off.

"Tragedy is they only grazed him. If Pordill is to be believed—and I do—it set off something of a stampede. Must have happened just after you cut to the wind, for he and his, all swift and addled, came upon my towers scarce an octave from what must have been your crossing. And today? I am weighted down with other letters telling of still more noble houses come crashing on my shore."

Ivon drew grim indeed. "Pordill—how fares? Is he here?" And this, as it carried, seemed much echoed in the other knights' looks. Even Vardick cast an uncertain eye.

"Thick with thirst, and mad with curses for the Bastard and fool-Ibin both, but otherwise well. He shall meet us when he is well enough to ride anew. The Bastard, I fear, shall not wait so long."

Another knight—some loyal lord of Witold's beholden son—dared speak then. "By all that is good and right, some enterprising lout should put him down while he still stands."

Scheyer drew on him dark as a winter storm. "Fool, do you not hear me? There are none left to do it! All flee here! And my own men upon that country do write me now he stirs them to some dark purpose, marching, I tell you, not east, but toward our own border."

They march on their own home? Roswitte bristled at that. The thought of Imperial men burning Imperial homes, bloodying hands on neighbors for some vengeful fool's thought of right made the blood chill and the anger rise. She looked to the Brickheart, still as a stone, but for him, it was in the eyes. They no longer looked aside. They burned on Scheyer—through him, even.

All men are dogs.

"Madness," Ser Lorenn muttered.

"Birds and riders are going mad out there, and the plains are littered with skittish flights. And I cannot imagine the Bastard marches here to turn himself in."

"I don't understand," Ivon said. "How…why? What does he intend?"

Scheyer stared at him like one might a child. "Are you daft, lad? You stab a fellow, he tends to hold a grudge."

"But Effise and—the men," another of Tessel's knights—Ser Ombert—stammered. "Why should they follow him? If he strikes at their lords—"

Scheyer barked, "He speaks to their base natures. And he speaks of plunder. How long has it been since any of them have been paid? The bulk of the booty has long since headed back for Anscharde, and their own homesteads, and all they see in us are traitors and cowards. It is a mess. I can only hope to muster my own men before he arrives—and that the Effisians pick off his scraps. I've sent letters to Othmann but—who knows how quickly he will receive them. Or if the Bastard even left him alive. Assal above, I hope he has."

"If this is true, we must be off swifter than ever, ser. We have lost precious days here. I know not how my own lands fare. Witold must be warned," Ivon said gravely.

"We need to ready additional levees," Lorenn added. "If the Bastard is allowed to move unchecked—"

"You'll do no such thing." The margrave's eyes glittered like dulled diamonds. They focused on Ivon, but they swept the room, making sure every soul heard him, and took measure. In that brief instant, Roswitte saw a flash of the man Scheyer was supposed to be. The guardian. The hammer. "You'll stay with me," he continued, less harshly. "Send a letter to Witold, see if he can't scramble those levees here before the Bastard arrives. His army's swollen, starved, and wanton. Rabble. These are the gates, Ivon. My lands. If we are to stop him, we shall do so here. My banners will be shortly set to gather their troops, as I set an eye on that one. All we need is fresh bodies, and we'll smash him at the gates.

"They call this my home, you know. My seat. Do you know this is only the third time I have even seen it? Fighting, fighting, fighting—it's all I'm for these days. But someone has to be. The Emperor—winds carry him—put me here so men like Witold wouldn't have to fight."

"My lord—"

"Could you imagine that fattened old toad with a sword in hand?"

The margrave pshawed, the warrior in him devolving into something less—a child, or a pup. Roswitte winced. He did not see how his taunt dug at his own guests. All five were Witold's men, after all, and some closer than others. Kasimir would have rattled this margrave with the back of his hand, but Ivon only stood, poised and seething.

"The man doesn't know war. *We* know war. My knights know war. And we'll teach the Bastard how to wage it."

That he danced between the pair of men, surely none had missed. Yet the margrave slapped his palm upon his chair and all but roared his boast, and seemed to stir to the thought of his own glory. He did not share the looks the other men scattered between, saw neither the fear, nor the loss, nor the loop they seemed to place upon his neck. Tessel's army was meant to break nations, and he knew, though Scheyer could not see it, precisely how to wield it. Between them, they had a province, and too much confidence to bear.

That night, she straddled the sky. It helped. Sometimes, she forgot how fortunate she was to have been born by water and shade. As she looked over the tops of the trees that harkened east, and bore her back across that distance, she thought of what it was to hide. Here, and to the west, as far as the eye could see, there were plains. Vast. Empty. Fertile, perhaps. Soon they would teem with life, writhe in it as men stabbed men and forgot who they really were. For all that land, they would never be able to run far enough.

Such was the way of war, she knew. Not from experience, but from the stories. The things old men told younger men, to prove themselves and dishearten the rest. Verdan had been a town of such men—soldiers and soldiers' sons, putting their hands to other ventures. They had earned their own blood killing Surinians, when Surinians still fought back. Then Surinians had become Effisians, and Matair and his soldiers were no longer needed.

And the rest? Battles kept churning, but the places changed. The faces, too, but the people? No. She could not imagine it was so.

The Brickheart was eager. He said as much, in those quiet moments when the soldiers gossiped and the nobles dined. In his eyes, they would smash a traitor and return home, simple as that. There was no need in him to be a hero, she realized—not like the margrave, certainly—but simply a desire to do his duty. That done, life would be as it was. In his eyes, everything would simply go back to its natural cycle.

Not for a minute could she believe that. The others drew strength from it, but not she. So many were gone. Fallit was dead. Kasimir, too. His house was emptied, his family scattered, and worse—two sons stood at opposite lines, and though neither would put thought to the fact, she had no doubt their swords would grow all too heavy at the sight.

And where am I in all of this?

Wind received her as she leaned a little deeper into the night. The windows were open, lacking the glass panes moneylenders and their like had begun to boast for their abodes. It must have been terrible cold in winter, but on nights like this, it was divine. Others might have shied away from the height—plainsmen had that tendency—but not she. She had climbed the tallest trees and dove the deepest depths of that wild Jurree, and she had never found a place so content as in the wind.

There was something about it. A secret men were not supposed to grasp. Sometimes, she wondered if it weren't the world's way of whispers. What secrets might be learned if only they listened?

It caressed her. As Fallit once had.

And she frowned because of it.

Some people dreamed. Their personal hells came back to haunt them by night's embrace. But for Roswitte, waking *was* the nightmare. Sleep was just this empty thing that wrapped her in its arms. Then it, and everything else, just went on. Time had not diminished this. Merely, it dulled her reaction to it.

When she woke, Fallit's ghost was still there, waiting. Even dead men did not appease him.

She had done her best to put Fallit's death behind her. To simply…well, not forget, but certainly not to dwell. In the camp, it had been easier. There were always things to do. If not hunting, then patrolling, or anything, truly. She found she missed it. These nights here, kept like a bird in a cage, she found herself too much in her own mind. An addled mind. One she found herself dreading more than anything.

But how could one forget? The way he held her. The way he smelled. Little things. Pleasant things. She sighed a little, and clocked her head twice against the sill. How she longed for those little things. There was no one else—no one that could love her as honestly as he. Few that would even try. Even Verdan did not appeal to her so much now, as it did to Ivon.

But so long as she was alive, she had to keep moving forward. It was all one could do. Pain was inevitable. Wallowing in it was not.

War, she decided. *Best to lose myself in that.* She tried to focus, but the night was dark and the candlelit city forgotten beneath the clouded sky, and all she saw were faces. Essa. Her very name meant star, and she could not see them on this

199

night. Leaving her alone hurt worse than most things she had left behind. Though she was not often one for fellow women's company, the girl had taken on something of a special place within her heart. Perhaps it was the hurt, or her own loneliness—she was not one for reasons. Only realities.

And the reality was that Essa had been hurt. She knew not the whole, only that Rurik was somewhere at the heart of it. And Voren. No doubt the baker's hand was in there somewhere. She frowned. She did not like the little sucklefish. But he fawned on Essa—perhaps even depended on her—in ways that Essa herself needed to get her mind off whatever it was that troubled her.

If only the girl had opened to her when they had a chance. Now she was surrounded by those mutts—the Gorjes—and that thought gave Roswitte greater horror than any. She had killed one, one the girl had been stupid enough to let get close. But now she wasn't there.

Would it happen again?

No sense worrying about what you cannot change.

She was here. Now. With new worries, and new dogs, and as little to do about it as ever she could. That was a whole other bag of infuriating.

"So what do you think?"

She nearly leapt from her skin. Thankfully, it was one of those rare moments where neither dagger nor bow was near at hand, else conversation might have ended before it even began. For his part, Ivon smiled wanly at her confusion.

How long he had been standing there, she could not say. Nor did she like that fact. She was not one to be caught off-guard. And when had the others gone? Only Jörg—Ivon's would-be shieldman—remained, and he for a fever that put him to his bed.

"Not me place to say…ser."

Ivon shrugged, and moved in from the doorway. "Then I shall. I am bewildered by the Bastard, and furious at our lord margrave, and if I had the stones, I'd smash their heads together until their faces made as little sense as their minds."

She stared at him. He stared back. The man had never spoken so candidly. Nor should he ever.

"That would be…a solution."

"Or something. Vardick tells me the margrave is a good man. Father always spoke highly of him. So why is it I see only a headstrong fool?"

These were not questions she liked put to her. They had the uncomfortable ring of equality—of two voices, devoid of rank, set together as men, and that was not normal. "Couldn't say, ser."

And when did dusk turn to midnight?

"And the Bastard—all those bodies. All that land."

"They did try to poke him, ser."

Ivon bridled. "Yes, and I do suppose I would act the same way if I were in his stead but—an Imperial decree? If it has gone so far, this could not be the first inkling he has had of ill wills. And to march on his own, well, he is as mad as a dog in heat."

Or madder. But who is sane anymore? She had to wonder. Her own lord took them to a midnight ride at the inkling of a notion she still did not perceive.

"I only wonder if we can put him down so easily as Scheyer would have it. We have the right of it, but a force so large—could they truly march against their own homes? What manner of man would do such a thing?"

She shifted uncomfortably on her perch. Her lord's words had the unpleasant reek of a man possessed of self-conversation, not one seeking advice. A sounding board, as it were. She looked out at the darkness a moment, watching as the flames danced with the apparitions of patrolling soldiers.

Whether he actually sought her counsel or not, Roswitte resolved that at least one man needed to hear the truth. She looked back to her lord as he rounded the table, lost in thought.

"Starved men. Thirsting men. Unpaid men. We're all but men." She paused there. "So's to speak. And they admire the Bastard. Look to him as one o' them."

Ivon twisted on her with a sudden steel in his look. "And they would turn against their lords for this? Do they not know the meaning of treason?" But this only steeled her own convictions. She swung her legs back into the room and hopped off her perch.

"And that's why they don't trust you. Think it. What'll you do? Kill them all? All them able-bodied menfolk. Tell me, how you figure to get your crops this spring, you go and do a thing like that? Your fine wines? Isn't nobles what pick the earth, lord, or put your homes up all pretty. And you wonder why them Farrens is so popular?"

"You stop right there," Ivon said very quietly. His voice tremored, despite the rage that ran clear beneath it.

"Equality has a certain appeal. All I'll say. And the Bastard's one of them, so I think things is sure to be bigger than all you lot think.

"And what would you advise, then?"

"I think His Grace Ibin had the right of it. Kill him in bed with a sharp knife—but afield? Bring prayers with you, ser. You'll be needing them."

There was nothing more to be said. A woman could be beaten for less.

Ivon made another round of the table before he slipped silently back out the door, bobbing his head in—*In what? Defeat? Uncertainty?* A shade of doubt crossed her as she regarded it. It was not a color that looked well on her lord, and she could not help but wonder if she had pressed too far.

Oh, she had. There was no doubting that. One was not supposed to address their betters as such but…it needed to be said. She maintained that. She only wished it had been someone else to make the observation.

She caught Jörg's fever-lidded stare. "Little bear," he grumbled. "Shut your hole to rest," she snapped clean back. And so he did, with a sickly smirk.

Turning for the window, she leaned out once more into the damp chill. It invaded her lungs and drew heavy across her skin, with a shiver of goosebumps.

But it was quiet. So quiet. If she had screamed, it might have carried across the plains for miles, like the echoing crack of thunder. So she had to wonder: how far would the Bastard's own cries carry? Hundreds of miles and hundreds of years stretched between the Empire's boundaries, built its walls, and tamed its wild plains. There were hills and forests, even mountains to the south. They stretched between two oceans, and basked in the wonders of a continent.

Words. They were all just words to her. It was almost comical how whimsical one could become on the promise of power, or providence shared—yet she had seen none of it, and never would. She knew the woods. She walked these plains. If they burned, what would be left for her?

A little girl's face drew to mind, and only then did she feel the chill. She was not sure Idasia was wide enough to smother the coming cries.

The night would be long.

Chapter 10

Relatives, as Leopold saw it, were so many roaches. They always came
unbidden, pretended as though they stood taller than they were, and never
seemed to notice the boot pressing on their backs. Too tough a shell or too hard a
head, a man was hard-pressed to say. Though even in this reduced family, one
had to suppose they noticed. They just didn't care.

Hard-headed.

Figures whirled before them all, to the light and life of the dancing glass.
Flames caught within the chandeliers and dangling paper lanterns, to cast each
corner of the room in a different, fairer light, such that one might think
themselves transcended from the bare mortal coil.

Memory may have been key, but forgetting, Leopold had found, was always
easier. A few pretty lights, some dancing girls, and the world could fall away for
a few hours at a time. Eyes saw what they wanted to see and turned away again,
leaving him to do the Lord's work in the shadows. Or his own. He liked to think
they were as one, oft enough. But if not, well, at least he was entertained.

Sadly, not all his relatives could be so easily amused.

While his younger brothers, Matthias and Rufus, had each taken to the floor
with wife and dame, and their youngest sister Kanasa stood defending herself
against the sharks of the nobility, Leopold's closest attendants remained his
closest brother—Heinrich—and the fop's sagging wife.

They touched him on the arm and dropped voices to the weight of steel, even
as some Asanti trollop contorted atop their table, the gold links of her outfit only
accentuating her ample gifts.

"Two months he's languished in the tower, brother. We cannot let it lie.
Mauritz stands a fierce man, and a good uncle, but if he can do it to his
brother…" Heinrich droned, even as the woman's back arched.

It was the penultimate ceremony, the culmination of an octave's debauchery,
in honor of news that had lit the whole city. On the morrow, he would address
the Empire for the first time as Emperor Leopold, the second of his name, master
of all that was and all that ever should be. Already the crown sat upon his head,
the coronation done, but this would be the moment he stood before his people
and became something more.

"His troops march through the streets. His troops watch the palace. And his troops have bidden us remain, for our protection. Are you so blind?"

A flicker of a snarl lunged up through his throat, but he drowned it with wine. Instead, he cast back over his shoulder, leering through the chattering crowd of performers—both those in masks and those in silks—to the robed figure beside the wall. There, his children played, fussing with others and with one of the castle dogs. It was a well-groomed bitch, he had to give her that, being sleek of body and possessed of a fine sheen of reddish-brown fur. A smile wormed its way up from his knotted bowels at the sight of those smiles mirrored on their own flushed cheeks, but sank quickly enough with the reality that certain things simply could not stand.

He was a man that would do anything for his children, but even he recognized there were some things emperors should maintain. To see their children with the beasts of the earth, well, that was not a thing for public.

A snap of his fingers drew up the robed man's attention. With a nod, Bertold's slender form leaned low to the pair of children and shared words. Then he reached to take each of the Imperial heirs by the hands. Leopold's eyes never left them as they began the slow navigation of the room.

"What of your sister, my lord emperor? Your dear father had so many hopes for her, and she is getting so…so very old, now." Marren, Heinrich's wife, paused with brandy upon her tongue and a finger pressed to her lip. "I could recommend a few. But do not wait too long. A peach such as that, left to pass her prime, well…the withering is swift."

So far as Leopold was concerned, Marren had withered long before she ever married his toad of a brother. He longed to tell her such, but even he still had the grace to hold his tongue. As to his sister—eighteen hardly seemed the age of fright and spinsterhood. Maker be good, his own daughter would be well into her years before that question ever confronted her.

Sharing was not one of his strong suits.

"I think the lady does just fine at her own." His wife's words were like music to his ears. She loomed over the table, emerged from the chaos of the party with a train of women at her side, and all the starlight of the heavens twinkling in her bejeweled hair. Forbidden or no, he would make the world *know* she was an empress.

Beyond her, Kanasa touched hand to breast and smiled a moment with one of her more attractive suitors. Some baron or something. Leopold glanced at his sister, let his eyes mark her. She certainly had the look. Between the hair of chestnut and lace, and the face of angels, she would never have trouble with the heart. No, it was children's duty to play a while before true duty beckoned. He would let her have a little time. As head of their house, the others would respect it.

"With due respect, it is not becoming, Your Majesty," Marren huffed. Still, she drew in her lip and smiled on the Empress and her handmaidens, raising her glass to all. "Ladies, ever a pleasure. And my lady empress, a most bounteous feast. I could think of no better way to celebrate your coronations."

"I could," Heinrich grumbled. "It is not unheard of for emperors to celebrate with certain freedoms. You could—"

"Perhaps my lords would be more comfortable upon the floor," Leopold's wife graciously interrupted. "We shall soon begin the Fassa-dance, and I know myself shall not suffice."

Heinrich stared at her, letting his anger blossom into a smile. "I am sure that is not at all true, majesty."

"Well. It would give us a chance to rescue your sister," Marren added, looking pointedly into the crowd. "Ladies? Would you join us? Leave our new masters alone a moment?"

They fled with all the proper rituals, Ersili curtsying to them as they made scarce. Leopold sufficed with a bitter nod, but might have given more if he wasn't immediately assaulted. Even as his wife's lips opened to speak, there was a loving shriek that formed around his name, his preferred name that is— *Papa!*—and then everything was pain as a child-body launched into his lap. He startled, nearly losing his drink in the process, but his wife scooped it from his grip in the knick of time, and saved him for his subjects, and his children.

In due time, both son and daughter had scrambled to his side, his daughter pulling herself up his lap even as his young son circled it. He kissed their delicate heads and fussed their hair, to laughter and to false anger both. He held them close, and asked earnestly after their evening. All the while, Ersili waited to the side, the grim specter of reality poised within their little corner of delusion. More than a few eyes wandered his way, but no one said a word to him. There were advantages to being the Emperor.

In Leopold's life, there was no pleasure so great as family. He recognized the irony of this, of course, in how much he hated his father's, but there was a difference. *Family you make, relatives someone else makes for you. The one you pick, the one you don't.* Perhaps he might have felt differently if he had ever known the latter, but what he saw he did not particularly like.

Still, his wife made sure to put him in their company. In turn, he made certain his children attended him at every juncture, as much distraction for him as for them to learn.

This, all of this, was his wife's doing, however. "The best measure to win a place is to distract its people with light so bright they cannot even hope to see the dark," she said. The ceremonies in the palace were echoed in the streets, where the littlefolk would bask in bawdier revelry, and the Church cried out his name, and every merchant for miles descended for the chances of a lifetime.

In these days, he had met so many people he thought his eyes would surely soon begin to bleed. Foreign dignitaries had borne gifts of gold and silver and ships, and one—some Tajali fool, no doubt—had even brought them tigers. "One woman, one man," he had said, a little smile tugging at his dark face. "Being as it is right." Leopold had taken them with awe, and his wife with grace.

In truth, he could not abide the Tajali. *Eastern fools, nigh as low as Zuti.* Traders and abacus-men, all. Best they be back to their donkeys and their elephants, where they still claimed some heathen dog for god. Assal, they cried, the great devil—well, if it were so, he would send them to Him one day.

Dukes and counts and barons, priests and merchants of the highest order—all had come into his city at the height of the greatest trains, following him first to the church at Blassenberg, then through the capital's ancient gates for the festivities. So many names and faces he had never known, and wanted even less to *ever* know, but all praised him in equality, and all made the days what they could, such that at times, he felt there was nowhere left to breathe. Every inch of his palace seemed filled with some fawning face, and the streets, though broader, would be no less cutthroat in the honor.

Even common guild masters came to him—and he could not but wonder why the peerless should speak to him, for it seemed a task for one of his simpering ministers—and they bowed low, even as they sought to rob him blind. This one sought reparations for a flooded port. This other reminded him of debts so soon to due. "Remind me," he told a duke—his young cousin as it turned, the Duke of Dexet—"who makes demands of an emperor?" And they slunk away, all very good ser, yes ser, very good ser.

Nobles danced about him. The older ones, they spoke of his father and the war, lost in what was. The younger, they groped him and they measured him in histories all the same. They chattered at trade and dispositions, flattering, flattering, until he heard nothing but chattering.

He knew the game. But he was too tired to play it. Would have told them all to stuff it if he might, but his wife would surely end him.

Only a handful of nobles had not attended, and these were perhaps the only ones whose names he did remember. Cullick being foremost among them. Sara and that bitch Surelia close behind. Loved or not, such days were supposed to be for relatives—for family—as much as anything else. That sister and Empress Dowager both had seen fit to snub his ceremonies, well, tongues would wag. Already they did, for what had come instead: the crowing of binds to come between that one's whelp and a Cullick whore. Done precise, no doubt, to sap some mirth from his grand day, for it arrived at just a goodly time.

Hold mirth tight against your breast, but answer every injury with bladed heart, Zelnig had once told him. A lesson he never forgot.

Instead, he drowned his bitterness in wine and focused on life's little pleasures. His daughter squealed as he bounced her on his knee, and his wife made a dancing fool of their son. Emperors and empresses. That is what they would be one day. He knew it to be true.

But outside, the hour grew late, and the stars dark. All pleasures had their end, shame as that was to admit. He loomed over his daughter and wondered: *How much do you and your mother share?*

"Have you done as papa asked?" Fiore nodded eagerly. "Have you played nice? And have you watched?"

The little girl stared upward, toward the light, before blushing into a smile. Her head shook far too fervently from side-to-side. "It's hardest to see when everyone's around."

"You will be fierce, I think, when you are older," he said with a laugh. "Will you eat for me, before you go to bed?"

"Don't want to eat. Don't want bed. I want to play!"

He held her just a little longer, before he offered both sweetlings up to Bertold. He would see them fed and off to bed, and there would be one less worry to Leopold's evening. All the same, he watched them go with a gentle smile, to know such bliss could be given. That was the true secret of life's circles, so far as he was concerned.

A touch upon his arm drew him back, to wife and to duty. She plucked him from reverie and pulled him toward the floor. "Duty ever beckons, my lord. Let us have the measure of it before we turn to pleasure."

* *

All people are bound, in their way. Some are bound by bonds of blood, and others coin, and the multitude might as well be bound by steel, whether oath-borne or readily borne against them.

For Charlotte, the bounds of hearth and home were supposed to be the all-encompassing. The only oaths that mattered. All other things were fleeting. Even the power they scrabbled for was less necessity, and more a means—a means to the family's end. Every decision was supposed to advance that end. If they did not, then they were poor decisions altogether.

They were playing the long game. So when Charlotte looked back and thought a while on the moons that had passed since she had taken it upon herself to snap the bonds of Isaak's imprisonment—the physical bonds, at least—the patient woman in her cautioned ease. Neither sign nor sound of the wayward Matair had graced her ears—and how she hunted for a sign!—but so it was.

She had to tell herself that Isaak was a hunter, and hunters had a habit for taking their time. Not to mention she had not exactly equipped the man before she set him to his task. Perfection took time.

But she preferred to *see* her puppets dance. Call her vain, or impatient, or what her father would, but if she was going to stick her neck out, she wanted some way to *know*.

Without, she could but wonder: was it the right idea? The right plan? It was her father's, in truth—were it her decision she would as well have left the man to his cell—but she was the one he had looked in the eye, nails dug as blades against his daughter's throat.

A daughter whose life still balanced between those nails.

Laughter drew her off. Isaak's little daughter, Kana, wove beneath the arms of her watcher—her young aunt Anelise—and tumbled flailing across the floor. Even in captivity, the mind could find its moments. The key was to find other people on which to dwell.

But no, that wasn't right. One needed only themselves. Reliance bred weakness and weakness could be exploited. Exploitation was one thing she could not abide, though it was the very basis of politics.

Perhaps that more than anything was what upset Charlotte about this whole situation. Not the children. She did not so much mind exploiting others to get her ends, but the thought that her father continued to do the same to her, to make her his pawn, now to games she had never even thought to reach—her nails dug into her leggings and it was an effort not to draw blood. This sort of control was the very reason she had taken that Matair boy to bed in the first place. The very reason the rest of his family now found themselves their guests.

Funny, in its way, how one decision could sweep aside so many little lives.

She leaned against the frame of the door and tilted her head to the children. Anelise lunged, catching the tiny Kana in her arms, and bore her up to excited squeals. Around them, three guards stood at grim attention, already chastised once for lax watch. Little girls the two may have been, but Anelise had nearly smuggled them both out a window. If one of the archers on the wall hadn't caught sight of them, they might have gotten away.

Or tumbled to their deaths.

Of course, the real trouble of the matter was her own brother. He had been with them at the time. A not-so-humble request from son to father. Gerold saw children of an age, and he wanted to play. He did not understand the concept of a prisoner—not in their truth. Charlotte had taken care to watch, and she knew the secret of that night's little venture, but she would not tell her father. For Gerold's sake.

Children were only children, after all. They still believed in drakkons, and the heroes that quarreled on their mounds of gold. They could be sweet-talked. They could be charmed.

She had taken care to separate them since, restricting the boy to his other friend: dear Emperor-to-be Lothen.

Her future husband. Barely out of swaddling clothes.

"Dwelling on what it may be like?" Sara's voice rang her out of her disgust.

She twisted with a start, to find Lothen's half-sister—nearly perched over her shoulder. Sara looked almost childish, hands clutched behind her back, smile spread wide with all the wetness of a candied bite.

Though her brother's death had addled her, the woman remained a vision at each passing of a glance. Her hair ran in golden waves, and her eyes grew greener pastures than most forests could boast. More than a decade her elder, they might as well have been sisters, so far as she was concerned. Soon enough, they would be.

"On what?"

Sara's grin split and gleamed. "To have children of your own, silly thing."

For some reason, the very notion left her bitter. She found herself unable to bite back her retort. "I was not aware a child could beget more children."

The princess leaned back, her smile fading to a frown.

Charlotte sighed. "Apologies. I find myself vexed of late."

"As do we all, dear child. Think nothing of it. This is the beauty of marriage. You shall have many years to grow into it."

As if you would know, Charlotte wanted to cry. This she bit back, however. It would be a step too far. She knew Sara meant well. Fact remained; she had seen her time at the hand of arranged marriages already. Sara Durvalle had, at the tender spinster age of 32 years, outlived two husbands without a child to call her own. The first had gone to plague, merely a year from their wedding day. The second, already her elder by many years, had lasted half a decade more, only to die in his slumber. She had a third, and nominally did still, though the secret to their contentment likely remained in how little they saw of one another.

Some dared to call her a witch for such. Charlotte would have plucked their eyeballs from their sockets, if they had said it to Sara's face.

Sara slid an arm through the loop of her own and sidled close. Her eyes followed the children, who had paused to sit themselves within a corner, that they might watch this new arrival. *Let no one say they are not observant.*

"What brings you to these western wings?" Charlotte asked.

"A friend, I suppose." Sara smiled sweetly back. "And word. Your father seeks for you. Something about your ward." Her nose scrunched and she gave Charlotte a pointed squeeze. "Speaking of which, why have I never met this ward of yours? I have seen the guards, and caught some whispered words, but surely there is more to her than whispers?"

She sighed. *How to even begin. Oh she is nothing. Merely a witch that quests for your own heart's blood.* Best to avoid it entirely.

"There is little to her. An ill child of Banur. She suffers the seizes those old fools call devil's play. It would break your heart to see."

"Goodness. I had no idea." Sara looked legitimately crestfallen. "My deepest sympathies, sweet child."

You have no idea. Which was reminder enough to sort away for later remembrance. It had been too long since Charlotte had checked up on that girl, but she had taken ill in ways yet stranger still, and Charlotte had done her best to find other matters for attention. Yet word had come, as maids would, that she quieted. That she drew still. *Too long, perhaps.*

Across from them, the children still watched. Whispering some word of warning, the eldest of the pair rose and started for them. Charlotte flicked an annoyed glance to the guards. They stiffened, but made no motions, lest they guess wrong at her intentions. The girl approached, and Sara leaned forward, deliberately pulling Charlotte along as she made to receive her. The girl stopped a few feet away, crossing her arms over her chest as she stared them down.

"Well aren't you the sweetest girl-child," Sara mused.

Nothing like acknowledgement crossed Anelise's long, skinny face. "Well, aren't you Durvalle?"

Sweetly, Sara answered, "That I am. You know us, child?"

"I know papa served you true." The child's eyes hardened at that, and twisted angrily on Charlotte. "I would know why you give yourself to snakes."

"Child," Charlotte snapped out her warning.

Sara let the hurt show plainly on her own fair features. Even that did not diminish her. "A cruel thing to say, dear girl."

"They killed papa. They sent my brother away. And she..." Anelise's face scrunched in distaste. "She is to be a princess, yes?"

Sara exchanged a look with Charlotte, a questioning thing, before she turned back to meet the girl's inquisition. Cocking her head, she gave a most regal lashing of her eyes and said, "That is truth, fair child. By whence did you come of that?"

But the child was as a statue before them. Fearless. It was a look Charlotte felt in the pit of her stomach, for in that moment the child never looked more the ghost of her father. "You know she did things with Rurik." It was not a question.

Those eyes. That tongue.

There were few times Charlotte honestly considered the worth of striking a child. This was one.

Sara had to stifle a laugh. "Your father did bad things, child. We did what was right before Assal. As to your brothers, I am certain they had good reason."

"Then you are a fool," the girl said matter-of-factly. Then she spun on her heel and stomped away, blatantly turning her back on royalty. Others might have struck her for that. Were she a few years older, she might have even faced a blade for that.

Sara let it roll off her shoulders with as little care as she greeted all such darkness. She stood back up and tugged Charlotte with her out the door, calling over her shoulder, "A pleasure to meet you, child!" To which of course, there was no reply.

They were scarcely to the hall before Charlotte let the venom drip. "Still think I long, dear sister?"

"One cannot fault a child for such."

"They are but little versions of ourselves. If not them, then whom?"

The princess pursed her lips, and for once in her life, guarded her silence well.

As they issued down the hall, trailed by Dartrek and a pair of Sara's own guardsmen, the scattering of small feet alerted Charlotte immediately to her brother's presence, long before he could ever to have hoped to flee. She thought of calling out to him as he darted down the corner and into shadow, but she doubted it would have done any good. *Children do not learn,* she thought bitterly, to the sound of Sara's muffled giggles.

Neither did she bother to question the red-faced guardsman at attention there just how long the boy had lurked. Gerold had been as a ghost to her since the

213

scolding. Sara's as well, though in that, she also supposed some childish infatuation factored. Like most his age, he was a creature of the heart. The mind—it factored little into his foolish motions.

That Sara indulged him in this was a pitiful thing, but perhaps, a boon to both their weary souls.

"A shame to think," Sara added, as they greeted the specter of the boy upon the steps.

"What?"

"Say what you will, dear sister, we do what we do for the promise of our youth. Yet it is always they who scar beneath the points of daggers." There was a measure of her deep as diamonds raining down that stayed her there, on the border of things. "Guard him well."

Perhaps that, she mused, had something to do with her joy at the marriage of friend to brother. *What fiercer bond?* For friend alone, perhaps, she hoped a lioness would fight for that child as her own fair cub. But was it fair? *Ah, that word again.* She hated herself with every use of it. Fair, she had always been taught, had little to do with anything. It was to be stricken from her repertoire, but there it remained, something neither praise nor scorn nor lash could suffice to scourge away.

Was it not fair for the lioness to ask for a lion in turn? Yet all that stood within that den was a bird still fresh from egg, too young to fly, or speak its own fair song. The lioness could not even be serenaded. She was to walk beside him until he could fly.

And then?

Perhaps the lion at the head of them all would ask that lioness to devour the song before it *ever* might sing. Then, perhaps, the plains would be bared.

They went on in muted character, following their feet to the vaulted terraces, and down the corridors of her father's labors. It would never be said that Vissering was not a lovely place. It was a manse, first and foremost among its galleys, and a mighty fortress second. When spring bloomed, it bloomed with them, from its crawling vines to the bounty of its petals. The arms of its halls stretched wide the artistry of the Empire's very best, and revealed to all that power lay not alone in strength of arm, but strength of coin, and brush.

It was a lie, and yet, it was home. She could not help but wonder if she would miss it at the end of days. That it would be gone was not debate—it was fact. Emperors and their brides lived in the hallowed halls of old Anscharde, where the illusions reached the peak of the weaver's loom. For there, history itself was born, to whatever colors men might wish.

Would it be so different? She thought of the sprawling streets, the markets fresh and full of all the brightest wares in all the land, and she could not help but feel a little sick. They would no longer weave strands into the tapestry, they would become the tapestry, and all the strands would weave into them.

When they spoke, it was much shallower than this. Of the beauty of this thing, of the health of the next, or even, the beauty of a passing manservant, lost quickly to lowered eyes. Neither liked to speak to the other in such terms—the uncertainty to their commentary told as much—but it was their way to voice displeasure. Freedom only went so far.

It served its purpose still. By the time they entered into her father's solar, she was sufficiently deadened inside to deal with him as daughter to father should. Her father sat with uncle and nephew and Boyce alike, sipping at the afternoon's cups. She curtsied to him across his pale bounty, even as he nodded to her accompaniment—and secretly, she thanked the Maker for the gift of company between them.

"My dearest princess," Walthere said with all the measure of a serpent's tongue, "how kind of you. Surely our servants should have found her."

Sara flitted with a huff. "It was no trouble, ser. Any moment at your daughter's pleasure is a pleasure well received."

As princess and father descended into their formal circles, Charlotte spared a glance for the others. Her uncle, as ever, laid things plain upon his face, and served as warning for the coming words. He made sure she caught his eyes, and gentle shook his head. Something was fouled, then. She locked that knowledge behind her own steeled gaze. Her nephew Amschel, ever the formal one, raised a glass to her, and gestured for the seat beside him. He was a sweet thing, and nothing at all like her uncle, she thought. But perhaps war would change him. Or a bride. Youth. It was funny to think how man and woman wore its mantle so differently.

Perhaps it had something to do with Walthere's plotting in the capital. The shadow man. Too many hours she had devoted to prying that truth, but of it, nothing ever came. It infuriated her. What they needed was the other Farren daughter of the crown. Not more ways to kill.

As her cousin held a chair out for Sara, Charlotte slid in beside her uncle and kissed him on the cheek. "Old Maynard," she whispered close, "do we intrude on war?" At a time, his belly might fair have shook for that, yet her uncle only patted her shoulder, and turned a weary eye upon his son's own shape. As she turned for it, she gaped, for the bandages his stoop exposed, pressed tight about the chest. Thick wrapping, that, and not lightly done.

Amschel caught her gaze as he limped from out behind the princess. He smiled slightly, and retreated heavily, lowering into another seat. Even pain, it seemed, did not quaff his manners. Nor did it prize an answer from him.

With the pleasantries out between them, the air took on a decidedly uncomfortable haze as Walthere turned upon their spymaster. "Overlong, is all I say, Boyce. Remind the good lord of his duties when the rest is done, and debt will be as ever it was—words upon a paper." With that, he made his dismissal, and Boyce, nodding to the queer instruction, took it upon himself to depart with but scarce words for his ladies.

Debt. Ever a weapon. A nation was, to a certain degree, built on debtors. Her father made a habit of knowing them, and buying up the more savory debts. It was a solid, vicious way to capitalize on other men's misfortunes. Unfortunately useless to her queries. Too many held the title usurer for any great narrowing of prospect. It merely tightened the noose about a plot.

"What calls me to your side, dear father?" Her eyes remained upon her cousin. "I was about the children."

"Time with your good betrothed, coz?" Amschel countered quickly— deflection's haste.

It was chill, what she flicked on him, but it was Sara who answered. "My brother, I think you mean," with tone sharp enough to redden him, "and prince, to be certain."

Walthere ignored their bickering. "A foulness. Your cousin was grievous struck, and I fear it for an omen."

It happened like this. Amschel and Maynard had been out upon the country with nigh a hundred men, hunting bandits near the northern fields. There was conflict there, as ever there had been, for though those borders were old, the men that settled them held grudges far older. Religion had only furthered the disputes, as men to the crown's side of the border tended to the Orthodox, while those of Usteroy took to their master's Farren nature. Blood came and went.

As they had made their rounds, Amschel, as the young were oft to do, broke off with a score of his men to ride ahead. With night, they had taken shelter in a tavern rather than head back for their camp, and there, as they drank, another troop of men had come upon them. These men, recognizing well the marks of Usteroy, announced themselves for officers of the Emperor, charged to arrest brigands. Naturally, they named Amschel for one of those brigands.

"They offered me no papers and they bore no badges of their office," Amschel spat. "I took them for Lievklaus's fools."

When Amschel had refused to lay down arms, a fight had broken out. Though the so-called officers had been driven from the tavern, as Amschel and his men had plunged after them a cry went out into the night, and crossbowmen, hidden among the stables, loosed on them. Three of his number had been struck dead, and in the same volley, Amschel was speared through the ribs.

Still, he had rallied his men and charged the crossbowmen, slaughtering them before they could reload. The original assailants joined the fight, and they fought like animals in the yard. Died like them too. Only two men managed to flee, taking horses in the confusion and striking back across the border.

Word of the fight had drawn Maynard there by morning's light, and doctors saw to Amschel's injuries. Broken ribs and a few broken fingers, at the end. Of their attackers, however, seventeen men lay dead, and from their captain's pouch, deputizing orders were pulled. To hunt brigands, indeed—at least one man bore a white cloak, and he, charged to demand the removal of the royal family from Cullick's hands. It was Ser Darrow, lately of Prince Joseph's own entourage, and a member of the Imperial Guard.

"I need not tell you why this is poor at any time, but why it stands so poorly struck now," Walthere concluded with a grimace.

"I do not understand," Sara shuddered. "Ser Darrow was with us when we made our decision. He, of all men, should know it was our own choice to remain."

"An emperor is advised by many, but beholden to none, and the Imperial Guard, beholden only to him." Maynard said, carefully eying his son. "And he knew Amschel's look. I've no doubt. This was a trap, if ever there was one."

"A trap?"

Charlotte leaned toward her friend, patting at her arm. "The crossbowmen. They knew someone would ride there. They hoped to provoke something. The charge of banditry—but an excuse, perhaps even one they started."

Sara's face fell. "They knew you would not surrender," she said, turning sorrowfully to Amschel.

"Just so," Walthere sighed. "In killing a knight of the Guard, we will take much ill will. The people love them. And now, Leopold will have claim against us for holding you—for now he has corpses to point to, to say we killed those men that sought to bring you home. We become the provocateur." His look was wistful as he tapped his chin. "A smarter man than I gave him credit for."

"So…"

"So I need you to deal with this, Charlotte."

"I?" She looked between the lot of them, all but scoffing at the notion. "Am I to be a gift for this royal? It was my thought I was already one prince's present." She did let a smile go when Sara lightly slapped her wrist.

Walthere snapped, "Silence, child, and listen well. The only gift you shall be is to the people. You and your fiancé both shall give letter and give voice to our family's own apology, and offer recompense. You will promise to go the capital at the Emperor's pleasure, when you are man and wife. Yet in the same breath, you will denounce the lawlessness that has befallen that corner of our country, and hold up your cousin as circumstance's victim."

"We stall?"

"We stall, and plead, and massage this problem down. Sara, I ask you do the same. Your mother, I think, we shall send south, with Bidderick besides, lest he be called upon here, and forced to his own sworn duty."

Politick. Diplomacy. Ever, and always, she remained the final card to be played. She shook her head, but Sara answered for them gently, showing such faithfulness to the task as one might begin to wonder who was daughter, and who, friend. They shared a smile, those two—Sara and her father. Charlotte did not like it.

"That will be all. Get to your boy, and see it rightly done, the three of you." Walthere ordered, as he took his feet. Then he moved to usher them out.

Charlotte let him take Sara's arm, and her ear, while she tarried a moment with her better-beloved family. She kissed her uncle's other cheek, and bid him well, and turned swift upon her cousin, bending to take his good hand. "The Mummer Knight," she whispered, seeing his uncertainty.

"If I had known him for Ser Darrow, I should not have killed him." The boy held up his left hand, showing the wrapping that now bound the fingers straight. "He had his mace. Broke my hand with it. Would have broke me, but…" He looked away, darkening. "I slipped in the blood."

"But all the same, you broke the Mummer Knight. Be proud, cousin. Above all else, be proud. Many a man have fallen to that man's club. Great is the soul that can kill a great man in open fight."

This seemed to cheer him, and she left him with both that and a hug, turning at last on her father as he parted from Sara. The princess went ahead as Walthere guided Charlotte out by a chin's flex of will alone.

"I will expect a draft by the end of the day," he chided.

She stopped him before the door. "And this other plot you fetch? Can you yet tell me whilst it lies?"

He took her chin between his fingers, and smiled where her defiant gaze met his, but a shred of light, he offered not. "Concentrate upon your coming nuptials, my dear. We shall make a proper woman of you yet." Where his touch caught skin, it might as well have been a slap. Yet he left her on that note.

Rage bubbled to a boil as the doors closed to them. Ustrit and Hacket, her father's shieldmen, did their best to seem oblivious as she watched the room disappear. *Come here. Go there. Do as you are told.* Some lion, she. *More a dog, like these.* She all but snarled as she turned past Sara, and surged down the hall. Yet Sara followed all the same, and in time she slowed for her friend's own sake, trying to conquer her fire.

"I am sorry for that," she said.

Sara dismissed it with a smile. "No, no. Order and chaos both. They find us all."

Logical, if annoying. True enough, though—the tasks would come. Best to address them. "Will your mother part so willingly from Lothen?" It was, she thought, a good question. Since the other princes' untimely demises, Surelia had scarce parted from her son. To be told she was being now sent away—she could not see it ending well.

"Truth be told, I do not think so. Yet if she thinks it will help him…I do not know."

Thoughts skipped, as they, upon the long halls. "I wonder how long it took my father to convince her—the Empress Dowager," Charlotte spoke hastily. "Do you think it took convincing at all? The greatest families of the faith, reunited at a wedding vow. Do you think we shall be a story one day?" She tried her best to keep the disgust from her tone.

"Excuse me?" Sara's face drew slack.

It did not become, to begin playing the fool now. Charlotte shook her head. "Apologies. My thoughts are—I wander. I meant Lothen and I."

"Oh, no doubt," Sara clucked. But the trouble would not leave her face. "But—your father? Dear, sweet one, it was not your father's suggestion. Not alone, at the least."

"My mother's?"

"Mine." Her look made a puzzlement of her features—a human question of a woman that seemed to earnestly wonder how Charlotte simply could not have understood. "You aid us. I should see it rewarded. And it will be the best of alliances for the both of us. Your father is not alone in planning for the future. Besides, did I not tell you we should be as sisters? Now it should be in fact, so well as words."

She missed a step, and stopped dead in the hall. Sara carried on a few steps more, before she stopped and turned to meet her. The lion, they said, was but a crest, but truth be told, Charlotte could feel it rising in her veins right then. A growth of fur, the bestial roar—if she thought hard enough, she could almost picture the nails of her claws.

She suggested it. The last act of the stolen life. This was precisely the reason one could not trust. So much given for duty. Could she not have but this one

220

thing? Fair. Yes, that was a word, but mere notion—that this woman who had known the greatest of deprivations at the height of duty would so willingly cast it upon another—this was the final betrayal.

But her eyes were dead, and cold, and leant none of this to her guest. Yet she could not keep the bitter from her voice.

"If you've such interest in youth, friend, why not marry my own whelp blood, rather than making me your proxy?"

Only then did the smile truly die.

* *

Hours turned to so much dust before his eyes. One of the princes of Ravonno nearly earned his wrath for daring to bring up trade rights before the best vintage could even be inspected. Exclusive rights, he wanted, to some of their wine country—country, the man had argued, that once belonged to Ravonno. Perhaps they thought him a prelate still before they thought him an emperor. The man certainly looked on him as one might a child. So he put the man to rights gentle enough.

But all anyone spoke of was the former empress. The Bastard too loomed like a cloud over the festivities, but there was nothing to be said for it. The man was like a bad dream—if they woke enough to the daylight, they all hoped they would not have to face it. Those who did assured him such treason would be crushed.

"But Effise?" Duke Turgitz had shook his head sorrowfully at him. "A shame to say, I think your greatest coronary gift will also prove your greatest loss."

He drank a glass and tilted his head with the gentlest of murmurs.

"Othmann is a most loyal man-at-arms, Your Majesty," another count and his attendants reminded him. "What the Bastard forsakes, he will return upon your plate."

He drank a glass and thanked the men for their insights.

"The real problem is the Farrens, lord. With a true man of Assal atop the throne now, I hope you will sweep them all aside," a baron chimed.

Even before he had finished, there were wives clucking like so many hens. "I heard they sacked the church at Weidekopf. Did you hear? And some supposedly make pilgrimage to see the Empress Dowager—can you imagine? If she was wise, she would turn them away."

He drank a glass and pretended they were so much dust.

"And did you hear? They take their filth to the Aswari camps now. As if those savages have souls to sway. Northerners, of course! Those keeper lords that allow such madness, well, at least we will know them for the traitors' blood."

He paused at that, and chirped an uncertain note. Aswari. That was one devilment, at least, Ravonno no longer had.

Foreigners offered gifts in one hand and asked for gifts with the other. They spoke of battles he did not care of, and men who did not concern him.

Ambassadors bowed to him. Oh, fine day, they said. All of Idasia shall benefit your wisdom. Now surely you would remember your friend, surely you will recall those blackest words this other lord has lain against you, yes, a fine day, fine day indeed.

Guests from Lorace spoke of Zuti probes along their border, and of war bands resurging. It would not be long, they said, until war resumed. To listen to the lot, one might think the world itself were crumbling. Of course, they knew Leopold's horses would protect them. Or so the game went.

The Asanti offered arms to help put down the Bastard—"A man cannot suffer treason in his country, or the people would suspect a fool. The important thing is swiftness." But he would brook no outside armies in his lands, save those of the Church, and he would not be made a weakling in others' eyes for taking thinly veiled bribes.

Still, the night's worst moment came when he nearly swooned into the back of Count Ibin, busy chattering with his wife. They parted to receive him, and fortunately made as if the fault was the count's own. It was an explanation Leopold readily accepted.

There were four of them, in all. The Count and his wife, Rufus—a nominal count in his own right and Leopold's youngest remaining brother—and a dark-skinned beauty whose name escaped Leopold's stilled tongue. He made a clumsy bow of himself to the woman, taking her hand in his and kissing it with all the grace of the town fool. But he straightened before her reddening cheeks and glared openly at any that looked affronted, Rufus foremost among them. Leopold's wife ignored the gesture.

Naran, the woman was. The count introduced her. The daughter of their ambassador—or at least, the old court's ambassador. The Narans had long since capitulated to the Zuti onslaught, their king losing his head in the process. What remained were few enough, but men and women like this ambassador and his daughter—these were the true inheritors of that kingdom, the rightful heirs of a lost land.

This one veiled herself in the colors of their country. A hundred tiny bells rang against the bright silks that named the place of her birth, each bit of metal, he was told, a marker of another eight-day lived. He marveled at the custom. Their skin was darker than most, though not so dark as the Zuti. The colors of her silks brought it out nicely. Lean and lithe, she had the grace of a ballerina, but the eyes of a woman. When she spoke, it was with but the slightest of accents—an infatuating roll of the tongue that drew his thoughts elsewhere—and words tumbled from her with the command of a man. A feature that reminded him all too powerfully of his wife.

He leered openly at her.

The men spoke of war, the ladies of religion and of fashion, and Leopold's dear wife effortlessly straddled the line between the lot. He remained largely quiet, until laughter left an opening with the ambassador's daughter.

"Do you find this place palatable, lady? It must be so different from your own climes," he blurted.

She turned on him with the measure of a child, a false but pleasant surprise, and the demurred nod of one pleased to be noticed. "Not so different—but I left when I was very young." The lady pouted her pretty painted lips. "We are lucky, to have such kindness here. And I, in your lady wife."

"Is that so?"

Ersili pursed herself into something vaguely resembling a smirk. "I have taken Alejandrita into my house for a Lady-in-Waiting. I find her eye for such matters of the cloth too entrancing to ignore. And I suppose it should set the other ladies tongues to wagging."

"Fashion is well and good," Count Ibin added. "My wife should know. She spends too much of her time at market, and too little in church, I think, praying for my debauched soul."

"The world could put themselves to such a task, my dear. It would not help."

223

Ersili chuckled. "So long as you gird yourself in the true faith, I have faith Assal will take his mercies on you, Your Highness."

"I dare say it did not much aid old Portir." The count snorted with clear glee, even as his own wife paled. "How is the old bag, anyhow?"

"He rests quiet until his trial," Ersili answered swiftly. "It is a source of our own great distress, and we have taken care to make sure his every need is met until that day."

But the count quirked a wary eyebrow at his empress-to-be. "And what of the Empress Dowager?"

The thin line Ersili made of her lips creased into the faintest of smiles. "We love our mother dearly, and wish her swift recovery."

Almost lazily, the count then cast about. "Yet I note you are also two knights shy this eve. All know where Bidderick dallies, but where, pray tell, might Darrow have gotten to? The rest of the family is here, after all."

Why that had anything to do with anything, Leopold had no knowing. Surely men had to piss. Mayhaps he had stepped outside to rut a maid—they called him the Mummer Knight, not the Chaste Knight. Yet it did seem to vex his wife.

Ersili left shortly thereafter, after accepting formally a request to take the count's daughter in as another of her ladies. Tragic as it was, Alejandrita took her arm, and the rest of her ladies took up her train, that all would know who passed through the crowds. They parted for her like waves in the sea, though her eyes graced none but his own, lingering a moment at the door before slipping out to bed.

Without the shield of his wife, Leopold found himself descended upon first by his brother Rufus, then all the rest. "So," the man said, as the others would echo, "what lies in our majesty's nearest future?" It sickened him to think on it.

By the time his knights waddled him to the door, he felt faint, and his stomach churned with the night's pleasures. There was a tune in his heart and a world before his eyes—too glittery, for the moment, and much too unstable, but nothing a long night's sleep wouldn't cure. He longed to take his wife in hand, but she had gone before him. A whine welled up in his parched throat, until he thought a moment on their bed.

He giggled, sharp and high, and nearly skipped a step straight into the wall. His knights gathered closer, and they began to ascend.

At the top of the steps, another figure waited for them, however. They paused only long enough for Leopold to realize the man was someone of import. He squinted in a vague attempt to steady his gaze. It brought a smile to his lips, for though the man was but a shadow, it was a shadow he knew well. A phantom nearly as old as crowned ashes on the wind.

Another uncle, or close enough. A bastard with his father's visage, and the greatest sense of the webs that surrounded his corpse. A balding, unassuming figure, he bowed low to his emperor, without mirth.

"I would have words, Your Majesty. And a gift for your coronation."

Their words were short, but to the point. By the end, he felt as though he might stride on air itself, and wrap himself in the fabric of the clouds. The Guard fanned themselves out against the door as he slid into the soothing darkness, rolling head and body to the sounds only he could hear—not in tune to the merriment still raging below. He nearly stumbled over the threshold, but another sight stayed him.

Upon the bed, his wife, bared wide before the eyes of Assal and man alike. Her hands touched the fullness of her breasts, as yet untouched by time, even as some foreign git, still full in the freshness of youth, ran fingers across the flower of her nethers. Nay. Not any foreign git—a Naran. Forgetting at once the buzzing in his ears, he stirred to the sight. He shed both cloth and sin, and hastened for a taste of heaven.

* *

The halls of the castle were quiet in this late hour, the merriment done, its spaces occupied by the wraiths of men, walking with spears and blades never meant to be unsheathed.

There were men that would speak of "real" men—of honor and right and other terms man-made yet indefinable. Men could always put a face to the term, and this face would come to define each to every one persona.

But if honor were so subjective, how could it be defined as anything *but* a notion? Poets and wordsmiths gave birth to such illusions, while men were left to wallow in mere reality—a concept that would send most those pretty pens scurrying back to their pretty puckered holes if it ever brandished an honest tooth at them.

The reality of honest and upright men was not that they were either honest or upright, but that, often enough, they controlled the means to cast themselves in a considerate light. Fire, after all, burned only where God or man deigned to give it breath.

And still the people will make their illusions.

The people, he thought, *well, the people are ill-suited to the intricacies of notions. Orthodox men, they'll say, this empress, she is the devil born, she hounded our mother to the grave with her spells and coaxing looks.* Never mind the Mother was a woman nigh seventy years from her first name day, decades older than most women should hope to get. *Meanwhile, the Farrens take you aside and say no, no, a devil, no—she is a saint upon the earth, a celestial made flesh. And they'll fawn and they'll swoon and they'll tell you how the Patriarch, far away in his palace in Ravonno, he made the crops fail or a son's nose grow too big, because all men gain power in the pursuit of wrongs perceived. It is so.*

In his forty years at court, Vollny had not met one man he could be forced to name chivalrous to the fettered confines of his own pauper heart. To their faces, of course, any man could be a knight that asked the pleasure and offered up the coin—but as he said, reality was another matter. Vollny had met liars and thieves and murderers and more than his fair share of whores—and lain with them, oft enough, in the golden bed—many of them men of cloth or steel or even a crown or two, but none virtuous. None that were anything but names whispered on all too fleeting winds.

More than a few of his whores had paid his way into the graces of these virtuous men's perfumed homes. It was in this willow way, this shadowed path, that his own mere concept of man had become something else. Not more, perhaps, but less was best. Less a man was less to see, to name and to know and to kill.

Men of the shadowed path cast aside faith as an end unrealized. Faulty and fragile. They kept to what they saw, and made it their own.

Yet the fact of man was this: some were inherently larger than others. Years Vollny had lost to the walls of Anscharde's lords, but never so large a prize in so small a shape had he been tasked.

A crown was the notion; its taking or its keeping, well, that depended on him.

He came as a notion, steeled in the arms of grander men—or rather, of a man, gutted and left rotting in the city's broad canals. Become flesh again, the opaque form took new shape—one could walk amongst them without travail if only he bowed his head and mastered the routine. So long as he passed neither too close nor too far from the sun of men's eyes, with the purpose of the dead and the dreaming.

Other rats of the streets had helped him to this point, but now—now it was his path alone. The final call had been sent, and that Boyce had not called him off. Now he walked the halls to the door, the gate to a nation. A pair waited, chattering with none of steel's convictions. He put a smile to his face, and a hand to his own, and moved toward them.

They scarcely noticed. He made as if to pass them by before one ever began to *look*, and all that one saw was the pike as it rammed him through the unclasped jaw. The other—too young to know war's kiss or a woman's touch, did not even reach for his blade. Wide suns merely stared as Vollny's own dagger ushered them into night.

Yet no clatter went unheard. Not in such a place. The sound preceded the beginning of the race, and he fell upon it as the wild horse first cracked by a rider's crop. Sturdy doors would not give to boots, but they would answer picks. He took their shape, and brushed the last of his barriers aside.

Gold awaited him. It was just so, for it was not Cullick's coin. Not really. It was his coin. Cullick merely held it for a time.

The crown slept in silken sheets. He bared his blade to cut her free and cast back the illusion.

Each soul had a cage at the center of its world. Some were smaller than others, no matter how grand the life beyond.

Some shifted day-by-day. His blade clattered off iron, and a man rolled free.

He should have known a trap by its smell. But he certainly knew one by the creak of crossbows.

All at once the room was an explosion of noise—the clatter of metal and arms, all coming for his neck. They spilled from the hall and from the sitting room beside, shouting orders. There was no man alive that could meet such a horde and ward them with a dagger.

He twisted, turned, backing, ever backing, as the noose drew tight. There was one thing he could do. Silence—it was the one precious item in the brotherhood of blades.

The crossbowmen were quicker. Even as the blade touched his throat, the first pin cushioned his shoulder, and the dagger flung wide. He had only a moment to consider where he had done wrong. Then the men were upon him.

* *

Sometimes the Maker saw fit to bless his loyal souls. Sometimes it was a meager gift, and others, a bounty.

Today, Leopold had learned the true meaning of bounty.

"Blade in hand? Assal be good, man, you let him so close to her?"

His bastard uncle shrugged. In such close quarters, a man might have mistaken him for a prune. "The spider must be allowed to think it is he that spins the web, lest all our lines unravel before his eyes."

I have you. I have you.

"You are certain he is Cullick's man?"

"Majesty, with all due respect—he has his birds, and I have mine. Truth be told, we have his birds as well, and that is half the reason we have him. It is his creature. And if any doubts remain, we have put him to the question. In time, as all men, he will say whatever you would wish him to."

Even the thought of torture could not sour Leopold's mood. With an almost child-like glee, he looked out on the city now called home. It shone at night, but it glittered as a gem by the dawn's early light.

The carriage rumbled to the crooks of the cobbles, but no quake could rattle the vision. From the iron gates of the castle, it was little over half a mile to the city's cathedral, where Ingricus, Archbishop and Royal Confessor of Anscharde, waited to greet them. Dozens of streets crisscrossed and converged across that distance between hundreds of homes and shops, built of a medley of brick, stone, and sturdy wood. Old gargoyles loomed prominent from high towers, occupying the landings some doddering old fools still claimed once housed nests of gryphon.

Banners hung from end to end across the broad lane of the city's main avenue, bearing more of those gryphons, and styled in the colors of the crown, or even the blue of the Church. *Mark these*, he thought on a glance, *for these are the*

228

men that hid, the men that survived where heathens walked. A firework went off in the street ahead, urging several of their accompanying horses forward with scowls on the riders' faces, while the children responsible were swallowed in the swelling mass.

Anscharde was one of the largest cities in all the continent Marindis, and it showed. It lacked, perhaps, the vibrancy of stone and architecture of his southron home, but what it lacked in artistic grace it made up for in the colorful nature of its people.

There, beside the southron gate—the Plains Gate—one could find even Zuti pirates plastered to their wagons, bellowing out prices of southron diamonds. To the north, along their river port, Karnushian vagabonds swaggered alongside the oldest of the city's denizens, and the three thousand members of the city guard walked at their strongest, shoulders heaved against the swell, in gangs and bands, the short cloaks and tricorne hats that were their marker whipping in the same water-borne breeze that drowned snickers of the same.

Between the low, expanded walls of the city's interior that split the place in twain, Leopold thought that this—all of it—was a damp thing, and smelly, in the fashion of all such wealth of humanities, but it was an old place, swelling with murderers and thieves and even an honest man or two, and these were to be his people. This place—a marker of the country as a whole.

Win this and all of it is yours, he told himself.

Along the streets and alleys, the bodies already gathered. Thousands left their morning's paces, or the gypsies' and the merchants' haggling, came on by foot or horse, and dangled from the backs of carts and the sills of windows, to catch a glimpse of the man that would be their lord. Around his train, men of his own chamber fueled the interest with the routines of more southron courts— passing alms and bread and sermons to the fleshy sea, and being sure all praised Emperor Leopold for the honor.

And soon, every one of these people would know Cullick and the Mother Whore for the traitors they were. Every one. And then, soon enough, the Empire.

What's more: they would love him for it. Emperor Leopold, second of his name, His Most Divine Grace, they would say, who returned the Empire to its true path and ushered in a new age with a cleansing of the old. Not conqueror, but reformer. Not emperor, but sovereign guide. Father, oh holiest of fathers.

His name—his family's names—would ring with the tingle of this victory for a century to come. Hard to imagine it all began with a spider. He could not have kept the grin from his face if he tried.

"Take care in how you treat this though, Your Majesty."

He startled to find his uncle leaned toward him, thin lips pursed tight. "What do you mean?" What was the man about? Was he a devil's advocate, or merely one of those insufferable wobblers? Leopold frowned at the man. He thought he had marked him better. "We have proof! After today, no rabble will take that whoreson for a leader."

"Cullick? No. But the Empress, majesty. I can see it in your eyes. I should not speak out against her, if I were you.

The audacity! He clenched his fist against his robes and felt the smile falter. "And why ever should that be?" he snapped.

A hand fell against his thigh, patting his own. He twisted on his wife, but her gentle eyes disarmed him. A word came to grips, then fell away again. She shook her head.

"He is right, Leo. This is the long game we play. One piece at a time." She flicked her lashes and turned to the window, and to the crowds beyond.

The long game. He had to bite that one back. Yes, it was true, but he did not know what the long game was—nor did he see the reason to make a long game of something that might be swiftly done. Procrastination—that had been the death of more men than a headlong charge, by his own experience.

But an emperor should not have to ask why. True men should already know what he did or did not fathom—be there to answer, regardless, to save a man his grace. His uncle dipped his head in assent to Ersili.

"Heathen. Heretic. Traitor. Name her as you will, majesty, but many still love her as a mother."

"The people are fickle," Leopold interrupted. "Surely they will love my wife as mother, and forget her soon enough? Especially as her treasons come to light."

"You are both new—forgive me so—untested and unknown. Your gestures, they come with a certain foreign scent to which they are unfamiliar." As both their eyes fixed on him, the old man made an apologetic roll of his shoulders, but pressed on. "Time, in all things. A crown sets you as their head, not their father.

Too much, too soon, and they and the nobles both are like enough to see you as invader, not as heir.

"You can use the woman. What is she, after all, but a captive to her coz's whims? He holds her, and now he forces her son to marry—your own brother! Do you not think this a more palatable dish for the people than to denounce both nobles you've never met, mothers and brothers you've never seen, and announce war atop it? Do not be a purge, majesty. Be a redeemer."

"And so I am!" Leopold snapped. "True believers already despise her. Only heathens—"

A cluck of his wife's tongue cut him off. "True believers, yes. But I think there are many of the other, dear Leo. Else your father would not have made the concessions that he did." His wife's hand squeezed his, though her voice was hard, purposed. "All manner of men have sympathy for a woman wronged, and children bloodied into motion."

Their spymaster smiled—a glimmer of respect, perhaps, for his new empress. "A truth, at that. The people see what they wish to, majesty, and what we wish them to, yes, but the latter is an art unto itself, and not a thing to be rushed. Use her but do not accuse her. Let that one come. Unravel the thread alongside your people, rather than for them, and they shall love you for it."

He fumed in silence, in dread thought—the woman, that was who he wanted dead most of all. Cullick was a symptom, but she was the heart of the disease. Cut it out, and it would die. Yet he heard their words; it was a matter of repurposing them. He focused not on the woman, but on the children beneath her. Twisted their faces into his own. He saw them: bloodied, held, ordered to dance to this and that. His heartbeat skipped. No father could tolerate such woe.

A nation was built on the backs of such sentiment—of fathers and mothers and children.

Ersili, fussing with Anatole's tunic, counseled, "Make your speech, husband, and worry not of all the rest. Already Cullick moves to buoy its sentiments."

"What do you mean?" Something Ibin had mentioned the night before unnerved him.

"Ser Darrow rides with Imperial decree already, to see justice served. It will force Cullick's hand." Content at last, she leaned back from her handiwork, and smile broadly. "Keep your manners before the crowd, children. And thus, Leo, the man will no longer be the player, but the played."

Darrow. The name rang true. He sank to hear it. So she had sent the man without his own knowing. Already she played the game, and he had not even known it was afoot. Yet, no—even this, he would not let it ruin this day! Such scheming, yes, it would only aid them in the end. Force his hand, well—let it be so. He was ready.

The carriage halted all at once it seemed, and the Master of the Rolls was calling out, "Make way, make way." His wife's hand was in his, and the world seemed to come alive with sound as the guardsmen bared the door to him—and him, to the world. At the top of the steps, destiny waited beside a rotund priest, and it no longer wore a whore's face.

An uncle. A lion. A spirit. Children seemed to dance the lines between the lot, and as he rose to greet the sun, the crown perched heavy atop his head, he had to wonder which threat they would shy from, and which they would embrace.

* *

Charlotte winced with the rest of the room as a loud crack split Boyce's placating tone in twain. To the spymaster's credit, he did not let it unman him. He only stumbled a step, and let it turn his eyes to the floor.

Letters had preceded the man. Riders as well. One by one the flies buzzed through the web, shocked to discover the spider had only carved the illusive outlines of its figure—the base had snapped clean through, and all the threads come tumbling with it. Boyce was their little spider, and he was tumbling through the air without a perch to latch onto.

In Idasia, as in all civilized nations, there were few greater crimes to be found than treason against one's liege lord, for treason was not truly a crime against one man, but all that man embodied. For a king, that meant the betrayer had unsettled an entire nation. The punishment was, however, left to the lord in question: a gamut of tortures over the course of which a man was disemboweled, racked, and inevitably hung, or at his discretion, a simple beheading. Already they had dreaded the word of Darrow's death. Now this.

Her father rather prized his head, as she so prized her own, but the fact was that their new emperor now clamored for it, and after all of this, he would do so with all the backing of the Electors' and Lord's councils.

"Shall I read you the charges, Boyce?" It was not a question. Not really. The spymaster was too well-acquainted with his master to answer. Walthere raged on regardless, rattling the parchment in Boyce's downcast face. "This scoundrel is hereby branded outlaw in the lands of Idasia, his lands forfeit, his countenance stripped, for the attempted abduction and murder of Her Most Royal Highness, the princess Rosamine. Plotting against His Majesty, imprisonment of the Royal Mother, and—oh, yes—the dastardly manipulation and dedication of His Most High Personage, the little prince Lothen, his own god-son, to his own seed, for the forced betterment of his own dastardly person."

The man seethed, red-faced, ending his tirade by crumbling the notice and bouncing it off Boyce's face. "Is that all?" he hissed thereafter, plodding out each word with a pointed snarl.

It was a black temper, made all the more terrifying by how dreadfully unlike Walthere it was. *Call the lion what you will, he is a snake at heart, accustomed to barbs and plots so deep his own hands might never touch the shit.* Now it was up to his neck. As it was for them all.

Empress-in-Waiting. Traitor-in-Waiting. The one costs the mind. The other the head. She shifted her eyes to the floor with swift grace as her father's furious gaze swept over the rest of them. *Is there any proper way the coin can fall?*

When her father twisted on poor old Ser Luiginw, Charlotte took the moment to weigh the other men's gazes. She was the only woman here, of course—the rest were the inner council, Walthere's most vaunted advisors and confidantes. And of the baker's dozen hosted in these chambers, only two would not shy from her father's rage: her uncle Maynard, and the hauntingly hollow, sour-smelling specter of Baron Koenraad, a man so dreadfully jaundiced he looked more than half again his own age. The rest were a gaggle of knights and lords in their finest threads and at the peak of life—and not a one that had ever encountered a proper taste of war.

"...Idiots. All of you. And you, Boyce, do not think this is through with you," Walthere growled suddenly, rounding on his man. "How many dead?"

"Five in all," the spymaster answered swiftly, but demurely. "Our man with the blade, the three that aided him, and…a stable boy." He shifted uncomfortably, and dared to raise his eyes when he felt the questions in the rest. "Apparently bribed, to saddle a horse for our man."

"And Lord Iggersohn? He escapes this?"

Boyce shifted, not meeting his master's eyes. "By my accounting, I should dare to guess he was the one that sold us out."

Walthere's mouth opened, but no words came out, and gradually, it fell shut again as the veins blossomed across his features. His fists clenched and he swung away, beginning to pace.

"A fine mess. Fine mess indeed. The Old Guard will rally to that southerner's tongue, and hang us all for traitors. Sure enough, he's already set messages to his dogs in Ravonno. Mark me on that. And what of the Empress? Think of what will become of her when word reaches. Beside herself, I tell you all, to know we shall never have her daughter now. For I tell you true, we will not. After this, there will never be lax in her keeping. Civil war. Now. As the planting season arrives. And that Mauritz, he'll burn us all out, you mark my words…"

Walthere's mind was racing almost as fast as his words. Charlotte was not the only one dizzied by the procession, nor, from the looks she saw exchanged, the only one worried by it. These were the moments that made her father appear quite human, as only rage could carry him. It was rare, but the higher his heckles raised, the more he unmanned himself.

Panic. It was not a color any man wore well. Least of all a delicate schemer like her father. Worst of all was the fact that it was not without reason.

Their spies, such that they were, reported the Lord's Council was in session, meeting not with the Emperor but with his wife. Charlotte, as all the others, was unsure what to make of that. A frivolous, disinterested emperor, or a strong empress? They knew too little to answer in certainties.

Likewise, Walthere had attempted to call the electors together—for bribes, most like—but of course they had refused. Duke Rusthöffen had kindly reminded him the electors met only at the pleasure of the crown, while one still kept a breathing head. Dukes Urtz and Turgitz both were already removed for the capital, with full trains, and the rest of the counts palatine were simply gutless.

They saw where the wind blew and dared not sail against it. Theirs were positions given by the pleasure of the crown—they would not shake its bounty.

And looming over everything was the very poignant reality that no one, no one could fight at full strength now. The nation was sapped, its armies scattered, its stock of men depleted. Many lesser lords were left with their household guard, and only just. Many were already relying on sellswords to keep order afoot, or even on the old and the lamed of their lands—the men to which war no longer held attraction.

At last, Maynard inserted himself calmly into the otherwise one-sided discussion. "You speak of things not yet come to pass, brother. They will rally. They can field armies. They intend to descend on us like moths to the flame. But what is certain is that these things take time, especially now."

Similarly, Baron Koenraad took up Maynard's banner and came to his defense. "Think, my lord count. Your brother speaks it true, and you said it yourself: it's planting season. What army will come willingly to the field now? What army is left? So many now walk the roads of Effise. Theirs, as well as our own. But theirs," he winced to chance a smile, "more so than ours."

And what were they to make of whispers that the Bastard's army stirred back on them all? Oh, all knew the rumors by now. They hung, even here, as a pall above the room. They could call it distant, and play as though it might never chance their way, but it was a fool's thing to do. Another contender, at the least.

A civil war could well prove a war of many fronts, and not all the players or reasons were even clear. Muddled. It was all so muddled. *Mark it*, she thought with distaste. *This is a war that will be fought on foreign backs—or women's.*

A moment's span carried her into thoughts of the Old Gods, the hushed memories from the days beyond walls and crowns. Of the Huntress, in particular, whose women once tussled their hair and drew steel beside their brothers in Her name. Funny, but she pictured herself in that goddess's shape.

Perhaps she would commission a portrait. It would be good for a future empress. After all, even the Church had long declared those gods mere aspects of Assal. Let her form be as an avatar. She was only holding faith.

Yet some lacked such conviction.

"But not all, lords. Lievklaus's already leant support." Ser Kobulle was to be the bearer of harsh reality, than. A broad man, red of cheek and poxed from an unfortunate youth, he seemed the odd man out to step from the whistling of the reeds. "Letters were barely out afore he and his were pecking at the borders. You know it's the fields is all he covets, and he's two hundred men already perched at that border. If it weren't for Niediheide and the motte our lord Makt keeps there, I suspect they'd already have marched in to sort things out. They do, though, and that motte won't hold them long, and there's nothing else to stand those fields."

Apparently, one brave soul was all that cowards required to find their tongues. "We need to levy the taxes now, my lord. The people will understand. Levy them now, and we'll buy the swords we need before this so-called emperor might. We'll shore up old walls, man the borders anew," Lord Wielo chattered. Now there was a man as short of wit as hair.

"And from whom do you suppose to take these taxes? Already the people have been taxed; would you tax more of what they do not yet have? You take them, we lose the people. Lose the people, we already have lost the war," replied the more sensible tones of young Amschel, Maynard's own son. The youth practically scowled at Wielo as he did. "Reach out to them. Do as they have done. This is not about one person, but dynasties, nations, faiths. Do this, then concentrate our forces here."

"And leave the borders?" Wielo snapped, aghast. "Did you suffer blows to your head, as well? How do you expect to shore up here without the food we provide, whelp?"

"And how do you—"

"Enough," Maynard cut them both off with a look. The chill took them both to silence, but when it fixed on Amschel, Charlotte could practically feel her cousin shrink and did not envy him. Maynard, one-eyed and lame-legged though he was, still had a presence that could usher a room of armed men to silence. It was not a presence of violence, no, but something more—something more akin to the hunch in a wolf's stride. Respect. Weight.

When he had the floor again, her uncle continued, "Children bicker. Men find answers." He levied his heavy stare next on his brother, whom had lapsed into meaningful silence. Walthere had also ceased pacing, which Charlotte took as a hopeful sign.

"The men here are ready. We have prepared for months. I can have 1,500 afield within two octaves' time, if it comes to that. More, with the calling of the banners, I'm sure. And already we've more than enough to scatter that rat, Lievklaus. But I would suggest we use the Empress," and at this, the man swept the room once more, cutting off the protests that seemed to squeak like so many mice from the floorboards, "You have sent her south. Fine. Send her further still—we have but few friends there, but she has many. Give her a retinue. If not her, then Sara, but someone must go. The people love them both, and would heed another call to arms better from their lips than ours."

Walthere was very still indeed. He stood looking out the window to the city and the plains below. The light made cruel shadows of his face, deepening the harsh lines time had already carved. His posture was not its high-handed, certain self. It was wearied, drooped, but still. There was something.

Talk helped to center Walthere. The sound of his own voice. The tribulations and tatting of others. It gave him focus, things to hone on and sift through, and in that winnowing, solutions. Tension gathered heavy at his shoulders, but he leaned back sharply, as if to let the whole matter roll off him, and he turned his attention squarely to her. He lifted a hand and waved it in a vaguely dismissive gesture.

"So it is, so it is." He sighed heavily. "You are dutiful. As are you all. So now I tell it to you true, my lords, this is how it is.

"The prelate can call me what he will. I will walk the middle path, as ever. My lords, we are to call on nobles new and old in the days to come, and remind them of the trials ahead. To this familial guard, the voice of assurance: the Empress is not our prisoner, nor her son. Hells, keep them all riding, yet far from that sniveling little monk's grip, and make her seen. Make her bless the people. Just make her seen.

"To our Farren friends, you put the fear of Assal in heart—this man is a zealot, a bigot from the south, and he marches not to damn me, but all the Faith. I am the symbol, the point he would use to break us all. Rally, damn them. And go north to do it. Our brothers litter the coast, and if we have them, we have already found that zealot three parts surrounded—his dogs are all massed in the south, or at his feet, on their knees. We are, both of us, isolated. Let us play it true.

"But care is ever the key, and I'll not have this made a holy war—not on my head. Koenraad, sick your son on Ravonno. Put Fitz with him. I want someone at those courts that can assure the Patriarch we are goodly men of the Orthodox, each and everyone. Would much not be lost in civil war? Was it not we who paid for those most lavish statues in the Patriarch's new garden? Yes, yes it was we.

"And Banur. Ah, to hells, to hells…my wife will be to that. If this is to be ill for me, we will gently remind her brother king how close his family is to the flames. And, of course, what he stands to gain if he takes to the banner. He'll give us loans, if nothing else. Pawn what we didn't mince out from the Matairs for a bit more—and kindly remind those who benefited from that endeavor that if it's to be my head on a spike, that verdict and all its earnings is like enough to revert to the crown.

"For that matter, Luiginw, on your return I would have you dispatch a rider for our dear Witold post-haste, and remind that fool that his friendship is most valued in these troubled times…and that is why we so cherish his trust in allowing us to continue the warding of his own granddaughter." He paused, and seemed as if to choke—but as it turned, it was only a gnarled chuckle. "At least those Matairs will be good for something."

There was more to the rattle that followed, and Charlotte could see the lists unfolding in his subjects' eyes. Tradesmen were to be reminded of the Cullick family's patronage. The iron deposits in the south were to be jealously guarded, while seed was to be stocked. Bankers—those lowest of dealers—were to be hounded, be it for repayment or for loans anew. Riders for the streets, such that all the hamlets of Usteroy might know the trial to come. Letters for nobles. Horses from the ranches. Fresh water for the keep. And of course, the Springtide Festival would go on as before. He left nothing to chance when his thoughts began to stir. Paltry though some of his men may have been in spirit, there was not one there of lax mind. They would remember, or they would suffer for it.

The dismissal that followed was terse, but utter. Their lord gave them purpose and set them to it, and they went without question. Maynard lingered long enough to share a nod with his brother—there was more there, Charlotte noted, than a lifetime of words could suffice—and then he swept down on his all but castrated son like an eagle to the kill, plucking him by the shoulder and nearly yanking him out the door.

Charlotte watched with some small pleasure, always eager to witness the subtle terror of her uncle's fatherly rebuke. It was so unlike her own. To that end, she made as a cat, to pad softly after them, but all too abruptly found it her turn to be swept down on.

"And you," Walthere whirled on her, as if to snatch her arm before she could scurry away. "I do not care if the girl is weak. I do not care if she is unstable. She has lain silent too long." She tittered. So. Her lord father remembered their witch, then. She cast a long glance at the door. If only she had been quicker. His growl snapped her back.

"Rouse her from her thoughts and take her to heel. By month's end I want that thrice-damned family so stricken the world shall wail at their passing, and lament a family utterly forsaken by the Holy Maker. Do you hear me, child?"

"I do not think—"

"Do not even start. It is this simple: she will kill for me, or she will be killed by me." The indelicate bluntness of the matter took her off her edge. Her father never spoke to her—or anyone, for that matter—so keenly. "Even a sorceress sleeps, and I'll have Boyce do her in the dark, I swear it so."

Charlotte nodded, numbly, in her father's wake. There was no standing up to it, there was only praying it did not drown her in its passing. A breath, a curtsy, and she fled the room with the rest, trying to ignore the eyes that stalked her flight. Finally, she realized in horror, she had found some understanding of their empress. They were all tools. It was Walthere's lot merely to decide how he would wield them.

Chapter 11

He kissed me. An octave later, the fact had not changed, no matter how much Essa wished it so.

How to frame the tumultuous twists of the heart's best intents? She wished to go to him, to set things right again—to that familiar, safe harbor that was their friendship—but as the hours turned to days, she shamed herself to admit that she hid from him. Not in the same manner a child might take to the trees, or a scorned woman to shuttered homes, for there was none of that here. Days were a march and nights were tents and familiar faces—faces Voren was now among. So instead she hid herself in plain sight, taking care to never be alone.

Though the baker had grown bold in recent days, he seemed to take the hint. But his quiet discomfited her as much as her own. His seeming patience infuriated her. *What gives him the right?* Should he not have been angry with her? Thrown himself prostrate and foolish at her feet? It was what Rurik would have done.

With a sudden, irrational vehemence she despised even as she felt it, she hated him. For reminding her of Rurik. For trying to take a friendship away. None of it was his fault, of course, and she knew well the heart careened where it would, but she could not bridle the anger in her. It nestled in her heart and guided her of its own accord, as though the woman that was Essa was but a puppet on its strings.

Worse was that the others noticed the change of airs. There were days Alviss would watch her for a time, as though considering some counsel. Blessedly, he never took it beyond a look. He would stare a time, and turn away again, silent as a mountain. Whether he believed she would come to him of her own accord, or trusted her to do right, she could not say. Rowan held none of that care. By day he teased her as some courtly fool, and by night, as they lay damp and miserable on muddied sheets, he badgered her relentlessly for her thoughts.

Sometimes she ignored him. Others, she cuffed him.

Worst of all was the Gorjes. She and the rest of the Company watched them as foxes looked to wolves—two scavengers, intent upon the same meal and the same ground, with the wariness that one was great enough to add the other to that meal. Already they had worried about them. Voren, try as he might to be discreet, only added to those concerns.

The fact was they no longer had protection. Captain Haruld had perished in the nobles' flight. Deprived of Ivon and the Brickheart both, the men of Verdan, already chastened by Tessel, no longer guided the ranks of Witold's additions to this mad rebellion. Though the Company had shifted their camp, their accompaniment had grown beyond mere Gunther and Marvelle, the brothers fool, to include no less than half a dozen Gorjes at any time of day, and they took to these developments with a disturbingly keen eye, and a harrowingly sharp tongue.

These men teased Voren. He sat there and took it. There were times she watched them and longed for nothing more than to throttle the life out of them, but he was as a rock, and Essa could not understand it. Yet she feared they would see him for her own weak link, as their feelings toward her in particular were no secret to anyone with ears and the sense to use them.

For good reason, one night Alviss asked them all if he might go to Rurik, to prostrate himself, and plead help. He was a proud man, but a practical one. He knew what it meant to walk alone among the crowd. Yet she had denied him. They had to find a way.

So Alviss sought to shift their marching orders and add their number to other camps. Now that they no longer needed to shield Rurik's identity, they had no reason to hide. Tragically, few were eager to add more mouths to their own lines.

It was breaking down. The whole great matter. All the attempt on Tessel had been in effect was the final sundering. What walked in its aftermath was a slavering beast with no drive but vengeance.

Which, she supposed, was what all war boiled down to, but usually they were kind enough to dress it up in other colors. For king and country. Now that she could understand. It didn't make her like it any better, but she could understand it. Effise had been to this end, and she could forgive men killing for it. Now, she watched men wander fierce and distant, some naught but skin and bones, to no more purpose than murder for a man that had the great misfortune of surviving others' attempts to murder him right back.

Perhaps she was a bit bitter. It mattered little. There was no order now but Tessel. There was no army. Only a mass of rabid dogs, and she wanted no part of it.

So when Alviss's effort failed, she sucked up her conceit and went to Tessel's captains herself, with her Company and her pride, and asked for the morning's rounds on the northern stretch, with one of the scout patrols. Tessel had called for volunteers, yet the men scoffed until Alviss recaptured the negotiations. The thought burned her, but she swallowed it down and sufficed to win the small victory—even if Alviss had to be the one to speak her words.

It was not without conditions. They were assigned to one of the captains' myriad lieutenants—some fat, squeamish little Baharian friar by the name of Gedler—with twenty other scabs of men. These were the warriors with no other place, and no rank among their own—men who did this only because of the extra handful of tack it offered. Naturally, a dozen of them were sellswords like the Gorjes. It seemed she would never be rid of them.

Still, a morning's ride with Starlet did much to rejuvenate her. It provided a freedom long missed, and the cool breeze sharpened her thoughts like few other things still could.

The thawing north—which was now the horde's right flank—was more remarkable to Essa than most could hope to realize. When they looked there, Gedler and his cronies saw only a flat, fat waste. A wide open expanse from which any of the hordes of east or west could descend in rapid, unbroken fury.

Essa saw it for what it really was. Though the earth was poor for any long-term farming, ranchers had called this place home for centuries, and their own hordes, like great, furred nomads, picked over grass and weed for any of the hundreds of pockets of water that gave it life. Here, the land shifted not in miles, but in inches. One could see far beneath the blue sky, but it was a deceptive thing. Crags dipped unseen on the rolling, seemingly unbroken sea of green, often suddenly. Little chasms that could lame a horse's leg or suck a man down whole before he ever realized it was happening. It was a place of simple beauty, but also great care.

In the mornings, it was also frequently dampened by a haze that confounded most of her companions. Two of Gedler's men had gryphons, and they fared fine enough on the wily earth, but Essa was the only one with a horse. As such, it was generally the three of them sent to do the ranging. The others watched from afar and kept relatively close to the other ragged bands of marching soldiers. There were no lines any longer, merely cloisters, hoping to forage their way to another day. Desperate eyes quested more for that fools' dream—the untouched farm—than for any sign of danger.

Though she often returned far later than the others, and was lectured enough for it, Essa reveled in these moments because, most importantly, these plains were empty. Devoid of feuds, of petty men and petty notions, nothing but the sky and the earth. It was in places like these the old Aswari had made their homes. Ranging, growing, living off the bounty of the earth. Teaching men, in time, the wonder of the walled city. Her mother's people.

Gods, but I know so little about them! She steadied herself in her saddle, and looked out on their one-time home, and there saw what they surely must have seen: freedom. If only she could have ran to it.

It was not that she hated Tessel. But she did not trust him, nor his ambitions. Home. What was it with men and this stupid little notion of returning the world to how *they* wished it? He was a child grasping for toys long denied him, no matter what he told the others. If she could, she would have left his horde in a heartbeat—but what then? Then she would be in front of it, instead of with it. Staying was safer. For now.

The real question in her mind was why Rurik saw none of this. Since the attempt on Tessel's life, he had not been around their camp. *Probably busy kissing the Bastard's puckered asshole.* Neither was healthy for the other. But then, Rurik had a habit of throwing himself to stupid notions, while taking them for truth. He was an idiot. They all were.

She could think no more of it.

Out here, they searched for two things: deserters and Effisians. Too long had been spent in the lands around Pasłówska. The Effisians would have had spies and scouts watching them. In fact, the whispers around camp indicated hope the Effisians had done them all a favor and ridden down their fleeing nobles. Not that they had seen any such indications. By now, the Effisians would know they had broken the long winter, and were in retreat. An army was always at its most vulnerable when on the march.

The crags, naturally, provided the perfect place for an ambush. Be it wolf or man.

Even so, the majority of Essa's treks were uneventful. Once, they spied a band of highwaymen setting camp from afar. By the time they could march against them, though, the band had slipped away, to find easier prey. Other days found traders or herders come among them, offering to barter food for news, for shot, or for clothes. Only the vultures kept any sort of constant company.

Time dulled her, as it did all things. Where others grew lax, she remained serious, even taciturn, but in the drab morning, with miles spread before her, even her mind drifted. She felt the lure of the great, lonely land.

Essa rode out alone, breaking stride from the gryphon riders to cover more ground in quicker time. All kept in sight, but only just. She walked her pony slow, letting her pick at the grass as she would. It was another hazy day. The air itself clutched at Essa's clothes, wet and heavy. The clouds were thick, but there was no murkiness to them—she feared not rain, nor storm.

As she wove between two dips in the earth, she even began to hum. She stopped at the sound of a birdcall. Another answered, opposite the first. She waited, but there was no third. Starlet bridled, and shook at her as she set the horse rounding. *Am I imagining?* Silence. In the distance, her own people wavered as lines against the grey.

Had she been any less a huntress, she would have missed the shallow easing of the grass. The breath of a sword easing from its sheath. With a yell, she kicked her heels against Starlet and skipped her into a run. Even as those hooves struck earth, she heard them answered by a dozen more at her back.

She dared a glance over her shoulder only once Starlet had cleared the immediate holes in the grass. Three men pursued her, whipping their own horses into a frenzy. Two others were still mounting behind them. Of the lot, two had crossbows, and swords to boot, while the rest bore the long spears that were the hallmarks of their people. No doubt, they had spied the army from afar, and lain with their beasts in the sandy pits that formed the crags' base, eased and at the ready. It spoke volumes for both the men and their steeds if they could get the creatures to rest so easily beside them. True horsemen.

Essa was in trouble and she knew it, even before the first bolt skinned the side of her neck with its feathers. She recoiled, but clutched tight to her saddle,

244

ducking low against Starlet to present a smaller target. She howled to the distant figures that rushed to aid her.

They would not come in time. Against the Effisians' fleet-footed ponies, she knew she could not long outrun. Starlet was a good horse, but undernourished. Distance was her only advantage, but they closed it fast. Nor was Essa good enough in the saddle to fire and to lead. Especially not on this uneven ground.

From the west, she could see the white-bobbed figures of the gryphons closing. She looked again to the line of her soldiers, where her own Company would be coming for her. Safety. It glimmered like armor in the slanting light. Still too far. Instead, she turned west, and rode right for the gryphons. Another bolt snatched her hair as she did, but this flew behind her, and from the strangled cry, she surmised one of her attackers went down with it.

Starlet was not a skittish beast, but even she tittered at the prospect of a head-on collision with the sharp-beaked gryphons. At the last moment, even as the scouts drew sabers for the close quarters to come, she wheeled away and around them, letting them break the ponies' headlong rush. There came a squawking screech as something tore into one of the beasts. On instinct, she pulled hard on her horse's reins and whirled Starlet around, to twist back on the fray.

One of her rescuers was already down, while his gryphon rolled and clawed over top of him. He did not move. The other rounded for another pass and another clash with one of the horsemen, but the third rider had broken past, his now bloodied lance discarded, and a cruelly curved saber produced for her own unfortunate displeasure.

A soldier would have drawn steel, met another man to man. A mixture of luck and whoever knew their steed better would have proved the living man. A scout should have fled, tried to evade until the others could descend. That, or gotten far enough away that they could have peppered their armored opponents with arrows until they broke.

Essa had a bow, but no time to notch and loose an arrow. But she also had knives, and she put them to purpose.

She urged her heels against Starlet's side and spurred the horse to a gallop. Delicately, she tugged her right foot loose of the stirrups and twisted side saddle, all the while clinging to the reins for dear life. The man neared, and his steel rose for the blow. Essa leaned on the one stirrup for support, and snatched one hand back for a knife. Then, as the joust reached for the climax, she took her gamble. She leapt.

Only a few feet separated them, and her aim was true. With all the force of both advances behind her, she crashed shoulder and chest into the rider's armored body. There was a pop as she connected, and a great heat flared up her arm, but as the man's eyes drew wide and the air popped from Essa's own lungs, they both pitched off the back of his horse and tumbled across the plain.

Dirt and rocks alike tore at Essa's clothes and skin as she rolled. Yet when she found her feet, head ringing, she forced herself to retake the earth, staggering sideways a few steps before kumbering forward with knife leading. She threw herself at the still soldier, but as she yanked his head back by its hair, she felt the looseness to the neck. Broken. The man was already dead.

She stooped for his saber as the first shot resounded from their advancing rescuers. Effisians shouted curses and twisted in their saddles. The pair that had held back rounded once or twice across the plain, calling to their engaged fellow, but inevitably fled as the gunfire spooked their horses. Essa's fellow scout and the last of the Effisians rounded and cut, stabbed and broke. Each had scored the other bloody, and at the last, the Effisian finally fled after his fellows, leaving the gryphon rider to lick his wounds.

By the time the rest of the party swarmed over the plain, following Gedler's cries of "Victory, victory," Essa shook to the bones. She settled in the grass, cradling her arm and trying to right her head. The clearer things became, the brighter the pain burned. Beside her, a dead man. She closed her eyes. *It is alright. All of it. Kill or be killed.* That was what war taught, wasn't it?

Alviss stood over her, and then he was lifting her up, holding her close. *Like a child,* she mused. Some of the sellswords sniggered at his back, lingering where the others raced on. *Look out,* she tried to tell him. But the words would not come. Assassins in the wake.

There was a wetness growing in his eyes, and behind them, the crack of the guns.

There was blood in her head, rattling. She could feel it. She winced against it, against the feel of the blood beneath her fingers.

Look out. Look out.

246

The head cocked and the familiar arms tightened about her. Like a bull sensing danger to the calf. The moment shuddered out like the wick of a dying flame.

She was elsewhere. A voice cried not to look, but she could not look away. A girl unfolded before her from the blood to the flesh to the cowering of the skin, quaking in the stale air.

Stop it. Look at yourself. This isn't you.

A girl, just beginning to swell and shine with the onset of puberty, stood with her hands spread wide on his table. The old man stared at her—through her—and rapped his knuckles against the wood. He tilted his head back, letting another fiery shot dribble down his throat. Its bitter taste shook his body.

Hoarsely, she yelled at him—again. Gone was the force with which she started, back when he had replied to her pleas with something other than stone-faced silence. She could not take it anymore. Day in and day out. His life was split in two, and she never got to see the better half. He reserved it for the world beyond, for the people that judged through glances and glares.

Empty, the mug clacked against the table. Again he demanded quiet—she was worried over nothing and his head was pounding. Fetch another drink, he cried. That would settle both his nerves and his pains. The whiskey, though, was across the room, and it was debatable whether or not he could stand.

How can you let her hurt you so? What is this lingering knife? Is this why she left you?—left me? These were the questions she had always longed to ask him.

Suddenly, the girl rounded the table and lurched the rest of the way, seizing his stein. Yanking it back, she yelled again at the slack-jawed man. Worthless. A terrible father. It was no wonder his wife left him—if he could not control himself, how could he ever hope to understand marriage? His hand shook when she would not return the stein.

Twice he beckoned, and twice she rebuked him, and finally, turned to go. The chair grated as it pitched backwards, and the man staggered to his feet, leaving one hand on the table for balance. His voice rose as he made the demand again.

The mug. He wanted the mug.

"Give it here you little whore." The words burned, like alcohol in an open wound.

Whore, whore, whore.

In her ear: a whisper of Rurik's heart. On her lips, the wetness of Voren's kiss. It was not of the heart. Neither. The warmth was in her blood and in her hips and her father named her.

Whore.

She recoiled, eyes watering as her lips quivered. What would come was known. *The Beast.* There could be no escape. Still, defiant, she raised the mug and, as he watched, she hurled it at him, screaming.

"I hate you!"

Because you hate me. You've always hated me.

He ducked and it smashed against the opposite wall—two big pieces and a mountain of smaller shards. He stared longingly at the mess. When he turned back to her, however, his face was contorted and fiery. Fists clenched as he roared offensive slurs. Her father reared back, taut muscles toned by years of labor and years at the bow flexed before her eyes. She could not run, rooted to the spot by terror.

When the blow came, it snapped her head back, straining her neck and stabbing daggers down her spine. She pitched to the right and toppled onto the floorboards, skin split on the barbs of a dozen splinters.

His shade morphed. The fist led into the shape of Roswitte, and the bear woman crouched, pounding at Viveld. Gorjes blood. Gorjes screams. So much anger. So much rage. The body pitched, contorted, flailed—broken. A doll with no one to pluck the strings. She could still feel his hands on her. The taste of alcohol and musk. Who was she, that all should wish for more? The fists fell. Again and again, and she wondered if this was how it all would end.

Nothing lives long but the mountains and the earth. All the rest is air.

At the crossroads, a voice howled praise to the Bastard. It gave them away. But Alviss's hands were holding her up. She was of his body, and they were alone. The others raced on.

Marvelle was with the sellswords. He reached a hand for Alviss's shoulder, and Essa thought she heard a voice tell her it would be alright. "Such a thing, such a little thing," the man whispered through gapped teeth, and she clutched the dagger tighter. The man leaned in toward them and she hacked it across his fat cheek. The howls ran as rain, and the thunder of blades answered.

When the Zuti crashed into them, all was monstrous sound. The world tilted and the sky—the Blue Wolf, as Alviss named it—seemed to reach toward them.

I wonder, its whispers seemed to say, *what it takes?*

Everything, she sought to tell it, but she was still nailed to the earth.

It seemed an impossibly long time before the Zuti stood over her, nestled as she was in Alviss's lap, and pressed a hand to her head. "It hit, bad pretty." He turned to Alviss, sighing through pale lips. "The rest—they no let dis go."

So tired. Her eyes drew heavy on him, and for once, she saw him beyond the blood. Beyond the blades. His touch was almost human. *Lessons,* he always quipped. *Without the pain, learning is beyond.* She reached a hand toward his cheek and watched him nearly recoil in shock.

Almost as a mouse, she heard her voice creep out: "Why don't we learn?"

But the bald man only touched her hair, and for a moment she thought him a ghost, and he wiped at the numbness burning there. "Is okay," he said. "Breathe. Remember: you are woman. They see not this, and so…"

The world tilted again before she could figure what that meant.

* *

It was not the path they had taken in the depths of winter, but in the pale light of spring one would never know it. With the snow smoothed away, the plains of Neunhagen lay wide and wet before them, splayed like some camp follower's all too eager thighs. All was bare, a vast stretch of grass and mud whose only sign of end were the hills at their backs and the looming ranges of Surin's white-capped northern wall, far to their left.

Around camp, some men spoke of their procession as if a great wave, steadily receding into the ocean that had birthed them. It did not do it justice. Huddled against the bleached greenery, Rurik saw the truth of them: a lumbering stampede, gryphons or bulls or even calves, picking the blighted earth dry on a blind descent into frenzied nothing.

Somewhere, a cliff undoubtedly awaited them, which their hunters would hound them down. Be it of blades or honest earth remained to be seen.

For the first three days of their march, Rurik had to be carried in a litter. His bowels quivered without the least provocation. Time and again his stomach forced a stop to his advance, until he reeked of sick. So ill took he, in fact, that there was some small whisper of poison at those traitor hands'. But he knew it for what it was, and many shared his condition—a flu, only worsened by their dwindling rations.

In those days Tessel came to him only once, for he was scarce in shape for riding either, but he managed, if only to keep faith with the men. Nevertheless, he was nigh pale as a ghost when he entered Rurik's tent. They talked a while of nothing—each, it seemed, but grateful of the moment's respite—and parted with a single promise. When he left, Tessel assured Rurik he would not be set with the other sick, and he was grateful for it.

That train was as dead men, and they unnerved him more than he could give to voice.

Thus, left alone, Rurik turned inwards, and to the coin at his breast. At first it was the case that Usuri did not wish to speak to him. He talked anyways—not intrusive or demanding, but with the subdued gentility of the ill. The ill and the wronged. For once, he did not so much speak of himself, but of days gone by between them, and of Verdan, and of the Ulneberg, and never once did he mention his other great sin.

When we were children...do you recall? How you marched inside when my father was not receiving? They yelled. Oh how they yelled, but you yelled the louder. Do you remember? Prophecy, you said, waits on no man, and certainly none so stuffed up as him. And all those soldiers, they just stared and stared until—well, until he laughed. I had never seen someone speak to him so.

Kasimir had always held an unusual affection for the girl. When Rurik had first thought her odd, his father had cuffed him about the ear and demanded he make nice. When she repeated the gesture, and asked what took so long besides, he thought that he should never like that stubborn girl. Perhaps he liked abuse—Essa certainly another bit of evidence to that theory—or perhaps he was simply a child with a child's sense of anger; it had not taken long before they called one another friends, though they saw but little of one another.

It struck him a crime that he had let those moments lapse. No—worse—that he had taken them for granted. It seemed his wont in life.

Bit by bit, she yet proved capable of mercy. *"You always prattle,"* her voice beckoned from the long silence one afternoon. *"A curiosity in the ill; mere annoyance in the sane."* Insult was at least half of the relation, but it was an inroad. Gradually, he became accustomed to her sound again, and at times, swore he could feel a touch of her. There was ever a hesitancy to it, a numbed and beaten distance to the thunder of her tenor, but he took it all the same.

Then, on the eve of the third day, as a renewed strength began to writhe in his addled limbs, something changed in her tone. *"Sometimes…I wonder why I let them make dead men of my dreams,"* she said without preamble.

Already half-asleep, it stirred him groggily to wakefulness. *Who?* He croaked out the thought without even grasping the weight of it himself. Yet he had to know. *Who?* he said again, with a better sense of himself and the notion he had so long pondered. *Where are you?* She had hidden herself. This much he knew. Hid from the world, to injure herself or to fade away entire. For the death of one's world, he could not blame her.

It took her a moment to answer. *"Where the sun rises red, and foolery is the only prophecy."* The sound shuddered out, and for a moment he was left in silence. Then, hesitantly, she wisped, *"I am his ashes, Rurik. He would not know me where I stand."*

Your father? he guessed. *Your father loved you, Usuri. Who makes you think this?*

"Some run the cliffs, and set upon an eagle's wings. Others mire in the den, and once within, can never leave again."

Riddles. His mind grasped for the meaning and drew up short. Philosophy. He hated the debate of either, and so he kept his silence, hoping this bout of madness should pass.

"Your own father—he pitied me before he died. Do you…could you forgive me? I saw him but I could not—he would not…" There was a shudder to the words that set his own body quivering, as it rattled out a haunting note. His father. "Kasimir?" He gasped it, uncertain of what else to say. It made no sense, unless—had she been in Verdan? If she were there, he might have seized her by her arms. *Usuri? Did you see my father?*

With that, the tender string was severed. It was nothing so dramatic as a thunderclap, but it as if, all at once, someone had pressed their hands over his ears and the world drew muffled for it. He sputtered into the dark. He called out, but she was no longer there to hear him.

Once again, he accustomed himself to the silence, and filled it with a terrible wonder.

If he thought to escape it in his duties to the army, he was mistaken.

For now, their one small comfort was that they would not starve.

Their own stores had run their course, but the plains were equal parts breadbasket and range to Idasia and Effise alike. Though the mass had been reformed for the march, Rurik found that in the days of his illness the army had been sundered, again and again and again, until it was a writhing mass of parties and gangs, like a thousand writhing serpents. The need for pillage and plunder was paramount, and their loose confederation allowed for greater ranging. It left them more vulnerable to attack, but it eased the burden of attrition.

Yet it would come. Days governed any would-be crossing of the plains. Octaves, for an army so large and weary as their own.

In the fall, the plains would bloom in vibrant golds and ripe greens, birthing countless rows of farm-raised crops. Year-round, travelers found themselves sharing road and field alike with wild herds of white-coated sheep and milk-laden cows, of succulent pigs and the hard, fleet-footed horses that were Idasia's staple. They wandered largely free-range between the myriad of villages, farms, and wood-walled towns that made their home here.

Whether any of these places would welcome them was another issue entirely. If they did not, however, there remained little doubt they would—or could—be forced to acquiesce. The soldiers still called themselves the army of Idasia, but Rurik laughed and took it mockingly, for they were little better than thieves skulking through the night. Daily, Farren priests grew bolder, re-anointing those who yet clung to the Orthodox rings, and bringing a holy sort of fervor to their mission. Rurik begged Tessel to crack down on them, but in this, the general was stone. Men, after all, fought better when they thought the divine stood beside them in the thick.

Truthfully, as the world spread out before him, Rurik felt only dismay. For the people, certainly, but also for the land itself. He despised the openness of it, the broad nothing. He longed again for the trees, for the shifting trails and the whistle of wind in the boughs—not endless sun. From the glances he caught other men casting south, he doubted his opinion was alone.

Less anxious was he, however, to confront the specter of his brother. It tainted those trees now, as his father's tainted the walls of the home he had left behind. Ivon was not one to simply slink away. Not like Rurik wished he could. Whether it was on the plains or in the trees, it paralyzed him to realize that soon, all too soon, they would likely cross swords.

There was a very good possibility Ivon would not survive that day.

I lose family at an obscene rate. With a frown, he hitched his horse against the whispers of the wind, and nosed it out along the edge of the column.

At this rate, it would be another three days before they passed fully out of Effisian territory, he figured. Or rather, Essa figured, and Rowan gossiped. It had been his declaration the morning Rurik roused from his illness. Buoyed by his talks with Usuri, he had sought the Company out anew. He told himself it would be different. In his head, he repeated all the things he wanted to say as he stepped into their ranks.

Then he had seen what was left of his brother's camp. Once proud men moved downtrodden and beaten, no longer at the head of the companies from Jaritz. The Gorjes now seemed to hold that honor. The Gorjes! Nothing but cutthroats and thieves. No one helped him. Most would not even speak to him, but still he heard things—from Berric, mostly.

Stories of the dead.

Eventually, he came upon the Company among the northern reaches of the great migration. He, alone but for Berric, rode into their camp astride one of the few remaining horses expecting—what, exactly? Whatever it was, he did not find it. Instead, he found Essa laid up in her bed with the baker pressing a sponge to her head. There had been an incident, he was told, but Voren gave him no more than that. Even this, the boy seemed to think, was more than he deserved. From his scowl, it was also plain whom he blamed.

The others were more helpful. "Gorjes," Rowan told him. "Traitorous piss ants tried to kill her on a ride, and fix it with Effisians."

"They hurt her?" he asked, feeling the familiar tingling of rage. "They attacked her openly?"

Rowan shook his head. "Alviss was with her. And not open, no—they picked their moments right enough."

He turned to Alviss, groping for the right words. "Thank you," he eventually murmured, though for his oldest friend, he knew they could not suffice.

"No," the northerner grunted. "Thank Chigenda." Rurik turned to the Zuti, but the man remained a statue. "Half a dozen, and only one a Gorjes. He killed them. All of them." At that, the Zuti actually grinned.

Sincerely, Rurik did his best to thank Chigenda. He reached out his hand, but the Zuti only stared. He uttered the words, but the man only stared. When he offered reward, Chigenda at last broke, and only then to scowl. "He ask once," he said, referring to Alviss, "if rumor true. If I kill women. Children." When first they had met, such rumor had been all their company had to go on. They had tried to attack him, and only later, surviving Rurik's hotheadedness, did they learn the flexible nature of truth.

"No, I say you then. But these?" He drummed a finger on the point of his spear. "Is so. Is wrong. So they go." A shrug was the end of it, and the warrior— he was warrior, through and through, from the fierce scowl to the fervent violence that seemed to wrap about his fingertips—was proven every bit the man. Rurik, nodding to him, let it go, sufficing to thank him in thought.

To the lot, though, he pledged his aid. Unlike before, none of them claimed they did not need it. Indeed, when Rurik met the man to whom they now pledged allegiance—one of Narve's fool-priests—he all but set it as decree. He promised to come to them. He pledged a watch of men about them, and harsh punishment for any Gorjes man that stepped out of line. Better still, he sent them Tessel's own doctor, though the man complained ere long.

In truth, the only man he had to offer them was Berric, but Berric took the post readily enough. In turn, Rowan shared their news, and promised to send word of Essa when she healed.

The sooner they were out of Effisian territory, the better. It would be one less enemy to contend with. If the Gorjes proved anything, it was that control was slipping, and the enemies within were far more insidious than those without. Already they had lost serious time having to bypass the conquered city of Lieven—a ruined husk whose guardians their scouts nevertheless reported favorably answering to Othmann's banners. And he did have banners. Word was he had slipped Tessel's loyalists and was now rallying men of his own.

Two armies chasing one another back to the home from whence both had come. It would have been a comedy if they weren't stuck in the middle of the tragedy.

Already they were losing scouts to shadows, though be they crag deaths or Effisian hunters they hadn't the time to say. Several raiding parties had already probed their ranks, no doubt hoping to find some breach in the lines.

So they drew the baggage train deeper into their ranks, and hoped.

It was a funny thing, in truth—hoping to live, that was. For it was not the hope for living, but the hope for killing. To be granted life, that they might take it in turn. It was war, true, but it still left a pang in his stomach no amount of tack or wheat would fill.

About all he had left to look forward to anymore was sleep. At least there his only enemy was his own mind.

Already he knew where they would set their latest night camp. There was a certain place, the scouts reported, partially shielded by crags to the south and low hills to the west. It would provide some small cover, at least, and the hills would give them watch points for any motions that way, while the crags would hinder any probes from the rumors made manifest of Othmann's forces to the south.

It was a little after dusk, and the clouds grew swollen and grey above their heads. He hoped rain was all the night would bring, for the water would be well earned and well used.

There were a dozen different companies that would have spit fire at him for sending them uphill on a late night slog for the vexing details of guard duty. Instead, he sped back along the fore of the staggered column and gathered men to him that would welcome the chance for a change of scenery. He had no intention of sending others to do something he would not; Alviss had taught him that much at least, and as he saw it, it was past time he started to observe it.

Every man he took was a holdover from Verdan—thirty in all. At Berric's recommendation, Rurik dropped from the saddle and walked alongside them, taking his steed by the bridle. "When everyone's got to make the same slog, you begrudge only the man that eases the burden on himself," Berric observed with a none too gentle pinch of Rurik's leg. Then Berric let him off with true encouragement: "I've other babes to tend today. Don't stay up too late, little lord."

It took them nigh on half an hour simply to free themselves from the last of the lines, but from there, it was an easy march, as such things went. The land was pounded smooth—pasture, all—and they made good time despite the fading light. By the time they had reached midstroke up the hills, their eyes were adjusting to the deepening twilight, and only a few men stumbled over their feet.

One of his father's former house guards was the first up the ridge, breathing deep of the heady air. A few farmers gathered dead brush to fuel a fire, while another man produced flint to get it started. Truth be told, the hills were not terribly large by any standard, so Rurik did not suppose defending them would be any great trouble. Nevertheless, he intended to have five men cycling through the watch at all hours of the night. Every man had a long gun, and even without cannon, it was enough to hold all but the most determined bands of raiders from overrunning them.

A bird call squeaked and drew his eyes skyward. Already he was thinking ahead, two and three leaping steps at a time, past fortifications to the salivating potential for local herds the next day's light might reveal. The rearguard slipped with a shout. Rurik turned to bawk, and in the same moment, several of his men scrambled sideways.

Then the house guard crashed into a heap at his feet, and before a coordinated cry could go up, they were under attack.

Men sprang from nooks night obscured. At least a dozen. Several of Rurik's company had gone down before they realized what was happening, but the rest rallied, either using their guns as clubs or drawing knives and hatchets for the brawl. No flashes of steel stole Rurik's attention, but almost every attacker leapt for a different target, grappling them to the earth if they could lay their hands on them.

A mud-slathered pig of a man rushed Rurik in the same wild charge. Instinct thrust him back, where once it had frozen him stiff; in the same gesture, Rurik slapped out a gauntleted hand. While it cracked off the armor of the man's collar, it was enough to deflect his charge, and he careened for the next man in line.

As if summoned by the flurry of motions, orange light suffused the plains below them, ringing out in a foreboding wall enclosing the hill. Horsemen. He could see the horses shuffling beneath the light.

In the moment of panic that splintered through him, Rurik heard his father's voice. *Form up. Break the line and you break the spirit behind it.* It was all he could think of and it did him no good—the attackers were on top of them, and they were strung out in a line of wearied men still laden with their packs.

A shot went off from the hilltop. They were lost. Rurik knew it even as he drew his pistol, but he was determined not to be another whisper swallowed in the long grass. Next to him, one of his soldiers buckled under the pig-man, his long gun battered aside and the swing of a club visible in the dim light. Rurik drew back the hammer of his pistol and belched the weapon's fire, its spark flaring wraiths of men into real beings, frozen for an instant in time, before spoiling his night vision utterly.

From the cries, the pig-man wasn't dead, but he wouldn't be hurting anyone else. Blinded, from there Rurik did the only thing he could, and bent down beside his soldier, fingers grasping for the neck as Essa had once shown him. Checking for a beat of life. He could feel the breaths before he ever felt the beat, but it was the slick of warmth that concerned him most.

More footfalls pounded up the slope behind him. He snatched up his pistol and twisted on them, shouting, "One more step and I'll snuff the lot of you," as he cocked the hammer again for emphasis. He was crouched—a huddled black splotch against the murky mound—but he dared not hope the vague shapes of men were as blind as he.

Around them, the sounds of fighting were quickly dying. "Hold, hold," someone shouted, and even before his moment of destiny came, he realized the voices were not their assailants' alone. Some of his men had thrown down their arms. Most were prone. Voices and nebulous motions confirmed still more souls lurked, and no longer lacking steel.

"Easy lad. It is being over now. We are not here to hurt you none. No one needs martyr," a voice called from below him.

Were it only him, he should have fired. Yet better men than him had always made one thing painfully clear: a man's duty was to his family first, his brothers second, and himself last. Rurik hadn't always listened, but that, he reasoned, only made such moments of commonsense more precious. He dared spare a moment's squint up the line of his men—none, at the least, seemed to be screaming or rattling out death's final tunes. That might not be the case the next time he fired. And if he had his mark, these weren't bandits they were dealing with.

"I'll need assurances," he sputtered.

Effisian was guttural, like Idasian, but it slurred certain pieces together where Rurik's own mother tongue innunciated clearly. The hushed discussion between those below, followed by a laughter's bark, confirmed his beliefs. It was an ambush, probably laid just for them.

"Our assurance is we not did shoot you as you trudged up hill, little man."

Resisting the urge toward bitterness, he let the pistol fall. It did not take his assailants long. First they relieved his sword and his pistol. They had him flat on his stomach a moment later, hands bound behind his back and a foot on his neck, as others checked to see if the man he had shot still breathed. He gathered it was fortunate for his own sake that the man did.

He couldn't see anyone's faces, but the soldiers came among them and tied both the dazed and the wakeful. Then they patted them for any hidden arms and tossed them into the dirt like sacks of flour. For a long time after that, things were still. The Effisians said nothing to them, and as long as they kept quiet, they kept apart from them as well.

Horses stamped and paced and their hooves clattered on the packed earth. Eventually the Effisians gave way and others lifted Rurik by the scruff of his neck. He struggled, kicking out at the first man he saw with a blade, but the other hit him hard in the gut and he went slack, struggling just to recapture the wind in his lungs.

A few feet from him, one of the riders swung off his horse with an easy grace. Yet it was his sheaths that caught Rurik's attention. Curved sheaths draped across his thighs, hiding the curious blades that were the source of their own fair share of rumors. As the rider loomed, Rurik tried not to flinch as he peered out the man's face. A legend of the plains stared back at him.

A thin line of horsemen blocked them, massing on the hills entrenching their path. The threat was moot—such a force could harry, but never assault their own.

It would break them to try. That said, the fact that the Effisians had managed such a show undetected was troublesome—as were the banners they bore.

Their sigil was a rearing and fiery-hoofed black stallion on an azure sea. Prince Leszek's crest. Tessel called up the horse while his other captains formed their baffled troops into a spear wall. They drew the wagons deep into the column and closed ranks against a raid.

But the horsemen never moved. As Rurik had said they wouldn't. He had returned to camp at dawn, none the worse for wear, with Leszek's call for parley. They had returned his items in good faith, and even let him reclaim his horse, on the condition he return if Tessel rejected their terms. They were simple enough.

"Wants you, ser," Rurik had told the general. "You and four others, or he'll not make this a thing of words." True to his men's word, the Effisian prince hadn't killed any of the men he'd captured. Yet.

Tessel stared up the hill. "Who has Leszek sent?"

"He comes himself."

Shock actually eased the general's otherwise tense figure. "Leszek? Leszek himself comes to us?"

Rurik nodded, but it was only now that Tessel finally called for his horse. "Is this wise, general?" the others cautioned, only to be ignored. Mounting, he dismissed them with a curt chastisement: "Everyone seems to want me dead. He's been at it the longest. I think it only fair that we indulge him. Either fortune waits, or death. Either way, we'll have it soon enough."

Rurik was among the four that rode with him. As a group, they mounted and trotted toward the line. They crossed a little over half the distance before five of the Effisians, in turn, rode to intercept them. They joined in the shadow of the hills, the Effisians with their obnoxiously long spears, the Idasians with their sabers and pistols laid bare against their sides.

The man at the fore of the Effisian party dipped his head to them. "You honor us with your presence, general," Leszek greeted them in easy-spoken Idasian.

"As you do us, highness."

None of them had ever laid eyes on the elusive prince before, but the man was one of those rare legends that failed to disappoint. Nearly seven foot, if he were an inch, the man's slender grace held him high above most others, even on horseback. Black, unkempt hair spilled from beneath an equally black helm and coif, leading down to the tip of a pointed goatee.

A veteran of no less than twelve battles and probably thrice as many raids, with all the dents and scars to prove it, he had fought longer and harder in this war than probably any man still in it. Twice, to Rurik's knowing, this prince had been reported dead, and twice he had sallied from the very gates of Hell to harry them into bloody submission.

Even here, the man held himself with such calm one could not help but be a little unsettled. Rurik certainly was.

He cast an uncertain glance at Tessel, but the general's face was a steady mask itself. *A stone wall meets a wild horse for conversation*, Rurik groaned inwardly. *This can only end well.*

There was a long moment of studious silence as the men took one another's measure. Then Leszek shifted in his saddle, scratched at his stubbly cheek, and chuckled.

"I see you intend to leave us, Tessel. Do you find Effise does not agree with you?"

Tessel shook his head. "I believe, at this juncture, I have already sampled all that she has to offer. I would not wish to grow sick of her so swiftly."

"Pity. As I understand it, your own country's bland palate shall not be availing you much either."

Tessel just gazed at the prince for what seemed a long while. Then he leaned forward in his saddle. "Perhaps you would agree to settle this by duel? We are both young men are we not?"

The smile that slipped across Leszek's wry face was coy, at best. "Young, yes. But I would know age. It is a fool that would risk all on the head of one. Besides, I do not come to war, Tessel. Rather, to warn you of those who would."

Suddenly somber, Tessel drifted with his nickering horse as it side-stepped a pace from man and blade. He nodded, as if to accept the burden of the words to come. Enemy to enemy.

"Four days ago, a curious message came to me from my father. Talk of alliance, talk of war, talk of earth and fire and the bodies that walk them both. Talk of a priest, most of all, who would name himself beneath a crown. So too

came a bastard's name, and a proposal. Kill the one to know peace of the other."
There was no humor in the thin man's frame as he followed Tessel's ambling.

"Harry, harry, harry. That the dead man might tarry. I see the bodies
streaming across my country, and it gives me peace. But I am told this is wrong.
That the greater good is served in blood, as it has these many years past. My
childhood, as it were. And so: for king and crown. But I do this for a land that
has bled too much already. I would see you gone, Tessel. We both know you
starve. That the earth swallows your sick behind you. That this land bleeds you
dry. That there is nothing here but ash for you or I.

"You would go, with or without the order. I know this. And this is why I
warn you—I would see no dishonor in this end. This new creature, and my father
both, know not war. They do not understand its addiction, and that no note can
end so many ought years of blood. What leaves will come again in new form, as
soon as the convenience has passed. Vipers always do."

"You will not bar us?" Tessel asked beneath a thin veneer of calm.

"I? No." Leszek struck his hand across the air, as if to dismiss it. "But my
father would. His men would bleed you. But I would have you home, and to your
own battles. That we might reclaim our own, with neither string attached, nor
fingers at our purse."

"You make a powerful enemy in this, highness. Your viper may be a priest,
but he still has the venom of my country. If our return is ill-received, your homes
may still burn ere long."

Rurik looked to the man, aghast. How, and why, the commander would
seemingly try to dissuade the prince from their own safety—safety he had
proposed—was too much to bear. Did the man want blood? Behind them, where
anxious mobs howled, he knew there were men ready to die for Tessel, but what
they wanted was to return home. The general owed them that, at least.

"I am aware," the prince said brusquely. "But this is later. This is now. A
year of peace, or another tally to a decade of killing? All men need to breathe,
and the smoke is stifling."

"There is still Othmann, and Ernseldt. They yet have many men between
them. They may follow me into the flames, or they may remain. I cannot speak to
them," Tessel replied honestly.

"Ernseldt, now there's a proper beast!" Leszek grinned, bearing teeth. "But Czeslaw's run him ragged, I think, and if Othmann is all that remains to me? A good man, but too cautious."

"And you are certain that I, too, am no snake?"

Leszek leaned back on the edge of his saddle, gauging his opponent before shaking his head. "No," he answered quietly. "You are a gryphon. You will always do best for the flock."

A moment's weight gave way to a gracious bow from Tessel. "I am grateful," he preened, and the horses stirred around them. Nothing but air answered, and the men, so long given to beasts and blades, clung to its soothing howl as they twisted away, to camp and to hills.

At their backs, Rurik watched the Effisians drift into lines and canter away beneath the swell of the earth. Their flags drifted, snapped in the breeze, and sank from sight. A few moments later, the figures of his own men crested the hill, a few propped against fellows for support, but more or less unharmed. Then they were alone, even amidst the throng of looming figures, in this land they had sought to bleed. It seemed to stir at the hope, and so too did he. War could be avoided.

But as they neared the camp, Tessel's voice wound its way into his ear. "You wonder," it noted, "why I should speak so candidly with the man?"

Rurik stared resolutely ahead, trying to pretend the man had addressed another, but their other guards looked on in bare curiosity. The eyes demanded.

"He is like me, in a way. Neither of us fights for ourselves. We fight for others. Yet in so doing, it is those others that always suffer. My father was the same. But this creature that sits our emperor's throne now would kill us all for personal gain. He has no interest in this war. No care. He is a beast, and we are men." Tessel drew his head up high and kneed his horse toward his troops. "Men discourse. Beasts kill."

Chapter 12

Effise was an old nation, much of its troubled yet prideful history shared commonly with that of Idasia. Its people were even older than that of its neighbor, though the first empire rose far before the Effisians had ever dreamed of more than petty chieftains.

They shared land. They shared culture. At a time, they had even shared ambition.

Perhaps they would again.

King Bezprym of Effise struck Leopold as a kindly man, and a worldly one, who knew the worth of the word as well as the weight of a good coin. As his wife dictated the terms of Bezprym's reply, he could not help but draw a comparison between the failing old man and his own, so recently departed father. They were as two stars, fallen to either end of the shadows' call. Each had fought so hard for their beliefs, and what had it brought them?

Time lays low even the mightiest of men. Leopold would not make the same mistake. Could not make the same mistake. And in a few letters, he had solved two problems very dear to his heart.

Attentions, his wife had cautioned, were not to be divided. Not so early in the dawn. At the time he had nodded, not really dwelling on the matter. But she had persisted, and he had been forced to see.

A bastard from the east.

A greedy count and a traitorous Farren whore from within.

Plagues within were always greater than the plagues without. Set the wolves to the Bastard, and Leopold could freely deal with the real threat to crown and hearth. An empire, after all, could not stand with two emperors. No lives changed with the baying of another ill-bred whoreson.

Yes, Bezprym was a good man. A pious man. They could have a bright future, their families could, if he were to cut the head off that bastard boy. *Then, perhaps one day, a marriage even? Between daughter and son?* They could dissuade this whole nation of war, draining as the matter was, and again, in the stroke of a quill and the binding of hands, attain what a decade of war had not.

Men called Matthias "the Bold." They would call Leopold "the Wise." Or so he dreamed, when the wine kissed his cheeks at night.

But he drew ahead of himself. Wheeling in his chair, he lifted his drooping head and turned to his wife as the final word fell. Her eyes gleamed. This. All of this was hers. He was merely the name the world would attach to it. He smiled back at her. The heart of his family. His heart, truthfully.

By noon, the last of the letters were sent, with blissful tidings for the Effisian king and demands for the Idasian general—the Lord Marshall Othmann. For all Ersili's badgering, Leopold had nothing for his margraves—those gatekeepers of the east. Worried were their letters, and frantic the motions of their troops. His uncle's birds reported movements all along the border, mobilizing for the return of their own brothers and sons.

It was a reception from hell, to be sure, but he had already assured them he had the problem in hand. There was nothing more that he could do. There were other battles to fight.

By evening, Leopold managed to break away from the badgering of the Lord's Council for a stroll through the castle gardens. It had fast become his favorite place, not for any great vibrancy to the flowers or vast wealth of scent, but because it was one of the rare places in Anscharde a man could find himself alone. Sometimes.

He sank heavily onto one of the benches along the walkway, plucking idly at his robes. For all his time in Idasia, he could not seem to shake the old style. He found that the more binding and expressive finery of his nobility did not suit him. It itched or it bunched; offered no freedom of movement. Let his wife play the doll. He would wear robes until the day he died, and know freedom for it.

Besides, the court girls were fond of telling him how their own husbands had begun to consider robes. An emperor was more than just a leader. He was a fashion setter.

But some things were never in fashion. Reaching down, he rubbed at a swollen ankle—a memento from an earlier fall. It swelled under the broad weight of his steps, not unlike certain other troubles.

Cullick.

Even here, a man was never truly alone, and the ghost of that scoundrel shattered what calm he hoped to find. Between the trees, drab figures in white led a solemn vigil. They were less than they had been before. Another white cloak had come from the south. Darrow was dead. In that, Ersili rejoiced. It was, she

264

declared, better than they might have hoped. Leopold contented himself to prayers. Sacrifice had never been his realm.

For all Ersili's words, though, Cullick somehow pulled some small loyalty even from this disaster. Defender, some few voices dared whisper in earshot. That was what they called the man. Like some avenging relic of brighter days. Even the whispers of the murder attempt on the whore's daughter had only darkened it so much. It had swayed the devout southron nobility, drawing the rank and file from their homes among the plains, but the north—those lands so dangerously close to the crown's own borders—remained unmoved, and the people with them.

Just as well. The southerners were real Idasians. God-fearing creatures. They shared their borders with Ravonno, and so their devotion was his gain. Already, he was told, some of the Patriarch's soldiers gathered with sellswords and marched across their mountain border to swell their alliance's ranks. *Between Mauritz and them, what hope does that isolated cretin have?*

Let the Empress Dowager ride on his behalf across the south. Let that dowager spread her legs and take a thousand men into that traitor's embrace. Leopold had her daughter, and as far as the nation knew, kept her safe and sound as any goodly uncle should. The mother he would kill at his convenience—an assassin's blade in the rush of a crowd, perhaps.

Soldiers lingered at the edge of the garden, watching him carefully. Palace guardsmen, lacking the subtlety he would have preferred. Not like Mauritz's men. Yet their subtlety was for a lack of presence. It had been half an octave since Mauritz had rallied the majority of his own army and bore them from the city.

"One cannot wait for siege. Wars are won by the bold," the man told him.

That word again. He cringed from it, kicking out his ankle and letting it rest in the soil.

"My lord?" a small voice beckoned. He flinched. Startled into seeking out the source, he found it at the edge of the trail behind a pair of round, monkey-like eyes, made bountiful only by the touch of Durvalle green.

Dear, sweet Kanasa. The sister that remained. He smiled to her as brightly as he could, and extended a hand to the space beside him. She swelled at the gesture and stepped boldly forward, pausing only to call to someone off the trail.

"Come here, child."

He froze at the pitter-patter that brought the girl into her sister's lamplight. It caught in the amber and made a woman of the child, another dirty bastard of the crown. His mood sank deeper into its bleakness. Kanasa merely took Rosamine's hand and guided her forward. At their backs, two of the Imperial Guard stepped off the path and into shade, clutching their staves tight.

Somewhere, his bastard uncle would be lurking. It was into his charge the girl had been given, after all. *A bastard for a bastard.* At times, he seemed surrounded.

"Your Majesty," the girl murmured as her half-sister prodded her onward. For an instant, the tiny voice almost reminded him of his own daughter. It only hardened him further.

"What is this, that I should deserve the bounty of two such lovely ladies this evening?" he tried to answer as jovially as he could.

He imagined a blade, lingering at the girl's neck. If only they had left her in that room with that assassin.

But then, he would have a martyr instead.

"I thought some air would be good for the girl," Kanasa said, sounding proud of her assertion. "Even these walls can prove stifling. And when I saw you, I knew providence had struck. We are both children of the gardens, I see." Her fingers tightened around the girl's shoulder. It was enough of a gesture to give Leopold pause.

Perhaps not so sweet. *Must even she have some game afoot?*

"All of Ravonno is a garden," he answered, longingly. "It is pleasing there is at least one place here that aspires to the same."

Kanasa's lips thinned. "I should like to see it one day. And its princes, I understand, arc most gracious."

So that's it, then. He might have laughed. *So simple a thing, some women's wants.* And he had been worried?

"But our young sister here had a question for you as well, majesty. We have heard so many things. It would be kind to know the truth of it."

"Ask, and I will do my best to answer."

At this, Kanasa made another nudge at Rosamine's shoulder. The girl clung to her, but the delicate touch gently dislodged her, and she stepped before

Leopold with a curtsy. She kept her eyes to the ground, but when she spoke, it was quickly. With a child's obsession.

"Some of the washer ladies said that mother walks the south. I-I was wondering when I might go to her. I miss her." Her eyes flitted to him, and quickly back to the earth. "Majesty."

It was a struggle to keep the smirk off his face. "Is that so? Well I've heard no such thing, my dear, but I assure you, if there is a grain of truth to the tale, I shall send men for her at once. I am sure she misses you at least as much as you miss her. Any mother would." For a moment, he considered reaching out to touch the girl. But that, he decided, might have been too much.

"Truly?" The hope in the girl's eyes could have broken a weaker man's heart.

"Truly. If it were in my power, I should let you go to her, but alas…"

"Is it not?" their sister chimed in, otherwise as featureless as a mouse.

The firm of his jaw set against her. "Indeed. Do you know what would happen to you, child, if I did? Any manner of men might scoop up a little girl like yourself and bundle you off into the night. And even if you reached her, would you truly want to end up like your brother?"

"Lothen? You know where Lothen is?"

"Oh yes. It is to our greatest horror both have been held so long by that wretched Cullick. Did you know that he's taken your brother in hand, and forces him to marry an old maid?"

"Godfather?" the girl seemed to perk up.

"Oh yes. But there is nothing godly about him, I assure you. If you were in his clutches…" He spread his hands in a placating gesture and shook his head sorrowfully. "Your uncle looks out for you, child. He would not have you harmed. But that man has deceived your mother, and would do us all wrong."

Though the girl faltered a step, obviously unsettled by these aspersions, the words seemed to sink in. She nodded, as a good child should, and twisted like a reed in the wind. *Lost little bird,* he mused. *Mind your sounds.* His attentions shifted up to Kanasa, who drew the girl back and sent her scurrying into the flowers with a few well-placed words.

Then the youngest of the pureblood Durvalles drew beside him on the bench, and met his gaze with none of her otherwise childish qualities.

"If you want the south, dear brother, truly want the south, you will need Duke Urtz. Did you know he was once betrothed to Cullick's daughter?"

He gaped at her as she plunged on, unabashed. "He is bullheaded, and driven by wine. Easily tamed, by the man that knows how, and he is already predisposed to us—you dealt well with Portir—but if you are to be for him, you will have to limit Mauritz. He hates his great uncle almost as much as he hates his grandfather." She spread her hands against her skirts and leaned her head against his shoulder. A little girl gone to confession. "I bedded him once. He is not so talented. But his friends are. Especially those in Asantil. And you know, I've always fancied an Asanti noble."

"Excuse me?" It was as if he was talking to an entirely different woman.

"Oh come now, brother, this is another game you must learn to play. Father would have had me married to some Banurian slob, or Walim's delicate duke. I detest the mountains, and I cannot stand a man that looks and acts prettier than I." She rolled her head up so that their eyes met, and the almost comical quality behind them returned. "Help me, and I would help you."

Can I trust no one's appearance in this damnable family?

"And how could anyone in this family help any other?"

"For starters, you could extend your church's blessing on me, dear brother. All know our father brought his heretical curses on our heads. There's not a one of us that doesn't need absolution. And be it devils or blades, something hunts us in the dark."

"I don't have any idea what you're talking about," he said quickly, hoping to avoid the topic entirely. It was enough his wife so often turned to that witch and her...tricks. Enough that he had begun to think he might actually require Bertold's particular talents.

Spirits. That was the last thing he needed.

Kanasa frowned. "As though you do not know. People say this family's cursed. That we've fallen out of favor. And the poor old chancellor..."

"Men drown. It happens." He countered roughly. "I've seen no tragedies since father's death. Have you stopped to consider it was not your spirit it was after?"

"And Joseph? And Molin?"

Long had he dwelt on those too. Longer than she or any other might have realized. It was enough to strangle his voice into a fleeting silence. *Joseph. Dear, angry Joseph*—such things, they had planned. The one brother he had truly known, and loved. In Cullick's hands, he had long placed that death—a death that, had it not been, he might yet be far from all this nonsense, aiding, but never held within the torchlight of this foreign soil.

Joseph had been a careful man. His guards were plenty. Yet Leopold had ever held the assumption that these facts merely indicated an especially skilled assassin. Men could always find a way. Even Ersili, however, had thought different. What assassin did his work with flames, and slipped away from a full cavalcade of soldiers on an open plain?

"Had they not just come from Cullick's estate? This specter, whatever it is, I am certain is a creature of his own creation." In this he was steadfast, but still the woman shrank. A tenderness ate at her, and gave her fears life. So he took her hands, eyes trailing the little girl moving through the flowers. Half of all life was lies anyways. "But fear not, we have seen to its solution. A shadow for a ghost," he said, gesturing across the lawn. The girl's eyes followed his motion, to the other robed figure stalking the periphery. A magus. "And words of benediction for any that would bedevil our souls. This place, this home of ours…it is safe, dear girl."

But sometimes, when his wife's witch whispered, and dear Ersili cast about in the dark of the night, he could not help but feel the tingles on his neck. The hair that would not fall. Like a man watched.

In those moments, he had to wonder what other gifts his step-mother might have left behind. *Farrens, after all, are creatures of Mordazz.* The Fell God. Demons were his cohorts, his agents, his lovers. *Who but they could seek the destruction of those who would not convert?*

Kanasa listened, but he was not sure she heard him. She nodded, absently, and patted his hand, rising a moment later to gather Rosamine for departure. In the same moment, Bertold slid fluidly from the shadows to Leopold's side, watching the pair head back for the light.

"We should follow. The hour is late and a chill clings to this air," his guardian said softly.

"And is it any warmer in there?"

Bertold lowered his head, studying the earth a moment longer than seemed necessary. "No, my lord, but your wife lights the fires. And I know the evils there better than those fleshen things that stalk these lanes. One way or another, we are not alone."

Even in the gardens. Even at the heart of the world.

How he longed for Ravonno.

* *

As Charlotte stalked around the cross-legged visage of the witch, she found herself marveling at the simplest fact of life: time works in mysterious ways. Such was why a thief, presented with the choice of death or imprisonment, would always choose the cell—one never knew the chance, the bounty, that time might present. Though that said, thieves received a blessed bounty compared to such a sentence as this.

Which made the witch's latest turn of character all the more puzzling.

Usuri tipped her head back to look at her, smile bright and easy on her wan and hollow cheeks. Even the Naran's dark skin had begun to pale from her long incarceration. Still, the change was not one of skin. In truth the change was one of fingers. They moved with purpose between the lanes of food Charlotte had provided, snapping up bits of bread and chicken like a monk renounced. She feasted, as she had not in whole moons.

When the servants had come to her with word of the witch's sudden change, Charlotte had not at first believed. Who would? Before reporting to her father, she intended to see the truth of it, and so she had. That first day, the witch had still been of few words, but she went about her chambers with a purpose, cleaning herself and the darkest corners of the room with a vengeance. When food and drink was taken to her, she dined freely. Gorged herself even.

Feeding the suicidal was a bit like tossing bread to the flames. Even if it ate, it would only fuel their passion for destruction.

That first night, the servants told her Usuri took ill from the lot of it.

Three days had since passed, and Usuri seemed only to be improving. It would please Charlotte's father, no doubt, but Charlotte herself was not sure what to make of it. This quiet grace was unbecoming of this creature which had, otherwise, presented herself as something of a monster. A ruse, she suspected. It thus became a matter of determining what, exactly, the witch was angling for.

With the silence between herself and Sara, it was not difficult to find spare moments. So Charlotte went to her, day after day, playing the part of the dutiful attendant.

And there, she watched.

Humming, the witch turned on her with those stormy eyes. Trouble cracked like a thunderbolt within them, and yet the clouds seemed calm. An unnerving revelation.

"Little bird," the witch whispered, "when will we fly anew?"

Always the same question. She wanted freedom, it seemed, where before she had only desired the freedom of death. If she was all that she had seemed, could she not simply take it? Surely Charlotte would not have been able to stop her. Not with these hands. Dartrek, hovering in the corner, or the soldiers outside the door, perhaps.

She smiled for her. "Soon, Usuri, soon. You do seem to be regaining your strength."

Usuri watched her for a moment before she shook away, playing with a doll she had pieced together of wood and string and cloth. At its breast, the only sign of extravagance—some old coin strung taut against its breast. It was a sad thing, but between its long hair and thin countenance, Charlotte could almost see her own figure in it. *Speaking of unnerving.* The last time she had seen such a doll, a man had burned—burned alive.

"I have decided, you know. Kasimir told me not to. Father would not have wanted to. And Ru…" The voice trailed, growing faint as Usuri pulled somewhere deep inside. Then she popped back, brandishing her doll like a torch. "No man alive could love a creature what so wantonly does as I."

Charlotte leaned forward, disliking the portents this brought. Rurik. *Had he something to do with this?* Since Kasimir's death, since her father's last lectures, she had thought the boy's trouble was at an end. Perhaps it was good, after all, that they had sent the brother to deal with it.

"Do you find yourself in need of love?"

"Are not all creatures?" Usuri's doll pirouetted by its strings, making a dance floor of the witch's lap. "Even your shadow. We do our worst, and our greatest, for the shadows of that shape." The doll twisted and swam at Charlotte. "You ask an odd question for one soon wed."

271

So she had heard. It remained a mystery how the girl learned half of what she did. Likely some loose gossip from the hags that attended her. But then, who knew with magic? "Weddings rarely have anything to do with love, Usuri. But more to the point: what is this of Rurik? I thought you had put him from your mind. With his deceptions, and his fickle heart," she spoke, feeling her father's repetition in the words.

"He speaks to me. In the long night." The figure halted, gesturing, it seemed, toward Dartrek. His dark eyes beheld it, and he grunted in annoyance. The doll's arm waggled. "In whispers no one but this head can hear. Oh coin of coins! Whereby your glitter might we shine? Might not your light yet lead us home?" She giggled at herself and pulled her doll up high. "He is troubled. As I. And the world shifts with him. Marching, always marching. But men, I suppose, will find themselves in war."

War? Riddles stalked the girl, but they knew where he was, and if war stalked him...*Does she speak of Effise?* A tingle rode the thought. If there were a way to have at information beyond the beck and call of riders or birds, then they could move with that much more reassurance.

With care, she kept that enthusiasm from her words. "What do you mean? They march?"

"It draws near enough to home. Dreads it, he. Longs for it. And the girl and he, they walk through different paths, as the blood descends. The Company is sundered."

"The Company? You mean the army?"

"I mean *his* company." The doll drew still in her lap, and the witch stared it down, brows scrunching tight. "He does not speak of them. It is..." Usuri blinked and the train of thought twisted. "But the army, soon, I should suppose—the weak and weary masses, they march toward no end. And the margrave, I think, will soon know what the Effisians know..."

Charlotte fell on her then, coming about the front of Usuri and shaking her by the shoulders. "Speak plainly, girl. What is this? What army? What moves?"

A frown darkened the whole girl's face. Dartrek took a step closer. "A kiss to king and country." With effortless grace, the witch leaned forward and planted such a kiss on Charlotte's cheek. "A count is not the only one what sees a crown unjustly laid. And a little bird is not the only one that would sing the petty-pretty song of rule." Then the kiss fell on the other. Charlotte let her hands fall away.

Usuri's doll rose before her eyes. "You will all bleed yourselves dry. What need is there for I?"

With a quick snap of her wrist, Charlotte sent the doll sailing. "God damn it, witch. What is wrong with you? Every day I come here, listening, watching, and always with the riddles. Some new brand of insanity. Your father dies. You maim and maul. We push too far, the threats turn to our own heads. Endangered, locked and barred, you turn the pain unto yourself and now…love? Happiness? Where do you conjure such senseless grace? What are you?"

The witch stared after her fallen creation, and for a moment, it seemed, the depression of prior days descended. Bare feet twitched once—fidgeted.

"Why…?" Her voice fell nearly as low as the earth. It was pitiful. "There is no why. But a broken mind. Broken creature. Conjure? I *am* senseless. But all of you are so much…so much…" Her eyes wrenched on Charlotte with a wet and sudden fury. "More." Before Charlotte could backpedal, the girl sprang without so much as a scream, and those dirty feet and those clawing hands were on her, and they scrabbled in the dust.

Then they were away.

An army marched, in step. A boy watched from afar. His eyes, they searched a woman out of the gloom, but she bled in the dust. Why, why, the crows seemed to cry as the very sky darkened. Drums of war. Drums of nations. The banners marched not east, but west.

The same boy sat at the opening of a tent, whispering words into the cradled visage of a coin. Coin. Charlotte knew the coin. Saw its rust. Once, twice— where had she known it? He spoke of love, and the heart, not because it was what he felt, but because he had nowhere else to turn, and the heart was second nature to him—the escape when the world did not provide. He was alone. Like Usuri. Lost and alone, and therein lay that fabled attraction.

Fire burned her hair and Charlotte stood cracked as a statue, naked in the grass save the crown atop her head. A snake curled around her. Feathers, everywhere the feathers—serpents dined on birds, did they not? The storm was in its eyes, and the fangs bared themselves back wide enough to form a face, and a woman, pulled from its sinewy depths, coiled about her and laid her bare.

Little bird. Little bird. Don't you hear the word? There are no strings to pull, for the mind is all so null.

She saw a forest, fraught with rattling banners. Gryphons hurdled across the branches as horses pounded battle tunes upon the dirt. Dust hung heavy, mingled with the kiss of blackest smoke. Nothing was clear. Nothing was sensible. The coin rattled and the whole vision shook, and the boy, hardened though he was, could not keep his sense. It was too much. He did not want to *be*.

The touch was on her and she rasped. The snake-girl delved, and sought the taste of their own night together—woman and boy. The night he fell to pieces, and Charlotte broke her father's heart.

It's not yours, she cried, and the walls struggled against her. But the fangs sank deeper and deeper, and drew them out like a poison.

The dance. The bed. The laughter. Rattles of chain with morning light. A father's cold eyes.

His kiss drew to her kiss, and the witch's eyes flared. *Do you like this, whore? You see: we both are creatures of destruction. The mind is yet so brutal as the body...*

A shadow gathered at the edge. Usuri fled it, but the thing persisted, prodding all the earth for trace of ash and dust. It knew. It knew what she was and what she had done. But where—where had it come from?

In the distance, a town burned. He saw it. His heart quailed for it, and Usuri, drawing Charlotte up by the hand, let her taste the ash of it all. Then the girl was behind her, wrapping arms about her waist as her chin rested on her shoulder.

The smoke, you see, is everywhere I walk. It and I—we are nothing without.

Then Dartrek had the witch by the shoulders, throwing her off Charlotte with a shout. She bounced off the stones and fell silent beside her bed, her short hair hiding nothing of the brutalized face. Imagined lips, still and full, lingered on Charlotte with none of the childishness of a boy emperor. Thunder resounded in the eyes—and this was what it was to know.

As did she now. A name fell on her lips, and Charlotte knew her vision's distant plain. She knew it well. "Neunhagen."

"My lady?" Dartrek asked, as his hands slid beneath both neck and waist. He meant to carry her. Was she so weak? "We shall have her chained again. She strikes you ill." For all the silent years, the humble giant's eyes burned, and suddenly this, too, she knew.

Even shadows.

Whatever the source of the witch's magic, it had always struck Charlotte ill. For their family's betterment, or worsening, it seemed to her a wretched thing— one that burned those that used it as readily as those in its path.

After their encounter, Charlotte spent the better part of a morning abed, dutifully attempting to sleep away the migraine pounding through her head. Exhaustion nipped at her, and she could not shake the feeling of that wild woman's skin on hers. Not for the first time, either. Her claws were quick, and they knew precisely where to strike. In body and in mind.

The sensation of being played like a fiddle was unique, but far from enviable.

Dartrek came to her, but she turned her shoulder and would not answer him. Only the stubborn dedication of a kitchen waif was finally enough to rouse her from her sluggish morn. News rode the girl's tongue—as it seemed to ride all those of such position—like birds upon the wind. Charlotte knew her; she had used her many times and made it known such work was much appreciated. Boyce had his webs, and she had hers. Little Millicent likely carried the word between them both, but either way, the word had value.

And the word was that the staff was preparing something extra, for a meeting between her father and some unknown number of attendants. Even the most delicately shrouded of cabals had to eat. Just as the worn and weary must one day rise. Charlotte bore herself up, and sent the girl off with thanks weighted in coin.

Locating the meeting itself was no hard feat. Secrecy may have been a virtue, but as careful as Count Cullick was, he remained a creature of certain habits. She came on them in his solar, already to wine and cigars. Some musical foolery, undertaken by their house's jester, Dogbee, entertained the little ones in another room further down, loud enough to drown out whatever words might go astray. Ustrit and Hacket, her father's bodyguards, let her in without trouble.

All but Walthere rose at the sight of her. The air of the solar burned with the acrid stench of their talk, but she drew it deep into her lungs and let it take

275

sleep's place, curtsying her way through her greetings and slipping as carefully as she might into the conversation and a seat.

There were five men in all—the youngest of Baron Koenraad's sons, Saelec, as well as his bastard brother Fitz, familiar faces among them. Given their empowerment as diplomats and departure for Ravonno less than two octaves before, their quick return did not bode well.

The other pair were not difficult to parse out. Both were well-shaved and wore their hair short to the scalp. One bore the blue robes of a Visaji priest, and the other, the rich cape and tunic of a Ravonnen gentleman. Diplomats, likely, in turn.

After introducing her, Charlotte's father folded his hands on his lap and leaned genially back from his well-fed guests. It did not take long before the priestly of the pair lay his hands on the table and leaned genially toward the lot.

There was, in truth, a lot of him to lean.

"You must forgive my impertinence, highness, but I fear we have little enough time for further small talk. As I told your men—and might have sufficed for you, I add—it is not our decision to change. What is done is done, and we would be to our other duties before that decision spreads."

Charlotte quirked an eyebrow to her father, whose fingers stiffened with constrained fury. He did not look back at her.

Walthere jabbed a finger at the table. "And I say merely there is no history of such a…harsh measure, without warning or evidence. It is ungentlemanly. I ask you to dine with us this evening, that I might see more—"

The priest held up his hand as if to make the Lord's sign. "The Patriarch's decisions come from the Maker Himself. It is not any man's will to question. We know you for Farren, highness, and heretic thus, and I would leave it at that. Your people will sort out the rest."

"Farren?" Charlotte gasped.

The priest's eyes flicked sharp and probing on her. "And by the sins of the father, so shall the child be condemned. Thus are the words of the prophet Ademius. Poor girl. If you put yourself to monastery, you know, the Lord would be forgiving." His look turned ravenous.

"Mind your tongue, priest," young Saelec cut in bitterly. "And mind your place."

"You know this house serves under the pleasure of the Empress, surely?" Walthere added, calmly.

"We do," the other Ravonnen countered with a haughty roll of the eyes. "And the Patriarch knows you offend the Emperor, with your attempt to bind your Farren heresies to the crown. Which do you think holds more worth?"

Not long after, it was Charlotte's duty to show the men out. The nobleman brushed by her without so much as a glance, stirring dreams of daggers and testicles, but his priestly counterpart was just the opposite, taking her hands and clasping them tight. "Remember," he said, "the Lord is forgiving. Repent, I beg you, for your soul—it need not join your father's."

In that moment, she found not the heart for politick. "To become your sister?" A scornful laugh rose high in her throat. "Only priests should benefit then. Get you gone, man, before my husband hears of your suggestion." She wrenched her hands from the man as though he were a snake, and he left at her good day, shaking his head in true pity.

Zealots. Everywhere, yet never bearable, in any form.

"Bastards," Fitz summed, almost as soon as they were out the door. He was a blunt one, Fitz was, but also a wise bastard—in noble company, he never would lift his tongue until he knew it might be sought. It was a quality both father and daughter admired in the man.

Saelec looked far more sullen, and far less certain. "Shall we still make for Ravonno? If we could gain audience, surely we could still…" But the words trailed, and the thought with it. They all knew better.

"Unless we offer to polish the Patriarch's boots with our own tongues, I dare say he's moved a touch beyond that, if he sent such ambassadors as those," Charlotte countered. She sufficed herself on Fitz's carefree chuckle.

"Aye, at that. Those two, as you noted, were coming here at a leisurely pace before you struck on them with the grace of Assal. Ahorse, and at haste, it would have taken octaves to cross those mountains. This was an old action, already set to motion." Indeed, for the distance between Ravonno and Anscharde, it had to mean the Emperor and Patriarch had already exchanged by way of bird. Given Leopold's nature, it stood likely they had never been beyond contact. "We can assume they move in tandem," Walthere summed, drumming his thick fingers across his table.

"So sticking those two wouldn't do us no good?" Fitz piped up. "Pity." And in his pity, he thrust his dagger through an apple.

"You would stick a priest?" his noble-born brother asked in only partial surprise.

"A priest is just a man, and holiness doesn't ward good steel."

Charlotte shook her head with a small smile. "No wonder they call us heathens."

"And so they know," Fitz shrugged. "But I should take it for the release it is."

Walthere rose and paced toward the window. All eyes stalked him as the serving girls appeared to remove plates and cups. Charlotte watched them all, wondering which were spies. At the least, she knew all of them were gossips. Fortunately, so did the others. Talk fell to the side until the women and the leavings were removed.

It was Walthere who broke the silence. "Fitz is right. I should have preferred some security on our southern front, but in truth, I had not counted on it, and this will offer us more mobility. We need not slink in the dark and bandy words as the middlemen we have always been." He paused, to let the words sink in. "We can actually take a stand. A public stand."

"It will earn us enemies," Saelec countered, lamely.

"We already have enemies. It will but entrench them more deeply in their convictions—yet it will convince potential allies we are not cowards," Charlotte added.

Walthere nodded. "Just so."

Saelec began to fiddle nervously with one of the rings on his hand. "What of the Empress? And Sara? Should not one of them be made privy to this?"

"Sara," Walthere sighed. "Yes, the princess should be told. She will craft some sort of response from their end, no doubt—and we shall need to pull her mother back to our gates or…" He turned to Charlotte. "Better still, we shall send her with your mother to Banur."

Since her outburst in the hall, Charlotte had seen neither hide nor hair of Sara. Though the thought of losing her friend pained some repressed part of her spirit, another part rejoiced for the silence. It left her to her thoughts, to regain some small part of herself. That was the problem, she whispered between the lot.

She had not had time to breathe. Every spirit needed some small time alone to regenerate the colors time would surely dull.

She had overreacted. In time she would apologize, even. But not yet. If that infuriated her father, then all the better. *Let him stew a while as well.*

"Kings do respect united fronts," Fitz said.

"And the safety it provides will remove another fear. But…what of the young Emperor-in-Waiting? Charlotte?" Saelec's head spun to meet her. "Will he not go with his mother?"

"I am not my fiancé's keeper," she spat, and surprised herself with her own bitterness. Thankfully, her father answered over her.

"I will deal with the Empress. Fear not. And we will take the opportunity with her son for what it is. Time with your…keep will do you good, Charlotte."

The look they might have shared was venomous, but Charlotte struck it away. For her father, she remained the picture of modest grace, dipping her head to his command, and settling her curling fists against the folds of her skirt. "You know best, father." With small satisfaction, she kept a sarcastic twinge at the end of her submission. His thinning lips told her it was not unnoticed.

Fitz loudly cleared his throat. "If there is nothing else—"

"Wait," she clamored. "There is something. Father, if I might—regarding the tower?"

She had yet to share Usuri's revelations of the morning. While she might have sent a servant, she had deliberately waited. It was news, surely, but it would be held wild by the regards of most. She hesitated, for she hated the thought of being wrong, but then the images returned to her unbidden, and she knew it would not do to leave them.

Walthere took her meaning, and dismissed the others. Neither Fitz nor Saelec knew of the witch, and her father preferred it so. "Tell me," he demanded as soon as they were gone. So she did, from its beginning to its end, leaving no detail unturned, save Usuri's seeming fascination with her night within the Matair boy's bed. Plainly alarmed, Walthere pushed back from the table as soon as she had finished. She stood with him.

"Are you certain she speaks true? Boyce has said nothing of this."

"Does Boyce keep men astride the border? He is much distracted otherwise, father." Indeed, the spymaster had been all but exiled in recent days, wandering the halls but no longer at his master's heel. His failure remained a sore spot in Walthere's mind, and while Charlotte was no friend to that fool, she did not disrespect him—nor wish to see further harm upon his name. "I am certain she speaks truth. As certain as anything. After what she showed…" She shivered.

"Hells," Walthere snarled. He rounded then on the door, and the servants beyond, shouting, "Bring me Maynard! And Boyce—I want the damned fool here now!" As feet pattered quickly beyond, he turned back on her, and drew a steadying breath. "Is she useful? Or not?"

"Father, you should send word to Anscharde," she cautioned. "Surely they already know, but if the Bastard has the army at his beck, it should be sufficient threat to ward a civil war."

"It is the court he shall strike for, if it is so," he countered, obstinately. "If we united, who do you think they should turn on next? Best to wipe them out while they might be distracted."

He did not see the obvious. "And if he comes, he comes through the north. Where your allies lie. If they are distracted, and we are left to the southern powers…"

Everyone would burn. Yet she dared not give it voice, lest it be given strength.

"Charlotte. The Bastard's troops will be starved by now. They will have been harried half to Hell by Effisians, and of those left, I do not doubt a great many will fade away in the night. They will be met by a steadfast wall of experienced troops, and even if they break through Momeny, who do you think will aid them? They have no supply line, and no aid. They will be chipped and isolated until they can be surrounded and destroyed. That is fact." With a sudden fury, his hands slammed against the tabletop. "But what none of this tells me is whether or not that girl can be trusted."

Charlotte drew still. Still as prairie grass, wilting beneath an arid sun. Then she leaned forward, placing her hands on the table to imitate her father's stance, but with slow and purposeful poise. It was a steady eye that met his.

"I pray you think on the girl a moment, father. Let her example stand for the Bastard's folk. Battered they may be, but what will the survivors be? Killers, with all the fat sheared from their bones." She patted the table with her palms, then leaned back again, crossing her arms about her chest. "The witch is as well as ever she was. She no longer hurts herself, it is true, but there is a madness bred deep inside her, and you knew that when you took her. Will she listen? Yes. If you are asking, will she kill? I cannot say. She has at least the peace of mind to know she hates what she is, and I cannot tell you why she willingly aids us. I would not, in her place."

For a span of heartbeats, her father held her gaze. "Lock the girls up. If you see Boyce, voice your concerns to him," he finally spoke, dismissing her.

There was no challenge left to him, and for all the heat of the discussion, she detected no sense of malice or offense. He dismissed her because he was done with her. That was all. Another person might have pressed, might have given the lion's roar and leapt out with a fury to shake the very earth, until their voice could be heard. It was not the way she had been taught. When she was younger, there had been moments, but now?

She left him there, passing out the doors and heading for the children's play. Dartrek waited there, but as he saw her approach, he started, and moved quickly to bar her path. "My lady," he announced himself, and promptly broke character to take her by the arm. She was too stunned to respond, but Hacket, at her back, saw this and called Dartrek out. The hand promptly fell, but Dartrek leaned disturbingly close.

"Some of the women was talking, while you was aside. Sara's lady came—not sure o' her name. Well, see, she joined the talk…"

Recovering some measure of composure, Charlotte leaned away again with a stern frown. "Is there a point to this?"

"Sara went to the witch's tower. She wanted—"

The rest was lost as she began to run. A terrible coldness seized her, but her only recourse was to spring. *Maker be damned!* Curiosity had at last gotten the better of the woman. She knew it; it need not be explained to her. From the very first, Sara had wondered at the mysterious ward they kept in their tower, and they could not rightly keep her a secret. So she had gone at last and walked straight into her family's greatest enemy, and if Charlotte did not reach her first she did not know what would happen, but she knew it would end in death.

Servants and men-at-arms howled as she sprinted past, her hitched skirts fluttering behind, and all sense of dignity momentarily stricken. As she reached the tower, she took the steps two at a time, feet lost to a flurry of fabric. From behind, Dartrek's huffs scuffed the clatter of that frenzied ascent, until both clambered to the witch's door. Would it be death or salvation? Effort. That was what would matter in the end. The guards shambled aside for her, looking on dumbly as she asked, again and again, who had come and who was within, and all the while the lock slipped and Charlotte nearly bolted into the room.

What she found there was more unsettling than any death might be.

Usuri sat as peaceful as a lamb, needle set to thread and the long sheet that served as her bed covering draped across her frail legs. She had been whistling at Charlotte's entrance—a sound that cut sharply with the squeal of the door's hinges.

"So soon?" she piped.

Breaths came heavily to Charlotte then, unaccustomed as she was to running. Yet she forced her back straight and her head tall as Dartrek wavered in the doorway, eclipsing it with his outline. "I come when—" Charlotte began, eyes making little skirts of the room. There was nothing but the three of them. "When I choose," she concluded, with no small confusion. And relief. Had the gossipy wench been wrong? If they had made her run for nothing, there would be blood.

Usuri arched a brow quizzically, and crossed one short leg over the other, leaning forward against her makeshift quilt. A budding bruise yellowed a bared shoulder, where Dartrek had seized and cast her down.

"She talks with voices, bodiless, with bedside manner—yet still the bird, at times, can make her wonder at the nature of the mad."

Then there came a sound so foreign to the little woman it was unsettling: a short, sharp giggle, with all the pitch of a mouse's squeak. Charlotte was not sure what to make of it.

"Would you have a seat? I should apologize for the last chirping. It was…" The witch's lips pursed and seemed to struggle to form around the word. It eventually eased out in a sighed, "wrong."

"Wrong?" Charlotte said. *A game?* she suspected.

"Would the shadow come and sit? He need not hang in portals. Someone should mistake him for a door, and all too crudely grab his handle." The witch's face scrunched up. "And I suspect the thickness would not remove their suspicions of the door."

Dartrek started forward and the witch shied back ever-so-slightly into her quilt, but Charlotte dismissed the threat with a gesture. Hesitantly—a trait she did not like to see in her killer—he drifted back to the door and pulled it nearly shut. Nearly. He did not, however, leave the room. Of the moment, she found that irritating for some reason.

Something rattled as the woman drifted back to the edge of her bed. Charlotte's gaze twisted back on her, roving for the source, but beneath the quilt, she spied nothing. When she bent down, the witch bent with her, and the little bare feet pulled under the patchwork blanket, but the rattle confirmed suspicion.

So they had chained her after all. *And what good will that do anyone?*

"At last, it seems, illusion dies. No door nor blanket should suffice. The chains dance from dreams and catch the flesh to quick," the girl noted, almost sadly, her eyes abruptly falling from her benefactor.

Charlotte shook her head and eased back to her feet as gracefully as she could. "You attacked me."

"Aye? And how many blooded sots before you?" The eyes darted back as swiftly, and had the sharpness of blades behind them. "They had not the pleasure of a personal touch."

"Pleasure?" She could still feel the silver-eyed serpent coiled against her flesh. *It wasn't real.* "Dear girl. As ever, you prove the mad thing. You think your act would spare the boy's heart for you? By Assal's blessed balls, woman, haven't you a sense in your pretty little head? Fictions or realities—are you that dense?"

For once, she found the witch stricken speechless. Chapped lips parted, strained around some retort, and struggled into nothing. She fidgeted, and Charlotte remembered what happened the last time the girl had done so. There was only so far one could push her. So she turned to go.

"Had your jibes? Is that all I am? A killer and a sounding board?"

Perhaps, she supposed. But to two different people—and that was twice what some could offer.

She did not answer, regardless. Yet even as she reached for the door, she heard voices without. *Not now. Please, not now.* A frown moved her. The door opened and bared for her a princess.

"Charlotte!" Sara beamed, her sing-song tone carving the very legs out from Charlotte's gripping terror. Ducking the posted guards, she darted inside.

One of the guards moved into the doorway, as if to shield them. "I tried, my lady, but Her Highness insisted…"

The witch's head lifted as if to drink. Charlotte could mark it in the ruffle of the cloth. From the storms of her eyes a spark glittered, then widened with knowing. Then the set of her jaw tightened and the storm narrowed to the points of its strike. *Assal be damned.* She knew. They were dead.

Charlotte shifted to set skin to stone, and as by an ill wind, the door slammed all too abruptly in their path.

Assal nothing. Chains be damned as well.

Sara startled, but Charlotte's fingers immediately clamped around the handle, giving it a hard tug. A hand tapped against the door, and one of the men outside called to them. She refused to look at the witch. She could feel the smile boring into her back. The question in her friend's own eyes.

From the way her shoulders slouched, there was an unusual heaviness to the princess's bearing. "Charlotte? What on earth are you doing? Not even a good day? Am I so monstrous?"

"Are not we all, lady?" Usuri answered.

Charlotte flung the coldest glare she could muster over her shoulder, even as Sara turned to face the witch. Usuri had bent forward and laid a hand against the stones, but she retracted it as the others' attentions adjusted to her.

"Goodness. And this is your ward? She is a mess." There was a low lilt to Sara's voice that perked up sharply. "But a Naran mess, and that—well, now that is rare enough to be a prize, my friend."

Usuri clapped her hands together. "Web descend and spiders fend, but to the flighty flies to mend—such weight, such weight, how can mere ripples sate?"

Riddles and rhymes and flickers of insanity. Just what they needed.

If Assal be good, if Assal be great, if Assal be anything more than wisp and smoke—come, please Maker, come down and stop this now. Charlotte yanked at the door with renewed purpose, but it had no give, and still she pulled, until she flitted, wild-eyed, back to Dartrek, his great brown eyes gone dark with purpose. His hand had gone to his sword, but she slapped her own against it, and shook her head to dismiss the anger welling in him.

Sara stepped away from them both, toward the witch, to the sound of another question: "Is this a test?" Dartrek relented and, all the while, took Charlotte's arm and handed her a dagger, before stomping for the door himself. Slipping the blade tight against her forearm, Charlotte turned to find that some flies, however, did not grasp the web to which they had been bound.

Sara stepped forward into the very trumps of doom, and bent a knee before them. How many could say they had the pleasure of looking their murderer in the eyes before the end? Perhaps, Charlotte thought for the first time, gunpowder was actually merciful in this way.

The fly offered the spider a hand, and smiled as she did. "Hello," the fly softly spoke, "my name is Sara. I do not believe we have yet had the pleasure of a meeting." Even as she spoke, Dartrek's bereaved grunts echoing at her back, Charlotte put a hand protectively around the princess's oblivious shoulder and sidled alongside her, fingers tight to the grip of her blade. She did not want to do it, but if she had to choose between the pair, she would not hesitate.

Thoughts of before were cast aside. No, she would not let such harm beset a friend.

It was like a twisting of the tongue. Her eyes flicked between the princess and the witch. *Friend.* A word she never thought to spare.

Usuri smiled wolfishly back.

"It is a princess!" *A mote in the eye.* "Fair in stature, Durvalle in nature."

The princess's smile faltered with uncertainty, just slightly, and another head tilted. "Smart child. Few can see a person's nature."

"The eyes gave it away."

Sara turned her smile on Charlotte with what could only be described as a childish sort of glee. "Such a smart girl you have been hiding from us, Charlotte dear! A disservice, I should say." It was like a girl that had discovered a stray cat. How dare the world keep it from her.

"Truly, I am so regretful of that error." The blade felt heavy in her grip, but Charlotte's eyes never left Usuri. She did not even bother to make the words sound genuine.

"Have us a hand, then."

Usuri released her quilt for the first time since Charlotte had arrived, offering both hands palms out to the princess. Sara looked delighted at the offer.

Then again: how often did someone actually offer to touch a princess? Commonsense was a fine barrier. But not for Usuri. Not for Sara, either. The portrait of porcelain drifted earnestly into the muck and earth. Steel drifted nearer all the while.

"Is it a game?" Sara peaked, as their flesh met.

"Game?" Usuri stirred. "No game, no. Merely a touch. Silly people." At this, she turned to Charlotte. "Always you assume so much more of a touch." It fell away, with nothing more, and nothing lost. Charlotte could not lower the blade. She looked between the pair of them, uncertain what to make of it. Sara, for her part, merely folded her hands against her own dress, and quietly regarded the girl for a moment.

"I know you, do I not?"

"What creature here could know a Naran?"

"Does she always speak like this?" Sara put to Charlotte.

"A curse of her people, I am told. Their passions sometimes get the better of them."

"Oh." The princess turned back to the ward, uncertain again. "My condolences to your people, child. For everything."

Silence reigned for a moment, before the witch dipped her head and offered in reply: "And I for yours." But without explanation as Dartrek's shadow swept over them all.

"Perhaps after our own war. After this madness…"

Charlotte squeezed her friend's shoulder, but looked to Dartrek as she did. The man nodded back at the door, his face a veritable feast of confusion. "Madness is a regenerating thing," Charlotte offered, nodding toward the door as well. Dartrek shrugged, and made a motion to indicate it was open. "Like a phoenix, when one strand dies, another burns anew."

"But if—"

Shuddering, the witch closed her eyes and drew back her legs. A pale sheen shivered up her flesh, and sweat beaded at her forehead. "Oh no," she moaned. "No, you do not understand—the dead, the field is littered with the dead."

"What?" Sara gasped, scandalized. "What field? What dead?"

Charlotte already knew. She saw it when she slept. The woman had taken her there, when the clouds of ash still rose to distant cries. Neunhagen. The New Field burned, and suddenly, their war was much more complicated.

Chapter 13

Men were adaptable creatures. Time made of them the greatest of creatures, where it had ground others to dust and cobwebs. Yet time was a fickle thing. It had to be coaxed, and loved, and treated fair. Those who sought to seize it rarely ever saw its potential. Adaptation was, after all, part of time, and even men were not so great as to rush its sweet embrace.

On average, Tessel once quipped, an army could make 25 miles in a day. This was a sound pace, a purposed but unburdened pace, by spring's gentle light and easy soil. Pushed to the edge of means, the same could make more than 30, but they would hate their master for it, and would never see a battle fresh.

Words, Rurik realized. They were nothing but words. Even as he sagged in his saddle, he pondered their nature, and that of the man behind them. The honorable man, laid bloodied and stricken with his own lies. This man, so unlike the kindly general of old, ground them down for what must have been 35 miles or more a day for the better part of an octave. An octave of anguish.

He sensed the taint of ambition and he did not like its taste. It was the taste of death, and more than its share of bodies had dropped in their wake. Whether exhaustion claimed them, or probing Effisians, or even the foul dog desertion, dozens vanished by the day, and Rurik could not find the heart to find out more than that.

It had been his hope that the pace would cease when they finally crossed that invisible line only men could call a border. Those hopes died unseen. He had not even realized they had crossed the border until he did the math, and the first of Momeny's line of stone watch towers loomed before them.

By then, it was too late to howl for reprieve. By then, it was time to worry for the war that was sure to come for them.

Horsemen began to shadow them from afar. It did no good to chase them. They were always gone before anyone could reach them. Thus watched, and worse still, groping blindly onward, tensions mounted to a fevered pitch.

Yet Rurik kept himself aloof of the meetings, the plotting, and the squabbles that went with both. He rode the lines and watched as the men pillaged and stole and begged, even, for what they needed. He dipped back with sorties into the rear to ward off rumors of the Effisian pursuit, and to see the many parties of their great whole gradually drift back toward the center as their destination loomed nearer.

Not once did he see any qualms in the men's eyes for what they did. Alms or arson, they did it all with the same resolved sort of necessity every man seemed to have fallen into. It was pitiful, and disgusting—and more so, that he could not bring himself to prevent it.

They might have killed him for trying. And for some reason, that thought still terrified him.

The unfinished, perhaps. He could almost hear Verdan's sweet song calling from the south. Tragically, it always sung with Essa's voice.

It had been all he could do not to run to its reality when Rowan had brought him word of her waking…

Nothing good ever began with: "Before anyone else tells you…" First had come the fight. Then, it seemed, the flu—much the same as it had decimated him.

And what had that sudden fright led to? Voren. Somehow, the Company had failed to tell him the baker was one of them now. The sight of Voren stooped over Essa, laid against the dirt and the sheets—perhaps he was a violent creature by nature, but he had wished nothing more in that moment than to clobber the whoreson.

She met his gaze then, for the first time in a long time, but she did not speak. It was the baker that stood, cocking his head back with an arrogant swagger. Rurik might have hit him. The greedy sneer the creature heaved on him hadn't much helped either.

"She mends, Matair. Have you not had enough of her already?"

But Alviss had seen to that problem. Even as Rurik's foot lifted to cross the threshold, Alviss had cuffed him like a bear did its cub, and drawn him off before any could speak a word against it. When they were far enough away, Alviss shoved him away by the back of the neck.

Rurik rounded back on him with a feral snap. "Is she with him?"

The Kuric was still. "What matters?"

"You—you know why it matters to me. She's always on my mind. Every day. And when I see her with him…I wasn't half so scared when they were pulling knives on me, Alviss."

Empty palms turned out to him. "All boys feel such. You want not to hear. Fine. But fact is this: her life is hers. It took great hurt. Let her make choices." Rurik started to interject, but Alviss held up one massive hand to stay him. "Are you sure this is love? Not lust?"

"Alviss! I of all people should know the difference."

"You of…" The giant shuddered once, then barked out a single laugh as dry and biting as an arctic wind. "Boy, you are. These things…you say, muddle? We see what we want seen, all true, when someone else has them. Calm. Treat her as you always have. Inside, she knows it was not you. She will come around." He stared over Rurik's head, watching shapes move in the distance. Rurik longed so badly to turn and to look as well, but he could not help feeling this was a test. He fidgeted. "Or she won't," the Kuric said at last.

"I can't accept that, Alviss."

"Then more fool, you." The Kuric's gaze leveled back on him, heavy as a weighted pike. "Choice, as I say, is not yours to make."

He had made sure Rurik did not come back, either.

Pitiful, perhaps, but it gave him more time to focus on other things. His family, for one. The army. And Usuri, of course. Their whispers in the night were a comforting thing. When nothing else could be. And she was opening to him. Night after night, when he could reach her, the walls gradually wore their way to cobbles, and the path led back to the old ways—to the time before all this madness. When both had been something more than orphans.

Then again, what good did it do to cling to the past like this? It did not hide one from the present. She knew it. He could sense it often enough in her voice. She wanted to escape, but even magic could not change her horror. Every time he felt it, the hurt in his own heart deepened.

Fortunately, in hours like this, when it was naught but he and Berric and the endless, ravenous swarm of steel, it was easy to fall into the routine. War demanded just that. All of them were orphans, in truth. Lost. Adrift. Desperate to feel. If only he had made different choices.

He looked to Berric, the russet-haired spring of man's best nature demanding a smile in response, though hunger had wasted it nearly to the bone. Was this what they fought for? What they would die for? A nation of ghosts, stalking the peripheries of nightmare. How one could keep such a smile, he did not know, but he did know that if the day came that Berric ever lost it—that was the day the world would finally end.

Giving his horse the leave to meander through the plains grass, Rurik could not help but give his thoughts voice. "How do you do it, Berric?"

All his loss of decorum earned was a chuckle from the older man. "Losing faith already, ser?" Berric made a wave with his hand. "Have you tried a life for others?"

"I worked in a company before. Of friends—family, near enough. The ones you…but I-I lead men now." His voice lacked weight. Berric, catching the horse's reins, guffawed at him.

"Do you really?"

His silence was answer enough.

"Everyone wants to be a leader—such trouble! Such drama. What is a soldier, at heart, but the purity of devotion? We listen. We answer. We act, for the other."

Was not his whole life for others? Essa, he had once thought, was bread and butter, life and limb and world. He would have done anything for her, and as soon as she had offered him something he wanted—or so he thought—he had taken it without second guess. Family? Where were they now? And his friends? A means to an end, perhaps, used for coin and life and laughter but…

That was for me, it seemed. The thought harrowed him. *Used, always used.*

They marched a long way through rocky ground, up onto the poor reaches of a downtrodden farm—the last before the trees. A score of pikemen had preceded them to the pasture to feast on goat cheese and milk, under the shade of a distant tower. Flickering shadow, for the fire atop had gone up, and the truth of war with it. Not long ago, another man had perished in the flames.

Do I use Usuri as well? It was only as they neared the cowering farmer that Rurik found reply. "And when it all abandons you?" The heart of it. The fear. Two dozen eyes were glued to him, and not one would have qualms against cutting out his heart. *Exile.*

His friend touched his shoulder gently and motioned the farmer forward with the other. "I think you have this all wrong, Rurik. It is the young who are supposed to be optimistic. It is not your land being eaten up."

There it rang again: the call of the south. He looked across the plains, following the line of mountains to where he knew a river bled into the soil. Verdan. Nestled in the bosom of the trees. Far from battle, but not far from war. He felt his breath quiver: *Not yet.*

In the days that followed, Tessel put the forced march mercifully to its end, and split his army still further, leading the horde in arcs around the line of towers Momeny, and its father Idasia, called the Eastern Gate.

At least, parts of them did. Their army grew scattered over miles of open land, each segment as careful as the next to avoid the vast specter of Hanschleig Forest. Had they not, they should have never found themselves again. As it was, for days Tessel allowed them free range across the plains, Rurik suspected, to pillage and plunder and burn the province's margrave into foolish action. Rurik could not fathom how they would be brought together in any form of cohesion again.

Still more demoralizing, at night when the horsemen had gone, any illusion of war's evasion remained picked apart by the flames the watch had lit. All along the border, it was as if their families called them home to feast. It was a bitter taste.

Then the moment came. Some farmers—whether pressed, or earnestly intrigued—brought them news of the enemy call to arms. Of a mustering in the trees before the city Oberroth, the province's second and only other settlement worthy of the name. It was a place existent only for the benefits of trade the border should have offered. Nor was it far.

At the news, Tessel thankfully put out the call for order, and the army set to march anew. For one night, if one night only, the general let them sleep. As exhausted as the day's duties left him, Rurik was, naturally, one of the few that could not manage to partake. Yet that night he held himself back from beckoning Usuri. He rolled his coin between his fingers, tipped his head against the poles of his tent, and kept his words to himself. These were not things to trouble her with. Not this.

"This is the moment." Unbidden, Tessel told him such that very night. "Oberroth will be the first step. It will set the path to which all others shall fall in line."

None saw it as Rurik did. Neither Tessel nor any other soldier wished to think of the ghosts. When they had joined battle at Leitzen, they must have had nigh 30,000 souls. Now, on the soil of their homeland, between disease and attrition, desertion, battle, and the old winter's chill, the roll calls put them at less than half that number for all the battles to come.

And all he could think was this: *For what?*

Madness was the only answer he could find.

The following day, after a late sleep, the army begrudgingly roused and marched to a more defensible spot a mere ten miles to the west—a forest-eaten place dotted with little lakes and smaller tributary rivers. Trees swallowed them up, and the mass finally began to pull together as the shadows descended.

Rurik closed his eyes and breathed in the piney musk of spring. For the first time in a long time, he felt as if he were home. A pity they would burn it all down.

Oberroth was somewhere in that mess, and it took them another day before they stumbled across it, as well as the army their informers had spoken of. Where the denseness of the underbrush broke and some manner of maneuverability opened in lanes of high green grass, points of fire struck the night, and gave the men away. *Like fireflies*, Rurik thought with little mirth. To the Idasians, fireflies were, after all, the messengers of the dead.

By daylight, they slunk from the trees like the draugar of legend. The two armies massed across from one another, rows upon rows of men, a grey blight on a green land. Sunlight slanted off mail hauberks as pennons and banners hung limp in the dead air.

Then the clamor began. Officers cried out commands, barking at the Bastard's army until the whole great beast began to churn forward. Cannons wheeled forward and the ground roared as the first shells sundered saplings and quaked the canopies above their heads, but all fell short of the enemy lines. Bawdier men hurled curses and raunchy jests, calling the men of Momeny women and whoresons and cowards, and some merely screamed, brandishing flesh and weapons both as they closed the distance with their foes. Rurik scowled at that. Months without the spoils of war—without any piece of war's release, in truth—could do that to an army.

Where Tessel's men looked almost eager for the fight, however, Rurik could see no signs of such impatience in their foe. Near their center, beside the flag of Momeny, Rurik spied the banner of a black goat, and he knew the first twist of fear's dagger in his bowels. His brief time with Baron Pordill had taught him one important lesson about the man: he was a master of discipline. That fact was reflected in the rigid lines of men at his command, stone-faced, pikes and rifles seamlessly shouldered. Whereas Tessel's soldiers milled about in a fashion more befitting a mob than an army, the Black Goat's men might as well have been an iron wall, patrolled by silent captains. Not one of them shouted back, or broke rank.

Despite the fact that Tessel's army dwarfed their own in number, the Black Goat's flock did not seem so much as rattled. While he could not spy any sign of horses among their ranks, the thought did not rest well with Rurik. But as Tessel rode out to address his troops, Rurik called Narve and his men to arms, and drew close to enough to bid the Company be ready, for he would follow as the Bastard commanded. He owed Tessel that much.

The wall of Momeny grew nearer and nearer, and he could feel a thousand eyes on him, waiting. The all-too-familiar weight in his stomach threatened illness as the trumpets blared. From the growing stench, others had not managed to contain it. Signs of the "honorable" deaths to come.

Naivety is a fact of childhood. Colors enter the world pre-tinted—the rose of a mother's praise, or the blackened horror of a particularly lumpy food. Staunch are the lambs in their presumption, but time batters all.

In his youth, Rurik had seen war as such trumpets, as armor glittering in the noontide sun, as men, all of a father's stride, scattering the villain like so much chaff. And this, from a boy that heard naught but truth from his father's own lips! How quickly, how horridly, true war annihilated that prospect. He had seen blood. He had watched men die. He did not wish to see it again. He could not understand how any of these mangy fools could either.

But boots marched in only one direction: onwards, ever onwards.

Their soldiers came on like a plague of grasshoppers. They hopped and howled and sprang, and every few seconds a long gun fired without order, and smoke belched, and even as Tessel cried for order, Rurik knew they did not hear him. Then he was among them, and the all too familiar chaos was his again.

The defenders saw no need to march for them. Even in the face of cannon, they ground spears and pikes and shields into the dirt and peppered the encroaching horde with arrows and bolts. When enough bodies drew within a few hundred yards, those same men retreated behind the shield lines, and from that entrenched mass emerged a scant few hundred in lines of three, to rotate through an effort of kneeling, crouching, and standing. It meant there would be no downtime for reloading, as they bore long guns, and from them the lead poured on with the horrid cry of its victims.

Rurik watched, dead even to the crack of the fire, as the first line of corpses plummeted to the earth. The priest-captain Narve, rattling his saber like a madman, was among these, and even at a distance, the boy could spy the instant the shot burst through the intestines and rent the man's life out with a scream. A mammoth pile of human fat and blood heaved to the earth, and was no more.

Rurik watched a man slip in another's brown water and felt his mouth go dry. Berric, at his side, cantered forward, twisting round about with his cavalry saber held high. "Forward! Forward!" Another line crumbled under the fire and more scattered as a handful of light cannon were rolled forward, their shots bursting among Tessel's ranks.

"Captain, we must be to the fight!" Around them, others were rolling forward, eyes already dead. Rurik turned, found Tessel wandered still along the lines, shouting orders and encouragements, a dozen shots no doubt primed for his head, but sufficing to whip by without so much as winding him. "Captain!" Berric, shouted, louder still. "It is time for blood."

If there were words, he did not know them. He had no encouragements, no condolences. Behind him, a paltry hundred men shifted uneasily, hands touching to the myriad weapons their motley band called to the bloodshed. Rurik raised a hand, weakly, and flitted it forward, and they moved to its motion. Berric cried out, "Glory to Assal," but Rurik could not tell if it carried or was swallowed in the inferno. He urged his horse forward and drew the pistol at his hip.

Only a few still had horses to call their own. Beyond that, there was nothing to call cavalry in the whole of their great horde. Nothing but infantry, and a few dozen scouts arrayed upon the vicious claws of their gryphon steeds. These Tessel held aloft, roving the edges of the lines. Rurik caught glimpses of their white tufted bulks darting through the trees. Tessel would spring them in the case of a rout, to hunt stragglers. So the people were left with nothing but a march. Bodies unto bodies, and all that would come of it was blood.

Rurik's horse stepped over the broken bodies of fellows, their faces gray and lost. They drew close enough to taste the ash on the wind. Then with a sharp cry, Berric raised his sword, and he and the men lurched forward through the splinters of bark and shards of stinging dirt.

Kicking his heels into his horse's ribs, Rurik spurred the beast at a trot, and hastened to join his men in the thick of it. As honorable men fought.

Gunfire continued only sporadically from his lines, but their heavier cannons pounded true. Rurik rasped as a cast iron ball surged through the air above his men, causing him to lean forward with the force of it, and he watched as that shot thudded into the dirt between the lines, only to bounce once, twice, and through a row of legs that simply disappeared beneath it.

When they drew within a few yards, the pounding of cannons stilled. Long gunners fired their final shots, then either turned their guns to clubs or discarded them for the weapons at their hips and at their backs, while reinforcements marched from behind, a wall of pikes and swords and axes moving to bar the widening lines of the march.

Due to the wearied but frenzied nature of their forces, Tessel's whole plan seemed to lie in their numbers—theirs was a three-pronged assault, arcing to cut into the much smaller forces of the margrave from three sides. Yet Scheyer, whatever else someone might say of the man, seemed to have realized this would be the case, and formed his people into an armored square, a formation Tessel called "the turtle." Those long gunners that withdrew from the frontlines made swift return to the corners of that square, to guarantee no side would go without support. Perhaps not the most morale-intensive position, for the sight it brought all sides, but deadly effective.

We will crash against it. Even as he watched, the first ranks struck the lines and the whole length of it seemed to shutter. Like a hammer on a breastplate, the mass reverberated, bent, but held. Then the blows traded. Shields heaved forward and the men of Momeny stabbed out.

We will be smashed against the walls and drown in our own fluids. Rurik drew his pistol and breathed through his mouth to escape the stench of shit and blood and saltpeter. All the margrave needed was this first move, to watch and to wait out a weak spot in their flailing.

"They need more men," Berric crooned in his ear. He only grunted in reply. They could see the place of impact then; they were within a stone's throw.

"Arms, to arms!" Berric cried, for Rurik had no voice, and he still was not sure they could hear him. He felt so small in the mass of men—could anything be heard in this? A final look about him showed faces etched with as much fear as resolution. These men would fight and they would die, but they would piss themselves doing it. The tongue near shriveled in his mouth.

Then his horse pitched up with a deafening whinny, and he felt his bladder shift. It reared, and he bucked against it, Berric shouting something to him and then—then he was on his back, staring up at the clouds and the leaves.

There was a boy there, in those leaves. Children flitted around him, naught but shadows above, and he knew that he was done. Ended. The girl stood over him, legs bowed to leave no part of him uncovered as she leaned to lock eyes. *"You know. You're always a little slow."* He tasted autumn and ginger and felt the blood of youth on his back. Some memories no creature could outgrow.

It was Berric that stood over him, and his loyal lieutenant seemed to flit to and fro between the shadows of that world, in some strange dance. "What…" he croaked, but his throat was dry. There was a weight on his leg, he realized, and all too slowly he saw the shape of his still horse, his own body awash in its lifeblood, and Berric—Berric wielded his saber in his dance, warding any that drew too close to Rurik. The crush of steel was so close.

Then he came again into the dew and grass, older, no wiser, stripped from waist up. The same girl, older, every bit as beautiful, though the body more so with time, lay tussled against him, plucking at the sparse hairs of his chest. *"These make you a man?"* Her face screwed with mockery. *"Manhood is quite the brittle thing, isn't it?"* He swatted at her, but she batted him off. *"Perhaps that is why women are the stronger,"* she said, swinging a leg about to straddle him. *"Our age comes in blood. Yours is naught but flakes."*

When he opened his eyes, there was nothing around him. No one, save a few bannermen crouched like squatters over what he assumed to be his corpse. They pressed at the horse, and he could feel it through throbs of his leg. There was wetness on his cheek. His hand rose and fell—too late, he realized: tears. His head rolled and he tried to sit up.

One of the men loosed a little shout and took him by the arm, helping him to rise. The other pushed the last of the horse off its master's leg. "Ser? Can you hear me, ser?" He blinked over the man's shoulder—he did not recognize his face—to the trees. Shapes flitted through the murk, and the fires belched black clouds into the sky, lit still further by the splinters of bark. Yet the lines had moved far beyond him, and only one banner fluttered between those shadows.

The two-pronged gryphon of Idasia, the crown still bright and gold atop its writhing heads. Sunset's purples and oranges caught the colors of its threads and made them shine, and he knew then that somehow they had won.

Stragglers were loping away into the west to lick their wounds. A tide of gryphons swept after them, descending on men with beak and claw. A great cry went up as the last of them scattered, leaving their dead and their dying behind to bloodthirsty swords. Pockets held out, but only pockets, and they were swept away before the tide. Rurik watched this and whispered a prayer to whatever spirit might take it, sinking back against his sword in the dust.

The soldier snapped his fingers before his face, then blanched at some new and distant terror. He retreated, as Rurik wrenched around to see what shade had come to take its dues.

Alviss caught him, but Rurik only smiled up at the man. He wanted orders. Reassurance. But Rurik had neither to offer. Only silent exhaustion stirred as the army turned its eyes to the open streets so near at hand. Through the smoke, he could see the outlines of buildings. Oberroth. The hollers rose to a fevered pitch, but all Rurik could think was: *He did it. He actually did it.*

* *

Essa was already in the streets of Oberroth—a name she had taken off a merchant fleeing with all his possessions—when the rest of the army began to trickle in.

She and her fellow scouts—Rowan among them—had flanked the whole of the battle, picking skirmishes where they could, but kept purposefully from the thick of it. Gedler had been wroth at the prospect, wanting to fight and to die with what he called "the fury of the divine," and had taken most of their band to Father Narve's collection of the horde. Their loss had bothered Essa not at all. As the direction of the battle became apparent, Rowan suggested they lay an ambush in the town, where they might intercept any soldiers seeking to shed arms and armor and blend in with the populace. It had been a sound plan, though none of the enemy obliged them.

Residents barred their doors as they swept into the streets. It was not a large place, Oberroth, but large enough to host the region's market, if not the walls that might have spared it. As Essa picked her way through empty streets, she found that it reminded her of Verdan, only with more sunlight. That thought disturbed her more than she knew it had reason to.

When the soldiers came, the others at first rejoiced, and went to them with open arms. Essa dared a smile with them, for the victory, if not the men at its helm. *We are here,* she dared to think. *We are here at last, and even armies cannot deny us.* Rowan threw an arm about her shoulders and hugged her tight, and at first she thought it was for the same reasons she smiled.

But the men came on like something out of scripture. Like rabid, howling dogs, or some orjuk horde. They weren't soldiers anymore, only beasts. They fell upon the streets of Oberroth and began to tear it apart.

Before the march, Voren had held her hand. It seemed a sweet gesture, so unsuited to the bloody work that was to come. It was all he had wanted. To hold her hand and tell her…tell her…but she had not let him. In his tender mercies of days prior, he had done enough. She kissed his cheek instead and promised to return. Then she had left, not knowing if that was a promise she could keep. Nor what that kiss would mean to the addled baker.

How could she reconcile that, and this?

She watched men sunder doors and set thatched roofs aflame. Men she had served beside for months on end, drawn steel with, suddenly turned that steel upon wood and flesh, and pawed at anything that glittered. Coins were carried into the street. Necklaces. Keepsakes. Women wailed against them, as men fought or fled their coming. Children were skewered in the dirt. The streets flooded with the misguided—the ones who had remained.

Blood stirred with the bodies in the street.

They were people. Her people. Their people. Not that it mattered whose they were, but the thought that they could do this to their own—it turned her stomach.

Is this war's truth?

"By Assal." The man at her side blanched, his all too green fingers shuddering on the hilt of his mace. "There can be no mercy for this."

She turned on him, finding a sudden fury inside. "And that is how we know there is no Maker, fool. Come on." These others followed her as wide-eyed lambs to slaughter.

There was a notion stirred in her. *Blood,* that little voice cried at the back of her head, *they would drown our earth in blood!* A savior, perhaps a martyr, that was what they needed—was not the Church always on about such things? She sprang between the houses, set to a frenzy, and made for the first band with whom she locked eyes.

They had broken the shutters off a simple log home and forced their way inside. Since, they had emerged, tossing wife and husband before them. They laughed as they pulled at daggers, and one in a flopped cap clicked back the hammer on his pistol. How she wished that they were Gorjes! She searched for sign, but nothing marked them—their clothes were ragged, their faces varying through the lines of age, in every way mere men, save the darkness that haunted their eyes.

So close. She raised a shout, and drew within a few yards. Before she realized it her dagger was in her hand, and one of the men had turned to meet her, eyes clouding in sudden uncertainty, but the others had not noticed. The woman, a townie wife by the somewhat finer patching of her dress, she threw her arms around her husband as they circled him, and begged them to spare his life. *Please, no!* Essa could hear the echo of her own scream, but it mattered not. Laughing, the soldier with a hat rested the pistol on her shoulder, and where it touched her husband, shot the man dead.

So near belched the flames that they scorched the sleeve of the woman's dress, mingling with the blood her screams answered. That same foul beast kissed her next with the pistol's butt, and should have descended on her prone and weeping body, clutching still to the fleeting lifeblood of her husband, save that Essa cleared the last few yards.

The youngest of them stumbled from her path, and in the clear, she hurdled her tiny frame into the far larger soldier's bulk. He let out a startled shout as her legs connected and he was flung over his victim, clipping the dirt face-first. He was up quick, for a man of graying years, but Essa was right behind him, foot to his groping wrist and dagger at his rasping throat. She might have cut. The voice screamed at her to cut, but she held that beast back.

That was what separated her from them. She realized, too late, she had left her back exposed, but at the huffs of her own approaching companions, she lost whatever fear remained of these startled men. The old man fidgeted under her steel, and carefully drew up his hands.

Her eyes darkened to the point of storms as she demanded, "You would take them? Your own countrywomen?" The cries still lit the air—and more wails, growing all around.

The thought—or her tone, more like—seemed to sit ill with the soldier. He began to squirm, but he still managed some small act of defiance, reminding her: "The men take it as part of their battle right. To the victor, as they say." When Essa's fingers tightened against the hilt of her dagger, the man edged back. "It's true, mum! Ask any man."

"Get from my sight," she spat. The dagger lifted, though the little voice howled. The man was fortunately quick to oblige.

In his wake, she raged, taking her wrath upon the nearest crates and all within. *Property. It's all just property*, she thought, as her foot smashed open a crate. The tent, the camp, and even the women. It wasn't rape if they had earned it. It wasn't rape if it was their property.

When a hand touched her, she whirled, ready for a fight, but as the hand fell away, Rowan stood before her, his own face lined with grim portent. She felt her resolve crumble—briefly—and the child within remorse, but she would not let it out. She stiffened and pulled back, demanding what he wanted. But her cousin only shook his head. He looked to her companions, brandishing blades as the rapacious soldier sauntered off, shielding the grieving wife. Then Rowan turned back to the town, as if looking for something. Some sign.

Essa snarled and twisted on the still prone woman. She took her by the arm and forcibly lifted it from her husband, shaking her as such. "Get gone, woman," she said—too harshly, but nothing else would be heard. The woman, broken, only sobbed the louder. "Get you gone, if you've any sense in your head. They'll be back, or others. Leave him. This whole place is soon for the torch; he'll not be left for the worms." If the woman heard her, she gave no sign, head rocking back and forth to the murmurs of the dead man's name.

With some small cruelty, she thrust the woman at one of her fellows and asked him to get her to her feet. She did not need to ask twice.

Her dark gaze swept over the rest of the street, judging the best spot to intercede herself. The question of standing aside, of disengaging, was not even in her mind. That would make her something less. An accomplice, somehow. She scarcely noticed that Rowan had turned back, eyes carefully fixing her.

"Should we tell someone?" another of the scouts—a paunchy, moss-bearded hunter named Gregor—asked. Words did not even seem worth the effort of calling out his ignorance. Who was there to tell? Who was there that could not possibly already know?

Accomplices. The world is filled with them, in silence or in shouts.

Yet the words were enough to shift her gaze. Just enough to catch the tightening of Rowan's knuckles, the paleness so sheer it might have been snow. "By God," was all that uttered. The world widened around her, though she was scarcely even aware of Gregor's flight.

It wasn't even rape. What they beheld went beyond that. Men stood about the body, framed in back by the logs of a tenderly built home. Cedar, perhaps—whatever was near at hand—yet the wood, while firm, was haunted by the rot of flesh before it.

On the ground, the boy could not have been more than ten summers. His hair was a wisp of blond, his cheeks still smooth in the way of babes and blades. A whole squad of ragged soldiers had stripped him and tied him to the shaggy legs of what could only be a plow horse—his own family horse, most like. The horse's legs pranced before the menagerie of iron, sensing and not wishing what was to come. It was in the beast's eyes. The fear—fear echoed in the mismatched pleas of that boy's own. Such vivid color.

She had known it once before. It twisted in her gut and before she knew it she was forward, daggers leading.

When the nobles played their games, it was always the nameless who suffered, but this—this was too much.

Rowan caught her, wheeled her back to face him. "They'll kill you, you stupid girl." He snapped. "Can't you see he is already dead?"

When had the cries gone soft? When had the horse whinnied with the cut of the hot iron? It bounded through the street, circling the place both had once

302

called home. Men, or visions of men, they did but laugh. And red was the only color.

She started, but he drew her close, wrenching at the wrist that held the dagger. "I won't," she hissed, but his grip only tightened. The dagger wavered, and so did she. Pleading, she looked at him, and saw the tears answered in his own eyes. He caught her and drew her close, shaking his head as if to a child's frantic question. He drew her close, into his arms, and held her as he had when she was but that child, and all this blood, but another blackened eye.

"Turn away, Essa. There is nothing for them now."

* *

Ash drifted through the trees, coating the bark and the soil with an unearthly pallor. Men gagged on it as they loped toward the heart of the flames. Yet they could not give this to war. This was something altogether darker.

It gagged Rurik. As he shuffled nearer, supported on Alviss's shoulder and in step with a dozen other wary and excited faces, he tasted the flames and shuddered for what they meant. It was the same smell that clung to the figure of their guide—it draped from the moss of his beard and ran in reams from the rolls of his arms. Pig—it tasted like pig. Yet as they neared, buildings naught but dancing lights between the brush, the reality drew so much worse.

They were inhaling people.

Oberroth was not like Hell. It was the model to which all others aspired. Not sated by plunder, several men had stripped three girls naked and tied them across barrels in the village square. Laughter—that vile sound!—dared drift between them as they did it. Still, it was the silence that haunted most. The silence and the cold, dead looks. As if screams and tears alike had been drained from the women's battered forms, they lay still as men hitched mail and breeches both to grunt into them.

The banner of the twin gryphons wafted in the ashes of its homeland, bodies scattered beneath its wings, and the men cheered it on. *Is this vengeance?* Tessel's voice called through memory—*"the first step."* Then what is the end? He shuddered away, retching, but his cohort went on as if in trace—all save Alviss, who stood at his side and never left. Likes times of old.

"She is in there, you know." Alviss's voice carried like a mother bear's mournful growl.

303

Essa...Rurik wiped at his chin as the queasiness ebbed. "Is there anything we can do?"

"Rowan is with her."

As if that answered everything, Rurik nodded regardless, shambling to his feet. *Oh Essa, Essa, what will this sight do to you?* He could not watch this, but Essa—Essa had proved she could manage her own affairs. She would emerge. She had to. Yet the guide waited, red-eyed, waving them on.

At the edge of darkness he could see them, child and protector, colors muted by the drifting shower.

He looked to her as the heads rose. Was it hope, they saw in him? Or something less? The eyes were hollow now.

"We tried to stop them," the hunter-guide explained.

When they were near enough to be heard, Essa looked him dead in the eye for the first time in many moons. Death clung to her hair and made a swamp of her features. "It is time to go." A voice, so soft he could scarcely hear it. Like it had nothing left to offer. "Will he let you?" she asked, and he was uncertain, for a moment, if it was a wraith that now stood before him.

Dead men moved the living. A woman wailed, to the crunch of many boots.

"We are not slaves. We can—we can..."

A small cloud descended with the shaking of her weary head. "Aren't we?" The words set a quake to his frail shoulders. How long had he missed this voice? "This is your bed. And you will do what you will with it. You always have."

Say my name.

"He would burn it all. You see that, don't you?" She bit the edge of her lip, held back the sound that dwelt there. Rowan's arms enclosed her tighter, but her cousin's eyes bore sharp into Rurik. Condemnation dwelt there.

Where once there had been fire, this man's hair and voice, too, had been laden by the ash. Still, the power beckoned: "Long ago, you made a choice. Do you even remember it now?"

"He knew not," Alviss began, but Rurik held a hand to his words, and they fell away.

Absently, he noted a few of his men had trickled off, moving to join the ruckus. "Essa." Her eyes lowered from him, and from herself, deep down into the earth. The others closed a protective ring about them. "Essa, I have tried. You won't listen. He won't listen. Everyone changes and—and I have never asked you to listen to me, to follow me, but, I just…" The weight of the world and all its false promises lay upon his shoulders. In his long silence, he had let it rise. Rage and bitterness so deep he could not know if it was for her or the bodies or Tessel or the whole goddamned mess of a world before his eyes.

This woman stood before him—a woman he had known from scraped knees and climbing trees—and yet he could not say what he wanted to say. It was all muddled in so much waste. Words could not suffice. It was to this they had come. Yet still she asked: would the Bastard let him go?

There was nothing else. Nothing but that little town, somewhere to the south, where a boy and girl still played across the fields of memory. He took a step back, and another. Silence unmanned him.

He twisted around and ran for Tessel's banner as swiftly as his throbbing leg could manage. Pain no longer seemed to matter.

* *

Blood was a sinister thing, ever plotting escape from its bodily host.

How many more scars? Roswitte swatted at the relentless cloud of black flies that attacked her face and neck. Yet the gesture aggravated her side, and soon she clutched it anew, feeling her own life ebb warm and wet against her fingertips where the shrapnel had caught her. *Goddamned swamp.* If only she had time, she might have found the needle and thread it would take for her to bind it.

As things were, infection was the least of her worries. At least the bullet had missed her. It was the trees that seemed to have it out for her.

She could not stop. *I will not stop.* There were no breaths to take. *I will not stop.* It was a limping gait, but dead men would rise before she would be left behind. *I. Will. Not. Stop.* Ivon and the rest were lengths ahead, but she could still see them.

When the shield wall had broken, it had not been so clear. Screaming hordes struck like battering waves, but these waves had crumbled the cliff. Traitors swarmed over the gaps in the lines, and forced them wider, and still more came, sweeping away men and banners both. They had been strong. A clutch of dust for all that gathered before them, but they had been strong, their ranks stacked tight, and then they shattered into pockets of men desperate to fend off the spears that hungered for them.

Those in the rear ranks began to flee. She and the other archers remained for one final volley, and the air had thrummed with snapping strings as barbed, triangular broadheads tore into their enemy. At such a range, they could not have missed, and many a traitor had made their final prayers whistling through an arrow in the throat. Some men, by then, had dragged up mauls and axes, and made to give a final stand, and Roswitte might have joined them, save for her lord's voice that beckoned her from the field.

Then the shot, the splintering, the searing choir—and flight.

Simply: they had lost the battle. All the rest was detail.

Now she scanned the trees, silent between the leaden green. Shapes moved, some near, some far, and the voices carried—the echo and the clouds, they were too great to establish truth. It had been the same since the start of the battle, when Ivon had whispered praise of her to Scheyer, and Roswitte had stepped forth from the lines and joined the other bowmen for the opening shots. A woman. A soldier.

There had been hope, then. Foolish, on reflection.

All the while, Ivon had said that Witold was coming. Witold would reinforce them. Yet Witold had not come. No one had come. Only a messenger, bearing word that Witold and all the rest had stopped at the edge of Jaritz's borders with Momeny, and slunk back, as if to save themselves the slaughter. So the levees of Momeny had fought and scattered alone.

She wanted to hate him for it, but Ivon's only fault was hope. She could not begrudge those that could still summon such a thing.

Yet all it came to was this: dusky figures streaming through a smoking hell. Sometimes crying out, all too often dying in silence.

A distant crackle of saltpeter spun her, searching. "To the south," Ivon shouted, but which way was south? There was a nearing ring, the shrill peal of armor. Somewhere to the right. Coming. Her head lurched and, cursing, she sought out the moss at the bark of the trees, but they were bare. A stick cracked. Something shuffled quickly. She rounded, bow notched and leading. There were shapes, too near for comfort.

She cried out, but at the same moment, their hunters sprang. Leather-clad men with crossbows and steel had gotten ahead of them, and they moved to surround Ivon's group. Nearly a dozen. A sharp bark from Vardick sent the others reeling to meet the threat, but even from where she stood, Roswitte knew it would be the death of them. Crossbows did not miss at such a range; best simply to take as many as possible before the hour fell.

Muscles straining, she pulled her bow back to full draw, and stooped to a pained crouch. Then she whispered a prayer to a certain little girl, too far away, she hoped, to know this breed of madness. She could still see the brightness of little Anelie's face the night they told her a brother had returned. It warmed her, when little else could. *Was it he that brought this curse on us?*

When the ringing turned to her, with the sharp, rhythmic rattles only a horse could muster, she spun in place, tracking the sound. There he rode: Death himself, shouting, clad in mail and shield like the knights of old, blackened to the point of pitch by the smog of gunfire.

Funny, she thought, *I did not know the Bastard had any left.*

"Put up your arms, men!" Ivon boomed through the confusion. "We mean no ill. Listen, we only—"

The little bear of Verdan let a slender bodkin fly. Aimed not for the armored man, but for his modestly clad steed, the arrow tore into the horse's expansive shoulder as both hesitated at the sight of her, and drove both horse and rider crashing forward. The horse squealed through its death throes, but the man—the man gave only shocked grunts as he tumbled through the woods.

The crack of iron's welcome issued behind her, and Roswitte leaned up first on one leg, then two. Trading another arrow for a knife, she advanced on the fallen figure mere feet away, a heap of armor prone in the fledgling flowers. As she came over him, she flicked out her skinning knife and kicked up the visor of his helmet, meaning to make it quick—and in his end resolve another nightmare that had so long tormented—when a gauntleted hand flashed out and caught that very leg. Her other hip—the wounded one—could not compensate against the sudden imbalance, and with a shrill bleat, she crashed beside the knight.

Dead. The fall stunned her just long enough that the flash of metal took her by surprise. She howled at the madness—the blooded rage stirring in her breast—when it lay flat against her heart. *By mercy, be swift, damn you!* A panting, dirt-streaked face slithered upon her, visor still askew, and the knitted brows, the bright blue eyes—these became the beacons of a memory she thought dead. Blade tapped flesh and the cracked but full familiar lips parted around salvation.

"You killed my horse," the dust knight said. Sprawled in the dirt, she mused, the dandy finally looked the name.

The knight looked sharply on his fellows and cried: "Sheathe! Sheathe! There is no blood to be had here, damn you."

Still there rang a strangled cry, and then the grizzled voice of the Brickheart seized the field utterly: "Let her go, and let the lord go, sellsword. Then I won't need this boy-child's neck."

Bayer. She pressed off her back to take the scene in cross-eyed. Bayer was the boy's name. A page, or like enough. She remembered him from their travels to the field at Leitzen—an idealistic youth, pepper-haired and quick with a drink. Less than sixteen summers, and now he and his skittish tongue knelt at the edge of a sword, whimpering, his own pig-sticker of a blade knocked far and wide. All the while his brothers in arms tightened their circle about the uncertain band of refugees, itching for an angle on Vardick. There were at least two of her own down that Roswitte could see—only wounded, she hoped.

"She is not my prisoner, nor are any of you, fool, so he need not be yours. Damn it men, put down your steel, for Bayer's sake!"

The dagger lifted, but before the Asanti dust knight could spare another breath, Roswitte slapped him away and snatched up her skinning knife. Men at war—all were too far gone to trust, no matter what the word or face. Flexibility—that was survival.

Ser Ensil, shadows framing the contours of his square jaw, looked startled by the sudden turn, but it passed swiftly into sorrow. His own blade kept to the earth, and he sufficed merely to lean back, offering precious inches from Roswitte's knife. For the moment, she allowed it.

His voice was low as it came on again. "You are hurt, lady. As are a great many others here today. But say what you will of the man—the deed is done, and the battle as well. If you hold me so, my men will do you nothing ill, as well you should know, but I am not the only hunter on these fields."

She let the inches between knife and skin shrink, but the man did not flinch away a second time. It was a weary speech, but not one of which she cared to be reminded. Better the killer at hand than the one afar. *One must take each man's motives to the scales, and weigh them on the merits of the moment. To measure on the merits of our own self—the ends may never reach the same.* Kasimir had taught her that.

Longing grew keen at the echo of that memory, and pulled taut the chains of her limbs. She looked at Ensil through grim shades indeed, for all that he had done for her. She could feel the blood worming its way out. If life was longing, perhaps the blood longed for freedom as well.

"You kill a man's horse, then you—"

Some shadow of the man's warrior nature flashed through that hard voice. She knew many that would have shuddered under it. But Verdan was a town of hard men. What was one more old soldier?

"Yes," she answered quickly, softly. "And don't think I wouldn't stick you, either. As you say, the battle's done—and we've no desire to linger in it longer than blood's already demanded." She thought of his smiling face peering down at her reflection in the well water. The gentle touch. Concern. How his eyes had fallen at that first mention of Fallit. *So long. So long.* "Thank you, ser, but need you minding that your blade and mine stand firm at opposite lines?"

"Roswitte!" came another, louder bark. Ivon. "Get to your feet and get to us. We would best be served in leaving now."

"Scurrying off again with your tail between your legs?" Her eyes flitted sideways, to track the spearman brandishing his weapon between her comrades and the trees. Bulbous chin, but tempered body. Cranst. Another dust knight. He would not let them go on such a note.

Even though her gaze turned back on Ensil—she could not give him opening—she could hear the shuffle of grass that likely spelled out Vardick's motions. That or one of Ivon's knightly friends. *Knights and their honor. It never does any of them well.*

Ensil quirked an eyebrow as she struggled to rise. He even offered her a hand. "Well? Does Cranst have the right of it?"

To Verdan, of course. She thought it, but did not say it. He did not need to know it. But they would be gone. They would see their own trees again or they would die for the effort. Condemnation or no.

For all the sternness to the knight's voice, his shoulders rolled and his back sank slightly. Roswitte caught his wrist and let each have measure of the other's strength. She felt the muscles of his forearm stiffen—weighted by years of sword and armor—but there was no flex to measure ill intent. His eyes looked her straight, perfect and blue. Not hazed, as Fallit's had once been. They almost dared her hand to conclusion.

On her feet, she anchored herself behind the knight and drew Ensil up, taking, for the first time, a full survey of the scene. Of the two men down, one clutched his side, and the other lay still. The one that still lay among the waking gritted his teeth and seemed to breathe only in little puffs, but his armor had likely spared his life. As she prodded Ensil forward, her blade quavered at the sight of the second man. A soldier. An honest soldier. He had followed them all the way from Verdan. A son of soldiers. Too young for this. The blood ran from his head and pooled about him like a halo.

One could never forget the enemy at hand.

As they crossed within a hair's breadth of the ring of dust knights and sellswords, Roswitte lifted her dagger to their leader's armpit and let the threat hang. It was not a long blade, but it was long enough. It did not take much, with matters of the heart.

The men split their attentions between the boy who knelt at the end of the Brickheart's blade, and her. They were like little points of light, deepening the shadows. She pressed closer to Ensil, and kept their steps short but quick. Things could turn too easily.

For all the danger, though, Ivon stepped readily—nay, pressed—from his own ring of fighters and crossed to her in two easy strides. Every vein in the Brickheart's neck seemed to bulge at that, but Ivon did not seem to care. He laid his hand on Roswitte's wrist and pressed it back, while standing but a pace from Ensil. The two men watched one another cautiously, but Ivon's words were for her alone.

"You are brave, old friend, but this is not the moment. Down, down, I say to all—or this will worsen before it betters."

Ensil nodded and addressed the others even as Roswitte's arm fell to her side, chastened. "He's the right of it. You heard me before. I will not repeat myself." And with one sweeping look, the weapons lowered for the first time. All but Vardick's, anyway.

"Vardick?"

Verdan's personal ogre grimaced. But for him, an order was an order. He snatched his blade away from the boy's throat, but gave him a hard enough boot to the back that Roswitte was certain a few cracked ribs would come of it. *Better than death.* Some of his fellows caught him. About him they formed a wedge, but their weapons stayed lowered. For the moment.

"You are a curious ambusher, dust knight," Ivon said, wheeling back on Ensil as soon as the boy was freed. While the lightness of his breath seemed to pull some of the tension away, his hard eyes, and the slightest lilt of tone in the utterance of Ensil's title still secured humanity in him—for therein lurked a petty sort of disregard. "You hound us, and we rush into it, yet…as soon as your horse stumbles," he added with a knowing glance to Roswitte, "you call it off. Not the actions of the wild and hungry few. Not the actions of a sellsword."

Ensil inclined his head in slight deference. "Ser, sellsword or knight, not all minds bestir the same notes. I meant you no ill. Not once I knew you. Not—"

Peace or no, few things stood before a madman's charge. Roswitte looked up in time to see Vardick's lumbering stride. The red face. The wild eyes. She winced at what was coming. Ensil's words cut off abruptly as Vardick thrust himself between lord and knight, catching the dust knight by the arm and shoving him back. One hand still clutched tight to his sword, and Ensil's people shuffled forward more than a few paces.

"That why George bleeds? Bolt to the head. Seems awful ill to me."

He puffed up his chest like a challenging bird. Roswitte felt her own fingers tighten about the hilt of her knife, but she knew not why. Reflex, she told herself. No soul tangled willingly with the Brickheart. Ensil only looked away, not meeting his gaze. Yet Ivon had enough, and his shieldman as well—a frown anchored Jörg's pale cheeks down even through the braids of his beard as he shoved Vardick back, to the soft-spoken tune of Ivon's: "Enough."

Something exploded through the bark of a nearby tree. *Long gun?* They all stumbled, all scattered. Composure crumbled and they ducked low, circling away with eyes to the shapes in the gloom. No one neared, though many drifted through the periphery. They needed to move. The others, coming swiftly to the same conclusion, put aside war for a moment and glided forward, deeper into the woods, like shades.

The dust knight fell in behind her, a hand to the small of her back. She tried to shrug it off, but it returned a moment later. His eyes were on Ivon, but he guided her forward, helped her to keep moving despite the ache in her side. Leaves scattered across the ground crunched underfoot; soot and pellets had smothered the earth with them. She looked back, into the haggard faces of the dust knight's people. She would have fallen behind, among them, or further still, if he had not helped. The thought infuriated. The thought stilled. She did not like the contradiction.

"Where are we going?" the Brickheart asked.

"West. Just keep moving west," Ensil said.

Yet Ivon, twisting them about, proclaimed: "South, you fools. We go nowhere but south. Let the west be to your people, knight. It already forsakes the rest of us."

Ensil stood a moment, uncertain. He followed Ivon's gaze, then turned back toward Oberroth. To the battle. His lips drew taut and he nodded slightly. "We will take you. So long as you never again call them *my people*."

So it was decided. Cradling the wounded between them, the party was slower than it ought to have been. Light came in slants through the boughs and smoke, and made the path hard to know. More than once they had to draw low, waiting for one band or another to skitter shrieking past. But Roswitte trusted Ivon. He knew the land as she knew it, and he had the head she no longer possessed to work it. She closed her eyes. Everything seemed to spin, just a little, but time would not freeze.

Still, the wails in the distance. A woman's wails. Sounds that rent the blood to ice.

"What are you doing here," she snapped at the dust knight, letting the sound of her fury cover all the rest. "You cannot convince me the Bastard has enough to pay your purse."

It seemed to startle him. It was in the hesitating flinch before words came, the uncertain creak of the next forward step. "Pay? Lady, it has been longer than last we met that I have known the bliss of weighted coin. Or my stomach, food." He shifted his hand, to take it a little further from her bloodied side. "Yet where else might we have been? Our other options, I am afraid, fled quite sudden in the night—with all the horses, at that."

She would not look at him. "You might have come."

"You might have told us. Then…" The rest need not be spoken. But at the time, what other choice had there been? "What would have happened had we chosen flight by foot? Traitors, you see, they meet the long end of the spear. We would not have been the first."

"Perhaps. You did have *a* horse."

"A?"

"One."

Ensil smiled. "Ah."

Another scream. Growing further away. She could almost taste the blood in her mouth. Long moments passed of frenzied running. No sounds but the rattle of mail and the clatter of boots and leaves in the golden light. Somewhere, there was an edge to all this. Then they would need horses. She thought of the horse bowing to her arrow. If the nobles had pilfered the horses in their own flight, then that steed was more valuable than she might have imagined. She brushed Ensil's hand away anew.

After a moment, he spoke again. "What they do in Oberroth—it was not the first." His pale eyes kept forward.

"No?" She spat in the dirt. "Well, we did keep all the horses."

"And left us war. You cannot judge men the same in war. Not for a horse. It is not the same."

Not the same as Fallit's face, carved into the bark. Every knot seemed to conceal those haunted eyes, a silent testament to their flight. Perhaps he knew they returned home. Perhaps it was an omen. Another woman might have told herself "if only she had been stronger." Yet in those terrible moments, Roswitte only wondered how much farther until home. Their home.

Too long.

Chapter 14

There was a pair of horses by the river. Witold's men. No colors stuck to the saddles, or the men beyond, but the hunter knew them. For the way they moved. For the way they dressed.

But they were not his prey, and he moved on. Smoke slithered through the trees above his head. Hearthfires burned low this time of night, but they always burned in Verdan. Some said it was a soldier tradition. Others Surinian. Folk superstition was all. Still, one could not dismiss it. The world was not made for logical men.

Tracks were many. His tracks were few. He paused a moment at the trumpeting of a rooster, and squinted high through the trees as if waiting for the sun to spring. After a moment, he bundled the fur of his cloak tighter against his shoulders and continued on.

Witold had not been in Gölingen. Paltry sums of men scraped the walls like ghosts haunting the memories of their lives. People had not been kind, nor open as once they had been. They kept their heads tucked and hastened down the thin lanes without voice. When pressed, they spoke only in half-whimsical terms of some terrible army sweeping out of Effise.

Hellspawn. Little men claimed the Effisians had made a pact with Mordazz. He had scoffed at the time—half the reason, perhaps, their hospitality was so small—for they could weep that it was vengeance all they wanted, but he knew as any sensible man knew that Effise had nothing left remotely capable of such a feat. War had already been decided. They merely set about flags now.

Still, he had not been careful enough. At the gates, Mariel had awaited his return. It was not finery that gave Jaritz's Master of Words away. It was the hollow pits of his eyes. Dark rings. The mole on his cheek. Dressed in simple wool and cloth, head covered by cap, neither clothes nor motions gave away anything. He moved with the crowd, never against, as he had once taught an all too eager youth. When he came he simply seemed to slide from the crowd, and Isaak was caught before he ever knew he was stalked.

What followed was confirmation: Witold had headed north, but the final, confusing word was that his armies held at the border. As if pressing beyond that invisible line would commit them to a place from which their flesh might never find home again. The Bastard's army, or the Holy Army, as the whispers of peasant Farrens had begun to call it, marched roughshod through the northlands.

He had felt a stirring at the name, though his heart was as blank to it as a heart could be. Closer, was all he recognized. If one was closer, than so was the other.

From Gölingen, he had headed north. Frost lingered on the trees, left them moist and chill even this far into spring. Beech and pine, weeping ash. There were memories here. Too many. He locked them away for another time. As all things. He peered through the drooping boughs of their present, to the house where the hearthfire burned low indeed.

Though he circled the town, its silent streets as ample ward as any wall, he would not go within. These people were known to him. Their successes. Their struggles. But human was human, and though hospitality would be forthcoming, the tongues would wag. It was the nature of people to gossip of things more interesting than routine. He would not linger. There was but one thing he needed.

In Gölingen, that had not included his wife. Longing had compelled him forward, but he knew it would only distract. Lead astray. That, and every time he thought of her, it issued forth such an ache in his heart to think that neither she nor her father had fought for that little girl—compartmentalized. Lost. He had shared his words with Mariel, and then he had gone. Mariel had asked after the hunter's daughter, and he had told him. Isaak did not ask about Nesse.

The army was what mattered. Where was it headed? Even Mariel had not known that. There was talk of a battle to the north, of discontent to the west— "Be careful," the old spy had said, clutching his arm like a wayward youth. "Remember to whom your loyalties lie." They had parted on that note, and only farmers and caravans had painted him clearer imagery.

The Hammer of Idasia had broken. The Bastard still walked. And brothers and bastard alike turned south. More the traitors, for it. For what man would lead such madness home? Yet when he closed his eyes, he nearly choked on his laugh. It was all Rurik had ever done.

The garrison at Verdan was depleted. Whether it was for lack of a lord, or supplication to a token show of Witold's own, the manse beside the river was all but empty. Ghosts on ghosts. A handful of men walked the walls. He scaled them and came inside unnoticed. A few torches burned, but the darkness seemed to suit the place now. He took one from its holds and steadied himself for what needed to be done.

One could never forget, but one couldn't let past guide future. This was a necessary evil.

A dozen heads lifted to meet him as he stepped inside, but not one bayed in fear or alarm.

By midday, the servants stared at the remnants of stables and pen alike. It must have seemed Mordazz Himself had swept the gates by night and stolen forth the animals. If the Brickheart still reigned there, he would have had every man on duty flogged. But he was gone. They all were. The hunter ran his hands through a wolfhound's fur, and turned back into the trees, heading north.

* *

Voren sat at the edge of darkness, the tanned skin of his arms illuminated in the flickers of the dead. It made him shudder in waking. There was no chance for sleep. When the dreams came—and they always came—dead men reached for him, weeping even as they pulled the flesh in strips from his bones. He shared their tears, but it seemed they were deaf to any but their own pain. It was like they horded it, shoring it up for the final feast.

When he came back into himself, he found the stub of his pinky throbbed. Ghost pains. His father, too, had known them, before disease had carried him away for good. But he had never known such horror as this.

Men and women burned on the pyres. Another lay at town's edge, having crawled from the field, picking and shoving his own guts back toward the wound from which they had spilled, as though the end were a cleanly thing. He would die cursing. They all did.

"What you looking at, baker boy?" a drunken soldier roared from the nearest pyre. "Get to it, then. Dead don't strip 'emselves. And they sure don't wobble 'em ownselves to that afterburn."

Robbery of the dead. Among the most heinous of sins. Yet he bent himself to the task and dragged another corpse to the fire. Any that had not fought were put to the task before they could eat and drink. They would labor all night, if need be, while the killers grew fat on their spoils. He was thankful for gloves, as he was thankful for the distraction. Though the stench made him ill, and the touch, the sight—nauseated as he was, he never could have kept food down. No matter how hungry.

Perhaps most disturbing was that time seemed to render even this evil null. Hours to the repetition, and he felt almost nothing. *Mayhap you already walk the fields of Hell.* The thought struck him more than once. Then the dead finger throbbed anew and he knew it could not be so.

Did war break men? Or did it merely shed those outer layers—knead the thing into its purest, darkest form? Voren didn't know anymore. They were all dying bit by bit, food and drink aside, and he thought that by simply not fighting he could spare himself, but his soul was shedding with them, moment by moment. Sometimes it was a struggle just to breathe. Few were the things that kept the breaths flowing. But they were there.

All of these people—they deserve to die.

When he had shoveled the last of the pile into the flames, he passed the soldiers without comment. Blissfully, they let him go. Some sot had found seven casks of untapped beer in the basement of a local tavern. They did not care to argue any longer. That they had killed the tavernkeep and driven off his help—no matter. Knives made short work of the barrels.

He walked along through this desert of forsaken souls, trying not to choke on the stench of human waste. *A necessary evil.* This was what he told himself when it all became too much. A child, dirt-caked, stood at the edge of his vision. Dark-haired, brown-eyed, Idasian to her core. He stood a moment, watching her in the hazy remnants of a town, and he wondered: *what have we done to ourselves?* Necessary. He repeated the word like a mantra, but he could not believe in it. It lacked conviction.

Then again, what convictions could a starving man truly muster?

He wandered like this, ethereal, apart from the goings on yet compelled to them, until the shadows grew long on the earth. At some point, he stripped his gloves off and bent to the rocks, scourging his hands against them until the skin reddened and tore. When he looked up again, he found dirt packed into the scars of those hands. A tent stood before him. Rowan crouched low before it, watching him, and Voren sat, blinking the red-haired fool into existence.

There was no mirth, even in this creature, any longer. He had been in the worst of it. The screams. Voren closed his eyes, breathed. "Are you alright, lad?"

Voren shook his head. Everything below the neck worked fine, certainly. *How might a man ever remove this stench from his nose?*

The Zuti came along a short while after, placing a hand on his frail shoulder as he settled onto a stump beside him. The fencer scowled at the Zuti, but Chigenda seemed to choose not to notice. Voren, for his part, could not will himself to shake off the gesture. Now, more than ever, they were all killers. What did one more touch matter?

"Careful with the lad," Rowan said.

Chigenda snorted. He patted Voren on the shoulder once and ran a hand over his own bald head. Sweat slicked off it like drops from a leaf. Or tears of a child. "He work. I see. Is..." He seemed to struggle to find the word, then stared off toward the buildings. The tents, seemingly in an effort to remove man from carnage, had pitched well beyond the boundaries of the ash and blood. "...Bad." The Zuti frowned, and his eyes slipped down into the mud his spear prodded. "Dey did no let me handle bodies."

When Voren looked up, he saw Rowan's brows scrunched. Wonder. The same thought: had the Zuti honest feeling?

The pole of the spear ticked off three more strikes into the dirt. "Imp-your, say dey." Dark eyes twisted back on them, hardening.

Solemn, Voren drew up to meet that look. "Do not worry at the words of hypocrites. There is nothing pure here. Anything, or anyone."

They both seemed to quiet at that. *Just men,* he reminded himself, looking between the two. Skin was everything, in the mind of so many. He winced. In his own mind. Yet humanity reigned between both. Even killers could flinch. They had. There were no jokes here, and no one seemed to know what to do with the aftermath.

He looked away, to another tent and to the great ogre looming within. Even removed from sight, the Kuree's presence was felt. Guardian. Protector. For all his efforts otherwise, he had gained nothing but respect for the barbarian in his days at their camp. No matter how the bearded fool distrusted him. For more than anything, he could see, the man cared not for himself. Not for health or gold or any of the like. He cared only for these killers. These killers and that one, rare flower, its roots withering under the weight of blood it drank.

Voren could not help but wince.

"Go her," the Zuti mouthed after a long moment. Voren startled, turning at the sound. The Zuti's eyes were on him, unwavering, with the same tone as one might carry to war. "Better dis."

"To her. He meant to her," Rowan clarified. "But I don't think…" Rowan stammered, only to let the words fall. He did not know. None of them did.

Voren looked between the pair. "Are you sure?"

It was a question that needed no answer. And neither could say. After a long moment, and a sigh, he stood up and started in. The canvas fell away, and the eyes were already there to greet him. The green of trees. The blue of oceans. One could travel far on such lines. Farther than this moment—yet he could never leave.

Alviss rose without a word. The bearded hulk nodded to him on his way out of the tent, pausing only to squeeze the prone girl's hand. Voren watched him go, then redirected himself to Essa. She did not look well, but then, from all he had heard, he should not have expected more. Heart hammered in his weary chest. She blinked up at him once, twice, and shifted onto her elbows. Between wan, rough skin and sunken eyes, she had all the look of one that had broached death's own bony touch. Even the wildness had faded from her. Not to docility just…

Numbness. He knew it well. Dreaded it.

He crouched beside her. Took her hand as the barbarian had. She blinked again and made the slightest of smiles. He patted the skin, but said nothing. Words could have accomplished little. At her side, though, the hours grew long, the minutes swift—warmth still trickled in the flesh. It only needed to be coaxed.

Eventually, he fell asleep there. The world grew heavy and the skin grew warm and the tent, well, the air—it grew all too oppressive. Body slumped, mind departed. He was carried away, to another field, another place. A boy watched him. Nothing more than a child. He scowled, even as he held out his hand. A river rose high against his neck, and higher, higher—it threatened to drown, threatened to steal them all away. Lips moved, but he could not hear the sound. Just the mismatched portions, the disarray. Brown and blue, they cried, and he knew fear, even in the depths of darkness.

Some threats never went away.

When he stirred, he lay against her. Something rustled outside. He was groggy, his head spun, and his stomach growled with the hunger he had deprived it of relieving. Their hands were still clenched tight—tighter than stone, he mused—but the dirt had given way to cloth, and Essa had curled herself into the warmth of him. He blinked. Another dream? Some men had dreams within dreams. They spoke of them with almost prophetic horror.

But the finger still ached. He sighed. *All the better for it.*

She seemed to sense his waking. Whether she was already awake or stirred to his own motions, the green eyes levied on him anew. Something shined in them. New. Bright. He squinted, smiled. Something old, perhaps. A figure of a girl, before the woman. Fingers clenched and the skin sang. He pressed his head against hers, savoring the warmth. *So close…*

"Thank you," she said meekly.

"For?"

"Just this." Full lips reached out and pecked his cheek. He nearly shuddered, but restrained himself instead. "You have put up with so much, Voren. Seen so much. And we…" Her face twisted, the blankness twining into sorrow.

"I know."

"We cannot stay here. Not anymore. If ever this was something—well, it has long lost its way."

And Rurik? the little voice whispered. He ignored it. Would not lend it sound. Gingerly, his other arm enwrapped his friend. He expected rebuke. Instead she nestled deeper into him.

"What remains when the silence breaks?"

No answer awaited her. Only bewilderment. He kissed her cheek and tightened his hold. He never wanted to let go.

Then the tent flap opened, and so was he forced. Men in armor strode through the glare of the daylight, hands on hilts. He flinched, where he thought a man should have risen. Essa snapped out of his grip, practically snarling. Crouched, slanted, fingers arched—she looked every bit the predator, ready for a brawl. Against that wall, there could only have been death, though. Only one could squeeze inside, but Voren could make out three men in all, all armed and iron-armored, grinning like coyotes. They seemed to ignore the howls of Rowan behind them.

They fell on her before she could truly come into herself, struggled through her thrashing hands and bore her back down beside him. He shouted, and she crowed, but they were not cowed, were not even put off. He shoved at one, kicked at him, but the man back-handed him, and he cowered into himself, holding his swelling lip.

"Voren!"

Love went skyward, kicking and screaming. He recognized the face. A sharp, short beard. Limping gait. Gorjes, no doubt. They wore not the colors, but sellswords rarely kept to organization anyways. Gold teeth were enough to make the man, though. So too the vacant stare as he slung Essa over his burly shoulder.

One of the other men loomed over Voren, holding his hand back as if to strike another blow. "If you even think…"

But what was there to think? He only saw Essa, borne away as if by an avenging wind. He longed to ride it, to force it out, but it would not even let him stir.

"What," he croaked, reaching a hand for the girl that the Gorjes slapped away. "What are you doing?"

"Sorry bint, eh?" the man said as he pressed a finger into Voren's chest. The baker sank back, growing still as a dormouse. "Fine piece to go to waste, I know, but she done a no-no. And even you's got to respect that."

"A what?"

"No-no. A wrong. A bad. Stepped across her own men. Beat 'em in the street. Not good for morale." The man straightened, removing his finger. He sighed as he stepped back. "No good for anyone, really. And we was closest."

The fear tightened in his chest. It became harder to breathe as he heard her scream. Heard Rowan chasing after. *Where is the Kuree? Will he allow this?*

"Look, baker, I wouldn't get involved. Bastard says she gets the lash. Not the only one."

"The…" His mind reeled. "The lash?"

The Gorjes' eyes dropped. Even he looked pale. "Look. I'll not say she's wrong, but—there's war and there's morals. Neither lasts long in the other's corner."

When daylight spilled inside the tent again, it was the Gorjes' turn to look surprised. Rowan panted, and though pale-faced he was, veins stood out prominently against his neck and knuckles. The sellswords exchanged concerned looks, and steadily, the pair of them and the fencer circled one another, eyes dark and blank as a slate, until the two of them had gone from there, and Voren lay alone, so alone, wrapped in the sheets that only moments before had covered his friend. His lady love.

And there was Rowan, staring down at him. He couldn't move. *The lash?*

"What…" The mind—it faltered in such moments. Shock.

"She stopped them," Rowan whispered, staring out the flap of the tent. Staring after his cousin. His sister, beyond race and blood. "Took a knife to them. Saved a woman's life. But in war…"

Rowan twisted on him sharply, as soon as they had gone. "Run," he ordered, and the shrill grate to his tone left no edge on which to argue. "I will follow them. To delay and debate. But you—get Rurik. He is the only one of us that can stop this."

A heart in turmoil drew suddenly still. He might have choked on those words. As it was, "Rurik," was all he managed to squeak.

"Now!" Rowan snapped, his balance lost. Slithering back on a hard breath, the man looked around, as if to hit something, then he swept back and away before Voren could think of any reply.

And then it built. Reality: they meant to kill her. On orders, no less.

If salvation began in death, then how could it possibly end?

He stared a moment longer. Unblinking, as if held in trance. *Rurik. The one that…* He had tried so hard to evade that creature since that night. To keep Essa from him. Steadying breath. His hand shook. *Rapist. Murderer.* Then: *aren't they all?* Rowan was right. There were many men like him in such positions. The place of lesser men was to navigate them as such, with the care of a white water river. Rurik was the only one who could help.

And most importantly: he cared about that woman. Had nearly broken himself over her.

Rurik was the only one who could help. If it could save Essa, then Voren could even grovel. *Pride is but a notion. It only slows one down.*

Outside, he cast about for any sign of the fool Rurik had set about their camp in days past, but he was nowhere to be found. There was no time to hunt him down. Voren took off through the tent city as fast as his legs could bear. The others were gone, but he knew the way. By the time he had reached Rurik's tent he could feel the burn in his limbs and the shortness of his own breaths. A pair of soldiers outside, deep in conversation, watched him with some confusion, but they made no move to bar his way. The tent flap drew open and he staggered inside, panting as the mismatched eyes took his measure.

Don't look weak. He drew up straight, like the soldiers did, but instantly knew it was a poor decision. He innately spoiled for a fight that would not help him. He looked aside. *Remember: think of him as another noble.* Hands folded and head bowed, but the words, the pathetic words, spilled out of him regardless.

"They took her." He hated his voice. Eyes lifted. The boy came into focus. "You have to stop them. They took her and they'll beat her, and if that happens—"

"Woah, woah," Rurik hesitated, leaning forward on the palms of his hands. "What is it? What are you on about? Who—" He licked his lips. Blinked. "Essa?" There came a hint of feeling—a flash of raw, mortal fear.

So we are both of us human, after all.

The explanation was rushed, but he left nothing aside. As he went on, Rurik's face blanched. Before he had even finished, the young lord had snatched up his pistol and was outside. "Berric? Berric?" he shouted, but no one answered. Voren followed, but the inflamed lord easily outpaced him—as well as his own guards, who shouted after their dust.

It was funny, in its way, what fear could do to a person. As Voren looked around them, he began to recognize signs. Signs that might have turned his legs to so much paste had not the fear for Essa pulled him. The camp always built itself up along certain lines, and even the drunken wake of victory had not changed that. So Voren knew they headed for its heart.

Voren had made it a point never to visit the place the men called "the pit." A barbaric notion, long past its prime but all too prevalent in their oh-so modern army. Everywhere they camped, a new pit—nothing but a bare patch of starched grass, really, where the most people could gather for a show.

It was the punishing grounds. At the center, five poles were daily raised, not so unlike the Springtide Poles, but to these were hung ropes threaded with the barbaric hunger of men taught to wear emotion far too close to the surface.

At its edge, Rowan sat glowering up at the gathering crowd, hands bound and lip bloodied. With no sign of Essa, Voren watched as Rurik shoved his way through several hapless soldiers, pivoted frantically in place, and at last settled on the cousin as well. Knuckles white as snow clutched the boy's pistol, earning more than one hesitant whisper. He looked back to Voren, as if for some reprise, but Voren only shook his head and nodded to their bound friend.

"What is this?" Rurik cried, voice breaking at the strain.

A cluster of men stood guard over the fencer, at least one of them a Gorjes man. They exchanged knowing looks before one among them shrugged. Rurik stepped toward them, but if he meant to cow them, it was an empty gesture. They stared, blank as posts. Probably twice as dumb. At least one snickered.

"I demand to know why you hold this man."

The Gorjes snorted as he stepped towards the boy. "Not your call, I'm afraid."

"Excuse me?"

"Bastard's call," the Gorjes sighed, losing interest in the debate already. "This one's to be held till the beatin's done. 'Is own safety."

"We'll see about that. And just who are you supposedly punishing?"

A toothless smile. "Y'know damn well, lordling."

For the fleeting breadth of a moment, Voren thought there would be blood. Though the armored hulk towered over Rurik, the boy's hand quivered to the tune of his taunt. A flick of a trigger, and another day of chaos might have reared its ugly head. Despite himself, Voren found it stirred a chord within his own head: *Kill, kill, kill.* All he had was a kitchen knife, but he was sure if push came to shove, he could bury it in one of the sellswords' throats.

Red-faced, Rurik shoved at the man, though it hardly moved him. The smile remained and laughter echoed behind it, and Rurik—Rurik let out one incontinent scream and swung back towards the baker. "Come on," he snapped, though he did not wait to see if Voren followed.

They made it as far as the edge of the gathering crowd. It was splitting down the middle, making room for a fool's procession. Armored men led three figures bound to a line by ropes, while two bare-chested Gorjes took up the flanks. None held weapons drawn, but their hands did not linger far from hilts. At the center of this procession was a disheveled Essa, eyes wild and alert, but otherwise as yet unharmed. Neither of the others were in such fine condition. She was a star swimming through darkest night—and he wondered how much longer she could shine.

He side-stepped the lord, darted through a few lingering bodies toward the line. He emerged to the left of the lead man. Essa seemed to catch the motion, for she locked on him instantly, gaze widening, eyes pleading. "I don't—" But that was as far as she got, for the Gorjes man at her side swatted her as though she were no more than a fly. Voren cried out with her pain, though she did not, and flung himself forward, overcome with the sight. He bundled his fist, even as he railed against his own idiocy in mind. The Gorjes turned, grinning and then…

Another hand caught his, and he was all but wrenched off his feet. He struggled, helpless as the Gorjes took Essa by the arm and hauled her back on her feet. Someone hallooed a cat call, and a dozen other voices answered. Voren raged against the grip, twisted on it—and found Rurik, stalwart, staring back at him.

"This does not help."

Voren pulled one final time, the fight if not the rage going out of him. Rurik let it go, but his stare—sympathetic, almost—did not waver. "Then do something," Voren cried bitterly. The boy nodded and his twisted eyes scanned the crowd. If the Bastard had ordered this, would the villain dare to survey his own handiwork? He rarely did.

"Back, all a ya's," one of the Gorjes said, with a shove to a soldier not quick enough on his feet. Voren tittered at the poles, wringing his hands. He knew what happened here. *So much blood.*

It reminded him of another day. Never before had Voren spared a wayward thought for the father. For Pescha. But he saw the drunkard then, bound up at the stake, on parade for them all. He looked to Essa and felt the sweat roll down. *Could she really take such a thing?*

When he turned back, Rurik was gone. It took him a moment to find him again, and then it was only his back, shoving forcefully through the crowd. Shapes broke at the passing, and he trailed the figure up to what he assumed was the destination—gryphon-headed flags, at least half a dozen flapping to the breeze of one. Though he dreaded the thought of leaving Essa alone, he dreaded more the thought of leaving Rurik alone.

He glanced back at Rowan, still as a blade of grass upon the earth. "I'll be back," he spoke softly, but the fencer did not hear him. He turned, regardless, and stalked after the boy. Their hope.

It was not nearly so easy for him to navigate the crowd, for though he did not lack the will, he lacked the body and the name to make the people move. He brushed alongside them, rather than they along him, like water crashing on the rocks, until he burst out the other end, stumbling into the clearing Rurik had marked as his own.

A dozen men stood in a throng about the boy. He looked outmatched, naught but his pistol within a mass of steel. These were men that were never off-duty. Not since the assassination attempt, at any rate, and they were all of them built like bearded statues. Career soldiers, he had no doubt. And at their center, the Bastard, with that fool-man Berric, listening to the boy he called a friend.

"…nothing wrong. In point of fact, the moral man would say she did all that was right."

The Bastard's expression betrayed no toil, nor mirth. It stood as stone itself. "After she attacked her own men? On this, law as well as commonsense are clear."

"Commonsense? She is not a soldier!"

The Bastard's lips curled into the thinnest of lines, giving him a dreadfully wearied look. "She bears arms. And she walks beneath these banners. We sent the camp followers home months ago. If not a soldier, my friend, than what is she?" Someone whistled, but the Bastard did not smile. At least, not with his lips. He flicked Rurik's disjointed stare aside and took a step forward. "Must we continue to make this such a show? This is best discussed in private, Rurik."

A shudder went through the boy, but even then, Voren could see some of the fire had gone out of him. *Don't you…*

"You have already made it a show. This is—"

"None of your concern. Your dedication to your friends is commendable. But this is beyond you. Punishment comes." The Bastard's voice seemed to falter on that last, and his hand absent-mindedly brushed against the scar at his hip. Then, sharply, his voice rang with a marshall's clarity, drowning out the crowd. "To one and all. Now take your stand. I would not drag this out any longer than need be."

And that was it. *Coward*, the voice in Voren screamed. He stood, fists clenched, like a child confronting a bully. The Bastard brushed by them both, and when Rurik turned, the fire had been replaced with naught but ashes. Chill and damp with the spring rain. *You coward. This is your fault. Do something!* Berric drew close to the boy, and said something in his ear. Rurik looked down. Neither bedeviled eye would meet his own, yet he lingered under Voren's scowl a moment longer, as if his own personal penance.

Then he too walked away. Following his bastard. His master. Like a faithful hound. Voren spat on him as he passed. "She trusted you," he snapped, but the boy only sank a little lower, and continued on. The fool-guard shouldered Voren as he passed. Rowan called out Rurik's name. It, too, fell on deaf ears.

No, this one is no Matair. He had to remind himself of that. *Something lower, yes, something darker than even that foul name. This was what we depended on?*

He twisted back on the processional, honing in on Essa. The wild eyes, in turn, had focused on the boy. Searching. Yearning. It broke Voren's heart. She still hoped, some small part of her, that there was some good in that creature. Rurik slid in behind the other soldiers like a snake, and stood shuffling his feet in the dust. A sergeant put out the call, and the prisoners were bound to their posts.

"Rurik?" The weak voice broke. Like a whisper in the surge of cheers. Both youths winced.

Blood was the only recourse. His eyes followed the boy, downcast, as he let the soldiers unravel their whips. *Coward. Traitor.* She looked to him, and back—trying to maintain the stoic disposition. Failing. A child's whisper in the haze of unknowing. The boy would not look at her. Not as the soldiers stepped forward and the charges were read. Not as some other man's dirty hands tore her tunic and bared her breasts. Not as the whip yanked back and the leather sang its airborne snap. He winced, as Voren did, with the crack. And the whimper.

She did not cry out. Not for them, or for any other.

The leather drew back and he looked away, unable to meet her gaze. It snapped, and the sound—it was terrible for its intensity. Wet and slick and echoing with the fleshy slap. It came again and again.

Hands swam before him. How many others wondered? He paused, breathed—had to remind himself to breathe. *They will weep. They will hate. Hell, they all hate. That is the nature of war. They pour that hate out onto others lest it turn unto themselves.* One could not bottle it. Only destruction lay within that path.

When Voren's eyes opened, there was but one body they honed on. Rurik looked away, watching the trees, or the smoke of the town. Nothing. In that moment, watching the hands revolve around themselves, and the purpose lost, he knew—Rurik Matair, the lieutenant, the lord, for all that he was and all that might lay yet within his stars—the lieutenant had to die. And in the night, the rest, they had to slip away.

When they were finished with Essa, her should-be savior did just that. As if sniffing at the vapors of Voren's thoughts, he slithered away into the mass of others and left her lying there in a puddle of tears and blood. The crowd gave way more gradually, loitering like vultures to the leavings. They inhaled the scent of pain, as if Oberroth had not been enough. In disgust, Voren pushed beyond them and into the ring where her blood still settled.

With a cry, Rowan sprang past him. He fell to the earth and clasped at her arms, trying to draw her in, but she shook him off, the gesture leaving little tremors as echoes down her frail frame. Pale. She looked so pale. Voren twisted to scowl at the loitering guards, but those that had bound her cousin had receded with the rest, content that their doings were only duty.

Bastards, he spat, and might have shouted, but sense still appealed somewhere inside. He went to her in turn, and Rowan's eyes turned to him, wild and wet with a boyish sort of uncertainty. It unsteadied him, nearly drew him back. But the eyes—they pleaded. He sank, shivering, beside them, and drew the modest cloak from his own shoulders. *What more will they do to you, oh star?*

"Take the cloak," he said. He was shocked by the hoarseness of his own voice. *When did it grow so dry?* His hands shook and the cape trembled over the scarlet mud. *Or so unsteady?*

"So much blood. Essa, you need to, if only…" Rowan looked to him, and to the retreating crowd, then back to his cousin. He blinked, licked his lips, and seemed to try to pause for time. But none of it could be blinked away. "Swine!" He bellowed sharply over their heads. A few turned back at the cry but, losing interest, turned quickly away again. Even though he hallooed it again, none turned at the second. Cracked hands swam through reddened hair, and reached to rub at his cousin's own. "Essa. Can you move?"

She shook her head. The lips opened, but fell back, as if the words were too much strain.

"The cloak," Voren repeated. "It will sop the blood."

"The blood?" Rowan blinked again. He looked up sharply, as though the shaken mantle had resettled, eyes honing to a darkened purpose. "Yes, yes the blood. Give it here. Essa, you should take it." Voren did not fight his hand as it ventured for the offering, but Essa's own snapped to take it. All three winced with the gesture.

"Foolish child! Do not open the wounds any more. You are—are bloodied enough," her cousin said.

She shook her head. Soft tresses tumbled with the motion, hiding her face. She could not look at them. Voren wished nothing more than to wrap her in his arms and bear her away, but she was insistent. Her hand would not loose the cloak until they loosed it to her, and then, with all the poise of a child tying her laces, drew it about her bared, stained back and tightened it across her shoulders. The fingers, rough-hewn though they were, moved like needlepoint, and settled as feathers when the deed was done. Thus covered, the head finally twisted up to them and bared its pain through every ashen patch of skin on that bark-like flesh. It had been harder to break this one's flesh than most, but they had done it all the same.

"Oh my coz," Rowan whispered.

She caught his touch on her hand and rubbed it gently at the palm. Then she turned to Voren, perched still as a statue beside. *An observer and nothing more,* he thought. When that gaze touched him, however, he felt the blood stir anew. He faltered. She did not. Her face, tightening, implored of him behind its mask. No gesture was required.

When it came, her voice was mouse-like in its utterance. "Bring me home." That was it, but it was enough. They did not question; they obeyed.

It was no easy feat to move one so scourged. They set her to her feet, only to become her shadows. Despite her words, Essa still tried to take the steps on her own, and though they lingered close at hand, neither man dared to take her in hand until the pain seemed prized to pluck that last shred of dignity, and the ground loomed. Every inch she took was every inch hers, and though it was not far they moved, they moved all the same, until a stray footstep threatened to buckle her. Under a dozen itinerant eyes, Voren surged beneath her as she lurched, and steadied her by the waist. She said nothing as they took that first step together, nor at the second, when Rowan stretched a hand to join them.

They moved slowly to ease the burden on the wounds themselves, but this only dragged the pain out longer, and by the ending paces, Essa begged them to haste. Though her eyes were wet by the time the familiar tents crowded into sight, they heeded her.

Alviss and Chigenda stood sharply at their approach, forsaking the bowls of dinner left to gather chill on the sodden earth. From Alviss: "What has happened?" But he already moved to meet them at their utterance, closing the gap in a few long strides. The normally cool face, nigh featureless beneath the coarseness of beard, grew hotly animated, twitching through the range of pity and disgust and agony the likes of which one might expect to see in a parent's eye. A storm stirred there. Of this he was certain. It reminded Voren of home, and it made him shudder to think how serious all this blood could truly be.

Between them, they set her to the earth. All the while, it fell to Voren to explain. He spoke of the soldiers and the beating and all of it—save Rurik's part in it. Much as the thought of him stirred blood to the fore, he knew that too much pain on so old a heart might only serve to break it. For whatever else lay between Alviss and he, it did not mean him cruel. The old Kuric, for his part, took it all in with sagely nods, and when he was finished, brushed the baker away again as easily as dust.

He sank beside Essa as she bundled against the damp. Her eyes had drawn shut, clenched and flinching every so often. Rowan whispered soft words in her ear as he petted her hair and held her hand, but it was Alviss that demanded: "Show me." Uncertainty blinked the emeralds back to life, but she need only look once into her guardian's eyes, and Essa left all play at pretense from her reply. A shift of the shoulder dropped Voren's cloak just enough to bare the scars to light.

A dozen lines crisscrossed her back, set almost so rigid as lines of wheat at harvest. Dry crusting had begun to take the edge away, but the wounds themselves still blared bright and red, and the edges quivered with the remnants of her flesh. Alviss took her cover and drew it tenderly back over her shoulders, settling his hands about them as he finished.

It was said her mother's people had skin like bark. Rubbish, he thought then, or that runaway had done her daughter wrong in gifts of birth. Flesh was flesh and blood was blood.

At the sight of the blood, Voren cringed away. *Don't look, can't*—Yet he found Chigenda sidled into his space, and he flinched away from the southerner, but if the dark man paid him any heed, he made no outward sign of it. Unlike Alviss, this one still showed no break. Cool as the wind he stood, and moved light as a mouse to ground. *Does nothing move you?* Still, in his posture and the way his hand settled in caress against the hilt of the machete at his belt, Voren saw a hint of protectiveness. For whom, though, stood the question.

"It will need stitch," Alviss laid plain. "But it may escape scar. I need ointment. Child?"

It must have been a difficult request for the old man. Positions suddenly reversed. Essa was the doctor of the group, if they were to have one at all. While the intricacies of apothecaries, perhaps, evaded her, the lighter pieces such as this came easily to her. Yet now she could do nothing for herself.

She shook her head at the question and seemed to shrink deeper into resolution. "We've none," she answered. "The last was taken for the scouting's misdoings. The camp—"

The rest passed unspoken. Alviss looked to Rowan, and the fair-haired mess clearly quailed at the thought of leaving his cousin. Yet he went all the same, saying, "I will scour the medicus till medicine sets in hand or my arse is thrown from their door," and fleeing headlong for the safety of action. It would do him good. There was wisdom in the sending, for there was nothing else he might have done for her anyhow.

"Backer," Alviss said next, twisting to him. Voren stiffened at the word—the Kuric's poor attempt at pronouncing his family's name—and duty. Yet he saw no malice in those eyes. Only the same concern. "Come. Sit with her. Press the cloak tight." He relaxed at this, bowing his head in deference before sliding down beside her in the muck. He looked to it, felt the brief and terrible surge of doubt that always reverberated from such mess, and then he looked to her, and felt nothing. He hesitated only to see if she would deny him, but she only watched with a child-like curiosity as he drew his arm about her, and drew cloak and warmth both close.

The Zuti slid after him, stepping between the group at an angle. Fingers still drummed against the hilt. He looked at her, then to Alviss. There was a spark of something in the shuffle of his feet. It drew even Essa's gaze up, where normally her eyes would not venture. He met her stare, and nodded sullenly, thin lips drawn almost into non-existence against his skeletal face. Where light caught, it made a phantom of him, dark and broad and terrible. A warrior.

"This…punish?" His lips seemed to struggle around the word, and he hesitated at its utterance, as if fearing it were not the word he wished. It was a question that set Essa's own brows furrowing, lips parted, but drifting—uncertain how to answer. Chigenda growled at his own encumbrance, adding: "For town? The—the sight?"

He meant the bloodying work, surely. The very thought seemed to dull the flickers of light in Essa's eyes, and she nodded limply to the fact. This was perhaps worse than words could offer. The simple madness of it seemed to reach even the Zuti, his cold dead eyes fixing abruptly beyond them, the world bearing itself in color to him. Voren knew the look. Had seen it in soldiers' eyes.

It was not one he cared for.

"Dis fair?" Chigenda's face had darkened to such a raw nerve of emotion, Voren thought he was for a moment in danger of becoming human. The dark earthquakes that became his eyes rippled out as he straightened. "I show fair. Is more de bloody."

A hand snapped out, catching him by the wrist. He looked as startled as the rest of them to find the pale skin led back to Essa, her hard eyes boring up into his own.

"Don't."

Chigenda's jaw firmed at the word—surely not one he was used to hearing—and his eyes still searched, but when the tension parted from his shoulders, Voren knew he had broken as surely as the rest of them, though he would not put it to words. "You have…" The Zuti reached for a word, only to give up a moment later, saying, "Fight. Spirit. Body. These are…strong." The hand fell away and the Zuti, looking suddenly uncomfortable, receded from it. He made excuse, and slid out and away as quickly as possible, on Rowan's heels.

They sat like this a little while longer, the baker and the barbarian and the tortured girl between them, head cradled against her knees. Then she flicked to

Alviss and dismissed him as well, saying: "Go with them. Lest they find trouble."

The great bearded father hesitated, and Voren wondered if Alviss thought it was his departure at the last such asking he sought to blame for this, but there was some quality in her voice that none could shake. He took her hand, folding it between his own, and kissed it, tender as a newborn babe. "I would have stopped them," he said hoarsely, but this was meant for him, not her, and she knew it to be so. This seemed to wither some of her own resolve, but he heaved to his feet and left them both before word or deed could dissolve entirely.

Then they were alone. Alone, and he with nothing to say. Apologies curled on his tongue. Anger died there too—it seemed somehow ingenuous in the face of such resolve.

But in the silence that followed, he watched that resolve crumble like the paper wall it truly was. Essa choked on a sob and shuddered, such that Voren snapped to her side and put his arms around her to steady her again. Her head twisted just so, and he caught the glint of scarlet at her cheek. Spatter. It chilled him.

"What have I done, Voren?"

He looked at her askance. "Done? You don't mean—"

"These things. They keep happening and I can't seem to stop them and they just—how much is one person to bear?"

"Es!" His fingers dug against her and he became acutely aware that the pair of them hung as if dangling on open air, mere inches from one another. "You have done nothing. No one deserves what has happened to you. No one."

"And yet…" The words came up like a morsel one gagged on.

There was a moment when her breath caught and she seemed to close her eyes tight against the evils of the world. He knew she questioned whether it was her own fault. There was no reason for it, but so it was. He longed to tell her she was perfection, she was devoid of fault, but he guarded their silence, for he knew those words would only strengthen her guard and draw her further into doubt.

Then she sobbed and he felt the last shred of him break. A picture of that boy turning away from her bleeding body came fresh to mind, and with it the thoughts came: *How can a man turn from this? How could you let it come to pass?* His hand shook, he knew, wild and uncertain, and gave his wrath away. *If only you had drowned yourself in drink and left her to her own.*

It all came back to that. None of it. None of this would have happened if not for him. The sages—they often said a breath could stir storms, as a man could change the world, and Voren could see this was the case for Rurik Matair, though no change for the good had ever stirred from his foul breaths.

He tried to hide his shaking from her but, being Essa, she caught it even through the veil of her own depression, and looked sharply back at him through it. The look stilled him, for through the pain he felt the breath, and the steadying thought that welled there.

"Do you remember the day my father was whipped as I?"

He would have preferred not, but he did not have that luxury. A nod sufficed—he remembered it well. Though none of the townsfolk were allowed at her side during the punishment, he had gone to her after, and held her, and offered her bread for the pain they both had suffered.

He thought of Pescha and how the fool, like Essa, had seemed to breed problems by the score. Yet Pescha made his own, where she only had them set upon her shoulders. Pescha had been the first to do so, in truth. It had been the booze, then—as it always had been. The man had been huntsman to Lord Matair, but he had slipped too deep into the drink. Even a loyal man could not turn from it by the end. So he had paid by lash and laceration, and made his daughter pay in turn.

The young did not understand crimes. They merely suffered their results.

Then, as now, Rurik had stood to the side. Then he had said it was his own father's doing that bid it. A child, he supposed, could host excuses. A man had nothing but his actions. Rurik, perhaps, had never grown past that tiny creature.

"Aye. A terror, that. Second to worst day of my little span."

"He cried out."

He looked at Essa crossways, trying to figure what she played at—the flow of thoughts. "Aye. Terrible, in its own turn. I remember watching, watching you and thinking—oh, Maker, I know not how you lived with it."

To her credit, she did not turn from him. "He was a drunk and a fool. He brought it on his own self." The dull tenor of her conviction was almost worse than the tears.

With its passing, he made the connection at last. These were not the random thoughts of a broken mind. She saw herself as a continuation of the failures he had wrought. That the pain, though she could not understand it, might have somehow been deserved. How she lived with it, indeed! How anyone could bottle up so much guilt, so much fear, and go through their days with smiles and courage to spare—he stood more in marvel, and terror, of her than ever before. This was no girl. At the least, he owed it to her to try and break this atrocious connection.

"You are nothing as him, you know."

"Did I say I was?" Though phrased as a question, there was a bitter sort of knowing in it. Nothing like the woman he knew.

"The seed bears not the stains of the father. Each is their own life."

"Then why—"

"Confuse not the poorness of luck and chance and the doings of others with wickedness, Essa. You are not your father." He almost bit his tongue, but he had come so far—he let the rest spill out, and be damned with the consequences. "Your father was a fool and he was a monster. The only good thing he did was bring you into this world, and he spent the rest of his life punishing you for it. It wasn't right and it isn't right that you blame yourself."

This, however, turned her aside. She swallowed hard and focused pointedly on the earth. "I'm not pure," she added momentarily.

"Is anyone? That doesn't mean anything. This pain—it should not be yours to bear."

She made a little sound as she straightened. "Second. You said—you said that day, that it was your second. What is—that is…"

"A consequence: the day you left."

It was a long time before either spoke again. Then, quiet as a mouse, the breath leaked from Essa's lips: "Sometimes, I hope him dead." Had he not been so close, he never would have heard it. A wisp of a thing, as though the very mention could sunder the world.

He gathered her a little tighter, cradled her head. "Has he ever tried to find you?"

"No." The gap after this was long enough that Voren thought the conversation left at that. Then: "Only once. It wasn't more'n a month after he took me to Rowan and his. I heard them quarrel. Rowan and him. Peeked out at them through the window. Papa said he was sorry. So sorry. Like he always did. But Rowan and his papa—they said he weren't welcome around no more. I think he knew it then. Realized, or something. Because something changed. He looked spoiled for a fight and then—then he just slunk away.

"I suppose he might have come back one day, but who knows? Rowan and I left not long after. To find our own way. To hide from him. To…to…" Her lip quivered, stilled.

"Essa?"

"My mother," she said, when she found her voice again. Exasperation lit it, and another cool tear rolled against his arm. "The dancing. The singing. The travelling. It was all well and good but—I wanted to see if I could find my mother. Stupid, isn't it?" She shifted in his arms, twisting to look up at him. And for the first time, he beheld her eyes as through a looking glass, the wavy character of her tears not reducing her, but making her all the more powerful. She was not afraid.

Solemnly, he shook his head. "Did you find her?"

"What do you think?" The words, apparently more bitter than she intended, stopped her own self cold. Gingerly, she reached out to touch his hand and sighed deep. "She was Aswari. Who would care to know? But I have a notion. They used to have a camp. Not far from here, really. Beyond the trees. It was burned, years ago, when they moved them all west. From what I understand, a lot of them—a lot of them died."

There were few places worse than the Aswari camps. People liked to gossip about them. Noble men, paid for the charge but scarcely noble in its execution, had long been given the duty of guaranteeing the Aswari life and lands within Idasia while at once keeping them from any of its proper citizens. Like penned animals, Voren's father had called them. In the foolish wonder of youth, at the time he had asked: were there no free Aswari?

"As there are wild dogs, and Orjuks," his father had bellowed. "But all find their way back."

It was an unpleasant thought. "You really think she would have gone there?"

"No? Yes? Who knows. I didn't know her. But I have to think I'm like her, and if that's true—I would choose family over Pescha any day. For better or ill."

Would that it were never for ill. It never had to be again. This was the moment. This tender, open thing. So unlike her, so telling. It sealed everything for him. For once in his life, the baker knew and was resolute. He stroked her arm, as he often had the grains of flour strewn about his kitchen. There was too much pain in the world. It was time he took some of it away.

This was the bridge across which there could be no return. A devil waited at the other end. A devil with eyes of water and of earth. Lies it had whispered too long to the wind.

* *

Say my name.

Damp yet fragrant, the air was of pines and water and curls of smoke. Nothing remained of the corpse-fires. They had burned themselves to ash and left the earth in peace. Yet there could be no calm. Not in the face of madness. Flames burned still as campfires, and in the flaring sparks there was not a man that should not have seen some familiar eyes staring hauntingly back.

Movement and muffled voices full of anger. They shuffled beyond the baleful boundaries of canvas, in the light, where they made ready to leave.

Without him.

Rurik knew this, and so he made the gesture. Night had confirmed everything, in the horror of dreams. The madness in the shadows that stalked him. He had too long walked the streets and trees, looking for sign of his brother. Then this. He could not close his eyes against them. He fixed his eyes on her, still at the opposite end of the tent, wrapped in the gloom like a cloak. One last try. It was all he could do. If only she would…

Say my name.

"Will he let you?"

Bodies stirred the camp to motion. Dead men moved the living. Dogs wailed, to the crunch of boots. There was no nobility left in these man's hearts. Nor in his.

"We are not slaves, Essa. I can go…if I wish."

She snorted, but even that jerk of the shoulders brought her up short. The blood, he knew—it burned in the whip's wake. "You aren't? So you say." Softer, then: "So you say."

He felt the quake in his shoulders. Alviss had nearly barred him from the tent. The old giant had taken him by the shoulder and wrenched him back so hard he thought he was for sparring. Yet he had said nothing, offered no resistance, and the Kuric had steadily bent to him, knowing he would not leave. It was to be quick. Fleeting. They thought, perhaps, he had come to say goodbye. Could any of them forgive him enough to allow for more?

The Bastard had led him astray. As deluded misconceptions of Rurik's father before him. It took his focus from the present, to future and past and anywhere but what mattered. He had seen the blood it led to. He wanted no more of it.

"Would you have me stay? Assal above, is that what you want?"

She would not even look him in the eye.

"You will do what you will. You always have." Her head shook him aside. "It began in Verdan, I suppose it only right that it would end there. Go along. We will follow if you choose it, *lord*."

The false honorific bit harsh. There was no mirth to it. Lord. If he was a lord he was the pettiest of them all, lord of the mayflies and the lemmings. Not a man. Not even the boy he once had been. He knew it to be so.

Say my name.

For once, he realized, there was no ring of steel in the trees. Mud had taken it. Ash and mud and all the rest.

"I don't ask you to follow me. I just…" There was hate in him. He could not even begin to describe. This woman sat before him—a woman he had known from scraped knees and climbing trees—and yet…he could not say. Words were not enough. This was what they had come to, and it had been his own doing.

"He would burn it all. You see that, don't you?"

She bit her tongue.

"Look around. Take this and turn it on the nobles, Essa. All the nobles. Who would be left to support him? To keep the other nations out? The fool has spoken long of right and vengeance, and godliness, but they are just words. Same as any other man. He may talk it up—the cry of the people, of the Farrens. But there's no right here. It would all come to the same end regardless. The squabbling would just lead to more—more claims, more conflicts, more revenge and—"

"I wasn't rejecting the logic," she said sharply. "Merely—never mind. I know."

338

"Essa…"

"What? We leave with or without you. If you come as well, perhaps there remains some chance for your twisted soul."

She looked at him levelly, with a stare that could have turned a dead man in his grave. There was finality in it. Rurik said nothing. He shook his head and waited for the tent flap to shudder back into its place. Eyes waited ravenously for him. Voren shouldered past him before the light had settled in his own. Not even a backward glance. No friends here, in the group that he had made. He had forsaken them. Such favors were always returned.

And she never said his name.

With an offering of what passed vaguely for a nod, Rurik slipped away. For a time, he wandered the streets, wondering without care how long it would take for an escort to catch him up. This was, after all, nothing like a victory camp. Where one might have expected to lose themselves in noise and lechery, there was only silence. A few haunted ghosts of soldiers ghosted the lanes and peripheries, but most retreated to their ramshackle quarters, in vain attempts to blot out what they had done.

It was one thing, he knew, to kill in war. To burn and to pillage from faces they had never known and would never need to see again. Different for a neighbor. Family, perhaps, for some. He thought again of the face he had searched the field and its infirmaries for, and gave a silent, thankful prayer that his fears had not been borne out.

A shadow crossed his path not far from Tessel's own tent. He looked up to meet it and found Berric staring back at him. Time had rendered the man gaunt and waxen-faced—in the lightless mourning night, he looked almost skeletal. They shared no words. Rurik turned from him, and his shadow fell in against his heel. They kept a distance between them, and in that uncomfortable air Rurik knew that he was not the only one haunted.

Would that he could have confided in the man. But he could never know if Berric was his own man, or Tessel's. He knew only that Tessel had been the one to offer him up, and at the moment that mattered most, it had been Tessel to receive Berric's voice, not him.

In times past, Rurik had kept close to his commander, by order and by choice, that he might be indispensible to his effort, day or night. Now they wandered to the furthest reaches of the army, and to the tents pitched as far as possible from the burnt husks of Oberroth. He could not stand to look at Tessel. Not since his dismissal earlier in the day. Not since the cracks of the whip. Each one had rattled him to the very bones.

He glanced back to be sure that Berric still followed. The faithful shadow stopped where he did, and cast a wary look about them. He, too, had stood by while the guiltless had been delivered into the others' guilt.

There was nothing for Rurik in this camp now. He began to fidget. A dream was dead. If ever they returned to Verdan, he knew, it would not be as liberators. It would be as murderers.

"Is there something you need?" he asked belatedly of his shadow.

The man tightened up, but did not shy from confrontation. "The general gives message."

All one need do to see Tessel's message was to look at the bodies scattered about the boughs. Even so, he inclined his head. "As you wish."

"He would speak with you on the morrow. With marching orders. And to extend his…apologies, for the day's blackness."

He felt the twitch in his eye, but did nothing to hide it. "Which part?"

"That business with Essa. It was poorly done. But you understand confronting him there, like that—he could not back down then, not in front of the men."

That was enough. In disgust, Rurik spun from him and made for his place at a fevered march. No footsteps stalked him this time, but at his back, Berric called: "On the morrow, than?" But he did not answer. He drew up beside an empty fire-pit and cast himself against the dirt. His cloak he took for a blanket, and earth his bed. He did not bother to pitch a tent. The air was cool but not unpleasant, and he was too restless for the excess. At his back, he felt Berric shuffle a while in indecision. Then he, too, slunk into the night.

So I am to be an exile again, he thought with bitterness. *Perhaps it shall actually teach this time.*

Two years he had been on the road. He would not have wished them on anyone at the time, young and foolish as he was, but he had not realized their kindness—warm friends and warm beds, if not an excess of coin. He had seen places he might have otherwise never seen, and he had never had to dread the coming of a night truly and utterly alone.

Yet he had taken in none of it for what it was. The youth of him was concerned only with the word: exile. It burned with indignation, like a brand on his heart. Drove him round and back again, and into blood. Everything that had come to pass was his fault. All of it. Eighteen winters now, and this was all he had. And the thought of bearing it alone—it was enough to break the gentler soul. As it was, he felt himself exhausted, without any hope of sleep.

What is sleep with nothing to wake to?

But there was something. Someone, still—distant yes, and broken as he, but there all the same. He tried to frame her in mind, the wisp of a girl and the bright, thundering eyes that had always shone for him. The listener. The wanderer. The fellow wronged.

Something struck him at the whisper of her being. A cascade of force nigh drowned him. He could feel his thoughts turn and quake and the semblance of himself begin to fall, all becoming hopelessly adrift and death's dark maw looming through it all, cackling mad as a burning village, and he cried out as the coin toppled from his hands.

It took him a moment to muster the courage for another try. Tentatively, he touched the rusted bit, daring not to place it in his palm again. He had the feeling of being watched, and he squirmed against his blanket, feeling his throat go dry. It had been like a raging storm, that moment, but he steeled himself and called out to her again. This time, he could feel her spread around him, and the tingle of the connection, and then it was as if she had made a cloak of herself to spread about him.

"It cries," came the whisper.

What was that? The storm. The madness.

"Murder by the child's own eyes. It makes no sense." He had a semblance of her somewhere in a dark place, groping about for something in the dust. *"But it strikes up lines she sought forget. Ah, she—I—we cry for the world, dear Rurik. Do you also, and for her? She would set you right, that there might be one pillar still…"*

It was a long conversation. One-sided, but long. He told her all of it. Told her all the things he had held back so long. Of Essa and Voren and all the rest.

His loneliness and his mournfulness, his hatred of Tessel and the regret of son for father wronged. His incapability. A rant, by its end, nigh raving, and when her voice trickled back from wherever it rang, he barreled over it, letting the pictures form in his mind until he himself felt nothing but the hard-hearted desire for the drink, to carry him away and never let this feeling return.

Love. That was all he wanted. Essa's love. Friends' love. A family to have and to hold and to take the pain away. *I am a child. A needy child.* He was such the child, ever and always, and he despised how he sounded, yet he could not help but offer his true heart, to for once honestly unveil the whole of its sundering.

What was bundled was loosed, and by the end, he felt all but empty in its wake.

After a long while, he realized she had not spoken. He called to her, somewhat unhappily—had she goaded him to speak, only to offer nothing in reply? Had he not listened in days past, and done the duty of friendship? He called again, louder this time—or so he thought, for it rose with his anger—and felt, for the trouble, the weight of the cloak about him grow thicker, pressing him down. As though Usuri clambered upon his back, and knelt. He rasped, groping for a mug near at hand, but feeling her presence grow with a thunderous tremor.

Could she come to him? Had she not done it before? No—or so he thought—that had been a trick, for she had followed them, and even magic had its limits. Or so he hoped.

"Oh, how it cries." The voice drew bitter and tremulous, storming through his bones as surely as his head. *"How it cries—for itself. Lament! It seeks to use, does it not? She should have known the voice was just a ruse. A child lost to shadow—oh it bleats! Does it not hear? Does it only speak?"*

Usuri, he choked, feeling the weight of her surpass him, bearing him down to the earth by the throat and all but tearing the world from his knowing. It was unnatural. He tried to rise, but he was caught as if in a vice. *Usuri, it wasn't about you, please, I know you hurt, and I just—* The words ran ahead of him, but he despised the known truth: just trading an eye for an eye.

"Well she knows!" And this—the thunder—it nailed him quivering to the earth, a drunk fool laid low by a wild man's cudgel. *"Name me, father, for a fool, and leave me dead. They all burn and burn, and never one to know the thoughts*

342

that fuel. Oh Rurik, the things you see and do, oh child, can you not hear greatness' call? Can you not see what looks you in the eye? No. Perhaps not, and nevermore. It fuels, but does it do?

"Leave me. Leave me to the memory. Leave me to the murder. Leave me to Usuri, and the names that should name her. Loneliness—do you know what it truly is? Name it Usuri, name for the stars—it knows not you, nor shall again. Die, Rurik. Die—for all you do not see. Simply fade, and greet me another shadow in another time."

And it was gone. The drunk man surged to the fore, rasping wild and weary for the drink so long denied him, and he thrashed in his sheet with the coin naught but a weight against his hand. It was cold, as he was cold, and the night was long—he shuddered against it and lay still. She was gone. Another voice to silence, another memory buried, and not for the first time, he wondered at his own seeming predilection toward self-destruction.

Greater still, the question: what murder had named Usuri? It seemed likely it would be his own.

Morning was groggily rendered, and the night's events left his mind detached and wandering far. He could not say whether he truly woke, or merely breathed.

For their hard-fought victory, and a far-deadlier march, the Bastard rewarded his army with a day of rest and relaxation before the order to move would be issued. It had been Rurik's intention to slip away with the Company while the rest of the army dozed, yet even as he wandered to his erstwhile companions, the mailed figures of Tessel's personal staff made themselves plainly known, and intercepted him. Berric was among them. So too was Orif of Kellsley, and his orjuk dog.

For a fleeting instant, Rurik let his hand fall to his sword. He thought them assassins, come brazen by the daylight. Yet it was Berric who did the talking, and reminded him of Tessel's command the night before. After that, he acquiesced quietly enough, letting them surround him like an honor guard as they marched for the heart of the camp. Back to the place where innocence had gone to die. Few onlookers would take him for the prisoner he truly felt.

"You mean to leave, I hear?"

Bundled in the stifling warmth of his tent, Tessel did not even wait for the honor guard to dismiss itself before he addressed his once-lieutenant. As it was, he sat hindering, rather than aiding his page in the removal of his muddied boots. He had been out riding. Either that meant him set for good spirits or in dire need of distraction. Given the sidelong snarl he leveled on Rurik, the former seemed doubtful.

It would not do to bandy words with the man, he knew. If there was one thing to be said for Tessel, it was the bluntness of his approach. That, at least, had not changed with ambition. So for once, he made his feelings clearly known.

"After what I witnessed yesterday, ser, I realize I do not have the stomach for this. Not this bloody thing. I know not if you ordered it, or simply let it come to pass, but the sort of madness as seen these days is not justice, nor even revenge; it is plain and simple murder that need never have been. You might have taken their food. You might even have pillaged the homes. But this? Such wholesale rape and ravishment—I tell you there is not one soul that shall not have this massacre on their lips by month's end, and you shall find yourself very much alone.

"You can tell me that soldiers will be soldiers. It's true, ser, I've seen it. And I know the sort of insanity that starving drive can bring. But Assal help you, I know your place with the men. Know that if ever a soul could have stopped such mindless bloodshed it was you. You let Scheyer get away, and Pordill, and instead, you took it out on their people.

"I have heard you call yourself Farren. A new man—well, that may be so, but what is to be said of new men that act the same as the old? And how many fellow new men do you think lie ashes in those streets now, when they might have opened their arms to you as brother and friend?"

Though Tessel's eyes flared and twinkled in their courses through Rurik's speech, it was to Rurik's own credit that he never once tried to interject himself. If the Bastard had, he knew, he would have faltered, and the whole thing would never have emerged. The Bastard's page ceased his struggles with the wayward boot and stood gaping at Rurik, the fear stark in his young eyes. The boot slid off of its own accord.

Tessel waved the boy off and shifted up straight to an arrow's point. Neither smile nor frown creased that point, but still the eyes burned. "So. You are certain this has nothing to do with the girl?"

"My lord, I—" The nervous page edged back as he spoke, but Tessel rounded on him sharply.

"No. Remain. There is nothing we would share here now I think the rest should not shortly know as well. Please, Rurik."

The boy huddled back from them both, and Rurik pitied him for having to witness such as this—and resented Tessel, too, for keeping others to bear it witness. Still, he did not let it deter him. Resolutely, he said: "Did I say this? Decisions, as you told me once, should never be singly delivered. Factors are innumerable, and all point from here. And I resent you think me so short-sighted."

The last earned a teasing smile from the general. "Of course. As you say. I merely thought to dwell a moment on history. Yours." A dismissive wave of the hand made a mockery of the thing's removal from his mind.

"With your leave," Rurik replied, turning to go. He hadn't crossed a foot before Tessel beckoned him back with a cry of "wait," and the pikes beyond the door crossed to enforce it. Sighing, he turned back to face the hollow glint of a man denied.

"Excuse me, lad. This whole business has left me bitter—I see it well as you. But you hear me out, for what you once bore me. Please." He gestured to the chair before him, and Rurik reluctantly slid into it, to meet his general eye to eye. After a moment, Tessel continued in softer tones: "Haste is a virtue we both share, I think. A blessing and a curse. It can make a man short-sighted; apply that to those with grand visions atop it and it is a recipe for disaster.

"I am for war. That is not about to change, and I'll not apologize to you or any man for it. I neither brought it, nor desired it, but I'll surely see it done. But what happened today, this whole mess—you have the right of it. It is not war, and while no man can be everywhere, every general knows that it will be his fault, down to the smallest man that sins within his charge. It is not a sin I intend to allow again. It will earn us no friends. And I shall need many where I walk."

"No doubt." Skepticism colored Rurik's words and left them grim. "But how can you possibly expect to move forward? There is no sanctuary for you. Here, or anywhere in Idasia."

The general's eyes rekindled at that, and the smile widened. "Oh ye of little faith! Have you fallen so far, Rurik? By Assal, we need no safe harbor. The Maker Himself set us here within His divine will, but then he stepped away, and left us to it. There's no man has a safe harbor in this world; merely illusions. These northern 'scapes are Farren. They need but hope to rise. So I march south, to give it to them."

And so he saw the madness of man come full into its bloom.

"Do not make this a holy war, Tessel. I beg you. It cannot end well."

Not least of all for Verdan. He did not say it, but in that boast of southern march, it was the only word that rang through Rurik's head. And it made the most sense. The forests would cover Tessel's march and offer game. The river would provide water, and mountains terrain to manipulate against any hunters.

But Rurik would not see it bleed. Too much blood had colored that land's history. *Let it end. Let the shadows of Ulneberg grow no deeper.*

"It is a war already drawn!" Wielded like a cannon, the anger snapped plain and fierce through Tessel's voice. Even the page flinched from it. Though Tessel shook, he made a gradual withdrawal from this lack of control, settling into a morose sort of whisper. "Drawn when some foreign priest tried to have me butchered. A man that never even knew our father would dare to guess his will. No, Rurik. This I cannot promise you. But I say you this, now—it is you who should be asked: where can you hope to go?"

"Home," he answered swiftly.

"Home," Tessel repeated, seeming to weigh it before dismissing it outright. He shook his head sorrowfully. "I worry for you, Rurik. Often. Many are those who wonder, how does a boy survive his family? But I see it in you, true enough, that a boy who survives his whole family has not survived—merely dies a slower death."

Rurik felt the shiver up his spine. His voice spilled out near breathless: "Meaning?"

"You think Cullick lets them breathe? That Ivon would look at you after all this?" A dry, bitter laugh caught in his throat. "Come now. Do not be naïve—that is not why I took to you. Use your head. By all rights, you are lord of Verdan. And of the Ulneberg, if I should have a say in it. You are the only noble blood I need, Rurik. Do you not remember that? But I do need someone with a name to support me. You may not think yourself loved, but your name is known, and it gives me cause against greater bloods than ours. The Emperor. Cullick. I have asked you before—would you not see yourself revenged? I am the only path to that. You must know this. On your own, you cannot hope such things. They will be snuffed between your hands like the flicker of a candle's flame. And you will die penniless and alone, knowing that everything you could have done, all the wrongs you could have righted, were left to rot at road's edge.

"Go, if you wish, but know that, and know that if you leave so too leaves any hope of protection this place has brought you. Think you that the assassins and their ilk have left you be simply because of war? Simple child, nothing is so simple. I tell you this: take up sword with me, or strike it up against me. There is no middle ground. No neutral party standing silent as a reed whoso lives within our lands. When it is a matter of empires, it can be no other way."

His gaze narrowed, then lessened to a rounded, gentler note, and the Bastard, seemingly exhausted, sank back into the crook of his chair. A long, steadying breath took him, and he dismissed Rurik, saying: "I give you the day to think on it. By time we move, your sword must be steadied to one side or the other."

Guards bundled him outside and tossed him into the waiting teeth of sharks. The honor guard had dissipated, and a peering twig of a youth remained in their place, though not for long. At the first glimpse of Rurik he made not even the pretense of disinterest. One look and he fled into the lanes.

One of the sentries followed the boy with his eyes, muttered something under his breath, and turned to Rurik as he neared. None of the honorifics of days before still settled on the edge of the tongue, however, and Rurik went to him as one man to another.

Unfortunately, the man did not ease his concerns. "That one?" the man scoffed in answer to Rurik's inquiry. "Little shite of a thing. Thief he is, but those sellswords took him on. He's a quick one, I'll give him that, eh?"

A shiver of dread crawled up Rurik's spine. "Sellswords?"

"Aye. Southerners, the lot. With them falcons for sigils." The man made what seemed a sign against evil and shook his head aside. "Your woods breed queer folk, ser."

A falcon. The crude sigil of the Gorjes. He nearly felt the point of a knife at his back. That made the runner Orif's creature, and if the man wanted knowledge of his departure, than his skin was surely to be the cost. *Will they find me in a ditch or strung from a tree?* Briefly, he considered asking for accompaniment, but even those that hadn't listened in on Tessel's parting words would be hard-pressed to leave either post or merriment for him. So he sufficed to thank the man, and bundled himself off toward the Company's camp.

The way was paved, one way or the other. Despite the looming threat from Orif and his bloody band of idiots, Rurik felt lighter both of foot and spirit to know that soon he could go and make some effort to turn things to what they once had been. Only the air above and the grass below, and all the world before their feet.

Thoughts of home tempered it. This time of year the ranchers would be leading their beasts abroad for the fresh grass, while the hunters set snares for the rousing creatures of the forest, still fat from winter's hording. The whole forest would come alive, as it had not since the snow began to fall, and all of them, caught in that land of ageless grace, would treat again with life, in place of death.

All save one empty home, with hollow halls and memories. No, he thought, slowing to a crawl near their ring of tents, there were some things that would never be the same.

Nor should he have presumed to think the rest would be so neatly done. Wolves, after all, never came at a man straight on. They circled and tore the flanks to pieces.

The Company's tents had been pitched at the base of a bent, double-trunked pine at the western edge of camp. Their tents circled one another, a canvas barricade against the outside, their perimeter a mass of other outcasts—individuals and broken parties, men that belonged to neither group nor land, and bore only what one saw before them. No allegiance, and hopefully, no vendettas.

Yet among the lot, sitting pretty-as-you-please beside the Company's own fire pit, was Orif of Kellsly, along with his man Gunther. There was no sign of the boy, but from the way their eyes crossed Rurik's expectantly—almost keenly—there was little doubt of his having been.

Rurik paused mid-stride to take in the scene and to make some sense of their play. Circling at the periphery was Rowan, hand loose on the hilt of his blade in a manner Rurik found in him unlikely: anxiousness. The others, resting, dined on scavenged bread, in a scene any other man might have taken for the old hearth greeting. Sitting across from the Gorjes, Essa barked something low enough that Rurik could not hear, and Gunther drummed out his own harsh laugh, turning away from the nearing prey. Neither she nor Voren, legs tucked beneath him and with an arm held defensively—and familiarly—across her backside, shared it. Orif consented to a sardonic smile, but his eyes never left Rurik. He even dipped his head in greeting.

In his hesitation, Alviss followed the Gorjes' gaze and caught him stiff. The look the old man shot him made him feel every bit the child again, caught prodding a feral dog. With a word of excuse to the others, Alviss rose from the place he held beside Essa and headed straight for him. Every voice in Rurik's head told him to move, but his legs felt bound by bog's mud. He looked to his former guardian and carefully lowered his eyes as the giant filled them.

It was in the shadow of the man's feet that he began to wonder: where was Chigenda?

"We move to be away from these. Now you bring them to us?" There was a terrible fury in the man's voice which only age and discipline contained. Rurik all but shivered under it regardless, and would not meet the man's eyes.

He stammered, "No. I—"

"What do I tell? Caution. Always caution. Never…" The voice trailed, and Alviss's tone with it, drifting into a sort of whimsy one might expect from a dreamer or a poet. Hesitantly, Rurik looked up, but Alviss was not watching him either. The man was fixated, further than he cared to question, until he caught Rurik's eyes upon him. Alviss grunted. "He waits you, boy. See him swiftly gone."

The northman turned and loudly proclaimed departure on excuse of water. Yet all the while Rurik noticed how his head twisted just so, and none of the muscles of his neck settled. He looked beyond the camp, to something—and there it was. Rurik cursed himself for not noticing sooner. The orjuk stuck out even in the colored multitude of the nearby tents, but there were others—Gorjes, all—that walked with club and knife both tapping anxious beats, watching the proceedings with all the subtlety of bulls on the plains.

They had been circled. This was not a man's threat, but a pack's.

Alviss shouldered past him. Several men, trying to appear a part of some ailing soldier's company, broke from their place and hastened after him. Rurik whispered a silent prayer for the Kuric, and turned his attention back to Orif. The Gorjes' captain hadn't as much as moved a muscle, aloof if not ignorant of the barbs being traded about him.

It had been some time since Rurik last had cause to give the man a second glance. Hard months had only drawn the slight man slighter still, but his teeth gleamed like a shark's, which was well, for he had lost none of the sharpness to his features. Lounged against several of the Company's packs, forsaking the grass the others contented themselves with, the man sprang like a jackrabbit at Rurik's approach. "Rurik," he cried as though old friends, crossing the feet between them in easy, luxurious strides. A hand snapped up Rurik's own, though he had not offered it, and pulled him close.

"To what—" was all he got out before he was all but yanked off his feet. Then, more cautiously: "To what do we owe the pleasure of your visit, Orif?"

The man pulled back, smile wide enough to swallow the lot of them whole. Beyond him, Rowan had drawn still as an addled man might, and their eyes caught. There was something there. A longing. Rurik drew aside from it.

"My boy," the Gorjes' swine of a leader boomed, "is it not manners to see a lad off? Surely war hasn't taken all our traditions?" Bells rang sharp through Rurik's head, and he angled for a surer look beyond the smarmy man. In the cast of his net, he spied Essa also stock still, her eyes fire on the both of them.

"And any protection this place has brought you," Tessel's voice echoed hauntingly. *Surely even he would not go so far…*

Trust. It was a fleeting thing. And men like Tessel—soldiers through and through—they knew that a pragmatic man used anything they might to see need met. Rurik's own weakness was only too apparent.

He cringed as he tore his hand back. "The day you learned manners—"

"Ah, ah, easy now. Wouldn't want to offend, aye?" Orif leaned close enough that Rurik could smell the wine on his breath. "Not your escort, I'd say."

"Escort?"

Orif threw his arms wide in a dramatic gesture. "Why, you're the general's chosen. He's not so heartless as to send his own off unaccompanied, nor I, for all those services you rendered. There's bandits in the woods, you know. And unseemly folk too, I'm told." He was enjoying himself.

"You need to leave."

Orif shifted his gaze sideways, as though addressing another beside Rurik. Someone who took his words no more seriously than he. "Ah-ah," he clucked absent-mindedly. "Now that's a might unseemly." He gestured out at the orjuk and the threat it implied.

If he could have throttled the man, Rurik would have. They were so close and he, boy that he was, still had a head on Orif. The first swing. That was all he would need. Instead, he tried not to choke on his tongue.

"That shouldn't be necessary, I'm sure. He must needs every man about him, and we are capable."

The corners of Orif's lips twitched at the last. "Oh, so he does, and that's why your loss does hurt us so." The man leaned back on the balls of his feet, hand tapping a gentle beat against his heart. "Perhaps I'll send a letter to Witold, yeah? Tell him the boy-lord's headed home, with Tessel's own blessing. Send someone to meet you, I'm sure."

He started to object anew, but as seemed the running case for this conversation, found himself once more cut off.

"Oh, but it *will*." All at once, all semblance of the smile dropped and the leer that became the sellsword emerged. "You just be sure and keep that girl real close now, you hear? Escort or no, I hears to tell we're headed south ourselves. And as you seen—accidents do happen." With a parting pat on the shoulder, Orif slid past him at a whistle. It took but seconds for the other Gorjes to snap to and come nipping at his heels. Before they were quite out of earshot, he could not resist one final gibe, calling out, "The very best, dear lordling!"

Rowan, standing as a reed amongst this sudden river, watched the flow of mercenaries with sunken eyes. He followed them long past the lengths of their threats, hand never once leaving his rapier. He never offered a glance to Rurik. Not like Voren. That one's eyes, still firebrands, remained fixed on him, as if by sheer force of will he might commit Rurik to the flames.

The promise of his blade was tempting, yet it was a temptation best resisted. Orif was swine, but one didn't get where he was without a few tricks. That, and the utter ruthlessness to see them done right. Between him and the orjuk, Rurik would have found himself little more than a thin paste smeared across the dust.

And Orif was one of those that rarely stopped at an eye for an eye—not that Essa needed help in riling this lot.

As it was, people were staring. Prying the nails from his own palms, Rurik twisted back for his would-be companions. Idle threats, he knew, were not the Gorjes' way. Nor Tessel's—and no man, even those cutthroats, would dare move so brazen without the Bastard's consent. It was to be blackmail, than.

The only noble blood, indeed. Tessel played the game with the best of them, it seemed. If only the core were a different man, Rurik might have followed him gladly to his end. But the man was a force consumed—he would burn or be burned in turn by the people, but never a blooded man or circled one to strike him a knee.

Essa scowled at him over the lip of the fire, sparing some sharp word for her faithful baker. Would they hate him for his weakness? Or for what he dragged them into? More important: could they ever forgive him, and see that he did this for them?

For her, at least, he thought he knew the answer. This, too, was his fault.

Hesitation held him at the edge of the tents. It no longer seemed, for all the warmth contained within, a place that he could cross.

Once, moons ago, a bastard-general had said that all men had a choice. So too did Rurik, and he saw it plain. Thus did he turn away now and leave the Company to their questions. Even Alviss, on his way back with bucket in tow, eyebrows raised in question, received nothing but a tip of the head. The stride came heavy, but it was not difficult to retrace his steps.

Conform or die. This was the decision laid at his feet. Tessel had never been kind to traitors. Perhaps the others would have chosen death, but Rurik could not choose it for them. It would only be a slower death for him.

Life was the only gift he could give, and they would never love him for it.

It was this they whispered in the dark hours of the night: he was the puppet on Tessel's strings. And how he danced.

The tent waited, and the blight within, growing longer in the twilight.

They would remain. *Assal help us all.*

Only two things held fortunate: the weather and their master. Both made a swift southern march of the days that followed Oberroth.

Agruil, the month the farmers quietly—for fear of the old goddess herself—referred to as the "fickle time" for its penchant toward indecision, dithering as it did between sudden, violent frosts and refreshing, windy blossoming, proved remarkably steady for their march. Nights were brisk, but morning quickly flooded the world with sunlit warmth. Even the sharp rains seemed to abate themselves, save for a few, scattered afternoon drizzles that served little more purpose than to wet the trees' thirst and cool the sweating men.

It also served to keep the Jurree within its banks—ever a problem in such early months. Already swelled with the thawing snow, any torrent might have flooded the banks and left the army trudging through mud and debris—something the raging river was always full with. When they reached it, however, the river was as placid as it could get, and cautious merchants were already taking advantage to peddle wares. Most fled before them, no doubt adding knowledge of the invaders' movements to their list of goods.

Tessel, in his turn, seemed to settle into the contentedness only a purposeful march could bring a soldier, partnered with the boon of a full belly. He left Rurik largely to his own devices, and rarely called on him for counsel, but in the same vein, he had no doubt kept his word regarding the Gorjes. Those mercenary hounds seemed almost stark in their absence in the aftermath of Rurik's decision. What few times he encountered them, they gave him room, and though they did not meet his eyes, he could feel their scowls burning into his back. Only Gunther put in any real appearance, and this amounted to little more than his usual calls on the Company.

For the moment, the swine were kept to pen. Yet it only confirmed how deeply linked they were to Tessel's own decisions. A moment's change of thought and Rurik might have found himself dining on a dagger's tip by breakfast. Fortunately, Tessel had never been an impulsive man.

In that same vein, the villages and hamlets, stray merchants and isolated ranches they encountered remained somehow, remarkably, unharmed. Though many men would have eagerly worked their dark deeds—by light of day or dead of night, Rurik reckoned—Tessel seemed to have regained some of his former soldiers' pride. What contact they had was civil, and aside from the setting of flags and a few posting of bands for watchmen and outriders, Tessel kept the interactions with "the new territory" to ambassadors—his captains—that often went to these places for pledges of allegiance, offerings of the Bastard's own word, and appeals for anything to aid "the pilgrim's march." This last disgusted Rurik, for it was merely extortion by another name, but he held his tongue.

All around the camp had spread new banners, following the influx of some small train of tailors to the camp. Gone were the gryphons, save of course the Emperor's own banner. In their place were seas of brown marked by the white, twisting mark of the "double infinity," some making of Tessel's curious mind, held aloft by staves.

"A symbol," the man intoned one night over a mandatory dinner with his captains and noble prisoners, "is as powerful as the thing itself. We make ours so the people mark us. This is, after all, a journey they shall share with us."

Rurik had kept to his cups that night and never shared a word, knowing that one day soon that flag would likely soar over his own hideaway in the trees. Yet another asked the very question he had pondered: "And what does our symbol mean?"

The Bastard's eyes seemed to glimmer at the telling. "Hope, of course. The hope of eternity, tempered by the simple earthiness of the shepherd's staff. We are born of the people, the ones left behind while the nobles play. Let them keep their beasts and their crowns. We, as faith itself, are born of the people, as Farre himself once said. Let us show them what it means to us."

What it meant to Tessel were bodies to fight his war. Anywhere they went, the Orthodox men shied away from the light and kept their families to their homes. The landed men among them often paid the lion's shares of a place's dues, and no few souls found themselves playing host to Tessel's hungry soldiers. But the Farrens moved with a vigor Rurik had never seen before. Some offered gifts at the gates of the morning camps. Some offered their arms to Tessel's cause. One adamant farmer even gave them three cows and a rather skinny chicken. The officers had feasted well that night.

Through it all, Rurik pondered: *How do they not know of Oberroth?* Clearly some word had gone before them, but it was Tessel's word, or some other fancy.

Truth died in the wake of greater things, and all the while, divided the ones that listened. In Emperor Matthias's day there had been tension, true, but the people were first and foremost Idasian—the heart of religion came after. Now, in Tessel, Rurik saw the beginnings of other loyalties. It broke his heart.

They never met another army. Twice, in small encounters, Witold's people probed their lines. The battles were short and indecisive—neither side lost many, and both withdrew as quickly as they were able. For the count's own part, locals said that he wandered further and further south, deeper into his territories at nearly the same pace as Tessel.

Running, most of the soldiers declared with pride. Biding his time, Rurik thought more likely. The old man was no fool, and he knew his land, proud hunter that he was. When battle came, Rurik had no doubt, it would be on his terms, and in a way that used the terrain to its full advantage.

So it was that they came to the very doors of Verdan. By nature, Verdan's people were folk accustomed to the harder matters of life. Life existed there, same as any other, but the people—former soldiers and soldiers' sons, wives, daughters, and the hard-set explorers that always journeyed with them—were accustomed to strife, and not easily intimidated. The surrounding farmsteads and logging camps, it became readily apparent, had deserted their posts and fled into the town proper, such that when the army's scouts returned to camp, they came with stories of a gathering several hundred strong, replete with the budding semblance of earthen walls. For all intents, they seemed spoiling for a fight.

The place itself was quiet. Even the animals fled before the deafening of their marching steps. Winter had not halted the logging, and more of the town lay bared to the light than ever. It made Rurik strangely self-conscious, as though the world itself were steadily breaking down the gates to his last bastion.

The others went to this place with only the outlook of soldiers: another conquest. Another place for rest. For food and drink. Women to warm their beds.

Rurik was sent ahead, with the remnants of Verdan's own levy besides, to take the town's measure and return to them as lord and master. He asked for the Company of the Eagle, but Tessel was no fool. Rurik compromised, and gained Alviss for the trouble. They went afoot, shunning the gryphon Tessel had offered Rurik. What's more, Rurik went to the place in reverence, for it was more than a place to live: it was a shrine to memory, to the toils of the heart and the foundations of the mind. So different from the last.

Soldiers met him at the outskirts, skittishly eying the army at his back. But they recognized him soon enough, and loudly so. It drew up a smile to see them, these opposites—the very youngest and eldest Verdan seemed to offer. Those men time could not align for war.

"It is good to see you, young master. And Alviss besides," one of the elderly said warmly. He addressed Rurik, but his eyes were for the northman, and he made no qualms about offering him a hand. Kuric though he was, Alviss was a figure here large as any other—and a place like Verdan was slow to forget its legends. No doubt they had mourned more for his loss than Rurik's, when the day of exile had come. "Your sister'll be beside herself when she hears you are about."

The word struck the false smile clean from him. Rurik all but sprang at the man in his eagerness. "My sisters? Anelie? Liesa? They're here?"

"*Sister*," the old man repeated. "Lady Liesa, begging your pardon. Or her erstwhile ladyship, as the good count does call her. She's been kind to us, lo these months—that business with your father aside. My condolences on that, lord—you have heard, yes?"

"I—" He knew the words he wanted to say, but it was as if he had suddenly been stricken dumb. Rurik nodded and turned aside. *Your ghost,* he whispered to his own grim mind.

One of the younger guards stepped in, apparently discontent to leave things so civil. "If only you had not brought an army with you," the youth said blandly, "you might have met your brother as well."

"Isaak?" *He lives?* How his heart leapt at the thought. Tessel had named them all dead—how had so many survived? Cullick was not so generous.

"Nay. Ivon. He sat your father's house, till the arms' rattle grew too near. Headed south—to spare us, says he. But Liesa stayed, aye. Someone had to, says she. Brave lass. Braver than some."

He let that slide. *Ivon.* So he was alive too. *A day for good news all around.* Rurik thanked the men for it, trying to keep the tormented bliss from his voice, and looked out on his town. For all the life within, Rurik knew, still one ghost walked its streets, waiting for him. He closed his eyes and spoke to a man too long beyond him.

Father. I'm home.

Chapter 15

The world seemed, for all its promise, to be bearing down on the house of Durvalle. The court was in chaos, and the courtiers with it, and so they turned that chaos on Leopold and his family. From terrified peasants to petty lords and even the high dukes, everyone seemed to wish a pull on the Emperor's ear.

He knew not what to make of the reports he was getting. There had been skirmishes at the border with Usteroy—some petty lords getting ahead of themselves, no doubt, and it was said that there were already reprisals springing through the villages of the heartlands. The Empress Dowager was in the south. The Empress Dowager was in the north. No one knew where the Empress Dowager was. Everywhere the song of Farrens and the howls of the Orthodox. Blood ran in the streets and man or woman, religious fool or noble dog, they blamed their emperor.

And why not? He was the father of the nation, and they his children. Even where his eyes did not reach, nor his hands touch, it remained his fault, because he had not guaranteed his eyes or hands could reach there. Leopold was in over his head, and though Ersili met daily with the council to try and stem the tide, no amount of words seemed enough to stay the madness.

Opportunistic fool that he was, his father's bastard had ridden in on the chaos like an avenging wind. Neither Othmann nor the damnable Effisians had caught him, and now the council quaked from what he had brought to the shaded copses of Momeny—that easternmost hold of the Idasian Empire. Decades in the building, and in one fell swoop the Bastard had smashed the Hammer and scattered Scheyer's forces to the wind. Oberroth, that last bastion of civilization, was said to have burned like Kimlia of old, with worse atrocities committed in the flames.

Only two goods had come of it. Such barbarity had been enough to unite the beleaguered old nobles behind their emperor, and sufficient to divide the Farrens. Where Tessel had been hailed as vengeance incarnate, this atrocity had—through word of mouth aided by royal messengers—colored their views of him. Some still drew to him, of course—peasants mostly—but the great northern lords, the merchants, the craftsmen, and those newly ennobled creatures Matthias had once called his "faithful few," still leant their blades to Cullick. All Leopold had to do was guarantee the two men never met, nor saw the benefits of clasping arms.

If they did, Idasia would surely burn, and his household with it.

With that in mind, he had at last recalled the Idasian navy from its blockade of Effise. Hopefully, they would be enough to crack open the northern cities and restore the lifeline of the river Klein. If not, it meant at least more bodies for the defense of the capital. A matter of days and he would know one way or the other.

At the council's urging, he had put away the old emperor's littlest daughter into safer hands than his. There was no mention of it to his wife—she would have simply killed the girl, out of sight and out of mind. Their own children, against his own heart's cry, were sent to the church at Blassenberg, and through it, south with the Inquisition to the border of Ravonno. The south was loyal. They would be safer there. Away from this nest of vipers.

Away from the visions of the huntress—the curse men whispered of on starless nights.

For more than a month, he toiled at his so-called duties, trying to make sense of it all, and not always in vain. Armies were at the march from Ravonno, arms and supply from Walim and the isles of Karnush, while sellswords swelled in from the world over.

If only that old fool in Effise had done his duty and caught the Bastard early. Then again, I suppose it's no good wondering at what might have been.

If only the dreams had not tormented him so, he might have been able to deal with the lot. As it was, he hardly slept. When his children began to whisper of the same—of dreams of some shade, wreathed in fire, hunting down the old gryphon—the final line was crossed. A feeling his so-called family apparently shared.

Long before, his siblings took to flight. For all their oaths, they would not remain within Anscharde. It was too close to Usteroy, they said, too indefensible and too close to the war. They would retire to the coasts, to their scattered holdings, or south and west to Dexet, and their great nephew there. None whispered of the ghost that seemed to cling to their castle, but it was there all the same. They feared blades, but they feared the darkness all the more.

Promises, promises. Everyone made promises. Few kept them. They had their priorities and that was just the way of it. Men could say many things, but they meant few of them.

It was different with the witch, or so Leopold's beloved claimed. His wife stood beside him at their table, holding his hand as this latest witch spread her hands across the fabrics she had laid. She smiled at him, mouthing assurances through the silence. But for Bertold and the witch, they were alone. Leopold smiled back at Ersili and let her certainty ease him.

Magic, at least, was something real. Perhaps not something that could be tamed, but something real, and something powerful. Bertold was proof enough of that. With luck, the witch—Duša—would be as well. Let the Church and his fellow priests damn it all they would. It had its uses, in moderation.

As now, in the guarantee of a life: his.

"Are we ready to begin?" Bertold asked, face locked in a perpetual frown.

Leopold nodded, gripping his wife's hand a little tighter. The excitement was dizzying. Never had he done anything like this before—that is, before the procession of witches. At first, it had seemed silly. Almost pointless. What man feared when steel and stone could protect? Yet he was no fool. Three brothers and a chancellor all dead under mysterious circumstances. It could have been a conspiracy. Others had whispered of it. Truth be told, it had haunted him every step of the way from Ravonno. The Empress Dowager certainly had cause. Her, or Cullick.

But even he felt the darkness lurking about their halls, and it bore no human shape. Ever since the first has-been of a witch, the first séance, he could almost feel it on his shoulders. Waiting. Watching.

The spirit. Or whatever it was. Something stalked his family. It was stalking *him*. Bertold had felt it, though he never said as much—like a good hound, it was in the way he tensed his shoulders at certain moments, the tiny eyes rounding about his person. Some men might have put that off to nerves, or something lesser. Leopold could see the truth, though. He knew when things did not add up, and Bertold had confirmed that much, at least.

As the witch bowed her head, he thought of Joseph and wondered. They said a fire had taken him. In the middle of nowhere, a fire had swept his flesh away and left him a husk. Mere ashes in the soiled snow. *What could do that?* Nothing human. Nothing real. He glanced to his bodyguard and back to his wife, and tried to breathe. This witch would fix it. Or they would turn her out as they had the others.

Then he could deal with real things. Like a bastard overstepping himself, and a Farren whore threatening his nation with damnation. The Patriarch's letter lay still crumpled on the floor. It called his very capabilities to question.

For all that, he wished for nothing more than to be able to scratch the itch on his forehead. Bertold had actually slapped his hand when he tried. Soot stained that flesh now, as it did all of them, and he could not help but feel juvenile for it. In the priesthood, of course, one was accustomed to having all manner of things smeared across the flesh, but there one had the added benefit of spiritual connection, and the knowledge that it would be only a fleeting show.

The only guarantees he received here were via his bodyguard's icy looks. "For the magic," the grouse assured him of the soot. Surelia actually seemed charged by it. Less so when Bertold began to smear ashes on the walls, too. Leopold smiled as he patted her hand. It was the little things.

Like the bath that will be necessity after this. If these northerners might be troubled to draw one.

Bertold wove his wards about the room, stepping around the table as Duša began to chant. Only once did his concentration break, as the witch's eyes moved to him, and there, then, Leopold caught the barest, fleeting hint of a scowl. Bertold did not approve of their choice. He would never say as such, but for all the things that Bertold was, Leopold could read him like an open book. The man put too much stock in his own power. Too little in others'.

Soon, even he would see.

"Breathe, Your Majesty. This is very important. You must clear your mind of distraction," the witch said, bobbing her gray head.

He swallowed. "Stop…thinking?" That seemed unlikely.

"Take my hand—and your wife, the other. The three of us will use one another. Our spirits will wash through one another's flesh and use the power within to channel the spirit here. If you are distracted, the effort will be for naught, and at best, your spirit will ignore us."

Leopold opened his mouth to say something else, then stopped with a furrowing of the brow. "And at worst?"

The witch coughed. "Are we ready?"

Ersili gripped his hand, looking him in the eyes as she answered, "We are."

* *

Something changed in the woman. Charlotte glanced up from her reading, to the woman on the bed before her. Meditations, or dreams, had carried Usuri away, somewhere far beyond the mortal coil. She had been knitting a scarf—they finally had begun to trust her again with sharp objects—and stopped, abruptly. Charlotte scarcely minded. Frankly, she felt the need to watch, but she preferred it when the woman kept her quiet. Of late, since the whispers with her coin had ceased, the woman had seemingly retreated into a shocked sort of stillness. Too many of her nurses had been scared off by such ploys. Charlotte would not fare the same.

Not when Usuri had finally seemed to be talking sense.

Yet the woman's sudden lurching startled her nerves to waking. Usuri bolted upright, eyes wide. She seemed to look across the room without seeing anything there, and began to shake. Charlotte set her book aside and rose to her feet. A tap on the door saw the guardsmen enter. She feared the woman was moving toward another attack.

But Usuri only stared. Pale fingers dug into the folds of her skirt and her body shivered.

"What is this?"

Inquisition was Charlotte's nature, but commonsense held her back. Something had the woman, though there was nothing there.

"What do you want?" the witch whispered.

Charlotte might have thought the question directed at her—but for the scream that followed.

* *

The witch reached out her hand, palm open, only to crumple it into a fist of ash. Duša barked some strange tongue and spasmed under the pale light. Ersili watched her with knowing eyes. Even Bertold acquiesced to some degree, his pacing ceased beside the door. He wanted no part of this circus of freaks, as he deemed it, but he could not look away.

The witch's head rolled and her mouth opened, ever-so-slightly. Even that grungy Loracian skin seemed to descend into a sudden pallor. Shoulders rolled as a low moan broke the silence. It sounded like she was choking on her tongue. No more words uttered. They seemed lost to the flames she had sparked.

"Stop this," Bertold barked sharply. "This is no spirit and she knows not what she—"

A force thudded against Leopold's chest. Something rippled in the air.

Leopold might have leapt back, if his wife hadn't held him firm. He looked to the witch, but that woman remained—head tipped back, eyes closed. Only the slightest of shivers gave any indication to her continued breaths. Ersili's eyes were locked on the air before them, though, in the same spot the ripple had issued from. That drew an easy breath. At the least, Leopold realized, it meant he wasn't insane. Whatever it was, she could see it too.

But it was Bertold that worried him. The magi's face had all the color of a child marked for death. Fear dwelt there, where there was supposed to be nothing. Yet he stood frozen, as if he could not comprehend what he was seeing. His eyes, too, had drifted toward that point above the table. The left hand twitched, in a sign Leopold knew well from the superstitious south.

A sign against enchantment and evil.

Then the room began to shudder. Even this, Leopold might have passed off as something else—if Duša hadn't chosen that moment to speak.

* *

Charlotte twisted from the shriek, clapping hands tightly over her ears. More men would come at that. They wouldn't be long. The scream was, however, and it flooded the room even as it seized the witch's body. Eyes widened and she seemed to go stiff, even as she clamored for her feet. They were begging eyes. Uncertain eyes.

"No more! I won't! I won't!"

Dartrek stomped forward to cut her off. "Not again. Sit you down you—"

She made it perhaps a step before the shaking carried her away. White eyes rolled back into her head and she plummeted toward the stone. Had she struck it, she might have broken something—but Charlotte was quick. She caught her even as she fell, and gently laid Usuri down. Then she called out, fighting to hear herself over the babble that broke the woman.

When she looked down, she saw only a woman lost—shivering against some unknown winter. Usuri's eyes were open, but she did not speak. Not words, anyways. It was babble, save one thing.

"See," she said. *See, see, see.* Dartrek and the others had the binds in hand. Still, Charlotte pulled her head into her lap, waiting for someone that would know more, and she tried not to worry as to what would come of this. The woman haunted her dreams—made the familiar terrifying. Imagination could scarce suffice for what lay inside Usuri's own head.

Yet the woman, dragging her nails along the stone, would only whisper of devils. From the sounds of it, they had little interest in her life. In this, they shared her wardens' opinions.

* *

She was there. Suddenly, violently, she was there.

The magi's hands surged into action, tearing a pouch from his belt and casting salt into the air. It struck out in a ring. A circle. *Maker protect us.*

There was no shape to her. Nothing to distinguish a person, let alone a gender. But he could feel as she pushed into being—a break in the essence of their world. It was the scream that gave her away. At first, it felt like the stones had begun to hum. It sparked a primal dread in him. The witch began to sweat. Then she gargled, as the room quivered, and the very air with it.

Something heavy battered at it, rolling in waves through the air. Then the ripple reverberated in turn, striking the walls and ricocheting out. Screaming, on and on. There was no voice, but the thing shrieked through them all, and there was not a soul there that did not buckle beneath the pressure.

For Leopold, it was like someone had beaten a drum through his ear. Rapid beats drilled the questions from his head, bloodied the body without ever touching the flesh. He stumbled, and his wife shrank beside him, as she shouted in surprise.

Such power! He found himself shrinking, pulling away. *Is this what stalks me?*

"Let go," Bertold shouted. Never had his voice risen to such crescendo. The man surged against their bond and feverishly tore at their arms. "Break the circle. Break it now!" the magi cried.

It was not that he did not want to oblige. Leopold yanked back, startled to waking by the sound of his guardian's voice. He yanked back and tried to pull free, but his wife began to shout, and the witch would not release him. "I can't," he shouted. "She won't let go. She won't!" It was like he had been caught in a vice of iron. Even his wife's nails, digging into his skin, felt as if they were searing into his arm. As if some invisible force had bound them.

"The fire!" Duša began to weep. "Dítě, dítě, turn back, I pray you still, ustat!"

As the woman fell into her foreign tongue, Bertold cast back as well, howling, snarling words Leopold could not identify. It was a language, surely, and though pieces seemed to borrow from Rovennan, their intonation was far darker, and the core was lost to time and space. From his touch on the floor, the salt and ash smeared across the walls began to bubble and shimmer. A dark cloud swirled over the walls, swallowing them, and that voice grew further away. More and more of the air warped, contorted, rippled in the dark, such that Leopold began to panic. It was as if the air itself began to bubble around the figure taking shape within their chamber.

He tried to shake his wife free, calling to her, but she would not listen. Someone pounded at the door. "It's here," Ersili whispered, almost crying. Pain creased her beautiful face, wracking them both. He kicked at the witch, but something—something more than those old bones—would not let go.

Air flickered to life, and he could see the barrier. It strained and became transient, like paper held before the setting sun. In that moment, he beheld the labors of Bertold's sweat. Something swirled beyond it. Waiting. Bertold's words seemed to flare the light to life, but the inky apparition hammered it, thunderous and terrible, like a battering ram. The magi stumbled, crying out. Muscles strained, though he grabbed at nothing. His face set to a purpose, and Leopold might have sworn something crimson surged through his robes—down, down into the earth. He muttered. He strained. And the world strained against him.

Please, Maker, Leopold cried, closing his eyes against the madness. *Let this be a dream. Let it all just be a dream.*

When the wall finally broke, and Duša screamed aloud, Leopold's eyes opened to the shape of her, lines of black and grey hair weaving into the very moulds of the stones, even as her eyes crackled lightning into the sky.

The room became her, and everyone and everything beneath her was consumed in her essence.

"Pomsti nás z plamenů," the witch cried out abruptly, jerking against the force of the presence. "I can see, I can see…"

The earth began to shake.

* *

Half a dozen men pulled them apart and dragged the still babbling witch toward the sheets. Charlotte twisted away as Dartrek seized her.

"Stay. Enough you have done," he demanded, splitting his attention between them.

The witch began to buck and shake, crying out as she clawed them. The guards took her by the hands and bore her down, but still she fought, unconsciously striking at any close enough to touch. "Bind her!" someone shouted. Every part of her edged out, as if the very world bore down upon her. "I see you!" she screamed. "I am the Inquisition! I see you!" So loud, that one of the guards called for a rag with which to gag her.

Blood dribbled from Usuri's nose, lapping at the flesh like a babbling brook. Skin paled as she contorted, writhing—something seized her.

Flesh bloodied against the iron and leather of her captors, but the woman struggled as if against the world itself. They clapped her tight, and still she raged. Charlotte could feel the reverberations, even from the other end of the room. They left her breathless—the air, heavy. Usuri was not with them. She could feel that much. Somewhere far away, and they were all the better for it.

For that presence, heavy as it was, left no light in its wake. What it touched, it consumed, and the air, numb, drifted in its wake—a forgotten presence, devoid of all that gave life breath. Charlotte placed a hand against her chest, trying to settle her thoughts, but they raced with the power of it all. It surged, through air and stone alike. It pierced walls no flesh could touch.

They needed to wake her. Blood flashed, bright and copper through Charlotte's mind, and she knew that this was the only recourse. Only destruction lay in dreams.

* *

Somewhere far from either ghost a boy came awake screaming in the night. The girl sang through the coin and through him, and even then he knew.

Something had broken.

* *

He held her. Bertold held her, but for how long Leopold could not say. The sorceror drew the full weight of himself against the ram of her presence, crying out his dark tongue as he crumpled under the pressure. Sweat beaded and descended his increasingly frail shape.

There, in that instant, Leopold could see that he was greater than they had ever known. There was more substance there, more presence, than even eyes could hold. He was a force in a world of motion, and he pressed it all into a single moment, hoping to batter one force with another. For a moment, it seemed as if it might work. Air rippled and strained against their effort, flaring and fading in time to some strange song Leopold had never known.

So long ago, they had taught him, the Lord moved in mysterious ways. Though his work remained unseen, the efforts were there for all to bask in.

Now Leopold saw the motions, as well as the ends. Everything quivered under the weight of their magic. Not just them. No—he could see that. Another man—a holier man—might have cried out to his god in that instant. When the lines of the world itself began to strain, they would have praised the Lord for showing them the very threads of earthly being. Yet Leopold was not that holy man, for he did not see the world at work. Rather, he saw the lines of the world struggling not to break. He felt flesh and spirit strain, bend, and fold beneath the tugging of its core.

Then, he felt it tear.

"What is it?" his wife called. "I don't understand."

One didn't have to understand to see. It was like the air itself was ripped asunder; to the shrieking tune of metal, rending. Ersili screamed. That seemed at last to rouse his wife, her hand and his peeling apart. Too late. The circle was broken, but the circle was only a catalyst. Bertold screamed and the light—the beautiful light that encompassed them all—rolled along the lines of the air and shattered as it clattered against the stones. Breaths licked darkness and everything rolled. Leopold's stomach shuddered under the impact. He felt ill.

And through it all, Bertold continued to scream.

Somewhere beyond the pale, the door also shuddered. With shouts and steel. Men had heard them. They clamored at the entrance, trying to force their way in. Yet he could not have wished that on anyone.

As flames wisped and subdued, something solidified in the air. His wife pulled him back, retreated across the cobbles. The witch's hand scored him as she called out across time, but his hand seemed to slip easily from her, at last. Bertold curled inwards, crumbling against the stones. In the salt, he writhed as a man possessed. Something broke in him. Leopold glanced from his guardian to the witch, and the eyes consumed him.

They lurked behind the witch's, watching his every step. Her breaths were in the air as he ran, shoving his wife onward toward the door. An axe splintered the boards and men hurled against the hinges. Yet this devil's anger was in his heart long before she ever gripped him. It screamed and everything seemed to rumble away. He gasped, for the power of it. It was like an avalanche.

"What are you?" he shouted, trying to retain some semblance of sanity. Trying to gasp. Ersili begged him not to look back, clawed at him, pulling him toward the opening door. But he could not look away.

She spread into being. Translucent, uncertain, her hands burned in some unseen tumult. Duša whispered her name and rocked against the stones as her hands reached out and her eyes nailed him to the floor. He was exposed. Fragile. He could see that now. He felt naked before the judgment, and cried out to Assal in a way he hadn't since he was a child. She wrapped her arms around him and he staggered. They were cold. So cold. He rasped as nails dug into his mind.

"You," the spirit called across the din of space. Then he could see her, as if she stood before him. Flames bubbled around her, and he knew of father, friend, life. It all boiled away. His own wife called to him, tearing at the men pouring through the gap, but he could not move.

"You would consume me. You all would," she said, and he knew it was true. He saw a child, only a child, and at last he wondered why.

Then she reached into his heart, and all the wondering ceased. *Assal,* he wept, as the world began to tear him away. *Have pity on us. We have sinned. We have*—a prayer to the tune of his wife's own cries.

* *

The flesh sank in surrender, though the mind remained. The guardsmen hesitated as the witch went limp, many of them boasting scratches from the throes of her tantrum. They did not know what to do and they looked to Charlotte for a resolution.

Though they had bound hand and foot to the bed, Usuri fought against them with as much fear as she fought against the flesh. When the moment of quiet came, it was as sudden as the fit had begun. She simply opened her eyes and sagged against the feathers of her bed. Ceased struggling. Ceased screaming.

Then vomit spilt from the witch's mouth and several soldiers vaulted back to evade it.

A terrible cough rattled her as she uttered, "I am used." Focus seemed to elude her eyes and they sank instead into the cracks of the floorboards. There was a phantom there that would not abate, carving lines beneath her eyes far deeper than the other deaths had wrought.

"Father. I am not fit. What good in this? What good?"

Usuri had been mad before. But taling to a dead man? Charlotte lacked the words to lend it shape.

She knew that drawn look. The ghost of flesh. Magic—there was no doubt of its part in this. Yet the woman held no trinkets, and so far as she seemed, had not stood compelled against another. Not in that moment, anyway. And the violence of it—she was normally so detached.

A horrible thought bloomed. Had someone else attacked *her*? If so, how could they have known of her? An old grudge—personal—or someone from the Court? Surely Sara hadn't said a word of the girl's presence. Where anyone could have found another creature like her to do it, though…it wasn't as though her father hadn't looked. Hadn't hunted.

Walthere had to be warned.

One of the soldiers had already gone to fetch Charlotte's father. Dartrek kept Charlotte sequestered off to the side while his fellows did the work. She stared over his shoulder, but said nothing, knowing the futility of that fight. The rest stalked the bed like vultures awaiting the final moment of surrender.

The witch began to rant. "He falls. She falls. It slips through the fingers and the world, it watches, knowing nothing of the grains upon the wind—just sand. Just sand. We wash away. That's it. We wash away and we are gone.

"The grain turns to another, says: I'll cast you out for that grain you tossed up last octave. And he throws him. And the wind howls dirges to the dissolution of the grain but—he's gone. The others don't notice. The wind howls again, and another goes the next day. Meaning is…is…"

Fear remained in the soldiers' eyes. They had seen too much of this girl to trust her insanity to merely that—insanity. So had Charlotte. She saw their fingers linger on their cudgels and wondered if, finally, this wasn't the moment. If death would not be sweeter for the girl than this. Something had happened, but then, something always happened.

Usuri's voice cracked, wavered, and trailed into silence. She cast this way and that, tossing her head as if to shake some foreign beast from off her back. There was nothing to say. A pang of guilt struck a chord in Charlotte's gut, but this was just case and point. The woman's madness had gone too far.

Long moments passed in the candlelight. It framed wrinkles about the witch's drowning face that made her appear far older than she was.

Gently, fingers once lost to frenzy brushed against the straps that held them. Without a word, in those places where rope met flesh, the threads unwound and snapped, brittle as ice. Thus freed, as the crowd gawked, she reached down and made the same work of those threads about her legs. Kicking them off, she stood abruptly, to the startled cries of her guardsmen, and headed for the door. Charlotte called after her, but the witch ignored it.

"It hurt. It always hurts. They round you and they rake you and…" Nonsense peppered the witch's steps, but Charlotte slowly rose to follow it to its course. Like a piper's note. Dartrek held her back, barking orders, as one of the other soldiers lunged for Usuri's shoulder.

And Charlotte knew fear.

Seeming in that instant to finally remember where she was, the witch stopped. She blinked as she turned to face the soldier's grip. While denouncing her for hellspawn, without hesitation the guard struck her down with a cudgel. A little rush of air was all she gave. Blood dripping from the side of her head, the dazed woman rolled onto her belly as the man stooped over her, cudgel rising, and began to dig at the floor. Usuri rubbed dust across her face, across her hands and gown. She piled it between her fingers and cupped it to hold out to the soldier. The man ordered her up as the others hedged in, but she did not obey.

"Hit her!" one of the others called. "You saw what she did to the rope."

Gone was the pain. Her face drew formless, empty. "Dust to dust," she whispered so low Charlotte had to strain to hear it. The guard's shoulders loosed with a sigh, his lips mouthing a soundless "What?" to Charlotte, with all the interest of a man jailed.

Usuri opened her hands as he did and flung the dust into the stale air.

It exploded.

When Charlotte pulled back from the noxious roar, the world ripped asunder with her scream. For her, there was only air. One moment, she stood in it, feared in it, and the next—the overwhelming sound.

It burned through her like a cancer. Limbs froze. Eyes watered—filled to bursting and broke. Her body twisted and croaked on its own breath. There was no sound to loose and only blood to taste. Everything went rigid, and launched her burning down a long, dark corridor.

She woke in it. One long, deep rasp. Then the coughs racked her. She sat up, wheezing, feeling—chill. She called to Dartrek, but the words seemed to ring hollow in her mouth, and all that greeted her was ash and more damnable dust. Something burned. Needles lanced through every motion, and she found she was not the only one so pinioned. There was a pile before her, all broken bodies and mangled limbs, and no one moved but in wincing.

Men armed and armored had been scattered as if by cannonfire. At their center, Usuri lay as though asleep—peaceful, almost, but for the broken murmurs and the pale, lidless stare.

She did not see—not them, anyway. The blood matting her hair was the only color left to her.

I am not here. A guard crawled through the doorway. Shouts in the hall—a maid calling for help. For the blood. *There is no blood.* She could feel it on her skin. Like water rolling cool fingers down her cheek. *I am in my room. I am running my fingers through my hair and—* It was muddled, distant—the sound. It had carved through her like a scythe, yet the chaff remained. Hunched, groggy. *I do not know this woman before my eyes.*

Blood had crusted where her fingers touched her ear. It ran the side of her face and stained.

"My lady?"

A spider scuttled at her shoulder, immaculate among the carnage. There were boots in the hall. All rang with the sound, such that she winced. *Weakness. There is no abiding weakness.*

She felt sick.

Boyce looked it.

"You're bleeding. Assal above—get the medicus."

Figures shuffled. They spun. She swooned, thought better of words, and leaned against the ground. It felt solid, anyway. Yet the witch laid on it as if adrift. Mumbling to the sea.

"It burns. It all burns. You and I and everything between. Only the lioness, cradling the gryphon in her arms, should ever kiss another snow. We are…"

There was a dagger in his hand as he moved on the witch. Charlotte blinked. Boyce's face gave nothing, but the hands were poised, even—eager. He moved between the bodily lanes until the shadow of his being put him over the source. Boyce did not blink. He lifted the dagger under her chin and made to push.

There was a weight on Charlotte's legs. She couldn't move. Into sight, the body flickered, and she knew it for Dartrek, still as a felled tree, covering her.

Tears stained the cloth. "No, no," Charlotte rasped, struggling through the croak of her voice.

The sound of hesitancy. The spider bent against its prey, attention rolling back along its web. Hard eyes held no remorse. But hers did.

He slid the dagger back up its sleeve and cast the witch to the floor. She never moved. Then: "As you wish, my lady."

It would end in blood. As she breathed against the stone, the silence whispered that to her. Insanity was useful. But only when leashed.

Chapter 16

A person can suppress hurt, but they cannot destroy it. They can try to put it from their mind, but the beast is an insidious thing. It only squirms between the fingers, wiggling deeper and deeper beneath the skin until the mind no longer hunts it out. It waits.

So it was with Rurik.

The night Roswitte told him of his father's death, Rurik had felt what little piece of his heart remained shatter into fragments. He sank into himself until the frost was all he knew. But he wouldn't face it. Not truly. Instead, he fled into winter, leaving the beast howling amidst the winds of his subconscious until he could harvest some semblance of himself.

Reconcile began in the concept that his father was the same man that had exiled him. This was the same man that caused Essa to leave with her own drunk of a father and robbed Rurik of love for all those years. It came in visuals of a hard man, a quiet man, a distant man. It regurgitated itself in memories of a child, motherless, unattended—a father turning a blind eye in favor of other, brighter seeds.

At first, he tried to pretend death didn't matter before such things.

Then he convinced himself he hated the man, and for that too, death did not matter.

Lastly, he tried to convince himself that he had moved on.

Pain always outed the lies. When the empty streets of Verdan loomed, it all surged back to the fore.

For all the trials and tribulations that family might put one through, there is a longing deep in the heart of every child, for the acceptance of their parents. A love that lies beneath even the darkest turns of tongue, the deepest cuts to heart. It is why, in fact, those cuts reach so deep—for they, as no one else, command a place reserved within.

As Rurik looked on the home he had once known, he realized that place was empty now, deprived by an act of sacrifice. He had spent so much time on hate, and yet, his father never had. Kasimir Matair had beheld his son before the flames and pulled him back before they caught.

But the act had, in turn, left Rurik utterly alone. Essa. Kasimir. His mother. Even his siblings. All, in one way or another, had been undone by his own stupidity. He knew it. Kneeling in the dirt, he knew, in the way of old men faced with the long and final sleep. For all that he had wrought, he had nothing. An army stood at his back, steeled arms and voices filling the void of their victory, and it was all so meaningless.

Yet men did not cry and he could not bring himself to do so there. Instead he drifted from house to house and street to street, as if upon a dream. No one moved to stop him.

Nothing stood barren before his eyes. Though uncertainty hastened steps or gathered peering eyes at the edges of the town, people still moved along old lines. Loggers put back to axe and struck trees to earth. In counter to that splitting note, the ringing chorus of the blacksmith echoed hollow and shrill, each bleat hammering as a nail. All the while the old women fussed over equally old tales—other armies, other horrors, and other trials—as they plucked and sewed and cooked and cleaned, those little ones not otherwise occupied listening in with eager ears.

After the initial tension of the army's arrival the day before, the people of Verdan drifted back into the cycle of routine. It was as though nothing had changed. As though the death of a good man meant nothing, and the people could simply forget. Perhaps they could. Yet Kasimir's ghost moved everywhere among them. The very lanes to which they moved had been built along lines he laid.

From every nook and crag of the nurtured earth, the smallest of voices whispered to him: *This land holds your father's bones. Never surrender your father's bones.*

At some point, Voren, following silent as a ghost himself at the back of their little train, departed with as little notice. Rurik twisted back only at a touch from his once-guardian, and the boy nodded, half-realizing, but not truly caring. That one, at least, still had family to attend. Family that waited anxiously for word or body. This could not be begrudged. Every man followed their own trails to their ends. Would that Rurik's led anywhere but a dead man.

Kasimir had ever been a strong man, for all the injury he bundled under his cloak. Winter had passed, but Rurik could still spy his broad strides leaving pits in the snow-strewn lanes, his black cloak brushing the earth behind him, snapping orders to men at the watch. Where to dig. Where to kindle the fires. Where to let it all drain out. It was a silent phantom now, but still he moved, ignorant of the little boy leaping hole to hole to try and catch his footsteps.

He followed those old ways, through the streets and along thatched and slate-struck foundations to the field beyond. The field had grown wild, its grasses thick, save where horses rode them still to ground. No one had ever been allowed to make pasture here, along the road that connected manor to town. Rather, soldiers had always been here to cut it down or grind it. Here was where they trained—not locked behind high walls, removed from the families for whom their swords were taken up.

They were gone as well. Ridden with Ivon or hitched to the Bastard's army, and some, they still lay scattered over foreign earth, never to return. Prayer could not have sufficed for them. They were gone, and he remained, and all a living man could do was wonder why.

Alviss shook his head here, running a hand through the long trails of green. "Shameful," he muttered. "Any snake could slither unseen..."

An old saying. Kasimir's. *Let the land about my home be bare, that even a snake should not slither unseen across my threshold.*

The man had seen everything. Rurik moved before Alviss and off the paved lane. One of his father's guardsmen moved with him, muttering, "Careful, careful," but Alviss only nodded. Rurik turned about. Like a sliver, the light fell through the distant trees, casting streams and shadows on the empty pasture. A boy had played here. So too had a boy trained here. A younger Alviss stood beside him, the threads of his beard still gold as the spring light, hand axe snapping at the youth's weak thrusts. A poor fighter even then.

A heavy hand laid against his shoulder, and they moved on. He tried not to think of those times, for the boy, feeling only the pain of landed blows and wounded pride of his own poor showing, had seen this as first among the signs of punishment. Of an uncaring host, putting him off to other men. Other concerns.

The manor sat as an untouched peak amidst the wild. What vines and ivy claimed the low stone walls had ever been there. Its gates, never tested by war, lay open to them, its ramparts manned only by a single sentry—a nodding husk of a man made skeletal by the girth of his armor setting at the winch, a lonely man set to a lonely duty. Rurik slowed, but the man did not call out. The eyes were on him, but his were all for the yard within. Several servants trotted up to the gate and stood waiting, receptive. As though to receive a lord.

There was a reason he had evaded this house until now.

The last time he had visited this place it had been by dead of night, slinking in like a mouse through a hole, hunted, unnoticed, and brimming with a fire that no one here had earned. It all seemed a dream now. A night of heavy hands and quick blades. A night of kind words, undeserved. It was made all the more unreal by how quickly it had ended—shuffled out again like prisoners put to march, and never again to see a father's face.

"Go on. I will join you shortly," he said to the others.

There was some hesitation in the guardsmen. No doubt they had their orders. Yet they went, as such men would, when they were sure he would not vanish. He stepped off the trail again, to the wall, and peered through the gate cross-wise, as a child stole into their parents' secret places. Alviss waited with him longer, watching until at last he too went, and Rurik could hear his voice rise at some near sight, which set Rurik's own hands trembling.

This was a mother's domain. Tenderly raised, painstakingly imagined. The father stood as but a caretaker, and it stood in memoriam. This was the heart, he knew, in the teeming greenery, the simple beauty, the shadows that pulled at a person night and day. In their wake remained the man, still as a statue, and this was how Rurik should forever remember him: not some pompous lord, but a man without extravagance, stark, thin, and tall, staring out wordlessly at the life around him, though his own face betrayed no hint of that existence. One never saw the limp here. Nor heard the whip-like voice. They saw but a soldier at his home.

Cold blue eyes turned to him, and in their place there stood a living vision— one he had never hoped to face again.

His sister was poised within the courtyard, hands clasped demurely against her skirts, but great pains taken to present the image of nobility through the braided hair and the flagrant color of her dress. "Liesa," he mumbled by way of greeting as he inched into the yard. For a fraction of a moment, she guarded her silence well. So well, in fact, Rurik feared she would not even grant so simple a bounty as her voice.

Alviss crossed behind her, and the passing shook her with the touch of ghosts. Then, like the cracking of a dam, she wavered, broke, and ran to him with his name on her lips, its sound born of tears. He opened his arms and took her tight against him as the sobs heaved to a fevered pitch. There were words, but they were lost in the torrent, so he contented himself to gentle whispers and still gentler caresses of her hair.

Then he saw it—the burned husk that stained the visions kept. Blackened beams lay strewn across the yard where the stable had sat, the ground still bearing the scorch from their collapse. Horses nickered from a pen nearby, pecking at the grass and hay that survived the harrowing. Nothing might have stilled him swifter.

It was a long while before either moved. She was the first, pulling away from him, but not so far as to allow his arms to fall from her. There was more of the real Liesa in the look that met him then—puffed and tear-torn, yet possessed of a tempered fire waiting for its moment.

"I did not honestly think it would be you, brother." Even through the tears, her look appraised him. With a frown, she slapped his arm. "Even thinner than before! I thought war put muscle to a man's bones."

"Such things do, in fact, require the food to see it done."

"You starve?" Concern flushed a dark veil over her. "Foolish boy—and you Alviss, fie on you!" She twisted on the old man sharply, with all of a mother's scorn. "This one has been your charge. Starving…" A sincere apology tipped Alviss's head, and she nodded grudgingly, accepting it as she turned back. "Come, come, we'll have the servants set us something, and I'll be sure you eat the better half of it while you tell me of this war of yours. Alviss, would you—?"

"Family," the Kuric offered in explanation as he stepped aside from the door.

Another, grayer man stood beside Alviss, buried under his shadow, and from the way Alviss looked from lady to scrawny servant, Rurik knew them for old friends—and knew, too, they meant to talk. Suspicious, Liesa quirked an eyebrow, but shrugged at last and left them to it. Rurik looked back, but Alviss gave him a knowing nod. They both had things to attend, it seemed.

Willingly, Rurik followed his sister's quick-step to the manor and the promised supper. Her tone, after all, had brooked no question, and he was not yet so great a fool as to refuse her graces.

The servants were quick, too—no doubt the dinner had not been as spontaneous as Liesa made it seem. Likewise, it granted her ample time to recover from their greeting. They were barely at the table before fresh bread had settled at their laps. It was to be a loaf shared for, though the long tables of the manor were set to host dozens, Liesa took the chair beside his. She tucked her legs beneath her as she had when she was little, and laid her head against his shoulder as they ate.

And he tried not to wince, for it reminded him still of younger lives—of another sister, still lost for his indiscretion. Anelie.

No doubt Ivon had already told Liesa anything she needed to know of the Bastard's little war. Even so, Rurik gladly offered up his stories—as much to unburden himself as to sate his sister's curiosity. Nor was it difficult to tell where the brothers' stories diverged. From the point of Tessel's stabbing and the massacre of the nobles, Liesa drew upright and watched with a certain gleam, picking all the while at the pork the servants had brought for dinner proper.

"Alas they missed," she concluded, hardening. The vehemence behind it startled even him. "Good man or ill," she added, tempering it, "it might have saved us all unnecessary woe."

Of his own questions to follow, the first was also the most obvious—one that had stalked him from first glimpse of the yard. "The stables. Did our men…?"

Liesa's face warped in scandal. "Stars, no! This was days past, before even Ivon. Merten says one of the boys must have left a candle alight. A candle! The whole thing went up like one big piece of kindling, I fear."

"And the horses?" Their father had loved those beasts. As had Isaak. Raised and meticulously bred them through generations.

"Fine, thankfully. Only one remains elusive but—so too does its body. Likely one of the ranchers took her in. No. The real loss came from Isaak's pens. Isaak will have my head." She frowned into her cup.

It went unsaid: if she ever saw Isaak again.

"The kennel? The whole kennel?"

378

"A good deal of it. We've had some back but…" The rest need not be said. Strong animals, but how they took to the wilds would be any man's guess. It was not as if, in the midst of all this—especially with the brief loss of horses—there had been any time to look for them.

Rurik let his own thoughts go unspoken. Liesa may have been right. All this could have been the workings of a stray spark. As she noted, "late winter fires, dry as all is," could be vicious. To him, though, it still reeked of arson.

But for the moment, there were other concerns. Like Ivon.

"Sister. I hate to turn things but…"

"Ivon?" She countered, on a teasing note. Rurik nodded uncertainly. "Here two days, truth told. Like a whirlwind. Took most what of the fighting men remained and headed south. For Witold, of course. I barely even…but then, when I told him of the edict, and poor Lotte…"

Unstable ground. He squirmed in his seat. It was not a place he could yet walk. "Of course," was all he said.

"You," Liesa paused, considering her words. Then she lowered her head and let the subject drop. "You only just missed him. He's worried about you, you know."

Words, he supposed. Dry air to fill the space between knowledge. Nothing real.

There was some discourse, thereafter, as to a brother's love. Of certain less than manly activities of youth one brother had ostensibly undertaken for the other. Rurik smiled, or occasionally parted with a sound, but otherwise let her go—Liesa could be an accomplished storyteller, when she wished it. In her words even he might have hoped, for a moment, but the world was as it was.

Belatedly, he stirred her back to the present, querying, "And why is it you did not go with our brother when he left?"

She sipped her cup before answering. "It is my right to see both my brothers, Rurik. And more to that—Verdan needs someone guiding it. They may have given Merten the manor for now, but he is, that is to say…"

Merten. Kasimir's old steward. The man in the yard with Alviss. What did she mean, "given?"

Liesa tossed her head thoughtfully, roving slowly about the room as if seeing it for the first time. "It grows lonely. I could not let it lose more."

"You'd no way of knowing Tessel should have sent me. Did you hear of Oberroth? It could just as eas—"

"Tessel would not be our first wolf," she spat bitterly.

"Only the biggest," he finished for her. "Who else? Cullick?"

Her stare hardened on him before she shook it off. "Do you even…? No. And yes. I suppose. Our neighbors. Witold held them off a time but we no longer sit this land, Rurik. Not by Imperial grace. I am a lady only so much as these people look to me as one. So the vultures peck."

"Have they come here?" When all he wanted to ask was: how did you come here, than?

"No. Nothing so bold, but Rurik, I…"

A sudden rattle at the door drew them off, to find an old servant—Michel, Rurik recalled—standing near breathless. Before they could ask, he rattled off something about guests—of Rurik's, no less—come in all their pomp and station and forcibly setting places upon the walls. Soldiers, the leader of which sought to join their little audience. Rurik cursed under his breath. He might have known better than to think he would be trusted for a diplomat.

"Tessel," he said through clenched teeth, answering his sister's unasked question.

The servant was sent to fetch his lady's caller as the siblings brooded over the remnants of their meal. *Even this small time, Tessel, you would have me owe you?* In a greater house, for a greater family, there might have been another room in which to receive the lord. To stick him with sweet things and put him off a time in waiting. But this was Verdan, where lord and peasant were not so far removed, and this was Tessel, who needed and who knew no nobility but his own.

There was scarcely enough time to caution. "Liesa, know that this man is no friend of mine, and certainly—"

Then he was there. The doors clacked and Merten entered to announce him, with Alviss a towering attendant at their backs. These were the only ones to enter, though Rurik spied Berric's shape snapping orders at guardsmen left to the hall. With a gentle dismissal from his mistress, Merten slipped away again as quickly as he might. Neither Matair rose to greet the remainder.

Even so, Rurik watched the mask clamp down over Liesa's face. Studious eyes ran Tessel's gamut, sharpened with Rurik's warning, and smoothed effortlessly into the glossy countenance of the proper noblewoman their father had always hoped she would be.

Likewise, Tessel made his most gracious bow and tempered his tone to such a patient note that Rurik scarcely recognized it. "My noble Matairs—excuse me for interrupting, but Rurik, you well know, patience is neither of our greatest virtues, and my lady, I simply could not put off meeting you." He rose on a smile and flicked a hand back to indicate Alviss. "I hope you do not mind. I know how close the lot of you stand, and I found the goodman…" He paused here, letting the note linger as he grasped for the name. A stark look from Alviss painted another picture all the while—calling into question whom had happened on whom.

"Alviss, yes," Tessel concluded at last. "Simply wandering about. Given the situation, I assumed honor would demand a blade present. I could think of none better, for either of us."

Liesa accepted this with the barest dip of the head. "You are welcome, ser, though you do come with a most unusual train."

"Sadly they simply cannot do without me," Tessel said with a little more teeth. Then, more earnestly: "You have my pledge as a gentleman that while they are here, they shall be on the very best of behaviors, though I would formally request quarter for my captains." He kept his eyes trained on Liesa, but there was something in his motions, and his tone, that told Rurik they were not all meant for her.

"This is acceptable. And I should so hope. But I meant these vagabonds here."

Tessel barked a laugh, and some of the rigid formality fled from his mantle. "Surely so did I, lady."

She gestured across the table. "Please sit, ser, and tell us what it is that sees you to our door—and my dear brother returned to us. And you as well, Alviss. Sit. For a man your size, you have ever eaten as a bird; there is surely one's fill left here somewhere."

"You are kind, lady," Alviss answered for them both.

After they had sat, and dinner resumed, there was some small talk as both masters of the table struggled to take something of the other. Tessel prodded at word of Witold, the forest, and even delicately Cullick, while offering condolences for what had been wrought on their family by him. The Bastard tactfully evaded the looming topic of Ivon—no doubt word had already reached him of his traitor's short stay.

Yet Liesa brushed off all notion of Witold either and played the woe-struck lady to its fullest—though a lady still, hounding dates of departure, and numbers, as well as the scope of Tessel's intent, all the while reminding him that the Matair name remained master in this place.

Yet there was something she wasn't saying. Something Tessel's placating smile seemed to know, and Rurik could only guess. He did not like being at a disadvantage.

"Frankly I must say it surprises me that Witold would be so gracious as to allow you to remain," Tessel cooed at last, folding his hands in gratitude over his empty plate.

"Should he not?" Alviss piped up, before Liesa had the chance. "Matair land. Matair home." His sharp gaze flicked to Rurik with a stiff nod. "Fought and bled for. Right-earned."

Liesa blushed appropriately, looking down before casting demure glances back at Tessel. "Alviss is right. He was one of those to fight and bleed for it, after all. And Witold—he is an old friend. The oldest, perhaps."

"To defy Imperial edict? He surely must be."

This drew Rurik rigid. "What?" Liesa sat stunned beside him—how could she have known how blunt the Bastard could be? He looked to her, his face pleading, but it was Tessel that continued.

"The Empire is not kind to ones it deems traitors. Hence my condolences—"

"They are no traitor," Alviss growled.

"No, no. Nor I. I never said they were. I said ones 'the Empire' deems traitors, old fellow. Your people, too, must be very loyal to have allowed you back in after all that. Though I note few soldiers to your banner—"

"What is your point?" Liesa bit crisply back. A sympathetic glance for Rurik was all she could spare. It promised answers—but when, he could not say.

"Dear lady, I think it time we come to the heart of the manner. You have noted my trains outside. They need not be seen as some raging war band, but as liberators." He dipped his head in a show of grace. "We would liberate you and yours from bondage."

"Bondage?" Her voice raised a note, then stilled. Delicate hands shook against the table before disappearing into her lap. In practiced grace, emotion fled her. Liesa smiled. "I know not what you think, Ser Tessel. But I assure you these lands—"

"Are not staked by other banners in the woods? My scouts tell me Insley men, among others, flee them in lands you supposedly hold. Might I be so bold as to ask what they do there?"

"They are Witold's creatures," she murmured.

"Of course. My apologies. And the rest of your family? Where are they? I have met two of the Matair lads. I should surely like to see how the third turned out."

Liesa's smile became the thinnest veneer—a viper's curve. "I think you know."

"Cullick is a divisive creature. I know him well. Your brother has been good enough to tell me much of the man. A pity he uses the true religion to enhance his own image." Tessel's face pinched into a scowl. "A despicable thing. And among his other crimes—something that shall be dealt with, I assure you."

"You are…" She swallowed, looked to Rurik's stunned face. "…too kind. During your stay, I hope you will accept Verdan's kindness at its—"

"My lady. Let us not dance around this anymore."

A grim gaze nailed Liesa to her chair. Meanwhile, with a butcher's ease, Tessel folded his knife against his plate and eased his hands against his belly. Rurik rested his on the table, waiting. His eyes strayed to the door and back. If Tessel were going to summon his people, he would have done it already. Nothing could have set him more ill-at-ease than Tessel's gentle manner, though. Given how Liesa's foot rocked, he supposed it had infected her as well.

"Verdan is yours. You know it and I know it. I would only make it official— but I am a lord, as any other. I need shows of faith. I would bleed to the last for you and yours, if you would but sign an oath of allegiance."

Alviss snorted, watching the man crossly. Tessel, seemingly amused by the less-than-noble gesture, met it with a smirk, asking, "Something wrong, Kuric?" The Matairs' one-time master-at-arms met him boldly at that. "Yes," he said, "contract. Like any sellsword. What goes unsaid—if you lose, a traitor two-fold."

An insult to Tessel's honor. Men died for less in the courts. "I will not lose. Think you so little of me, Kuric? You are, after all, a sellsword yourself." Tessel waved a dismissive hand and shifted back to the young nobles. "It is standard, as you know. A lord needs shows of faith from his vassals, and in turn they are as his children. As my army is so. I will not neglect you."

It was a challenge for Rurik to resist leaping the table at the man. As it was, he tapped a carving knife against his leg, pondering the chances he could make it. "How good of you to care of our bodily health, Tessel. You are ever so kind."

The general's gaze twisted with slight confusion. "Bodily and spiritual, Rurik. As an emperor should."

"Spiritual?" Liesa gasped.

"Of course. Too long has this nation spent its time unnecessarily yoked to the burden of Mother Church. My father saw that and sought to change it. I would continue his example—and it is the young voices, the eager nobles like yourself, that shall help me to save this country so. Tell me: what are your thoughts on the Divine Will?"

"Assal is…" Liesa hesitated, glancing between her guests, face scrunched, as if trying to parse out what the Bastard wanted to hear. "Assal is everything. The Emperor masters through him. The rest, we can but…" An eyebrow arched and she leaned forward pointedly. "…listen?"

Tessel laughed aloud, a sharp, biting thing. "It is one thing to have the divine rule—it is another to hold it. Divine Will is nothing without stout hearts and sturdy steel behind it. And men—divine or no—bleed. If they shirk their covenant with men, they falter and fall the same as any other.

"And after, men will say, well clearly he did not have the divine favor, for if it were so, how could he have lost? Fickle. It's all so fickle. I have my faith, but I put it first and foremost in steel. It is the truest religion any man might know." Tessel leaned forward as well, clasping his hands together in a show of unity with his own words. "Assal watches, but men are his tools. His greatest and most terrible works. Faith rests on our own shoulders."

"Great pains smother their young."

Tessel turned once more to the Kuric, sitting calm as a willow. "What is that?"

Alviss looked him dead in the eye, any hint of mirth gone from him. "Proverb. My people's. Means: in great pain, those small are forgotten."

"And this relates…?"

"If your war is this, it is war against self. Gives life illusion of being…a hollow march, its ends naught but tragedy."

"*Hollow*?" The word tightened in the Bastard's own throat, and Rurik could bear out the slightest hint of red to his cheeks.

"Religion, if it exists—it is man's. Not men's. To force is to paint it false."

Liesa sighed, rising to talk over them. Before blood spilled across her table. "And if I were to say I am already of the Farrens, ser?"

It was hard, but Tessel managed to pull his sneer back from the Kuric and to settle hands and hearts and eyes to the matter at hand. Jurti. It was the way of things. "Then I should say you would have no troubles signing letters to this end."

"And the people? As Alviss says, not everyone stands the same. You cannot expect that everyone here—" Rurik intervened.

"The people follow their lord's example. If you declare it, so shall they follow. But if some Orthodox fools wish to cling to old superstitions…" Tessel shrugged. "The faithful will deal with them as they may."

"Meaning?"

"What do you think I mean? It is not a thing for polite discussion." Tessel's eyes hardened and locked on his former counsel. "I shall expect you to enforce these things, of course."

"Excuse me?"

"Who better than a native son? I have no doubt you can keep all of these in line." With that, the Bastard pushed back from the table and came to his feet. Alviss stood with him, though Tessel saw not the threat in it. He smiled at the man and tipped his head. "Good baiting words with you, goodman Kuric." His eyes alighted, losing the harshness to their fire, and they adjusted to Liesa, settling on her hand with kindness as he bent to take it up. She offered it wordlessly, letting his lips grace the cool flesh. "A pleasure, lady. My attendants

385

shall be along in due time with the necessary papers. You should make arrangement, such that your goodly townsfolk will be there to witness the signing. Rurik," he said lastly, as he made to depart.

But Rurik did not rise. Tessel was halfway to the door before he noticed, but it halted him rigid as bones. "Rurik?" he repeated.

"I shall remain for now, ser. My sister—we have scarcely had enough time to catch up on…on everything."

Tessel's lips parted to speak, then fell tightly shut again. He looked to Liesa and she only nodded, saying, "It would be a kindness, ser. We have lost so much time." Even a man as cold as Tessel had to have been moved by the sincerity in the wetness of her tone. He shook his head in regretful assent and promised someone would be by on the hour with the papers, as well as to collect his men. Goodbyes exchanged and the Bastard slipped back out the door through which he had come, taking most—but not all—his guards with him.

As soon as he had gone, Rurik rounded on his sister. "Anelie? Isaak? They are—they are still in Cullick's hands?" She nodded sullenly, and sank as one defeated into her chair. It felt as if the water had drained from Rurik's own throat. "I…Assal. Liesa, you have to go."

"Excuse me?" She shot up sharply. "I will do no such thing. You think he scares me?"

He took her hands in his. "There comes to be few and fewer of us, Liesa. If he doesn't scare you, he rightly should. I have seen what he and his will do if he does not have his way—sometimes, even if he does. There is honor there, it's true, but also anger. Great anger. And the anger will win out. You would be but a pawn to him, as I have been. You need to go."

Kasimir had, for all his faults, sought one thing above all else: for his children to have it better than he had. But for Rurik, the point had come and gone, and he had made it clear—at some point it was not better at all. He had failed his father and his name. Months had brought him to this moment, years, even—perhaps all the years of his life. As he stared his sister's stubbornness down, however, he saw a chance to go beyond his nature.

So many lives had been broken by his childishness. By his inability to grasp at what it meant to be human. He would let no more of his family blood be shed for the flaws of his own nature. Even if that was the last—the only—thing that he could do.

"And leave our people to rot?" Liesa snapped.

"They shall suffer either way! At least this way, he cannot make you his martyr, and these—this way they will make their own choices. They—I will take you, Liesa. Away from here. But we must all go. Tonight."

She ran a hand along her face, smothering her annoyance before it flicked back on her brother. "Is that right? Can you not come to this house and stay more than a single day, brother? Not once?"

He ignored that. Could not deal with it at the moment. Instead, he rounded on Alviss, whose surprise was plain across his own bearded face. "We will remain for now, Alviss. They will expect this. But you—you need to get the others. We must all go. I'll not leave anyone to bleed, and by the Maker, Tessel will find someone to bleed if we do not."

"And the Gorjes?"

"Let them threaten. Let them howl. They knew where we went before, but now—this is our home. We know it best. And Essa…Essa will know it better than any. Let her be your guide. But find somewhere to hole up. I—I think it best we travel separate. It is me he will seek. The rest of you can slip away."

"And leave me with the hunted man?" Liesa squawked. "Oh, lovely. Chivalrous, brother."

Chivalry, he longed to tell her, was dead. It had died with the last of the knights, buried in the ashes of a distant plain, where the gunpowder crackled and the golden earth drew sundered by the fury. He was no knight. He was just a man—and he would do what he could, as he could. He was beginning to see that was all anyone could do.

Alviss, without a word, went from the table and left them to it. Then the siblings turned to one another and Rurik tried not to flinch from the tears that awaited him.

Father. Give us strength.

* *

Stars formed shimmering novas through the canopies of leaves by the time the Company made good its flight.

By then, the night patrols had made their rounds about town, and all but the most dedicated watchmen and wastrels had given way to sleep's inevitable call. Chigenda, whose regular late night wanders placed him beyond additional suspicion, was the one to make certain of this. At his silent word, the others made good their escape, foregoing their tents, lest wary eyes noted too quickly their abrupt departure. With only what they could carry, they hastened to the northern edges of the camp and slipped away into the trees.

Only two stops delayed them: to collect a baker from his home of thatch and wood, and to bid a friend farewell. This last was Essa's decision, for it led her to Starlet and the stables. A long moment guided her hand against the trusted pony's side—then she loosed her reins and bid her ride, which Starlet did only with the greatest reluctance, taking to the south, and away.

Let them follow her. Let them howl and curse and scorn their chase until all that remains to them is a riderless horse, free at last, as nature intended. Yet let no one ask me how it feels.

Fortunately, they all had such sense of mind.

After Chigenda guided them outside the boundaries of men it became Essa's place to lead. She took them on a hard slog, shying away from either the merchants' road or logging trails for hard earth and thick brush. The rockier the better. So, too, in careful leagues, did they drift toward the rumble of the white water Jurree, praying its roar would cover any excess noise their progression might leak. If luck were on their side, they would not have to cast themselves into the river's depths. Spring it may have been, but the ice still flowed heavy down the river, and its deep waters bit as chill as the harshest wind.

Best not to be seen.

Essa herself was as a ghost among such places. It had been years since she had known the trees, but her feet remembered, and they beckoned her on as old friends. She knew, too, that Alviss and Chigenda could be as deer—swift-footed and sure, with a concerted alertness toward any sense of excess. Voren and Rowan on the other hand floundered hopeless as fish on dry land.

The going was rightly slow. Purposely so. When they were far enough to render voice a softer threat, though, Essa called a halt—by way of rounding on departure's instigating figure. "Where is Rurik?" It was the question she had wanted to ask since Alviss first stalked back from the Matairs' manor with his orders.

It had been time. There could be no other. No point to question it then.

Alviss, caught between her fury and the blackness of the trees, found no reason to lie. "He is not coming."

"Not coming? What do you mean? This idiocy was his idea."

A harsh shooshing took them both as Rowan swept into the line of fire. Pine needles and stray twigs had insinuated themselves in the flopped remnants of his plumed cap, making his shrill words almost comical, but the tone ended that. "Is this really the time?"

Essa's eyes lit on him. "If they should find us so quick, I should welcome death to be rid the shame."

The Kuric's own were a pointed blankness. "He remains. As we should not."

"He sacrifices himself?" There was a certain rising note within the baker's tone—hope? "A noble end, at least."

"Noble? Always dis say," came the rasp of the Zuti's harsh voice. He had circled once as the others spoke, scanning the trees. Reassured, he strode back with all the glamour of a creeping snake. "Is strong. Yes. But fool. Self is…" Alviss shook his head, and the Zuti let it go. "Is."

"Merely he walks another road," Alviss concluded at a deadpan.

"No doubt a broader one than we," Rowan said through thinned lips. "Please. Already the ground rests too dark beneath our feet."

Essa held her tongue, for the moment. She did not wish to, nor did she wish to take the hand Voren offered her. Instead, she took the trees for company and left the others thrashing blindly in her wake. It seemed a small and venomous justice.

Their way was a winding one—brushing the river and receding, winding to a boggish strait where the earth dipped and the stars all but vanished from the sky. And Rowan with them. Pulling her distraught and shivering cousin from the muck by a handful of lace, Essa backtracked them to a thin line of soft dirt—small enough for a deer trail, though far less apparent to the eye. She, at least, knew it well.

It had been her father that set its boundaries.

At the mouth of this crooked trail lay a broken pasture, surrounded by trees and scrub and weeds, and covered in vines too long left to the damp. In the heart of this stood a crumbling cabin scarcely fit for holding its own roof. Stray limbs from wind-swept trees had collected against portions of it, while the vines and weeds encircled the rest. The door was ajar, and so were the windows, the canvas flaps that once covered them now long since nibbled away.

How to describe the sensation? It smelled of old fires long set aside. It had the shape of a father's rearing hand—and a bottle, oh yes, a bottle that ever drank the man down. It even possessed an owl's eyes, and the stare that watched, forevermore, never leaving, never shifting, only piercing straight to core.

She shuddered despite herself. Voren, mistaking it for cold, slid up behind her and offered his cloak. She countered with her best, placating smile, and let it go.

"What is this place?"

It would have to have been Rowan that asked. She turned, the curves of her smile drooping to a more demure sort of remembrance. Would that she could ask the same. Cousin the red-haired fop may have been, but he had never come here. Family, until exile took its hold of her, had been little more than a distant notion—a fleeting thing that took her father's shape, and no other. Perhaps his family had known. Known the character of her father's ghosts.

"It is her—" Voren stopped short, spared a pained look for her, and looked aside, continuing more softly. "Was her home." He stared off, until the touches of light struck his lips again. When he turned back, he pointed to a knot of stumps among the field, where apples used to grow. "We used to read there, remember? The Vorges…"

The Holy Text. But more than that: salvation. The light glinted through her own heart, and threatened to straighten the curves of her lips again. Then it shuddered out again as quick. Many hours had been spent at that sad little knot of wood with Voren, teaching him the shape and tone of language. Yet before she consented to teach to others, it had been Rurik's gift to her.

Chigenda moved as a tiger across the field toward them. "Is good. Bog light—make east de treachery. Trees be tick, and walls…" He grunted, nodding to the old cabin. "Dey will hold de evil wind."

390

"But the river is loud here." Alviss appraised, eyes roaming the field with a commander's precision. "It will cover approaching feet, as it covered our own."

She opened her mouth to speak, but the two fell to bickering at the details. Pointing out this and that to make for cover, or to set aside their tracks. Down from her feet, a voice thundered, years in the passing, and a hand took her by the hair. Little girl, little girl—she had not wished to go. Her father too spoke of cover and the hunt, and of all the things that had made this place so dear to her mother's heart. Then, all too abruptly, the lash, the voice, the wounded pride.

The baker, beaming as a child, stepped toward her and began to quote. "I know not what waits for me beyond the Grey Hills, but I shall go there with song in heart, for where e'er I go, its beauty shall transcend all others, and I shall lay me down and know such peace as I have never seen before. And so shall I lie, until the trumpets of eternity call me home once more." He remembered. Her focus narrowed, and the man and boy were as one.

The past destroyed men as sure as any blade.

Without voice, she took his hand, feeling the pulse quicken in his wrist. But she shifted to the men beyond him. "Why did he stay? You owe me that, Alviss."

Conversation stilled. The pulse slowed. The bow of Alviss's head was like the withering of many willows. "And more, child. Calm. He does this for us. You know Tessel's threats. This is the Gorjes."

"So what? He led them off? A sacrificial lamb?" And in her hardened heart: *does he think this changes anything? That it will redeem him? Fool.* Redemption was the hope of fools and the divine.

"He does." The man shrugged around the question. "As he always. As he will. If he can save you, save too that child that calls herself lady…"

Chigenda bobbed his head, considering. "Is brave. And fool. So close, both."

"But," Voren said, hesitating on that note. He chewed at his lip, averting his sweating eyes as their own swept him. "But he, that is to say—if Tessel watches him, if this is about him, what makes you think Tessel didn't watch us? Isn't watching him now?" His gaze rose reluctantly, to pleading saucers. "They could know…"

"What? What does he know?" Essa all but spat. It cowed the boy back down as she snatched her hand away. Her patience was worn too thin to care. "And what right does he have? Who, who has he ever saved? The idiot orders. The idiot takes. But what does he ever give? Trouble, and I'll not—"

"Enough." That one word carved clean through her ramble and drew her up short as a startled animal. Not a deer. Not a mouse. Mere animal—undefined. The look that joined it kept her there, transfixed, uncertain.

"Don't talk to her like—"

"A boy would lecture of boys?" The Zuti all but laughed.

Alviss only shook his heavy head. "You do ill, girl, and you, boy, and I'll have no more of it."

"But he—"

"Find us kindle." Even before the words had concluded, he turned from her, dismissing her as effortlessly as a noiseless night. "We speak when your head finds earth again."

A moment passed before she moved. It did not come easily, or without fire, but she clung to it, forced it back, drinking pride and torment as she stormed off into the night. She did not stoop to earth to gather sticks, but rather, headed for the bog, still fuming. It was not long before she heard the unsteady and rapid patters of feet behind her. She turned, all ice, but her hand never so much as breezed against her daggers.

"Are you alright?"

Voren stood before her, panting. There was a naked fear about him—pale, sorrowful thing—and she knew that it was for her. Whatever scathing word had sat on her tongue fled before that miserable image. It left her to recede, back into the ashes.

"I am fine, Voren."

He took an unsure step toward her. "This—none of this is what you pictured, is it?" She shook her head. "No, how could it? And my mother, I know…"

That afternoon, when they had attended the old woman, she had all but cast them from the bakery. *Like a harpy, that one.* She could scarcely think of a time someone had used more—and more creative—curses before other ears. Treestriding harlot was probably one of the kindest hurled on her alone.

She could not understand it. The bakery remained untouched. From what she could tell, the woman looked healthy enough. What's more: she had regained a child. A dependable soul. It should have been enough.

To think most of the abuse had been for Voren, her own son. His only crime? Leaving her alone.

A bitter old woman. A broken old woman. *But then…who ever wished to be alone? Too much has been caused by that bitter end.*

"She was upset, is all. We all deal with the silence in different ways. She'll settle."

"There can be no silence around her," the baker grumbled stubbornly. "Even the echo of her should not let it settle."

"You are too harsh, Voren."

"Would it be different if she had struck me, Essa?"

That did it. The chord was struck. She could see it in his eyes, feel it reflected through her own heart. Deeper she shrank, and he fell after her, mumbling rapid apologies. If she had been as Essa's family, he had meant.

"I didn't mean…"

"You did."

"But I—"

"Stop apologizing!" She snapped a scowl at him and waited for him to wither. There remained something there, some wiry strength she had not seen since the night he…and the kiss…He stood before her and did not wilt. Bathed in the shards of silvery light, he stepped close to her, and reached out his bony arms. "Voren…"

"We cannot choose family. I will stop my mumbling but I—I am truly sorry, Essa. You suffer too much. It is not fair that I heap my own…"

She squeezed his hand and twisted away, careful to step around the noxious peat. Like a faithful hound, the boy followed dutifully in her wake, matching every stride. It was a time before they spoke again, and the fumes of the bog were receding behind them, the river surging blue and dark before the glittering points of their eyes. It was a point of grounding. Familiarity. She breathed in its thick, wet scent. Few things felt this way anymore.

"We are all of us alone, Voren. Do you know that?" Her patch of voice was all but lost in the tumult of the surge.

She could sense the maw of him open in objection, but nothing came out. Wisdom, perhaps. She closed her eyes, let the darkness in deeper. "There are points of light, little flickers of flames that light the way, but the path…it is shadow." What was she trying to say? She grimaced in annoyance at her own lack of voice. "Apologies. I am not the one for words, but your mother only fears the dark. As my own, I hope, so feared."

"That does not justify it. Any of it. Not yours. Not mine. Not Rurik…" A soft step drew him near.

That word. "And Rurik." She held it there a moment, let it coat the air between them. Her eyes opened and she found Voren looking warily down at the waves. "He too does what he does for fear." It was hard to speak it, but in its utterance, she knew it for truth.

Something tightened in the boy. He turned to her only slowly, and for the first time in that haunted place, she thought she could see the man he might become. A shape of things to come.

The raw venom in his expression startled her. "What he did—there is no justification."

"We all fear the dark, Voren. Loneliness."

There it was again. The hand. It clasped her arm. First one, then two. They slid, captured her hands, and through some magic she could not identify, drew her eyes to his. They were of a height. He—battered, beaten, yet untainted. She—bloodied, old before her years—and still his hands folded around hers, and he looked as if he were at the verge of tears.

"Not all of us have need to be."

Silence followed the weight of that. It was not that there was nothing else to say—but that there was nothing they needed to say. They walked on, along the bank, and through the trees, Essa watching everything but themselves, and Voren with eyes for nothing but. There were moments, then, when it seemed they were but children again, wandering the trees with the same lack of care. Then others came, where she saw that there was nothing of the old remaining, save the loyalty, and the kindness—there was nothing to the shape of it or to the motions of their bodies that were as things once had been.

Years before, her mother had abandoned her in this place. Not a human, surely not a woman, that she would do such a thing. Then her father had turned her from this spot, flushed with the fury of other men, and cast them both into exile. Now it was a place a boy became a man and friendship, the last vestiges of thread tying her to this place, became…

Something else. She could not say what. For another boy walked still beside them, and even in her darkest hours, she wept inside for all that was. What had the eyes not seen? What lay hidden?

They were nearly back to the cabin when Voren gave her arm a halting tug. "And the kindling?"

She hesitated, then with the gentlest of exhales, let a rub of a smile drift bare. "Yes. Let us not forget the kindling."

* *

It was all behind them. Childhood. The awkwardness of youth. He said a prayer, and for a long time, he would not close his eyes.

They slept entwined beneath the old boughs, tickled by grass, the smallest vestiges of fire to warm them. Clothes were not shed. Base passions were not indulged. Yet something joined them, and he knew, holding her as he did, that this—this was everything.

Sleep came easy and dreamless. The sleep of babes.

Emergence was warm and breathless, rough arms cradling him close. Dawn was still a notion, silver light creeping through the slots of the leaves to rain across the field in shards. Their fire had trickled to naught but embers, and even the smoke had dissipated, leaving nothing but her scent. Wood. Dirt. And Woman. It stirred his heart and blushed his cheeks; it felt, for a moment, as if all the others might look on him and know.

As if that mattered. Here, away from people, from coin and nobility and all of society's wanton mechanisms, with her and her alone, he knew he could be happy. He could find a way. *To hell with mother. To hell with the rest.* Let him have a touch and he could find a way.

Feather-light lips pressed against the back of his skull and he stiffened, thoughts of bliss scattering swift. *She wakes?* He tried to turn into her, but the arms held him fast, and she mashed against him, as a child against a doll. His cheeks burned. So too, it seemed, did the sound of her voice.

"Restless?"

She pinched him, and he yelped to a squeal of her own girl-delight. One of her hands clapped over his mouth, but she pulled him with her as she sat upright. To his horror, Alviss sat squat across from them, head bowed but eyes like hot points of iron. *If ever looks could kill...*

"I swear there's not one of you ever grows up," she whispered in his ear. The blush deepened, and he squirmed against her, but this only drew a deeper laugh. She shook her head into his shoulder and let the motion still him. Steadily, her hand fell from his mouth.

He swallowed. "How—how long have we been…?"

"Not I—"

"Perhaps two passing notes of day," Alviss answered for them. His head rose and revealed the bags of sleeplessness beneath hard eyes. His voice was hoarse. "Chigenda has your watch."

"How kind of the Zuti…"

From behind them: "At least someone has a sense of kind. Darkness, children. Must we make so with the chatter?" Rowan groaned as he rolled onto his back. "Bad enough we take the earth for beds when there's a house right there."

"With bugs enough to make your skin right-crawl, I'm sure," Essa teased.

"And you think the dirt lacks for them? Maker, you're a cruel lot."

"Were—were you all awake?" Voren chirped.

The silence was deafening. The proceeding laughter more so. It stilled only as Alviss, rising at a stretch, reached out to kick their dead fire and knocked a few stray sparks to light.

Birds scattered as a gun clipped a hole in the night. A bright, fierce hole that flared the trees around it into being, and sank away again as the wood splintered at Essa's side. Of preludes, there was none. Even she froze, she with a wolf-hound's hearing, and the light touched her, making ink and tendrils of her hair. For an instant, she was as Voren knew she would always be: a girl made of darkness. Not a thing of the light. That clarity receded into the uncertain mooning as more shots rang out, and the wood cracked all around them.

There was a second of indecision, splintered only by Rowan's bewildered cry.

Shapes sprang through the trees, little more than inky blotches in the profane silver of the night. Weapons drew tall by the shadow, only to be drunk away again by the smothering dark. There were no whooping cries, no declarations— only murder and the means to inflict it. Smoke drifted aimless at the figures' backs, making monsters of them.

Demons.

There were two more patters in the wood before the earth drew still, and Alviss swung up roaring at his assailants. Without another thought, the Kuric snatched at the axe discarded beside him, and flung himself headlong to check their rush. Quavering, Essa fell back before her cousin, shocked still beside Voren, both watching as the swordsman who had draped himself across them as the shots rained down, now recovered and stepped to meet the advance by cold steel. Voren sagged, frozen. Absently, he felt through the ashes for a log club. It was all he could muster.

Essa's hand was on his arm. Everything reeked of saltpeter. The sky was black. This was all he knew.

They advanced in pairs. One man dropped as Rowan's thin steel sunk its kiss against his breast. Others ambled aside at the turning of Alviss's axehead, only to swarm on the backswing. Sparks traded between them like a dance of fireflies. Before them, all fell to the chaotic squabbles of the night.

This was not the battlefield. No organization. No rules. Each struggled to kill the other, and through any means. A figure lurched through the dark to tackle Rowan, and both went shouting into the dust. This at last seemed to strike Essa, and she lurched after them, pulled from Voren's groping hand. He saw the knives flash from her belt, the raging in and out, and darkness spray. Another rounded on her; she lurched back from a strong backhand.

Alviss head butted a man—Voren knew it only for the fact that it was illuminated in another flash of saltpeter. Yet the only thing to crack was a man, not near but distant. Voren threw about like a man possessed, and bore witness to a shadow slinking in the trees beyond. Another—longer, thinner—darted from its wake. They were not abandoned. His night-bled eyes could see others, the long guns raise, but not to them—to the hunter, and the long limb flooding from his back. Only then were there shouts.

A demon stalked the trees.

The man that struck Essa lurched back as her boot found that sweet spot between his legs. Even as Essa clambered to her feet, Voren found some inner font of strength, and in the man's weakness, swept behind him with a sharp and fevered cry, to bash him across the skull with his club. He toppled like a bag of wheat, and the air eased out of him just the same.

Voren stood shivering, even as Essa cried out to him. He blinked. He had hit a man. Broke a man. What more could she—the pain took that note away. The elbow that ended him landed on his neck.

Then he was on his belly, head lolling, desperate to make his limbs do anything more than tremor. In the dust and the dirt, the dirt-dirty-dirt, he quavered, and the shade drew long over him. Something gripped his hair. *Not now*, he prayed. *Not now*, chanting it like a mantra. Not when he finally had something. He reached up, scrabbling at the hand in his hair, and just in time to see Essa blunder forward.

A blade lanced over her—he saw her flinch—but her feet were true, carrying her under its arc and into Voren, crashing into him, and he into his foe. There was blood in his teeth, and he squeezed his eyes shut despite himself. Someone cried out. Others shouted. Feet shuffled and the blood ran hot and hotter, burning as it dribbled against the skin. He shuddered.

Not like this.

"You." The word dripped like venom off Essa's tongue. Voren's eyes flashed open and found the hand on him limp, and the body beside him still. Above him, a ghostly sort of play took shape as Essa grappled with another man, neither more than silhouettes. It was a macabre thing of jerking arms and quick feet, lit only by the sliver of the moon. How he longed to name it for a dream.

Yet the cry stirred him. The man had good armor, and a good arm besides, and his strikes were true. Essa coiled about him with a dagger in either hand, but he had the range, and he used it well. He feinted and she fell to it—took a step to close the gap, and took a slash across the calf for her trouble. The cry echoed across every vision of her. Time itself drew bloodied. She limped back, and the man followed her, prepared to dispatch her on his follow-through.

Then her cousin was there, as an avenging flame. It swept her aside and drew stiff under the sweep of the assailant's blade, catching it. The man jabbed him in the gut all the same, and yet, the frail swordsman grunted but held firm, jamming a free hand into his attacker's eyes. The brute howled, and Voren, aware suddenly of how close it all was, snapped out his good hand to catch the killer by his boot. Then he pulled.

It was enough. The man snarled as he stumbled, trying to use the momentum for a hard swing, but Rowan was quicker, and he drew his blade short to stab him under the armpit. The man fell forward, but he would have kept his feet—save for the knives that awaited him. As Rowan stepped around him, the man fell to Essa, and she caught him swift by both the neck and the cheek. Lines of liquid slicked black through the dance and stained the earth where they fell.

Voren scrabbled back. Some last defiance gargled out of the man, and the blade rose, flailing. But he was sinking as this happened, sinking down not merely to earth, but to death's embrace, and he heaved at Essa's feet, collapsed before Voren's eyes, and reached one final hand for Essa's boot before the life finally eased from his body.

Mere feet apart, Voren realized at last there was some sense to the face. Not a silhouette of a man, but surely a shadow of one—the grubby face of Gunther stared back, and with it, the other silhouettes took on falcon-like proportions. The Gorjes had spread their wings.

"Alviss!" Essa screamed herself hoarse.

He twisted in time to see the giant of a man go down, speared through the back. The offending lance snapped off as Alviss elbowed its bearer, but the giant took to a knee, and the spark of him seemed to shudder under the circling bites of the remaining hunters. Only the bardiche held him up, and its threat kept the others still at bay.

The Kuric staggered and swung, and like a candle's last guttering flame, his eyes seemed to flare with a brilliant fury, before sinking into the dark. He was done. Voren knew it to be so.

Yet night had not disgorged its final miracle. There was a whooping cry the like of which Voren had never heard—too high to be human, too low to be anything but blood induced. It looked like a branch had sundered and taken flight. It whipped across the span of them, skidding a running Rowan to a halt, and pierced one of the twisting Gorjes through the shoulder. It let him twist still, but around the other side, and took him less than cleanly off his feet.

The other, horrified—Voren imagined—turned in time to meet what appeared, for all intents, no man, but the basest of beasts. It scurried across the earth on hands and feet alike, but sprang up onto those feet as its victim loomed, with all the grace of an eagle's flight. There were swipes of iron, and the shadows melded in the dance. The demon seemed to stoop between blows, the blur of his footwork kicking leaves and needles between them. Something short but sharp flashed up, and with it, the demon began to thread the man to pieces.

They scrabbled, and scrapped, as Rowan limped to Alviss and bore him back, but the blur of them halted as the invading demon caught the mere man's failing hand, and by fist and knee tore its bladed limb bloody from the Gorjes' hand. There were shouts, until the demon brought the hilt of it down again and again. They died out in inches, until it was the ears—not the eyes—that bled at the scene.

The demon stepped furiously toward them, and there was not a one of them that did not put guard against it in such aftermath. In the cool light of the moon, however, and the reflected pools of blood that framed him, the demon melted into the visage of Chigenda, and a face that was not at all wicked. It seemed to pool into the very visage of distress, and all of it, Voren saw, fell to the old man being lowered to the ground.

"Alvo," the stooping darkness whispered, "where bleed?"

The shift was sudden, and every bit as fierce as the bloody struggle. The others were over him, questioning, prodding, and in the eyes of cousins, tears, through some trick of light vibrant for all the darkness around them. The rest were silent. The dead, after all, have little to say.

Voren could not bring himself to move. For the first time since the opening pop of gunpowder, he came into awareness of himself again. Then he felt it, hot and slick against his skin. There, vivid against his pale skin, was the blood. The greatest stain. He felt his body shake, and he heard Essa's questioning voice. He blinked at her. These things never went away.

"The blood," he whispered. Then all went dark.

Slumber was not long, but in his mind's eye, Voren saw them howling after him. Spirits of the dead. All of them wore masks of Gunther's skin and rattled his own with his mother's yellowed teeth. But the shout—it was always in the Zuti's voice.

"I see! I see!"

What he saw first on waking was the emptiness of sky. Dawn lit it anew, and though the sun had yet to crest the trees, clouds formed long trails of its blood across the sky, dripping in thin, clear lines that made him think of the promised end of days. No shapes. No sound.

He slid up, wincing at the stiffness of his neck. Fear of solitude went unrealized. The others were near, huddled around the rise and fall of a heavy chest. Alviss. So he still breathed. Voren tried to catch the Kuric's face, but it was in vain, for Rowan blocked it, crouched over him as he was, with a bowl of water clutched in his hands. There was life. Essa would surely be relieved.

Chigenda, too, kept quiet vigil, eyes flecked with devotion so fierce it changed the very nature of his face. Voren did not think it could be the same man.

Yet one was nowhere to be found, and it was she that mattered most in waking. As his eyes sought her out, though, something else became apparent: they no longer remained in the weeds of the old cabin. It was no longer even in sight. Long grass and rotted boards had been traded for the trampled, muddy contours of the forest floor, patches of snow still clinging to its deepest shadows.

"Where…" It was all he could muster before the coughing took him. His throat, he realized, was parched—it burned like the stench of sulfur itself. "Where is—"

"There," the Zuti answered, nodding to the trees. Chigenda's eyes did not soften to him, nor did Rowan bother to turn. "She watch. Waits. While others—dey sleep."

Hostility was bare in the tone. Voren did not press it. He nodded his assent, and the Zuti's gaze slithered back to the stilled giant. Voren moved from them, though on unsteady feet. He hobbled, and the world spun such that he had to lean against a tree for support. The blow to his back suddenly surged to memory's fore, and he felt sick.

Assassins. The Gorjes had sent assassins. Or the Bastard. He breathed a steadying breath, but sureness did not come. Their so-called savior, it would seem, had failed.

"Voren."

The shape of her swung down through the lanes of the trees, flitting on light feet. She came to a stop before him, and there was something there—a fear bright as the rising sun. *More assassins?* He tried to rise, to appear strong before her, but she caught him and anchored him back down to the earth.

"Essa," he murmured. "I was worried."

"Hush, hush now," she said, pressing a finger against his lips. Her gaze swiveled out, but softened as it struck the prone figure of her guardian. The others watched her now, though with none of the intensity. "Has he woken? Can he move?"

"I would not recommend it," her cousin said. The Zuti shook his head in agreement.

There was a flicker of doubt in her, and she nodded away from them. "I see. But we—we need to go back."

"Back?" Even Rowan twisted at that, a frown pulling his whole face down. "Are you mad, girl?"

"His blood is dark. That means they may not have pierced his lung, but he will die without treatment. We need their doctors. And we need to warn Rurik."

Warn Rurik? Voren all but choked on it. He reached out for her, but his shaking hand fell without purpose. He stared, blank and dumb, trying to disbelieve what he had heard. Not after all this. *That boy—this is his fault. What does she mean to "warn him"?*

"If Rurik has half a brain, he should be three provinces to wind by now. Let him be." Rowan turned away again, stirring at a rustle from the body beside him. But Alviss did not wake.

"Is strong, de boy. He know." The Zuti nodded to himself, but he was rising to his feet. "They no will find him, me tink."

A flicker of doubt took Essa's face, and she let Voren go. He groped for her, but he only brushed against her hand. "It's not Gorjes that worry me," she said. "There are men in the woods. And coming down the river. Witold's colors. It's not some petty raid, neither." She glanced back over her shoulder, as though the lurking ghouls might emerge at any moment. "If it's the Gorjes that struck us, Tessel knows, and if Tessel bothered with us, Rurik remains. If he remains…"

Chigenda shook like an oak waving in the wind. "Fight?"

"Fight," Essa said.

"Witold is not likely to spare a thought for someone he thinks a traitor, especially when his own brother thinks it." Rowan's voice was scarce above a whisper, but the forest was dead around them, and even this came as a roar. "I suppose we owe him that." He looked up at Chigenda, and something profound passed between those warriors then. "Chigenda, will you wait with him? I must go with my cousin."

I can go. But the words did not come.

The Zuti nodded and clasped the man's hand. Together, they raised one another to equal ground, and Essa, tearing her eyes away, stooped over Voren. *Please don't leave me.* He rose to meet her, the pain flooding away into a terrible sort of numbness. *Every time. Every damned time.* His hand reached out to her, and she caught it, to pull him up.

"My hero," she whispered, but in its depths he heard the bitter seeds of mockery. Childhood resurged, and with all the petty vengeance of a child scorned he smiled his sweetest smile as he told her: "Let us go to him. Let us make this right." If only she knew what that would entail.

Chapter 17

Fever made a crossroads of the flesh. Iron bound it down. Iron, after all, was the ages old remedy for witches' magic. Or so the old wives claimed.

Sweat made a sheen of her olive skin, sun and stone her only companions. And the woman, hovering at the edge of it all. Charlotte could see it through *her* eyes, yet she had the prescience of her own sight as well. Abandonment. This was all that remained to her. Even the keep would not hold the witch now.

Clouds bled the horizon of its precious light. She sat among the rocks, watching as the distant sky lit with nature's solemn trill.

She did not remain to listen to Usuri's own tears fall.

Days before, the thought of such an image could have been no more than a whisper to her.

Truth be told, they took whatever whispers they could get. Thanks came only in one form: the mother had not been there, nor the hound that was her knight. Yet gossip claimed the halls like a thousand chattering birds. It would wait until she returned. None of it would fly south with the winter.

The witch was dangerous. Too dangerous. From the window of her room, Charlotte could look out on her still, but there was nothing left to the witch's designs. Not even a prison of a room to call her own. They put her in the field like a criminal to the stocks, in a pasture on Walthere's own land, where none might wander save on pain of death. Soldiers watched her, but only at a distance—fifteen feet, some arbitrary man decided, and it was done. All the rest was rock and dust and chain.

Neck, arms, and legs. All shackled. All tight. A rag, shoved into her heathen mouth, would keep them from its poisons.

No one believed it. But they had to do something. This was a creature they had stirred. Their weapon. It was out of control.

Sara came to see her, as Charlotte lay among the coddling sheets. She blinked up into the pale light, sweltering down to her very core. The woman cooed over her and touched her head, prescribing this and that to all of her physicians. As if she knew.

They might have talked, but father was always with her. He hung at her arm like a slavering dog. When he could not be spared, she knew it was a train of clever spies, flatterers and philanderers all—men who could hold a princess's eyes and whisper their sights into Cullick's waiting ears. Men like Martel and Kamps. It was a heavy blanket over the warming days.

So Charlotte buried herself under them and slept.

Weakness, her father had told her child-vision, lurked in the limp hand. Good or ill, choice made a man. Apathy—there was no fouler death. Yet she found it comforting.

Somewhere in the dead of it, a tiny hand snapped the murky threads and tugged at her skin. "Go away," she tried to say, but the hand held her. Guided her. By the time she woke, the little boy was already retreating, but she could make out the bobbing gold of the crown. Longing eyes.

Her future husband. There was a hole in the pit of her with the thought. It drank of her, and drank deep, pulling her down hard into the darkness. Sleep could not return quick enough.

Yet when she slept, there were only nightmares. For some reason, Dartrek was there, no longer a hovering shadow. A man, tall and long-limbed, in a fashion some might call gangly. A ghoul, she thought at first. He paled before her, and his dark beard hung off him like grave moss. Flies made up his eyes and his hand, reaching, seemed to point into the core of her.

He never said a word, but she knew. It was a ghost, haunting its killer. Wronged men—they could not forgive and their specters consumed the living that wronged. Sometimes she tried to apologize, but the words always seemed to be sucked away, sometimes by a distant cry, and the thunder of a scream, and sometimes by the choking silence of her own swollen tongue.

There were only two things about him she could never figure out: why he was naked and why he had the Matair boy's bedeviled eyes.

It was four days before her fever broke. When she could rise again, she made a grave attempt to put off her maid and to ask to see to Dartrek, but one could be certain her father's sparrows waited for the word. A door opened on Sara within the hour, and at her heels, Walthere strode in with a boy on either arm.

One, a brother. One, a laughable entreaty of a lover.

"Highness," she managed, with her most gracious curtsy, but she was the only one to stand on courtesy. And only just. Even that made her light head swoon.

Sara, alone to see this, caught her by the hand and helped her up on a friendly guise. She shared with her a knowing smile, and took her on her arm, patting her hand against Charlotte's own. "Ever the lioness, dear. But there are moments…" It was more a tease than a lecture. Charlotte even smiled, despite herself.

The boys rushed to her legs, and in moments, each was pulling at her skirts, vying for the attention only boys could crave. If it wasn't questions on the "vile witch," it was protestations of honor, and the churlish claims of youth that already thought themselves knights.

But there were moments. Moments when a child's whisper drew her close, and asked, in all its quivering form: "Did she hurt you, my lady?" Absurdity, from one so young. But noble. And well-crafted. She might have suspected Sara. It was too sweet to ignore. She kissed her husband-to-be on the head—crouching to do so—and whispered, "No, no sweet prince, your lady lives." When her jealous brother tried to shoulder in, she laughed and touched his head as well, ruffling the feathery strands of his hair.

Children.

"With knights like these, I think the world itself should not suffice to do me wrong."

It was the moment her father sought. She could see it in the way he beamed. For once, there was no fiction to it. Save the actual act of the smile. Tenderly, he pressed a hand against her shoulder as she wobbled forward, the children swept around him like tiny waves. "I have been here every day, my dear. Every day. But you are a Cullick true, I see." The smile widened to a lion's mouth. For a moment, she could but wonder if it would consume her, too. She bobbed in gratitude all the same.

Little time did it take for him to draw her aside on some pretense of her health, entreating her to his study. Sara—*Maker be praised*—would not be pried from her for any reason, though. When Walthere suggested it, she brushed it off, claiming a walk would do her every bit as well at a friend's side as it would in daylight's care. Walthere was practiced enough not to let his distaste show as anything more than the slightest twitch of the cheek.

Servants and guardsmen alike shuffled quickly out of their path as their train wound its way down the keep, first for the kitchens, and inevitably on toward the central yards, where the blossoms of spring held fast. Even with food in hand, the conversation was cordial to a point. Formal. More was given between the words than in them—the way Walthere talked after Sara's step-mother, or the space between the talk of lords.

Even Charlotte's husband-to-be could not escape mention in the side-talk. It was in the words. Oh, they all sounded well and good put together, describing how the boy had visited her daily, and wept for her, but individually, the descriptions beckoned a weak character. A moldable character. An orphan. Sara, if she noted it, had the grace not to comment.

It was only when it became apparent that no matter the time involved, Sara had no interest in abandoning her friend—particularly, Charlotte gave thanks, when she made plain how much the seat outside comforted her still-recovering form—that Walthere stopped talking around the issue, and came to it at a head.

It was about time.

"I wished to speak with you of…well…" *So close.* The man's hard eyes showed none of the hesitation his voice did. "The obvious, I suppose."

"Apparently, witches are hardly that," Sara retorted dully, clinging protectively to Charlotte's arm. As though a frail thing. A little sister. Charlotte looked sidewise at her friend. *Are any of us so broken?* "I had her mistaken for a simple girl—and might I add, not a portrait entirely of my own painting."

Walthere's chin wobbled with a purposeful cough. He looked apprehensively away. As though he were actually troubled. "You will forgive us this one indiscretion, highness. All families have their skeletons, as it is said. We did not wish you troubled nor, nay, your name tarnished by knowledge of her person here. We faithful—it is a burden to bear." He held up his hands, helpless, as though to say: "But some things are unavoidable." Sara's lips thinned with pursed distaste, but said nothing.

Above their heads, among boughs from plains as distant as alien Zutam, the birds sang a dirge. It caught in the smoke from the city to the west. It carried on a dry wind and grew muddled by lack of the singers' accord. Confusion. It was in the air.

At her father's urging, Charlotte's thoughts drifted back. "What of her?"

"I think it time we considered a parting of ways."

"Oh, but father—surely she has barely begun to work." Idly, she fiddled with a scorched strand of erstwhile blonde.

"Or perhaps she works too much. You might have been killed, Charlotte. And you would not have been the only one."

For a moment, she weighed that. On surface: truth. That scream echoed across memory. In darkness, the stillness of Dartrek's face. Yet there was something else. To her, all of them had been as ghosts. Notions, not flesh. Madness, or insight into a battered soul. She considered telling her father of the presence she had felt there. That weight that seemed to bury the witch. In front of Sara, though—too easily put to dreams and illness.

"She had been doing better," she intended defensively, but only mustered lamely. Then she changed tacks: "Where is she now?"

Walthere hesitated. His gaze flicked to Sara and back. "Outside. The mushroom grove by Badur Hill. Amid the circle, bound in chains."

An old place. Both for ritual and execution. "The standing stones?"

"She remains?" Sara grasped at her own neck. "Maker above. What would possess you?"

The look Walthere shot her next was one of bland fact. "She has had her uses in the past. I think it best you content yourself at that."

"And mother?" Charlotte asked, changing tacks again. "I do not recall seeing her at my bedside." Had she known of this, come hell or human hand, she would have been there. Waking should have been a smothering of old beauty.

"She is away. To Sayerne, in Banur. I thought it prudent. We need more from your skittish uncle, and you know well as I she is no good in madness such as this."

"And your excuse for my uncle?"

She felt bold. Prideful, even—and dangerous. Something clicked behind her father's cheeks, and it echoed on his tongue. Respect or loathing. They were much the same in a Cullick's hand.

"How your mind races!" Sara piped. "Do not forget to breathe."

"There was a battle at the Three Ponds. Lord Gallas led the loyalists. Led them right into a pincer. Old fool." He smirked, and the years toppled from him. "I am told only a few dozen escaped—though, there were only a hundred or so to begin. Your uncle took Gallas, but the affair did keep him and your cousin afield. Otherwise, I am certain they would be here…attending you." This last was not entirely devoid of sarcasm.

"Then I think, on the morrow, we should ride to attend *them.* And show our support." Charlotte was certain to share a glance with Sara on that note, leaving no doubt she meant the both of them. Witold, like a gathering cloud, loomed forward as if to storm, but a heavy knock on the study's door drew him off.

"Enter."

A bareheaded little man dipped repeatedly with his entrance. For all that, the breastplate over his tunic marked him for a soldier. He spoke only when asked. "My lord, ladies. I come with word from Messar Boyce." At this, he glanced up, waiting until Walthere bid him on. "It is the witch, my lord." The room grew deathly still, shuffling the man onto his other foot. As if he meant to flee. "She asks for the lady—for, for Charlotte."

Only Sara offered the obvious: "I thought she was gagged."

It was the second time Charlotte visited the witch that they actually spoke.

Smoke-filled eyes looked to her—to the one they had scorched—and receded. There was almost light, but the clouds swirled, and the haze thickened, and the witch sank gasping from them, a husk of life. She had not been so bared since the day the soldiers dragged her to the keep.

Would that they never had.

Lips starved purple and thin drew a soft breath to declare: "I have had a vision."

"A vision?"

Charlotte wielded the words like a curse. Lightly, she stepped around them, as she did the circle of stone and mushrooms—the faerie circle, as the old ones once called it—though she feared neither. It merely seemed wrong to humor the girl—to give to this witch that had taken and burned any shred of human comfort.

This stunt she could greet only with suspicion. There was magic and there was prophecy. Two threads, perhaps, of the same tapestry, but rarely intertwined. Too much for one soul—and even Usuri, in all her rage, had never shown hint of that capability.

Not like the father. Not like he that proved even foresight could not stave off fate's hand.

"You have never suffered such a thing before."

"My father—"

"Is dead. So much for the gift." She leaned against one of the standing stones, waiting for the girl's head to rise again. The witch chewed at her lip, but did not oblige. Like a cowed dog. In a moment's introspection, it reminded of a dream months before, where this very witch had stood upon a rock and cast her down. It made her vicious. "Witch and prophet. Each was its own. Now, suddenly, you take the Sight as well? Desperate waif, why should we believe you?"

Usuri's reply was a soft note in a bitter wind. "Already you speak as woman crowned…"

"I am leaving," Charlotte said simply, and turned to go.

"Wait!"

The head lurched up at last, and Charlotte smirked for that small victory, but turned with nothing more than contempt. Arms crossed about her chest, she—despite herself—whispered a prayer as she crossed the lines of the circle. Eyes stalked her from every long-stretched shadow. They wondered, useless and mortal. Feared. She would not let it infect her.

Usuri's arms were drawn to her naked chest, her legs forced to kneel, the whole of her drawn taut. Iron-bound.

The witch had to strain her neck just to watch her. "It—that is, my vision—it *is* his, bird."

"Do not call me that."

"You are afraid."

So dry was her laugh it drew even the witch aback. "Of you?"

"Of life, lioness. And that—that makes you wise." The eyes lowered again and the girl shrank against her bonds. "You shall surely care. Oh, listen, listen, why do they circle? The birdy and the witch so foul? Oh, she might have burned

410

her. Might have plucked a pretty hair and done her wrong. World burst, and yet, was there any scar but sound? Yes," she added, with rhythmic, manic tapping of her finger on the chain. "It is a vision, lady, and it gives us sight of *you*."

This sounded too much the old Usuri to be anything passing comfort. "Me?" Breath caught in her lungs, an icicle-laden drag. She felt as still as bodies in their graves. Still, she took another step.

"How long have you known it?"

"How long the mind did set to flight? Call your father, b—lady. Call him, and let him know. It should not hold it any longer. I am no worthy bearer. There's too much…too much…" The witch's lips tittered around the coming "b," and would not let it out.

"If this is a trick…"

The final step was the easiest of all. Charlotte stood over the woman again, and as the small shape of her began to shrink into something terribly human, and frail, the hand rose. It swept the air and heaved blood to the fore of the witch's rolling cheek. For a moment, Charlotte thought that action might have drained what remained of her own weakened body. She held. Her hand tingled in the air, reverberating with the girl's own hurt, and she held.

"Even witches sleep. And I've enough of your waking."

A Witch's Vision

The Gold Sunrise wilt meet the Green Descent.
Fire rages through earth and sea, should threaten to consume—
a child, lost within a family's shadow, shall turn it all to dust.
Oh ashes, ashes, Idasia!
We have seen you smothered in the gore,
consumed by swords of retribution—forgotten, lodged within your spine.
We hear your lamentations, though your people be proud, your walls be high
the shadow will be higher, yea, your weary chick shall take its flight
in reddened sun retire, where leaves and herbs grow green
watered in the heart's ambition, the distant untouched dead—
therein, the Lady Fair, who at her tips the storms, the life
this slanted earth, scorched beneath the fiercest strife—
though nest be sundered with the call for death

411

north and south shall take refuge in the lion's mouth
tax and blood and cruel, cruel war
shall settle by the choice, where heads wilt bow before the door.
But by shackle-rattle hear it now
the enslaved people shall not bow
but shall ye bow, that does not of the blood relent.

At Charlotte's behest, they rode out the next morning, for the Three Ponds and the company of her uncle. Herself, Sara, and a dozen men-at-arms between them. There had been enough "good" news over the past evening. Something was to be said for the simple honesty she knew her uncle could bring.

It was about three hours' ride to where Usteroy's army encamped, open terrain already jewelling at the touch of the springtide sun. Foot traffic on the cobbled roads was heavy, swelled by farmers, merchants, and afflicted refugees alike, and more than one village's bells rang with their passing, though whether to bark in warning or to beckon traders to Sonntag market was anyone's guess.

It had been suggested—or feuded over, more like—that the ladies take to coach for the journey. For Charlotte, though, the sun was full in a crystalline sky, the grass stretched long against the memory of rain, and she could think of nothing better to suppress the rigors of previous days than with a vigorous ride. Sara, ever her proxy now, was likewise adamant.

So they rode, setting at times a furious pace. For Charlotte, it was about putting as much distance between her and "the lion" as possible. What was little more than fantasy to her had given that one wings, and all evening her father had reared himself about the keep as though Providence itself had settled about his shoulders.

"Don't you see," he cried aloud in joy, "these are the words! It was shards of these that burned him, that brought that whisper of that woman to my ears."

The witch, it seemed, was no longer to be removed. Rather, she was to be given into Boyce's care.

Which was to say, the question of her removal remained very much unclear.

"Is she really a prophet?" Sara asked at one point. They rode side-by-side, reluctantly confined to the middle of their column.

Charlotte fixed on the dipping land before them, and the smoke of the fires burning up the sky. "The father was."

"Was?"

"The Inquisition burned him."

And that was that. Sara nodded, absently paling at the thought that the Inquisition would no doubt do the same to her, if given ample chance. They had done it to other Farrens. Other heretics. Perhaps it even struck a chord of sympathy in her. Regardless, Charlotte saw no good in adding that the burning had come at the old emperor's own approval. No need to make his daughter anxious.

They arrived just after midday. The camp at Three Ponds was a solemn, simple thing, regimented to strict military standard and devoid of the pomp and polish of grander campaigns. Lines of tents staked out a small patch of land to the east of the aforementioned "ponds"—small, freshwater reservoirs nestled among the fertile soil of Usteroy's western fields, from which local farmers and ranchers made ample wealth. Stakes had been hammered into the dirt to mark perimeter, while a long, thin ditch had been dug around, encircling the camp.

Of this, Charlotte had no doubt, the wandering ranchers and sheepherders would not be pleased, come war's end.

For all its starkness, the camp grew lively at the sight of them. Only a few hundred men were afoot, but all doffed caps or struck a knee, some crying out: "The Empress's favor upon us!" Sara waved with a practiced poise, but Charlotte only blushed. Moderately. Appropriately.

They savored it.

Few looked worse for wear. Beyond camp, at the heart of the ponds, there remained little sign of the recent battle. What bodies remained had been put to fire far afield, the equipment gathered from their bloodied hands. There was no sign of cannon, no scorch or blackened lame—truly, she would later learn, neither side had boasted any. It had been what her uncle called a "good little war."

Belligerent Lord Gallas, hoping to chase Maynard through the ponds and therein bottleneck him, had in turn found himself caught there, with nowhere but through the waters to flee. It had been a pitched thing, of cavalry and sword-arm, and little entry even from the muskets. Arrows cleaved the air, and the fleeing men drowned in the puddles as they should.

Trapped, Gallas and his retinue had flown the white flag before the hour was done. They sat now dour-faced at the center of camp, in a hastily-erected stockade. The last time Charlotte had seen these men, they waged a battle of a different sort—sycophant nobles, she knew, built for parties. Not war. Not one among them offered the grace the soldiers gave their ladies now. Too far gone to care. In the weight of all that armor, it should have been no surprise.

Devoid of politick and the yammering of the court, Charlotte's uncle was not the awkward, formal creature her friend Sara had come to expect. Having no doubt heard of their coming, Maynard was there to greet them, and as soon as they were bundled out of sight of his men, the bear of a man twisted sharply and caught his niece up in his broad arms. Sara looked scandalized. Charlotte only laughed. Over his shoulder, she spied her otherwise rigid cousin grinning back at her.

"My dear, dear girl, the things we have heard here," he said as he set her back to her feet. The first breath after was a heady rush. "About the…" His concern folded into a decisive frown as his one wary eye cast Sara's way. "Well, you know. You are still pale as a sheet. Your illness is better, I trust? Or is there a doctor's neck I must wring?"

"Should it be so, I should have already done it, ser," Sara chimed happily— and honestly.

"How now—none of that, uncle." Charlotte tapped him once on the chest while twisting a playful look at her friend. "The war could hardly spare you."

"Then I would send the boy to do it," he grunted.

She rounded back on him. "And Her Highness already knows."

Walthere wouldn't have flinched. Maynard all but gaped at the princess. Yet his son did the only thing available to the lost and confused—he quirked a brow and looked between the figures of this new conspiracy, awaiting one or the other to welcome him in with open arms.

None did. Rather, they fell to discussion of the battle. Of troop movements, for the lord Gallas's partner in crime—another neighbor to Usteroy, Ser Lievklaus—had not been caught with his men, and stood at large, whilst word said Duke Urtz was nearly arrived from the south, hoping to join the Loyalist forces of Mauritz gathering in the southwestern farmholds of Corvaden—the crown's lands. Gallas's raids, Maynard suspected, had been but a feint, to divide the army's attention.

And still there had come no word from the northern lords.

They stayed until evening, Sara even so bold as to allow herself to be talked into surveying the troops. "No one," she said later, framed under the guise of the Cullick lion and the Farrens' wheel and eye, "could be so blessed as my brother and I, to have so many men as these before us." They dined, and turned to more distant things—to wandering mothers and ambitious fathers, and even to a marriage. Charlotte found little enough appetite by that time.

It was only as they made to go—buoyed by certain spoils of the battle, and an extra escort besides—that Charlotte's uncle broached again the topic of Usuri. "The witch," he asked, "has she been ended?" Disappointment was heavy in his beard as she assured him of the truth. "There is no master in that one. Remember that. And this last, I fear, in the timing…"

"Timing?" Sara said, perking. She had an ear for gossip, that one. Charlotte felt only a lump in her throat.

The presence.

But her uncle's eyes swiveled to her cousin, and the boy, staring openly—and admiringly—at Sara, blushed at the sudden attention. The bearer of ill tidings. Amschel cleared his throat, but would not look above his sodden bread. "I found a rider on the road a few days past. He said…there had been an accident. In the south."

"In the…" Charlotte felt the breath sucked from her. "Oh, no."

Sara cast about. "What? What do you mean?"

Maynard sighed deeply. "The Empress Dowager."

The sound of Sara's choking rasp was all but deafening. Tears bulged in those beautiful green eyes before the addendum ever mustered itself: first among the witch's victims, if victim she was, to have at least survived. A carriage had apparently broken away, as she delivered a speech. Before a crowd of southern peasants and Orthodox nobles…and one faithful knight.

Someone had spooked the horses—a loyalist, the crowd had decided, when all was settled. Ser Bidderick had run the man down himself, the rider claimed, and dueled him in the road. A riot nearly did the rest when he ran the poor fool through. Later that very night, however, Bidderick himself was said to have been killed, and all knew who to blame for it.

But the information had been held, at least, until they could confirm it. How any of this had eluded Boyce, Charlotte did not know, but one thing seemed certain at the telling. Even between Sara's bitter—and relieved—sobs, she knew this was not the witch's work. Mercy was not in Usuri's bearing. She said as much, boisterously, when the princess made threat against the witch's life. Why she mustered such defense she could not say. Death would certainly be easier.

"And how do you know?" Sara bleated back, sharply. The pitch in her, the raw emotion—it nearly unsettled Charlotte. "How do any of you know?" she repeated more softly.

But Charlotte kept her voice level, and the point drove home. "For I have seen her. And I tell you this: she would not do this." Not entirely a lie.

It was, however, the death knell of conversation. After, it was hurried farewells and uneasy silence. Sara wished to be home. In recent months, she had seen too much tragedy far too close to bear. Charlotte wished nothing more than to let her sleep.

By the time they returned, light trickled down into points of window-side flames, and nothing more. Walthere had retired by then, so Charlotte handed her uncle's trophies over to his steward. Then, parting at last from Sara's company—though not without necessary assurance as to her own health—the Lady Lion took a pensive stroll through Vissering.

Everything was different at night. Halls, bustling and breathless by the golden bars of light, drew long and empty with the passing of that brightest star. She lit a lantern, and save for the guileless pair her father had left to lope after her, the only play about the halls were the shadows and her own sure-footed taps.

At last—quiet.

Almost.

At an apex of stairs, watched over by the hollow eyes—soulless, it seemed, where the lantern struck them—of her own painted family, Charlotte's little group came upon a spider pacing from the other direction. With the shuffle of their steps, the man lifted toward them, but it held none of the disinterest, nor even the false smile that was his wont. It was an empty look. The bland bow that followed was every bit as lacking.

"My lady."

"Boyce."

They took the measure of one another, as they had a thousand times before. Yet this time, neither seemed to have the energy. The man's body slid to a somewhat slumped posture.

"It is good to see you well."

They might have left it at that. As it was, they ambled through the uncomfortable nature of their meeting a moment before Boyce himself made to brush past and leave it all be. She stepped aside to let him, cursing all the while for the words that would not come. There were a hundred questions she might have made of her father's oldest pet.

And every one of them ended in a witch.

She hastened to catch him before he had gone too far. He was rounding the hall as her quick feet caught his ear. Mirthless, he half-turned, and was most of the way into another bow when she gasped, "What is to happen to her?" The phrase seemed to rock him, but as she breathed she did not regret it—there was no politick way to ask.

"You have read the Vorges," he countered, wielding that stony phrase like a shield.

She knew what he meant, but it couldn't be—not that. A moment wavered in indecision, broken only by Boyce's sigh.

"Tell me, lady, have you seen Dartrek yet?"

"Dartrek?" She perked unwittingly. She nearly popped forward on the balls of her feet, but caught herself in time. More guardedly, she asked: "What of him?"

"If there is one thing we should take from the witch, it is that those things common to us—overlooked—may slip all too swiftly by. You should, you know." His eyes lowered, as if toying with some distant thought. A hand reached out toward her, hesitated, and drifted back to its place behind his back. Then he made to go. "The witch will live," he added in passing. "Much as I regret it, your father commands it. I but bleed her daily, to keep her wiles at their weakest."

"And what of that other dark creature?" she called after him, drawing a stern review. "What of that thing you brought here? What is his purpose?"

The man's tongue clicked disapprovingly, and then so did his head. "Loose ends. You should not worry so about the witch. I cannot understand the fascination. Not after all this." Almost as an afterthought, then: "Pray the pair do never meet."

"And why is—"

"The Vorges, my dear. Strike up your bedtime stories."

Then he was around a corner and away. She did not pursue him, though his words sapped some of the fire from her. *Will not one of you take me to confidence anymore? You would make a queen! Why then, do you take eyes to me as so much the pawn?* Setting her jaw, she turned on her heel and started the way she had begun, breezing past her guards like they were not even there.

A name called to her from the lower levels of the keep, but she pressed past the stairs, headed for the nobles' secluded wing. If pawn she was supposed to be, then she would show them what happened when one drew the leash too tight. *Husband, dear, is it past your bed time?* No doubt the boy-king lay curled in his blankets, swaddled in the plush security of one of their station. *Never to want, that one. Never to hope, or care, and certainly not to think. Not for a king, oh no!* But the question of the king was who would stand behind him, who would be the voice through which he spoke. It was a mother's role, perhaps. But mother was gone.

Men would make a puppet out of her. Well, let them see how much more the puppet, they. It was the man who swaggered before the crowd, and the man's voice that flooded the stage. Pity how few realized it was a woman who wrote the lines.

What she intended to do, she did not rightly know. All she knew was her wrath, and the feeling of it all slipping between her fingers. Usuri. Her father. And Boyce, too—*thrice damn him to Hell!* She saw it all, and what could she do? But this boy, this boy—as the boy's door loomed—she could be as god and master. Life needn't be something that happened, but rather, something that could be...

Controlled.

Three guards stood at the ready. They started at the sight of her, stood rigid and pious before the coming of the night. She loathed them. Immovable statues. Everywhere they worked, content in their nothingness, content to do nothing but serve. A penny for the dozen, and they were there. They did not complain—to master's face, at any rate—and took it all, for what meager reward they were given. Or worse: on faith. They came and they forced their way into another's life, insinuating themselves into something irreplaceable, and then they…then they…

She vacillated on her heel, faltering to a halt. Men were such frail things. And women, no better.

"Sister?"

Charlotte turned but slowly at the sound, as though it stood so frail as to break at the sharpness of motion. By pale candlelight, the ghost of Ser Gerold looked sheepish and uncertain. His bright little eyes watched her, weaving between the flames and watering with sleep's call. She stood before his friend's door. Her future lord's. And she had walked past his own unnoticing. Was this the duty of a wife?

Tresses dipped with her head, to hide her face. "Nightmares, little brother?"

The ruffled brown head shook vigorously. Tiny feet padded nearer. "Did you come to see me, sister?"

Opaque faces watched them. By morning, their father would hear everything. The statues that were her fiancé's guards were intractable, unmoved. Every word sunk hollow, somewhere between the bodies and the act. It reminded her of another shadow, too long in the dark.

She reached a pale hand to him, and smiled. "Of course, Ser Gerold. What maid could resist?"

Together, they went away from that place, from all the glamour and pomp, and moved into the darkness of lower halls, where the servants dwelt. It had been so long since she had been here. The cloistered space, the heavy air—it stood familiar, and yet, it rang tinged with a voice that haunted ages. It spoke in father's tones, though it was not one voice, but many.

This is no place for us. Man and woman. Master and servant. The Lord made all separate, and he made it thus for a reason. The voice always spoke in a high language, away from simplicity. What it really meant: *There are lines, there are always lines.*

Her brother's eyes never left her, just as his hand. At last she leaned across the divide of them and made to speak, but he beat her to it. "If you came to see

Lothen, that is alright," he said seriously. "You don't need to walk with me, just because…"

It was a tone she could not match. "Is that right?"

He smiled back, but said nothing more.

There was a certain door, though it stood indiscriminate from the rest. Their guardians looked as puzzled by it as her brother did. Yet she saw it through a little girl's eyes, though she did not know she still possessed such things. Wide eyes. Fearful eyes.

Staving off any questions, she put a finger to her lips and shushed her brother forward. Then she asked their attendants to wait outside. Only because they lately realized whose chamber it was did they oblige.

Inside was a stale room, rendered oppressive by the dribble of smoke from dangling censers. Gerold wrinkled his nose but stepped onward all the same. The place was nigh bare, boasting little more than a bed and a stool, for it was little used. Dust, however, did not cling to the floor. Recently cleaned, no doubt, when the censers were carried in.

Charlotte followed her brother in and clapped the door shut behind. Only the points of their own light hung here, and they made phantoms of the smoke.

Charlotte stopped before the bed. It was a small thing, too small, with scarcely enough straw to support a chicken at roost. Spread across it like so much mulch was the pale form of one she knew well. The cheeks had hollowed and blistered, and the flesh drawn wan against so much sleep, but the lungs rose and fell in determined strokes. They pushed on. As they always would.

Dartrek was a husk, withered by flame. Not the shadow. Not the idiot hound. A human husk, perhaps finally unveiled.

Her protector.

"…like you did."

She blinked. She had not realized her brother spoke to her. Her attention shifted to him, but he remained at Dartrek's side, leaning over the edge of the bed to catch the man's breathing. As though, in looking away, he might condemn him to cease.

"Pardon?"

"He looks like you did," her brother repeated. "Like…like Kana does when she sleeps at night." He blushed, and caught himself, quickly twisting back toward her. "Not that—I mean, you know, you all look so peaceful."

She made a mental note to check in on the girl, but left it alone for the moment. Gracefully as she could, she slid forward to the stool and settled in, letting Gerold's fear slip away with time.

Gerold looked warily back at the slumbering giant. "It was so odd to see you without him. We call him Ser Hollow, you know." When Charlotte started, the boy added a bit guiltily: "He—he always looks so alone, you know. Like Lothen."

A smile forced itself upon her. It had, perhaps, been too long since she'd had a serious conversation with her brother. Too easy to forget that even children were not always children. More difficult to think her stoic shield had anything in common with their emperor-to-be.

"What do you mean by that?"

The boy reached out and pressed a cold hand to Dartrek's forehead. From whatever darkness held him, Dartrek shuddered, and Gerold shrank back swiftly, all but hopping to his sister's lap. "He…" He trailed, haunted by the sleeping man. "He is very lonely here. And you—he talks about you like you're the most beautiful woman in the world." Then his nose scrunched. "Even when I tell him you're my sister."

She hesitated. Lothen, he surely meant. *Why would Dartrek…?* For a second, she considered laying a hand on her brother's shoulder. Instead, she clasped it to her lap.

"And why should our young emperor be lonely? He has you, does he not?"

"Of course!" Then, proudly: "He said I could be one of his knights. Just like uncle. But…everyone else, he says, they're always there to tell him what to do, but they never listen. Even when they smile and nod and go away, he knows they're only pretending. I told him you're not like that, though. How you listen, and you always try and, and…"

"You are a good friend."

He blushed, losing his words to her praise, but gaining new life in them. As only children could. Then: "Do you think Dartrek will wake up?"

Would that she could say for certain. "In time, little one. It takes more than magic to slay a Kuric."

But this did not seem to cheer the boy at all.

"Does this not please you?" She asked, sincerely puzzled.

"It's just…when you woke up, Charlotte, we were there to see you. Waiting. But I don't think—does Dartrek have a family?"

It was a thought, admittedly, she had not considered.

"No, Gerold."

"No papa?"

"No, Gerold."

"No mama?"

"No, Gerold."

His eyes flickered down, and the sallow light made pools of them. Pools that dribbled over his feet, wondering. "Is that why we came here?"

Was it? She sat back on her haunches and twisted her eyes to the sunken picture of a man defined by his faith. Not in some faceless god, but in a simple ideal, and in flesh, set before him. Not a blade, but a shield, a watcher that never turned from those about him. She tried to picture him as the child had, so long ago, but it was impossible. This was Dartrek, as he had always been. But now…

It was a child's turn to play the watcher. No one should ever have to wake alone.

Night stretched into the restless blackness of pre-dawn, but she came to Usuri again. A certain jumpiness—a heightened uncertainty of the world around them—seemed to possess this shift of guards, standing as they did in the very throes of the witching hour, and they did not wish to let Charlotte pass. But all things bend. Before the sun was a mote in the Maker's eye, she bent them to her iron will, and walked as a lion would.

The witch knelt—what other choice did she have?—as if waiting for her. No doubt, it was exactly that. Yet the mind was elsewhere. It hung at the edge of a coin that Usuri cupped between her palms as tenderly as a newborn babe. Shoulders slumped, head bowed, it seemed there was no light at all left in this child of fire. Charlotte felt some of her own go out of her as she slowed before the somber figure, a sliver of torchlight all that stood before them and the dark.

"Father always said that pain schooled a soul. For that, he said, we Naran should be the oldest, wisest souls of all." The chin lifted, though the eyes remained, as though Usuri could not pull herself away. "Yet the soul bleeds. A word can set it off again, where years of scarring sought to heal it. And you know what that leaves us with? I could die. I could kill. It's nature—I've seen others do it." She paused. "I've done it.

"And you know what I have realized? For all the hurts that come upon us, all the ends we come to face, so much of it leads back to our own self. A word unspoken. A deed unrealized. Visions whispered for the wrong eyes…" A shred of a tear bubbled in the girl's eye, and threatened to fall. Instead, she blinked it into air.

"So…" The girl murmured, at least some of herself returning to that mouse-like body. "Your father knows of the lion?" Charlotte nodded, uncertain which aspect of the witch she now faced. "In earnest will he move, to make it so."

"Self-fulfilling prophecy? Aren't those a little tired?"

"Quite. But not all of it is so. Not all of it is a lion's share, after all."

"How do you mean?"

Usuri's eyes sank, and the body with them. A tired sigh eased out of her like old wind. "Prophecy is words. No more. No less. Alterable. Lions, you should know, are indolent creatures. Self-indulging. They sit on the labors of others, even to their mates, and reap a kingly title from the bones. This vision—it is not about lions, lady, but the fairer cat."

Charlotte betrayed no hint of surprise. Rather, she gently kicked the shoes from her feet and let the dew play between her toes as she stalked nearer to their so-called prophet. So soft, the grass. It carried her away from the walls raised about her. So frail. Like the witch's mind. Like her own skin. She peered down at one dainty limb as she let it fold beneath her. None of the roughness of Dartrek's hands, no. It lacked the experience.

She ran her fingers along the witch's chains. Cold iron. "I suspected."

The witch actually smiled at that.

"Tell me. Why do you not just burn it all? These chains—they are surely nothing to you. And for that—why did you not finish what you started, in your quarters? Not a one of us might have stopped you. As you say—a prophecy is but words. As are the people in it."

"But I like those words," the witch countered coyly. "Tell me. Do *you* act now, as once you might have?"

"It does not change what we have done to you. What we—"

"Hush."

When had the hands slipped their bonds? The witch leaned forward, and as she stretched Charlotte beheld, clearly, the bruises her father's soldiers had left her. She winced where the witch's fingers graced her cheek. Felt herself grow smaller and smaller within the lion's shell. A word. It was all Usuri need utter.

"I am nothing. But through me…it is the mantra of many men. I remain because for all the pain, there is something to be seen. An ideal or a spirit. I will die a thousand times for it, and I will suffer for it, because I know that for I others may suffer less. Odd to hear from a murderess. From a mad woman. But so it is.

"So tell me, little bird," and the hand pressed more heavily against Charlotte's flesh, nails coiling against the rings of her hair, "Do you think *your* death will do this?"

Something flared beneath her skin, and Charlotte—the lion, the wall, the little bird all—shed her masks for a whimper.

The night was long, but it made the sun brighter for it.

No one should ever have to wake alone. Not even a witch.

Chapter 18

It was dawn, and the light streamed bright and clear through the trees, tingeing leaf and earth alike a ruddy scarlet. Men were not long in waking, though the cocks had already crowed the waking anthem. Not even the loggers had yet set to their tunes. Verdan was at peace.

For a moment in time.

Trumpets scourged the ears with frantic notes. The men staggered from sleep, but with the fury of the fearful. Someone shouted for the gryphons—what cavalry they had needed to be saddled. Powder was rolled out. It coated the earth and its bearers' hands black where it leaked.

Then the first crack of gunpowder shattered the vision. In the trees, it seemed to echo all around them, and the frightened men grew frenzied. Shouts broke, scattered between layers of canvas. Another trumpet blew, but its note bit off into an echoing death rattle. Arrows swarmed the aftermath of the confusion, fletched with death.

A man's sweaty palms wavered on her wrists, looking for purchase. She would not look him in the eye. Not him, and not the general that had sought their end. The Bastard stood low before Essa, for all his height. Sunken eyes turned east to the river, as the men about him crouched and shuddered away with pleas and plans. Tessel knew, in that moment. Knew she had not lied.

And she knew he hated her for it.

Lips smacked behind her as the sweating soldiers fidgeted away. He wanted to run. She knew it. Almost prayed he would. Tessel swung sharply on their jailor, and the man drew still. "Cut them loose." The dark eyes swiveled, taking the others in. "I'll not be caught in robes again. Arms, all of you. Arms and to me, and we'll see what these frogs can belch up." They flicked over her, dismissed her at a look, and turned away again with nothing more than a grunt. No thanks. The mind was elsewhere.

Soon, so was he, and the guards with him.

Voren stumbled to her, taking her hands in his and trying to get around to her gaze. "Are you alright? If only the fools had listened..."

Three figures had stalked along the flushed dawn, the only ones that knew what crept as wolves into a shepherd's pasture. Yet the wardens had barred them at the gate. A man there knew their faces, and named them traitor. Long guns. So many long guns, all pointed to their hearts. A flourish of Rowan's steel, but the guards were many, and they were deaf. A messenger ran as the others dragged her cousin down. Hands bound. Eyes set to earth.

Scowling, the wardens told her what she could not have known: that Rurik still was not returned to camp. Yet Orif of Kellsly was, and soon enough, he descended on them like a black wave. "You!" he roared, for surely he knew their presence meant the death of his own men, and he would have killed them if their guards had not feared Tessel's wrath all the more.

By the time the general came, they were decided. Voren's blubbering convinced no one, and Essa's stony silence only seemed to egg them on. But Tessel listened, though he did not speak. The runner he sent—the niggling fear of confirmation—was all that gave his camp the briefest warning call it managed.

Now she stared at the baker. Words spilled at a flood from him, and she blinked at the sudden feeling in her wrists. Bodies skittered away. The clamor rose. She winced against it. It rang in her head and heralded the flesh's end. But Rowan—Rowan had been borne away. There was only Voren. Frantic, she searched for any sign, but Voren gripped her, crying, "No, no," he had seen him, and he fought her to make her know it. Tessel's men had taken Rowan, not that swine.

When he talked her down, he held her bow to her, and she took it reverently. It felt foreign to her, the wood rough where it should have been smooth. Something like ash graced her tongue, and she shifted it around the words. If Rurik had not returned, then Rurik might yet survive. Perhaps he had the sense to flee after all.

But good sense, the roiling pit of her stomach beckoned, had never been any of their strong suits.

"Essa. We need to go. He's not here. Surely, we—"

He did not see what she saw. Men pushed out, away. Where the tents butted against the plain, where war met memory and children fled the dust of it, she saw them blossom into men, and these men, as a dark and terrible scar on the sun-dappled field, pushed toward the violence.

Essa need not ask if the boy was among them. Her stomach heaved in answer, regardless.

* *

The first pop of gunpowder was little more than a crackle of fire before a sleepy dawn.

What Rurik, as so many others, only belatedly realized was that the raiders did not come by land. No one had thought to watch the river, and least of all he, the native, for anyone could guess this time of year that bloated, raging beast should have been a haven only for the crazed. Witold was apparently that. His men were already among the Bastard's camp before they ever realized something was amiss.

Only later did he learn the camp's own watchers, many slumbering, were slaughtered beneath the mists of spring, or fled, such that none were able to give voice.

What he heard was fire. It was enough to rouse him from slumber, but not enough to move him. The mind, hazed, flitted with the question of why someone should strike up so great a cooking fire, but it could not wrap around the answer. It was dulled by blankets, by the feeling of solid floorboards beneath his back and the sister that lay curled beside him, as if it to loose him might be to condemn him to a thing of phantoms. As if he were smoke that would flutter away.

As the door to the sitting room snapped wide, he realized it was not so far from truth. Both started, and he, putting himself before his sister, flailed for the pistol off his belt. Liesa flinched. He, too, froze to see the thing finally rest before his eyes.

Men had entered. They screamed things at him until the noise turned to words again, and he to a man, settled in the taut flesh of the starved and weary soldier. Night had nearly given him humanity again. In an instant, it was all but stolen, and even as he turned to his sister's pleading eyes, he felt the darkness seeping into everything that was him.

Screaming soldiers pulled him toward camp by the first shudder of a cannon. Liesa groggily stalked him to the walls, and there both saw it. Blazing, billowing smoke. Pale ghosts flooding through the trees.

His parting words to his sister, made in the haste to arm, were thus: "Make for the trees, with all you trust. Bear the white flag. Speak to none but their master." Then he was away, swept into the fields by the terror of Tessel's soldiers.

Essa and the Company had escaped. This, in his heart, he knew. So too would Liesa. He held no regret as he shifted the pistol in his hand. As the smoke enveloped him. For him, Hell would be a blessing, and fitting.

All war was chaos, but this—anarchy. In the streets of Verdan, many formed ragged bands of bucket crews, children rushing to the river for water, men and women battling to keep the flames at bay. The ground was damp, and the trees, too—it was the only thing working in their favor.

At the edge of camp, the cry of his name spun him, but whoever cried out was lost in the swell. Here was the source of the fire, and it swept through the tents. Even in daylight, he could see the bobbing of torches, like so many cackling spirits. He only hoped it did not reach the powder magazines, or they were all done. Every one of them. Men moved not in ones, or twos, or Tessel's beloved columns, but hordes—some fled, axes and swords nipping at their heels, while others scrambled for the river and the sounds of battle. Orders were but shouts in the wind.

Yet here, Rurik found a voice. With a bevy of men at his side, alert, all spoiling for a chance, he presented a sort of calm in the storm. Thought, at least, put him a step above the animalistic flight about him—a point of normalcy to which the many could flee and find chance to breathe. Forgetting his hatred of this place, and of the one that commanded it, forgetting the threats and the pain and thinking only of the terrified, breaking mass, he called to Tessel's soldiers and formed a block with which to advance. Then they pushed forward, all the while reaching out to any that would have them.

The closer to the river they pushed, the harder it became to breathe. Smoke drew thick and murky, and the dry canvas went up like kindling. Among the screams, the ghosts of Oberroth stalked. This he knew. It did not matter.

I will never walk from this alive. Whatever the reason, that thought gave him a greater clarity with which to strike. For with it died fear. *Watch me play soldier now, father. I have done all that I could with the rest.*

They had nearly reached the river when the first assailants fell on them. A squad of them came howling from the dark, their weapons gleaming like beacons from the oily smoke. They came roaring cries of "Idasia!" over the ash and bodies, whipping their maces and axes in a blood hazed fury. Those not skewered on the pikes of Rurik's wall died as Rurik and the second line stepped in to carve them down with cold steel.

As these died, another group—some of their own, Rurik realized almost belatedly—rushed past, shouting rallying cries. For Assal. For Tessel. For Freedom. Rurik stared after them, as they thrust themselves on a band of soldiers scrabbling to shore from a raft. Too late, he noticed the other rafts sweeping down the current behind them.

"Shields!" he cried, and the men around him sank to a knee with practiced purpose, casting bucklers to the sky or simply cowering into the smallest targets they might. Arrows fell like barbed rain along the coast, and more than one man in Rurik's own party cried out as they fell. One bolt took Rurik off his feet, when the man beside him toppled under his meager shield.

When the sprinkle of death was ended, however, and Rurik pulled himself from the heap, he found his own men only lightly touched. A few walked or limped away with new scars, but none had been killed outright. The party that had rushed ahead was not nearly so fortunate. Only a few rose, bloody and uncertain, and these—stranded along the river's edge—sank soon after as another raft bobbed near, and wobbling bowmen picked them off.

Bodies choked the river, but as they regained their feet Rurik spied the rafts forming a beachhead. While teams of Witold's men had already dispersed amongst the camp, to sow confusion and madness, these later comings were organized, forming a shield wall while boat-borne bowmen provided them the cover to hold it. Time and again smaller bands of Tessel's followers broke against the wall and were repulsed. Neither wounded men nor promised booty would draw the staunch defenders out, and they watched the myriad smaller battles breaking around them with only a passing sort of satisfaction.

"Ser," a grey-haired veteran called from Rurik's right, "If they take the bank, we will never throw them back."

"Push," another cried. "Push now! We have the men!"

Of that, Rurik was certain they did not, and the longer they remained in indecision, the more of a target they made for the paddling bowmen. Near frantic, he cast about, trying and failing to force the strangling sounds of the wounded and the dying and the oppressive heat of the flames from interfering.

When a cannonball snapped apart a nearby tent and scattered his men, however, that thin concentration fractured.

Dirt searing into his cheek, the winded youth twisted to the opposite bank, where he plainly saw cannons and men now gathered. Boats merely shuffled between, cast out from the shore.

From Surin. A white dread seized him. Witold had utterly outmaneuvered the army. It was not simply the river they had mastered. Surin had so long been enemy to Idasia, surely no one could have thought, but Witold had always cultivated friends among the petty nobles of that foreign shore. To cut the raids and bandits in peacetime. And now, this.

If they had firing positions there, it could mean a massacre. Tessel had no men on that side of the river, for he had neither wished to provoke the Surinians, nor deal with the petty banditry that stalked its shores. Thus, Witold now held an unassailable position.

They needed their own cannons. Few of Witold's men seemed to bear long guns, but their own camp held them in abundance and…Rurik's thoughts halted and his eyes alighted on the barrels left along and adrift among the crumpled tent beside them. A dead Asanti cannoneer lay bloody and black amidst the leaking powder of the kegs.

Perhaps there was a way. "Puncture those barrels! To your feet, men, to your feet, and grab me a torch." Bodies heaved the toppled barrels. More than one man looked horrified at the thought of dragging the powder so near, but no one disobeyed. "It's downhill, fools—cast for the shore!" And his plan suddenly became clear.

Then five barrels of gunpowder were sailing down the bank toward the cloistering soldiers. Men had returned with torches, and even as Rurik took aim with his pistol, they cast them to the powder as the barrels clattered off the gathered soldiers. Looks of confidence disintegrated into sharpened horror. Someone had just begun to cry out for the river when the flame took hold and Rurik's shot split the morning.

It seemed an instant. Then the fire sparked, and the air with it. Powder screeched and the earth thundered every man about the beach clean off their feet.

Everything ached. From his back, Rurik lurched with his stomach as something wet touched upon his skin. The air, he realized, had grown heavy with blood. It choked him. Yet there was no sound, save the distant ringing.

Witold's men no longer held Verdan's side of the river. Those who remained wandered or swayed in a bloody daze, but many more would never leave the dust, scattered in bits and pieces where the explosion had torn.

If only he could find his head again, it was the chance they needed.

"Push forward! Forward!"

At least, that was what he hoped to say. He had no idea if the words actually tumbled off the end of his rattling tongue. Feet lurched under him and hands seized him up. The sensation of the lift set his head spinning even more. He squinted, then blinked through the reeling world. Only slowly did it right itself, but he remained focused on the point before them. The shambling and the broken. He shook, clawing for purchase on the world, but all he managed to shake off were the hands supporting him. Using the momentum, he stumbled forward, and the men, soldiers that they were, had no choice but to follow.

When had they so grown? Dozens of them stepped in line on his mark, and not as the howling horde that had dragged them here, but in line, in formation, the clap of their boots setting a haunting undercurrent to the gargle of the river. Ghosts stared up at them—wrecked, bloodied husks—some missing limbs and others vainly struggling to regain their positions, but Rurik's force marched forward unphased and unturned. Whatever the nature of the men, these raiders had sought to kill them, and for it, they would be driven into the icy water.

Something popped. Cries of "to me, to me," echoed at their backs. It startled Rurik, for the low thrum of its repetition broke through whatever barrier surrounded his thoughts, pierced the numbness and the hum of clustered feet to beckon back the sound. Yet he had little time to revel in it. Everywhere, the little battles gave way as other columns reformed under competent commanders, and pushed the same as Rurik. On the far bank, an explosion toppled an oak that sent men scrambling as it careened across the river. One boat, unable to turn quickly enough against the current, gave up a heavy sigh as it crashed against the bark and sent its passengers swimming.

Rurik twisted back just long enough to see the camp's own cannon—larger cannons than Witold could bring to bear—rolling into position. The world began to stink of sulfur.

We will do it. The bodies were forgotten. *Father, do you see? I'm not hopeless.* The haunted faces. *I can—I can...* The scream of neighbors as they were cast into the waves. Red became all. He did not think of his name being shouted.

Somewhere, a father's voice echoed: *"Steel your heart or lose your mind."*

There was cheering on the bank. Swords rattled. Even Rurik felt his heart leap, for knowing what salvation could be like. It wasn't about Tessel, or the Farrens, right and wrong or anything else. It was a victory of the self. A knowing affirmation.

Until his father's eyes arrested him.

No—not a father. A brother.

At the far bank, the one he had so long sought stood among the shadows and the sand. Their eyes met. A hand faltered, then chopped down. The cannons had twisted, now trained on their position.

Fear had a second to trickle through realization. There was not enough time left to that instant even to cry out before the world sundered. Heat engulfed him. Flame licked his arms and he felt himself hurled like dry hay, engulfed in the screams that so suddenly, so horrifically returned to him—only to cut once more into that rising, ringing nothing.

He struck something. Rolled. Rock seared the already beaten skin. Something rattled—him, or his chains. There were no bodies. No people. Only silhouettes. Bones felt nothing more than clay, and every bump struck like a coiled fist. When everything stopped spinning, though the ground beneath him thrummed, he tried to lift his head. He felt the slickness—something licked the hair damp to his head.

Then.

The darkness.

He was not in a war. There was a girl—pale-eyed. Her tears filled an ocean, and the world was at peace because no one could hear any other scream. No fire. No emptiness. Because the entire world was shifting all around him. Her hands reached out to him, and he saw only then that she wore two faces.

Waking was not painful, nor wearying. The only word he could find for it was: heavy. He tried to move. Again the slickness, the pain. A face loomed over him. It burned into his eyes. They too were heavy. With ash, he supposed.

I'm dying. He tried to voice that, but his words were smoke. Something brushed him, and the words found a scream.

A caress on his throat. *"Let it go. Let it go."* Storms capsized the whole of him. In the waves, there was no forgiveness.

When he entered into Rurik again, the world was moving. He could feel it under him, and see it shift through half-lidded eyes. But slowly. As though it all bore a great weight. Bodies all around—so many, many weights. His head lifted from them and, strained against light, looked to salvation. He expected his mother's eyes. Or father.

Instead, he found a wisp of a baker. "Thank you…" He did not hear it, so much as his lips formed around it. The muddy eyes flickered down, abruptly uncertain.

It was then he began to wonder at the fire in his side. It seemed to burn the world away by inches. His head lolled. It was Usuri's hand, and her scream. *In the coin?* He longed to reach for it, but the fire burned hotter and the smoke choked it all away.

The darkness.

Just a girl by the sea.

Sweat drowned him. It lapped at the flesh and submerged the mind, drawing back only piecemeal the man, drenched in the agony. Crusted and heavy, the world revealed itself. Focusing hurt. It was all a blur and his eyes strained to take it in. Wavy. That was the world. Something burned in him to such an extent it drew the rest of him cold. He shivered despite himself, reliving the depths of winter tight against the length of him, without fire for reprieve.

"You're awake? I didn't think—no matter. It is what it is. Does it hurt?"

He narrowed the scope of things, to the point dangling before his eyes. A human point. *Is this it?* The girl was gone, and the waves by the sea. Instead, Voren rippled over him, above him, fingers roaming over themselves like nervous spiders arrayed against a backdrop of wood and peeping rays of sunlight.

They were in a cabin. Dust filtered through the air. An old cabin. He tried to move and felt through the needles of pain a solid weight beneath his back. The world did not swim around him, but he was not level. A table. He blinked, remembering the battlefield and the swirling hell it brought. The heat. The smoke. There was none of that here. Only an old home and a splint-ridden table on which he lay. It seemed to wobble with his motions.

A flush of air galloped across bare skin and he gasped for it. Ash still touched it, dirtying his lungs to the point of a rasping cough. As he heaved, and invisible nails drove deeper into his spirit, his jerking motion brought the whole into view, and made the point of flame burn all the hotter for it.

His tunic had been cut away, his armor discarded. Sweat beaded and descended into pools, burdening his mere humanity and staining the wood beneath. Most vividly, though, stood a blight against the flesh—a deep, jagged slash bit into his side, pulsing with every subtle shifting of muscle and oozing the colored flash of life out and away. Something was jammed in it. Wood, he thought at first—a part of the table. Yet it shone in the ragged light and some distant part of him named it metal, while his soldier, by widened eyes, named it for what it was: shrapnel.

Bile surged in him and the wound pulsed, sending another wave of fire running ragged through him. He fell back howling, and only as the numbness carried him back to the low, murmuring moan did he beg. "Water. I-I need water…" It felt as though the cool drink were all that might draw out the flames.

The mind receded, to deal with the pain. It too narrowed, heavy and blind to the roar beyond. It narrowed to a baker and to the nature of reality. *Is this real, or do I dream?* It felt real. Dream pain—it was an abstract thing. *But this…* The baker was the crux of it. Would that he could cry out! The baker—the baker was supposed to be gone. Voren was an enigma. He existed only in the land of Essa, and she, in the sanctuary he had carved of his mind, where his was a noble sacrifice and they, at last free of his imbecility, and free of all that man might use to do them wrong. They had fled.

If Voren were real, then so was Essa. Her face cycled through the flames and the smoke and rasped as if for air, but it was own throat that choked. *Be free. Assal above, please be free.*

434

Then the water struck his face and removed any doubt. Wretchedly, he wrenched back to the land of sight, and to the baker clutching a canteen above his now sopping head. Therein, he saw the first true glimpse of the boy, and it made him shudder worse than any piece of metal.

"I need you awake, Rurik. Focus. Can you hear me?" He nodded only vacantly, reaching for the canteen. Only lately did he realize it already hovered upside down, the contents lost. "I had thought you dead," and Voren receded on that note, pulling the canteen with him. "It would have been easier if you had died."

What would have been easier? It seemed Voren meant to stitch him up. The hands returned—the smooth, yet heavy hands. They wrapped about his throat and he wretched as they pulled him back to tie something taut. His own hands jerked up to take hold of it, but the baker forced them down, hard, and snapped the fight from him. Rope, he now saw. It chafed the bare skin, but it held him fast. Voren was no doctor. *Is he with Witold?*

"Voren…" He could not think of what else to say. The baker, though, drew back on the word and stared at him through eyes lidded by grief.

"Rurik. Do you…" Voren's eyes darted down almost fearfully to the wound in Rurik's side, before they settled somewhere below his own gaze. They would not meet him. "Am I a bad person?"

Only a mad one. "No, Voren. I don't think—"

"Well that much is true," and the voice turned venomous. "You never think. No, you never do that. Fly, fly, little ones, you say, and play the noble fool. And what does it do? It engrains you more. Endears you more. Raises you above the filth you play at every other moment of the thing." He stepped forward, so that above Rurik there was nothing *but* his leering, soot-stained face and those beady, hate-filled eyes.

"Why? Why can't you just forget? You have had everything, don't you see? Moan, whine, complain, oh—how the world is so cruel! It takes and takes, but you—you don't know a damned thing about the reaping! And you sure as Hell can't let it go." His hand on Rurik's collar shook. "The pain you bring to others. To her…"

Essa? He tried to lean up, even if only an inch, but the ropes held fast and the wound sapped the rest. He moaned, fearing for what had happened in the dawning.

All men marched toward death as soon as they were born. Yet at the thought of Essa's demise, Rurik saw the other half of that truth: that for those who outlived those closest to them, death was something that settled over them and blotted out the light. One still lived, but they might not see it.

"Is she…?"

The baker blanched. "How could you even…? No! She comes for you, you twit. There was the forest all before her, and life, and light, and what does she do? She comes back for you. After your assassins came for her. After the dark."

This, however briefly, focused him. It pushed the pain back. "My…?" *The Gorjes.* He knew it without even asking. *But how…?*

"You don't think, Rurik. None of you nobles do. You give orders, sure. You act, but you surely don't think. No-no, don't try to talk. You're too weak, too weak." The baker's hand pressed him flat as he squirmed, and the eyes softened of their fury. "That's for us, isn't it? Do, do, do. Listen. Obey. And you reap all the rewards. Do you even realize how lucky you have stood? Oh, poor lonely boy. Misunderstood. What do you know about it?

"You're an idiot, Rurik. An idiot, and all you do is hurt the ones that try to help you for it. I tried. Oh, I tried to understand, to let you go, saying, she'll see in time, she'll learn, and him, he's not so bad, not so bad, if you just take that one single point away, well, it will all work out. And they can drift, side-by-side down the riverbank, and there, we can be content. And then…

"Alcohol is a dirty drink, Rurik." Something squealed, sharp and hollow. It took Rurik a moment to realize it was Voren, biting back a sob as he twisted away, trembling. "It wasn't for you. Not a drop. Yet there again—what can a man do to turn a woman's eyes away from the flame that will consume her?" This last he said into the floor, shaking his head slowly from side to side. Rurik stilled, the words revolving around him like a flight of pecking crows.

The alcohol. A certain night. Suspicions, long pushed to the edge. His lips shaped around words, and lost them. There was something terrifying in honest evil.

So many times he had wished to give it voice, only to hold it in check saying no, no, it couldn't be, but now it overwhelmed him. "You drugged her? How could you—"

The wrong thing, apparently. Something squeezed his side and the world dissolved into a shimmer of screams. He had never known sound could take so vivid, and bloody, a picture. He panted in its wake, a caged dog thirsting for relief against a summer heat.

"Even this…you found a way. And you hurt for it. Always. Hurt them all. They'll all be better off without. And I, surely, I." The baker turned back, cheeks wet with his own decision. He saw it then—Voren was not lecturing him, not truly, but debating with himself. There was a dark decision in that malevolent gaze and he was working to it in leagues. The pit of Rurik's stomach churned at the sight. "If you live, Rurik…"

This was all a dream. A terrible dream. "Voren. Please."

Yet Voren simply talked over him, as though he heard not a word. "I tried to be like you. To talk like you. But the lines—they just can't be erased, can they? A peasant is a peasant. A noble is a noble. How could I ever compare myself to you? I come with obligations and you with freedom. You offer adventure, and I? I offer a bitter mother, unable to leave her husband's deathbed."

"Let me go, Voren." *Like me? Assal avail me of madmen.*

The books Voren had learned from Essa as a child. His letters. The hound he made, always following at their backs. Unable to let go. The pieces went round about in Rurik's head, forming a gradual chain down to this extreme moment. The realization: was this simple jealousy?

"You don't know what you're talking about."

"Oh I don't? I don't?" The baker's voice snapped like a whip and for a moment Rurik feared he would strike him again. "You're blind as a bat. I love her. As a man should love. Not like you, with your bitterness, your shortsighted—no. I'm not like you. Not like that. All I ever wanted was to give her the world, but it was never mine to give. It was yours. And theirs. Men like the Bastard. Like your cold-hearted corpse of a father. You don't deserve her. But then…"

Love. He felt as empty as a flake caught on a winter's breeze. The boy could stand there, talking about drugs. About pain and death and all the rest, and lecture him of love? Voren wasn't just a fool. He was insane. But inside was still that scared child. He knew he had to reach it. Cow it.

He let pain settle in his lungs on a deep breath. It was necessary fuel, to sober him for the assault. Without it, the boy might yet come out the other end a man.

"Is that it?" The words seemed to startle the baker. Rouse him. "You drag me from the field, just to tell me your heart? That you love Essa? How? How can you love her? And how do you think she can love you? If this is what you are, I tell you this, she surely never could. You dwell. You whine." *Why do you think she could not love me?* "You're pathetic. You drug her and you call it love? What kind of a sick love is that? No one that loves a person could do that.

"You know nothing!" The boy screamed, and he kicked the table, jerking the wound in Rurik's side and leaving him rasping. "You don't know what the emptiness will do—what it can drive a person to. You've never had to go without."

"Coward," Rurik sputtered through gritted teeth. Again the table shuddered.

"Monster. You're no friend to anyone but yourself. You don't know love. But you masquerade, to get what you will." The baker leaned forward and spat on him, square on the chest. "You deserve to die. Let the worms have you."

Perhaps a different tack. Rurik's tone softened around the agony that split him. "Listen to me. I never meant to hurt you. I—certainly not Essa." He had to try to reason. "But I'm—I'm dying, don't you see? I'm already dying! If you—I just need water. Please. That's all I need. Just give me water. Do you think Essa would want to know you for a killer? I'm a killer, and look where it has gotten me. Please. You're better than this. The pain, if you just…"

"Shut up!" A hand flashed across his vision and snapped his head sideways. The baker shrieked and drew back like a startled child. Then, in the silence that followed, he crept back by inches, peering over the edge, into the abyss that waited. Something changed. "I'm not like this, Rurik. I'm not. But you—if you just die, you won't be able to hurt them anymore. And they won't kill themselves for you."

The sting in Rurik's cheek stole away the rest of the pain, but only for a moment. It took his breath, and when it returned, so too did all the rest. "Voren," he said again, more softly, trying to fix his pleading gaze on the boy, to speak to

438

whatever human thing remained with him. "Voren, look at me. This isn't you. I never meant…"

The boy grew still indeed. "No. You didn't."

When Voren had acquired the dagger, he could not say. It took him a moment to realize the blade now brandished in the baker's hand was his own, no doubt pilfered from his belt when the tunic was cut away. It dangled between those pale fingers, uncertain, but its threat was palpable. Bright eyes glinted in it, watched it as if captivated. It hung in them and danced in them, and only slowly descended. Where it touched his chest, there was only chill.

He pleaded. He pleaded until his hoarse voice cracked. Even though Voren looked as pained as he, as pale and as broken, the blade pressed in, and he howled as a line curled its way across him in little beads of scarlet. The knife retracted as quickly as it went in, and the baker hovered over it, transfixed by the blood. He dabbed it with the end of the knife and flicked it away. He would not touch it himself.

"I'm not sure how this…"

The blade bit again, this time at the arm, where the muscle was most tender. Tears took Rurik as this second flesh wound was dealt.

"Is this what war is like?"

Lower, this time. As the blood scrabbled against the air, Voren's hand grew steadier in its butchery, and uncertainty's dark lines withered from his face. Horror refined into a horrific expression of curiosity.

It was in that instant Rurik remembered a lesson his brother had taught him many years before: Man was not born to kill. He learned it, and inch by inch it possessed him.

The blade arced in and slit a long, deeper line down the length of his arm. Rurik's shouts wavered, for they struck at the dryness of his throat and burned him all the more for it. He could breathe, and yet, he was being cut to pieces. Voren's blade flicked again and again, sometimes lighter, sometimes deeper, without pattern, but growing bolder and more quickly wielded with every triumphant carve.

"Is this what you do to people? How you soldiers get your kicks? Mother, she always said I'd be too weak for a war…" The blade tapped against the first wound again, already crusting over. "Just a baker, you know. Nothing so like a man. Can't even get the other boys to play with him—they'll break him, they say." The blade danced in and laid it open anew.

By then, Rurik had run out of pleas. He felt only the sharp pain, only the dulling sparks of the fire. Thought of dying and killing in the same breath. Killing Voren. *What is this monster doing? He drugged Essa and now, what, because he couldn't have her, he...* but the thought broke on the memories of a boy far beneath his notice. The little baker boy, but a shadow of the girl from the trees. What had he done? What had he said? Always nothing. *Like everything else.*

Yes, somehow, somewhere in all the pain, he found the strength to turn to pity. *Poor boy. Poor little boy. Doesn't he see?* But the anger remained, even then. So much anger.

The blade hovered over Rurik's throat when the rage snapped forth again. "Do you expect me to feel sorry for you? You stand here, carving up a bound man, and you moan? Poor boy, indeed. Just a boy. A stupid, jealous boy that will never have what he wants." He winced, but knew he had to force himself on. The blade held, and he felt a bit of the killer recede at the sudden outburst. If he didn't have out with it now, he probably never would. Life ran with the blood, out onto the floor. "How many children like you? How many let it eat them up and grind them down to this? You're just a scared, miserable little shit. Maybe I don't always think. But if you don't act, if all you do is think—all you get is what you are, Voren."

He punctuated the last by hocking a glob of phlegm on the baker's hand. Never had he seen a thing recoil so fast. Bäcker screamed and struck the affronted hand across Rurik's leg. Then he turned the blade to his own affronted flesh, and as Rurik looked on in dread, sliced across the skin. Blood oozed and the baker's eyes teared anew, his blubbering reaching a new peak.

"It's your fault. It's your fault. It's your..."

Voren scowled behind the tears. Then, in shaking hands, he took the knife and slapped it against his heart. Rurik tensed, feeling the words lost. They had done nothing. This was madness of its purest sort.

"You have never cared, have you?"

The blade dithered, one final time. *I'm so sorry, Essa.* Then it began to sink.

"Voren."

The word hung like a curse in the stale air. Gradually, it took shape. Red hair and cap. It took the sound of steel and the crack of a boot. Ash billowed in behind it, spilt from an open doorway. In that portal stood a man and a sword. As one.

Rowan did not say the boy's name again. Its blood hung in his silence.

The baker spun from his charge, the dagger still in hand. Caught at the act, he became only a boy once more, naked with the fear of death. It seemed sound wished to beckon from his slacking, fumbling lips, but nothing issued. The wild eyes darted, first to Rurik, and away. A step bore him back. And another. Always, his eyes kept coming back to Rowan.

The swordsman's gaze flicked from him only once. It found pity in the form of Rurik, but Rurik lay still, and could only mumble his pleas. In every breath, death pressed a little more air from his lungs. There was nothing left to give. It hurt too much. He dared not hope.

The eyes, though—they twisted back hot as the dagger point. Then Voren fled.

Bodies propelled across the little space. "How could you?" Rurik craned to see—the blade, the body, the little voice. It screamed out, seemed to run with the shape of blood where Rowan pierced him through the side. Like a piece of cannonball.

Too late, they caught the motion of a fire poker. It cracked Rowan across the head and staggered him to the floor. The sword fell at a clatter, and Voren, howling, plunged into the night.

It took a few moments for Rowan to right himself. Breaths came as fumes as his hand touched his head, and when he pulled it away little red mirrors of himself came with it. Collecting his rapier, he staggered into the doorway, but Rurik already knew the man would find nothing. Voren had gone.

But his anguish—that remained.

At a shamble, Rowan returned to the table and began to cut him loose. Like a mantra, the swordsman kept repeating: "It will be alright." It seemed more for Rowan's own self than for him. There were no tears in his eyes, but his friend was pale as a ghost, and his hands quaked where they touched Rurik's bonds. When Rurik cried out, for the rattle one snapped bond set off, Rowan all but faded away. Only his touch on Rowan's hand set him moving again.

Rurik wanted to reassure him. To tell him it would be alright. The words wouldn't come. Fire trickled to a tedious throbbing, and with every bead of sweat he could feel a little more of the heat trickle out of him. Mind wandered lonely and adrift, but Rurik still had the sense of self to try and focus on the pain. To focus on the hurt. The mind begged him stop, but he knew what lay in acceptance. He knew what would happen when he ceased to feel.

Not now. Assal above, not now. He had to tell them. "Voren, he…" But Rowan shushed him, told him to keep still. The mantra broke, and it was Rowan that assured *him* it would be alright. It could not rest. *What if I do not wake?* "The whiskey. Rowan. It wasn't me. It wasn't me." The hands slid under him and faltered just a little with the words. *Please believe me. Don't make me die a liar.* Fingers coiled, heaving him, and he screamed in spite of himself, for Rowan was not large enough of a man to bear him straight, and the wounds curled deeper as he bent.

He thought of Voren Bäcker, of the words the baker had said, and felt them dampen the light of it all. Lies. Truths. So many people, fighting so many unnecessary ills, all because they dreaded the silence.

Who am I? Why do I deserve that beautiful sound?

They were nearly to the door before Rowan replied. "Be still now. I know, little lord. I know."

No sweeter words could have rang out from the dark. He wanted to thank this man, but he was too tired, the wounds too deep. Strength flooded out, and where the grip faltered, he sank against his friend, letting the words repeat, but in his head it was no longer Rowan he addressed.

In a white field, a little girl waited for him with nothing but the stars as guide. She turned, drawing the years about her like a cloak, and the green fires burned through all the mirrors of herself. No longing, anymore.

A voice called to him. Somewhere, a head rolled across limp shoulders. There was no darkness.

Chapter 19

There was no path but forward. No destination but away.

They saw. They all saw the blood. Through a fop's hate-filled eyes.

Branches snagged and snapped both cloth and flesh, tearing little corners out of the soul that remained. Trees and more trees. That was all he ever saw. All he ever had a mind to see. Winter had done little to halt the overgrowth and spring had returned it to full bloom. Vines, branches everywhere. Even the sun only slanted in at angles. That did not matter. If he could not see, then they could not see him…right?

There was never consideration that he was not being chased.

He stumbled over a root. He threw up a cry against his fall, but while quick feet saved his pride, the sudden jerk tore at the wound in his side. Its very edges seemed to crackle as he stilled, rasping as he steadied a hand back against the flow.

The whole side of him was dampened, stained. It made his head spin to watch. There would not be water enough in all the world. Dirt was getting in. *Dirty-dirt.* Shreds of the world. All the while, he kept leaking out.

They can't see me. They can't. But it seemed like all the hounds in Hell were nipping at his heels. Every shadow held ghosts of footsteps. Whispers.

They would kill him when they caught him. Oathbreaker. Killer.

No, he could not even do that right. The blade was still clutched claw-like between his fingers. He could not seem to let it fall. It was frozen. Frozen in blood. Cries of pain still rattled in his head. That face, that horrible face—burned forever into the back of his eyes.

He should never have spoken. That was his downfall. *Damn my tongue! Luck flees when unlucky men moan.* So help him, time had proved that bit too readily true. But you couldn't kill a man like that without teaching him his sin. Otherwise it was just…just…

Murder.

He wasn't a murderer. He just wanted them to be free. If he had done it with an army at his back, would they have called him a murderer then? No. Slap armor and a few long guns on them, and they would be naught but heroes. Hypocrisy. That was all the details understood.

And Essa. Oh, Essa. What will you think of me when they lay this at your feet? Were it anyone else, he could deny, deny, deny, but now—not her cousin. Not that brother from another flesh, no, she would never take a kindly word from any over his. This was enough to slow him—that and the lack of breath. Rowan was not a bad man. Would he understand? *Couldn't. Idiot.* The blade. The ropes. *No one could "understand" that.*

The world was spinning out of his grip and there was nothing he could do to stop it. Suddenly, he could not breathe. He came to a halt, gasping for air. The trees rose up around him and the shadows were long, and everywhere there were bugs forming columns, like little soldiers at their wars of infestation, creeping-crawling their way toward him at a whistling tune.

When his hand came away from his side there was so much blood. It wouldn't wipe away.

Yet the whistling did not go the way of other fancies. It, like the blood, remained even as the bugs dissolved into a prickling sensation along his neck. He swooned and caught a branch with his arm, pulling himself forward bit by bit. Eyes lay in the trunk. They were everywhere, all around.

I'm sorry. He wanted to shout it, but there was no use in it. He did not even know what for—the effort with the knife, the pain he brought to Essa's feet, or failing. Pride—the soldiers always said it was the sharpest blade.

Something snarled from the dark and yanked him forcibly from the eyes and whistles of the world. There, before him, was no bug. A dog. Wild thing, surely, bowled over with a layer of fur so thick as to make a shepherd jealous. He took a step back, and it stepped after him, padding one long leg among the needles and bearing its heavy jowls. Foamy breaths dribbled from it, and the growl came again. It possessed him and seized him still. He could not bring himself to cry out. No one would have come to his aid, anyways.

And if this thing rose up on two legs, we might strike ourselves a conversation. Not that the beast looked particularly inviting to that prospect. He might have had better luck with a wolf.

There wasn't even a rustle to announce the blade that came so effortlessly against his already screaming side. It prompted him to give it voice, but when another tapped against his throat, it trailed into an agonizing murmur. *Trapped.* He dared not look back, but the sight of the dog lowering itself on its rear legs only drove the frenzy higher. These two Hells—they moved as one. The hound was nothing but the pet. *Not so wild, after all.*

"Please." The word had scarcely left his mouth, however, when the dagger tapped his wound flatly and doubled him up.

"Ah, ah," a dark voice ticked, admonishing him. "If I wanted to kill you, doughboy, I might have shot from afar. You are no deer. But that does not mean I'll permit sound."

When Voren nodded—vigorously, at that—the blades slithered away as quickly as they had come, to be replaced by a firm boot to the back that sent him flailing into the forest floor. In a panic, Voren twisted wild, scrambling onto his hands and scooting back as many feet as the shadow-man seemed wont to let him. The man's tone had the amusement of a cat's contented purr, but when he looked up, half-expecting to see only leaves and silhouettes, he found a man true enough, but one without any mirth beyond a stone's capacity.

For a moment, terror of a different sort held him. Prayers began to dance at a fevered pace across his bewildered tongue. A ghost stood before him, and he knew he had wandered far indeed—passed from the forest into some faerie's glade, straight beyond the mortal circle into some other dreaded coil.

This Matair was dead.

Dead men without heads, however, did not regain them with their end. The Church was clear enough about that.

He bit the dogma off as he forced himself to focus—to look beyond the initial thrust of dread's spear. To the perfectly attached head. To the limpless leg, propping the unsightly slender figure—for his breed, at least. That, and the lightless haze of green that marked but one of that family told him this was an altogether different demon. He knew this man. Not by face, but by name. And then, he dreaded all the more because of it.

There was no menace in the way Isaak Matair moved toward him, but there never was. Emotion never touched this one's blades. Not like Voren. Not unless he needed it for something else. Yet the threat hung about his very airs, weighted down with the force of rumor and blood.

"You walk with the camp, boy." It was not a question. "And you walk out of it. Tell me: does my brother take the same fool's path?"

Another step, another inch closer to the end. Voren stared at him, blank as a slate. He could hear the dog panting, but his eyes seemed incapable of parting from the man to find it. He knew he should run. He tried to will himself to do so. But he couldn't. Fight. Flight. Truly, he knew what the deer felt like when they beheld the creaking of the bow.

If a banshee ever took your name, the village wives whispered, they held your soul beyond the lines of life's spheres. This man knew him. Not just as another boy, but to his core. His servile, cowardly core.

He knew not what else to say. "I-I can take you to him. Ser, he lives, please, if you'll just allow me. I can."

The man did not move another step. Merely, he leaned a little forward, tilting his head to catch the light just so. "Yes," a fleeting patch of voice erupted, "you will."

* *

A band of them hunted through the forest. For game, or stragglers. Either was as good as the other. Patchwork colors, but well-armed: brigandine and hardy cuirasses, with sturdy tools of war to match them. They had learned the perils of their long guns—powerful, terrifying, but useless at a range, and all but worthless in the quick, ruthless skirmishes of the forest. So the fiery limbs lay stretched across their backs. Silent, unassuming.

All around them, the ghosts of the forest rose to stalk them. They did not even realize they had gone too far. Yet so like a deer, possessed of that last moment of prescience, one of them lifted a head, hand to his axe, and peered out at them. He tensed.

So too did a little bear, except that she tensed with the pull of a bow. The creak of it thrummed in her like the beating of her own heart. Muscles strained. No wind to speak of. Only two cool, dark eyes, shining like torches through the gloom. They said to kill a man was nothing like an animal. In truth, it was no different. Each fought death with every fiber of its being. Her whole body sighed with the loosing of grey goose fletched death. Another arrow was already in hand by the time the first struck home.

They had thought themselves the hunters. So like animals, the unsuspecting pack knew terror in that moment. As the first went down, the others panicked. One barked out orders for a circle, but by the time the words had left his mouth,

446

half a dozen others followed that first into death. The rest trailed shortly, not one having ever cast upon their foe, nor even fired a shot.

A perfect hunt, she thought mirthlessly. When the men's deaths drew to certainty, a high-pitched whistle bounded off the trees. Only then did Roswitte and the others shuffle from their concealment.

Ten lay dead. Quickly. Cleanly. Their killers stood admiring their work.

The battle at the river was a thing of intimidation. Nothing more. Its purpose had been to show the invaders fear and taint their southern march with it. This was how the people of the Ulneberg fought their battles. Such a mass as Tessel's was good for playing proper war. It could not cope with the buzz of a hundred little skirmishes like these.

"Collect their sticks. Salvage the armor if able. Strip the bodies and leave them for the wolves."

Fear was a powerful weapon. Couple it with exhaustion and one could sap even the greatest of hosts. The dead would be a warning. If Tessel were wise, he would heed it. If not, than the earth would feast.

She plucked her arrow from a dead man. His wide, gulping eyes stared back at her, and she wondered if they, too, had known the sundering of hope. Or if it had clung there until that final, rasping moment. If he had known a family.

"I killed him," Ivon had confessed to her in the aftermath of Verdan. "I saw him and still I trained the cannons. I could do no other, but it makes no difference. I am kinslayer." But weren't they all, in one way or another? All men walked the same path. All were brothers in the journey. Yet the arrows fell indiscriminate and uncaring among them, and the bodies were many.

Even so, she had never seen that soldier so shaken. She shifted uncomfortably and knocked the dead man's eyes away. *Let it not be so.*

For her, every corpse was Fallit's. She did not wish Ivon to forever after see his brother among the dead. To look up from a kill and see naught but sunken eyes and wispy threads of memory walking silent and alone among the broken and the burned. As for the boy, what madness, that he would come so far only to die at the very gates of his home. She did not long to tell Liesa.

Did you get to see your blood one more time, at least?

Perhaps. *But not little Anelie.*

This last tricked her step as she moved away from the site of the ambush. That child had so little. Wherever she now stood, this news would break her. *Let it not be so.*

After looting the dead—"May Assal forgive you," their party's leader quipped, "for no man shall suffer a traitor to live"—they struck south and west, skirting the perimeter of Tessel's relentless searches. They were nearly to the rendezvous set with other likeminded parties when they happened on another treasure. Before them, a resplendent train of folk cast about the woods as if searching out a spot to dine. All were armed, but not one had drawn.

Their leader drew his fist tight and all fell back a pace, crouching, watching, debating, but Roswitte knew the colors of the banner this strange party flew. What's more, she recognized the stark look and black hair of their apparent leader.

So like the mother. Only Liesa, after all, would march a train of soldiers into the trees, glowing like a torch in all the colors of her station, rapier unused at her hip, and never pause to wonder at the oddity. Though, in truth, the only wonder about this picture was how the group had come so far without getting themselves feathered by another of Witold's war parties. White flag or no, most would not have hesitated.

Roswitte made no attempt to conceal her approach. Voices hissed after her, and her party's leader tried to grope for her arm, but she hopped aside and hurried out. As though merely returning from a stroll, she marched straight into the embassy's midst and struck a knee before their hopelessly bewildered leader. *A pity, child, you never took to the trees as your brothers did.* She kept her eyes raised to the woman, for all her show of deference, for Liesa would not have had it any other way.

How she had loathed to leave this woman behind, days earlier, when Ivon had fled the army's advance. Some people were intractable. Admirable trait, if it didn't get them killed.

Their exchange was curt, and while the men cloistered about her stood aggravated and uncertain, Liesa cut straight to her point: Witold and her brother. Given that was where they were already headed, it was easily done. Another whistle drew Roswitte's own men out—though no few of them caught bemused scowls from the Verdanites at the sight of drawn bows. Liesa herself looked little surprised. She merely offered Roswitte her hand to help her up, along with some quip about shots in the dark.

Careful as they moved, it was nearly an hour to the rendezvous. From there, buoyed in number—though less than they had hoped—they trekked swiftly south, in a line straight for Witold's temporary reprieve this side of the river. It took another few hours, by the tracking of the shadows, but they reached the place without incident.

The soldiers there were only a loose confederation of Witold's own household troops and a smattering of the same from his banners, as well as what foresters, hunters, and rangers he could sway from local holds—which was to say, whatever men remained in the aftermath of the war's great leeching. Some small number of Surinian sellswords were afoot as well, distinguishable by the thick mustachios and dark eyes their people seemed to breed in abundance. Some petty baron's meager scraps, no doubt, there to guarantee their masters' shares of whatever loot Witold won. Roswitte welcomed them with the suspicion only a generation of river raids and thievery could evoke.

As the old adage rote: there were no knights in Surin.

Yet all seemed to know the lady Matair, and what's more, none seemed terribly determined to bar the Little Bear's path. Soldiers might have been a superstitious lot, and distrusted women with a blade because of it, but they were also practical. Many here had seen Roswitte fight. Many more knew the deceased Matair patriarch, in one form or another. Messengers were scuttling about before Roswitte could even find her lady a seat.

Eventually, they were taken to the heart of Witold's staging—a grim but study old shack of thatch and poorly shaped timber, likely used by hunters and trappers when the seasons called. It could scarcely fit ten men, but Witold, counting as he surely did for at least two of these, hardly seemed to mind.

The Ulneberg's count surged to his feet at their entrance, smile nearly as wide and bright as his open arms. Verdan's liege lord was not at all what one might expect. Presiding as he did over such lean and hardy folk, Witold himself was a broad man, thicker about the middle than the arm. A substantial double-chin waddled when he spoke, with a wire-thin peppering of beard doing its best to cover it, but he was otherwise well-composed, with a hard voice but a clear, jovial presence that left even the bitterest guest feeling as if they had his undivided attention.

This man was a politician, not a soldier, and for that Roswitte could not bring herself to trust him, even though it was a weakness the man himself knew well. This was a man that built himself up on an alliance of skilled advisors, generals, and meticulous planning. At the least, he knew what he was doing, and she had to give him that.

To Witold's left stood Ivon, bedecked in the artifices of war and looking utterly out of place. He stepped forward at his sister's entrance, and gallantly kissed her hand in welcome. *Good,* Roswitte thought. *No sign of despair.*

To Witold's right were a handful of his captains, a certain dust knight among them. A smile gleamed for her on that latter's face as he touched hand to shoulder in a grateful bow. She ignored it utterly and scrutinized instead these others. A short man, a wide man, and a white-haired man. She grinned inwardly. *Stumpy, Pudgy, and Snow*, she decided.

"My lady, it pleases me more than words could suffice to see you safely here, away from that madness. Though I should have preferred you sooner," Witold said to Liesa, with all of a father's seriousness.

Liesa, taking up her brother's arm, let him guide her around the small skinning table they had taken for a map-holder. Her eyes flitted across it, noting the pegs on the board with a hunter's clarity, before settling back on Witold.

"I had to see my brother. It was as simple as that."

"Had to…" Witold paused thoughtfully. "Then I suppose that you have seen him? He is well?" It was masked, but in this, Roswitte saw only politick care from the man—he did not care about Rurik. Not for a boy that had only been embarrassment to him, and lately stood a traitor. Friend's son or no.

"He was. Before that horrific show this morning. It was he that helped my flight." At this, Ivon fidgeted. It was a brief thing, but it was there. Those words shook something in him. "But you may thank Roswitte of Verdan for seeing me safely here."

Witold's heavy stare shifted considerately to her. When she realized she still slouched, Roswitte drew up taut as a bowstring.

"We owe you a great debt then, goodwoman." To Liesa, Witold added, "And your enigma of a brother—I should like to speak with him, if he emerges from this unpleasantness."

Liesa bowed her head. "He will." In those words, there was not a shred of doubt.

Witold had the grace not to rebut. "So," he said, casting expectant looks around the room, "what brings you here in such haste?"

"The plans to retake my town." Liesa's eyes shone hot and fierce at this. "I will not leave it in the hands of that sanctimonious monster. He could make Cullick look a saint."

Snickers went around the room, save to Witold himself, who whitened considerably at that mention. Already, Roswitte had heard why. Children were the world to Witold, and Isaak, a son. The thought that Cullick still held his granddaughter compromised his character as a leader. He would be, in many ways, as broken as a roped calf. Any normal person would, she supposed.

"Let us not—"

"After today," Ivon said, cutting off his lord with a courteous gesture, which Witold only belatedly returned, "I think it should not be hard. Tessel will surely watch the river now, but he will see the folly in remaining. Especially since his only token to legitimize his occupation has now fled." At that, his grip on his sister visibly tightened. "It's not as if the place stands a breadbasket."

That was not, however, entirely true. "My lord?" All eyes flicked to Roswitte. They made her shift uncomfortably. But someone had to voice it, lest they go too far on presumption. "If Rurik is still with him, he may seek to use the boy."

"An exile?" Witold's head perked.

"A bastard," Stumpy pointed out. Witold bobbed to this, staring deep into his map's heart.

Ivon's lips tightened with a suppressed sort of outrage, but it was Liesa that replied. "He is not."

"How can you be certain?" Witold's head did not rise.

"Because he hates the Bastard. He told me so himself."

"But at the river…" Ivon hesitated. He could not finish the thought.

His sister twisted on him, a wolfhound scenting blood. "What happened at the river? Tessel's soldiers bundled him there, when he sent me off." Ivon looked to her, but the words would not come. The eyes could not hide it, though. They offered enough to know. "No…" Liesa shrank, eyes wavering. "You—you don't mean…" But his own, hollowed by the long hours dwelling on that bitter scene, did not falter. She let out a moan of such utter devastation that no less than two of Witold's captains started forward as though to catch her.

Instead, she rounded on Witold, snatching her arm from her brother's grasp. "We must go back. And soon. We—we can't…"

"Tessel pulls his scouts back," Snow offered. "Like a turtle retreating to its shell."

"It's true," Roswitte said. "He will be wearying and wary of our ambushes."

"But if we could lure him out…" Witold's head bounced agreeably.

Then the dust knight stepped forward. "My lords. You do not see the crux of this thing. With respect, Tessel is a soldier through and through. Your ambush worked once. But it will not again, and if you face him in force, he will smash you utterly." Looking around at the hard stares that met these cold truths, Ser Ensil put up his palms defensively. He had no friends here. "I mean this as no disrespect to your prowess, but it is fact. I have seen him fight. Likewise, his host is too great to take through these shadow strikes alone."

"Cannot fight him by shadow. Cannot fight him by light. Do you take him for a god, ser?" Stumpy said bitterly. "Are we to just lie down and die?"

"No." At this, the knight turned to the table. "If I may?" Witold shuffled aside, to allow him room. He stared a moment, then pointed to the mark that indicated Verdan. "Not all shadows are yet exhausted. The host may never be consumed in them, but this one man—let a small group go. Find a way to penetrate his camp, or draw him out. That host holds together only by his binding thread. If we end him, the rest will sunder."

"Assassination?" Stumpy blanched. "Dishonorable."

Roswitte all but laughed. A dry, mirthless chortle. "Had you seen Oberroth, you should not be worried of that." No amount of time would relieve her of that bitter memory, and the knowledge that these very men might have been there—should have been there—and might have turned the tide.

Given how Witold's face thinned into darkness, she thought better of that remark—and any more like it. *Too much time in Kasimir's company.* That was one lord that encouraged the habit of speech among "lessers."

Liesa turned her a look that summoned images of mothers reaching for a wounded child. "Believe me, sers, I am all for Tessel's end. Yet Roswitte brings a clear point. We cannot simply ignore Oberroth. If you tell it true, and that horde stands so tenuous a thing without Tessel's guidance, I frankly dread what will come to Verdan at so sudden a removal of his influence."

From the uncomfortable silence that traded space about that stodgy map, she was not the only one to see the possibility. It was enough to make Roswitte beam inwardly. Good to know there still stood Matairs that could leave a room breathless.

When the silence snapped, it was Pudgy that at last offered some words. "We must lure him out." *Ah. A toady, that one.*

"I volunteer," Ivon immediately replied. Otherwise, he was as still as a statue.

Pudgy looked dubious. "To lure him out? What makes you think he shall answer?"

"For all of it." His face betrayed no emotion, but the others more than made up for it. There was much stirring, and more than one uncertain breath. "By now, Tessel has no doubt heard of my presence at this morning's attack. His honor and his pride are beasts of burden—as they are for many of us. By now, I should think my actions have put more than sufficient burden to them. If he thinks I move against him, I guarantee these same beasts will not let me pass another time. He will put himself to the hunt. My lords, if you would so oblige me?"

Witold's nod was curt. He accepted the logic and he trusted Ivon. Liesa, however, clawed at her brother's arm as though it were the last bit of wood in a raging sea. The anger, the hurt, flaring but moments before, had died as quickly as the notion of losing a second brother had risen. "This—this isn't about Rurik, is it? You don't…"

But he did. They could all see that. Ivon shook Liesa off, though his hard eyes rested only softly on her. "No, my lady, this is of something else entire." The man might have been ice when it suited him, but all his stoicism did not make him a good liar. It was in the way he tensed. The shoulders and the eyes. A brother for a brother. A life for a life. Roswitte looked away in disgust. It made little sense, though it was hardly the first time.

The sister, however, would not give up. She cast her wild gaze out at the other men, looking for aid in any corner, but they averted their eyes from anywhere it crossed. Emotion—especially a woman's emotion—had ungainly effects on such men, the Little Bear had found. They liked to hide it behind crude humors.

"Surely," the lady Matair stammered, "surely aid comes from the west? They cannot let the Bastard do as he will."

It was Witold to speak to this, and he sighed heavily for it—clearly a thought that had been weighty on his own mind. "I am afraid we *are* the aid, lady. The Empire is depleted and what little remains wastes itself between a foreigner and an idiot. As far as they are concerned, the east stands alone." Alone among the men in the room, Witold's eyes met hers directly. "I am sorry, Liesa." Then, almost as an afterthought to Ivon: "Take whatever men you need. I will see it done."

How Roswitte longed to go to her. Without support, Liesa looked as pitiable and alone as ever a creature could. Her haunted eyes roved between the lanes of men, pleading, but it was a child's cry in an empty wood. Roswitte longed to lead this child from the room, and to hell with these men and their grim news. Yet she did not. She remained, as ever, too well trained. Funny. That might have comforted her once. Like them, she looked away.

"My lady? My lord?" To Roswitte's shock, it was Ser Ensil that stepped forward. Liesa's hope rekindled on that goodly shape. Witold turned to it, however, with only a slit of a gaze. "If it please you, I should like to accompany Ser Ivon in this. If men he needs, mine will be glad to join us as well." The words alone seemed to earn an inward squeal from Liesa. Were she any less composed a lady, she might have flung herself at him right there.

"That is not…" Ivon started to say. Liesa slid her wrath round to him, and some of his fire ebbed. Her brother shuffled from it. His eyes, now, were the ones to search, and they measured the others, lastly coming to Roswitte. Without planning to do so, she felt her head dip. Affirmation. Ser Ensil, she knew, could protect this man. With a sigh, Ivon came back to Ensil, and dipped his own head into the barest of acknowledgements. "I should be honored for your aid, Ser Ensil. Your party's reputation precedes you."

A smile grew on the sellsword's face, too bright and innocent, Roswitte thought, for any man so battle-hardened as this one to possess. It made her stomach churn. Apparently she was not the only one incensed by it. Snow scoffed openly, earning a sterner look from the knight.

"What should prompt you to this, dust knight? You're not even Idasian. It's not as though you have anything to gain in this."

Ensil stiffened as though struck, but the breath that left him was easy, if pained. "Ser. Some matters of honor have nothing to do with country nor coin." He did not elaborate on what those things were. Roswitte had an idea all the same. Some men lived with codes that bore nothing of a nation's influence. It was her suspicion that his did not permit such a thing as Oberroth to pass without a stain on his own character. Not while he still drew breath.

"I should also like to bring Vardick of Tarney with me. He was my father's man, and none may doubt his prowess."

Roswitte cleared her throat loud enough to be sure no one took it for simple hygiene. "Ser? With respect, Vardick's injury won't stand it." She had been beside him at Oberroth when it happened. A spear thrust through the leg. True to form, he had killed the man that did it and fought like a mountain lion through the aftermath, hiding it even through the early throes of their march, but by the time they had made camp that first night, the extent of the injury had been plain. Infection had followed—a deep, pus-ridden affair. For a time the doctors had feared the loss of the limb.

Not the Brickheart. "It's a wonder he's rallied so—I should not think it wise to risk a fever resurfacing, or the slowing of your party by it." The way Ivon shuffled uncomfortably, she knew he recognized the truth of her words. That his shieldman, Jörg, had also perished in that madness, she knew weighed on him as well. *So many good men now unable to aid him.* "I humbly request to take his place."

It was, perhaps, to their credit—and the wellness of their person—that none of Witold's captains snickered at the last. More than a fair share of soldiers would have, noble or common alike.

Ensil traded a glance between them. When Ivon held himself aloof, he offered: "She does know the woods, ser."

"Aye, that she does," Ivon conceded. "Very well, Ros."

Witold nodded sagely, though his eyes crinkled with only a weary sort of mirth. "Best of luck to you all, than. I shall see what we can do to aid you from this end, of course. But be wary. I tell you, take care. I think you are not the only ones for the hunt."

Ivon's puzzled look asked the question his lips did not.

"I wished to tell you before but, as you shall be leaving us, I cannot hold it any longer. I'd word from Mariel the morning last. You Matairs seem to be trickling back into these woods at a gryphon's pace." One fat finger wiggled before Witold's face, and landed with a thud on the marker of his capital, Gölingen. "We had a vague shadow of a Matair about, asking for information on the lot of it. Though his interests seemed…pointed."

"Isaak?" Liesa squeaked. "That's…not possible. Cullick wouldn't release the last male at his hand. Not—not when he wouldn't give him to you." Her brows knitted, calculating. "Why?"

"Does Witold fear the Bastard as well?" Ivon's cold demeanor cracked just a little with the mention of another brother. Another chance, Roswitte supposed.

Witold sighed heavily, legitimately sinking away from their questions. Unease. "Not…that. No. And Kana is still…still in Cullick's hold. That much I know. For that, I reason him to be Cullick's creature. Mariel said there was an eclipse about him, of person and of purpose, and feared…" He trailed off, turning his pain pointedly on Liesa. "Your brother may have something to do with it."

"Myself?" Ivon asked, incredulous.

"No. The other. The one you fear…well. Yes. I think we all know how little love Cullick spares the boy."

A little sound broke from Liesa before she spoke again. "The dogs," she said breathlessly. Some dark image seemed to glaze her eyes. Roswitte quirked a brow, uncertain what she meant. Yet the girl quavered. "You don't mean…Why? How could Mariel know?"

Ivon inched a hand toward her, but did not touch her. "She is right. Isaak would not give his purpose if it was…so."

"What's more, why would Mariel care?" Liesa spit this last carelessly, and it earned her a spiteful stare from her brother. But not from Witold.

"Mariel loves your brother dearly. As I do: as a son. For all that, the greatest character in my Mariel is his loyalty. However little a thing, I know it. He fears for your brother, and rightly—kinslayer is no easy burden to lift."

A burden that hung on Ivon's own shoulders like a noose. "Then our effort gains a double purpose. I will find him." There was no hint in his tone of what he might do if that man did not look on him with the same brotherly care, however.

"Alive?" Liesa's voice was little more than a whisper. "Please, Ivon. Soon there may be none of us left."

"I will do my best."

It was all any of them could do, in truth. In the pit of her stomach, however, Roswitte felt a familiar lump. *Would that it were enough.* She doubted it would be, and Liesa was right. They were running out of Matairs to save.

Chapter 20

Circles moved the world. Mad men told it true. Circular motions, round and round about. Routine, they called it. Predictability.

The shadows breathed it. The air. The sound. Like sweet summer rain. There was nothing but the people. Guards stepped along the parapets, the darkness in the halls. Silhouettes. Routinely shambling to the coin that sang. All men were sellswords at heart. Some merely charged more for the pleasure.

It was just the two of them alone. Moon rose and eyelids fluttered. Mortal coil yawned to the twilight mumblings of the soul. The bedded one thought he was alone. Lonelier than the loneliness of they. Like children, settled down between the sheets, he crooked arms and legs in tight and sought to dream stone walls between the sheets to guard him from the world beyond.

Guards. Walls. Shadows. He knew them. He held them. He thought they would protect him. The Routine bid it so.

The shadow tensed, breathing out life as he slipped from the rafters. Grounded, grounding—the world was real again. Present. Shoeless feet made no sound on the old wood.

Below, three guards waited in a small room. All cards and chatter. Within the hour, one would rise for the privy. Like clockwork. An old board on the second step would give word of approach. Stone stools would grate. So were they set, alarm to the bedded soul; it would serve in turn to the shadow and the cry.

He stretched, savoring the warm trickle through numbed flesh. Tingles lanced the delicate step.

They did not write of shadows, merely the forms they stalked.

Caution there. Five beads to the draw. Bone and string dangling from the very rafters. Chill made the boards' squeal extra firm. Caution, bred of routine. The slumbering master knew. It would not aid him. Where starlight cracked the window, steel broke its sheath. Come one man or twenty, gold spent was blood earned. Some called that anarchy. They knew little. It was not duty, no, but they could not understand it could be something else entirely.

Nothing drove him but the coin? Endless, aimless collision. Who could say that was the world?

It had not been coin that turned him on the woman's dutiful hound. The bloody clash! The knowing look! The anxious creak of will! Coin—what madness indeed!

Skin often tensed just before a blow. Even if the mind could not register its passing, the body reacted—to sound, to motion, to the subtle touch of change. So it was with the sleeping man, chest panging with the chill of the blade. Only then, the mind realized. Only then did routine's veil slip.

He knew. They always knew.

Blood shot the eyes as they fluttered open. Breaths gasped for life, but the shadow clamped a gloved hand tight against the wriggling hollow of his being. The blade worked through flesh as it did through silk, carving a line up the contours of a caving chest. The whole of the man heaved. Hands quaked—too weak to rise. Another sound, pattering past the gulping quivers of his heart's descending tune.

It did not have to be slow. He considered it a courtesy for one of his own craft. A lesson, that he might learn of his errors for the next incarnation on the circling descent into eternity.

One could hope.

Wrinkled skin quavered. The feral eyes grew grey. Bare skin, paled in the restlessness of a killer's dreams, slicked the laxing face. Only the mouth—that eternal portal—remained open to the silence. Even in death, the soul sought to scream.

Only then did Aurinth lean back. He made the courtesy of closing the eyes. Another gift for shadows. There was nothing else. No silk. No gems. The room, save for the bed, was all but as barren as a tomb. Even those that killed for duty knew: the pompous earnings only drew you to the light, and the light was far more deadly than the dark. Spymasters and assassins were no different. Only the targets shifted.

This one breathed it in. It was not all he breathed. Another scent, airier, yet heavier, scorched the halls of this place. Hate had burned it deep, and he knew it well, for he had smelled it once before.

There was a woman in a place not so far from here, and the world was wings and chains alike to her. It rippled through the very nature of her. It stained those she touched. No scent quite like it. His mind drifted to a note, one of many. A lion's scribbled clawing. Oh, Usuri. The Many-starred. The Many-ended. Let this be done. Then it would be for her.

A thought to savor.

Then came the whimper of the dispossessed. He breathed. They had tried it one way—the lions and their spiders. Rattled and roared and rotted for it. When they sent the bird, they had resolved to the final course. It had begun with the great mother. Could not even see him, she couldn't, not with so many suckling at her breast. Horses could be such skittish beasts.

This one saw, too clearly. She had the mother's look. She shied away, curling into the shelter of the corner. Too late to know: it offered her nothing. The little girl…

Just a step. A very little step. Whole worlds below.

About the Author

Chris Galford spends his days as a freelance journalist and editor. Writing, in all its forms, has been his passion from a young age, but fantasy and science fiction are the sparks that give his nights purpose. A native of Michigan, in his spare time he can usually be found wandering the lake shore with a camera in one hand and a pen in the other.

The Hollow March, the predecessor to *At Faith's End*, was his first major work, based on a series of short stories he wrote in the summer of 2008, titled *The Company of the Eagles*. Another short story set in the same world, "The Child's Cry," was published in the Twelfth issue of *Mystic Signals* magazine.

Visit his website at: http://cianphelan.wordpress.com/

Or contact him directly at: shadowedwolfe@gmail.com

Printed in Great Britain
by Amazon.co.uk, Ltd.,
Marston Gate.